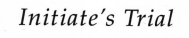

Initiate's Trial

Janny Wurts

INITIATE'S TRIAL

The Wars of Light and Shadow

VOLUME 9

FIRST BOOK OF
SWORD OF THE CANON

HarperCollins*Publishers*
77–85 Fulham Palace Road,
Hammersmith, London W6 8JB

www.harpercollins.co.uk

Published by Harper*Voyager*
An imprint of HarperCollins*Publishers* 2011

1

A catalogue record for this book
is available from the British Library

ISBN: 978-0-00-736212-7

Set in Palatino by Palimpsest Book Production Limited,
Falkirk, Stirlingshire

Printed and bound in Great Britain by
Clays Ltd, St Ives plc

MIX
Paper from
responsible sources
FSC FSC™ C007454
www.fsc.org

For Abner Stein

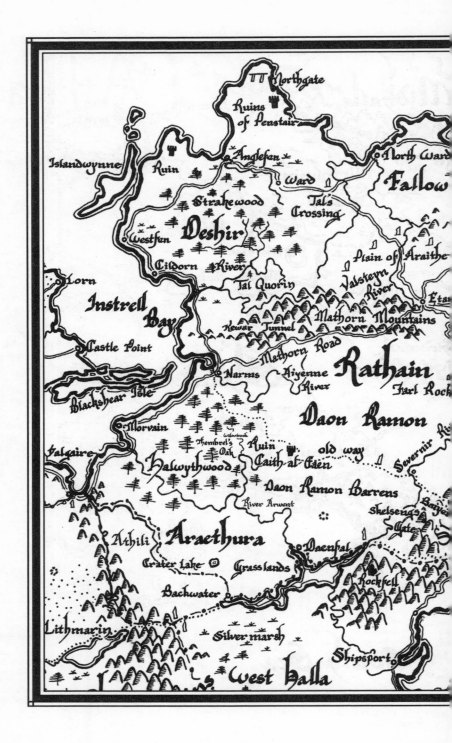

Nidhalla

Mariac Mountains

Mirthlvain
Swamp

Orvandir

Methisle

Methlas Lake

Methlas River

Ishli

Ganish

Six Tower

irdmark

Shand

Atchaz

River Ippash

Forthmark

Sacred Well

At Royal Sceress

Junish

Desert of
Sanpashir

Ichish

Ruins

Mountains

South Sea

Alestron

Acknowledgments

My grateful thanks and steadfast appreciation goes to the following individuals for their invaluable support and assistance:

Jeff Watson, Andrew Ginever, Lynda-Marie Hauptman, Gale Skipworth, Charles Whipple, Angus Bickerton, Teri Wiegand, Stefan Raets and Sandra Jacobs

Jonathan Matson

Emma Coode, Sarah Hodgson, Jane Johnson and all of the Voyager Crew

and above all, my husband, Don Maitz, whose constant love and unflagging support exceeds all words.

Contents

I.   Imprisoned....................................1

II. Vagabond......................................35

III. Change..69

IV. Dispossessed.................................113

V.   Mis-step......................................155

VI. Haunted Wood.................................193

VII. Confrontations...............................233

VIII. Trial..265

IX. Throes..305

X.   Reversals.....................................343

XI. Upheaval......................................385

XII. Bind..425

XIII. Double Bind..................................465

XIV. Conflagration................................515

Glossary..553

Third Age Year 5922

Declared Under Interdict:
THE KINGDOM OF HAVISH
For crown-sanctioned liaison with Darkness,
as the iniquitous haven for Old Blood Talent,
and for armed defense of Heretical Practice.
Henceforth, no True Sect Faithful shall traffic therein,
or flout the High Temple's Trade Embargo.
—decreed by the Light's Conclave, Erdane
3ʳᵈ Year of the Canon • Third Age 5686

I. Imprisoned

All of his days began the same way. He awoke without any memory. Nameless, he knew nothing at all of his past. Search though he might, his thoughts churned in circles. He encountered no sense of self-purpose. Nothing beyond the fact, *I exist,* that might endow him with a future.

Eyes opened, he surveyed his featureless surroundings. The place did not appear to have walls. Which deception perhaps prompted his first recollection. He understood that the silvery, reflective enclosure was a prison, woven of impenetrable spells. Colourless, textureless, the barrier enveloped him in a suspended state of neutrality, neither hot nor cold, apparently without a ceiling or floor, as seamlessly sealed as a bubble. Bland, like the clothing he was given to wear: a white shirt and dark breeches stitched from a nondescript fabric, fitted comfortably to his slight frame. His diligent keepers, whoever they were, did not wish him to suffer indignity.

Unable to view his reflection, and with no outside window to relieve the monotony, he began with a survey of his own hands. Their structure at least prompted the insight that he was individual, with a claim to both history and character. His fingers were refined, almost delicate, the bones cleanly sculpted beneath his lean flesh. The left ones were tipped with calluses. Insight suggested the wear had been caused by repeated deft pressure to stop off taut strings. First epiphany, he recalled the joyful making of music. But not how he had acquired the scars.

Tentative, uneasy, though he knew not why, he traced the whitened welt, gouged across his right palm and snaked in a half twist up his right forearm, to end at the elbow. The shudder raised by his tentative touch roused an unpleasant recall of searing fire. That burn crossed other weals, surely older. Disturbed, he found that both wrists, and his ankles, bore the chafe marks left ingrained by steel shackles.

Rage stirred in him then, a formless awakening arisen from a prior trauma. Someone else had taken him captive before this. The visceral remembrance of freedom denied and the resurgent echo of rebellious anger shuddered in recoil through him. Still nameless, he knew he had broken that chain and those manacles.

Why was he here? Who held him caged, now?

But his fogged memory refused to unveil the hidden face of his enemy. The record of past violence written into his flesh failed to account for his straits. He remembered no crime, no offence enacted against humanity, to have earned him this punishing state of incarceration.

His questions chased themselves into holes, stubbornly uninformative. By then, the explosive surge of his fury lashed him onto his feet. He paced. Every day, like the trapped tiger, untamed emotion spurred his frantic steps. The blank, silver prison swallowed up his dire restlessness. Its forces encapsulated his person and absorbed his aggression without a ripple. His ire blazed deeper, an unstoppable torrent that stripped his nerves livid. How he hated the fact he was helpless! He was given no target to savage. No captor appeared on which to salve his ravening grief for the loss of his being. He had no means to wreak vengeance for the outright theft of the *person* he had been, and rightfully should be, since he was kept living.

When the edged intensity of his temper peaked, the old woman always appeared. She came, swathed head to foot in a violet mantle, sewn with nine scarlet bands upon her full sleeves. He never observed her arrival, had no way to detect the means or the moment that permitted her soundless entry. The primal urge to close his grip on her throat always died when she offered him the lyranthe.

The instrument consumed his attention. Seductive snare, its promise bewitched him. Fourteen silver-wound strings and polished wood woke an ache, unrequited, that glimmered with love beyond hatred and freedoms untouched by captivity. Music, he knew. The structure of melody, cadence, and song framed a power instinctive as breath. Magnetic attraction broke his resistance. He succumbed, every time, and accepted the gift although, beyond question, it came from the hand that abused him. Though such acquiescence should seal his downfall, his innate desire won out. No other choice existed, for him, shut in the unending horror of isolation, except to die without the courage of harmony, bereft of his last human grace.

Imperative instinct silenced his questions as he took the instrument into his arms. His trembling hands caressed lacquered wood. Beyond words, he stroked shining strings with the desperation of the addicted. The brilliance of their sound endowed him with solace. Music opened the channel for healing and lent his last foothold on sanity. Or perhaps the cold stir of true memory served warning: if he failed to ply his art without flaw, he could fall to mortal danger.

Sweet longing transformed into shocking need. Now hurried, he tuned the strings quickly. Shaken, all but undone by foreboding, he broke into a sudden sweat. A prickle lifted the hair at his nape. Then a ranging, unpleasant chill chased his spine.

He remembered, now: thousands upon thousands of days just like this one, each filled by terrors that flitted, unseen, and challenged his innate survival.

His struck notes had seeded a perilous change. As though a tossed stone had crashed through a pool, the ripple broke the stilled tension. His prison was no longer seamless, or safe. An uncanny rift opened up underfoot, letting in an inchoate void that now stirred with purposeful movement. Dread lurked in its shadow. Though the eye could discern neither form nor shape, an unseen invader was stalking him.

He recoiled a step. Fingers flying, he plucked a spray of harmonics, then cranked the drone strings into stinging, true pitch.

Sight still showed him nothing. Warned onto his guard, he trusted the inner panic, that he was not secure, or alone.

Something uncanny had been let inside, though it ranged beyond reach of his senses. The intrusion flicked him as a breath of cold, then jabbed in pure malice and tested his stance, prying to thrust its way into him. The first tingle of etheric assault laced his skin, sharp as the teeth of a starved predator. Anything that possessed life-force was prey, and in this place, he offered the only available source of nourishment. The old woman had gone the same way she had entered, and left him to his own devices.

Sometime, somewhere, he had gained a master's initiate discipline. Those trained faculties responded to primal fear. Bristled into a state of reflexive defense, he needed no trappings of lost personality to recognize the opening throes of a fatal conflict.

A free wraith battled him for possession. Countless millions of others had done the same, prior to his encounter with this one. He knew what to expect. As its ungoverned whirlwind of hatred sought to unbalance him, his own fervid terror would break him. The entity could feed on his leaked strength and vitality. To sate ravening hunger, it would wring him until exhaustion drained his resistance. Then its ferocity would sap his will and supplant his natural awareness. Against the invasive threat of possession, the only weapon he had was the lyranthe and the empowered expression of music.

Peerless talent, he plied his command over fret and string and unleashed a blazing cascade of bright harmony. Jigs and sprightly reels burst from the suppressed well of his deepest longing, first driving him to stamp in madcap rhythm, then lifting his heart to let go and soar. He played music that cried out for laughter, a consummate fusion of tone and bright artistry woven into boundless exaltation. No intrusive attack might swerve his rapt focus. His fingers carried the dance without stumbling. Aggressive oppression must bow to such banishment. He let no hostile thrust of vicious dissonance raze through his exacting discipline. Dread and ruin could not mar the deathless flame he rekindled from inspiration and hope.

Unaware of a mastery that once had commanded the stature of a formal title, the bard tuned his very being to light. Sound gilded his spirit, then forged him, whole, behind an unbreachable bastion. For as long as he played, he could not be tamed. Spirit, raised to an incandescence of joy, could not be caged, or broken to mindless suffering. Remembrance poured back, as phrase upon phrase of melody took wing through the matchless skill of his fingers. He had weathered assaults as perilous as this one; sublime triumph had brought him the victory.

His safety lay in defining the wraith's lost identity. He must achieve this before, Name-forsaken, the howling emptiness of its ferocity beat him down into subjugation.

Cruel desperation guided his tactics. Before he tired, he must find the single, true line of song that could bind the wraith into sympathetic entrancement. Once, before trauma deranged its identity, it had been born enfleshed and human. It had possessed a mother, a father, a family, and a best beloved. More, it also would own the individualized spark of the greater love that sourced its original being. Gently, with tacit tenderness, the musician expanded his range. Poised with single-minded intent, brave enough to extend his most vulnerable sensitivity, he struck the testing, delicate notes to tease out the first flicker of emotional response. Straining, he listened for the pulsed echo that signalled a harmonic confluence.

He would sound out the wraith's obscured self, his tune led by the resonance of its genuine being.

Note for clean note, it would fight his discovery. Blandished by his music, it still would seek to hide, sundered past sanity and shattered by surly fury that rejected the concept of solace. Cut off from reprieve, its hopeless despair perceived no other option, far less understood any balm great enough to ease its deviant existence.

But the bard possessed a relentless compassion. Cued, measure by measure, he stitched a haunting descant above his foundation of ineffable joy. He formed the darker phrases that whimpered of pain: themes of crippling loss that had cankered, unanswered, amid endless vistas of loneliness. The wraith was affirmed, first of all, as it lived, but without criticism or judgement. Where the deep, questing tones brushed against its true pattern, the musician extended his chord and laid claim. His structured invention raised a forgotten beauty from dissonance and reclothed ancient wounds with love's purity.

He refused to recoil from hideous ugliness. The most horrific shriek of torment must not haze his sweet measures into retreat.

4

Immersed in a melting sequence of song, the bard let the wraith's deathless rage become mirrored: gently, terribly, unflinching in honesty, he described the balked need, then the hurt, raw enough to devour all resilience of spirit. Human himself, he acknowledged the hollow agony of separation. Captive as well, but unbroken yet, he encompassed the cry for requital that festered the wraith's insatiable need.

His music wept the river of tears that purposeless emptiness forgot how to express. Unreeled as a thread of glittering gold flung downwards into the void, he probed the wrack spun by the wraith's blinded misery. He sifted, patient, through veils of dread fear, and chipped at the tarnish of desolation. Beneath the bleak chasm of alienation lay the buried gleam of forgotten identity. He must plumb the pit and shape the wraith's Name, before its crazed torment wore away concentration and turned at the last to consume him.

Harmonics spiralled into the air and woke other tremors of insight. Touched by echoes of his own buried memories, the bard encountered themes from the essence of his very self. Bright flashes of resonance sprang from strengths he had once expressed in full cognizance. The unconscious awareness shimmered within him, until the aching tremors of stifled experience stormed over his nerves in sweet waves. *He had known a forest clearing by night, ringing with cascades of unworldly harmony played upon crystalline flutes. Partnered in matchless love, he had cherished a woman with such bonfire passion that the land's flux had ignited to burning. His own aroused flesh, ablaze with hers, had scalded them both, incandescent . . .*

Even the suggested memory of *her* evoked longing beyond all threat of danger to bridle.

Loss followed hard on the heels of epiphany. Fast as his fingers spun song to recover her, *the gift of her being no longer lived in his mind.*

He tasted the cinders of absolute grief, and pain great enough to seduce him. The glass edge of torment nearly made him let go: how easy to embrace the blind ease of oblivion. Surrender beckoned him towards the numb absolution of apathy and promised the end of intolerable sorrow – which *was* the same lie proffered by the wraith. Almost, he had been lulled to forget the stalking presence of that lethal danger.

Bare-fisted courage braced the bard's rocked commitment. He firmed his purpose. Determined to ride out the rip tide of unrequited futility, though the cost left him weeping forever, he unleashed his yearning of spirit until his trained fingers howled his agonized emptiness into grace upon silver-wound strings.

Too late, he realized his effort went wrong. Unstrung past recovery, self-betrayed by the diabolical mistake that had tripped him, he realized the quickened voice of his past had wakened too many powerful echoes. Taken in, he himself had succumbed to beguilement. The pattern played into structure belonged to no starveling wraith! Waylaid by his own searing mastery, he discovered, stripped naked, the strains of his own Name resounded upon the loom of creation. Left with every guarded boundary undone, he stood shieldless before this antagonist. Of the countless thousands of ravenous entities his talent had peeled down to vulnerability and redeemed with tender compassion, this one did not seize upon his disadvantage. It did not rip hungrily into his essence, hating the blood and the bone of him. Rather than savage him in his defeat, this intelligence met his terror with a gentle pity that steadied his measures to haunted wistfulness. Shocked soul deep, he found his tears streamed for a pain all his own, with himself, the bird caged with clipped wings.

Immersed, he could not tear his rapt focus away. The net of his true Name surrounded him without struggle, soft as a caul, even as the ringing chords under his hands sealed the framework of his imperative summoning.

His wily contender was no wraith at all, *and on this day, never had been.* Enthralled by the gift of his own nature, he beheld the trickster at the last, illumined by the living force of his music, now upraised to the beacon flare of true magecraft. He faced another veiled crone, not the same who had delivered the lyranthe: that one was never his friend.

This woman wore no shimmering violet mantle. Her cuffs were not banded with scarlet. Instead, a single ribbon of white silk shone moon silver against her plain robe of grey wool.

Initiate discipline quelled the shocked reflex that urged him to stop off his strings and unspin this illusion of substance. Blind rage could at least seize that destructive outlet, even at risk of unravelling the most vital part of himself. Yet before his lightning reflex forced annihilation, she tilted her veiled head and spoke.

'Choose wisely.' Voice she had, tender enough to wrench his exposed heart-strings.

Wracked foolish with dread, all but paralyzed by fear of the price he might pay if he dared to listen, he fought the dark pull of his agony. Dispossessed, he owned nothing else but his music. Will defended that talent. Although sorely afraid, he cherished the strings, infallibly striking the notes that refined the connection, strung thin as a cobweb between them.

'You are finished with banishing free wraiths,' the crone said with ineffable gentleness. 'That hideous trial is over.'

But he heard the clear warning she left unspoken, laced through his echoed counterpoint: that his future course of confinement extended without the fierce solace of the lyranthe. The other hag in her purple robes well knew that his gift for song might be turned to forge the key to wrest back his freedom.

His pealing cry of resentment retorted: repeatedly he had tested the enspelled barrier that hemmed him! Whenever he tried to break through, other forces would answer, bleeding him until he lay helplessly prostrate. The silvery walls of sealed spells locked him down under twisted skeins of revilement. If he ventured too close, he trod a verbal bed of live coals that burned him to humiliation beyond endurance. He crumpled, each time, savaged by accusations that pierced without mercy: '*You have destroyed the woman you loved, left her forgotten and abandoned. Ruin walks in your footsteps. Behold the days when you trampled down hope. Come forward, only to suffer again! Walk your scarlet-soaked battle-fields and acknowledge your legions of slaughtered dead.*'

The veiled woman wept in sympathy with him. While his music transmitted the relentless sting of his cringing nerves, she did not spurn him with scorn. As if he was not wretched, or defiled beyond bearing, she answered with consolation.

'You are not all they say. Truth has many facets, and your eyes have borne witness to more depths than most. If anyone claims that you sold yourself out, and betrayed every love you once cherished, I say otherwise. Your past never followed the ruinous path, as your captors claim, to your detriment. Oh, you have wept! You have survived horrors. Truly, you have suffered all measure of grief, your inner heart cannot lie to you. But emotions can be manipulated to extract an undue toll of cruelty. Never bow to defeat! Not once have you forsaken the ground you stood with steadfast integrity, and even bled to secure.'

He let his notes answer, distrustful of words. What facts supported her bed-rock assurance? Against the conditioned responses he *knew,* her contrary statement meant nothing.

She did not disagree. Would not belittle the terror that clamoured, racing his breath until the black-out pall of self-hatred threatened to crush him.

'Doubt frames the walls of your prison,' she said. 'Some of your uncertainties hide deeper truths. Others mask distortions and outright falsehoods, crafted by design to break down your spirit and finally destroy you. Are you alive enough to fight back?'

Battle, he knew. His bitter contests with uncounted free wraiths affirmed his hard-won experience. No matter how often he tasted defeat, his core fire would not stay doused. He might not *remember* his history, or the deeds he had written by choice, under Name. But through his skilled hands upon the lyranthe, his defiant joy shouted, undimmed and unbeaten.

Behind her grey veil, the old woman laughed. 'True as the line of your birthright,' she mused. 'Never let go! Not until you reclaim the blood-born right to your whole being.'

She extended her hand and dangled before him a shining white crystal, strung on a silver chain. 'This quartz holds the spell that imprisons your spirit. Sing for your liberty with passionate grace, and the matrix that binds you must shatter.'

Urgency thrummed the strings under his hands. His rushed pulse chased the reach of his terror. Yet no hesitation remarked the shift as he changed the intent that founded his next measures. Where, before, his shaped art aligned outward to seek the Name of another, now, he pitched his quest inward to ignite the lamp at the source of himself.

The first clear notes he struck from the heart collapsed the sensory web of his perception. Falling, he tumbled. His aware grasp on the lyranthe dissolved as his balance upended.

Then a *snap!* ripped through his tumbling frame. The old woman vanished, along with the featureless, dreary envelope that sealed his long-term confinement.

In place of the null grip of emptiness, he stood, ankle deep in muddy loam. Disoriented, utterly, by the nip of brisk wind, he smelled damp leaves, and the tang of hoar-frost on thickets and grasses. The sudden shock of concrete aware-ness smashed over his uprooted perception and shattered his equilibrium. Dizzied by the abrupt transition, he crashed to his knees. The jar of firm ground jolted his bones and snapped his teeth shut, while panic spurred his raced pulse and tensioned his breathing.

Who was he? Where was he? No memory of the bodily self he inhabited explained how he came – *from where* – to awake as though dropped from the void into this sere autumn garden. He stared, benighted, and left at a loss.

Grey mist dripped off a tangle of grape-vines, laddered up a weathered trellis that leaned on a ruined stone wall. The chill in the air suggested daybreak, thickened by the mouldering fust of turned leaves. Whiskered ice silvered the vegetable plot where he shivered, distressed and disoriented. The last hardy stems and a few runners of gourd still hoarded the green bestowed by the last kiss of summer. A wooden rake lay fallen nearby. Sweat laced his wrists, and mud stained the patched cuffs of his shirt and breeches. As if all along, he had laboured to mulch the tough stubble left after a late-season harvest. He had worked the earth here – who knew for how long – to tidy the rows of a field bedded to lie fallow for winter.

Which situation made no living sense, disconnected from all that he knew of existence.

He traced the coarse, callused skin of his palms with a shudder of stark disbelief. These cracked nails and chapped knuckles *had not, in this place, ever wrought superlative music on the fret and string of any earthly instrument.* Every artful line of his own refined melody deserted his cognizance, lost to him as though hurled to oblivion.

Nameless, rudderless, homeless, he wept shining tears for he knew not what – perhaps he ached for gratitude, perhaps for grief, perhaps for a talent he may never have owned, except in the fled echo of dreams.

Or maybe he cried for the merciless hurt inflicted by bewildered confusion.

The only congruity left was the scars, graven into the chapped grain of his skin. They alone marked the frightful proof of a history that *some event, or someone* had snatched away, then left him bereft. Beneath a brightening sky, buffeted by a southerly wind that forepromised the misery of cold rain by evening, he shook off his distress and reclaimed his feet. A resiliency he had forgotten he possessed raised his courage to survey the landscape. Ahead, a wrought-iron gateway led through the crumbled wall. The barred portal hung open. Chafed mad by confinement, he kicked clear of the furrow that mired his toes. Whether the way out was a baited trap, he welcomed the reckless risk. Though the impulsive presumption should kill him, he assayed the first bold step towards the overgrown lane, that led towards the unkempt fringe of autumn woodland beyond the gap.

No one's hand stopped him. When no outcry arose in alarm, he tried another stride, then another. Then he stumbled headlong into a run, upon legs that felt clumsy and strange, bearing his ungainly weight.

He never sighted the lady in grey though she observed his terrified departure. Concealed in one of the tangled thickets that bounded the deserted garden, she took extreme care not to draw his attention. Motionless, she watched his panicked spurt down the carriage-way, once in antiquity paved with white gravel to welcome refined guests to an earl's summer palace. The ancient woman relaxed her clasped hands and sighed in grateful relief.

Blessed she was, to assist the release of a spirit intact and unbroken.

For the prisoner just restored to liberty had endured an incarceration far longer than any mortal being should ever be made to withstand.

Once his flight reached the tree-line, barely moments after his lonely form vanished from sight, the crone knelt amid the browned stems of wild thorn. She opened her clenched and bloodied palms and buried the smeared fragments of shattered crystal and broken links that remained of the sigil-forged chain that had bound him. Tears of bitter anger striped her withered cheeks as she rammed cold earth overtop the unpleasant remnants. For his life's sake, no more could be done to assist his escape without danger.

Her fugitive must be left alone on the run. To survive the long reach of his enemies, he would take the harsh road to rediscover himself. If he had been granted the most slender chance to foil the deadly pursuit of the captors who soon would be hunting him, she could not spare him from the brutal whip-lash of consequence: *the obliteration of his identity provided his only protection.* No friendly hand could shield him from the blow, when in due time he encountered how sorrowfully he had been sold out and betrayed.

The crone's prayer was not empty as she turned her back on the man whose charge had encompassed her life's work. 'May Mother Dark's powers lend you the strength to stand your firm course through the maelstrom.'

On the very same crisp autumn morning, already saddled with troubles that threatened a crofter's mean livelihood, two brothers worked side by side, set at odds, as they hitched the yoked ox to the wagon shafts. Neither guessed, at the time, what that fateful market-day trip into Kelsing would bring. Except for the unusual, fierce pitch of their argument, nothing about their hard-nosed, haunted quiet seemed out of the ordinary. The bushels of apples and crates of runt poultry bound for sale had already been loaded. Square jaws clenched, their seething rage crammed into hurtful silence, Efflin and Tarens both struggled, and failed, to bury the axe resharpened by their wounded grief.

The toll taken by last summer's outbreak of fever had been too swift, and their losses, too tragically recent. No more would their badgering nephews pull pranks. No filched lengths of garden twine, strung underfoot, tripped up the feet of the unwary. No rash little hands misdirected the buckles and entangled the harness, or exasperated them with the endearing hindrance, as hysterical poultry flapped free of mischievously unlatched crates. Never again would their chatterbox aunt pounce into the fracas, or tuck in loose shirttails with floury hands. Adult males and wild offspring alike would not wince as she scolded over their foolish laughter and larking idiocy.

Which hurt that much worse, when the shouting match over the surly bull's fate devolved from scorched language to fisticuffs. Big men, as honest with fights as they were with the stewardship of family assets, both brothers now puffed, grazed scarlet as schoolboys, stiffly nursing the sting of scuffed knuckles.

'Could be we'll regret not keeping yon beef on the hoof to ease the pinch at midwinter,' said Tarens. Tenderly, he fingered the bruise that swelled into a noxious, black eye. Not the price of his brother's mulish punch, but from a headlong bash into a fence-post, caused by the cantankerous, four-legged creature his argument still defended.

'Be claimed off us for our unpaid taxes, first!' Efflin snapped, shoulders hunched, with his back turned. Leaf brown beside his younger sibling's blond fairness, he scowled under his hat brim and waited. Since the snorting, loose bull still rampaged at large, not yet ready to settle and graze, he declared, 'Sell that brute for a breeder, we could pay off the debt. Maybe have a little left over. A brace of coneys could set young in time for the feast over solstice.'

'Without corn to fatten them? They'd just grow ribs.' Tarens braced himself upright, forced to maintain a resentful stand-off while the parked wagon propped his shaky legs. 'Shadow take the damned coin and the rabbits! We can't brazen through a live sale since you know the randy calves by that bullock would be hell-bound to suffer abuse.'

Efflin rounded, fists cocked to strike, when their younger sister Kerelie burst, railing, out of the cottage door.

'Leave you to yourselves, and here's both of you, trading blows like two frothing theosophers!' She snatched her embroidered skirt clear of the frost-rimed mud. A wet dish-cloth bunched over her stout forearm, she thrust into the fray with a raw slice of meat robbed off the hook in the pantry. The cut was too choice to succour a sibling, never mind one whose daft habit of sentiment had lately laid him out cold in the barn-yard. 'Here's a fine supper, wasted! Aren't we burdened enough, without you louts bickering fit to break your necks?'

The work and the winter would not forgive the fact they were drastically short-handed. Still huffing, Kerelie tossed the chilled meat to the reeling victim.

Then she laced into her unrepentant older brother, whose level good sense had flown south since their untimely inheritance placed him at the head of the household. 'Tarens is right! 'Tis a hazard to breed that cantankerous beast, and no! You will not sell it dear for its ugly temperament! That's cruelty. The dastards who buy such rogues use them to bait their vicious dogs for blood-sport wagers!'

Efflin tipped back the lumpish felt hat that lent him the semblance of an unsheared ram. Eyebrows raised, without sympathy for his battered younger brother, he stonewalled his sister with a stoic shrug, wiped a blood smear from his split lip, and that fast, caught the black bullock. With its nose ring roped fast to the tail-gate, the brute pawed and gored the stout slats, unaware it had wrecked its last claim to long life and a docile maturity.

The beast snorted yet when the wagon rolled out, dragging it towards the stock-yard and slaughter. The brothers perched side by side on the seat, their broad shoulders rubbed by the jounce at each bump. They winced with the same hissed breaths as the vehicle swayed to the rake of the furious animal's capped horns. The bone-jarring journey to Kelsing market promised them no respite from their ill-gotten injuries. A stupid predicament, which once would have made them the butt of their uncle's banter.

But the care-free family of those days had gone. Truth brooded amid their sullen silence: that the bull's sale might buy a month's time but not turn the tide of bad fortune. Rigid tradition still ruled in the westlands: a married man always left home to increase the prosperity of his wife's family. This moment's immoderate pain was a pittance against straits that could force them to sacrifice their remaining measure of happiness.

The wagon rolled into the morning's choked mist and turned north on the rutted trade-road that wound through the wood. Already, the maples had shed their foliage cloaks of bright russet and flame. The crabbed oaks wore drab brown, shorn of acorns. The spoked wheels turned, sucking, through the ice-glazed puddles, and grated where frost crusted the verges. Only the mourning doves' doleful calls fluted through the overcast gloom.

Determinedly buoyant in his muddy clothes, Tarens started to whistle, while Efflin clutched at sore ribs and withdrew, his scowl ingrained as chipped wood. The patience that had been his virtuous mainstay had disappeared with their burned dead. Soon enough, his tense brooding would drop a wet blanket back over his brother's vivacious spirit.

Like Kerelie, Tarens refused to dwell on the problem, that the croft demanded more coin than they owned. Half of the harvest rotted in the field for the lack of strong hands to wield the scythe and hay-rake. The milch-cow in the barn was too aged to breed, which a healthy bull's service to a neighbour's dairy herd might have done something to remedy.

'The pair of you ought to be facing the butcher's knife, and not that savage wretch of a beeve, who should've been culled as a yearling!' The puckered scar on her cheek shadowed under the rim of her pert straw bonnet, Kerelie wrung out the dish-cloth and gave up her effort to dab the stains off her holiday finery. The spatters of meat juice already set, without lye soap and a pail of hot water.

Her grumbled oath made the jaunty tune pause.

'Forget that we never asked for a nurse-maid,' her cheerful brother pointed out, reasonable. 'Are you going to geld me to settle the score?' Tarens liked his risks spicy, though usually not by acting as shield for star-crossed, recalcitrant livestock.

Efflin risked a baleful glance sidewards. 'More of somebody's bloodshed never did gag a woman hell-bent on a scolding.'

'I ought to whack someone's bravado, straight off!' Kerelie shoved a strayed wisp of wheat hair underneath the delicate row of blue flowers stitched into her headscarf. Flushed pink, she gazed fondly at her brothers' broad backs, alike in size and yet so different in demeanour.

Of course, the belligerent idiots behaved as though neither had just hammered the other to pulped flesh and cracked ribs. Tarens returned a wolf's grin, brazen calm flaunting his innocence, while Efflin goaded the plodding ox with his felt-cap jammed down to his ears. The odd little goat-bell some past affectation had tied onto the band gave sweet tongue, belying his sour expression. The tucked feather, sported for the courtship that, somehow, he never found time for, defied the low cloud that threatened a drizzle.

Kerelie attacked, moved by fierce affection. 'A good thing you bumble-butts have no children to hobble the next generation.'

Where Tarens's gleeful insouciance failed, Kerelie's nagging at last lifted Efflin's grim mood: the brothers exchanged pointed glances from equally guileless blue eyes. Having made rueful peace, in sore need of distraction from their hitched groans of discomfort, they vied to see which one would bait their sister's flaying tongue first.

'Stubborn? Me?' Efflin snorted. His flicked finger jingled the ridiculous bell, mocking her fire-brand common sense. 'I can't take that prize, sweet. Not since the time you kissed the neighbour's mule on the muzzle in an attempt to make friends when it bit you.'

'Once!' Kerelie howled. 'I was three years of age!' Would anyone ever mature enough to overlook that blighted mistake?

As Tarens's broad smile renewed the embarrassment, Kerelie slapped his wrist, then masked her rioting blush, bent in half, as a squabble among the crated hens drew her repressive notice. More than one stabbing beak sought to rip the rush baskets and peck holes in the harvested apples. Through a shriek meant to shock thieving poultry out of their natural appetite, she buried the branding humiliation: that her face was grotesquely spoiled, no matter how neatly the village healer had stitched her ripped cheek. She cringed to count the grasping suitors lately chased from the door with thrown pots. None of them had trampled the garden-path muddy before Uncle's death left an inheritance.

She would be forced to marry. If her brothers remained too kindly to speak, they must broach the sore subject, and soon. A croft in dire straits for the lack of grown field-hands could not stall for long while she pined for a love match.

'Folly lights up no candles, dear girl,' Efflin soothed, wisely quick to dismiss the mishap that marred her porcelain complexion. 'And Tarens won't sow anyone's moronic by-blow, today. The strumpets will snatch coin for his kisses, up front. Unless, with that toad's mug, he plans to hide his licks at the butcher's?'

'Why would he?' Kerelie shot up straight in offence. 'Most women turn into simpering idiots shown a damned fool with an injury!'

'And you never dote on the lame ducks, yourself? Then I don't smell cinnamon bread in that basket, and we all never noticed how much you loathe baking.' Tarens's snorted laughter transformed to a cough, as her toe poked into his banged ribs. Sobered, not chastised, he ploughed ahead, 'A bashed eye from a bull is no hero's fare.'

'The damaged tomcat better make himself scarce!' Kerelie turned her unmarked cheek and warned, 'Forbye, who said the basket was brought for your sake?'

Tarens laughed, boyish dimples and handsome features rugged with the sunburn peel on his hawk nose. 'Never claimed, did I, that you had good taste.' Sheepish, he ducked Efflin's fraternal cuff and avoided being knocked off the wagon seat.

'You randy louts!' Kerelie shrieked. 'Your manners alone will wreck my last hope of netting a decent husband!'

But Efflin wheezed because he was chuckling. The three of them never could stay at odds for long. 'Doused in beef juice,' he quipped, 'your smell's about right.'

'To impress someone's hog? Good thing, then, we need to,' Tarens said, suddenly serious. As his sister glared back, fair brows pinched with outrage, he winked. 'Lure ourselves a stud pig, that's the issue, directly. Her highness at home's stopped producing.' Owlish, he added, 'That's been true since the night Efflin downed uncle's stash of rye whiskey. Did you know he mistook the stall with the cow? I caught him shoved in with the farrow, his lewd mitts busy squeezing the sow's udder.'

The chickens were left their free take of the fruit as Kerelie groaned, giggles muffled behind her chapped palms. She tried not to imagine what might have prompted that odd bout of maudlin drunkenness.

'Oink,' Tarens gasped, then dodged like a weasel, aware he had earned another black eye from his brother's punitive fist.

But no trouncing rejoinder hammered him flat.

Efflin was too busy, hauling back on the reins to slow the yoked plod of the ox. Abused leather harness squeaked in complaint. The trundling wagon slewed in the ruts and jerked the bullock on its short tether. Through the bucketing creak as stout wood took the strain, the vehicle ground to a stop just in time to avoid the odd fellow whose aimless stance blocked the roadway.

'Light's grace!' exclaimed Kerelie, above the distressed cackle of upended hens. 'Is that someone's lost child?'

But the drifting mist unveiled a grown man, mistaken by his slight stature. Back turned, unaware that his loitering obstructed traffic, he wore a laborer's seedy clothes. The hard-worn cloth had been repeatedly mended, the original color lost beneath a tatterdemalion motley of patches. His stained knee breeches, napped hose, and holed shoes were dirt-caked, their style beyond recognition. Filthy hair nested with snapped twigs and leaves hung in snarled hanks to his shoulders.

Efflin's shout did not chase him out of the thoroughfare but raised a flinch that near startled him out of his skin. His unkempt face turned. An unshaven black tangle of beard buried most of his features. Not the whites of his eyes, distinct with alarm as he stared in blank shock. Despite his sad state of frightful neglect, his manner seemed too confused to be dangerous. His empty hands dangled, unthreatening.

Nonetheless, Efflin reached for the cudgel wedged behind the cart's buckboard.

'That's no marauding bandit.' Tarens's urgent grip on his brother's wrist checked the move to brandish the weapon.

'You're that sure he's not been sent out as bait?' Brass chinked, as Efflin tipped his hatted head towards the wood, where late-season briar laced the dense undergrowth, dank with fog, and impenetrable. 'If that's a tinker, then someone unfriendly's already lifted his pack.'

'Here?' Kerelie scoffed, too riveted to brush out the hen feathers snagged in her sleeve. 'Don't be a fright-monger!' Astute when it counted, she gestured towards the tipsy stone finials that loomed through the murk a stone's throw to the left. Those moss-splotched markers were well-known, even feared, where the overgrown track branched off the trade-route.

Efflin's ruddy face flamed. The site was no place for wise folk to linger. Travellers avoided the tangled lane, which led into the ancient ruin. Oftentimes, Koriathain practised their uncanny rituals there. When the enchantresses pitched their silken pavilions amid the tumble-down walls of the grounds, or if birch smoke rose from the crumbled chimneys, the charcoal men who cut trees for their kilns did their rough-house drinking in taverns, safe behind Kelsing's brick walls. They spoke of queer doings in whispers, while the ivied remains of the Second Age hall were reclaimed by the order's sisters. Nobody dared to stray past the wood or till the rich soil of the fallow pastures.

This had been true well before the Light's avatar had tamed the Mistwraith's malevolence. Older legends held that the place harboured haunts from the days before Mankind settled Athera.

Like most Taerlin crofters, Efflin and his family were blessed for the Light since their birth. They went out of their way to avoid the wild places where the mysteries were believed to linger. Such arcane trouble as walked in the world was best left to the dedicate priests. Sound sense suggested their wagon ought to be set rolling at once.

Except the bewildered man in the way displayed no inclination to move.

Efflin shook off his brother's clamped hold. 'Why not make yourself useful? Step down and shift that seedy fellow aside.'

'I say he isn't right in the head.' Tarens flexed his shoulders to mask his uneasiness. Deliberate, as if nonchalant, he arose, ahead of the moment his sister lost patience and fetched him a kick on the backside. He slid to the ground. His solid build should deter anyone's urge to pick a fight or try robbery.

'Don't place undue trust in mild appearances,' Kerelie blurted, concerned.

'Who's the fright-monger, now?' Yet Tarens honoured her anxious prompt and lifted his quarterstaff from the wagon-bed. Step by easy step, as though stalking a poised hare, he closed on the befuddled stranger.

The brazen creature regarded him, motionless. Close up, his eyes were a startling green, brilliantly clear, and focused to a frenetic intensity. Drilled by that keen survey, Tarens felt the bristle of hair at his nape. 'Who are you?' he asked, cautious.

The stranger presented his opened hands. If he understood language, he chose not to answer. His fixated regard never left Tarens's face. Diviners who owned arcane Sight had that look: as though they could read a man, past and present, then project the unwritten course of his fortune and sense his future demise.

'Who are you?' Tarens repeated.

The man's uncanny regard showed him emptiness. As though human speech chased his thoughts beyond desolate, he seemed absorbed by an unseen inner vista that stretched forlorn and unutterably lacking. He might stand on two legs as a man. But the rapt poignancy of his expression suggested he grasped no firm concept by which to define himself, or anything else in the world he inhabited.

Tarens shivered. Distrust dissolved to heart-rending pity, he pronounced in swift reassurance, 'He's a lack-wit.'

The queer fellow listened, head tipped to one side, but without sign of comprehension.

'I mean you no harm,' Tarens added, contrite. 'I only thwap others who cross me, besides. Mostly, after my brother hammers me, first.' Aware that his purpled eye lent him a frightening aspect, Tarens slowly shifted the quarterstaff into the crook of his elbow. By nature, he was prepared to be gentle as he eased the odd vagabond clear of the road.

'Any idea where he came from?' Kerelie ventured from her anxious seat in the wagon-bed.

'No.' Tarens grasped the man's ragged shoulder. The unsavoury shirt was

15

too thin for the season, and the bony frame, disgracefully underfed. Outraged, he exclaimed, 'Wherever that was, naught can forgive the wrongful fact someone was starving him.'

'We're not hauling a stray!' Efflin bellowed, at once shouted down by Kerelie's protest.

'For shame! Would you turn a blind eye on misfortune? If the man's a simpleton, how can we not show him kindness?'

Efflin grumbled, unmollified, 'You're that sure he's not one of the ungrateful orphans, scarpered from the witches' protection?'

'Nonsense!' Kerelie batted his arm. 'Since when has a boy ward of theirs grown a beard?' Truth disarmed the argument. Koriathain always placed their male charges with an honest apprenticeship before they reached virile manhood.

'Worse,' Efflin persisted, 'we could be caught harbouring one of their order's half-witted servants.'

Which cruel guess was the more likely prospect. Rumors and grannies' tales said Koriathain coveted idiots for the brainless service of fetching and carrying. Coin endowments, word held, were awarded for deaf-mutes. Ones unable to read or write could not betray the order's secretive business. 'If that creature's stumbled away from such keepers, we're not safe assisting a runaway.'

Tarens overheard. Susceptible to soft-heartedness, he jumped at fresh cause to brangle with his older brother. 'I wouldn't leave my worst enemy, here!' If his prized bull must be condemned to the knacker's knife, he had never allowed better sense to abet any form of mistreatment. Nor would he stand for the callous abuse of a person luckless enough to be moonstruck.

Efflin understood well enough when to humour his brother's obstinacy. 'Lead the wretch here, then. We'll grant him a ride into Kelsing and leave him the coin to buy a hot meal.' He set the brake, resigned, looped the reins, and climbed down to restrain the bull, while Kerelie pulled the latch pins and lowered the tail-board.

If the creature had been a witch's familiar, he stayed docile as Tarens boosted him into the wagon. He curled up by the chicken crates, knees hugged to his chest, soothed by the ponderous rumble of wheels, and contentedly pleased to watch the autumn landscape pass by. When the ox-wain trundled into the sprawling farm market, shadowed beneath Kelsing's walls, he observed with bright eyes as Efflin hauled the ox to a stop. Before Tarens could hitch the draught beast to a rail, the fellow leaped out, saw where he was needed, and with no one's asking, helped Kerelie unload the baskets and poultry. His small size masked an unexpected, fierce strength. He hefted the heaviest crates without difficulty and arranged them as she directed for display and sale.

While Efflin took charge and untied the bull, Tarens dug into his scrip. The last silver left to his name, he placed in the vagabond's hand. Sadness struck him afresh, that the man's nails were dirt-rimed, and his palm, welted over with callus.

Peculiar, how those oddities niggled. Tarens had never heard mention that Koriathain worked the land or kept destitutes for field labor. He shrugged off curiosity, aware by the heat on his back that the risen sun burned through the mist. Already he risked being late to nose-lead the beeve to its fate at the butcher's. Loose half-wits were scarcely his problem, besides. At large in the open market, someone might recognize the mute stranger and claim him.

If not, surely the industrious fellow might find some sort of menial labor in town. Aware he was unwanted, he moved off unasked, to assist an old woman who struggled to lift hampers of yarn from a neighbouring wagon. Diligent as he seemed, the local tavern might hire him to scrub tankards and sweep.

'He will be better off,' Efflin snapped, and dealt Tarens a shove to break his reverie. 'Anything here offers much better prospects than blocking the trade-road for shiftless amusement.'

Hard Reckoning

The Fellowship Sorcerer entered the order's sisterhouse at Whitehold empty-handed, his purpose to close the terms of an ancient score, declared in an hour of bitter defeat on a morning well over two centuries ago. He came clothed in formality. His robe of immaculate indigo velvet brushed the marble floor, while the silver braid that bordered his sleeves gleamed in the early sun shafted through the hall's sea-side windows. Pale steel were his eyes, steady as he took the measure of the Prime Matriarch of the Koriathain, enthroned in state panoply to meet him.

Always dangerous, the enchantress sat above everyone else in the room. Her coquette's beauty was regaled in the deep purple gown and red ribbons of her supreme office, and her massive chair, atop a canopied dais, over-shadowed the initiate sisters selected to witness the momentous audience. Where the Sorcerer was required to stand at her feet, his immense strength leashed in stilled patience, she glittered in extravagant triumph. Pale aquamarine were her eyes, hard as her jewels of amethyst and diamond, and just as stone cold, while she savoured her moment to hound him to humiliation.

She had cornered his game, or so she believed. The flicker of gilt thread in the gloves worn to mask her grotesquely scarred hands all but shouted her defiant scorn. Peremptory, invigorated by the thrill of her victory, she gestured for him to open the proceedings.

'Prime Matriarch,' he greeted, too self-contained to sound cowed, though the grandiose hall with its stone-vaulted splendour had been staged for demeaning spite. Lean and tall though the Sorcerer was, the soaring pillars that upheld the domed ceiling diminished his upright stature. More, the silent regard of the ranked Senior sisters picked to share his Fellowship's demise seared the atmosphere to contempt.

The weathered lines on the Sorcerer's features might have been quarried, with his hawk's profile straitly expressionless. 'I have come in accord to confirm the reckoning owed by our mutual promise.'

Perfect with youth, though she was in fact aged, her vitality engineered by dark spellcraft that had repeatedly cheated mortality, the Prime Matriarch tipped her coiffed head to acknowledge his careful greeting. 'Asandir.' Her coral lips turned, a smile made cordial by poisonous satisfaction. 'We accept, by your presence, the promised acknowledgement that your Fellowship's debt is now due. The last invasive free wraith from Marak has been duly banished by Athera's Masterbard. The event occurred yesterday. This dawn, by the covenant carved onto stone in the King's Chamber at Althain Tower, the stay of execution your Fellowship demanded on behalf of Prince Arithon of Rathain is named forfeit. Our order's sovereignty requires his death. By the pledge held and sworn by Crown auspices to Koriathain, and sealed by the prophet apprentice under your Fellowship's oversight, we choose to reject a further hearing.'

Asandir said nothing.

Stung, perhaps, by his dead-pan silence, Prime Selidie sat forward and jabbed. 'My order will seize its deferred satisfaction! Did you really believe our initial demand would be softened by your past effrontery when you forced our hand?'

Malice spiked the Prime's anger. The sweet hour of ascendancy heated her blood, all the more rich since the vicious riposte thrust upon her by the Fellowship Sorcerers' underhand tactic: a deadly influx of wraiths unleashed on the world as their ruthless weapon in counter-threat. Unconscionably, they had gambled! The survival of Mankind on Athera had been callously tossed on the board as their bargaining chip, with the innocent populace placed at risk under a lethal threat to buy Arithon's chance for reprieve. Centuries she had waited for the deferred moment to exact her treasured revenge. She fully intended to relish this long-sought, moral requital.

'Such arrogance!' Selidie chided, drunk on the precedent that the Sorcerer stood at her mercy. 'Did you lie awake night after night, all these years, hopeful that time would soften our committed stance?'

Asandir only inclined his head, hair glinted white in the unkind glare that stabbed down from the lancet window.

'Well, our terms have not changed.' The Prime restated, crisp, 'I will have the Koriathain released from the tyranny of your compact. Grant our demand. Or Prince Arithon dies before sundown. For his life, and the continuance of Rathain's royal lineage, how will your Fellowship plead?'

'We choose not to plead,' Asandir stated, quiet. 'The old law that grants humanity's right to exist on Athera remains intact. And enforced! We stand upon principle. My dear!' he exclaimed, not amused as the Matriarch stiffened. 'Should my ultimatum surprise you? This world's future has never been mine to bequeath! Mankind dwells here by the grace of our surety. That interest is our charge to balance and never set under your order's purview to negotiate!'

Selidie's eyes narrowed. Her malice had roots. Beyond question, she knew: Arithon s'Ffalenn was the linch-pin on which the Fellowship's purpose depended; also, the cipher to leverage her gain. If Asandir would not bend his terms, if his Fellowship's stance remained obdurate, she would follow through. Arithon would be killed, and with no mercy, if only to void the old prophecy that forecast the failure of her succession.

'I live for the day!' the Matriarch pronounced. 'Your stubborn ethics have just signed the death warrant for your captive prince.'

Asandir raised open hands. 'So be it.' Like rinsed granite, his face, as he added, 'My course of noninterference is hereby confirmed. Expect me to remain as the Fellowship's witness. I will stay present only until the bitter ending's accomplished.'

Selidie regarded him, dissecting his manner to gauge the hidden depths of his discomfort. Field Sorcerer to the Fellowship, he would keep his adamant poise, along with the letter of his spoken pledge: no record in history ran contrary. Nonetheless, the air trembled, taut as a roughly plucked string. The breadth of raw power in his contained presence could have broken the natural rise and set of the sun.

Selidie laughed until the hall echoed. 'Your Warden should have sent someone more inventive! How the collar and leash must chafe your proud neck! Or is this a novelty? A twisted attempt to pique your jaded nerves? Are you grown tired enough in your dotage to find relief as a passive observer?'

'I am waiting,' said Asandir, clipped impatient. 'My word, struck in closure, is all you require.'

'Do as I say, and be done here?' Prime Selidie laid the swathed stumps of her hands on the purple silk over-dress, artfully draped over her lap. Her sharp focus heightened like a hunting cat's toying with a pinned mouse. 'Should I rush the moment? When every exchange made with you before this has demeaned our needs as a pittance?' Emotion leaked through, the first tremor of rage, transmitted by volcanic fury. 'How does it feel, now the tables have turned? Should I not enjoy watching your years of planned strategies flicked hither and yon, hapless as chaff in a storm wind?'

On an occasion less fraught with peril, Asandir might have smiled before he attacked. 'Glendien's bastard daughter threw a wrench in your works? Is it true, as I've heard, that every quartz crystal she ever touched became shattered to fragments? I could relieve your order of that embarrassment. If her natural father is condemned to die, you've no further need for a hostage to guarantee our share of the bargain. I would gladly accept on my Fellowship's behalf if the Koriathain would release Teylia back to us.'

'What! Leave you the means to extend your pestiferous royal lineage and seat a successor on Rathain's vacant throne?' Selidie gloated outright. 'Not a chance! Teylia was wrested away from your charge. Inept or not, even aged past senility, she may find a useful place in our order yet. No. Her loyalty stays tied to me. Unless you would care to rethink your position and release your ironclad grip, binding my will to your compact?'

The Sorcerer inclined his head, his large hands with their capable callus and the worn tracery of scarred experience now lowered and quiet. 'Impasse. I rest my case.'

No more could be said. He would not lie. Even by inference, he dared not tip his hand. His last wild card must stay invisible: that the secret truth, and all of the facts still in play with regard to Prince Arithon's issue, were not, and never had been, made known to Selidie Prime. Terrible, the self-restraint that checked Asandir's urge to speak his mind; overwhelming, his fury for the twisted practice that permitted the abomination he confronted on the dais to live. He capped his latent rage for the abhorrent abuses that kept Selidie's creamy skin smooth; smothered his heart's need to let fly with rebuke for her cruelty, which once had commanded the separation of a three-year-old girl from the arms of her widowed mother.

While Selidie drew out his agonized wait, well aware how her practice offended, Asandir checked his torrential emotions. His nerves must withstand the terrible course!

Exposed, he endured the grueling pause, as the Prime prolonged the climactic chance to snatch her long-sought recompense. Too viciously clever to act on rash eagerness, she expected to cede him a failure to trump the annals of abject defeat.

For her crowning blow, she chose insult. 'I shall not rely on your spoken word.' Unable to resist the temptation, she meant to bond him with the validation demanded of common petitioners. Her tight gesture encompassed the gleaming white marble that paved the floor under his feet. 'Seal your promise, Sorcerer. As was done before at Althain Tower, I would have your surety set into stone.'

An offence, past impertinent, fashioned to desecrate every clean ethic he cherished! Asandir bent his head. This was no time to give way to weakness.

'Do this on your knees!' Prime Selidie crowed, enraptured to vindication.

But the matter at stake did not stand or fall upon the blows to his dignity. Asandir knelt. His height made the gesture convincingly awkward. The long fingers he laid flat were a workaday labourer's, the strong, weathered knuckles strangely naked against the pale mineral. No artifice masked his humility as he begged the stone slab to grant him forgiveness. His requisite permission was asked with apology for the betrayal: that the quarried marble came from a mountain under the sovereign charge of Rathain.

Asandir braced his will. He must proceed! The past's cruel balance had to be served, despite the unknown course of the outcome. Nothing could be raised out of ashes if he failed to shoulder the crux. Under a loyalty commandeered by the dragons, his obligations had been fixed long before the dread purpose that brought him.

The quartz vein in the marble gave to his need, fearless in generosity. Into its patient suspension, the Sorcerer spoke a phrase tuned to yielding compassion. Light flashed. Between his spread palms, the firm slab blazed red and ran suddenly molten. No heat attended the empowered change. His flesh was not seared, while substance embraced transformation.

'Stone as my impartial witness, behold!' intoned Asandir, hammered steady. 'The terms of the Fellowship's stay of execution for Arithon Teir's'Ffalenn are withdrawn. Crown debt to Rathain, sworn at Athir, is confirmed. Koriathain are freed to determine his Grace's fate, henceforward.' The Sorcerer flipped back his right sleeve and bared a silver bracelet incised with runes. Deftly, he rolled the metal across the cherry red magma.

A swipe of his hand quelled the rouge glow. When he straightened, the paved floor underfoot subsided to its former polish: except the impressed string of ciphers remained as irrefutable proof of his vow.

'I stand on my word,' declared Asandir. 'The hour is yours for the reckoning.'

Prime Selidie's venomous gesture acknowledged the challenge that thwarted her passionate drive to claim unlicensed autonomy for Koriathain on Athera. Denied yet again, she would wreak the full score of havoc in retaliation and deny the Sorcerers their sole hope of requital.

'Bring me the closed coffer!' she commanded the enchantress in silent service behind her state chair. While the summoned Senior came forward, obedient, and proffered the requested item, the Prime's icy study of Asandir's face never wavered. 'Open the lock.'

Inside, darkened to black by the sigil fashioned to end life, rested a prepared crystal. The artifact radiated a halo of dire cold. Unfazed by its unpleasant proximity, Selidie directed her female attendant to remove her embroidered mitts and place the enabled jewel into the crippled stubs of her hands.

'Now, bring the filled basin,' she ordered, though usually others performed her brute work to spare the fumbling embarrassment of her deformity. 'I shall align the spell of fatality myself.'

Asandir looked on, eyes open, unbending, although the practice enacted before him wrenched horror and sickness down to his viscera. He held on, lips sealed against outcry, as Arithon's imprint was taken from a dried blood-stain, soaked out of a ripped scrap of cloth. The same shirt, torn off on the ruinous hour the prince had been run down and captured, now framed the foul means to target him as the Prime's victim.

By force of character, Asandir did not flinch though all could be lost! The moment brought agony as Selidie dropped the crystal with its lethal directive into the turbid solution swirled in the glass bowl . . .

* * *

Far to the west, in the garden of the ruined earl's palace where the shards of another crystal had lately been buried, a black ring of energy darkened the ground. The blight spread like ink, rippling outward, then stopped, contained by the hands of a hooded crone. She who still waited in steadfast vigil spoke no word of incantation. Shrouded in nothing else but fast silence, she let the blood heritage in her own veins intercept the vile binding, then absorb the spell's lethal directive. The hideous taint crawled up her arms. Its vicious passage blackened her flesh, then razed skin and muscle to instant corruption. Stripped to a cadaverous horror, she toppled into a grisly heap as the final breath left her lungs. Shortly, naught but a tangle of bones lay wrapped in the rags of singed clothing. Above her grotesquely murdered remains, the violent release of her spirit stirred autumn brush and rattled the frost-brittle grasses . . .

Within the grand hall at Whitehold, the basin exploded. Water whined into a cloud of white steam, and the spent crystal crumbled to powder. At Prime Selidie's shriek, her slavish attendant beat showered sparks from her hair and rich gown. The Fellowship Sorcerer observed her distress, impassive, his fierce eyes relieved.

'What have you done?' the Prime Matriarch shouted.

But, of course, upright upon bonded stone, Asandir had not lifted a finger: at his shoulder, wrapped in ephemeral spirit light, came the ghost of the departed crone. Gravely direct, his heart saddened, the Sorcerer bowed to the flame of her transient shade. 'Have I your leave, Teylia?' he asked, gently reverent. 'Your remains properly should be returned to be blessed by the Biedar tribe in Sanpashir.'

The crone's discorporate imprint smiled, fleeting, but like her wayward, importunate mother, without any shred of regret. 'Kingmaker,' she answered, 'look after your own. My birth purpose has been accomplished.'

She faded then, fully, her subtle light snuffed like a candle.

Through the chill vacancy left by her passage, the gathered sisters exchanged whispers sharpened by uneasy fear and suspicion. Prime Selidie glared above them, her soaked finery dusted with chipped quartz and glass, her volatile rage beyond perilous. 'We demanded custody of the child to vouchsafe your Fellowship's intent,' she accosted the Sorcerer. 'What did you plant by your endless deceit but a serpent into our midst?'

Asandir sighed. 'Your accusation carries no substance. Or did you brush off Sethvir's statement when you struck your vile contract and demanded a hostage of us, back at Althain Tower? Our Fellowship has never endorsed, or permitted, the parting of child and mother! Teylia chose to dedicate to your order. She declared her destiny with her first words, long before that unkind fate was asked of her.'

'As an infant, under three years of age?' The Prime Matriarch rammed straight, seethed to outrage, while her coterie of Seniors drew hissed breaths of stark disbelief.

The Sorcerer answered with unabashed sorrow. 'Don't play your line of indignant ignorance. Teylia was no commonplace child! What arts she possessed sprang direct from her birthright. Admit the straight evidence in your own records! I assure you, her advanced age was no fluke, and her fate, without ties of our Fellowship's making.'

'Spin me another false tale!' snapped the Prime. 'The woman was gifted by a precocious lineage and stubbornly wayward as well! You foisted her on us. Gave us bad blood, foreknowing such headstrong stock would never submit to our discipline! Honestly, tell me she would have suited your purpose as a candidate heir for Rathain!'

Asandir looked up at the dais, his steely glance harsh but not with pride or vindication. 'The body begotten amid the raised mysteries on that signal moment at Athir was Arithon and Glendien's, delivered by natural birth. But the spirit was purely of the old Biedar ancestry. Under the auspices of an ancient rite, Teylia's incarnate destiny was claimed by the tribal matriarch on the hour of her conception. Your sisterhood embraced that enemy's legacy at your own peril!'

But the bitter-sweet victory of today's ordained sacrifice never would console the deep ache of the Sorcerer's grief – for a small girl consigned, life to death, on cruel terms to an ignoble service: a child conceived in rare joy, brought into the world with prodigious talent, and sprung from an ancestry too mighty to tame. Asandir pressed onwards, left empty-handed, except to honour her steadfast achievement.

'I clearly warned your machinations would fail,' he told the Prime enthroned on her dais. 'So did Althain's Warden advise you with caution. Pretend you did not heed our words at the start, and I will have Sethvir recall the event, bonded under a sealed oath of truth.'

Prime Selidie fumed in her spoiled state robes. 'This will not end here! Our lawful rights have become stymied by premeditated manipulation. I demand my due forfeit. By your oath of crown debt, grant me the access you owe to my order! Give over the key to Prince Arithon's true Name.'

Now Asandir smiled. He gazed down at his feet, planted atop the runes just etched into the slab of cold marble. 'My dear, I am sorry. You have no grounds at all. I stand on my oath of noninterference, as witnessed by impartial mineral.'

Entrapped as the spider in her own web, Prime Selidie lifted her mangled hands for her diligent attendant to slip into mitts. 'Your Fellowship cannot side-step this obligation! I will take satisfaction. How dare you presume to forget? The Teir's'Ffalenn is still my kept prisoner, and through him, you shall suffer undying regret.'

'Perhaps,' Asandir allowed with dry irony.

He understood the unmalleable stakes. Upon his departure, the Prime would invoke the fury of her obsession. For hours, or days, she would seek Arithon's demise through an invocation aligned to his auric pattern. She would try and fail. For the personal imprint no longer existed, as sworn by the Mad Prophet long ago on the night sands at Athir. Arithon Teir's'Ffalenn had been stripped of that memory, along with his greater identity. Nor was the prince still confined by the Prime's power, not since the Biedar crone's secretive working at dawn smashed the crystal that constrained his consciousness.

By the earth-linked assurance, sped to Asandir on a thought from the Warden at Althain Tower, the man the Koriani Prime Matriarch would cry down for murder had just crawled, anonymous, under a tarp in a crofter's rattletrap oxcart. Precariously hidden from hostile eyes, he lay curled in oblivious sleep. As yet, no one realized he was there.

Arithon Teir's'Ffalenn was safe, for this moment. Until greater peril should stalk his location and fashion the ambush to snare him, the refugee slipped from the Prime Matriarch's clutches did not recall his own name. More, he had lost a daughter he had never known, or been told that his love had bequeathed to existence.

The Sorcerer bled with inward sorrow for that; and for the unparalleled courage that had sealed Teylia's silence through two hundred and forty-nine years of agonized secrecy. Rivers of tears should have fallen to acknowledge her selfless memory. No consolation might salve such a loss. Grieving, and saved beyond recompense by her monumental achievement, the Sorcerer tendered his final word to Selidie Prime. 'You will not threaten anyone further, today, madam! Above any faithless action of ours, your debt of constraint against Rathain's crown for now has been summarily thwarted.'

Autumn 5922

Tidings

The enchantress already knew, aware even before the visitation sent by Althain's Warden brought news. From extreme isolation, immersed in a healer's work from an old ice-cutter's hut shadowed under the aquamarine wall of the Storlain glaciers, she had sensed the profound change on the moment when shock stopped her breath in the pre-dawn chill. Her satchel of simples slipped out of her hand. All her rare herbals and specialized instruments tumbled down an alpine cliff, lost amid puffed explosions of powdery snow.

She had not paused to swear. Had scarcely cared, that her follow-up check on the trapper's wife's recent childbirth would be set back by the inconvenience.

Hours later, in daylight, after the long hike round the ridge to access the base of the vertical drop, she wept yet, whiplashed between unbridled release and bouts of joyous laughter. Gratitude overwhelmed her last grip on decorum. Never mind that her russet braid had torn loose. Or that her last pair of gloves became frayed to soaked holes at the finger-tips. She was heedlessly burrowing through rumpled drifts in search of her misplaced belongings when the shade of the Sorcerer tickled her presence.

A power to turn the world's course in his own right, he slipped in softly, a breath of deeper cold against the sharp chill of high altitude.

'He's set free!' the enchantress was first to declare, overcome once again. *Arithon.* She could not speak his name for the tears that spilled through another fierce smile of wonderment. The miracle rocked her, that she had endured: decades, then centuries, heart braced to withstand season upon season of unreconciled anguish. The onslaughts survived under crushing despair, when dreaming into the horrors he fought, she wakened each night bathed in

26

terrified sweat, gasping for mercy from every bright power that she might live to see the impossible.

A Sorcerer come hard at the heels of reprieve triggered her most fearful question. 'Whose help lent his Grace the chance to escape?'

A deep voice, wrought of wind, framed the Sorcerer's reply. 'The double-blind scheme was the careful work of the Biedar tribe of Sanpashir.' Which was no lie, except by omission. If the enchantress sensed the gravity of the particulars that weighted the statement, she was wise enough not to broach the dangerous inquiry. 'The tribe's eldest wise woman and her male dreamers invoked the world's greater mysteries,' the Fellowship emissary to Elaira hastened to qualify. 'Their reach extended across the veil and split time to achieve this triumph on Prince Arithon's behalf.'

'My Matriarch knows this,' Elaira mused, quick to wield her trained intuition as circumspect caution required. She straightened up, turned, a slender woman with misted grey eyes, but courageous past measure to face the discorporate being sent as the Fellowship's harbinger.

He stood, an illusion less solid than air, displayed before her as a dapper personage with tanned skin, and dark hair streaked white at his craggy temples. His extravagant dress was embroidered with lace, jaunty accents of emerald studs and silk ribbon agleam against elegant velvet. Orange satin cuffs set off his clever hands, expressive as his narrow, fox features and clipped spade-point beard: which aspects perfectly mirrored his rapacious preference for edged conversation.

'Kharadmon,' the enchantress greeted him, pleased. 'Always, the suave touch. This isn't an ambush?'

'Since Sethvir doesn't favour the vogue for snared hostages, no.' The image of the Sorcerer bowed, ever delighted to flights of dry irony by her tart wit. Their last meeting, of course, had been brusquely uncivil, her reproach the piquant reminder that once he had broached her close-warded cottage and disturbed her sleep while in her bed.

Today's underhand tactic of announcing himself from behind was also deliberate though not a discourtesy. His amused glance directed her attention downwards, where a zephyr winnowed the snow at his feet and exposed the strap of her buried satchel. His own flagrant flourish: a long-stemmed red rose, too fresh to seem real, pierced the pristine drift alongside. 'I'm not always ungallant. Or demanding. Or rude.'

'Intrusive,' Elaira corrected, and laughed. Flushed, she bent and accepted the bloom, her uncovered remedies left until later. 'Should I also thank your Fellowship for a scandalous hand in the prisoner's release?' Her cross-grained concern was not overlooked, however she strove to stay circumspect.

'We broke none of our covenant!' Kharadmon snapped. 'Would that we had, and years earlier!'

No need to expound upon his sudden rage: on-going for millennia, the sparring enmity between Fellowship Sorcerers and Koriani Matriarchs. A foregone conclusion, that the long, vicious pitch of the order's rivalry must entangle the pawn just wrested away from the covetous Prime's close control.

'You can protect him?' Elaira pressed gently.

Kharadmon dissolved into a self-contained whirlwind that whipped up a cyclone of ice-crystals. 'Asandir was forced to swear! He laid down an oath by the witness of stone, of Fellowship noninterference. Damn your Prime's machinations to Sithaer! The terms that completed her claim of debt towards the Crown of Rathain have extracted that ruthless stay!'

Which bad news delivered a blow to weaken the knees. Elaira drew in a bracing breath. Under the astringent blue sky of altitude, chilled in the pine-scented shade of the rock scarp, she fought for the balance to curb draining fear. If few staunch spirits could match her bold strengths, none equaled the depth of her love for Prince Arithon. Or her steel endurance, as she dared to challenge the turbulent fury repressed by the Sorcerer's shade. 'You cannot lift even one finger to help,' she accused in bald-faced distress. 'What of the Biedar? Will their shamans stand guard for your prince? Now he's freed, might they warrant his safety?'

The discorporate mage drifted to a freezing pause. 'Who knows what might move the desert tribes to act? In this world, who dares to try them? Biedar wisdom lies outside the compact.'

Elaira gaped in dumbfounded surprise. 'I never imagined! More tellingly,' she added the moment her paralyzed wits sorted consequence, 'has that sharp fact escaped the Prime Matriarch?'

'Oh, past question, she knows.' Kharadmon's image unfurled again, smiling with forthright malice. 'That sore point's a matter of recorded history, and no secret buried at Althain Tower. The Biedar people came to Athera before the terms of the compact were struck. They set foot in Sanpashir, just ahead of the Fellowship's promise of surety, which granted the rest of humanity's right to fair settlement.'

'How could that happen?' Elaira asked, stunned. She had never envisioned the paradox!

Kharadmon's grin displayed wicked humour. 'Their tribe's revered elders did not petition for leave through our Fellowship's auspices. Are you breathing? Here's the stinging fly in your Matriarch's cup! Her Biedar counterpart treated for residence directly with the Paravians.'

Staggered dizzy by her upended assumptions, Elaira required more than a moment to measure the implications. She felt as if mountains had moved at a stroke, with every familiar landmark thrown into radical rearrangement. Changed truth arrived as a blast of fresh air, that the latent power possessed by the tribes far outstripped the reach of the Prime Matriarch's bidding.

'A bit of a quandary,' she sympathized to the discorporate spirit, poised in rapt interest before her.

Kharadmon's corrosive manner turned fierce. 'Quite.' Even his Fellowship must be hard-pressed to reconcile the salient question of sovereign authority. Should Sanpashir's desert-folk choose to exert their enigmatic autonomy, the might behind their least action could throw any power on Athera an untoward wall of obstruction.

'You don't know the limits on the tribe's intentions,' Elaira needled, point-blank.

'Your guess would fall under the provenance of Sethvir,' the Sorcerer evaded with delicacy. 'Or else be found among the lore kept by Athera's living Paravians.'

But the creatures he referenced were lost to the world, and such knowledge, a quest of futility. Elaira smothered a frustrated sigh. The Warden of Althain was unlikely to send her the grace of his counsel. Sethvir's adamant silence had stayed unbroken since the desperate decision forced upon her on a lonely beachhead at Athir two hundred and fifty sad years ago. Naught remained to be said beyond dogged pursuit of what pressed Kharadmon to broach the indelicate point. 'If the Biedar cannot be trusted to act, how will my beloved defend himself against the vicious designs of my order?'

Kharadmon raised his eyebrows. He had no glib words. Nothing of comfort to soften the blow bestowed by his shattering news. 'There, rare lady, the inspiration was guided. The Biedar followed after the tactic his Grace himself used at the terrible crux, to spare you.'

'They displaced his memory?' Elaira cried, drained white, the rose fallen from her nerveless fingers. *'Left him blind to himself?* How deeply? To set him past reach of a Prime Circle's scrying . . . !' There, her appalled reason faltered.

Kharadmon stated for her, with terrible calm, 'Arithon's remembrance had to be stripped. Completely, without reservation. To stay undetected, safely out of sight, he could not have access to the least knowledge of his identity.'

She collapsed to her knees. 'You've thrown him naked before baying wolves with nothing but his primal instincts!'

'That, and his born gifts, which are not inconsiderable!' Kharadmon assured, beyond ease. A Sorcerer, and powerful beyond measure, he could but watch and wait, since that bleak encouragement brought no consolation.

Gloved palms pressed to her face, Elaira shuddered as though the pressure of the icy, wet leather might shore up her frail flesh. Some hurts plunged too deep. Alone, she battled for the toe-hold to assay the shaken first step towards recovery.

The Sorcerer's spirit ached for her struggle, insouciant sarcasm shredded away. Once, he had owned the warmth of human hands. He had loved, and known how to clasp a devastated woman and lend her raw tears the intimate patience of a warm shoulder. Helpless to offer that solace now, he gave her smashed courage his inadequate words. 'Dear lady. Handfast to Rathain, of us all, you must not lose your heart.'

For in fact, every hope of Arithon's hale future lay in this enchantress's unsteady hands. More: the very thread of Athera's grand mysteries could dwindle, or snap, or perhaps be raised to renewal through her tenacious constancy.

Kharadmon bore witness through her torment. He did not plead. Not while the balance hung trembling, and all that his Fellowship laboured to heal relied on a destiny yet to be claimed. An interval passed, filled by the wind through the snow-laden pines, and the ice-scoured scent of the Storlain glaciers. Inhospitable country, where a proud woman had nursed her solitary pain, clinging to hope with her hands tied. Unbroken then, she could crumble here, with no trusted ally to steady her.

Then Elaira contained herself. Possessed of a dignified calm that outmatched her diminutive resource, she unshuttered her hands and began to remove one soaked glove.

Before she bared her right hand, the Fellowship Sorcerer guessed her desperate retort. No poise could mask the wrench of her regret as she hardened herself to offer back what never in life, or bound service, ought to be returned.

Kharadmon spoke quickly to forestall a decision that could only launch a disaster. 'Lady! Don't do this. Did your best beloved not grant you that ring? And has he, since that terrible day, or in his hour of darkest despair, ever asked to rescind his left token?'

'No,' Elaira admitted, pinched white. 'But you know the Prime's use of me as her personal weapon against him was stopped when he bound his own recall of me beyond reach—'

'Hush!' The ghost of the Sorcerer raised a forefinger with admonishment. 'I've seen how you've suffered in his Grace's behalf. My dearest, yes, I know what he sacrificed for your sake! Althain's Warden has been party to all that you've borne through the earth-link wrought by the Paravians. If Sethvir were here now, he would tell you the future you dread is not written, besides!'

'Arithon doesn't know me!' Elaira cried, pained. 'He may never remember. Why should he not be set free of a past that is dangerous unless it stays lost to him? Where I have the bitter-sweet joy of remembrance, he has been left nothing at all! Is my love so small that I cannot let him discover anew what happiness life has to offer? Who will he have at his side, and what caring, unless he finds joy in another companion?'

Kharadmon applied reason, profoundly relieved that his status as spirit disbarred her impulsive appeal for requital. 'I cannot take charge of an object, except to unmake the thing, stone and setting, which would be a breach of the Major Balance. I cannot revoke your ring's reason for being, or break the purpose for which it was wrought.' As she stared at him, stricken, he added, 'Put straightly, the royal signet of Rathain will not cede me due cause by permission!'

She made a choked sound, but not in protest.

Kharadmon smiled, then. 'Elaira, lean on your instinct! That ring stays with you, with all it entrusts. Honour the covenant of Arithon's promise, and guard his intention as sacred!'

She stayed unconvinced. 'And if I should not?'

The Sorcerer's ephemeral presence gentled with compassion as he spoke the truth. 'If you honestly wish to renounce your heart's beloved, even the Warden of Althain cannot stand as his Grace's proxy. Should you resolve to cast Arithon off, then hear me! You must face him in person. A vow from a crown's heir may not be released. With royal heritage invoked, there is no other course, except to return his token directly into Prince Arithon's hand.'

Elaira stood up. Eyes filled with all of the day's blazing light, she regarded the high mountain peaks, white and cold as a sword's edge above her. 'You feared to add that our paths must stay separate?' Too well, she perceived the quandary that stifled her future happiness. 'I dare not meet him, or touch him, or speak, lest for his life's sake, he should he be prompted to recover his past, prematurely?'

Solitary, left only the shadow of their cherished passion for comfort, Elaira faced her core terror: for too many years, the ring's custody had burned her lonely heart with bright longing. The withering need for Arithon's partnership opened a constant wound of stark agony.

For how long? How many more unendurable days and nights must she tread a trackless path that led nowhere?

The Sorcerer's fraught silence did not presume to salve her with empty platitudes.

Kharadmon bowed, instead. He could do naught else. Ever and always, Elaira's female wisdom stayed infallible where Arithon's welfare was concerned. 'My dear,' the Sorcerer murmured. 'You are beyond compare. Among women, no other will match you.'

He recovered the perfect rose from the snow, slipped the stem through the flap on her satchel. And then his discorporate presence was gone, a tacitly bitter-sweet grant of the needful space for inviolate privacy: to weep, as she must, and to come to raw terms with the terrible trial laid on her. She had retreated for over two hundred years to the desolate hardship of these remote mountains. Held out and stayed sane, and endured the hurt of an inconsolable separation. For the world's sake, and for a crown prince's safety, Kharadmon could not beseech her for the exigency of his Fellowship's need or further burden her course for a cause he had no other choice but to champion.

Nothing rested secure. Not while the Prime Matriarch bade to unhinge the compact and grasp the reins of her unconstrained mission barehanded. Arithon, freed, remained the obstructive cipher that promised her downfall. The Black Rose Prophecy still governed his fate: by himself, quite unguarded, he remained the sole stay that promised the restoration of the Fellowship of Seven.

All over again, Kharadmon could not bear to watch as Elaira regrouped her lacerated spirit. As she chose to hold firm in the face of redoubled conflict and uncertainty, she must stand or fall on her own merits.

Changes

As Koriani scryers fail to trace the released prisoner, Prime Selidie rages across her defaced floor at Whitehold, 'Our arcane vision is thwarted, you say? Then we'll seize the True Sect's faith as our instrument in Tysan. Send a warning dream to the Light's High Examiner. Spur him with the notion his calling has come, that past evil wakens from dormancy. Show that a minion of Darkness moves abroad for his priests to destroy!'

Her healer's work finished by midafternoon, the enchantress Elaira repacks her satchel for a speedy departure: since the Fellowship Sorcerers have disbarred themselves from defending her best beloved, and given the news of the Biedar tribe's active meddling, she resolves to risk the journey to Sanpashir to measure their wild-card stake in his destiny herself . . .

'How can either party withstand the brute course? Worse, Elaira's just made herself a naked target!' Kharadmon rails, lately made aware that the Koriathain twist Asandir's oath to exploit the Light's zealot religion; from Althain Tower, Sethvir returns a dismal silence, too distraught to weigh the bad odds: which enemy faction will trace Arithon first, if not strike him down in the vulnerable gap, before he rediscovers his natural talent . . . ?

II. Vagabond

The last of the hens to be sold from the crate squirmed out of Kerelie's grasp. The rude creature bolted before her new owner clamped a firm grip on her struggling legs. Lest the customer grumble, or worse, accuse Kerelie as a thieving cheat, the coin just dropped into her cash-box was returned with her regretful apology. No use to pretend that sore need for the paltry half-silver did not matter. The Light's tithe imposed by Tysan's high priesthood already claimed the last revenue from the harvest.

Since Tarens was poking about looking idle, he became saddled with the thankless task to recover the runaway fowl. If the useless bird was too scrawny to lay, she possessed enough spiteful fight to take off as though chased by the fell powers of Darkness. Tarens pursued her cackling flight as she darted length and breadth through the stalls of Kelsing's packed market. Jostled patrons cursed in his wake. A hand-cart of pumpkins upset. Tarens leaped, skidding, through rolling fruit. He elbowed past the irate ring of gawkers. Plunged headlong into the havoc that disrupted the vested priest of the Light at his booming recital of doctrine, while the hen flapped through the audience to outbursts of laughter that upset all pious solemnity.

Tarens missed his next pounce.

Immersed in the impassioned delivery of warnings against the subtle practice of evil, the priest glared daggers down his lofty nose. The hysterical hen back-pedaled, trumpeted in alarm, and scooted beneath the gilt rostrum.

Tarens tugged his forelock with an endearing shrug and mumbled a shamefaced apology. Then he dropped onto hands and knees in the grass. His frantic snatch under the priest's white silk hem raised a sneeze on the cloyed reek of incense. Mortified beyond care how much he outraged the temple, the crofter damned the pea-brained wits of loose chickens to reap the fell gale winds of Darkness.

The fowl he cursed hiked up ragged wings, squawked like a jammed hinge, and indignantly pelted. Her flight skittered into the candleman's stall, with Tarens blundering under the rails, fringed with tapers hung by the wicks. Repeatedly clubbed about his reddened ears, he ducked clear, blindly sprinting. The bird raced ahead. She jagged shy of a helpful bystander's snatch. Plunged into the thick stand of trees at the verge, she vanished into the autumn tangles of burdock.

Tarens swore and ploughed after her, snagging up burrs and dry runners of thorn. If the silly bird thrashed beyond earshot, she would be lost for good. The fact his beset family needed her paltry worth forced him to keep on until dusk made the finicky bird come to roost. Once she tucked her head under her wing for the night, he climbed the tree and snared her barehanded. The shocked fowl emitted a curdling screech. Tarens winced, insulted by a squirt of guano that splattered his hair.

'Fiends rise and take you!' he snarled, then blasphemed in earnest as the sky opened into a downpour and drenched him.

Full dark cloaked the market field on his return. He slogged through the trampled mud between the shuttered wood stalls, dismayed to find even the tent merchants packed up and gone. Dripping and forlorn, their family's rig was the last harnessed wagon tied to the empty hitching rail. The bedraggled hen was furious still. Her beating wings and manic squalls set the huntsman's kenneled dogs barking behind the town-walls.

Efflin's vile mood had not improved. 'Should wring that bird's neck before we get nailed with a fine for disturbing the peace.'

Tarens shrugged. The sluiced rainfall at least spared his sister's tart fuss over his sopped clothes and slimed hair. Soaked and cold as he, Kerelie hunched with the open crate readied on the lowered tail-board. Efflin sneezed too hard for further complaint through the ruckus as the miffed fowl was caged. Throughout, the relentless drum of the rain pocked the puddles dammed amid the heaped tarp in the wagon-bed.

The vacated grounds lay felted with mist by the time Tarens clambered aboard. Efflin tugged the knotted reins from the rail, took the bench, and headed the steaming ox homeward.

Bone weary and shivering, no one had starch enough left for regret that in spring, their market days ended with two little boys curled up like exhausted puppies, soothed asleep by Efflin's baritone singing. Grief flattened the family spirits too much to lament that the bull's yield of meat had gone underpriced at the stock-yard. The meager coin hoarded in Kerelie's chest scarcely covered the guild fee paid for their license to sell. The land tithe owed for the inherited croft remained still indebted.

The estate possessed no more excess belongings or chattel to spare. Belts would have to be tightened, again. What cloth goods and staples they gained by straight barter had to be savagely scrimped.

'We could be facing worse,' Tarens declared in attempt to lighten the pervasive gloom. Town law allowed a year's grace in which to square the account rolls. A margin at least to assure them of shelter under the hardship of winter. 'Did anyone see if that crazy vagabond found a patron to hire him?'

'Can't be our problem,' Kerelie grumbled. 'We're too pinched ourselves to fret over another.'

Which should have left Tarens ashamed for the coin he had gifted in soft-hearted folly. If Kerelie and Efflin knew that such charity set him back more than a copper, they rightly would skewer him as he deserved. But guilt over untoward generosity did not resolve his anxiety over the strange fellow's fate.

Softened, Efflin peered through the drizzle that streamed off his drooped hat. 'Last I saw, your simpleton was muscling casks for the brewer.'

Tarens sighed with relief. Tafe Aleman was sympathetic towards beggars. Always gave wretches who free-loaded a beer, and ones willing to shoulder a few extra chores found dry lodging inside his store shed for a halfpenny.

'The man seemed willing. Didn't balk at hard work.' Kerelie blew a strand of wet hair from her lips. 'Careful too. He broke nothing he handled. He's likely to fare well enough.'

Dismissed, the subject lapsed into silence. The home-bound cart creaked through three more sluggish leagues, wheels sucking through dreary mud and frothed currents of run-off. Lashed in by the storm and a cruel risen wind, the lumbering ox turned at last through the painted posts of the farm-gate. The hooked lanterns swung, darkened on their chains. The cottage at the end of the lane had no cheerful aunt waiting, with a warm supper and candle-lit windows gleaming in welcome. No uncle stepped out to take charge of the reins, or hustle them inside to warm by the fire. Efflin did not pull up in the yard but drove the wagon straight through the open barn-doors and into the cavernous, hay-fragrant darkness. The ox huffed and stopped, bawling in complaint. Everyone piled out, too chilled for the burdensome chore of unloading. The barn was pitch-dark, and wax candles too scarce. The paned lamp must be reserved for emergencies, and the risk of a pine-knot torch was too dangerous in the draughts gusted through the gapped plank walls. Kerelie hefted down the hen's wicker cage. The dry goods, the crates, and the empty coin-box could wait until tomorrow's daylight.

Efflin squelched in filled boots to unyoke the tired ox. While he goaded its reluctant tread to a stall, Tarens dashed ahead through the downpour, with a breathless promise to lug wood from the shed. Hungry and cold, no one lingered. Battered by the frigid wind, Kerelie shoved outside and dumped the errant hen back in the chicken coop's pen. She fed the livestock and hastened inside to scrounge crusted bread and heat soup for an overdue supper. Efflin was left to hang up the harness. Since preservative grease could not be applied before the wet leather dripped dry, he stamped after his sister and never looked backwards.

The dreary night passed, and the icy rain stopped before anyone realized the heaped tarpaulin in the wagon-bed sheltered more than the goods fetched from Kelsing market.

Tarens woke the next morning with sun in his eyes. Or so he presumed, until he squinted and found that the dazzle that blinded him glanced off three silver coins, stacked beside his crumpled pillow. Dawn was well gone, the past evening's storm broken to a flawless blue sky. The shaft of clear yellow light through the window burnished the placed silver like gold.

He shot upright, dismayed, the oddity of the coins eclipsed by embarrassment. A selfish indulgence to have overslept, with the winter wheat-field to be tilled and sown before the frost hardened the ground. The family prankster who needled his conscience by leaving the silver could wait; but never their jeopardized stake in the croft, strung up by hard work and a thread. Tousled hair in his face, Tarens kicked off his blankets and slid out of bed. He snatched up his dropped shirt and breeches, jolted to a hissed breath as last night's damp clothes pebbled gooseflesh over his skin.

Arms clutched to quell the violent shiver wracked through his sturdy frame, he paused in disbelief.

Downstairs, Kerelie was busy cooking.

Plain fare, sure enough, in a house plunged in debt, and still muted by the grave-seal of grief. The upstairs felt quiet as an abandoned tomb without the boisterous yells of the boys.

Tarens bit his lip. Past was past. No use to dwell on what might have been. Quickly dressed, he grabbed his dank boots and plunged barefoot down the shadowed, board stair.

He slunk into the brick-floored kitchen, braced for a facetious scold from his sister, backed by Efflin's bull-dog bark.

Instead, Kerelie spun from her stirred pot and glanced up. As though shocked by a haunt, she dropped the ladle of water just dipped from the bucket slung by the hearth.

'Light's blessing, you startled me!' she blurted. Then her round cheeks flushed pink. 'Tarens! Lay off your quack foolery. You didn't wake up just this minute! Or else who's already tended the cattle and finished the chores in the barn?'

'Efflin, of course,' snapped Tarens, sarcastic. 'I notice the butcher's knife's gone from the peg. He'll have fumed himself black out in Aunt Saffie's rose patch, bent on an ambush to flense me.'

Kerelie dried her chapped hands on her skirt. 'Efflin's knocked flat with an ugly green cold. Which is why I'm in here, stirring up gruel to coddle him.' She retrieved her fallen implement and plunked on the hob, blue eyes wide and lips pinched with distress.

Tarens regarded her fraught state, amazed. 'What under sky's strapped your tongue when you ought to be yelling fit to raise the roof?'

'You men weren't the only ones laggard in your blankets.' His sister shed her awkward reluctance, and admitted, 'I snored through the sunrise, myself. We've all been bone-tired! I'd planned to surprise you and muck out the barn. Give your lazy bones an undeserved rest and let Efflin's sourpuss mood have one less target to savage. He's been such a wounded bear since our fortune's turned. Why won't he tell us what's cankered him?'

'He'll speak when he's ready.' Tarens treated her angst with the same stubborn patience that had argued the sale of the bull. 'What's upset you, Kerie? I'm too thrashed to guess.'

His younger sister sucked a vexed breath, her pinched forehead suddenly pale. 'Who's moved the ox,' she began, 'and the milch-cow's been taken—'

Tarens outpaced her slow explanation. Protective to a fault, he abandoned his boots, grabbed the fire tongs, and banged open the door. He charged outside, hackled to gore any thieving intruder.

First step, his brandished tool snagged a dangled wrack of frost-burned tomato vines. As dry leaves and green fruit yoked his lowered head, he yelped, 'Light avert!' and thrashed the pungent stems aside in annoyance.

The uprooted vegetables had not hung there, yesterday. Since Efflin slept, and with Kerelie barely shucked out of her night-rail, who had dug the plants from the kitchen patch and strung them from the porch rafters in the pre-dawn dark? Each year, his aunt had tied the yellowed stems upside down for late ripening, a last frugal harvest snatched from fate's jaws before winter. But Aunt Saff was dead. Two months had passed since the Light's priest settled her with the blessing of passage and torched her remains to sad rest.

Tarens shook off his wild-eyed startlement and bashed the straggle of vine from his neck. As the wrack slithered off him, he swept a frantic glance over the muddy yard but saw no tracks left by rustled livestock.

Broad daylight revealed only the pruned canes of the roses and the crude prints left by Kerelie's pattens.

When the dry cow and the ox raised their horned heads in the field, his glare confounded to befuddlement. The animals were as they should be: routinely turned out to pasture and chewing their cuds behind the shut gate. They had not moved by themselves from the barn, any more than a garden turned over its frost-wilted rows and laid down leaf mulch by itself.

More, the broken handle on the well's crank had been fixed, a skilled task Uncle Fiath bequeathed to his heirs by neglect.

'Fiends plague!' Tarens swore. No mischievous *iyat* visited mankind with the untoward kindness of miracles.

Thoughtful, the huge crofter padded between the mercury gleam of the puddles. Oblivious to the cold nip to bare feet, he entered the barn and paused, impatient while his sight adjusted to the dusty gloom. The fragrance told him the stalls had been mucked. The mangers also were forked with fresh hay. More, the ox harness hung set to rights on the hook, freshly oiled, and for the Light's sake, who bothered? *Even the buckles were polished!* Beside the whetstone's damp wheel, the missing butcher's knife showed the argent shine of a whetted edge.

Footsteps at his back, and a prim swish of skirts prompted Tarens to task his sister, 'The vagabond did this?'

'Had you listened and not belted off with the poker, I would have suggested as much.' Kerelie sighed. 'He must have trailed us back here on foot.' Her hateful cooking abandoned for gossip, she sniffed. 'Or else he snuck into the wagon. The empty bird crates were loosely stacked, and nobody tidied the tarp.'

'He's accomplished all this?' Tarens capped his amazed gesture with a chuckle of flat disbelief. 'One starved little wretch? Merciful Maker! The man would've laboured all night!'

'In the dark,' added Kerelie, uneasy and shaken. 'See for yourself. The candle stubs in the lanterns weren't touched.'

Sure enough, the horn lamp had never been lit. No spent reek of oil and charred pine bespoke the foolhardy use of a cresset.

Tarens scratched at his stubbled chin. 'Done us ten favours, we owe him that much.'

'Don't be daft!' Kerelie snapped. 'We can't possibly keep him!' Since her brother would argue, she slapped him down first. 'I don't care how hard the miserable wretch works. Another mouth to feed through the winter will strain us nigh onto breaking. We can't meet the croft tax on inheritance, besides. And why should a rootless man swipe the best knife from our kitchen only for sharpening? The fellow might be quite ruthlessly mad! Touched by Darkness itself and hell-bent on slitting our throats as we slept.'

The firm line of Tarens's sealed lips gave a twitch. His blue eyes widened and glinted. Sparked into sudden, inexplicable merriness, he stifled the laughter that would only fan his sister's volatile fury. She looked apt, as things stood, to make a quick snatch for his poker and brain him. Ever the sort to enjoy taunting fate, he outfaced her stormy reproof. 'I don't think it's our necks the bloke means to cut.'

Kerelie flounced. Heated enough to pummel the fool who played her for a dreaming idiot, she glanced over her shoulder just barely in time. Her large jaw dropped. 'You!' she exploded, burned red with embarrassment for her feckless outburst of unkindness.

In fact, the small fellow her words had reviled crept in silently, right behind her.

Evidently, the knife had been borrowed to shave. The barbarous straggle of beard was razed off, and the matted tangles trimmed from his raven hair. The loose ends were neatly tied up with twine, snipped from one of the lengths that had strung the tomato vines. Cleaned of wild growth and masking dirt, the features revealed showed a man in his prime, taut cheek-bones and brow line distinctively angled and nowhere ill-bred or unpleasing.

Inquisitive, piercing, his vivid green eyes surveyed Kerelie's blanched surprise. The intensity of that fixed stare ruffled her skin into gooseflesh.

Then the vagrant glanced down, disconcerted as she.

Kerelie recovered her rattled wits. Like her brother, she noticed the man's roughened hands. His chapped knuckles cracked from the setting of his snares, he cradled a brace of limp woodcock and a fat winter hare, hung by the hind legs from another filched string.

Then Tarens gripped Kerelie's shoulder and gently steered her aside. 'Sister, I believe we're blocking his way.'

The beggarman smiled, an expression so honest with contrite apology that Kerelie gasped, lost for breath.

Quick to seize advantage, the elusive creature slipped past, light of step as a thief, or a ghost. He crouched by the sharpening wheel, hefted the knife, and industriously started to dress out his game.

'The man will have breakfast,' Tarens said, calm.

'We still can't upkeep him!' Kerelie whispered, remorseful for the tight-fisted need to hoard their dwindled resources.

'We'll discuss that,' Tarens temporized. 'Inside.' The cold numbed his unshod feet, and coatless, his unlaced shirt made him shiver. Time enough later to broach the matter of coins: the gifted silvers left stacked by his pillow added up to a threefold repayment, though he feared the sweet little cache had been stolen.

As though the wary thought had been spoken, the beggarman stiffened. Though the distressed reaction was swiftly curbed, the subtlety did not escape Tarens's notice.

Recognition followed, as both men locked eyes. Then the vagabond drew an offended breath. He laid aside his half-gutted hare and gently set down the knife. Deliberate, he wiped his blood-smeared fingers clean on a twist of dry straw. Then he stood. Reproachful, his attention on Tarens's broad features, he cocked his head to one side.

The large-boned crofter was swept by raw chills. Raked over like prey by a raptor's inspection, Tarens tightened his grip on the poker.

But the beggarman only dug into the patch pocket stitched to his threadbare breeches. He fished out a creased paper. The unfolded sheet was offered to Tarens, distinct in respect for the threat of cold iron poised yet for a defensive strike.

Muscled enough from the plough to break oak, the blond crofter towered above him.

41

'What does the note say?' prompted Kerelie.

Tarens risked a look downwards. The inked scrawl was the brewer's, and the words a receipt for three silvers, paid labour, with the outstanding promise for a pint of beer at the Candle Mark Tavern.

The supplicant hand was a beggar's, the broken nails rimmed black with dirt. But the courtesy was not commonplace that tucked Tarens's fingers over the written proof, then emphatically shoved off his fist with the voucher nestled inside.

Crisp as any statement, the stranger's stung pride.

Shown an astringent reproof to strip skin, Tarens gaped, as awkward with shame as the sister caught aback before him.

Then the pause broke to the whiff of smoke wafted on the morning breeze.

'Breakfast!' yelped Kerelie. 'Plaguing fiends take it! I've stupidly scorched Efflin's porridge.' Skirt stoutly bundled, she bolted for the cottage, still railing over her shoulder, 'I'll serve a fourth portion. But over my last shred of common sense, yon shifty fellow's not coming inside!'

Tarens chose not to mention the snag, that her adamant boundary had been crossed already.

He grinned at the odd little beggar, then shared a wink of conspiracy. 'Don't make my mistakes, man. She barks and she bites, though you'll find her bluster hides a soft heart.' Just as mindfully fair, he placed his appeal for forgiveness. 'I'll wager your generous portion of beer that Kerelie'd bunk in the hayloft herself before she makes a destitute visitor shiver out in the cold.'

The stranger laughed, a strikingly musical sound that belied his feral appearance. Perhaps, Tarens thought, he was a born mute, until in forthright honour he touched his closed fist to his forehead. The quaint custom suggested disturbing origins. Barbarians who trapped for pelts in Tornir Peaks used the same gesture to seal their agreements.

Tarens frowned. The last dedicate purge to clear clanblood had happened before his sister's birth. She did not share his graphic memories from early childhood: of dead men roped by the heels behind horses; or the riders, who boasted the gory tatters of scalps cut for bounty, then sewed as trophies onto their saddle-cloths. The head-hunters' leagues still patrolled the wilds, though clan numbers had yet to recover. Everywhere persecuted by the Light's True Sect, the secretive few who survived skulked deep in the high country. They showed themselves rarely, and only in dire hunger, when their gaunt men dared the illicit trade of raw furs to garner provisions. The penalty upon capture brought them swift execution by public dismemberment.

Tarens gripped his poker with redoubled unease. Kerelie's fears were misdirected, not groundless: the cagy vagabond might play at speechlessness to conceal a clan accent. Certainly his practised skill with a snare suggested a forester's upbringing.

'How much are we at risk by your presence, my friend?' Tarens asked, very softly. Town law on the matter was ruthless: to knowingly shelter an old blood descendant was to risk being branded as heretic, then outlawed, with the forfeit of all goods and property bound over by temple decree.

His shaken question received no reply. Not deaf, perhaps circumspect, the odd man retired to his unobtrusive place by the whetstone. There, he bent to his diligent work, deboning the meat from his carcasses.

Tarens stayed reluctant to voice his concern on return to the warm, cottage kitchen. Amid the wax polish of Aunt Saffie's plate cupboards, surrounded by limed brick and the comfort of the faded braid rug patched with sun through the casement, his sister's sensible antipathy towards rootless beggary seemed uncharitable.

'We don't know what connection he may have with the Koriathain. Or why his own kinsfolk abandoned him.' Determined to worry the subject to closure, Kerelie removed the tin spoon from the pot of singed oatmeal, then stomped outside in prim displeasure. She left a scorched portion slung up on the meat-hook under the eave by the threshold.

She returned with a scalded palm wrapped in her skirt. 'Let that starveling bolt down the miserable fare with his hands. He'll learn fast enough we can't pay him for field work. I'd have him shove off to a wealthier croft. Surely it's better that his earnest work should receive a fair daily wage.'

She banged the door closed, shot the bar, muttering, and flung the clotted spoon into the wash-basin. Spattered by dish-water, Tarens collected his abandoned stockings and boots. Aware he rightfully should feel relieved that his sister's position stayed adamant, he sat at the plank table and gouged his soles with large thumbs to ease his numbed feet. Against his straight grain, he silenced his doubts, while Kerelie scooped a new measure of oats and ladled fresh water into the spare cauldron. She swung the replenished pot over the coals, stirring with fierce concentration. Sun through the window-panes lit her savaged cheek, striped by the shadows of the mulberry boughs outside the whitewashed cottage. Within, the awkward, sealed quiet extended, cut by the rasping cough that laid Efflin low in the next room.

'Divine Light keep us!' Kerelie snapped. Exasperated by the worry that cramped her preferred generosity, she grabbed a wooden bowl, dipped her ladle, and plonked the steaming gruel onto the trestle in front of her brother. 'I'm not being a pinch-fist! We've got to recoup from our losses and heal before we sweat over strangers!'

Tarens swallowed his food, left with nothing to say. Self-reproach made his limpid blue eyes seem accusing as his sister unsealed the last crock of summer honey and consigned it to the tray for the sick-room.

'Quit moping, can't you?' Kerelie sighed. 'The harder heart would have tossed that burned meal in the hen coop to fatten the poultry.'

She was right. Tarens ate and tried not to dwell on the penalties meted out to sympathizers who treated with renegade clanblood. Kelsing fell under the long shadow of Erdane, temple seat of the True Sect's high priesthood. Here, a man upheld canon law if he valued his family's prosperity. Yet hard common sense failed to ease his torn conscience concerning the wretch sheltered inside the barn.

Though today's breakfast might soon be a luxury, Tarens scraped his bowl clean without savour.

When he arose and tramped out to split wood, he found the black pot on the porch left untouched. Past question, the stranger had noticed the offering. In an irony much too pat for coincidence, his neatly cleaned meat swung beneath, hung to season. Yet the hunter himself appeared nowhere in evidence. Two hours later, the cut fuel was stacked. Tarens sharpened the axe. He strode to the shed to stow the greased tool and caught Kerelie, angrily flinging the cold, congealed oatmeal into the pen for the chickens.

Startled, he laughed. 'I see your rude table's been spurned by the starving?'

She glared. One meaty fist stayed cocked on her hip, while the other threatened to shy the scorched pot at her brother's insolent head. 'See for yourself.' She sniffed, her chin jerked towards the back of the barn, which cued Tarens to go and investigate. He encountered the ashes of a frugal fire, then the green stick lately used as a spit to roast the haunch of the hare.

'Resourceful wee chap, I'll give him that much. Goes out of his way not to take advantage.' Tarens rubbed at a crick in his neck, sunk in thought, when Kerelie arrived to a bustle of skirts and stopped at arm's length in distress.

'How do you throw out a squatter who's so damned resourcefully self-sufficient?'

'You open your door to him?' Tarens measured her sidelong.

But the lines fretted into his sister's brow stemmed from another quarter. 'I need you to go back to Kelsing and fetch a tisane for Efflin.'

Tarens's startled glance met her anxiety straight on.

She added, upset, 'His fever is soaring. Worse, that wet cough's settled into his chest with a speed that is dreadfully frightening.'

Tarens's blunt features drained, his bruised eye tinged grotesquely purple and yellow beneath his rumpled, fair hair. 'Can't be the same fever!'

Kerelie chewed her lip.

'Can't be!' Tarens insisted, rock stubborn. 'Efflin's always been strong as an ox. Surely he's just stuffed up and grouchy.'

Kerelie shook her head, then spun, blinking back desperate tears. 'Not today.'

Tarens stifled the surge of his helpless anger. Bad luck was too busy, and setting a clutch, if the malady that had reaped half of their family struck again and took their older brother.

'You know the Light's priests claim we owe retribution,' his sister said, muffled. She swiped at wet eyes, then knotted her damp palms in her skirt. 'Grace fled, they say, since corruption divided the faithful.'

Tarens slammed the axe into the top of a fence-post with the raw force to split oak. 'I won't swallow the doom in the priest's windy scriptures! Or their guilt, which wrings piteous offerings out of the masses.' He rejected the afflicted belief, that the blight of disease was justified punishment for the Great Schism caused when heaven's sent avatar turned apostate and denounced the blessed Light's doctrine. 'Cattle sicken,' he added, 'in years when they're stressed, or when a fulsome herd overgrazes their pasture.'

Other rumours sprung from barbarian sources claimed the ailments stemmed from the waning surge of the flux lines. The land's health, they held, was starved thin near the towns, where the flow of the mysteries no longer flourished. But no initiate talent from that ancient heritage dared to step forward or challenge the fires of rampant theology. Not with the practice of herb witchery and magecraft crushed under an interdict with a death sentence.

'Just go,' Kerelie urged, breaking off the debate. 'Tell the apothecary we also need a flask of syrup to ease a raw throat.'

Tarens cupped her harrowed cheek in rough hands. 'Calm yourself. Our straits will come right. I'll have the remedies for Efflin's sniffle back here before sundown. Just don't wear yourself to exhaustion, shut in with his carping complaints.'

'He's too sick to grouse,' Kerelie snapped, stressed enough to shake off his comfort. 'Take the coppers I've saved in the crock. We'll let Efflin haggle over the tax we can't pay after he's back on his feet.'

Since the oxcart was too unwieldy and slow, Tarens ran the errand to Kelsing on foot. He left their scant hoard of pennies untouched, and instead tucked the coins from the vagabond into his jacket. He covered the leagues by road at a jog, spurred on by brisk anxiety. Yet despite his diligent care to make speed, ill fortune delayed his timely return.

The muddy road froze iron-hard after dark, and a mis-step twisted his left ankle. He limped into the yard weary and empty-handed under the icy glow of the late-risen moon.

He expected a chill house, kept dark to spare fuel, as his numbed fingers fumbled the latch. Not the blast of close heat that burnished his face when he opened the door. The fire built up to nurse a fevered invalid clamped fear like a fist in his gut. Efflin's condition had worsened, proven out by the sick pallet made up in front of the hob. His brother lay limp as wax under blankets, with Kerelie's stout form stamped in bleak silhouette as she spun from his side in frustration.

'Tarens! What's kept you? The kettle is filled. Get that dose of cailcallow leaf heating. The cough syrup's no use. Efflin's weakened. His breathing's too laboured to swallow.'

Tarens faltered, rocked short, his desolate news fit to shatter her. 'I have no remedies.' Ahead of Kerelie's searing reproach, that he must have indulged himself drinking, he blazed, 'The Mayor of Kelsing's formally listed our family name on the debt rolls.' Which twist of fate meant no merchant in town had the right to accept honest coin from them before the treasury received its lawful due. 'I tried to bargain!' Dropped to his knees, Tarens closed his strong arms around his disconsolate sister. 'Folk believe our luck's left us. My plea was not heard. The apothecary slammed his shop-door in my face. When I argued, he claimed that his cailcallow stores were too low to waste on a grown man with a sniffle. The new leaves won't sprout in the wild until spring. There'd be babes with the croup far more needy. Could I guess? I'd have battered my way in had I known Efflin's straits had turned desperate!'

Further lament would not stem the crisis. Kerelie's tears were not frightened hysteria. The laboured rasp of Efflin's clogged chest ripped through the thick, humid silence. Four times before, that sound had heralded death for a beloved relative.

'You're shivering!' Kerelie chided at due length. 'Light above, Tarens! Take care for your health.' She pushed him away, the surge of her anger turned to drive off futility. 'Doubtless, you won't have eaten a thing. Bless your vagabond friend. We have him to thank for the gift that tonight none of us will go hungry.'

That moment, belatedly late, Tarens smelled the aroma of wild leeks and savoury stew. Astonished, he blurted, 'You let that shiftless rascal inside?'

Kerelie dabbed at her wet lashes, defeated. 'I had little choice, didn't I? By afternoon, Efflin was unconscious and shivering. Someone needed to help me shift the mattress and move him in here by the fire. Your crazy fellow spent the rest of the day by the well, washing himself and his clothes. He's too thin.'

'He was naked? In this chill?' Despite harrowed upset, Tarens snorted and grinned. 'How long did you stare?'

Kerelie slapped him. 'And I should have fed all the livestock blindfolded, while the imp stitched the holes in his breeks with the harness awl?' She added, 'I looked the other way, best I could. He's shameless as a creature born wild. But not uncivilized. He also scoured the scale off my pot. By the time I finished up in the barn, he had diced up his game and hung the filled cauldron on the pot-hook to simmer.'

Tarens inhaled in appreciation. 'Rosemary and sage? And fresh leeks? You hate cooking! Aunt Saff always claimed you couldn't tell a sweetening herb from a grated red pepper!'

'Your scampish guest must have scavenged the lot,' Kerelie retorted, offended. 'Who knows from where? He was busy foraging. Somehow, he found plants that the frosts hadn't touched. Just hope his filched cache was honestly abandoned.'

'Resourceful of him,' Tarens declared. While his sister treated his brother's clogged chest with goose grease and a hot compress, he unfolded stiff legs and arose to help himself from the bubbling cauldron. No one would profit if he should fall sick. Neither could a weary man get himself warm on a rumbling belly. Somehow, some way, he would find the means to reward the stranger's persistent kindness, though at the moment the odd little man was not present to receive his thanks.

Through a savoury mouthful, Tarens accused, 'You didn't send the poor vagabond packing? Or make him sleep out in the hayloft?'

'I didn't,' cracked Kerelie, stung to reproach. 'He left on his own. I brought him a blanket to bed down in the pantry, but if he understood, I've not seen him. He slipped off again and made himself scarce since the sun set.'

Tarens considered the fellow's rag clothing, and shivered. The night was bitterly clear, the freeze lent a harsh bite by the wind since the rain-storm. Unkind weather for a thinly clad wretch, turned out of doors without shelter. But a search at this pass was not practical with a sprained ankle, and the chill that still gripped him bone deep from his errand. Kerelie looked thrashed. Her sore need for relief could not wait. Tarens begged her to rest straightaway, then rose from the trestle, tossed his dish in the wash-tub, and shouldered his turn with the invalid.

Nothing prepared him. Even Kerelie's urgent distress failed to brace his nerves against the sick-room fetor of purged broth and excrement. Too well he recognized the sunken cheeks, waxy sweat, and flushed skin of the dying, tucked limp in damp sheets. This was the face of the fever that killed, with the terrible, clogged rasp of breath the sole assurance that life had not fled untimely.

Tarens's fortitude failed him. Crouched by the mattress, he gathered his brother's slack, clammy hand into trembling fingers. 'Efflin, Light save us, don't bring us to this!' If his brother did not know he was loved beyond measure, he must recognize he was needed! The croft would be forfeit to Kerelie's marriage if her blood family could not provide two adult hands to manage the fields. As things stood, she must wed before the spring planting. Her scarred face already spoiled her chance for a comely match. Let her not be forced to the joyless choice of a suitor who preyed on the fact they were desperate.

The night passed as it had too often before, fighting the malady that had reaped aunt and uncle, and cruelly robbed two young nephews' exuberance. Tarens changed his brother's soaked bedding and hung the damp linen to dry. He plied Efflin's forehead with cold compresses in a tireless, vain effort to draw down the fever. Left nothing else but to stroke the screwed hair from his brother's furnace-hot temples, he tried to banish the creeping fear that such diligent effort was useless without stronger remedies from the apothecary. Efflin would waste away until death, with another pyre and body laid out for the True Sect priest's final blessing.

Bitter, as the hours wore on, Tarens rested his cheek on crossed arms, help-less to stave off the turn of Fate's Wheel. No older brother to stand at his shoulder would cripple him worse than the loss of a limb. Tarens covered his face with strong hands, unable to stifle his anguish.

Soft footsteps arrived. A comforting hand clasped his shoulder. Kerelie pulled up a stool and sat down, a fresh bucket of ice set between them. She retrieved the damp rag left draped on his knee and methodically started to refresh the cold compress.

'Tarens?' she said, hushed.

He did not turn his head, taut fingers in place to hide his sudden, useless tears.

'We can't give up.' Kerelie rearranged the damp hem of her night-rail, huddled into the mantle thrown overtop, sharp-scented with outdoor air. The sheepskin slippers on her large feet were caught with moist leaves from her foray to skim off the bucket left by the well.

If Tarens believed the fight was not lost, his black despair whispered otherwise. Their late aunt had insisted the bountiful luck had deserted the croft years ago, when their father was conscripted to bear arms for the Light. No word of him had ever come back. No letter to say if he survived the harsh training, or whether today he still served, sworn to a dedicate's term of life service guarding the sealed border of Havish.

'We will weather this. No matter what comes.' Kerelie's chapped fingers tucked the packed cloth into folds and plied the wrapped ice to Efflin's flushed forehead. 'I'll call if I need you. Best sleep while you can.'

Tarens lifted his tousled head and regarded his sister's profile. By the seeped light from the fire's banked coals, her unspoiled cheek wore the sweet flush of youth. Her upturned nose bespoke the light humour and innocence remembered from better days. Tarens chided gently, 'Did you rest yourself?'

She sighed. 'I couldn't.'

'Then I'm sitting with you,' Tarens insisted. 'I'll be at hand's reach because I know you won't leave Efflin's side to ask for assistance.'

'Ought to help yourself,' Kerelie retorted. 'At least strap that sprained ankle. Draw down the swelling, or else, come the morning, you won't manage to pull on your boot.'

'I'll borrow your slippers.' Already stiffened and not inclined to move, Tarens slept in the end, propped against the oak hob. Because he was peaked with exhaustion, his sister could not bear to roust him.

Kerelie nodded off also in the bleak hour before dawn. Despite the best intent to kick her brother awake to look after the livestock, she never opened her eyes until sunlight streamed through the casement. The astringent scent of cailcallow and wintergreen scoured her nostrils and shot her up straight.

'Tarens!' She reached out to shake him, only to find he had risen ahead and gone outside to mind the chores. Efflin languished, still gripped by high fever. But his tormented breathing had eased just a bit. An empty pan and a spoon at his bedside suggested that someone had dosed him with a strong remedy. The reek of herbals wafted from a second brew, brought to a low boil over the fire.

Kerelie paused and made certain the sick man's sheets were not clammy.

She tucked the blankets up to Efflin's chin, then straightened her night-rail and crossed to the hob, prepared to return the profuse word of thanks to the charitable neighbour who had sent the bundle from town.

But no kindly matron's unpacked basket rested on the kitchen trestle. Kerelie saw none of the apothecary's phials of oil, and no string-tied packets of purchased herbs. Instead, the boards were spread over with root-stock, cut fresh from the bush, stripped of bark, and pungently grated. Also wintergreen berries and leaves, several rose hips, shredded willow bark, and two other twiggy plants that her country-bred knowledge failed to identify. The collection had arrived at the cottage bundled inside a frayed rag. She still stared, overcome by surprise, when Tarens ducked through the doorway.

He had been mucking stalls, by the barn reek breezed in with him. He also carried two muddied shoes and a bunched wad of damp, tattered clothing, which he unburdened into her dumbfounded hands. 'Hang these up to dry.'

'They belong to the vagabond?' Not indignant so much as undone by the strain, she scolded, 'Tarens! You didn't –'

Her brother cut in, 'Yes, I did. The fellow's wrapped up in my second-best shirt. Asleep. I gave him my bed. Kerelie, be quiet! We owe him that much! He stayed out all night to bring Efflin those simples. You know the creek's swollen too high to wade over. He must've stripped down and swum! I found him frozen nigh onto death, burrowed into the oat straw stacked in the hayloft.'

'Where did he find these wild rose hips?' Mollified, Kerelie ran on as Tarens stamped to the hob and shrugged off his cloak. 'While you explain, give the pot a good stir. Use the wooden spoon. These rags must be wrung out before they'll dry properly.'

'I don't know where the man found any of this,' Tarens said, willing to do as she asked with the remedy but otherwise stiffly reticent. The apothecary had held his dried cailcallow dear, since the bush would not leaf over winter.

'This paragon tracks down rare plants in the *dark*?' Kerelie's nagging sharpened in pursuit of the uneasy discrepancy. 'Where under sky do you think he was trained?'

'I have no idea.' Tarens added, 'He's got a field-worker's hands. I saw that much.' The horn callus left by the scythe never lied. 'The fellow's mowed barley. And he's got straw cuts from tying up corn shocks.'

'Well, he's done a countryman's labour, perhaps.' Kerelie eyed the worn garb in her arms, too concerned to let sleeping dogs lie. 'Yet he wasn't born to the life. Whatever mother gave birth to him, the specialized study of herbals is not common knowledge for farm help.'

Tarens kept his mouth shut, in dread of the day she encountered the shackle scars that marked the fellow's ankles and wrists. Since Kerelie's prying overlooked that detail, he might keep that questionable bit of the stranger's personal history quiet. But the dangerous threat to his family's security forced him to broach his earlier concern. 'He might be clanblood, perhaps, from the deft way he snares wild game.'

Kerelie tossed the dreadful rags on the bench. 'Look again!' she demanded in withering scorn. 'Tarens, you mean well, but are you stone blind? No clan-born ever wears woven cloth! Why would a skilled trapper not have deer-hide breeches at least, or a jacket of cured fur at this season? These shoes were not cobbled by free-wilds barbarians. I know my sewing. Have you found the seams in a field-hand's dress done in a whip stitch? Or a shirt collar and fitted cuffs, laced with a pattern as these are? More likely we're harbouring a simpleton servant, escaped from the Koriathain!'

'Efflin needs him,' Tarens insisted, hunched over the steaming pot. 'Whoever he is, wherever he came from, I won't run him out. If you aren't willing to mind his wet clothes, I'll handle the problem myself.'

'I'll waste time drying nothing,' declared Kerelie, in her way just as mulishly stubborn. 'Those shameful rags aren't fit to be worn. You'll throw them into the midden at once. Then find me something of Uncle's that I can cut down to size. Stay out of my hair, and I'll have the work finished before your pet visitor wakes up.'

Autumn 5922

Caller

He awoke, still without recollection of name, and discovered that somebody thoughtless had taken his only clothes while he slept. The virulent sting of his anger surprised him. If the meddler's intentions were kindly meant, his sorry rags had been everything that he owned in the wide world. Surely worse, the pathetic possessions provided the last link to the wretched existence that only the wear on his body recorded. Practised instinct endowed certain knowledge by rote.

The croft proved as much. Without ever touching the tools in the barn, he grasped their function and use. His rough hands insisted he had worked the earth. The calluses welted over the scar on his palm told of the scythe, and a lengthy acquaintance with rake, hoe, and ploughshare. He knew how to preserve jam, dry fruits, and weigh the measure of salt needed to pickle vegetables. He had smoked butchered meat into jerky. From habit ingrained by the seasonal cycle, he had endured a hermit's existence, scratched out in the ruin where he had recovered awareness.

Husbandry kindled no passion in him. His acute craving burned beyond hunger, that such country wisdom did not tap the greater part of his experience.

Whenever he listened too closely, his refined senses unfurled and extended. Too far and too fast, he dropped into perceptions that frayed his awareness of self altogether. Or else he lost his inner balance and tumbled into deepened Sight that tracked mental engagement as colour and light, and grasped the drift of emotional currents distinctly as an unreeled melody.

Shaking, afraid, all but unmanned – *he did not know why!* – he became overwhelmed by the force of sheer gratitude. The mere touch of warm sunlight fallen through the window-pane shocked his skin with ecstatic intensity. Upended again, almost hurled to delirium, he shut his eyes, hard. Frightened, he grounded himself back into the texture of solid surroundings: the coarse weave of the linen sheets and wool-blankets that covered his maddening nakedness.

Unmoored and desperate, he affirmed what he knew as a recited litany to impose calm: he was in Tarens's bed. Clad in a shirt too large for his frame, cut from cloth that smelled faintly of lye soap. Unsure of his voice, he silently mouthed the name of his benefactor. 'Tarens.' The unspoken syllables let him savour the thrill: that he might have a friend although his tongue felt too clumsy to dare attempt speech, even in solitude.

Once, he had loved music. The vague recall tugged, as estranged as a language elusively veiled beyond meaning. Perhaps even, he had been a singer. The idea terrified him to goose bumps, and contrarily, eased his sped heart. The galvanic dread gripped him, that if he found the nerve to try sound, he would utter no better than a rusty croak.

The grotesque possibility of such a failure slammed him back into paralysis. To shake crushing anxiety, he reopened his eyes. This time, his survey encountered the breeches. Facetious female generosity had left them for him, folded on a nearby chair. The loss of his own garments stung him again. What other clue did he have to reveal the person he had been?

Too late for regret, that weakness and sleep had relaxed his wary defenses. He could sulk and stay naked, or else bow to the straits that forced Kerelie's high-handed charity.

If he must arise vulnerable under her roof, he intended to stay unobserved. In adamant privacy, he tested his untrustworthy senses one cautious layer at a time. *Gently,* he reined in the torrent that rushed to burst through his restraint and strand him in dizzy bewilderment. Control did not come easily. Somewhere before, he had faced dangers that demanded an exacting degree of tuned reflex and receptivity.

But whatever shadowy perils once stalked him, in whatever forgotten strange space, their spectre stayed hidden. Nothing untoward lurked here in this cottage. Only quiet lapped against his awareness inside these homely white-washed walls. Around him, the empty room was unthreatening, the air still in the silk fall of sunlight.

Tarens's preference enjoyed rough-hewn pine furnishings, either whittled with whimsical animals, or else adorned with jaunty charm in painted patterns of vine-leaves. The floor-boards were gouged where he scuffed his boots. His sturdy clothes-chest displayed spirited dents inflicted by his quick temper. But the fierce, loyal eddy of Tarens's bright presence was not here to safeguard a stripped stranger's dignity.

The purposeful clatter from the kitchen downstairs bespoke the defensive sister. Immersed in her habitual prickly noise, she ransacked a cupboard like a butcher who had misplaced a favourite knife. Her bustle sang of annoyance and worry, but no longer streamed the rank copper taint of fear from the evening before. Therefore, the bout of illness that threatened her older brother would have improved. Tacit listening confirmed this. Efflin's hacked cough emerged muffled, removed from the kitchen fireside to the downstairs bedroom. Though the sick man's being rang yet with the fraught overtones of high fever, he no longer gasped for every clogged breath. Yet the dark vortex he carried still weighted his heart: the core flame of his vitality stayed wrapped at low ebb, sapped by a secretive bundle of pain.

Snagged in the midst of this tight-woven family, the upstairs visitor broke his tranced reverie. He tossed off the annoyance of the itchy blankets. Acutely ashamed of his burdensome presence, he placed slender feet on the floor-boards and rose. Soundless in movement, he fingered the pair of brown breeches given for his use. The homespun wool had been cuffed at the ankles to suit his shorter stature. Kerelie's neat stitches hemmed the turned seams. Her delight for needle and thread touched his spirit, a dance of harmonics that soared far above the range of natural hearing. He stroked the cloth and also sensed the whispered urgency of her unease: that some later short-fall might wish back this old garment to mend a brother's torn jacket or patch up a moth-eaten quilt.

Lip curled at the thought of wearing such chafing anxiety next to his skin, the destitute supplicant dressed himself. The breeches, made for a much broader build, threatened to slide off his hips. He would need a string to secure the loose waistband if the household insisted on decency. His beard stubble prickled; his jet hair hung tangled. Yet he had been offered no comb and no knife, far less soap and basin to shave. The napped hose provided at least had no holes. Since borrowed shoes appeared nowhere in evidence, he padded into the hallway on stockinged feet.

A narrow passage with creaky, pegged floor-boards led him to another bedchamber. Dust filmed the thresholds of two more rooms with shut doors, both shadowed and uninhabited. Too respectful to pry, he ventured the stair towards the kitchen, determined to right his disgruntled pride and amend his overlooked grooming.

He was halfway down and still masked in gloom when the sharpened ripple of an inbound disturbance flicked over his sensitized nerves. He froze, unsettled by split-second warning: another *person* strode towards the cottage, not expected by the known family inside. Survival reflex prompted him to expand that initial assessment. Still strange to himself, he quashed that fierce impulse: locked down the swift expansion of his perceptions hard and fast, before he lost his grip. Unadorned hearing already informed him that the caller was not a close neighbour. Through the hearth-fire's crackle and the on-going rattle of Kerelie's heedless industry, he picked up a stamped hoof and the restive jingle of harness bells from outside. A carriage and team handled by a groom was being tied to the pasture fence.

Nothing like Tarens's straightforward tread, the passenger's step minced along the mud path, then thumped up the porch stair from the garden. Then that someone, *unknown*, and bullishly *male*, knocked at the kitchen-door.

Kerelie's skirt swished, a brusque rustle that bespoke surprise as she passed the pine trestle, crossed the braid rug, then scuffed over the slab at the entry and lifted the latch. The squeak of the door-panel's crooked hinge was followed by *speech*, enlivened by recognition.

The listener's ear ignored Kerelie's greeting in favour of tracking her tone: she was annoyed, even felt imposed upon, which tagged the fellow as *invader*. But perfunctory courtesy obliged her to invite the unpleasant caller inside.

As her platitude brought his unctuous acceptance, frustration spiked the rampant dislike she smothered behind genteel manners.

Shameless, the eavesdropper poised in the stairwell chose not to retreat. Since the secretive vantage provided him with a covert view of the kitchen, he settled down in cat quiet as the pushy visitor shoved into the cottage. The man's fruity voice and deliberate gait foretold the portly build that shortly emerged into view.

Pinkly shaved over his pouched chin, he claimed the only padded chair from the trestle, and buckled the rug in his grunted effort to haul the seat onto the slate apron before the hearth. There, he settled, oblivious, or else uncaring, that his planted bulk blocked the heat that kept the rest of the croft cottage cozy. His clothes and tweed jacket bespoke country origins, a surface impression spoiled by the gleam of a tailored silk collar and gold rims on his oyster-shell buttons. He provided a gift. His fussy, scrubbed hand bestowed the package on Kerelie as though grateful acceptance was his rightful due.

Which presumption made the unseen witness bristle. Restraint kept him still, while Kerelie took the man's bundle of charity with clipped distaste. She unwrapped a glass phial of cough syrup, then a string-tied packet that faintly wafted the astringent fragrance of cailcallow.

The silent lurker understood herbals: somewhere, he had been well taught to know their virtues by their subtle essence. These dried, crumbled leaves had been cut under daylight in early summer, when rain and hot sun spurred fast growth, and diffused the medicinal efficacy. More, the plants had not been *sung to*, or touched by gratitude when they were gathered.

Unlike the stringently potent root-stock his own hand had collected last night, under influence of the autumn moon.

'. . . must have heard about Efflin's condition,' Kerelie was saying. Her thick fingers, most reverent with anything cloth, refolded the packet and knotted the string.

The little pause floundered.

Her caller shifted, then cleared his throat. 'I'd not heard your brother took sick, not precisely. Yesterday's rumour said the apothecary refused to accept Tarens's coin. You did send to Kelsing to fetch these same remedies?' A suggestively weighted interval ensued. When Kerelie said nothing, the visitor added, 'If Efflin's down with a cough, surely you'll need better help than a pennyweight parcel of herbals.'

The words kept the pretence of polite conversation. To the sensitive listener, such windy noise could be plumbed for the strains of true nuance: this *predator* had been stalking the family's rough straits, poised for his moment to spring.

'We have managed,' said Kerelie, bitten to a snap.

From the stairway, the vagabond shared her contempt. The pervasive, bracing reek filled the kitchen: of stronger medicinals already provided for the ailing brother's recovery.

'Efflin's sniffle's improved,' Kerelie dismissed. 'The winter wheat's being planted, besides. That's hard work aplenty to fill our day.' Her tart inflection meant anyone else underfoot clearly wasted her time.

'You'd begrudge me a stirrup-cup?' the caller pressed, although he had travelled from town, sleek under the comfort of carriage rugs. 'Saffie always boasted your late uncle's spirits took the bite off a brisk day.'

Cornered again, Kerelie sighed. 'We sold off the whiskey. As you've been aware. Or didn't I hear the complaint that your man lost the lot to the justiciar's house steward?'

The stiff quiet deepened, coloured by her regret, that the corn still also had gone to raise cash, which was why the family had not made the mash this year to ease their stark hardship. The lurker had noted Efflin's delirious rant, bemoaning the loss of the revenue.

'If you're chilled,' declared Kerelie at freezing length, 'I can offer you unsweetened rose-hip tea.'

The caller deferred with a smile that belied the miserly flint in his eyes. 'Your company might warm a man well enough. That's if you'd consider unbending for an hour's playful enjoyment.'

'Is this a courtship?' Kerelie banged down the pan just unhooked to boil water and glared fit to singe her oppressor. 'If so, then shame on you! My affection cannot be bought by a miserable bottle of cough syrup!'

A kindly man should have been taken aback. This one stood up, his shark's smile all teeth. Surly confidence carried him across the room like a blast of cold air. That frisson of chill brushed the furtive watcher. His rapt quiet turned poised, where he crouched on the stair.

'Must you stall until poverty leaves you as sour as a worm-eaten fruit?' The caller stepped close and crowded himself against the reluctant young woman's side. His covetous touch fingered the decorative garlands embroidered on her full sleeve. 'How long will you defer the inevitable, Kerelie, and face that you must accept marriage? Soonest is best for the sake of your family. Why suffer a lean winter when your choice can spare your two brothers from beggary?' Thick gold, his ring glinted, as he slid his eager palms up her arms to embrace her.

Kerelie's adroit counter-strike elbowed the water pail. 'Oh dear!' As her splashed suitor jumped backwards, she blotted her soaked cuff on her apron and surveyed the puddle that flooded her hem-line and seeped into her scuffed leather shoes. 'I'll just step out and put on a dry skirt. Do me the courtesy while you wait? Shout outside for Tarens to draw a fresh bucket. If you insist upon staying for tea, he'll certainly want to join us.'

Yet the caller refused to cede his advantage. 'Why this belated concern for propriety?' His expensive, waxed boots defeated her ploy: he advanced without scathe through the water, and captured her wrist. 'Your older brother's now head of your household. If his well-being's improved, as you claim, and if he doesn't favour a match, then why has your family's upright westlands decency left you on your own to receive me?'

But she was not alone. The lurker on the stairway uncoiled and moved, his timing impeccable.

Tarens sighted the flashy carriage from the far side of the field, where he muscled the ploughshare down the next furrow to till the last acre left fallow. He paused only to knot the reins of the ox. If the beast broke its harness and wandered at large, he would deal with that nuisance later.

'Grismard! You dung-feeding maggot!' The opportunist had tried worming in once already, before Uncle's corpse had grown cold. Swearing fit to scale a bagged viper, Tarens charged over the welter of newly turned clods, hampered painfully by his puffed ankle.

'If that creeping slug's laid hands on my sister, I'll wring his greasy neck!' Unless Efflin managed to totter erect first and gut the man's paunch with the poker.

Tarens gasped another breathless obscenity. Lamed, he could not vault the fence. Forced to take the long way around through the gate, he sprinted at a hopping limp to the cottage, scrambled up the stone steps, and bashed open the door.

Inside, tubby Grismard stood in a puddle, backed up with his spine bowed against the hard edge of the copper-lined sink. The vagabond faced him. At least a head shorter and one-third the weight, the fellow should have been harmless. All the more, since the hand gripped to stay his loose trousers disarmed any threat at the risk of buck-naked embarrassment. Yet the feral green eyes pinned on the disgruntled suitor drained the man's salmon flush to fish-belly white.

'Grismard!' Tarens opened in venomous delight. 'Don't you look like the bloke who just pissed his own breeks.'

'Who's your unsavoury visitor?' snapped Grismard, chins quaking with sweaty unease.

'That's the foot-loose vendor who sold me the herbals,' Kerelie smoothed over, shaken. The relief that acknowledged her brother's arrival stayed charged with alarm, that something beyond a straightforward brawl might erupt in her sensible kitchen.

Tarens traipsed forward, thumbs hooked in his belt. A grin pasted over his clenched jaw, breathing fire, he kissed his sister's scarred cheek. 'You've scrounged some old clothing the peddler wants in trade?'

As though cued, the vagabond stepped back and unpinned his discomfited victim. He raised one arm and displayed his oversized raiment as if pleased by an exchange for his wares. The ferocious edge did not leave his eyes. He stayed placed between Kerelie and the importunate caller, no matter that the breached door to the kitchen flooded him with icy air or that the ludicrous fit of the breeches threatened to strand him, half-stripped.

'I was planning to make tea,' Kerelie announced to stem a burst of wry laughter.

Tarens snapped up the dangling line, 'But at the moment, praise be to life's set-backs, your sewing claims the more urgent priority?' He strode forward, seized Grismard's arm, and steered him on firm course for the exit. 'Announce yourself, next time. We'll be better prepared.'

The incensed visitor jerked himself free. 'Best watch the quality you bring under your roof.' He shot his cuff, yanked straight his mussed tweed, then warned in thwarted vindication, 'Word's hot about town, or haven't you heard? The high temple examiner's dispatched his diviners to hunt down a minion of Darkness.'

Before the electrified clash of bravado cocked Tarens's protective fist, the vagabond moved. Snake quick, his slim hand skimmed the trestle and snatched up the abandoned packet of herbals. His gesture shouted scathing contempt as he tossed the spurned packet across the room. His aim could have been deadly, executed with force: the tied bundle struck the caller's broad chest at the heart and rebounded.

Tarens's reflex barely salvaged the catch before the gurgling flask tucked inside struck the brick floor and shattered. 'We've survived very well without any help from busybodies, religion, or charity,' he retorted, still on the muscle.

The browbeaten outsider wisely chose retreat and backed onto the threshold.

'Don't come again unless Kerelie invites you!' Tarens thumped the spurned gift against Grismard's jacket, shoved him out, then banged the door shut in his suet face.

No one spoke. The gloomy chill left in the kitchen hung on, even after the carriage wheels ground from the yard, and the fancy harness jingled away down the lane and dwindled, turned townward.

Kerelie huddled in uncle's stuffed chair, restored to the head of the trestle. Her chapped hands gripped the tea she had brewed after all, to soothe her rattled composure. Along with Tarens, she regarded the dark, bent head of the vagabond, who perched on the left-hand bench. The naked slenderness draped in her borrowed blanket did not belong to a displaced labourer. The unsettled quiet forced both siblings to acknowledge: the thoughtless dexterity of those slender fingers was too well practised at plying the needle and thread just filched from Kerelie's mending basket. Nor were the intricate stitches that retailored the trousers to size part or parcel of any field-hand's experience.

At length, through unease that failed to dispel, Tarens mused, 'Where have I seen work like that done before?'

Kerelie's glum spirits dissolved at the question like storm-clouds chased off by fair weather. 'Did you think I burned those vile rags with my eyes shut?' Her devoted enthusiasm for sewing gave answer. 'The tentmaker locks each stitch the same way when he fashions the seams in his canvas awnings.' Her shy smile flashed, surprisingly sweet, on the side not creased by her scar. 'Don't imagine that I haven't chewed over the subject until I remembered. The chap said he learned his craft from a ship's mate who once mended sail on a lugger.'

Tarens sighed, his loose hands as browned as the soil the plough had ground under his nails. 'We are a very long way from the coast.'

'Well, don't pretend Grismard won't keep his vile promise.' Her scowl resettled, Kerelie rapped a flaked chip of glaze from her tea-mug. 'How long do we have, do you think, before he brings your stray guest to the notice of the Light's diviners?'

'I don't care a hoot.' Tarens stood up. His crusted boots tracked muddy prints without reprimand as he banged open the wood box and laid a split log to build up the fire. His blond hair shone against the stirred coals, crowned suddenly in bloodied light by the sparks wafted up the stone chimney. 'I'll never cringe from the threats of a toady,' he cracked as he straightened. 'Or bow one inch to the pious demands of some whey-faced temple examiner! Such sheep may preen in their white robes and pontificate. But I say human beings have purposeful brains beyond acting like flocks of scared pigeons.'

Yet as the wood caught and blazed at his back, the sudden, fierce heat lent the unpleasant reminder that brush-fires seldom burned without smoke.

Autumn 5922

Borrowed Time

Elaira braced for the next frontal attack launched against her by the Prime Matriarch. The Sorcerer's warning, that Fellowship powers granted Arithon's plight no further protection, woke the urgent need to unwind the riddle posed by the Biedar tribes' intercession. Key to that answer lay three hundred leagues distant, amid the torrid black sands of Sanpashir. Already a renegade Koriani initiate, now determined to treat with the order's most ancient arch enemy, Elaira expected the sisterhood must actively move to defend their close interests. Every hell-bent resource they owned could be unleashed to forestall her safe passage.

Therefore, she guarded her tracks and took flight through the spine of the Storlain Mountains. Travellers avoided those rugged wilds, far southward of the ancient pass at Lithmarin and well off the established route that linked land-bound trade with the deepwater harbour at Redburn. The hardy clanborn who trapped in the deep vales never ventured the high country alone. Few beyond the Fellowship Sorcerers braved the fault-line that bisected the continent where the collision of tectonic forces wrestled with titanic violence.

From the gouged channel of Instrell Bay, and against the primordial vistas of lava that bubbled the steam pots that bordered Scarpdale, the buckled strata of bed-rock ramped upwards. Towering white pinnacles scraped the sky's roof, until the wracked terrain subsumed again and plunged into the reef-riddled fissure of South Strait. Where such mighty pressures shocked the earth's bones, explosive shifts whiplashed the flux lines. Quakes tumbled the weathered scarps into slides, and spurts of destabilized electromagnetics erupted as howling gales.

A lone woman afoot was an insectile speck, tramping these trackless wilds.

Overshadowed by clouds, or choked under the mist snagged on the vertical buttresses, Elaira journeyed where ice-falls and split rock keened to the savage winds. She laboured against the white-out blizzards that flayed her exposed skin like shot needles. Yet the same brutal elements also granted her a backhanded measure of safety. Storm and avalanche, and the roaring cataracts that tunnelled through crevasse and glacier produced the violent energy needed to confound the subtle venues of arcane surveillance. Enough to thwart even a circle of Senior seeresses, at least until she mastered the change imposed on her by Arithon's current predicament: the fragile defense that hinged upon the kept secret of his anonymity. He carried no recall of her existence. But she, who safeguarded the trust of remembrance, still endured the empathic channel that linked her with his intimate being. Infallibly, Prime Selidie's malice would seek to exploit that subtle connection.

If Elaira failed to seal off her unruly emotions before she left the Kingdom of Havish, all stakes would be lost. Packed light for speed, her cerecloth bedroll held only jerked meat. The spare shirt and a tin panniken in her satchel wrapped no more than basic healer's supplies. She slept in the open. A steel-shod staff tested her steps on the ice-fields, and the knife at her belt that shaved wood for kindling also skinned her snared game and dug tubers. One night, she bedded down in a cramped cave, steamed by the malodorous seep of a hot spring. Another found her camped on an ice shelf, bridged over a tumbling freshet. Always, she sought running water, or places where the tumultuous elements swirled with turbulence. She dared even those sites where the sprites, known as *iyats*, gathered to feed upon chaos. If their fiendish pranks broke her rest, the same interference thwarted the sisterhood's scryers.

The burning jab of their probes never ceased. Elaira lost count of the times she plunged naked into deep snow. Such acute discomfort broke off the assaults, which struck always when she was most vulnerable. Anytime her alert focus drifted, the Prime's spies thrust to rifle her mind. Over the course of two and a half centuries, such relentless pursuit had stalked her for an oath breaker's punishment. But since their coveted male quarry's escape, the old cat-and-mouse stalemate had broken. The prize became Arithon's tenuous freedom, with herself the game-piece to expose him.

Elaira rammed her spiked stave into the glare ice scabbed over a tumbling streamlet. She assayed the next precarious step, her breath plumed in the bitter air. As she edged down the jagged scar of a ravine scoured bare by a recent rockfall, the lethal endangerment posed by the terrain became a pittance beside the love that made her a target. The day must never dawn that the Prime's balked ambition should seize on the chance to use her again.

Once betrayed at such cost the true heart shrank to contemplate, Arithon had consigned that power of choice into Elaira's steadfast hands. For both of their sakes, her strength must shield him through his harrowing hour of weakness. Exhausted in the fallen silence of twilight, her feet sore down to the bone, she sheltered amid a stand of stunt firs, cragged roots anchored like a miser's clenched fists into the cracks in sheer rock. Possessed of the same tenacious endurance, Elaira huddled by a frugal fire, sinews limp as unravelled knit. Stars blazed above the snow-blasted summits, foil-stamped against gathering darkness. Here, no saving disturbance existed to upset the reach of a crystal transmission. Selidie's scryers might snatch that advantage to break her resistance. Elaira hoarded a store of dry wood. She would shove her hand into live coals if need be to deny the Prime Circle's intrusion.

Yet nightfall deepened without undue threat. Only brutal cold and astringent breezes whispered and moaned through the lopsided evergreens.

Elaira pressed her fraught hands to her face. Discipline never had tamed her inner bond with Prince Arithon. The instinctive alignment of magnetic rapport burned in her each moment, made urgent as breath by her solitude. Worse, Arithon's acute danger drastically heightened the already volatile interface. His emotions flared hers into flash-point gestalt without warning: vividly intimate as he brought in fresh game, and the homely croft woman who sheltered him attached him with a nickname not even a dog would have answered.

Worse, the flat twang of her town accent offended his musician's ear, coarse as ground glass to the lyric awareness once titled as Athera's Masterbard.

Through his eyes, Elaira captured his sly effort to thwart the irksome presumption. His laughter laid siege to the sternest resolve each time he deplored the address by turning his backside in clownish rebuff.

The by-play lightened the enchantress's spirits until his yearning, bewildered desire – *to be as he was* – sought relief from the desolate pain of his alienation. Quietly, Arithon flagged the fair-haired brother's more sympathetic attention. Then, with a bit of flaked charcoal, he started to write out his preference on the slate hearthstone. The first of his sketched characters wrung Tarens pale.

With the sister too preoccupied to take notice, the crofter's shocked hiss quashed that first earnest effort to establish a personal trust. The dropped charcoal, stamped beneath a rough boot, obliterated the crude writing. Tarens whispered, frantic, 'Light save us! If anyone realized you knew the old tongue? We'd be ruined, my friend, and you'd meet your death. Condemned as clanborn or else burned alive, executed for renegade sorcery.'

Alone in the brutal alpine cold, Elaira suffered the blow as a silenced witness, while fear and distrust quenched the tentative spark of her beloved's stifled identity. Buffeted by the cruel gusts off the glaciers, she gasped as the tears blurred her eyes. Her heart could break for the lifetime's trove of experience that lay sundered from Arithon's grasp. Without power to comfort, she ached for his outsider's misery as he leaned forlorn on the largesse of strangers, pretending to drowse while his trapper's fare simmered in the kettle slung over the flames . . .

*　　*　　*

. . . too anxious for subtlety, Kerelie kept nattering as though her subject were deaf, or born nerveless. 'Suppose the fellow knows witchery, Tarens?'

'What makes you think that?' The brother reseated himself at the trestle. Too poor for a lamp, forced to squint in the glow of a spluttering tallow dip, he resumed stitching a mend in the torn harness strap, broken after the folly that led him to tie the ox up by the reins. Rattled himself, and unskilled at pretence, he kept his head bent to his work.

'Well,' Kerelie temporized, her usual piece of fanciful sewing draped over her knee, 'you can't pretend that the oddities don't cling to the man like jumping fleas. He's gotten that scrawny hen to start scratching. You'll see she's recovered the gloss of good health. The grouchy bird follows him like a tame pet. Tell me you don't notice? The animals thrive something more than they should when he helps with the chores in the barn.'

Tarens shrugged. A fallen lock of fair hair veiled his face as he ducked her direct regard.

'You know that our ox dislikes strangers,' Kerelie pressured. 'If the brute doesn't tread on their feet or balk outright, it sidles them into a post. Yet your vagabond leads that beast hither and yon without the least roll of an eyeball.'

Tarens grunted, the plink of his hammer against the awl made the ready excuse to duck conversation.

Kerelie out-waited his reluctant stand and picked up once the hole had been punched. 'Someone taught that man knowledge of herbals, and not in a kitchen patch, either.'

'He's not *my vagabond*,' Tarens replied. 'What makes you think I have answers?'

By fretful habit, Kerelie scraped a knuckle along her scarred cheek. 'I say he could be an uncanny creature dropped into our midst.'

'He *appreciates* things,' Tarens amended. 'You feel that quality with his attention. Dumb beasts respond by giving their trust. Where's the mystery in that? He understands language, and if he's a mute, he doesn't need speech to make himself understood.'

Kerelie poked her embroidery needle through a fold in her loose sleeve. Overlarge for the delicacy of her stitches, her prim hands rummaged into her basket for the emerald floss to embellish a rosebud. She was not a mean spirit. Only frightened, and worried past peace for the brother who stubbornly languished in sick-bed. 'Koriathain prefer to take on mutes and half-wits. You don't think our stray served their interests?'

'If he did,' Tarens argued with rock-bottom certainty, 'the order would have done away with him. He picks up connections and details too fast. That's not a safe quality to keep in the presence of dark arcane secrets.'

The pause hung, sweetened with the fragrance of birch coals and the burbling of the meat stew. Kerelie knotted her hands and glowered at her brother until at last he was forced to look up from the harness.

'You were never thick-headed,' she scolded. Then added, persistently honest, 'Are you willing to risk our livelihood? More, would you gamble that vaga-bond's life on the chance that you could be misled? By tomorrow, we could face a temple diviner sent to probe for heretical practice. Do you truly believe the Light's faith rests its cases on anyone's heart-felt conjecture?'

'Those herbals are all that's kept Efflin alive!' Tarens snapped, riled by his innate sense of loyalty. 'Are you saying we should act upon groundless fear, disown kindness, and throw the man out?' Engrossed by his sister's well-founded challenge, and not least, by a shared anxiety, the big crofter also forgot the tucked figure, miserably stilled in the shadow behind the filled wood bin . . .

But the distant enchantress cried out, locked in empathy and unable to bear Arithon's quick stab of agony from her vantage in the Storlain Mountains. Loss of memory had not dimmed the acuity of his gifted talent. The bitter argument between brother and sister smashed his frail poise at a stroke.

As initiate master, his extreme sensitivity tracked every nuance of subtle distress. The captive centuries spent under forced threat, healing the crazed terror of free wraiths, had laid his heightened awareness wide open. As the blunt blast of blame and raw stress battered into his unshielded nerves, the shock hit like a punch to the viscera.

Dizzy nausea shot him to his feet. The notion his *presence* might cause someone harm woke the echoes of forgotten horror. The drive to avert cata-strophic misfortune lashed him to instinctive flight. He was gone, out the door in one silent move, both dinner and comfort abandoned. The latch fell. Only a chill swirl of draught marked the wake of his frantic departure.

While Tarens whirled, stunned past words of regret for the hurt bestowed by his carelessness, the distant enchantress encamped in the mountains shed furious tears. She raged at her fate, that the mate she cherished as her own flesh and blood should become so bereft! The prodigious, bright talent whose labours had dispelled the worldwide invasion by Marak's hordes of hostile entities should never have been abandoned to languish alone in such bitter ignorance.

Which quandary baited Prime Selidie's trap: Elaira dared not give way under pressure, no matter how vicious the consequence. She sucked a cold breath to rebalance her rocked poise. The signet ring of Rathain on her hand bequeathed her its burden of secrets. She was the defender of all that it held, and by Arithon's placed faith, must sustain the harsh crux with her eyes opened. Or else become broken by sheer despair and take her heart's beloved down with her.

Amid desolate rocks, by the glimmer of starlight, she shouldered the watch through another bleak night.

Yet this pass, far worse than a scryer's assault rattled her shaken defenses. As Arithon's headlong flight through the wood distanced him from the cozy croft cottage, he gave rein to his natural instincts. Elaira shared his acute stress and confusion. She also shuddered as his inner senses exploded. The same terrible onset raked through her like fire as the rogue gift of far-sight his straits had made him forget smashed across his rifted perception.

He whimpered, beset, while vision upon vision *of what soon must be* hammered into his shattered awareness. Overset, stumbled onto his hands and knees in chill leaves, he panted in traumatized panic while the incomprehensible blaze of his wild talent seized the posited threads of the future and unfolded them into simultaneous multiplicity. Drowned in that welter of colour and noise, he floundered, bewildered. The rushed assault of overlayered images flickered onwards like a meaningless storm. He found no bearing: until one view captured his focused attention and fused into a clarity sharp as cut glass . . .

By tomorrow's dawn, an official mounted in ceremonial panoply would invade the croft with a cavalcade. The yard would be cluttered by gold-and-white banners, while shod hooves chopped the neatly mulched garden. While the armed outriders circled the cottage, their glittering captain would crash his mailed fist on the door, under temple authority. Doctrine confirmed his lawful right to arrest anyone who resisted. A search by his men would toss through every room. Despite the genuine strain of dire illness, Efflin would be hauled from his blankets. The bed where he lay became stripped to the frame. Men with drawn swords would hack mattress and ticking to shreds. Yet the Light's avid talent would find naught to incriminate. None of the closets held any trace of the herbalist reported by an upright citizen's complaint.

'He's not here,' Kerelie insisted, past tears. She wiped her scarred cheek, undone with relief that Tarens was off to haul fire-wood and not underfoot with his ready fists. 'Since no one knows where the odd fellow's gone, your questions cannot be answered.'

'Nothing's been found?' the lance captain snapped to the temple's baffled diviner. 'No item sufficient for an arcane scrying?' Failure at last would press him to withdraw his men. While they trampled through the wrack of upended belongings and formed up outside for departure, he would leave the distraught woman with an emphatic warning. 'Keep your door closed to strangers. The high priesthood at Erdane says Shadow is rising. A minion of Darkness is wakened and walking abroad, we've been told . . .'

Shuddering breaths pulled between his locked teeth, the fugitive huddled in the icy wood as the bout of slip-stream vision tattered to smoke and receded. He grasped what he saw well enough to perceive the precarious veil of innocence that shielded his benefactors. If authorities sought him, perhaps he was a criminal, although he could not remember the enormity that branded him as an outlaw. At least his shoddy rags were untraceable, burned down to ash in the cottage grate. Nothing he owned remained behind for a hostile talent to seize as proof, or use to track his subtle essence. Keep scarce and stay hidden, and he risked no one's safety. Cold and privation could be surmounted. He had the resourceful, inquisitive intelligence to survive the bleak onset of winter. Steadied once more, in command of himself, he pushed upright to seek a snug bolt-hole for shelter and sleep . . .

But the haven created by his reasoned calm eluded the enchantress, cross-linked as his helpless observer. For her, Arithon's momentary, insightful vision lashed her to alarm: *the True Sect's diviners were unleashed to run down a minion of Darkness*. Initiate-trained, the Light's examiners dispatched their servants abroad. Primed for an arraignment, such armed dedicates would harrow the country-side, played on the puppet strings of their creed and the canon law rigidly enforced from Erdane's high temple by a susceptible priesthood.

Whose secretive ploy had provoked such a search?

Elaira suspected the Prime Matriarch's ambition manoeuvred this cleanse to root out her fugitive quarry. Worse yet, the Fellowship's stay of constraint gave free rein to permit that unholy alliance. The religion's fanatics subsisted on faith since their grand avatar's abdication. Wracked into factions by the theosophers' jostling debates, and pitched by self-interest to extend the firm reach of the temple's influence, the Light's zealots and their righteous, false cause lay ripe for seduction as Selidie's diligent tool.

Hounded already, Arithon could be hunted across Tysan anywhere he tried to flee.

Nothing might turn the relentless adversity he might be driven to face. Aching, exhausted, while her distant beloved also braved a frigid night, Elaira gathered her courage, dried her eyes, and wrapped herself in her lonely bedroll. More than ever before, if she slept, she must ward her dreaming awareness. Under stress, reluctant, she sought shelter behind the endowment left to her in Arithon's ring.

More than symbolic of blood-line and royalty, the white-gold signet had been worn by Rathain's crown heirs back to the lineage's founder. The inside bore the engraved inscription: *'To my sons, from their forebears, back to Torbrand.'*

Elaira cupped the emerald setting. Immersed in a seer's trance, she focused her faculties into the mineral matrix. The imprinted tapestry of the ring's history flowed over her opened perception. She sank slowly into the depths of the stone, aware of its multilayered legacy. Kings and sanctioned princes far and long before hers had stamped the whispers of their bygone lives in the ring. Unlike the focus stones wielded by the Koriathain, kept uncleared to preserve intact records, this jewel retained its past impressions under Fellowship precepts: its crystalline nature served human purpose by choice, in exact harmonic alignment. Elaira's descent through its lattice became a light journey, untrammelled by conflict. Not every aspect contained within the jewel setting was laid open to her inspection. Wise enough for respect, Elaira bypassed those boundaries set under Sorcerer's seals. The private memories from Arithon's forebears stayed beyond her purview to access.

Her deep reach instead sought the gateway framed by the emerald's inclusions, keyed only to her. A specific phrase, spoken three times by a man's unbounded regard for her unlocked what no other could access. Chosen mate to the Prince of Rathain, Elaira alone could match and complete the bias of calm that once had enveloped a sea-side cottage in the impassioned moment of Arithon's discovery that his pure feelings for her were returned.

She, only, recalled the arduous passage when the very same phrase was repeated: as a Sorcerer's maze reforged their joined selves and scoured out all false reflections, man and woman had blended again, inseparable in mind and heart.

Worse, Elaira relived the last time, arisen on the wrenching hour when a false liegeman had betrayed Arithon into captivity. The moment revisited her in darkest nightmares, as the same outcry unleashed in extremity became their love's bittermost affirmation. When Selidie Prime threatened Elaira's life as the wedge to break Arithon's integrity, third and final, his protest rang, still: '. . . *Give me torture and loss, give me death, before I become the instrument that seals your utter destruction. Of all the atrocities I have done in the past, or may commit in the future, that one I could never survive.'*

The echo, stone-graven, tumbled Elaira back into the moment she had faced death at Prime Selidie's hands. Defenseless but never resigned, she could not fault the tragic choice, made while the throes of unbearable torment forced a desperate act, in resistance.

Shattered, yet defiant, *Arithon spared her life.* Saved her, by remaking as hers all the intimate joy shared between them. He ceded her everything: each cherished thought and every gathered memory of her encompassed within his experience. That sweetness of presence, treasured and true, was surrendered into her sole possession. Emptied himself, his given will yielded the part of his core self that was hers alone. Cut off and separate, he ensured that never again could the Koriani Order wield her mortality as the sure weapon to break him.

Royalty's ring on her hand kept the record of Arithon's grace within its inviolate sanctuary. An artifact of Rathain's founding heritage, wrought under the sacrosanct auspices of Fellowship purpose, the signet's protection predated the crown's bond of debt to the Koriathain, which Asandir's witnessed oath at long last had discharged. Within its safe haven, Elaira could let down her guard and dream past the reach of the order's design.

The double-edged gift surrendered her senses to an unbearably vivid immersion. All that Arithon was, and everything they had been together enraptured her starved spirit and wrapped her in a state of exquisite tenderness.

Always, visceral sorrow reopened the wound. When night passed, and she woke to cold wind, snow, and solitude, the past remained hers, unsullied still. But the glory of the sacred dance was sundered, the unparalleled harmony of their union broken to spare her. If Arithon survived, he might recover the lost identity sheared from him to safeguard his freedom. Yet the part of his being conjoined with Elaira, sequestered for safety within Rathain's seal ring, could not become reconnected. His enchantress retained her forlorn charge of the fact his male existence had once celebrated his true match. Unless the stake held by the Biedar at Sanpashir lent fresh insight to resolve the quandary, her heart's future stayed hopelessly bleak.

Ripples

Warned by her balked scryers that Elaira's resistance seeks contact with the Koriathain's most ancient enemy, the Prime orders the enchantress stopped, at all cost, before she sets foot in Sanpashir; then she announces her boldest step yet to pin down the elusive fugitive: 'We'll engage the infallible use of a fetch and stir Desh-thiere's curse to dog Arithon's trail . . .'

The same night, torn from sleep in the Lord Mayor's suite at Etarra, a fair-haired man thrashes awake in soaked sheets, chilled by the shadow of prescient nightmare: shivering, alone in the dark, he fears most to stand his frail ground against the consummate evil coiled inextricably through his being . . .

Days later, still troubled by dire portents, the Light's High Examiner responds to the news that the search for the minion of Darkness near Kelsing turns up nothing but rumours of an elusive herbalist: 'He left no object for a diviner to trace? Even a flask or a tie-string? That's suspicious! Hold the croft that sheltered him under covert watch and deploy more dedicates to quarter the country-side . . .'

III. Change

E fflin's recovery did not progress despite the efficacy of the remedies that broke his runaway fever. Constant dosing with cailcallow infusions, and the use of strong wintergreen poultices eased his wet cough for a time, even helped soothe his laboured breathing. Yet each hard-fought improvement failed to take hold. Days of diligent care did not lift his spirits or unseat the entrenched grip of his lethargy. Night after night, his reddened eyes dulled, until the once-vibrant spark in them faded to absence.

Since Tarens could not win this fight with his fists, he vented his helpless rage in the field, where hard labour behind the ploughshare granted his fury a harmless outlet. When the ox balked in the traces past sundown, he returned to the cottage, sore and snappishly tired.

Kerelie shouldered the burden of nursing, as well as the tiresome task of heating the gruel and bread sops for the listless invalid. Mostly, the trays returned to the kitchen with their picked-over contents untouched. Desperation led her to swap a precious crock of summer jam for a marrowbone from a neighbour. She soaked barley meal in the enriched broth in a hopeful effort to perk Efflin's flat appetite.

The beef in the soup became equally spurned. Driven fuming out of the kitchen, Kerelie smashed the clay bowl against the back step in a fit of exasperation.

'He's not trying!' she ranted to Tarens, drawn by her noise at a breathless sprint, with a stick snatched up as a cudgel to beat off a hostile assault.

But the only rescue his sister required was respite from an onslaught of tears.

'Unlike you and me, Efflin's not fighting!' Swept headlong into her brother's embrace, she pounded his arm in despair. 'Why, Tarens? *Why?* He knows our family inheritance cannot be salvaged without him!'

Tarens held her close. Heedless of the barley mush strewn down her skirt, he pressed her marred cheek against a worn jerkin that smelled of sweat, harness leather, and turned earth. 'I don't know, Kerie.' He let her sob, quite aware of the clean spoon and napkin that told over the source of her grief. Painfully wretched himself, he had little comfort to offer. 'Efflin's not been right for quite some time. Not since the misfortune came on us. But whatever afflicts him isn't your fault, Kerie. He's a grown man. Maddening as his behaviour can be, as hurtfully as his wasting straits try us, while he won't speak, there's no helping him.'

Kerelie sniffed, caught aback by the hiccup muffled into his sleeve. 'I'd rather you whacked him outright with a fence-post for acting the brainless fool!'

'Chin up,' Tarens chided. 'I'd prefer to keep the pasture intact and just break his head with my knuckles.'

Clinging to each other in harrowed dread, sister and brother stifled the thought that Efflin might easily die of the rancour sealed beneath his stark silence. Life, meantime, would not pause for his obstinacy, nor would Kelsing's mayor forgo the debt set against their name on the town tax-rolls.

Kerelie's exhausted weeping ran dry. While thin sun bleached the frost-burned grass in the yard, and the gusts scattered raced leaves between the straggled stakes in the fallow garden-patch, Tarens sighed and circuitously broached the idea that nagged at his uneasy mind.

'Survivors don't quit without reason,' he said.

Somehow Kerelie sensed the root of the tension that upset his natural complacence. 'Don't even say what you're thinking!' she snapped.

When Tarens returned no argument, she pushed him off, angry, her raw cheeks flamed pink and her swollen eyes bright as north sky. 'You daren't tell me I've driven away the one person who might have changed Efflin's condition!'

Tarens set his strong jaw. Prepared in his way to smooth her nettled anguish, he pointed out, 'You have eyes. Tell me you haven't seen the same evidence? Or haven't you noticed that the scrawny hen we dragged back from the market is now eating her silly head off? She'd bring double the price now, restored to good flesh.'

'Doesn't mean the useless fowl will ever lay, or hatch a new brood come the spring.' Kerelie belatedly dabbed her wet lashes on the inside of her cuff.

'Well, the sheen on the bird's feathers belies that.' Tarens dug into his breeches pocket and offered his crumpled handkerchief. 'Here. Don't mess up your blouse. You'll bleed the dye out of your pretty embroidery, and if not that, we've all heard in steamed language how much you love ironing wrinkled linen.'

'You're dead right. I hate laundry, never more than while Efflin's flat on his back and quite busy wrecking what's left of our sorry lives!' Kerelie honked noisily, huffed, and shoved a frizzled wisp of hair behind an ear the chill had buffed scarlet. Then she pinned her critical gaze on her brother. 'How could we have hidden that vagabond, anyhow? Did you honestly think he was innocent? By the rude way we were questioned, the high temple's examiner sent that diviner to ferret the poor creature out. If we chanced to harbour a heretic, wherever he is, you have to agree he's better off gone and, safest of all, well forgotten!'

Tarens looked away.

Kerelie's eyes narrowed. Fists set on her hips, she stared at her brother until his blunt silence piqued her suspicion. 'You know where that man is!'

'No.' Tarens blinked through his unkempt forelock. 'I swear on the graves of our dead, I do not.'

'Then what aren't you telling me?' Kerelie crushed up his soggy linen and hurled it down like a duelist's thrown gauntlet.

'I've not seen the fellow, hide nor hair!' Tarens protested. 'Not since the evening we aired our crass fears bare-faced in his living presence.' Stung, he poised for a wary retreat: his sister in a high fettle was wont to clout back with the first handy object within reach. The soup-bowl was broken. Left nothing else, she would pitch the available cutlery at him before the innocuous napkin.

Yet Efflin's wasting illness had sapped the spunk from Kerelie's spirit. 'Tarens!' she pleaded, wrung beyond fight, 'at least grace me with a civil answer.'

She would give him no peace. Warned by raw experience, Tarens sat down on the step and laced his big hands over his patched knees. 'I don't know where the little man went. But you're right. He has not gone, exactly.' The admission emerged in careful words: of fences repaired in the dark of the night; of water drawn to fill troughs for the livestock and small repairs done in the barn; of the fruit trees and vines pruned with expert skill where the untended tangle of last season's growth threatened to choke the next harvest.

More, Tarens acknowledged the signs of a talent beyond anything known to farm husbandry. 'If you saw the mends in the hedge by the wood, you'd see he's got yew twining into itself with a purpose that's frankly uncanny. That's not done without use of the secret lore kept by the charm makers.'

'Few dare that practice, far less in the open.' Kerelie shoved the sick tray aside with her foot. Frowning, she gathered her splattered skirts and settled next to her brother. 'Why didn't you tell me?'

Tarens regarded her with wide-lashed candor. 'What would you have done, Kerie? Driven him out? Or could you lie to a temple examiner if one returns with more suspicious questions? Worse, could I lay us open to blackmail, that any unscrupulous suitor might pressure us for your hand in marriage? I couldn't abide the chance that might happen! But without Efflin's help, in flat honesty, I can't work the croft by myself!'

Kerelie stood. Tight with hurt, she spun and picked up the tray. The clean spoon beside the untouched cloth napkin sharpened her to accusation. 'You were risking our landed heritage, Tarens.'

'Set against Efflin's *life*? Does our titled right to till these miserable acres even signify?'

'More than our brother's health may be at stake,' Kerelie pointed out, tart. 'Or does the fact each of us was declared for the Light since our birth have no meaning?'

There, even her brother's mild nature lost patience. 'Your prim faith in the True Sect's canon serves naught. The temple preaches a loveless morality that cares not one jot for the plight of our livelihood. The priests are fat parasites, theosophizing on their rumps while folk like us break our backs, milked dry by their tithes and their rote obligations. Where does their doctrine show the least concern for our chance to enjoy the fruits of our happiness?'

Kerelie banged down the tray and confronted her brother, her work-worn hands as chapped as his own, and her eyes just as smudged with relentless fatigue. 'Do you honestly believe that mad vagabond has the gift, or the know-ledge to enact a deep healing? Even the Light's priesthood don't flaunt such arrogance! They warn against undue interference. Could you take the risk that an invasive power of Darkness might ensnare a man's defenseless soul? Or that a madman with a rogue talent could invasively damage a wounded spirit?'

'That fellow is not crazy!' Blushed under her censure, Tarens amended in heart-felt conviction. 'No, I don't know everything. The Light's policies confuse me. But if Efflin dies, our family holding is lost to us anyhow. Should we act on our unseen fears before the virtue of human kindness? Who's given us more, the Light's faith or that stranger? And if you choose to reject generosity, then what standing do we have left in this world, or in the hereafter, for that matter?'

Kerelie turned her back. Palms pressed to her face, her hunched shoulders quivering, she lashed out and kicked the tin tray. The spoon flashed air-borne and tumbled into the garden, while the napkin, wind-chased, fluttered across the sere ground and caught like a forlorn flag of truce in the rose trellis. A moment, she stood, her vulnerable fragility fit to shatter at the next breath. Until the surfeit of grief overset her distress, and she broke into snuffles of laughter.

'Well,' she gasped presently. 'I never did want to marry. Or bear the brood it would take to upkeep this sprawling place properly. If you think that scruffy creature might help, go ahead and try to find him.'

Late night made the vigil the hardest to bear, when the candle carved harsh shadows that rendered Efflin's wasted face cadaverous. He had not touched the stew brought for his supper. The sorry, cold mass congealed in the bowl, that hard straits and poverty saved to reheat for Tarens upon his return. Since the plan to seek help must wait for the vagabond to emerge from his hidden cover, the lonely watch extended far into the night.

Kerelie fetched a rushlight for thrift, and her osier work-basket. She stretched new linen onto her embroidery hoop, then snatched for the illusion of solace by plying her needle. Against the laboured breaths of a brother's decline, she sewed life: small birds, brilliant butterflies, and entwined summer flowers. The simple beauty that nurtured her delight bloomed under her hands in lovingly set, intricate stitches. Frantically as she sought to escape from her grief, the pervasive astringency of cailcallow tea and the bitter aroma of willow bark made the sick-room oppressive.

Religion had never founded her peace, but nothing else fed her stark absence of hope. She lacked the wisdom to tell if the vagabond was in fact a rogue sorcerer. Her prayer to the Light appealed for clear guidance, or lacking that, the gift of clemency. Should the human heart be asked to choose between a blind adherence to faith, or succour for a dying brother? Hours passed to the whine of the wind through the eaves and the bang of a loosened shutter. The northerly cold that brought in early blizzards seeped through the casement and flared the coals as the kitchen fire subsided to ash. Kerelie arose and piled on fresh logs. Almost, she wished Tarens would be unsuccessful, that the gall of her doubts might stay the brute course on known ground, without liability. Perhaps the refuge of belief was best kept unchallenged by troublesome questions that bordered on heresy.

The latch clicked in that moment of harrowed uncertainty. Kerelie met Tarens as he stepped in, bone chilled but triumphant. The disreputable vagabond dogged his heels, slight and graceful in step as a ghost.

Kerelie's start of jangled trepidation met green eyes, oddly sparked by ironic hilarity. Then the wafted stink brought indoors with him assaulted her nostrils. Her mouth, just opened to scold, snapped shut against sudden nausea. Hurled beyond dignity, Kerelie back-stepped, hands clutched to her middle.

For of course, denied any civilized shelter, the vagabond had been forced to survive on snared game. Necessity made him fashion his jerkin and jacket from green hides, skinned off the animals he trapped for sustenance.

Kerelie whirled, forearms braced on the window-sill until her shocked spasms subsided. 'Light's grace attend us!' she gasped. 'Your sorry friend will breed rampant pestilence, reeking of rot as he does!'

Before Tarens managed a heated response, she collapsed on the bench, flushed bright pink. She drew several taxed breaths, then abandoned propriety and curled up, not sick, but helplessly laughing.

'My fault, I admit, for pinch-fisted thriftiness since I refused to spare any other warm clothing for someone so desperately needy.' Her contrite change of heart came on as the spring storm, without apology and brisk enough to level pride and presumption. 'Tarens! Fetch in the wash-tub and draw water for bathing. Then ask that poor creature to strip to the skin! Burn his unholy mess of raw fur out of doors and throw the ashes onto the midden. I'll fetch the good soap and scrounge proper dress from Uncle's left things in the cedar trunk. Be sure of this! I won't let that appalling charnel stench anywhere near Efflin's sick-bed.'

Scoured clean by his own hand, also shaved and refreshed by the scent of lavender soap, the vagabond soon passed the sister's critical muster to be admitted to her brother's bedside. Kerelie ensconced herself in Aunt Saffie's rocker, once used to settle her infant sons after nursing in the late hours. Now, the worn cushion held a bristle of jabbed pins to take in Uncle Fiath's good winter jacket. Tarens tucked cross-legged on the window-seat, reluctant to rest and abandon the beggarman to his sister's prickly temperament.

Efflin alone showed no apprehension. Bone-pale, he lay lifelessly still, the smoothed quilts on his chest scarcely stirred by his shallow breaths. His cheeks were sunken into his skull, with his half-opened, flint eyes glinting empty and listless. He seemed to have drifted past Fate's Wheel already, with naught but a shell left behind as his sturdy frame wasted.

The vagabond absorbed the cadaverous flesh at one glance. Restless or driven, he retreated into the kitchen and slipped back out into the night. A taut interval passed. Before Kerelie loosened her guard in relief, and while Tarens wrestled impatience, the fellow returned with an armload of logs from the wood-pile. His hand-picked cache contained only birch. The sweet fragrance lightened the air as he built up the kitchen fire.

Once the crackling flames caught from the embers, the ruffian stood up and quartered the croft cottage, length and breadth. His industrious survey peered into crannies and touched random objects with an interest that ran beyond curiosity. His rapt manner frayed Kerelie's already rattled state of anxiety. She dropped the distracted pursuit of her needlework, stalked into the kitchen, and hovered over his shoulder, though Tarens chastised her rudeness.

'Let him be, Kerie! He isn't a thief.'

'What's he doing, then?' Trailed after the man's furtive step up the stair, she bridled as his brazen exploration turned down the second-floor hallway. Before he presumed the unthinkable and breached the shut door to the boys' empty bedroom, she called downstairs, benighted, 'Shouldn't somebody check to be sure he's not up to mischief?'

Which comment froze the snooping stranger at the forbidden threshold. His head turned. Kerelie caught the brunt of his razor-keen stare, charged by a contempt that prickled her hackles. Then, undeterred, he spun on his heel and invaded the family's most sacrosanct shrine. The room was pitch-dark. He carried no light. Since Kerelie could not bear the desecration, she refused the loan of a candle. Instead, she fled headlong downstairs and collided with Tarens, who captured her into his steadfast embrace.

'You know where he's poking his inquisitive nose,' she objected, muffled by her brother's warm shirt.

'Let him do as he must,' Tarens urged, also shaken, but unready to surrender his last glimmer of hope to the stifling shadow of grief. 'Everything that man's done has held purpose! I'd place my trust in the same goodwill that spared you from Grismard's clutches.'

Kerelie sniffed. She conceded the point, enough to suppress her outraged nerves until the intrusive, quick footstep re-emerged and descended the stair. Her stare still shot daggers for flagrant presumption. Worse yet, the glow from the kitchen fire brushed the tell-tale gleam of polished wood in the pilferer's hand.

Rankled, Kerelie shouted, 'He's got Paolin's flute! Efflin's going to be furious!'

Tarens clamped her arm, curbed his own blast of temper, and whispered a plea for restraint. 'Efflin's riled nerves might be for the best. Force him to take a stand and maybe he'll rejoin the living.'

If the vagabond noticed their umbrage, nothing deflected his course as he poked through the cottage kitchen. No pot and no spoon on the rack went unfingered. He laid his ear to the trestle, eyes shut, as if the scarred planks spoke like a book's riffled pages, scribed with the past layers of ingrained conversations.

While Kerelie glowered with prim disapproval, he moved on and ran a near-reverent hand over the contents of Aunt Saffie's dish cupboard. As if the tactile slide of bare fingers garnered the nuance of buried impressions, he lingered, drew in a satisfied breath, and savoured a pause before he pressed onwards. Glimpsed by the frangible gleam of the fire, his eyes appeared softened from focus. Bemused as a dreamer's, the slight tilt of his head suggested he listened to strains far beyond natural hearing.

Kerelie's impetuous tongue blurted outright what Tarens was thinking: 'Either your creature's as daft as the moon, or we're watching a sorcerer work.'

'I fear the temple's meddling examiners far more,' Tarens snapped. 'If harm comes to us by this man's hand, I'll shoulder the blame. But without a shred of contrary evidence, my mind is going to stay open.' Deaf to debate, he positioned himself to shield against his sister's untoward interference. When at last the vagabond made his way back into Efflin's chamber, the shortened candles cast fluttering haloes over coverlet and furnishings, and pooled yellow light on the braided-rag carpet. Kerelie beat a nettled retreat to her chair and retrieved her dropped mending like armour. Tarens stationed himself by the door, despite his stout claim of unshaken faith, poised to move fast if need warranted.

The vagabond drifted onwards to the bed and extended the hand-made flute, balanced across his open palms. There, he waited until his planted stance forced Efflin's blank stare to a flicker of confrontation. The moment faded. Indifference resurged, then subsided to flat rejection. The inflamed rims of the sunken lids lowered, sight shuttered behind adamant, closed eyes.

The vagabond bowed his head, not resigned. He laid the flute across Efflin's stilled knees. Left it there, gleaming atop the plain coverlet as he leaned forward and ran his expressive fingers over the bedstead: the same that Aunt Saffie and Uncle Fiath had shared through their eighteen years joined in marriage. He stroked the carved wood, engrossed: as if his engaged survey of another's belongings scrutinized intimacies that even kinsfolk had no right to rifle.

'Feels like an invasion of somebody's privacy,' Kerelie grumbled with self-righteous heat.

Her intrusive comment offended at last. The vagabond's chin snapped up from absorbed contemplation. His disturbed regard raked her soul-deep with reproach. The effect all but flayed skin, as he left Efflin's bedside and advanced on her chair, his stalker's step primed for a challenge.

Her fierce courage met him straight on. The fears that edged Kerelie's outbursts never had stemmed from concern for herself. Aware she would stand her adamant ground, Tarens looked on with choked breath as the vagabond squared off against a loyal sister's disapproval. The hands he raised could have belonged to an artist, but for his broken nails and chapped knuckles. Firmly, he tugged the bastion of fine needlework out of her defensive fingers. Then he gathered up her emptied palm, and cupped her own flesh against the old scar that disfigured her cheek.

His clasp guided, only. She easily could have yanked free. Yet as though anaesthetized, she did not jerk away, but looked upwards into his angular features. His green eyes captured hers, deep beyond measure, impenetrably calm and unthreatening.

And something inside of her burst the rigid dam that constrained a violent torrent of feeling . . .

She was three on the day the neighbour's cranky mule lunged with flattened ears and nipped at her arm. Open-hearted and innocent, she had leaned over the fence-rail to plant a kiss on its whiskered muzzle, eager to grant any creature who wronged her that earnest gesture of forgiveness.

Such a simple mistake to have scarred her for life. The pain as the mule's blunt teeth crushed her cheek had been brief, and the pinprick trauma of stitches, a pittance. The damage that crippled struck later, inflicted by endless humiliation.

Hurtful memories rushed through in a cruel cascade: of her mother's exasperated anger and resigned pity; then the remorseless jeers of the other children who poked fun at her welted face. She shrank into self-consciousness, then scourging embarrassment, as puberty delivered the blow that her blemish made her undesired by the young men. She endured the torment of her uncle's strained silences, then the helpless resignation that drove him from the room each time her aunt broached her dim prospects for a good marriage. The westlands tradition of chaperoned courtship made her teen years a punishment as she sat through the dances, or waited forlorn at an empty table. Shunned, she had watched the lit candles burn above the baked sweets that hopeful youth had laid out for young suitors who failed to appear. Or worse, she had struggled to make conversation, when callers were sent by their insistent mothers as a hollow gesture of conciliation.

Seared to her core, Kerelie ached for the flaw that could not, in this life, ever leave her. Her spoiled features could not be restored. She lived, day on day, as separate as though sealed behind a pane of marred glass. Except for her brothers, no one she met ever *saw* her: until a wild vagabond, chance-met on the road, had bridged the gap of her isolation. No person, ever, had soothed her raw nerves with the tonic of clear understanding.

The first sob tore from Kerelie's chest with a sound like rent cloth, coarse and alarmingly primal. Tears followed, a wracking catharsis of shame that alarmed Tarens to witness. The spate passed without incident. Limp, drained to emptiness in release, Kerelie made no effort to disentangle herself. Bent forward, leaned into the vagabond's support, she allowed him, *that gently,* to ease her soaked fingers back into her lap.

Now, his weathered touch cradled her scarred cheek directly. The drawn flesh with its whitened, hard knot of tissue did not repulse him. His contact stayed steady, an unpretentious acceptance beyond any banal word of comfort.

Unthreatening, tender, he lifted her chin. He brushed the brine from her lashes, and gazed into her eyes until the flood brimmed again, spilled, and emptied. *Something* uncanny quickened the connection: a bloom of spring warmth, or a balm on the spirit. The spark ignited change that rippled beyond mere sensation, too ineffable to be captured by language. As though she received the live pulse of his thought, Kerelie experienced a view of herself that transcended flesh and shattered the framework of outward appearance.

She experienced a redefinition of value, as if a veil lifted, or the dross had been razed at a stroke from an unfinished sculpture. Where strangers complained of her carping tongue, *this touch* spoke of a vulnerable heart, defensively guarding a family. She saw, in the stitches of her busy needle, a glow that whispered of happiness *so delicate,* she had never risked its fragility to outside expression. The caring she could not expect, from a man, was twined into her embroidered flowers and birds, and the ebullient scrolls of spring vines. These quiet gifts were bestowed on close kin, and more shyly, to the rare few who showed her a constant friendship.

No one before ever spoke of her grace as she moved. None mentioned her staunch strength, or complimented the confidence she brought to the mindful tasks of plain living.

Through the stranger's eyes, which mirrored her self, she saw her steel core and encountered the person she was: a being devoted to kindness, who would not forsake the living trust of another. The monstrous shadow thrown by her scar no longer eclipsed the inherent treasures of the virtues she brought to the world.

The bubble of startled laughter began in her chest and burst from her throat. Remade inside, she gave rein to the joy unleashed from the locked prison within her. Hurled into a freedom too large to cram back into her former shell, she revelled in the vibrancy of her wholeness. The mask people viewed was not who she was. Her inner light shone with a rarefied brilliance beyond any flaw to extinguish.

The vagabond quietly withdrew his hands. Deferent, he smiled and ducked his head to forestall her effusive thanks. He bowed instead to show honour to Kerelie, which restraint let the unfolded changes within her smooth into resettled alignment.

When Tarens's anxious query broke in, puzzled and sharply insistent, Kerelie answered, astonished to wonderment. 'Be still! All is well. I'm quite fine. More than that.' She paused, drew a breath, and tingled from head to foot with exhilaration. 'Now I know how your beggarman healed the old hen.' Hesitant, she touched her ridged cheek. The ugly scar remained as prominent as ever, but its blight on her spirit had lifted. The entrenched belief she was hideous no longer smothered her under the patent falsehood of unworthiness. The blemish on her self-image, which had strangled the fearless intimacy of her innate joy, was cleansed.

She pronounced at due length, 'If this man's talent is considered black sorcery, then the temple and the Light's priesthood are wrong to forbid us the benefits of such practice.'

'He might heal Efflin's ailment the same way, you think,' Tarens ventured, afraid to hope.

As fresh tears brimmed her luminous eyes, Kerelie nodded with encourage-ment. 'Let him try. I can assure the attempt is unlikely to cause any harm.'

The vagabond accepted her tone as consent and resumed his disputed place at the invalid's bedside. Efflin's eyes remained stubbornly shut. Inert to the life in his presence, he languished amid the unwrinkled sheets, motionless but for his slowed breaths. He seemed a being sucked empty: except that the dark-haired healer surveyed his slack frame with undaunted focus. As though attentive to registers too refined to be heard, he studied Efflin's unresponsive condition.

No word did he speak. No demonstrable feeling moved his expression. Yet after a searing, stopped interval, the vagabond reached out and claimed the wood flute.

The oiled surface had been polished by love. Beyond that, the toy instrument was unremarkably plain: a fancy fashioned by country-bred hands for a child, whose sprightly laugh and innocent pleasures had perished of sickness untimely. The drilled stops were spaced for a little boy's hands. But the stranger's slight fingers danced over them, silent, as if the wood sang, quite alive to the sensi-tivity of his inner mind. As Kerelie and Tarens watched, their strange visitor did the unthinkable: he raised the heirloom flute to his lips and sounded the lowest pitch.

The bass note that emerged should have been nothing special. Yet his extraordinary, expressive breath shaped a tempered statement that raised the small hairs at the nape. The vagabond's regard stayed riveted upon Efflin's form, dull and abandoned to listlessness under the blankets. The ferocious attentiveness brought to bear bespoke nothing else but an awareness of the uncanny.

The flute's voice dwindled like a cry into nothing. In fixed focus entrained upon Efflin's blank face, the dark-haired fellow paused once again, then uncovered the next hole and ran up the scale. The highest tone faded. This time the silence hung like blown glass. Head tilted, he engaged the small instrument, and by tentative phrases, began to unreel an evocative melody.

Ragged nails and rough callus had hidden the fact that those fingers belonged to a talent: his touch on the flute spoke, exquisitely sure, and laced calm through the stuffy room. The outlay of music refigured the senses, until familiar perceptions acquired a chisel-punched clarity. The neat, coloured petals in Kerelie's embroidery glowed, alive in the handcrafted counterpane. Fire-light shimmered like a warm caress over the quaint patterns carved into the pine bedstead. Moonlight glittered the frosted window-panes to opalescence, and buffed a sheen on the grain of worn floor-boards. Vitality became magnified, until the clean sigh of the onlookers' breaths flowed like spun silk, entwined and then braided by the intimate love expressed between them as a family.

The vagabond took charge of his composition and wove in the flicker of a sprightly lilt. All the while his gaze stayed locked upon Efflin's features. Change had crept in, almost unseen: the invalid's brow was no longer smooth, or the lips, slack with bitter indifference.

Soon the furrowed frown deepened. As if the happy lift in the tune somehow chafed, Efflin gritted his teeth with annoyance.

Like the hook of a burr, the musician seized his bold theme and expanded its rankling influence. His melody soared into foot-tapping joy, then took flight with grace notes that skittered with laughter. Caught up, then wound in and gripped by his spell, the listeners smiled as the tonal harmonics seized their hearts and flung open the gates of remembrance.

Swept away, they relived the forgotten cadences of better times, when an older brother's mature strength had worked the croft side by side with their uncle. The lost days of their childhoods re-emerged, before the high temple's decree had seized their father as a troop conscript. The ribald jokes, the wry pranks, and the long, summer days spent lazily fishing, while Aunt Saff smoked the beehives to harvest the honey, and the sun-drenched barley fields ripened to yellow. The crushed scent of greenery, and boiling jam, and the spike to Fiath's jack whiskey brewed in the cold snap of autumn – the ease of those gilded years flooded back on a poignant wave of nostalgia.

Efflin's eyes were closed still. But his wracked fight to stay separate now became a pitched battle that rammed his frame rigid.

The musician played on. Tempo quickened as he sliced golden showers of sound out of silence. His merry measures *described* Efflin's grace, until none watching could deny the sorrowful ache of a lifetime laid down by abandonment. The brother who wasted in bedridden inertia became an agony to behold. Kerelie fought the fierce need to shake him, and Tarens shuddered with clenched fists, raked by the urge to pick a rife fight.

But the voice of the flute raised a wall in restraint, fashioned to smother harsh action. Bright as the struck peal of bronze chimes, the notes quickened with shimmering urgency. To Efflin's being, as once he had been, the musician added a descant theme teased in counterpoint through the base melody.

Kerelie whitened, first to identify the uncanny source of the tune's inspiration. 'He's playing the boys! Paolin and Chan, do you hear? Light above,' she gasped, aching, 'Make him stop! I can't bear it.'

Her appalled shock only spurred the musician to seize on the fuel of her distress. He reached into that molten core of sheer agony and played love, his tender measures swelled to a shout that scalded with more brilliance yet. Two deceased children were respun from the grave. Vibrant, as though living – *almost!* – the eye saw them in etheric vision beside Efflin's bed. Their young spirits would have showed laughter and verve, unmarked by the loss of their mother. With all of life's wonder undimmed, their memory beseeched the grown man to open his jaded eyes and acknowledge them.

The insistent demand: to *be* what they were, must crack, through a fiercely kept isolation and loose the agonized grief kept imprisoned by steel reservation. The music commanded, until stone itself could have wept in unbridled sympathy.

The musician dared further. Theme and playful embellishment flowed into refrain, and resounded, more haunting yet. The pervasive gloom of the sickroom air parted before the sweet scent of Aunt's cherished roses.

Which lyrical impact raised Kerelie's tears and winded Tarens like a punch in the chest. But Efflin's response outstripped them both: quaking as though seared inside by hot iron, he bit his lip to the verge of drawn blood.

This time, Tarens unriddled the astonishment. 'Light's own grace,' he whispered, appalled. 'Efflin! Aunt Saff! For mercy, how deeply he must have loved her!'

As if his cry unleashed comprehension, the innocent melody that bespoke the two boys reached consummate pitch. All three of the musician's laid lines became welded into a harmonic nexus. Imperative artistry cascaded, peaked, and stripped bare an indelible truth: that Efflin's theme was the backbone that cradled the effervescence of both little boys.

'The children were Efflin's!' gasped Kerelie, rocked by the bolt-strike of epiphany. 'Paolin and Chan! Bone and breath, they were Efflin's!'

Facts fit.

With a sting like the snap of a brittle stick, the flute's call destroyed all reserve. On the bed, Efflin turned his head into the pillow and buried his ravaged face. He groaned, stricken through by stark anguish. Then his bent shoulders shook to a sob as though his very spirit had shattered. The sorrow never expressed leaped the breach, dredged up from his locked well of silence. He wept for a loss that no other but Saffie could have understood. His blessing, and his curse, that she had not lived long enough to share his distraught pain as he served the last rites for their two little sons.

Hammer to anvil, past memories reshaped: of Uncle's seamed face, eased from years of pent strain in the delight brought by Paolin's birth. Fiath could not have known. Saffie and Efflin had never been seen to touch hands, not within anyone's presence. But the hours spent whistling in quiet content as he hauled the mulch and manure, built and bent the arched trellis, and dug the beds for Aunt's roses: hindsight unveiled all of his secret regard, lavished onto her garden in tender devotion.

Tonight, shown the shocking depth of his wound, Tarens and Kerelie bestowed no blame. Aunt Saffie was not their blood relation, except through the kin ties of marriage. The indiscretion just bared to light could not provoke a betrayal. They knew Fiath's contentment had hidden no falsehood. His presumed paternity *never* had been under question throughout the boys' raising. No harm could befall the dead, after all. But for the benighted siblings left living, the course of bereavement changed shape. Shared grief emerged that broke like a squall and closed the familial circle. Sister and brother piled onto the bed. They held Efflin together, as if their clasped arms could bind up a fissure that, till this night, had been as the abyss, wide and deep and beyond insurmountable. The cankered sore that had tormented a bereft father no longer lay gagged under honour-bound silence.

Efflin wept, freed. Bonded once more into seamless fellowship, none noted the moment when the flute player ceased his infallible effort. Amid softened quiet, gently fire-lit and warm, the three siblings revisited their sorrows in depth, and together shored up the wreckage of a brother's unconsoled spirit.

'If my act was wrong-doing, no one took hurt,' Efflin murmured at due length, replete. His exhausted defiance asked for no forgiveness. 'Uncle never knew. Aunt Saff asked for nothing, nor begged a thing more beyond her sore need that pined beyond hope for the chance of conception. She had sensed my indecent feelings, I'm sure, although I never broached a word to her. When she realized her fertility might pass her by, she pleaded with me, and begged not to make use of a stranger. She was that desperate to give Fiath the children they both ached to rear. And for all our sakes, the croft demanded a secured future, besides.'

'Efflin, hush,' murmured Kerelie. 'No need to explain. With Saff and Fiath both gone, it is meet that we share your burden.'

Tarens swallowed, unable to speak. Embarrassed at last for his kinsfolk's breached privacy, he turned his head, first to notice the empty room at his back. The child's wooden flute, that Efflin had carved for a son who called another man *father*, rested abandoned on the window-seat. The stops were silent. Smoothed wood gleamed in the etched spill of the moonlight, never to sound the like of those piercing measures again.

Only the partially re-tailored jacket had been removed from the arm of Aunt's chair.

The night was the family's to rejoice in relief for the gift of Efflin's recovery.

The bleak hour before dawn brought the True Sect's temple examiner, arrived in a ground-shaking thunder of hooves with a lathered entourage of mounted lancers. Elite dedicates, drilled lifelong to bear arms, they poured down the lane without warning, polished to a frost glitter of armour and headed by the pomp of their Sunwheel standards. They carried a warrant to shackle the guilty, verified by a vested diviner sworn to uphold the faith. A blessed talent who served divine Light, he claimed to have sensed the emanations raised by a minion's dark practice.

Tarens wakened to the commotion. Still halfway clad in yesterday's clothes, he grabbed his boots and charged downstairs, just as the double column of horsemen crammed into the cottage yard. Indoors, the candles were long since pinched out. Ghostly in her night-rail, Kerelie poised in blanched dread at the kitchen casement. Tarens crossed the rug and peered over her shoulder, then swore through his teeth as the arrogant brutes trampled their shod mounts over the rose-beds. He yanked on his footwear, further enraged as they commandeered Efflin's trellis to snub the lance captain's makeshift picket line.

'You can't stop them, Tarens,' Kerelie said, frightened. Her alarmed grasp sought to restrain his tense wrist, shaken off in savage rejection.

Outside, the steamed horses jostled and stamped. Steel jingled to someone's brusque demand to form up a cordon. 'Quickly, mind! Strike to kill if anyone tries to escape.'

Efflin slept on through the upset. Dreamlessly convalescent, he never stirred as the flare of held torches speared through the front windows. Nor did he hear the marched scrape of boots on the frosted ground as temple guardsmen with ready weapons surrounded the house, then a smaller group detached under orders to move in for the shake-down.

'What should we do, Tarens?' Kerelie fretted.

A last-moment evasion was already futile, with Efflin too weak to stand upright. To move him at all would require a litter, and even unburdened, a hale man on foot would be ridden down as a marked target.

Tarens faced the bad call. His questionable traffic with the vagabond cornered them all, with barely seconds left to forestall the sure threat of disaster.

Flooded light through the panes juddered over the pots by the chimney as the dedicates' advance crunched up the garden-path. As their tread boomed in step up the planked stair to the porch, Tarens grabbed Kerelie and forcefully dragged her into the downstairs bedchamber. 'Stay with Efflin.' A snatched view from the window-seat let him measure the strength of the temple's invasion: eight sword-bearing heavies in gold-and-white surcoats flanked the entry, backed by two more bearing brands. At ground level, poised before the placed cordon, the talent diviner stood rapt as a ferret, his stainless white cowl and blazon lent a sulphurous tinge under the flame-light.

This was not a warrant for inspection but a company dispatched to seize custody.

The lance sergeant's fist hammered into the door. 'Open up! Or the Light's protectors will claim their due right!'

'Tarens!' cried Kerelie from Efflin's bedside, 'Unfasten the bar straightaway, or they'll break it.'

'More like fire the thatch in their zeal to flush heretics,' Tarens snapped, grim. He shoved from the window-seat and plunged back towards the darkened kitchen, still talking. 'Let them have their way. After all, what ugliness can they find?'

'Go after him, sister!' The rushed plea was Efflin's, croaked from the pillow. 'Whatever he's planning won't be to the good.'

'Tarens! Hold back!' Kerelie's appeal raised no answer, an ominous sign. Worried, she bolted a scant step behind her impulsive brother's intent. The banked hearth shed no gleam on his purpose. The sultry glow of the torch-flames through the mottled glass only dazzled her vision and swathed his quick movement in velvet shadows.

'Wait, Tarens! I beg you!' Her appeal stayed ignored.

Already, Tarens had flung wide the door. He hoisted the trestle bench as a shield. His other hand brandished the poker snatched from the hearth. Head down, shouting curses that blasphemed the Light, he clouted his way through the startled dedicates placed to secure the entry. Several crashed over, yelling. Their fallen weight staggered the torch-bearers backwards. Mazed in the swoop and flicker of confused light, the lancers left upright scrambled and surged forward to stop him, too late.

Tarens bulled onwards down the porch stair. His leveled spike gaffed the partridge-plump breast of the Light's diviner. Blood blossomed. The gush smirched the sacred Sunwheel emblem and spread scarlet over the spotless robes of divine office.

Kerelie's scream overpowered the stricken man's grunt of agony. Those lancers still astride roared in black rage and raked spurs to their idle mounts, while their foot-bound comrades charged to retaliate. Tarens moved faster, grabbed the speared victim, and hauled his collapsed frame upright by the collar.

'Spying scum!' The crofter jerked out the impaled barb of the poker and flung the gored implement end over end. The tumbling length of iron spun into the forelegs of the inbound horses. Half of the beasts shied, which broke and unravelled the concerted attack. Exposed, made the target of two dozen swords, Tarens dumped his grisly trophy into a sprawling heap at the feet of the horrified temple examiner. While the corpse writhed in the throes of fatality, the brazen crofter dropped to his knees in surrender.

Arms outflung, head up, Tarens's burly form invited the vengeful lance, or the punitive blade to strike downwards and finish him.

'No!' pealed the command of a ranked authority. 'Take the murderer alive!' Emerged to the fore, the speaker wore the hooded regalia of the True Sect's temple. 'He shall die for his crime. But the execution will take place in public as a moral example!'

Life dedicates trained to unquestioned obedience, the men pulled their steel. En masse, they slammed into Tarens and wrestled him prostrate on the frosted ground. Their captain attended the savaged diviner, whose blessed talent would track no more minions of Shadow for the faith.

While the men on the porch pinioned Kerelie's struggle to rush down the stair to her brother, Tarens cried, 'I'm the only one guilty! The others knew nothing.'

'I'll be the one to determine the charges,' declared the Light's Lord Examiner. A vigorous official, ablaze in white cloth and the rippling glitter of diamond-set appointments, he gestured. 'Set the criminal in manacles. He must face the scaffold, but all in due time. His kinsfolk will stand trial on their own merits. My official inquiry begins immediately.'

'You'll find nothing!' yelled Tarens.

A mailed fist cuffed him silent. Hardened to Kerelie's weeping, and rough-shod before Efflin's mortified weakness, the dedicates invaded the cozy croft cottage with their hobnailed boots and pine-torches. They tore through each room, upended the furnishings, and bashed over the plate cupboard. Smashed porcelain became ground into the braided rug as they raked kettles and ladles from their rowed hooks and slashed into the flour-sacks hoarded for winter until the puffed contents emptied. Against Efflin's desperate, sensible pleas, they demolished the larder. Jars of preserves were smashed to the floor, and the waxed cheeses pulped underfoot. When the exhaustive search found no artifacts of dark practice amid the litter of wreckage, men rifled the wood bin and barreled upstairs to kick through the contents of clothes-chests and closets. Room by room, the desecration proceeded, cloth goods and belongings savaged to destruction, and floor-boards mauled into splinters.

When the invasion burst into the sick-room, Kerelie's outraged language met deafened ears. 'Where is mercy? Have you no care for illness?'

Efflin's blanketed form was thrust into a chair. When his tattered bedding yielded no hidden cache of arcane talismans, he was forced to endure the further brutality as the lancers secured Tarens by stringing him up by chained wrists from the rafters.

There he swung, bashed and bleeding, worried by the point of the sergeant's sword at his throat.

He railed, nonetheless. 'Leave my family be! They've done nothing wrong.'

'Clap a lid on your noise!' the sergeant cracked.

Tarens spat, which earned a back-handed blow to the face that pulped his nose and set Kerelie shrieking.

'Silence that bitch!' snapped the captain, annoyed. His sideward glance cut through the turpentine taint of the torch smoke. 'There's a dish-rag? Then gag her.'

But Kerelie quieted, before being forced. Against the shocked quiet, Tarens unclenched his bruised jaw. Shaking, he spoke through the slur of split lips and the jet of streamed blood from crushed nostrils. 'My sister and brother are innocent! Until tonight, they had no knowledge I sheltered a fellow who trifled with sorcery!'

But his confession brought his siblings no exoneration.

Too haughty to soil his temple finery, the Lord Examiner served his rebuke from the cottage doorway. 'The Light's justice acts with infallible equity. Punishment only follows due cause, and mercy rests upon no one's insolent claim or false testament! Before you burn for a liaison with evil, you will bear truthful witness! Divine law also must vouchsafe the fates of your brother and sister. They will be condemned or set free only under the burden of proof.'

To the dedicate lancers, the Lord Examiner said, 'Bind the pair of them with their wrists at their backs. I will verify whether the works of a sorcerer were made welcome under this roof!'

'Don't fight them!' begged Tarens. 'Just give what they ask!' Shivering now, sick and cold and in pain, his voice cracked at last under punishment.

Efflin slumped, wrung limp, the glisten of tears dammed behind his shut lashes. He could not speak for the horror, that his younger brother had tried such a desperate measure to take the blame as their scapegoat. The croft would be lost. Westlands land law adhered to the True Sect Canon. But the fragile hope to spare the rest of the family from the fires of heresy might yet be raised from the ashes of a brave brother's sacrifice.

All their fates rested under the provenance of the Light's Lord Examiner. A fleshy man with sandy hair and cream skin, he minced across the breached threshold in his rich robes and jewelled insignia. Even in the dimmed kitchen, he glittered. Wrists tied, tongue stilled behind his locked teeth, Efflin winced at the heavy-set tread that chinked the sadly smashed fragments of Saffie's glass honey jars and painted plates. He reeled, wrung faint, unable to watch as the dedicate who had just clouted his brother moved in and vised Kerelie's face between bloodied gauntlets.

Tarens thrashed in trussed rage. His irate howls raised chilling indifference as the examiner's pitiless eyes locked onto his sister's pinned features. No matter whether she shrank in shame, supremely unconcerned as her bound body arched backwards in fear, the examiner bore in with the conviction of a man possessed. Cold rings flashed as he aligned his pink finger-tips against her pale forehead. A pause ensued while he intoned a prayer, 'Oh omnipotent Light, may the powers of goodness prevail. Grant my faithful service the humility to rise above all mortal frailty.'

Lips curved, but not smiling, he focused his talent. His temple mission to eradicate Darkness invoked the trained reach of a power enhanced far beyond the empathy of the born healer. The inquisitor's probe he unleashed lanced into Kerelie's personal memories. The raw violation made her cry out as shocked nerves exploded to sparkling pain.

He dug deeper, thrust past her vulnerable, raced thoughts and pulled apart layer on layer of her natural resistance. Deaf to her screams, he ripped through and dismembered the emotional tissue of her family loyalty. The relentless ordeal gouged up every nuanced scrap of experience her shrinking terror strove to keep hidden.

Sharp-tempered she had been, even prudently critical of her brother's impulsive charity. But nothing amid the shreds of exposed memory unveiled concrete evidence that she had sheltered the foot-loose beggar who dabbled in simples.

'Innocent!' the Light's examiner snapped. 'This woman has not pretended her ignorance. Her consent was not given; neither did she welcome the Dark's practitioner under this roof.' He lifted his touch. While Kerelie's head lolled, and her frame quivered in traumatized spasms, he stepped back in contempt, then gestured for the dedicate sergeant to sever her bonds. 'Obstructive defiance is scarcely a crime worthy of death on the scaffold. The temple does not punish fools or set irons on persons not guilty!'

Perhaps angered that his effort disclosed no overt wickedness, the True Sect's high officer spun and confronted Efflin with a narrowed stare. 'Your sister's testimony appears to support the claim that your bedridden illness kept you from involvement.'

'I submit myself anyhow,' Efflin demurred. 'As head of my household, and a man of true faith, I insist that your divine calling ought to make sure.' Tears streaked his cheeks openly. For grief, he shouldered the practical choice: if the loss of a brother could not be salvaged, reprieve must be secured for the sister who might still be saved.

Tarens acknowledged, with desperate relief, that his ruinous action had not gone for nothing. Through blood and hazed pain, his stolid calm bolstered Efflin's selfless courage.

The examiner's search was dismissively cursory, a corroboration less exhaustive than a ceremonial inquiry processed by a formal trial before Kelsing's temple tribunal. The sentence was read straightaway, the harsh quittance pushed through in the heated rush to bring Tarens's act of slaughter to punitive justice.

'This croft will be sold at auction,' the True Sect official declared. 'Of the proceeds, one-third share will go to the temple coffers as due forfeit for the guilty party. The other two-thirds stay reserved in trust for the sister and brother surviving, provided they shall be exonerated by the heretic murderer's sealed proof in confession. They will suffer penance. Let them serve the temple as forced labour for the term of one year and count themselves graced by my leniency. For the fact that their traffic with a suspect herbalist flouted the temple's authority is a misdemeanour that narrowly skirts the more dangerous charge of complicity with the forces of Darkness.'

As the sergeant bent to free Efflin's hands, the examiner snapped final orders to his dedicate captain at arms. 'Hitch up the croft's bullock. Load our wrapped dead in the cart along with the chained prisoner, and choose eight lancers as escort. A temple processional will meet their arrival at Kelsing's front gate. By then, I'll have the diviner's widow informed and peal the bells to honour her husband's passing. The murderer's trial will be held today, with the formal sentence by sundown and execution by fire at dawn tomorrow. This family stays in close custody, meantime. Let them bear witness to their brother's fate as a lesson against the taint of consorting with Shadow.'

The arms captain saluted. 'What of the rest of my troop? We still have a renegade sorcerer at large.'

'Dispatch them for the man-hunt, of course.' The examiner's words faded into swished silk and torch light as he made his way out of the cottage door. 'I will assign you another diviner and also requisition a league tracker with dogs. Quarter the district and find Shadow's minion. Drag him back dead if his viciousness warrants.'

Kerelie sank to her knees beside Efflin. Shock and terror left her in shreds. Her older brother's trembling arms closed around her, fever-thin and bereft of comfort. Too easily, their desperate stay of reprieve could lapse back into deadly jeopardy. Tarens had yet to surmount the extraction of his final confession. Sister and brother could do nothing but cling to each other, meantime, helpless except to endure on the chance their lives might be spared in calamity.

Naught could be done to ease their cruel anguish as the dedicates hauled Tarens away.

Man-hunt

Tarens fought his temple wardens at each step, once they dragged him beyond the porch stairway. Hope forced the necessity although for his own sake the struggle was futile. Even if he broke away shackled, the fury of eight mounted lancers would serve him a brutal comeuppance. Last desperate mercy, lost to a grim fate, he battled for need to be served that quick death before the last shred of courage forsook him. The frost-hardened earth muffled his tell-tale noise, and a shut door hid the grim scene from his family. More than their distress, Tarens feared to stand trial.

Not because of his guilt: a diviner killed to win a sorcerer's clean escape sealed his death on the scaffold already. The risk must perish with him, that the temple examiners might wring him to further betrayal. He wrenched his broad shoulders and dug in stubborn heels. Given a large man's manic strength, he yanked the paired men-at-arms who restrained him off stride.

One tripped over the low fence that rimmed the mulched garden. The other, clubbed by the swing of his chains, fell back with a broken arm.

While the dressed ranks of the escort recoiled, and strict order unravelled to shouting, Tarens ducked under a destrier's girth and burst into a hobbled run. But no welcomed lance-thrust skewered his back. No enemy's vengeful blade cut him down or spared him from the course of due process. The Light's dedicates responded with ironclad discipline, for all that he lashed out with kicks, even bit, as their mailed fists pummelled him to defeat. No one cuffed him hard enough to break his head.

'You're spoken for the fire and sword, once you've faced the temple's tribunal,' the troop captain snapped. 'Accept the harsh fact!' He bellowed again to quell his provoked company, then promised, 'We will hear you sing for the Light's examiners when they extract your confession.'

Tarens made the lancers drag him to his feet. No effort he made forestalled the brute muscle that wrestled him towards the hitched wagon, heaved him inside, and bashed him prostrate. He blasphemed. Spitting the blood streamed from his crushed nose, he cursed his unwanted survival. He had a sister's thread of complicity to hide, and the burden of Efflin's honesty. Give the Light's priests their chance to unravel his mind, and any small fact might be twisted for leverage to reverse the lenient sentence that spared them. Tarens sweated under shattering dread, that the canon tribunal might pry out the criminal evidence that his brother's illness may have been healed by dark practice.

His defiant bid to be dispatched beforetime devolved to raw rage and rough handling. Tarens was pummelled until the pain reduced him to gasps that silenced his abusive speech. Limp, bruised, and bloodied, he lay pinned half-senseless on the musted straw spilled from the poultry crates. No soldier sullied his immaculate appointments to clear out the cluttered wagon-bed. They ploughed aside the fruit-baskets and osier cages, and roped Tarens out straight by his manacles beside the tarp-covered corpse of the slaughtered diviner.

There, he shivered, stretched on his back, choked by the welled drip of his shattered nose. The gall of his failure gave way to despair as the yoked ox was lashed forward. The cart creaked and rolled from the rutted yard, while the biting, pre-dawn cold spread a murky, starless sky over him. Chills wracked his pulped muscles to misery, and the rough motion jounced his cracked ribs. When he cramped in hitched spasms that threatened a faint, his escort sent a flunkey back to the well, then doused him with a pail of water. Weighed down by chain and shuddering in soaked clothes, Tarens suffered in helpless straits for a ghastly journey to Kelsing.

His plight moved his escort to ribald amusement. Through the chink of spurs and steel weaponry, Tarens weathered the filth they heaped on his dead mother. He gritted his jaw and stifled back screams when the riders capped their verbal slangs with jabs from their lance-butts. When the game they made of his torment raised boredom, their derision changed to speculation that chewed over the latest fragments of gossip. Tarens caught snatches through his spinning senses, as their conversation threaded between the cart's grinding racket and the clatter of the restive horses.

'. . . haven't condemned a dark-monger to burning for as long as I've been alive.'

'. . . think we may face renewed interest in the stymied campaign at the border?'

'High time the court of Havish's king was cleaned out as a breeding roost for warped practice and clansfolk.'

'. . . surely would take a rising of Darkness to force the temple's flint-fist bursars to loosen their purse strings. How many years have they waited to fix the shoddy roof on our barracks?'

'Oh, they'll pay! Always have. But for vestments with diamonds. The excuse will pack some pompous chump off east again to remand the delinquent avatar.'

'A Light's Hope? For real? You're joking!' The speaker snorted, derisive. 'The high priest at Erdane won't quell an outbreak of Shadow through mummery! Or waste his devout talent for such a fool's delegation. The True Sect's more likely to launch their case to condemn the fair-haired fop the traditionalists still revere as the founder of faith. Who wouldn't bid to eclipse Lysaer's power? The high temple conclave's primed for the opening. I say they'll depose him, seize his mayor's seat at Etarra, and build up the warfront with the s'Ilessid treasury. Then watch how fast we'll break the locked stand-off with Havish.'

'Light's own grace! Watch your tongue! Might find yourself wrung by the temple examiner alongside this wretch of a prisoner.'

'. . . beyond all doubt the avatar's abandoned the godhead! That's if the Great Schism's not a flagrant myth, and the man ever wielded true Light in the first place!'

'No myth, boy. Don't mock history. My grand uncle twice rode as a guard with the Light's Hope. He's seen divinity with his own eyes. The Blessed Prince never ages.'

'You bought the legend for an old man's maundering in his beer cup? That's quaint.'

Tarens absorbed the by-play through his daze, too damaged to care about the old controversy that flared between the True Sect and the traditionalists. The tale held that the avatar once denounced his priests and barred Etarra's gates against his protesting faithful. Pleas to win back his loyalty encountered rebuff. When the Temple's delegation placed an appeal, the priests were kicked out with their banners in flames and their horses' tails singed to smoking.

The veteran dedicate shrugged off his peer's ridicule. 'Greenhorn, you weren't by chance signed on as a recruit to redeem your gullible relative?'

Through an indignant chorus, a louder voice prevailed, 'Don't cite the accounts in the temple archives. Likely some bored copyist got drunk on devotion and larked off. Who's to say the lines of early scripture aren't outright fancy? Nobody's seen the like of the myth passed down from the siege of Alestron.'

Other voices declaimed, until the stiff-necked officer in charge caught wind of the blasphemous chatter. 'Since the Schism occurred over two centuries ago, our priesthood defines the sanctity of the canon. Your job's to defend the Light's grace from corruption! Clap your lips like a virgin caught out after dark if you want your sweet shot at advancement.'

The grumbler protested from the rear-guard 'Service in the ranks is rude enough without bending to jiggle the butts of the Light's inner conclave.'

'Listen up, bucko!' the officer snapped. 'High Temple's secretive feud with Etarra has seen better men drummed out of their whites in dishonour.'

The freshened breeze blew further chill through the talk, with the mounted procession compelled to rein in to flank the slow roll of the wagon. Another league passed before someone's laconic check on the captive raised a bark to a lazy subordinate. 'Flip the tarp off that corpse and shelter this wretch. We'll catch something worse than a reprimand if he packs up and dies of the cold.'

'. . . this poxy assignment!' someone else carped. 'It's still black out here as a witch's twat! When in the name of the Dark will we see the first glimmer of sunrise?'

'Spooked by a few clouds, then?' ·

The round of jeers lapsed as a shouted call from the vanguard halted the double-file column. The oxcart's wheels squelched to a stop, to more steamed oaths from the duty-bound lancers. Hoof stamps and snorts pocked the frigid air as their curbed destriers tussled the hold on their bits.

Sapped to dulled wits by the strain on bruised sinews, Tarens gathered the pause concerned an unscheduled obstruction. A glow emerged through the felt blanket of mist: some prankster had lit a bonfire from green wood in the midst of the trade-road. The blaze piled up traffic in both directions. With none but the agile, mounted couriers able to surmount the ditch at the verge, an irritable pack of balked carters shook fists and shouted, while their discommoded draught animals coughed on swirled smoke and jostled to evade the whirled sparks chased up by the changeable wind.

The temple man wrestled the oxcart's reins, swearing, while the fidgety escort of outriders closed their skittish horses into tighter formation around the chained prisoner.

'This may not be a coincidence. Stay on the alert!' The lance captain's next order dismounted the company's two strongest men and sent them ahead to sort out the confusion.

'You'll extinguish those flames!' he called after them, anxious. 'Pull apart the smouldering logs, stamp out the piled brush, and back off those carters before their teams pitch a fit and some blighted hot-head starts brawling.'

The nuisance would impose a lengthy delay. At least until the raked coals cooled to ash, with the steep banks of the drain ditches on either side set narrow enough to break wheels, and no burdened draught animal in its right mind likely to be cajoled to tread over hot embers.

Tarens languished in the wagon-bed meanwhile, surrounded by jumpy lancers and the dedicate officer, whose unhappy subordinate paced in tight circles, both hands full, tending riderless mounts. No one passed the time in loose talk, with every man's nerves primed to face an assault by barbarian raiders, or bandits, or worse: an attempt by Shadow's collaborators to liberate the condemned murderer. Never mind that the wretch was secured by locked chains, with the temple examiner in sole charge of the key, and the suspect family constrained under guard back at the ransacked cottage.

Bound in supine misery, Tarens suffered the worse. Though the draped tarp cut the edge from the wind, his swollen contusions had stiffened. What marginal surcease he gained from the stillness was undone by his tensioned cuffs as the brisk cold settled through his clammy shirt and wracked his outstretched body to shivering. The torment did not stem his terrified thoughts. Horrors awaited him in Kelsing's dungeons, put to the question by the True Sect priests.

That pernicious dread colored the disgruntled change, as the two footbound lancers who dismembered the bonfire sprang back from their task with riled oaths. When their outburst cranked into yells of dismay, Tarens strained to see through the slat side of the cart. What seemed like a wind devil whirled aloft. The tempest sucked up cinders of ash and live sparks, gained momentum, then vindictively reversed direction. As the gyre raked over the row of parked vehicles, the lance captain had little choice but to spur ahead and take charge before further mayhem erupted. Two strides out, he cursed, almost thrown as his mount reared, wild-eyed, and determined to bolt. The beleaguered officer wrestled its frothed panic and shouted to warn the fuming subordinate left in charge of the rest of the string.

'Clear those horses off! Turn the oxcart around and retreat at least one hundred paces. We've got fiends!' Harried as his frantic horse crab-stepped, the dedicate captain vented a gush of relief for the nuisance. 'No surprise we're beset, given this lug-headed rash of hysterical upset.'

The volatile mix of flames and raw tempers attracted such bothersome plagues: the energy sprites, known as *iyats*, irresistibly fed on emotional frenzy. No rank outbreak of Shadow, this inconvenience would scarcely balk temple justice. The lancers' mounts all wore banes on their bridles, tin disks stamped with ciphers of ward to repel the mettlesome influence. But the shabby paint on the croft's borrowed wagon suggested that the worn talixman affixed to its shafts might have discharged from neglect. If its virtue had waned, the vehicle with its distressed felon aboard posed a fresh magnet for trouble.

'Does one of those carters carry a shovel?' the lance officer called, spun about in the tussle to quell his crow-hopping mount. 'Requisition the tool, then! Move smart, and smother that fire straightaway. Those fiends won't disperse until they're starved out, with no ready source to replenish themselves!'

Tarens endured, teeth clamped through the jostle as men goaded the balky ox backwards, then shouldered it into a clumsy turn. When the vehicle slewed at the rim of the ditch, more lancers were obliged to vacate their saddles and brace lest the wheels slide farther and mire hub-deep. Splashed muck stained their surcoats. Stung pride shortened tempers as they bent their backs to brute work beneath their lofty station. Jolted and bashed by the slide of the poultry crates as the muscled cart jerked and tilted, Tarens snatched only a fitful view through the side slats as the fire suddenly exploded. The busy dedicates who manoeuvred the ox had no other warning when the shouts down the roadway changed pitch to alarm.

Already, the fiends sowed their vehement havoc. Gouts of flame and pin-wheeling logs whistled air-borne. Mule-teams bolted. Incensed carters screamed as their startled teams scrambled, entangled, and crashed into their neighbours. The lancers caught amid the irrupted blaze flung their borrowed shovels and scattered, while the berserk draught beasts shied hither and yon, and bashed their handlers aside like thrown rag dolls. The rampage of panic set off the ox, which plunged and jarred Tarens to further torment. Pelted by rolled baskets, and winded half-senseless, he cried out in the turmoil, voice drowned out by the racketing thunder of the other stampeded harness teams. Crazed livestock and smashed wagons caromed down the roadway, chased mad by fiends irresistibly baited to feed on the effervescence of chaos.

The few lancers assigned to the prisoner's oxcart sweated and swore, hard-pressed to curb their bucking mounts. If they missed getting trampled, that triumph lasted only until the *iyats* streamed within range of the talismans sewn to their horses' head-stalls. Temple-wrought, the banes did their exemplary work: the sprites in possession of the fiery debris became forcibly stripped from their air-borne loads. The result hurled down a storm of scalding ash, flaming bark, and burning sticks over them and their milling bunch of riderless horses. Swept into the vortex of screams and confusion, gadded and singed by the maelstrom of embers, the escort for the prisoner collapsed. Silk surcoats ignited. Routed men dropped and rolled on the ground to snuff out the errant blazes, or else found themselves mown down in the melee.

The cart jockeyed clear of the ditch fared no better. A dropped log whooshed earthward and struck the yoked ox. It whuffed, plunged, and bolted. Eyes rolled white, tail curled over its bristled, humped back, it rampaged through the held knot of horses and ripped them free. Swept along as they galloped, the bucketing oxcart swayed and careened like a storm-tossed shallop. The jounced corpse fetched up against Tarens's strapped frame. Flaming twigs pelted into the overset crates and spilled straw, and flurried sparks lit the wrack incandescent.

The devout driver, who bravely wrestled the reins, abandoned his post, before roasting. He dived for the ditch, beating flames from his beard, while the untended ox and its bucketing wagon hurtled off with the chained prisoner and the slaughtered diviner, streaming a comet-trail wake of torched basketry.

Trounced helpless, Tarens laboured to breathe. Scorched, coughing smoke, he reeled from the knifing pain of his broken ribs. The stout rope that lashed his chains became singed, while the heat transferred through the metal shackles blistered his fastened wrists. He could not thrash off the smouldering tarp or escape the threat of immolation as the burning crates bounced against the spread mantle that shrouded the corpse.

Suffocation and fear rendered him nearly senseless when someone's urgent presence tore away the blazing fabric. A living hand bare of gauntlets snatched the pearl-handled eating knife sheathed at the dead diviner's belt and sawed through the knots that secured Tarens's ankles. A tug parted the charred ties that restrained his arms and yanked him clear of disaster. Then a sharp whistle pierced the crackle of fire that raced in red-gold sheets across the wagon-bed. The fluted note shocked a resonant vibration through Tarens's chains, reached crescendo, then snicked open the locks on his manacles.

The release came too late. His traumatized limbs failed to move. Tarens whimpered, curled up in wracked pain, undone despite the continuous prods that insistently bullied him upright. When his stupor persisted, the forceful grasp rolled him up like dead meat in the singed tarp. Another heave pitched him belly down, with his head dangled over the side of the cart.

Through blurred confusion, all shuddering flame-light and wheeling shadows, he captured the brief impression of spoked wheels churning through rutted mud. Then the tumultuous hooves of a runaway mule-team obscured his view and pelted his broken face with flung clods. He flinched from the sting. Too traumatized to hike his weight backwards, he flopped like a draped rag as the adjacent dray overtook the clumsier oxcart. Swerved together, the vehicles swayed side by side in the maelstrom. Sparks snicked from the bash of their iron-capped wheel hubs. Only the fist entwined into the tarp secured Tarens from maceration. Whooping for air, paralyzed by torment as the wooden slat gouged into his damaged ribs, he battled raw terror and dizziness. Then a sharp push upended his ankles. He pitched out of the oxcart and tumbled, not under the wheels, but into a saving pile of hay as the mule-drawn wain rumbled past.

His agile keeper dived in alongside him and burrowed under the thatch. Strangled on dust and poked by the tickle of straw, Tarens moaned. The sneeze he failed to contain ripped his chest. A callused palm swiftly muffled his scream, as his bashed ribs erupted to agony. The relentless hold gagged his noise, then let go as his abused stomach revolted. Limbs strapped in the tarp and torqued double by nausea, Tarens retched. The harsh spasms savaged him past all reprieve as the mule-cart jounced and clattered down the rutted road, with its team harried senseless by *iyats*. The haystack that cushioned him failed to stave off the sucking plunge towards unconsciousness.

Through dimmed awareness, dazed by the pain as the gushed blood from his fractured nose became blotted up with a twist of rough cloth, Tarens realized that no temple guard would have granted the kindness. Reassured that he lay in the hands of a friend, he let go and allowed the merciful darkness to swallow him.

Tarens surfaced again through a bright scald of agony, as if whole patches of skin had been flayed and exposed every quivering nerve end. A strip torn from the tarp crudely bound his bashed ribs. If the jacket and shirt overtop remained clammy, nestled hay and the warmth of the body beside him at least eased his desperate shivering. His crushed nose ached, stuffed tight with swelling. Both eyes had puffed to throbbing slits, and he breathed in shuddered gulps through split lips. Matted hair crusted his brutalized scalp, and everything else the Light's faithful had kicked felt bludgeoned to grape pulp.

Through ringing ears, he overheard a brisk conversation, conducted in masculine voices. The words stitched together the alarming discovery the mule-cart had stopped for inspection. Tarens froze. Before his frightened gasp made him choke on loose chaff, a friendly clasp squeezed his wrist. The assurance did nothing to quell his dread. He would be retaken: a thin cover of hay would never thwart searchers commanded by a temple mandate. Worse, the fugitive talent who bade for his rescue would share his trial as a murderer's accomplice. The brave ploy that had unfastened locked chains must condemn them both to a sorcerer's death. Boots scraped, close by. A shadow raked across the chinks of filtered daylight, and the clipped phrases acquired coherency.

'No bribes today, scoundrel!' An authority's tread took pause by the stack in the wagon-bed. 'We're placed on tight watch. Can't risk an exception. A chained heretic's escaped. Oh yes! Priests claim he's got a minion of Darkness as a collaborator. The pair's on the run somewhere in the district. Dawn this morning, we're told. Uncanny for sure, if they've outfoxed the best of the league trackers. Three temple diviners are combing the country-side to flush them out while we're saddled with manning this road block.'

The mule-driver lodged a fretful complaint.

Another official dismissed him, annoyed. 'Just a stray storm of *iyats*, you say? Well maybe that's true. High on a fresh charge, a fiend storm might spring a steel lock by chance. But a full set of manacles amid a live fire? That's much more than random mischief.'

Another protest, then, 'Well, yes! We'd rather be settled inside over mulled wine and breakfast. Except that some pious lance captain's pegged us to salvage his blunder.'

The mule's driver argued, hotly incredulous. 'If a felon dodged justice through a sorcerer's havoc, you wouldn't be likely to find such as them holed up in a wain-load of hay.'

'All goods get examined. No use crying foul.' A sheared ring bespoke steel withdrawn from a scabbard. 'One mewling yap from a True Sect dedicate, and it's hop, skip, and jump for us field-troops. They've rousted the garrison out in the cold, too, poking pig crates and tossing through farm-carts!'

A rustle of cloth, then a metallic whine as the weapon stabbed into the haystack behind the tail-gate. The point sank a span deep and thunked hollow wood, to a tell-tale gurgle of fluid. 'Contraband, is it? Grain whiskey, perhaps?' The foot-soldier laughed, while his fellows closed in and burrowed to expose the illicit cache.

'He's got barrels, sir. Ones without tax brands or seals on the bungs.'

'Too bad,' said the officer, unsympathetic. 'Looks like you're faced with detainment for smuggling.'

The mule-driver scarcely bemoaned his bad luck, but offered a bribe to evade the penalty.

'One barrel? Kiss my rosy arse! You'll donate thrice that number and grin. Count on it, my captain insists on his share. Not to mention the filthy provost's men skim. That's only sound business, to gag their stickler's consciences.'

The brazen bout of dickering finished with the busy slide of raised pins, then the creak as the tail-gate was lowered. A dog growled, caught up by the scruff and tossed into the haystack to satisfy duty. Its honest nose snuffled for fugitives, while the men collected their sweetening share with unrestrained greed.

Tarens cowered, too injured to stir, and petrified to bated breath. He recalled the knife stolen from the diviner and braced for the futility of desperate action. But the vagabond hidden beside him did not spring into tensioned sweat. His stilled clasp on the crofter's wrist stayed collected, even as the diligent hound whined and rooted. When the crofter finally inhaled, he nearly choked, membranes singed by the sharp sting of wintergreen. A genius stroke, as the industrious hound sucked the astringent herb into its snout the next moment.

Its explosive sneeze flurried the hay. Then it yelped and shot backwards onto its haunches, where it shivered and licked its nose, whimpering. No one took notice. The last unloaded cask thunked into the ground to someone's snap of impatience. The dog was seized by routine and dragged off the wagon to speed the smug rush to sequester the dunned casks. The mule-driver slammed closed his tail-gate and secured the pins. Released on his way, he clambered back onto the buckboard and shook up his mules.

Tarens lay trembling under the tarp. Limp with relief, he placed no innocent faith in coincidence: surely his clever friend had not fallen into a corrupt dray-man's wagon at random. Neither was the skilled penchant for skulking the habit of an upright man. Yet the puzzle could not be pondered under the misery of black-out faintness. Too shaken to think, Tarens let the rattletrap wain bear him southbound through the chill morning.

Noon came. More mounted lancers swept past, first one troop, then another, noisy with the martial jingle of steel and the snap of streamed pennons. A third, larger company of dedicates followed. The horn blasts of their advance guard warned other traffic clear of the roadway, and drove the lumbering dray to stop at the verge. Hay stalks whispered and winnowed to the backwash of breeze as the cavalcade clattered past at a canter. The muleteer and his load stayed at the side, unmolested. Whether the temple's elite lancers disdained to sully their snow-white surcoats to conduct a search, or if their officious captain avoided the bother of the delay, no rider dismounted to trifle with a farm vehicle passed through the earlier check-point.

The next batch at their heels reined in, but apparently only to breathe their hot mounts. The multiplied clop of shod destriers woke Tarens. Through febrile pain, he overheard the excitable gossip exchanged in response to a bystander's query. 'The hunt's out for the renegade sorcerer, yes. A practitioner in league with Darkness who unkeyed the locks on cold iron with spells. He's absconded with the confirmed murderer the Lord Examiner arrested just before dawn.'

'Oh, he left no prints to clue the league's trackers! There's truth,' a second speaker chimed in. 'Head-hunters' hounds so far have drawn a blank field, as if there's no scent to nose out.'

'Maybe he flew like a bird in the night. Shapechanged to a beast? Never saw such, myself. But that's what the priesthood is saying.'

'Claptrap!' another man added, and laughed. 'If yon skulker's that powerful, we're wasting our time. Such a paragon wouldn't stoop to a runaway's game, chased off like a thief through the country-side.

'They'll run him down through the use of diviners,' a fellow in the rear-guard assured. 'A wee knife was stolen from one of their own. If the object's still in the creature's possession, their blessed talent will use that to find him. If not, the next crafted spell he attempts will alert the temple's trained sensitives. Once they have him placed, we'll close in for the capture. If the twisted criminal isn't killed outright, rest easy. He'll be dragged to Erdane and put to ritual death by the sword and the fire.'

To that end, lance troops had been deployed from all points of the compass, with each dedicate captain primed for his chance to seize glory.

'We'll have eighty companies deployed before nightfall. No way the Dark's minion is going to slip through. Sleep soundly tonight, man, and thank the Light for the grace of the temple's protection.'

The mule drover mumbled an unctuous blessing, his gratitude more likely due to the contraband he slipped under the troop's righteous noses.

Then the horn blast sounded to signal the trot. Bits chinked as the lancers gave on their reins and spurred on their way. 'I do suggest that you roll straight through,' the last man in the column called over his shoulder. 'A curfew's been imposed after nightfall for safety's sake. Don't pause until you're snugged down inside the stone walls of an inn.'

The mule-cart ground onwards through late afternoon, with Tarens sunk deeper in misery. For each black-out moment he catnapped, the rude jolts of the hay-cart awoke him, gasping in pain from the grate of his damaged ribs. His untended gashes swelled into a throbbing crescendo of aches. Terror stifled his moans. He bit his split lip and endured without respite until the cold, clouded sunset brought the hay-wagon to its scheduled delivery. The heavy wheels rumbled to a stop on the cobbles behind the stable at a traveller's inn.

A changeable wind blew in from the north, salted with early snow. The hostler's boys who caught the team's bridles carped and blew on numb fingers. The driver flung them two coppers to unhitch his mules, then chased them off with the laconic assurance he would fork the hay into the loft in due time. The boys pocketed the coins, content to scarper without asking bothersome questions. The inclement weather defrayed any suspicion since a carter hunched at his reins with cold feet might well crave whiskey and a hot meal before he tended his load.

The cart stayed unobtrusively parked, removed from the torch-lit bustle that ebbed and flowed through the crowded front inn-yard. The dusk shadows rapidly deepened to felt. By night, someone was bound to come on the sly to collect the black-market kegs. Before then, the stowed fugitives must make themselves scarce, a pressing urgency that Tarens grasped even while beset by relentless discomfort. His companion helped free him from the wrapped tarp. The crofter forced his battered body to move, shoved off through the loose hay, blundered over the casks, and clumsily crashed against the fastened tail-gate. He struggled to hoist his stiff frame overtop. The effort went badly. He dropped, his feet jolted into the ground, and crashed heavily to his knees. Light-headed dizziness crumpled him there, shuddering with his forehead pressed against the frigid cobbles.

'You may have to leave me,' he groaned in despair.

The sound of his voice raised a fearsome, low growl from the back of the stable. Apparently the inn kept a mastiff to forestall sneak thieves and chase off any freebooters who sought to bed down in the hayloft. One bark of alarm, and a heavy-set bloke with a cudgel would be drawn at a run to investigate.

The vagabond forsook Tarens's side. The charmed touch that once mollified scrawny hens also settled the dog, which presently leaped on him, nuzzling. He scratched beneath its studded collar, then left it wagging its stub tail. He collected the furled tarp. A patience that did not seem hurried steadied Tarens's tormented effort to stand. Unbalanced, the large man leaned on the smaller. Together, they managed the agonized shuffle towards the rear door of the stable. No one challenged their entry. The bustle at day's end busied the staff, with the arrival of the public coach out of Cainford flooding the front yard with pitch torches and noise. A shrill woman scolded a crying child, while the head hostler's roaring invective chased laggards to unstrap the guests' baggage. Every groom not hot-walking outriders' mounts became chewed over for laziness. Amid the commotion to unhitch the harness team, no slackers sidled off into the unlit crannies to loiter.

Softly as the whisper of wind, Tarens was eased in careful stages through the gloom between the dusty, back rows of stalls. Past the straight slots used to quarter cheap hacks, and the boxes for the quality livestock, the hay driver's mules were tied up with the nags, munching nose-bags of oats. Across the aisle, a mountainously muscular bull jangled the chain that secured its nose-ring. Huge, black and furious, it pawed and swiped its capped horns, eager to trample all comers to mincemeat.

Which rampaging peril hooked the vagabond's interest.

'Here, let me,' Tarens croaked. The late darling consigned to the knackers made him expertly skilled with brute-tempered bullocks. Since death by goring seemed preferable to facing the temple's tribunal, he veered on unsteady legs and took up the goad he found hooked on a nail. Ceded the brazen initiative, one defensive arm clamped to his injured side, Tarens sucked a wheezed breath and staggered forward. He jabbed the bull's flank. When it humped up and plunged, he judged his moment, shoved into the board stall, and dropped into a roll through the straw. Impetus carried him past the beast's forelegs, then broke through a musty veil of old cobweb and fetched him into a huddle beneath the stout slats of the manger.

Just as agile, nipped in tight behind, the vagabond slithered into the fusty nook, still packing the tarp. While Tarens shuddered, vised helpless with cramps, his friend's resourcefulness lined their noisome refuge with hay, then fashioned a makeshift bedroll. He tucked Tarens inside to get warm, then took charge of the goad and ducked out to pursue the necessities of their survival.

The crofter laid back his sore head, at last granted a measure of surcease. While the wind keened outside, and thickened flakes drifted into the season's first snowfall, he gave way to the grief that seeped stinging tears through his bruised eyelids. Shortly, he slept. Or else unconsciousness granted its fugitive gift of oblivion.

Much later, he roused to the ice-kiss of snow, packed into a compress and pressed against the throb of his disfigured face. Shock drove the last gasp of breath from his lungs. Then the grate of his splintered nose drove him to whimpering agony. A warmed cup touched his lips. The vagabond gently coaxed Tarens to swallow a bitter brew of valerian mixed with willow bark. Drugged into a haze, he still had to be gagged to stifle his cries through the trauma of splinting. His crushed nose required reed straws and stuffed rags to redress such drastic damage. A skilled healer somewhere had trained the deft hands that ventured such bone-setter's work without flinching.

The after-shock left Tarens dizzy and limp. Sweating, he languished. The oblivious bull chewed its cud overhead, while the relentless, doctoring fingers moved on and unlaced his ripped clothing. His skin was toweled clean with a wet burlap sack. Past question, the handling was expert: each cut and bruise was assessed, then plied with the strong remedies filched from the hostler's stores in the tack room. The snow packs were replaced with a poultice of wintergreen mixed into goose grease and bound into place with the leg wraps kept for lame horses. The treatment was done in pitch-darkness throughout, quietly sure, without fumbling.

Legend held that born talent could see without light. The True Sect priesthood required no other sign to condemn any heretic charged with dark sorcery.

Tarens was too muddled to confront the dire proof or broach the issue of thorny morality. Whether spelled tricks or thievery had acquired the cup, or if dishonest practice had steeped the soporific tisane that eased him, the relief that dulled the mending sting of his cuts melted him into a stupor. As the braced flush of astringents soothed battered muscles, he swallowed the hot broth he was offered, then the second dose of valerian prepared to settle him. Adrift towards oblivion, he closed his eyes. If his soul had been traded for craven survival, his spirits were too low to care.

Deep in the night, he reawoke to the nightmare of searchers invading the stable with lanterns. This time in earnest, dedicates in white surcoats tossed through the straw in the horse stalls. Their shouts and commotion were joined by the clangour of the fire-bell, jangled to summon the hostler. The man shambled in, wrapped in flannel and beer breath. He climbed to the loft and kicked his sleepy grooms, until tousled horse-boys with hay in their hair tumbled, swearing, out of their blankets. Granted no chance to pull on their boots, they scurried on stockinged feet to fling open grain bins, lead out courier's hacks, and shift haltered mules at the whim of the diligent task squad. More urgent outcries and pungent oaths filtered in from the carriage yard. Evidently the innkeeper's outspoken wife fared no better in behalf of her rousted patrons as the temple's foray swept through the tavern. Her curses blistered ears to no purpose. Pillows and blankets were put to the sword. Smoke laced by the stink of singed goose-down rolled in billows as the inn's quilts and mattresses were torched in a heap. The fumes made the chained bullock bellow and paw. Its restive temper daunted the grooms, who cried blame on their fellows for the mislaid goad, inexplicably gone from its hook.

The troop captain gave their timid protests short shrift.

'That vicious beast poses the least of your fears. A minion of Shadow's at large in the district, and I'm under mandate to find him. Move that animal. Now! Or the ninny who shrinks will be put to the sword as a criminal collaborator.'

As the reluctant hostler shuffled in compliance, Tarens started to a touch on his arm, quickly followed by furtive movement in the stygian dark beneath the board manger. He had shot peas as a prank in his boyhood: often enough to know the sharp hiss of a reed being used as a blow-tube. Sliced light from a torch winkled out the flicked shine of a miniscule dart, let fly at short range.

Unseen by the guardsmen outside the stall, the missile struck the sensitive flesh of the bull's lower lip.

The split-second glimpse as the brute backed up, snorting, showed Tarens the ingenious invention: a sliver of metal, feathered with a snippet of goose quill, affixed with a bit of wrapped thread. One recalled the old jacket claimed by the vagabond when the shortened sleeves were unfinished. Both cuffs had been basted up with Kerelie's precious steel pins.

The insectile prick gadded the sullen bull to a maniacal fit. Its capped horns raked wood and gouged up furrowed splinters, while showered slaver and dust sifted through the sturdy slats of the manger. If the nose-ring and chain kept the maddened beast tethered, the violent force as it plunged amok rattled and bowed the stout planks of the stall and dissuaded the bravest fellows from entry. Someone helpful fetched the bull's owner, who also balked, however the lancers waved weapons and threatened.

'So arrest me!' he shouted, 'Whose dimwit blunder upset the beast, anyway? Send that man in, first. No way I'll risk myself to smashed bones while that bullock's enraged.'

The hostler agreed, persuasively reasonable. 'That brute's certain to cripple anyone foolish enough to challenge its viciousness.' He added, insistent, 'Don't think we'd have napped through yon dreadful noise! More, if your fugitives molested that bull, they'd be mangled meat, beyond question.'

The lance captain bristled, to no avail. His blustering effort to overturn sense met defeat upon the breathless discovery of the contraband stashed in the hay-cart outside. The bull's tantrum was dropped for the spicier prospect of nailing the errant smuggler. After the culprit was smoked out and arrested, the bother of splitting grain sacks and pitching more harness out of the tack room lost out to the prospect of stirrup-cups filched from the casks. The lancers confiscated the spirits and retired to wet their gullets and lounge in warm comfort inside the tavern.

The grooms were left to set the stable to rights and quench the hot gleam of the torches. Tarens lay wakeful long after the last chattering horse-boy retired to the loft. The dust settled also, once the rampaging bullock ceased goring the wooden manger. Suspended between rattled nerves and drugged torpor, he lay troubled, under the cover of darkness. The distanced carousing as the drunken dedicates burst into boisterous song did not quite mask the stealthy stir as the fugitive next to him slipped out of hiding. Quietly calm, with no fuss at all, the man plucked the stuck pin from the bull. The animal gusted one last surly snort. Horned boss lowered, it munched hay with supreme unconcern for the penalty served upon creatures who consorted with minions of Shadow.

But bovine simplicity failed to quiet the more vicious quandary of human uncertainty. Tarens never felt more alone in his life. Grief resurged, inconsolable. He missed the family irrevocably left behind. Savaged by loss and tormented by hope, he might never know if his rash intervention had saved their wrecked lives. All of his former choices were forfeit. He could not return. Whether he rued his impulsive strike against the temple's authority, his fate was sealed. He had bound his destiny to a stranger with a questionable past, and a future that followed a frightening course of unfathomable motivation.

Early Winter 5922

Afterclap

Dawn came in a pallid wash of grey light, to the scratch of straw brooms and excitable chatter. The stable-lads swept piled snow from the cobbles and whisked the last of the spilled grain and debris the past night's searchers had strewn in the aisle. That industry brought the ominous bent of fresh gossip to the ears of the fugitives hidden beneath the bull's manger. The beast had not been collected at daybreak. Because Shadow's rogue minion had not been found, nor any trace of the accomplice murderer, a True Sect decree extended the curfew that locked down the surrounding country-side. Only the head-hunters' league moved abroad, out in force to beat the brush along with their mute packs of hounds, their trap-setters, and their skilled trackers.

The failed man-hunt whetted the unresolved air of menace, all the more since the new snowfall yielded the searchers no trace of a human footprint.

'Uncanny, that,' the head hostler declared, ducked in to throw butcher's scraps to the mastiff. The horse-boys chewed over the scared round of talk overheard from the stranded travellers, or else fretted through their chores with naked unease. The curfew stultified the unsettled mood, with the Light's lance captain stationed in wait, his hard-bitten company poised under the grim instructions to ride down any person who left the premises.

Within the white chill of the stable-yard, or huddled indoors around a roaring hearth, the whisperers spoke in haunted dread of the Darkness and revisited horrors from the ancient massacres; the grisly atrocities at Tal Quorin, or the grim battlefield at Dier Kenton Vale that had seen thirty thousand brave spirits struck dead in a day.

The war hosts slaughtered at Minderl Bay and Daon Ramon perished again, recounted in heroic ballads sung by itinerant minstrels. Past evils received the lurid embellishments of bar-keepers and wrinkled elders, until hearsay carried the stature of myth, and wilder fancy described the Master of Shadow as a vile being with raven skin and monstrous features.

Others claimed his fell presence passed over the land as a wind, reduced over centuries to a bodiless haunt. A resurgence would turn the untrustworthy mageborn to minions and sow all manner of savage destruction. The riveting stories claimed Darkness himself snatched newborns from their cradles and leached their heartsblood in hideous rites of live sacrifice. If no one actually had lost a child, true relics remained from the campaigns fought against the servant of evil. Rusted swords were still kept enshrined, or sheaves of browned letters bundled in string, which told of the Light's standard raised for divine cause under the avatar, Lysaer s'Ilessid. Everyone honoured a forebear who had marched and died in heroic defense of the Light.

Woven into the fabric of folk-tales, or indoctrinated by the temple canon, the factual events that drove past and present had become lost in the welter.

But not everywhere. As morning brightened, both the frenzied stress of the leagues' stymied dedicates and the crippling discomfort endured by their cornered quarry drew the concern of another formidable power.

The Sorcerer who bore title as Warden of Althain might have appeared drifty and daft, immured in his tower eyrie amid the remote dales of Atainia. Yet his owlish stare masked a stature that soared. Sethvir had served as Athera's archivist for close to nine hundred years. Ink stains on his spare knuckles and the frayed shine on his cuffs bespoke tireless days spent inscribing quaint script onto parchment.

But the hour did not find him sunk in rapt industry, among the emptied tea-mugs nestled between the detritus of leather-bound journals and dog-eared old books. Instead, burdened with the world's most intractable problems, Sethvir had tossed aside his quill pen with fierce intent to tidy his cupboards.

Cobweb smudged his creased cheek where he knelt, swamped in clutter: tatters of silk ribbon and ancient strap buckles, the variegate egg-shells of song-birds, a grey wasp's nest, and a jam crock inhabited by a live spider lay heaped with a clutch of old river stones, boxes of corks misplaced from his ink flasks, two hawk feathers, and a flagon with a cracked crystal stopper. The Sorcerer regarded the shelf just raked clean, apparently lost in bemusement.

That innocuous vagary was deceptive. Sethvir's piercing acuity remained without peer the length and breadth of five kingdoms.

All events on Athera crossed the lens of his subtle awareness: from the doings of snails, to the hatreds of men, to perilous marvels unfurled like the pleats of a fan by the dreaming of dragons, both living and dead. *Sethvir sensed the footsteps of the enchantress, Elaira, descending from the frozen heights of the Storlains by way of the white-water gorge which thrashed into the port town of Redburn. He knew the Queen of Havish was dying. Her frail breaths reached him, as his colleague, Traithe, kept the vigil to ease her final passage. Alongside the hibernation of bats, and the first rickle of ice that closed Northstrait, he also followed the tracks of the desert-folk, erased by the winds from the volcanic sands of the black dunes of Sanpashir. He heard even the gibbers of Desh-thiere's captive wraiths, sequestered within the enspelled deeps of Rockfell Pit.*

The extraordinary range of the Sorcerer's sensitivity could trace the overlaid patterns unique to the vitality of each individual consciousness, and from them forecast the ripples of probability that streamed towards the manifest future.

When the Fellowship colleague just returned from the field found Sethvir's cloud-wool hair tufted up into snarls, the sight raised a signal flag of distress.

'You look like a sheep that needs carding,' Asandir ventured carefully. He still wore his leathers. Pungent from his arduous sojourn abroad, he brought the fust of horse and the smoke scent of camp-fires into the bookish miasma of ink and antiquity. 'Should I lay the blame on Davien, or the Koriani Prime Matriarch?'

Sethvir clipped off a shockingly filthy word: one better suited to embarrassed young men caught aback by the pestilent itch noticed after a toss with a harlot.

'The witch brood is hatching up a fresh plot,' Asandir surmised. But his rare laugh stayed silenced, and his chilly regard kept the bite of edged steel as he folded his tall frame into the squashed upholstery of the chair by the hearth. 'Which arena?'

'Where are they not meddling?' Sethvir laid down a ribbon fastened with tiny bells, once worn by a Paravian dancer. His disgusted sigh seemed heaved up from the soles of his feet. 'Like a plague of spelled rats, their Prime's got the Light's armed faithful scouring Taerlin and Camris to smoke out a minion of Darkness.'

Asandir steepled chapped fingers. 'Arithon's rediscovered the depth of his mastery and accessed the keys to grand conjury?'

'No!' Sethvir clutched his smutched temples, as if frantic to stem the torrent of disruptive images: *of zealot lancers, and grim-faced league trackers with hounds, who avidly quartered the grey-on-white fields and scrub oak for two heretic fugitives: quarry in fact huddled inside a cold stable, with one of them battered half-senseless and terrified.* 'I would bless the good news, if his Grace had recalled even the glimmer of partial awareness.'

'He hasn't?' Asandir probed with delicacy.

Sethvir dashed the forlorn hope, that the infamous s'Ffalenn temper may have singed the order's ranked Seniors into embarrassed retreat. 'By my accurate count, his Grace has recalled nothing, yet. He's worked no craft at all! Beyond a bard's turn of phrase with a flute, and the resonant notes to move iron, he's carried off his friend's rescue by straightforward subterfuge. A few darts made of tinker's pins, aimed with effect, and the mischievous instinct that knows where a strategic bonfire will raise tempers and draw in stray *iyats*.'

Asandir frowned. 'Then Arithon hasn't *yet* tapped the force of his born gift for Shadow?'

'No.' Sethvir lowered his fingers, limpid turquoise eyes widened by acute distress. 'Last night, his Grace moved at large in the yard of a travellers' inn with no more protection than a burlap bag used to hood his face.'

'It was snowing?' Asandir observed, thoughtful. A seasoned winter traveller, he knew that grooms often sheltered their heads with grain sacking under a pinch-thrift stableman. 'You don't feel the prince was cautious by restraint, in line with his sly touch for cleverness?'

The reluctant pause lagged. Sethvir picked up the gold-and-black hawk's quill with fidgety care, and said presently, 'Earlier today, a temple high priest claimed to have sensed an act of dark spellcraft disturbing the flux lines. But actually, no such deflection took place. The True Sect's examiner at Kelsing conducted the search of an innocent's home under that falsified testimony.'

Asandir raised straight eyebrows, coarse as steel filings on his weathered face. 'Ah.'

Sethvir's anger acquired a dangerous spark of leashed rage. 'More, that brazen lie marked an honest crofter for the scaffold and saw his family stripped of their landed inheritance.'

The logic required a beat to unravel. 'No craft was used. The lane currents were silent. Else we'd have had Koriathain themselves drawn to Arithon's refuge like crawling lice.' Asandir sat very still, sensitive to the myriad threads of inquiry sorted by the vast range of his colleague's earth-sense. 'Then whose poisoned suggestion tipped off the prying diviner?'

'A snitch with a rumour,' Sethvir answered, too tightly succinct. 'One inept, rebuffed suitor informed the temple those crofters had sheltered a ruffian.'

'Quite a long leap, to peg a mere beggarman sight unseen as an affirmed minion of Shadow.' The knifed lines of Asandir's frown intensified. 'How did Arithon raise undue attention?'

'The deep empathy he evolved to appease Marak's wraiths has entrained him to hear the nuanced pitch of emotion. A neat trap,' Sethvir said, 'exploiting the fact he still is quite defenseless, without a haven, and left with no secure route for escape.'

With all recourse hobbled in Arithon's behalf, the old set-backs festered like thorns in the flesh, that the temple's sway over Tysan remained absolute. The canon's long-standing doctrine of fear kept the ports and the borders locked under a Light-sanctioned chokehold. Which ironclad security had been what prompted the Koriathain to locate Arithon's spelled term of captivity at the ruined earl's court at Kelsing. If their brazen connivance also used the false faith as the sleeve to flush out their fugitive, the move seemed an ominous excess.

Asandir gauged Sethvir's raw nerves and probed gently, 'Prime Selidie cannot fear the s'Ffalenn penchant for vengeful fury at this pass.' Not if Arithon had yet to recall why he should bear the initiate witches a capital grudge.

Sethvir folded the sleeked hawk feather into a silk cloth, then picked up the gaudy flask. The indigo glaze, emerald vine-leaves, and scarlet birds glinted with gemstone brilliance as he raised the vessel up to the light and peered askance through the flawed glass stopper. His colleague knew not to press him. When the Warden chose to deliver bad news, his word often struck like the fall of a hammer and smashed every alternate option past salvage.

'The thrust has changed,' Sethvir allowed. 'Since Selidie's settlement rests our oath of noninterference, the Prime's decided she has the leeway to spin wider plans. I'm loath to suggest that Arithon may be of more use to her, now, as a gambit.'

'They're angling for Lysaer?' Asandir snapped point-blank.

'Let's hope I'm mistaken.' Sethvir tapped the flawed crystal. His finger touch sparked a blast of raw light. When the flash cleared, the crack that gave the glass character stayed: but the chip was erased, which impaired the stopper's integrity. 'Lysaer cannot be other than compromised.' Either by the roused influence of the Mistwraith's curse or through the born drive for justice instilled into his royal lineage, the Prime's exploitive stake in high temple affairs must engage the attention of its forsworn founder.

With the sinister upshot that the delinquent avatar well might fall prey to that lure. The sisterhood yet bore Lysaer's entrenched enmity. To thwart their machinations, and to wrest Tysan's religious populace free of their corrupt influence, he might well step in and resume his lapsed charge as the divine figure-head worshipped by the Light's faithful. Should the affray in the west-lands push him to try, he would flirt with a peril beyond his means to defuse: Desh-thiere's insidious geas never slept. Its subtle pressure would warp any action he took and distort even the most altruistic morality.

'Is Lysaer yet aware he may face a fresh trial?' Asandir ventured at length.

'Oh, yes.' The frightful back-lash could not be disowned, that Arithon's restored freedom inevitably renewed the murderous compulsion to destroy his half brother. Sethvir granted the proof of that horror without words and shared a fragment of image: *as nightmares had broken Lysaer's sleep, and wrung him to cold sweat and dread before daybreak.* The vicious dynamic resurged beyond quarter, with his cursed nemesis once more at large in the world. Already, the sterling strengths of true character staged the potential for a tragic relapse.

'We face a bad call regardless,' Sethvir admitted in gloomy assessment.

If, against weighted odds, the s'Ilessid sustained his avowed course and renounced his former posture of divine importance, he would leave the religion's false doctrine intact, ripe for other arcane exploitation. Lysaer's absence ceded the Prime a wide-open field to keep steering the True Sect's high priesthood.

Which naked threat made Asandir bristle. 'No chance the Matriarch won't pounce on the choice to leverage the Light's canon as her ready weapon against us.'

'The Paravians' return could shatter that web,' Sethvir murmured, deceptively wistful. But the diamond gleam behind his veiled lashes bespoke tears before dreamer's bemusement.

'Check, then, if not mate,' Asandir finished, tart for the venomous irony. For of course, with the old races lost to the world, the chore of house-cleaning such meddlesome spiders fell under the Fellowship's purview.

The Koriani Prime would launch her ambitious assault, with the impasse bought by Arithon's term of captivity broken at last. Marak's invasive wraths might be banished, but the Fellowship's hands remained overburdened. The discorporate Sorcerers Kharadmon and Luhaine yet laboured to dismantle the mighty wardspells, once fashioned to separate the rogue horde into single entities whence a masterbard's song could transmute them. A grand construct potent enough to dim the world's sun must be unravelled, each coil of energy harmlessly dispersed before the onset of explosive attrition. More, the life-web of two other afflicted worlds required to be mended and rebalanced.

Asandir's practicality never minced words. 'Either the Koriathain turn the might of the masses to shatter the compact, or we rend our own solemn oath by desperate means to prevent them.'

Sethvir picked a napped thread off his cuff. 'We're all too conveniently hobbled.' Cheerless, he placed the repaired vessel in a niche where sunlight would fire the vibrant enamels. If the gesture brightened the cloud settled over the library, no rainbow might ease the gloomy predicament that Lysaer s'Ilessid had been formally outcast from the protective grant made by the Fellowship for mankind's lawful settlement. An unmalleable point the Prime Matriarch planned to mine for her ruthless advantage. With Arithon's survival also bound under Asandir's pledge of noninterference, both of the princes stood at the cross-roads of deadly risk.

'Davien,' said Sethvir, 'would be having a field day if he were at liberty to offer comment.' Not least, for the back-handed reverse, that the traits instilled into Athera's crown blood-lines had bred so perniciously true. But, of course, no one dwelled upon Davien's hung fate, wedded to the perilous whim of a dragon.

The bleak pause after that might have gathered the dust displaced out of Sethvir's cupboard, but for the shuffled step on the outside stair, and the cursory bang at the library door that forewarned of another arrival.

'My unfinished business come flocking to roost,' the field Sorcerer observed, beyond tried, as the latch tripped.

A plump, brosy man with a salt-and-ginger beard shoved over the threshold with a laden tray. He wore a sober brown tunic, neat as a clerk's but for the haphazard knots that snarled his laces. The inquisitive dart of cinnamon eyes picked up Asandir's presence and narrowed.

'I wasn't told you returned!' the fellow accused, while several fortnights' freight of injured offence precipitated a minor disaster. Something crunched under his left-footed tread. Then he tripped on Sethvir's chunks of river stone and escaped falling flat by a hairbreadth.

'Hello, Dakar,' greeted Asandir. 'The bluebirds will lay a fresh clutch by next spring, and your stubbed toe will recover. Before you waste further breath in complaint, we could use a tranced prophecy telling us where the Prime Matriarch plans to wreak her next round of havoc.'

Once, the rebuke would have flustered Dakar scarlet. But tempered living and wisdom, painfully gained, at long last had established decorum. The tea-tray came to rest on the table without the crash of unbridled pique.

'Could I offer an augury without knowing the facts?' The spellbinder also known as the Mad Prophet snatched up a cloth napkin, bent his stout frame, and scooped up the pulverized egg-shells. He slid the offended rocks to one side with a genuine word of apology, then accosted the sore point headlong. 'You didn't invite me to the Koriani summons at Whitehold! Neither would Sethvir share what occurred or tell me the terms you relinquished to win the Prime Matriarch's appeasement.'

Asandir extended lean legs and answered the gripes in strict order. 'I didn't. He won't.' Reclined with his capable fingers locked behind his tipped head, the field Sorcerer trampled the incensed retort. 'You stayed here because, on formal terms at the time, you were no longer subject to my apprenticeship.'

Dakar shut his gaped jaw like a fish revolted by a distasteful morsel. Appalled, then suspicious, he shot a glance sidewards.

Sethvir answered, his air of innocuous innocence absorbed as he poked through his displaced belongings. 'You were signed off and sealed as your own master before Asandir ever left to square the debt held against the Crown of Rathain.' The crock with the spider was removed from harm's way. Benignly agreeable, the Warden added, 'Enjoy the autonomy. Pursue your own fate. All your Fellowship ties have been sundered. The parchment was formally entered in record, which means by my count, you've been free-loading here for two months and a day.'

A mild turquoise eye peered askance as though startled to catch Dakar dumbfounded. 'Do you wish,' Sethvir mused, 'to question the surety of the star-stamp I placed on the document?'

The high flush of fury drained fast as the impact struck home: Dakar faced his discharge from an eight-hundred-and-fifty-year term of formal apprentice-ship. More, the severance came vouchsafed under Sethvir's titled standing as Warden of Althain.

Dumped unceremoniously on his arse, the Mad Prophet leaped to pick a fight with his erstwhile master.

'No one informed me!' he fumed to Asandir. 'Why the blatant surprise? Is this some new test? Or, dare I suggest, a secretive manipulation?' Stung beyond sense, Dakar renewed his festering grievance. 'Since I stood for the oath you just brought to closure, in fairness, I should have witnessed the finish.'

'Oh, you started the dismal affray, beyond question!' Steel eyes half-lidded, Asandir let his former protégé squirm. 'If you thought I'd be lenient, Sethvir doesn't forget.'

Denial was futile. Dakar's maladroit usage of Fellowship auspices indeed had saddled Rathain's crown with the ruinous obligation to the Order of the Koriathain in the first place.

Asandir was not finished, though the accusation lay over two hundred years in the past, and nary a word since had broached the disgrace, or faulted the spellbinder for prior misconduct. 'The discharge of your jumped-up initiative at Athir has set Athera's future on tenterhooks and cost a gifted woman her life through an ugly act of self-sacrifice. Don't trouble to add the misery that a sanctioned s'Ffalenn prince has endured, caged in conditions of inhumane horror throughout centuries of captivity!'

'He's survived to win free,' Dakar argued, jaw set. 'You assured me that Arithon's mind was not broken.'

Sethvir's retort produced three succinct images derived from the earth-sense bestowed by the Paravians. *The first replayed the ancient memory of a bereft mother's tears as her only daughter left Althain Tower at three years of age, by adamant free choice bound to swear service to the Koriathain; the next displayed the terms of Asandir's oath, lately sealed by stone's witness at the Whitehold sisterhouse as surety for Fellowship noninterference on the matter of Prince Arithon's life.* The third image, concurrent, wounded the most: *of the world's most brilliant born talent, sanctioned as the last living heir to Rathain. That view showed Arithon Teir's'Ffalenn huddled under an ox manger, bereft of the natural recall of his identity.*

'What else could I have accomplished alone, that dark night when the crisis faced me at Athir?' Dakar blurted, culpable and defensive for his role in that ruinous past string of betrayals. 'You'll recall, at the time, your crown prince was dying! When Elaira, or I, tried to contact Sethvir, we were granted no shred of grace! No response came in that hour, and no succour arose from any other Fellowship Sorcerer—'

'What made you think that we could?' Asandir snapped across vain protestation.

It fell to Sethvir to respond to the Mad Prophet's interrupted appeal. 'Elaira wished me to secure Arithon's survival, a call that was not mine to make. Clearly so, Dakar.' Calm, ink-stained fingers carefully lifted the paper wasps' fragile nest. 'His Grace's free will was not compromised! Only his choice to live hung in question, and by the Law of the Major Balance, mortal death is not a matter under our jurisdiction.'

Dakar paled again, hurled backwards into the agonized recall of the untenable crux thrust upon him, hard on the heels of the ghastly defeat that ended the siege of Alestron. 'Don't claim your Fellowship planned to do nothing! Not after you held Arithon's blood oath to live, no matter the cost or the consequence.'

'We expected the Biedar would step into the breach,' Asandir corrected, ungently. 'And the tribe's eldest did that. But after you had taken rash action first, with the sorry result that the options thereafter were limited.'

Dakar looked worse than weak at the knees. His desperation found no handy place to sit down. Sethvir's displaced sea-shells crammed the cushioned window-seat, and stacked books occupied every chair. 'You might explain why I'm being tossed out! I may have created a grievous set-back, but I promise, my botched efforts stayed within form. No one who was conscious had their preferences compromised. I took care to secure the consent of all parties before the first ritual was undertaken.'

'Did you?' Asandir sat forward, quick as a coiled snake.

'I made sure!' Dakar insisted, tinged sullen by stress. 'You held the power to stake Arithon's survival. Therefore, I did not turn on him without grounds.'

'Then who is responsible for what happened at Athir?' Asandir probed like struck iron.

The silence turned suddenly dense as poured lead. Dakar floundered, aghast, while Sethvir blew the dust from the paper wasps' confection and restored its frailty to the cupboard. As softly deliberate, Althain's Warden listed the damning facts from a memory impartially flawless. 'Who hounded Elaira to make her decision? Or did you not make a sly pact first with Glendien, whose unborn child's betrayed trust in due course paid the ultimate price? Teylia was forced to salvage the brunt of your maladroit chain of ill consequence. Who else might suffer in further forfeit remains under question.'

'Merciful Ath!' Dakar exclaimed, trembling. His diligent years of rapt study *could not* be dismissed at a stroke for the sake of one bygone grievance. 'Why wait so long to bring this to light? What raised the issue at this hour?'

His anguished question stayed brutally dangling.

'The disastrous choices have been made already,' Asandir declared, unequivocal. 'My oath, set in stone, forbids further action on Arithon's behalf for the future. What you do hereforward is your own affair. You have been released to walk away, or to find the conscience to seek a redemption.'

Dakar accepted the severance, granted no chink for appeal. He was not crushed pithless. On his way out, he paused only to fling back a cruel dart of his own. 'Forget my thankless service! Best for you to fall back on your king-making touch to appoint the throne's shadow, in fact!'

At Asandir's startled glance, which all but cracked a legendary demeanour, Sethvir said in arch calm as the door slammed, 'On that count, no one is joking, dear friend. After all, Tysan is legitimately threatened. There, actually, Fellowship auspices can snatch the initiative and declare the next successor to the s'Gannley title.'

'Which branch?' quipped the field Sorcerer, too astute to be surprised twice on the subject. 'Or can you mean both at once?'

Sethvir's eyes gleamed with the suspect sparkle of paste, buffed to pass as a swindler's trifle. 'How far can we bend the dictates of old law and strain the frayed cloth of tradition?'

'Far enough,' cracked Asandir, 'to scald the naked pink flesh of our arses!' He reached to fortify himself from the tray. To one who knew him, the sadness and grief afflicted by Dakar's mean departure were poignantly visible. In truth, his return had been most tenderly expected: with faultless care, his discarded apprentice had catered to his personal preference. The delicacies of hot bread, and fresh fruit, so often missed in rough travel, accompanied Sethvir's pot of steaming tea. The congealed plate of sausage and pickled eggs, Dakar would have arranged for himself.

The light meal Asandir wished, while at leisure, would scarcely stand him in good stead as he braced for another hard journey. Already expected to crown the new heir on the death of the High Queen of Havish, he understood Tysan's explosive woes could not rest, shadowed under the deadlier threat of the Mistwraith's resurgent influence.

Asandir sliced a thick slab of bread, wrapped it over the plump link of sausage, then tucked in, determined, and ate. While the Warden fleshed out the rest of the news, he chewed fast, driven by need to commit his strength to two winter errands, one nearer at hand, and the other at extreme long distance. Both added tasks must be handled at speed, without rest amid inclement weather.

For Dakar, the harsh temper of training would hold; or else break down, to the waste of centuries of unstinted effort. Today's abrupt severance had been nothing less than a pitiless act of expediency. *Every* frail thread of advantage must be seized in the heat of the moment. For if a stop-gap net could not be spun to foil the Prime Matriarch's ruthless intentions, the Fellowship Sorcerers had no other avenue left to deflect the hurtling course towards ruin.

Early Winter 5922

Departures

While the Prime Matriarch pursues her intent to thwart Elaira's journey to seek Biedar counsel, her urgent design to trap the enchantress takes pause for fresh news from the lane watch in Tysan: that a sharp quittance by Asandir has left Dakar stranded as a free agent . . .

Alarmed by the uncanny failure to collar the elusive pair of condemned fugitives, the True Sect High Priest at Erdane suspends his enforced curfew, then issues a command to assemble a formal delegation to Etarra, entrusted to bear a renewed petition pleading for the reform of the Light's renegade avatar . . .

On the morning that suspended road travel resumes, an apparently surly, underfed groom weaves a hand-cart piled with horse trappings through a jammed inn-yard; but as a merchant's wagon filled with cured fleeces rolls out down the Cainford road, the dumped saddle-cloths are found in a heap, with the fellow responsible vanished, and no other to blame for one stable blanket gone missing . . .

IV. Dispossessed

T he driver of the cart-load of fleeces proved to be a man in love with his wine-skin. Between rapturous guzzling, he sang off-key, or mumbled obscenities in tones of encouragement to the back-turned ears of his draught mules. Stopped by the Light's lancers for questioning, he told raucous jokes. Oblivious to rolled eyes and glares of annoyance, he folded double and whooped himself breathless with laughter at his own cleverness.

The exasperated sergeant propped him back upright with distaste. Since nothing witnessed by a drunken sot could be counted reliable, the dedicates slapped the rumps of his team and sent him on his merry way. Better that, than risk being saddled with him when he flopped into a stupor and snored off his binge amid his rancid cargo. The minion of Darkness sought by the temple examiners moved over the land without tracks. Such a fell power would not need to skulk, far less stow away where the pungency of shearling wool left the hand that inspected it reeking of sheep.

Therefore, Tarens slept undisturbed, comfortably nestled amid the grease stink of lanolin. When the tipsy driver succumbed to his spree down the road, a small, black-haired man cloaked in a horse-blanket emerged from the fleeces, took over the mules' reins, and steered the cart southward at a brisk pace.

Hours later, the driver awoke, moaning with a bilious hangover. Naught seemed the worse for his bout of unconsciousness, except that his strayed mules had meandered off course down a derelict side lane and snagged their bridles in the rank overgrowth. The wind was rising. Lowered sun filtered through the bare trees, and a pewter scud of cloud from the north threatened to bring a fresh snowfall. Grumbling over his tender head, the carter extricated his team, muscled his stalled wagon right way around, and back-tracked towards the main trade-road.

He never saw hide nor hair of the fugitives inadvertently given safe transport. An hour gone, the pair pressed forward on foot down the unused by-way. The weedy wheel-ruts devolved to a path, embroidered with dense thickets of burdock and flanked by a leafless coppice. The wood opened at length where the tumble-down ruin of a settlement bordered the river's edge.

The rotted lathe-walls, broken fences, and moss-capped chimney stones had lain abandoned for years, roofless crofts and a caved-in forge overtaken by bitter-sweet vine. Likely the land's bounty had gone to neglect when the resident families fell to a virulent outbreak of fever. Tarens allowed that Efflin's case had been lucky. More often, those stricken succumbed and died. A village might be wiped out in a season, with the hale survivors too few to maintain the legacy left by misfortune.

The fallen beams stood open to sky. Nothing moved but the secretive pheasant, flushed squawking from the weedy straggle of stems left by kitchen gardens gone wild. Where there had been children and laughter and industry, only the rustles of drab little birds foraged amid the snarled briar.

Tarens ached, dispirited. 'What are you looking for? We won't find a haven, here.'

Head cocked to one side, his dark-haired friend continued to listen as if hope had not gone with the vanished inhabitants. Shortly, in the yard of a tumble-down cottage, he unearthed a dry root-cellar in decent repair. The nearby well had not fallen in. Though the rusted crank-shaft had frozen, the chain stayed intact enough to replace the rotted bucket with a discarded preserves jar. The drawn water stayed sweet. Plentiful hare grazed in the overgrown pastures. Summer-fat on the unmown hay, they were easily snared with a string noose. By nightfall, before the first snow blew in earnest, the vagabond's foraging provided a tasty leek stew, stirred with a peeled stick in a dented pot.

The frugal cookfire he built amid a cracked hearth vented almost no smoke, a detail not lost upon Tarens, who crouched in the lee of the collapsed foundation, bruised and pained by every drawn breath. At each turn, his friend's resourcefulness displayed a flagrant proficiency.

'You've done this before,' he broached at a hitched whisper.

The beggarman returned a luminous smile, unapologetic as he dished out two savoury servings into his scavenged jam crocks. Carmine-lit by the embers, he was raffish again, his dark hair in tangles and his sharp-cut features blurred over by several days' stubble.

Tarens accepted his portion, moved to trepidation by the messy prospect of eating while strapped in the dressing that splinted his nose. A touch on his wrist dispelled that apprehension: he was offered a wooden spoon, crudely whittled. Not by the artifact blade from the diviner but with a plain harness knife, too likely filched from the inn's cranky stableman.

'Thank you,' he rasped, grateful in spite of the suspect case of petty theft. 'You must have a name?'

The question incited a glance, with raised eyebrows. The vagabond set down his meal. He retrieved the stick implement from the emptied pot and scraped three antique Paravian characters on the slate apron. A pause followed. After a frown of intense concentration, he surrendered his effort, left a gap, and inscribed a last cipher with an irritable flourish.

'I can't read the old runes,' Tarens pressed gently.

The stick moved again, the inscription redone in the common characters used by town commerce. *'ARI,'* the string began, followed by the same annoyed space, then the dangling character 'N,' finished off with a flick.

'Arin will do, then,' Tarens declared, tactful enough not to stir the frustration behind the peevish omission. 'Unless you wish otherwise?'

An open-hand gesture gave resigned assent. Then hunger eclipsed the token exchange. Both men ate quickly. Before darkness fell, their coal-fire was doused, the swept ashes flung into the river. Arin smothered the blackened hearthstone under mouldered leaves, cleaned the jam-jars, and removed the one rigged to the well chain. Satisfied that no trace of their presence remained, he chased Tarens into the root-cellar. Huddled amid the chill influx of draughts and blind in the dank, cobwebbed darkness, the injured man wrapped up in the moth-eaten horse-blanket.

Nothing spoke but the outside whine of the wind, and the fitful scrape as dry leaves scratched across the overgrown entrance. Denied simple conversation, the crofter wondered what trauma incited his companion's reluctance to talk.

The elusive answer remained unsolved since Arin slipped back outdoors in pursuit of unspecified business. Nocturnal by habit, he might stay abroad until after the storm broke. Tarens was left stranded with his own thoughts, wakeful and alone for the first time since the fraught peril of his deliverance.

Crops had failed here. The awareness tingled through skin, bone, and nerve, from the finger-tips pressed to cold earth with intent to detect the drummed vibration of hoof-beats. But no patrol of white lancers pursued his battered friend. Not yet; the certainty that such searchers *would come* cranked a relentless tension through his viscera. The man who failed to recall his true name, for convenience addressed as Arin, expelled a vexed breath and stood up.

He could not have explained how he sensed the imprinted presence of subtle disharmony. Only that, between the snow scent on the wind and the rustled chatter of frosted grasses, a lingering blight threaded through the innate fabric of this remote patch of farmland. Like dissonance, some long-past event spun a kink in the natural currents that nourished the life in his surroundings.

He had no memory and yet, he *knew.* Once, long ago, he may have spun music to remedy such an imbalance. But not here: the pulse of this place did not rise in his blood though he could trace the stagnated eddies and define where ragged constrictions marred the rhythmic flow of its melody.

The upset was an entrenched affliction. Through the whine of the wind and the pressure of pending storm, he noted the absence of owls and the scarcity of the field-mice. The plentiful hare bespoke sparse herds of deer, which should have browsed on the unmown pastures in their drab winter coats. These fields were not, and never had been home to him. Still, if he let his attentive pause lengthen, the subtle symphony of deeper nuances gradually would be unveiled.

He shrank from the prospect. The stretch to access such uncanny awareness bristled him to instinctive recoil. Who knew what other dread fact might emerge? What firm assurance did he possess, that some ugly circumstance from his blank past might not resurface and shatter his equilibrium? *Someone* had chained him, once. He bore the scars. Trauma from an incorrigible imprisonment made him flinch, until the evidence haunted him: that somehow he might be a danger to others, and the cruelty of his past shackles might prove to be justified.

Fires never burned without smoke. The placid country-side was being swept to flush out a sorcerer maligned for foul practice. Frightened talk between the travellers on the thoroughfare had shared the same terrorized undertones overheard at the inn-yard. Worse, he had tended the hideous injuries inflicted upon Tarens by the brunt of hysterical consequence.

The inner dread had to be faced: his unknown past might hold criminal acts. If so, he deferred the crippling horror of digging for self-discovery. His gifted talent could not be denied. The evident power he carried, untapped, burned like molten flame under the skin. Scruple kept that frightful well-spring untested. He would not sound those depths. Never, until the kind-hearted crofter could be delivered to safety. That feat must be done on his upright human merits, if only to bear out an honest man's faith in him.

Therefore, his finely tuned senses searched only for warning of inbound lancers. No such intrusion disrupted the night. Pending snow whetted the air to shaved ice, and stiffened gusts clattered the branches. He moved through the ruin softly as a wraith, while the promised storm stole in like snipped lace and paled the darkness with flurries. Content for the nonce to wear Arin's identity, he combed through the graveyard ruin of the village for anything useful. He finished fast, stripped off his jacket, and wrapped up his picked stash of oddities. He returned to his chosen bolt-hole before the dusted ground showed his tracks.

The shelter enfolded him, pitch-black and silent, but not peaceful, as he expected. Instead his companion's inconsolable grief pounded with breaking force against his unshuttered empathic awareness.

Arin dropped his wrapped cache. Reeled as though struck by a mortal blow, he could not move, could not breathe, could not think. Only *feel*, quite helpless to stem the flash-point shock of the other man's raging emotion.

Entangled, Arin lost the wits to recoil. He had spent too many traumatic years pitched to the razor's edge, his survival pressured to split-second response through the soul-naked handling of free wraiths. His ingrained, urgent reflex sorted the wrack, already driven to seek the needful pattern to uplift and heal . . .

Images of family burst through in a flood, stamped with the loss of unbearable parting: a thousand desolate imprints of love wrenched into abrupt separation. Some faces he recognized. Beside Efflin and Kerelie, he picked out the two deceased children whose spirits once spoke through a borrowed flute. The sad barrage also encompassed lost parents: a boy's eyes watched a father leave home, conscripted to arms by a temple muster; this triggered a spinning, prescient rush into an unformed future, which showed Kerelie, convulsed with laughter while sewing a rich lady's ruffled silk dress. Then that image faded into another, of Efflin bent over an open account book. Both scenes yet-to-be stretched like gauze across the torched biers that had consumed the wrapped casualties of summer's fever. Amid the crackle of flames from past pyres, other layers of charred bones whispered through the endemic malignment that wracked the country-side to disharmony . . .

The paroxysm of visions flayed through as a rip tide that broke, ebbed, and stranded him. Arin came back to himself, his eyes streaming the tears of fierce heart-ache. He tasted the tang of death and despair, and ached for the bleak damage yet to occur. Once while caged in crystal, assuaging a wraith, he had translated such findings to music, then lifted the tissue of pain to a gentle requital through resonant melody. But Tarens was a being of flesh, prisoned inside the range of his cognizant senses. Lacking an instrument, speech only remained: and the stark terror of sounded words left the musician wretchedly paralyzed.

If he spoke, Arin dreaded the crushing discovery, that the singer perceived by his inner awareness might be just a wishful figment. To shatter a dream of such exquisite purity surely might wound his spirit deeply enough to destroy him. More than silence, he dreaded his flawed human voice might be found lacking in range and tonality.

Perhaps vicious uncertainty ripped a sound from him.

'Are you all right?' Tarens cried, from the dark. 'Arin? Save us both! Are you injured?'

'No.' The word burst from his lips, half gasp, half whisper, a cork unleashed by a torrent. Arin's concern could do nothing else. Only stem Tarens's poisoned depression before sorrow blighted the man's open heart and stunted his generosity.

'Listen to me!' Forced past reserve, the phrases burst free in a crisp, antique accent. 'Your sister was never content as a crofter! She will serve out her year's term at the temple, embroidering vestments and altar-cloths. Her fine needlework will bring her a skilled job at a quality dress shop. Your brother will never return to a farm. His loss of the boys cannot rest in that setting. He will find a new life as a clerk, enjoy songs with a circle of erudite friends, and marry a good woman for comfort.'

Tarens's staggered amazement was palpable. 'Arin! My friend, whoever you are, how can you claim to know this?'

The question floundered into tense quiet. The uneasy answer was not safe to broach since the truth implied seer's gift. Such had happened before: *prescient visions also had forecast the inquiry of the Light's diviner. Which suggested a faculty that out-stripped intuition.* Content to stay Arin, beyond fearful of Tarens's righteous distrust if such talent branded him with the wickedness of proscribed sorcery, he retrieved his jacket and rifled through its bundled contents. The flint striker and bronze clip were too easily found: more damning evidence of a breadth of vision unimpaired in the dark. Frantic to salvage the man's benign faith in him, Arin fashioned a rushlight.

He hoped that the wavering flame unveiled an innocuous presence: of a lean fellow with tousled black hair and green eyes, earnest with care and uncertainty. 'Friend,' Arin said gently, 'by all that I am, whatever that is, I promise I won't ever harm you.'

His assurance was not rough, or grating, or flat, but instead possessed a mellifluous lilt that all but unmanned him with gratitude. The elusive remembrance of a bard's ability might not be a delusion, after all.

The rushlight steadied. Its honest exposure should reveal the terror that shadowed his unknown origins.

Tarens returned an unruffled regard from a hideously battered face. He saw no reason yet to shy from the fearful thorns of uncertainty. Crofter, he had been. But his fighter's temperament sprang from a loyalty solid as bone. He said carefully, 'We found you where the old lane leads to the ruin of the ancient earl's court south of Kelsing. The Koriathain sometimes make use of that place for their private rituals. Have you an active connection to them?'

'If I did,' Arin answered, stung to leashed rage, 'I was held as their captive, most likely for an unclean purpose.' He shuddered, hesitant to broach the nightmares that troubled his sleep. 'By no means would I let them retake me.' Shown Tarens's appalled consternation, he added, 'Your question is forthright! But if I don't remember, I can't guarantee you don't walk in dangerous company.'

The awkward moment spun out to the hiss of the fluttered flame. How to account, that no recall existed? Or explain an experience that lurked outside reason, formlessly venomed by the latent horrors of a term of helpless entrapment?

While Arin struggled for tactful language, Tarens eased the tense pause with the innocence of human decency.

'Since you don't know what set you to flight, let's not rush to press judgement. You may be the marked quarry, but I've been condemned. Survival has joined our fate.' Before that recrimination could wound, Tarens added, 'I regret nothing, do you understand? In your own way, you took risks for my family. All of your acts have done right by them.'

Last gesture, the crofter snuffed out the rush lamp. In patent reassurance, he settled and slept, deliberately vulnerable to the busy works of his mage-sighted companion. Surely he heard, as he nodded off, the purposeful strokes of edged steel being honed across a scrounged whetstone.

At due length, three broken kitchen knives were refurbished as daggers. Arin's cut-leather belt wrapped the grips, with his oversized breeches retied at the waist with a braid made from scavenged string.

Stretched out to rest, tensioned yet by unease, Arin listened as the gusts winnowed the thickened snowfall outside. Musty air filled his nostrils. He could not shake off the haunted impression of another prior experience: that somewhere before, the hitched breaths of an injured friend had been sealed by a blizzard inside of a root-cellar. The cramped ambience spun him a gruesome dream, stark with the memory of desperate straits, and more vivid than uncontrolled prescience. . .

Then, the reiving cohort of lancers had worn black-and-gold surcoats blazoned with entwined snakes and lions. The innocent's cottage just put to the torch crackled in red conflagration, whipped under a white-out blizzard. In that day's frigid air, amid drifts trampled pink, sprawled the large, honest man their knives had tortured to find him. Heart-sore, he strove with his healer's skills to stem bleeding and bind riven flesh. The damage lay beyond any remedy. Even so, he rejected the dying man's plea for abandonment: *'For your gift of feal duty, my charge of protection; for your loyalty, my spirit shall answer, unto my last drop of blood, and until my final living breath, Dharkaron witness.'*

He finished the dressing for honour alone. 'You didn't betray me,' he told that wounded man, whose agony, suffered in his behalf, came to refuge in the comfortless chill of a root-cellar.

Amid winter's freeze, sheltered in earth-bound quiet, the reliving carried the same fetid smells: of breathed air and wrapped wounds, congealed blood, and the hounding dread of uncertainty.

That man's fatal anguish had wrung him to voice the bitter extent of his sorrow: *'You failed nothing and no one. I could name you hero, gild a plaque in your memory that proclaims the cornerstone for a crown that will stand on the strength of your sacrifice. But the truth casts down rhetoric. A man who holds hospitality sacred is worth much more to the land than a king.'*

'Long life, and my blessing,' said the ghost in his nightmare. 'The Fellowship Sorcerers are right to restore you.'

Arin wrenched awake with a gasp, shuddered by the throes of after-shock. Somebody's callused hand gripped his arm, and another muffled his screaming.

'Arin?' The concern was Tarens's, not some long-dead trapper. 'You shouted in your sleep.'

Carefully tactful, the crofter released him. Respect did not rush to ask probing questions. Yet the fabric of pretence had shredded. As fugitives roped together by destiny, one man understood that he was the sole cause of his fellow's hapless endangerment.

Worse, the relentless peril that stalked them trafficked in blood-letting stakes. Arin sat up. Arms wrapped over tucked knees, he rested his forehead against his crossed wrists.

Tonight's outbreak of recall suggested a history his spirit cried out to disown: chased as quarry before, he had survived because a strong man with great heart had died for him. More, his own peal of sorrow restated the lines of a prince's oath to a feal liegeman. Incontrovertibly, he had a past and a name: dangerous facts all but certain to drive the committed factions that hunted him. Though to the last fibre, he viewed such a royal legacy as abhorrent, for the worse, Tarens was already ensnared in the weave of that intractable heritage.

Scalded, Arin reaffirmed the past vow hurled into the teeth of his enemies. *'I don't leave them my wounded.'*

If the selfless kindness that brought Tarens to shelter a destitute stranger was not to share a dog's end, the misery of their cooped quarters must be sustained throughout days to come. Just as before, the diligent searchers would leave no stone unturned, and no weedy field untrampled in their manic furor. Therefore, no quarry's tracks must be found in the pristine drifts. With luck, under snow, the temple dedicates would overlook the buried depression at the root-cellar's entrance. For safety, the fugitives holed up inside must stay immured until the next thaw. The bare ground would have to be frosted iron-hard before they dared emerge, first to forage, then to move on.

As wretchedly plagued by the capricious onset of an early winter, only one person alive stayed at liberty to illuminate Arin's veiled past. Dakar the Mad Prophet sulked in shadow beneath the bleak spire of Althain Tower, buffeted by the cruel north wind. He needed no seer's gift to forecast the squeeze of the crisis: beyond doubt, his accursed role in Prince Arithon's past would run him afoul of the Koriathain.

Dakar had crossed their filthy agenda before, even quashed the wily gamut of their probes in his time as a crown heir's appointed protector. Under Fellowship auspices, in lawful standing as Asandir's agent, he had been the target of their baneful plots often enough to wring him to cold sweats. The fresh prospect woke the spectre of nightmare, since the thankless quittance of his apprenticeship stripped him of the Sorcerers' backing.

At loose ends, three days later, Dakar reeled yet. From outraged denial, to obstinate dragged heels, to packing his tinker's haul of possessions, he loitered outside the tower's shut gates, abandoned to his own devices. The warded locks were fastened, behind him. Ahead, the worn spur of the north trade-road seamed the barren wilds of Atainia; daunting, inhospitable terrain for a traveller stranded afoot.

Southward, the ancient track flanked the iced current of the Isaer, passed the massive node that harnessed the lane force at the Great Circle, then met the cross-roads at the crumbled Second Age ruin, where the river's head-waters welled from an underground cavern. Asandir's journey lay that way, en route to the mountain outpost that sheltered a persecuted clan enclave.

Fed to the teeth with the hazardous affairs of his former master, and festered to a grudge like a canker, Dakar turned his back and set off for the nearest town habitation. Weeds snagged at his boots. Too short-strided for the rough ground, he stumbled across stony gullies washed through the wheel-ruts. Few wagons ventured this desolate land, laid waste since the tumult of a First Age battle, with bleak, scoured hill-tops whipped to thin dust, and vales that whispered of keening ghosts, slagged yet by the glassine pits of past drakefire.

Solitude gave Dakar too much time to brood. Independence did not leave him care-free. His tuned awareness picked up the warped flow of the lane flux, unbalanced still by the echo of ruin a wrathful dragon had unleashed at Avenor. Disharmony and disease still choked the realm of Tysan, a condition unlikely to find a reprieve under the True Sect's doctrine. If such weighty matters correctly belonged under Fellowship oversight, Dakar had suffered the Sorcerers' company too long to stay blinded by ignorance. Aggravated, each step, he vented and kicked a loose pebble.

The spiteful impulse injured only his toe. While the missile cracked off a boulder and bounced, the Mad Prophet hopped on one foot and let fly. 'May Dharkaron Avenger's immortal black horses drop steaming dung over Asandir's field boots!'

The Sorcerer's footwear, likely as not, would walk scatheless through the encounter. Worse, the maligned gravel would imprint the curse, since the Athlien singers had vanished. The Mad Prophet yanked his flapping cloak tight and sullenly shut down his mage-sense.

If he must blister his tender soles and spend brutal nights in the open, he would endure the unpleasantness without the bother of a refined connection. More, if the crux of Fellowship need pressured him to *volunteer* to safeguard Rathain's hunted prince, he was older, and finally wise to the fact the position was star-crossed! Riddled with pernicious pitfalls and foes, with the man himself given to powers and strengths unimaginably dangerous.

'Damn all to Sethvir's manipulative maundering!' Dakar swore. The Warden's almighty earth-sense knew how keeping that post had wrecked the last footing for a friend's trust. Dakar could not weep. Not anymore. His recriminations were long since spent for an anguish that could not, in life, be erased. His unsavoury duty in Halwythwood, and again, after warning, at

Athir, had unequivocally served Fellowship interests through the betrayal of Arithon's personal integrity.

If the royal victim ever discovered the secret price paid then to win his survival, Dakar understood what his hide would be worth! In his shoes, the guilty party would run, never to shoulder the lash of reprisal from the infamous s'Ffalenn temper.

'Murder would be kinder,' Dakar muttered, and pumped on short legs to hike faster.

He reached Lorn three days later, puffing and tired, with chafed heels and both ankles blistered. The town was no place to cheer dismal spirits: little more than a barnacle cluster of dwellings attached to the rocky north-coast, sandwiched between a clouded, pearl sky and the pewter shine of the winter breakers. Dusk had fallen. Under the smeared smoke from the chimney-stacks, the rimed cobbles in the narrow streets sheltered the slink of scavenging cats, and the briny miasma of fish guts. The years since the revival of navigation had shrunk the port back to an isolate haven for mackerel boats.

The market lay deserted, where by day the garrulous matrons diced and salted down the dawn catch. The risen, raw wind already had chased their benighted gossip indoors. As eager for comfort, Dakar steered between the bleak, wharf-side warehouses and the netted thatch roof of the chandler's. The hot glow of lamp-light steamed the roundels of the sole clapboard tavern when he shoved his bulk through the squeaky plank door.

Conversation quieted before him, replaced with the owlish stares by which grizzled, backwater salts measured an outsider. Even the urchin stopped begging for scraps and turned round eyes towards the cloaked stranger.

Dakar surveyed the coarse company, daubed in the thick shadows from the tallow lamps slung from the ceiling beams. Unattached men sprawled at the trestles, flushed with drink as they elbowed to cuddle the barmaids. Others with wives and young children at home downed their pints and hob-nobbed with friends. The widows with black scarves tied over their hair, and the ham-fisted matrons crammed into the corner nooks, while the wizened elderly snoozed by the hearth, too arthritic to haul twine on the luggers.

The acquaintance Dakar sought was not present.

Aware if he ventured abroad that the doors would be closed to late lodgers, he waded inside over mud-brick floors tracked gritty with sand. The taint of wet wool and sweat was ingrained, and the attitude jaundiced as the offal dumped out for the sharks. Lest such contempt be mistaken for welcome, the muscular landlord propped against the bar priced his beer to fleece strangers.

His brew would be sour as pig swill, besides. Dakar might have matched the extortion with coppers spell-burnished to gleam like silver, but the clam stew with hard bread he wanted sold for only three pence. He seated himself on an empty bench, ordered supper, and ate. Talk of nets, sails, and weather resumed, pointedly directed around him.

He was not left to mind his anonymous business. Another woman tucked into one corner was equally shunned by the locals. Although she wore the same smock blouse and wool over-dress, her lily-white fingers had never flensed a wet cod. The sigil she pitched against Dakar's aura flicked his nerves like a scuttling spider.

The Mad Prophet choked. He blotted the chowder broth sprayed through his beard and slurped onwards. Apparently innocuous, stupid, and fat, he measured the execrable nuisance: Prime Selidie's rapacity wasted no time. Already, he was pinched in a trap laid by the Koriathain. More, the power that hounded him was no trifle. The witch had more sisters stationed nearby, equipped with the force to shred his defenses.

Cornered, alone, he was tacitly warned to accede in quiet surrender.

Dakar spat out a mauled clot of gristle and sopped up the last driblets of gravy. Bedamned if he meant to move before he settled his dinner. The enchantress could fume herself purple meanwhile. Tysan's dogmatic aversion to sorcery meant a sister reliant upon a quartz focus dared not wield her blatant craft in the open.

Inspired, Dakar belched, clutched his middle, and yowled. 'This vile soup is tainted! Does the house poison guests? I've been gouged before for the price of a bed when bad stew laid me low with a belly-ache!'

A smatter of laughter arose, cut by the inn matron's roar from the kitchen. 'Going to spew, are you? The gutter's outside! No refunds here for a whiner's gut, nor warm milk for a griped constitution!'

Dakar doubled over and moaned.

Nobody else who consumed the same fare took pity on his distress. The bar-keeper ignored him. While his enemy watched, Dakar ripped off his belt. He tossed the strap onto the trestle hard enough to make the looped coin pouch clash loudly against the brass buckle. Cloak shrugged off to puddle around his ankles, he unlaced and peeled his twill jerkin, then groaned and crumpled arse down on the floor.

Heads turned, hatted and bearded and weathered, amused by his histrionics.

Dakar shuddered and held his breath. When his pouched cheeks flushed to vermilion, he rolled up his eyes and flopped into a faint.

Evidently out cold, he lay like a log. Where a dishonest bumpkin anyplace else would snap up his obvious bait, Lorn's slack-witted brutes showed no interest. Instead, the burliest onlooker grabbed the suds pail from the tap. While he doused the felled landlubber back to spluttering consciousness, the beggar child *finally* dived after the abandoned purse. The predictable happened: his disreputable, grimed hand blistered on the spellbinder's wards as he tried to pilfer the contents.

The treble scream as the boy singed his fingers sheared over the rumbled laughs and snide comments. He was quite unharmed, beyond a few moments of painful sensory illusion.

But where conjury was anathema, the lad's cry raised a furor of panic.

While the timid backed into the corners and prayed, the brave brandished raised benches and bottles and closed in to trounce the unholy practitioner. The door banged as someone left at a run to fetch the town's armed authority.

'That's your sorry response for a lad caught out, thieving?' Dakar yelled through the commotion. Soaked to dripping, hunched over with belly-ache, he shoved erect in the jostle. Backed to the wall by a breastwork of benches, he pealed on through the bar-keeper's bellows and the child's roaring tantrum. 'Your snotty brat looks fit for work. Let him earn honest pay washing pots in your scullery and thank me for the sting of a timely correction!'

But instead, the harpy from the inn's kitchen barreled out with her meat skewer angled for blood. 'We don't take interference from upstart sorcerers!'

Dakar dug in his heels. Safe, he hoped, from the underhand wiles of Koriathain, he measured the angry fishermen who crowded to carve him in strips. 'Damn all to Dharkaron!' he railed in their teeth. 'And the same to the Light's idiot doctrine.' Only a suicide would blaspheme the True Sect's Canon by the name of Ath's Avenging Angel. Annoyed that Lorn's inept constable was tar-slow to collect blatant malefactors, Dakar ducked a swung fist. 'Why beat a sick man? Take that ne'er-do-well snip who shoved his sticky mitt in my coin-purse!'

Buffered amid the pummelling scuffle, with both eyes alert for the Koriani meddler, a short man tussled by a pack of stout locals failed to see the town's hastily summoned defender: one who gleamed, out of place, in the white-and-gold robes bestowed by the high temple at Erdane.

With the vested Sunwheel diviner came the immaculate armed escort, dispatched for the annual headcount of the Light's faithful. Dakar's rude discovery of the surprise entourage met the mailed fist of the dedicate whose righteous clout dropped him unconscious.

Dakar woke behind bars. A connoisseur of dark cells the length and breadth of five kingdoms, his nose broke the news that Lorn's dungeon outstripped the most noisome. He languished in fishy straw used sometime ago to pack mackerel. The stink threatened to kill him. Worse, clutches of starved rats rustled to feast on the rotted bits of fins and glued fish-heads. The slide of hairless tails and scampering feet tickled over him, while beneath, the floor stirred to an army of questing roaches. His nape throbbed, his eyelids were crusted, and the slob incarcerated before him had mistaken the water pan for a chamber-pot.

Nauseous, Dakar counted his blessings: he was not wracked by a hangover, or pulped by a bed-frolicking woman's crazed husband, or worse, brothers outraged by a sister's lost chastity. Expertly versed at survival in duress, the Mad Prophet knew how to upset a gaoler. Just by singing, he could make his presence unpleasant as nails pounded into the brain. Other wardens had thrown him out on his arse for drawing in plagues of *iyats*.

Lorn's square-jawed trusty escaped such grief, due to the predation of the Koriathain, and because temple authority left no heretic sorcerer to corrupt their horde of spiff rodents. Lancers in white surcoats collected Dakar by the scruff before his bashed head stopped spinning.

He played uncooperative and weak at the knees. Despite centuries of civilized apprenticeship, the Fellowship's cast-off spellbinder could belt out insults with dock-side flair. 'I'm too sick to move,' he finished off, douce, not faking the fact that the starch had run out of him.

Lethargy forced the hand of his captors. They smutched their white livery, heaved Dakar's bulk upright, and grunted his dragged heels upstairs, where the predictable jumped-up clerk surely waited to record the sentence.

'Don't promise me justice!' groused Dakar, en route. 'I've seen the facetious performance before. The magistrate's chamber won't be a turd-box for rats. No, their two-legged cousins like floors without muck. They'll expect me to wet myself for a gaggle of buffoons perched on a dais. They'll wear jewels and prettier robes than you lot, with chins brown as yours, because anyone jostling for a promotion always polishes backsides with puckered lips.'

The warden roared and cocked his mailed fist. Dakar smirked and sagged into a curtsey. While the muscle that propped him upright bowed also, bent over by his unstrung weight, the chap's armoured knuckles ploughed unimpeded into the stone wall. The screech of steel links made the most stalwart man cringe and caused Dakar to faint into a wad on the landing. The vengeful boots that kicked his larded ribs roused slurred mutters but failed to stiffen his backbone enough to stand up. There forward, he had to be towed by the wrists and ankles like a dead donkey. Onwards up the rough stair, then forcibly skated down a corridor floored with waxed wood, Dakar bemoaned the abuse until his sweated escort flopped him through the doubled doors into the chamber for judgement. Prostrate and panting, he exuded the reek of dead mackerel steeped in rat piss.

The Light's diviner scarcely blinked at the stench. A bald fellow with translucent skin, he sat enthroned beside candles that lit his livery to eye-stabbing brilliance. The town magistrate and justiciar flanked him like book ends, with a stool set aside for a bothered clerk, and a sparrow-thin orator who plucked up a list and wheezed through the verified accusations.

'The prisoner will stand for sentencing,' the temple diviner intoned, his accent from upper-crust Erdani origins.

Dangerous history had roots in that place, where the mayor's council once had been corrupted by necromancers. Though the cult was defunct, the shady influence still tainted the town's entrenched factions. Dakar peered through cracked lids and held his tongue. Jammed between two upright guards, unshaven and itching and irritable, he watched the snake in white vestments dispense with all semblance of judgement by trial.

'For the charge of blasphemy, you will be stripped to suffer ten strokes of the lash, followed by execution without appeal for sorcerous works and dark practice,' the diviner decreed. 'May the divine Light cleanse the taint as your wicked heart is pierced by cold steel, and your flesh is consigned to the fire.'

'Are you done?' snapped Dakar, revolted to nausea. 'Better tell your thugs to let me lie down or someone's sure to regret it.' Ahead of the officiously outraged recoil, he folded and spewed up his guts. Last night's sour meal spattered onto the dais and fouled the velvet slippers of his accuser.

Which lapse provoked an ear-splitting screech, and sealed his death at dawn, barely hours away.

'Break wind and pray all you like!' Dakar bared his teeth in a snarl. 'Your lash will not bite. Your sword will not pierce. Worse, the Light you invoke is a shameless fraud! Fire itself should disdain the dry wood you stack to murder the innocent.'

'Not so innocent.' Divested of his sullied shoes, one foot raised while the obsequious clerk knelt to remove his splashed hose, the robed diviner pronounced, 'I have not waived your right to a trial without reason. Before witnesses, you are confirmed as a seer. Not ignorant, but capable of prophetic fits and unimaginably dangerous! Lorn's warden and two guards overheard quite enough to confirm your damnation. By your own words you named yourself in league with the Spinner of Darkness!'

Dakar sucked a sharp breath, abruptly unnerved. Not by the dire incrimination, but from the nasty surprise that his upset stemmed from no head blow, but in fact arose from the queasy aftermath caused by a bout of tranced prescience.

Worse, the forevisions arisen through a black-out trance became fated. Althain's Warden himself never found an exception: such events were predestined to happen.

'This case is sealed!' The magistrate banged down his gavel and dismissed the guard. 'See the prisoner secured!'

Too facetious to detail the spurious vision foretold by Dakar's errant gift, his priestly accusers rushed ahead with their plans for a public roast. Lorn's dearth of a scaffold meant rousting the hands to nail up a makeshift platform. Lackeys dunned the fish-market smoke-shacks for wood, while the dedicates set the condemned into shackles and flung him back into the dungeon to languish.

There, the novelty packed a collection of gawkers against the cell door with craned necks. But the only Dark minion to face death in Lorn failed to satisfy their curiosity. He moaned on his back in the putrid straw, pathetic as anyone else who suffered the gripe from a crock of spoiled chowder. Eyes shut, he slept and snored like a walrus, which finally drove his nervous wardens to saunter away in disgust.

Dakar continued the racket, the rude noise needful to scare off the rats while he engaged his mage training and spiritwalked.

Immersed in deep trance, he projected his sensitized awareness into his outward surroundings: first into the straw, with its resident scavengers, until he could have identified every noisome rodent, cockroach, and louse maggot by Name. Farther, he expanded, through the forged essence of the steel grille, then the dank masonry that imprisoned him. Lightly as breath, he brushed past the two guards and the warden on duty. Dakar eased his boundaries wider still. Soon, he knew which clerks were diligent and which slouched at their desks as their quills scratched out copies of the summary judgement against him. No written account included the words he had babbled in prophetic trance.

Since a more active scrying could snag the attention of the Light's pesky diviner, Dakar abandoned the fruitless thrust to recoup the content of his blind prophecy.

Softly, he extended his probe past the ivied walls of the magistrate's hall. Beyond the cramped wing that housed Lorn's guild ministry, harbour office, and ramshackle customs shack, he paused where the gulls roosted with heads under wings, beneath the roof peaks and carved cornices. The dark streets below were deserted, except for a drunk who staggered homeward between two companions.

Dakar girded himself in transparent calm, then traced the by-lanes and shut houses, with their slate roofs and dormers smudged in smoke from banked fires. Patience showed him the warded calyx of sigils that shadowed his greater enemy. The Koriathain regrouped, poised to help the Light's priests fulfill their intent on the scaffold.

Dakar lacked the innate power to thwart them. A second attempt at diversion would spring an attack past his resource to counter. Since the sisterhood's amplified spells of coercion failed to recognize the Law of the Major Balance, he evoked his knowledge of natural order and melded at one with all things. As frosted air and chill stone, sleeping bird, and even the dark coil of enemy sigils, he slid his merged awareness into, then past their hostile boundaries without impediment. He widened his range: combed through the straggle of the fishermen's shacks, where honest families slept in their beds. Among them, the particular captain he sought sat awake, puffing a late pipe beside a lit candle.

Relief pushed Dakar's scrying outward again. He encompassed the pier at the harbour-side: ran with the cold surge of the tide, and splashed as the wavelets that necklaced white foam against the slimed rocks of the breakwater. He became the breast of the salty sea, rocking luggers tied up at their moorings. If each boat had similar clinker-built planks and workaday piles of fish tackle, only one wore the seal of safe passage bestowed by a grateful Fellowship

Sorcerer. There lay the spellbinder's hope of release if he could contrive the means to make a rendezvous.

Dakar stilled the expansion set into motion. Centred within the known sphere he encompassed, he gently loosened his ties to the manifest present.

Adrift in the shadowy realm of on-coming futures, his seer's talent sorted the overlapped images of what *could be,* and what *might become.* Trained focus breasted the ephemeral morass, and with consummate skill, traced the singular threads that concerned him.

Dakar saw the dawn, hard-edged with certainty; then a bled corpse on a scaffold of fish barrels, torched into flame. The alternate view, superimposed and much fainter, showed the unoccupied post and piled billets abandoned. He chose that branch, and from thence, viewed the fisherman of his acquaintance arise and eat breakfast, kiss his wife and three children, and stroll to the docks. Soon after, his boat with the Fellowship's blessing raised sail and scudded from the harbour. Dakar re-ran that sequence and noted which alley-ways held posted guards, and where the Light's lancers were quartered. He forecast at what hour the streets would become impassibly jammed with fanatical spectators.

Adept at his craft, he sifted the multiplied twists of event. As the probable thinned into the wisp of the possible, and the views of overlaid futures dispersed into fog, hazed over the glare of infinity, Dakar tested his choices. Through each posited frame of consequence, he selectively chose his best course. Then he woke to ground out his strained senses and reorient. Nerves steeled, he gathered his natural strength. Before the Light's guardsmen arrived to collect him, the condemned paid his earnest respects to the rats, who had forborne to gnaw at his finger-tips.

Then the hour drew nigh. The ephemeral shift that occurred before sunrise prickled through mage-sense as the flux reached the neap in the lane tide. Dakar slipped into trance once again. Not for an innocuous spiritwalk this time, but to garner the requisite permissions he needed to open his bid for escape. His arrangement began with such subtle stealth, just one aware mind on Athera took notice.

Kingbreaker

Winter travel and the fever-pitch tension of crisis saw Asandir in his habitual element. En route to the defended clan enclave tucked high in the mountains near the Pass of Orlan, he had left Althain Tower by transit to Isaer's Great Circle, then ridden fast and hard down the westward trade-road for seven days. He rented no post-horses when his mount tired. Bred to bear him as a cherished companion, the black stallion was a wonder among the world's mystical graces, too devoted to be put aside. The Sorcerer snatched sleep while the animal rested. Starry nights bedded both of them down in dry leaves, Asandir wrapped up in his cloak and reclined against his mount's side for shared warmth.

But even a Sorcerer's familiar could not travel at speed in the thin air of high altitude. The whipped drifts piled by the last blizzard bogged the pace where the old road narrowed down to a track folded into the buckled ramparts between the iced cliffs, and the high cornices swathed in white threatened the avalanches that broke away with a roar at the sound of a whip-crack. Experienced masters of caravans with their pack-trains of sure-footed mules never ventured the pass, facing winter.

Asandir went where Fellowship business took him, bold beyond care for the season. Yet this time, his iron strength and determined purpose laboured under the sorrowful heart-ache: that Arithon's plight had compelled the terms of Dakar's brutal dismissal. As a bone tossed into the shark's teeth of fate, the initiate prophet could stand with heroic grace, or else fall, wasted utterly, to the murderous wiles of the Fellowship's bitterest enemies.

Which painfully overdue word from Sethvir reached Asandir swift and straight as the flight of an arrow: *'Our wild-card cast-off is safely away from the ambush set for him at Lorn. He's escaped execution by the Light's doctrine and eluded pursuit by eight Koriathain.'*

The black horse stopped four-square in the road, though the rider's hand had not moved to rein in. The Fellowship's field Sorcerer bent his bare head. Stiff breeze tangled his silver hair through a moment of poignant humility. 'Show me.'

As he wished, images relayed from Sethvir's earth-sense unveiled the particulars from the morning's hair-raising triumph: *several dozy Lorn guardsmen had roused from a snooze to find they no longer warded the Light's condemned minion. Worse, the fell creature's evasion left every bit of forged steel in their dungeon, from locks and shackles to the grille on the cell, reverted back into crystallized carbon and raw clumps of unsmelted ore.*

Asandir might have laughed, had the True Sect's officious audacity not galled him to redoubled rage.

The next view showed the plump fugitive abroad in the dock-side streets in the icy darkness before dawn. By no coincidence, the spellbinder slunk down empty alleys and crossed by-ways while the town's watchmen found their eyes turned elsewhere. Like a hot knife through butter, Dakar reached the wharf by the simplest artifice: a neat scrying told him where to be and when, down to which of the tied dories to filch from the cluster tied at the stone jetty. Black-cloaked and unseen amid blacker air, he rowed out to the sole lugger in port whose fisherman would grant him free passage.

Day broke under clouds, with no staged execution to requite the Light's thwarted diviner. The vessel with her furtive passenger already had cast off her mooring and sailed. She clove through the bay's open water, while more quietly, the covert circle of Koriathain cursed the salt waves that eroded their quartz-wrought enchantments . . .

Rinsed in fleeting gilt sunlight as a veil of cloud shredded against the obsidian spires of the Thaldein peaks, Asandir drew a cold breath of relief.

Sethvir's laconic summary confirmed an outcome not fallen too disastrously wide of the mark. *'Since Dakar chose not to restore his defense of Arithon's person, at least he's arranged a spectacular diversion to confound the hunt pressed by Erdane's high temple.'*

Asandir coughed behind his wool sleeve. 'The priesthood is wall-eyed, suddenly saddled with *two* escaped minions to trace?'

Sethvir's pleased snort all but ruffled the world's wind. *'The Koriathain will have a tough time puppeteering their preferred agenda, since Lorn's diviner was given hard evidence. Dakar's confirmed sorceries must overshadow the spurious case that tags Arithon's heels in the south. More, our seasick prophet bargained with the fisherman for an urgent passage to Halywythwood.'*

Now, Asandir's craggy face broke and smiled. 'Ah!' Manfully dignified, he restrained a loud crow. 'Which of the owed debts to crown honour does the Mad Prophet intend to invoke?'

A tight pause ensued.

Asandir's smothered laughter did escape then, fierce and ineffably joyful. 'Oh, better!' Fur would fly with a vengeance in the clan chieftain's tent when the inherited burden of shame was called due for the plot that had brokered a crown prince's betrayal and capture.

'Quite,' Sethvir affirmed. '*Your master initiate appears to have handled himself on his own rather well.*'

Asandir's thoughtful quiet allowed as much. Dakar could side-step the Fellowship's constraint just by spreading the recent news. For the cogent fact Rathain's royal heir had been liberated must summon the realm's *caithdein* back into royal service.

When the Warden's contact continued, unbroken, the Sorcerer exposed to the cruel chill in the Thaldeins nudged with gentle heels to prompt his horse onwards. 'What else?'

Sethvir's sigh could almost be felt over distance from Althain Tower. '*There has been one set-back. Dakar blundered into a seer's fit that forecast the death date of Havish's queen.*' The loss to old age was nothing the Fellowship Sorcerers had not expected. But premature word sent to Erdane's high temple would sever the terms of a treaty and reopen the arena to renew a stalemated war.

'How long do I have to sanction her successor?' Asandir asked, resigned that his time for a hard winter journey had to be brutally shortened.

'*Prince Gestry must be crowned and invested ahead of the winter solstice.*' Sethvir added a poor consolation in parting, '*The outpost at Orlan expects your arrival. That should speed your errand a bit.*'

Thankful for any small favour amid a relentless rip tide of trouble, Asandir forged ahead. The clansfolk in wait for him would not be glad: never in their forefathers' memories had Fellowship Sorcerers brought them good tidings. Today's call could not spare them in that regard. Asandir stroked his stallion's neck with apology, then pushed the pace to outrace the blizzard that threatened to smother his passage.

The storm roared in, a dark maelstrom chased on by a gale that battened the peaks under snowfall as thick as a winding sheet. A welcoming party of two horsemen poised in wait, buffeted by the wind at the rise to the notch. Through the grey gloom, the formal gold trappings on their matched coursers shone beacon-bright, though the riders were not clad in the state dress that tradition would turn out to honor a prince. One wore undyed leathers, armed as a scout. The other, elderly, white-haired, and erect, bore the blue badge with Tysan's crown-and-star blazon as the realm's steward in royalty's absence.

Asandir drew rein before them. Despite the rugged hours just spent in urgent ascent, his stallion was not lathered or winded. By contrast, the Sorcerer looked beaten to rags, his horse's endurance sustained by the profligate gift of his personal life-force. He spoke his mind quickly. '*Caithdein*, Teir's'Gannley, crown service requests your third grandson, just come of age.'

The old man saluted, closed fist to his chest. Beneath the soaked pelt of a wolfskin hat, his seamed expression returned no astonishment. 'Our seer's vision told us. Kingmaker, the lad sits as my right-hand escort, already presented before you.'

Gold flashed, as the second horse tossed its blazed head, pressed forward by the ascetic young man, flushed with cold in his workaday leathers. Not brawny enough to excel at bearing arms, he showed the anxious edge of a restless intelligence. Flaxen hair overshadowed poetic brown eyes, while the rakish jut to his shaved jaw bespoke an unfinished maturity. 'What does the land's need demand of me?'

Asandir skewered him with a level stare from grey eyes that dissected him, body and spirit. Behind this youthful face, the Sorcerer saw others: predecessors with illustrious names, and histories that reached back to Iamine Teiren's'Gannley, who had in fact declined Tysan's crown for the choice to stand shadow at the first high king's shoulder.

How the Sorcerer read today's gangling candidate, or what fate hung over his unwritten future, no man knew. Saroic s'Gannley endured in silenced dread, straight and pale as an ash spear. He held, as he must, through that scouring scrutiny, while the ghostly sting of every insult, each jeer, and all the derisive clouts from companions who branded him coward flamed his cheeks scarlet.

Asandir pronounced with shattering brevity, 'Saroic s'Gannley, you are called forward by Fellowship prerogative to replace the heir apparent named by the clan council. When the hour arises, you shall inherit your grandsire's title as steward to the kingdom's throne.' The Sorcerer peeled off a black glove and extended his work-worn hand. His touch on the candidate's forehead imparted a silver glyph upon living flesh, the Fellowship's mark of surety that would fade within a moon's cycle.

Shock might have left anyone else disconcerted. Saroic vaulted out of his saddle, almost without turning a hair. Though helpless to banish his desperate fear, he keenly sensed the moment's exigent priority. He offered his fresh horse for the Sorcerer's use and volunteered to take the black's reins. 'I could lead your stud back to the outpost on foot and tend him myself, as you wish.'

Asandir's smile appeared like the sun through the whipped burst of snowfall between them. 'By your grace, I accept.' He managed to dismount without a stumble. Swung astride the handsome, loaned courser, he leaned forward and whispered into its back-turned ear. Then, with artless abandon, he curled up and slept on the horse's neck.

The bay knew its own way. No hand on the rein was required to guide its return to feed and dry shelter.

Tysan's most guarded clan outpost lay tucked in the secluded recess of a hidden gorge, the access defended by fortified walls, and a double gateway whose massive blocks had been raised and sealed by the lore of the vanished centaur masons. Inside, the arches that vaulted the dry cavern rose three times the height of a man. When not hung with tapestries for guest custom and feasting, the hall rebounded with hollow echoes: on this hour, conversation with the ominous overtones predominated as the Sorcerer's fresh news prolonged a precipitate session still in progress. The old man seated as Tysan's reigning steward leaned over a trestle draped with parchment maps. The rapt company with him included his war-captain, two elderly women, and three harried selectmen from the clan council. All wore fur hats and oiled-wool cloaks since the desperate measures of tightened security risked no fire to vent tell-tale smoke from the central hearth.

Asandir was no longer present at nightfall, when the young man who bore the fresh mark of heirship stepped in from his volunteer charge of the Sorcerer's horse. The blizzard by then closed down with vengeful force. Despite the mauling wind and choking snowfall, word of Saroic's changed status had blazed through the guarded settlement.

The off-duty scouts crowded him at the entrance, exclaiming with incandescent excitement. No Fellowship Sorcerer had visited in recent memory, far less to serve them with an upset to their clan council's choice of succession.

'Did Asandir say we'd battle more True Sect purges?' asked the puppy-dog boy, tagged at his heels since the stable.

Saroic shrugged off the rough back-slaps and questions. Still clad in soaked leathers, worn breathless from the chest-high drifts breasted on his return, he subdued his inquisitive friends without words, then left them silenced in his wake. Across the darkened, cavernous chamber, while the snap of his footfalls reverberated a ghost's legion of whispers around him, he stopped before the seated elders and clan chieftains gathered around the lone candle that lit the strewn charts.

'I'm not celebrating,' he informed the uncle the Sorcerer's prerogative had seen fit to supplant.

Older, broader, and mightily scarred from the fights that repulsed the relentless Sunwheel campaigns to rout out clan presence, the uncle rose for the traditional salute, his closed fist clapped over his heart. He wore the mantle of tested experience as war-captain, yet ambition did not stand between them. Elsewhere in seclusion, Saroic's mother and sisters would be weeping, consoled in their grief by an aunt, who shared in equal measure the tears of joyful relief for a husband's lot, unexpectedly granted reprieve. The *caithdein*'s post was an iron-hard charge bestowed on the best and the bravest. The call to that service could, and had, tried the stoutest hearts in their family's long history. Times when the succession was Fellowship claimed, a grim threat to the realm demanded the cruel sacrifice of necessity. That the inheritance had skipped generations foreshadowed a hard plight ahead for Saroic s'Gannley.

He would not break under the sudden shock, any more than the uncle who gave up his titled seat resented fate's blessing, which lifted the burden.

Saroic took the heir designate's chair too suddenly made his by right. The seal on his forehead a star in the gloom, he saluted the erect old man, who yet carried the mantle of lifetime authority. 'Grandsire, I hope years will pass before I'm invested. Surely the Sorcerer will answer my questions after he's fed and settled?'

Tysan's *caithdein* measured his young nephew's transparent uncertainty and sighed. 'Asandir's already gone. He left for the mountains on foot, with the promise his errand would upend every hair on the heads of the temple's diviners.'

Outside, the gale shrieked fit to knock the man down who ventured the exposed rock on the heights. Snow fell thick enough to blind and bury a traveller, then freeze his bones fast until spring. Yet no fury born of the world's wild elements might gainsay a Fellowship Sorcerer. The *caithdein* appointed to speak for the King's Justice in Tysan would rather have shouted against the raw might of that storm than venture one word of dissuasion. 'Asandir will be back before dawn to collect his black horse from the stable. He's said not to follow or upbraid the sentries if nobody sees him away upon his departure.'

Saroic met the set-back, wavered, then bore up. 'Did the Sorcerer mention why I was called forward, or what threat to the realm we'll be facing?'

'He told us the Master of Shadow has escaped from Koriani captivity,' the uncle admitted, moved down the trestle to accept his ranked place as the war band's commander. 'We must brace to expect widespread panic and purges such as our clan presence has not seen before.' The swoop and dip of the candle-flame shadowed gruff features not given to seams of uncertainty as he added, 'Already, Sethvir knows the temple at Erdane is calling up a fresh muster. The High Priest's ambition is bound to renew the Light's quest for the conquest of Havish. Your role is bespoken, Saroic. Asandir said you will come to uphold crown law as *caithdein* against forces beyond any precedent. Because if Lysaer s'Ilessid should fall to the binding influence of Desh-thiere's curse, he could try again to impose his false claim and seize sovereign rule over Tysan.'

'I'm expected to defend in this breach?' Saroic reeled, hands better suited to penmanship clenched on the boards to stay upright. Who possessed the main strength to sustain the onslaught? Aside from the zealot troops ruled by the temple canon, none but a sorcerer's power might curb a self-made avatar, birth-gifted to wield the direct power of elemental light. 'I am no fighter!' he gasped, honest in the wretchedness of his misery.

His grandfather's hand braced his unsteady shoulder, but not for false reassurance. 'You were picked as my heir for your clever intelligence! Force of arms cannot hope to win our salvation. The man who knows when to run can be wise, and for that, take your place at this council.'

The clans' beleaguered efforts would not stand unsupported: sprung from blood lineages, each endowed with a talent to safeguard the land, everyone present sensed the sudden change that unfolded as Asandir's remote work reached completion.

A sharp shimmer rippled the air, unbidden and fierce as a shower of light splashed over their perceived surroundings. The odd rush of sensation bloomed into sound, a clear note that chimed beyond hearing and sweetened the yearning spirit. All things that glittered seemed painfully heightened. The candle-flame suddenly brightened and stretched. The gleam of dulled steel on hard-used weapons and belt rings pulsed to blue stars of reflection. The clean scent of snow wafted in on the draughts gained a scalpel's edged clarity, while the shadows that veiled the hall's deepest corners softened to textured velvet.

Living flesh became flushed with heady well-being, as though lifted from dross by a tonic.

'Ath's grace, the Sorcerer's clearing the flux lines!' the clan's seeress gasped with astonished elation. 'The blessing we witness this night is beyond two hundred years overdue!'

No others found words. Within Orlan's clan outpost, no clanbred inhabitant withstood the rip tide surge that flushed out the stagnation of long-standing obstruction. Even the most sturdily grounded among them became whirled into rhapsodic, forgetful oblivion.

Outside, the storm winds keened and boxed the high peaks, then veered to a cyclonic frenzy of joy. As Asandir's power bored through the blocked channels, the released torrent crested to a flood that shook ancient rock and unravelled avalanches like trampling thunder. Lightning shattered the night silence as lane currents held trammelled for centuries exploded with frenetic force and burned clean.

Next morning dawned clear. The blizzard blew out to the pristine shimmer of ice and a lucent sky cloudless as aquamarine. Packed snow should have drifted the notch, with the way through the mountains impassable. Yet Asandir's horse was gone from the stable. When the outpost's mazed sentries regained their senses, and the recovered parties of scouts ventured abroad to quarter the high country, they found that Fellowship urgency had not been inconvenienced.

A track cleaved like an axe cut where the road ran. Unerring, paced at a gallop, the black stallion's hoof-prints carved down the centre, headed due east for the lowlands.

As the day's shadows lengthened, Asandir returned to the nexus at Isaer's Great Circle, forty leagues distant. The black horse grazed, stripped of tack by the verge, on green grass coaxed to grow out of season. No rime of sweat marred the gloss on the animal's raven coat. The rider sat on a fallen stone, back braced against a cracked archway. Absorbed with a meal of raisins and tough cheese bartered from a passing courier, Asandir did not appear as he was: powerful beyond mortal measure. The chill that settled as evening approached sliced through his travel-stained leathers. He felt the nip as keenly as any commonplace traveller unsheltered after a hard journey made in the open.

But unlike other wayfarers, a Sorcerer versed in the high arts could tap the land's flux currents and down-step the frequency to replenish himself. Collected and alert, Asandir licked the last crumbs from his fingers when the Warden of Althain's light contact addressed him.

'*Confusion to the enemy!*' Sethvir sent, amused. '*As ever, your timing's impeccable.*'

Select images followed, lent a gilt-edged flicker by the crackle of the heightened flux currents blasted clear by Asandir's labour the night before: *Koriani scryers who searched for their escaped captive were dazzled near blindness by flares amplified by their engaged quartz sphere, while their aghast Senior frantically scrambled to cover the crystal before the excess charge cracked its matrix. Across Camris, the True Sect's vested diviners were seared by heretical dreams. The priest on duty at Erdane's high temple fled screaming when a shrine collapsed during the nightfall devotions and doused the perpetual flame sanctified to the Light. At Cainford, the ranking examiner died, his weak heart stopped by a surfeit of ecstasy. While the lane flux lit Tysan from end to end, the seals laid by the temple canon exploded, leaving armed camps at the border wide open to infestations of* iyats. *The ruin of fallen Avenor chimed aloud as the slagged remnant of the stone foundations rang like a bell. Game quickened in the wilds. Clansfolk rejoiced for the change, aware the blight and the fevers that ravaged the unsanctioned country-side would be lifted; while far off, immersed in a state of awareness too distant for mortal hearing, a dragon whose will tangled a Sorcerer's destiny lifted her head and turned opened gold eyes towards the far side of the world . . .*

'Seshkrozchiel heard!' Asandir exclaimed, pleased. 'Any chance that Davien's made aware of our quandaries?'

'*He knows,*' Sethvir answered. '*Beyond what I'd hoped, though the knowledge does not leave him free to declare himself.*'

Asandir raised a glare like snap-frozen ice. 'Is that everything?' he demanded, alert for sly subterfuge since Sethvir's caginess often masked set-backs.

Althain's Warden capped his summary with more cryptic news. '*Your lost prince goes by Arin. He's cut past the abandoned farm-steads above Cainford, across country-side rife with pursuit. The river hems his course to the south. The shallows by the road where he might try to ford are much too heavily guarded.*'

Asandir arose. Sundown approached. Time he moved to achieve his planned transit. He whistled to his dark horse, and the animal came, head lowered to receive the bridle that hung braided reins, but no bit. The Light's priesthood feared the beast's single ghost eye, eerily offset by the irregular star and stripe, which slewed an oblate course through the left nostril. Asandir scratched the black ears, afraid to ask outright the last burning question before he broke off Sethvir's contact.

Althain's Warden rebuked the unspoken, naked hope gently, that the resonant surge as the flux current balanced might have wakened Arithon to recoup something beyond an intuitive grasp of his trained mastery. *'Whatever his Grace doesn't know cannot matter. Ath speed your course to Etarra.'*

Win or lose, the outside risk lay behind. The Fellowship's future course was committed beyond all regret. The back-lash stirred through Tysan's upset factions could allow their hunted fugitive to slip clear, or else come to hasten his helpless downfall.

Asandir resaddled the stallion. Alone in dusk's shadow, he mounted and wended his way through the scrub forest rooted over the ancient, concave pattern of Isaer's Great Circle. When the eventide lane forces crested, he would be bound on to Rathain by way of the beacon array that channelled the planet's electromagnetic currents through the ancient marker stones on the Plain of Araithe.

Dawn three mornings later brought the Sorcerer's unobtrusive arrival in the trade town of Etarra, his first return since the ill-starred coronation day that had failed to restore crown rule under the auspices of old charter law. A sad irony, that today the last true royal heir was pursued as a renegade in Tysan, and Etarra was governed by a lord mayor descended from Halduin s'Ilessid. Lysaer did not know of the Sorcerer's presence. The palace staff remained uninformed, and the townsfolk's absorbed complacency kept them in ignorance.

A rangy, silver-haired figure unrecognized in his wayfarer's mantle, Asandir paid in coin to stable his stallion at a quality inn with first-rate care. He rented a cheap room at the Goose Quill for himself, slept briefly, then spent the afternoon hours abroad in the grey, cobbled streets.

Etarra nestled within a doubled set of walls, defended by a private, armed garrison and a roster of crack sentries. The square buildings of brick, with their peaked tile roofs and ceramic chimney-pots, here and there through the years had acquired still more pretentious detail and ornate facings. The deep, vaulted cellar beneath the state palace that once housed the dread rites of Grey Kralovir held no more entrapped, tormented ghosts: only the dusty racks of rare wines, hoarded to appease the ambassadors who wheedled and aired their sullen complaints at the mayor's lush table. The crabbed trees of the region's famed apple-orchards were lost to memory, cut down since past campaigns against Shadow required a tourney field, a rambling barracks, and larger stables for courier's mounts and trained destriers. Crows wheeled, screaming over the middens. The flags that snapped in the gusts at the gate arches streamed the scarlet-and-gold governor's cartouche, once flown at the forefront of war in Deshir, and adopted ever since the Great Schism as Lysaer's personal standard.

In other ways, Etarra had not changed at all. Where the snarl of back-alley tanneries and knacker's yards reeked under the lour of smoke from the glue-pots, and in the clogged side streets where the craft quarter's industry loaded finished wares bound for Market Square, the metallic tang of the smelter's fires in the forges sometimes cleared, refreshed in changed breeze by the waft of perfumes from the High Street's fashionable dress shops. The old wineries flourished, packed with the languid dissipation of the pedigree dandies. Minstrel's song mingled with the staccato whip-cracks, where the ox-drawn drays of the overland caravans still cankered the subtle flow of the lane flux.

Yet Asandir had not come to temper the stew of Etarran politics. Not directly; he strode down prosperous streets with great mansions owned by merchants and guildsmen engaged in honest prosperity, pleased at least that Lysaer's fair rule had hazed out the old nests of corrupted practice. Clan captives were no longer sold for child labour, and brisk justice had banished the ugly business of rival feuding through hired assassins.

The Sorcerer paused in a winter-cold lane. Seamed face upturned, his lumi-nous eyes blank with thought, he appeared as innocuous as a maundering grandfather. But in fact, his honed senses were tightly entrained: to sound out every spirit sprung from the outbred, matrilineal branch of s'Gannley. He needed the blood heritage of Sulfin Evend, a name still reviled by the temple archives as the Light's most nefarious heretic.

The spirit Asandir selected stood out, hot as flame, from the pack of siblings and cousins. She was a pert creature, incorrigible, rebellious, and wild as a sparrow-hawk among pecking doves where she stood, surrounded by swank admirers and Etarran rakes. Asandir cornered her in the Red Cockerel's packed tap-room, just as she finished the knife throw that demolished five noisy contenders and won the purse their male prowess had wagered. Flushed with laughter, stylishly dressed in a laced-velvet bodice, full skirts, and ribbon-tied slippers, she crowed like a hoyden and twirled face about in the scintillant sparkle of her flushed victory.

The pirouette fetched her, pink nose to chest, against the tall Sorcerer's presence.

Daliana possessed her forefather's keen instincts. Tawny eyes widened, stopped short in her tracks, she tipped her chin upwards and gasped. Even in the dim setting, her truth-seer's vision grasped the implacable power leashed behind the seamed face that confronted her. Fearless, without artifice, she dared to speak first. 'Who are you and what do you want of me?'

'Do you not know?' Asandir's smile was lightning against thunder-head, alive with the force of upheaval and change. 'I've come to request a service befitting your ancestry. Though I daresay the matter should be broached in depth, under raised wards and in privacy.'

The quiet room let to patrons for close business was intimately furnished with a polished deal table and two comfortable, stuffed chairs. A tray of bread, cheese, and wine was provided, along with wax candles for the paned lamps that hung from bronze hooks in the ceiling beams. Under that refined light, Daliana's straight, dark brows looked severe, drawn into a frown as forbidding as any displayed by her distrustful forebear. 'Sulfin Evend was a captain at arms, skilled at weaponry, and, history says also, a master strategist.'

'You are his equal for tactics, I think.' Folded into a chair too squat for his stork's frame, the Sorcerer opposite looked more rumpled but not less imposing. Deep shadow accentuated a face time and weather had ruthlessly chiselled. His leathers were worn, but his pewter hair gleamed, spilled over immaculate, squared shoulders. 'You have the s'Gannley talent in full measure. Also an enviously quick set of reflexes. And courage to blister any man scarlet.'

From pale, she had coloured. Nerves showed in the tremulous flare of her jewels. Still, she had fibre. She had not interrupted his brutal account of the relapse fated to hound Lysaer's sanity since the Master of Shadow's freed status renewed Desh-thiere's curse.

Quiet, the Sorcerer sat back and allowed her to weigh her decision: whether or not to stand forward as her ancestor had, as a tormented ruler's clear voice of conscience. He would not pressure, or rush, or cajole. Asandir's lean hands stayed busy, and his strong teeth tucked into the tavern's plate of hot food with an appetite shamelessly ravenous.

As the weighty silence dragged out, he laid down the chunk of cheese wrapped in bread, poured a goblet of wine, and pushed the stem crystal between Daliana's delicate fingers. 'You would not, of course, rely on force of arms. Quickness, yes, and a glib turn of phrase, and also the most artful advantage of all. Your illustrious predecessor fought as a male. Never discount the fact you won't have to.'

Daliana stared back, arrow-straight, while the candle-flame rubbed cinnamon highlights into the walnut braid styled in a pinned circlet above her pert face. 'Lord Lysaer can't stand the sight of me,' she stated, stripped frank. 'That's been evident since the first day my mother presented me to his court.'

Asandir stared back, a bold glint in grey eyes that never stopped measuring. 'You remind him of someone,' he said. 'As you choose, you might press that advantage. Lysaer has never healed that deep weakness. You threaten him, truly, in places he prefers to deny that he's nakedly vulnerable.'

Daliana met the Sorcerer's cool regard, rapacious with innuendo. 'Would you care to elaborate?'

'I would not.' Without further rebuke for her indecent prying, Asandir attacked his meal. If he seemed pleased that she was not afraid of him, his words rang beyond chill, as he added, 'Sweet lady, you realize the boon I beg of you cannot be repaid with the promise of triumph or happiness. I am asking you, of your bravery, to shoulder a peril beyond reprieve. The charge would risk your life! Before, Sulfin Evend treated with me to bind himself for the love of a friend. Caught in the breach of a peace that could torch the known world into flames, he followed through because he was desperate. I come before you as the supplicant, this time. The need that commands me to appeal for your help could lead you to a bitter defeat, and a destiny cruel beyond imagining.'

'Sulfin Evend succeeded!' Daliana reminded with a whiplash snap.

Then she spilled her wine and broke into tears, while the Fellowship Sorcerer arose and bowed to her.

He knew! Ahead of speech, Asandir already sensed the heart that framed her commitment. Before he left the room, she would swear his great oath, and take on the spirit mark of his arcane protection: to defend Lord Lysaer from the recurrent threat of the madness raised by Desh-thiere's curse.

Extrications

Solstice eve in the town of Whitehold in winter still saw paper moons and stars cut by children tacked up in the candle-lit windows. But since tokens that honoured the night implied suspect association with Shadow, the wealthier mansions also burned Sunwheel lamps to acknowledge the supremacy of the Light. Bakers' girls sold caramel-nut pies in the square, while the jingle of harness bells, coming and going, wafted the fragrance of cut evergreen and spiced chocolate through the cold twilight streets. Birch fires warmed out the chill within doors, though no such cheerful flame burned in the icy gloom of the chamber where the Koriani Prime Matriarch retired under a mandate of seclusion.

Her mood was as veiled as the glint in her jewels, reduced to a fitful flicker in darkness as two burdened servants hovered at the threshold of the open doorway.

The Prime beckoned them forward. Not imposing today, she sat in a plain chair, dressed in a loose-fitted linen shift with a purple wool robe belted overtop. Her lofty station was not left in doubt: the red-ribboned cuffs displayed nine bands of rank, and the brooch that pinned her high collar was an intaglio amethyst, carved with the rampant crane seal of her office. No dimmed room or unassuming facade could blunt her predator's temperament, or her mood, galled by fresh set-backs and doubly dangerous. She had steamed with impatience for over three centuries to redeem the order's most compromised focus crystal. After a drawn-out, unbearable wait, the ripe moment arrived to redress the damage inflicted upon the Great Waystone by Prince Arithon's past act of sabotage.

'Set down the load. Yes, there! Where else but on top of my work-bench?'

141

The Prime gestured anxiously with the wrapped stump of one hand. 'Carefully, mind! I will not forgive clumsiness.'

The harried boy wards sweated with nerves under her eagle eye. Husky and muscled, almost grown enough for discharge to a craft-shop apprenticeship, they wished only to be quit of the Prime's peremptory bidding. Her coveted treasure gave off a bitter chill that hackled their necks with inchoate fear and plumed their puffed breaths as they grunted under its ungainly burden. Jockeyed on shoulder poles like a catafalque, the shrouded cask they unloaded nestled in its crate, packed in a bed of shaved ice.

'That will do.' The Prime inclined her head to a muted sparkle of diamond hairpins. 'Close the door, but remain outside at the ready until I have need of you.'

The boys bobbed an obeisance, then thumped in their sheepskin boots towards the threshold in hasty retreat.

No healthy male cared to be tasked with their post. Never, when the Matriarch engaged her advanced arts in secrecy. Selidie waited only until the shut panel pinched off the last gleam of light. Then she bared her teeth and tugged off the bindings from her crippled hands, aware she worked to an urgent deadline.

'Come forward!' Her curt order broke the stillness of what seemed an empty room.

Movement stirred like the night rustle of bats' wings behind the Matriarch's chair. Few left in the order remembered the name of the creature who answered. Enslaved to the Prime's most intimate service for two hundred and fifty-two years, the woman had once possessed stunning beauty, with glossy jet hair and tawny eyes, and high-bred, aristocrat's features. Unlined with years, her pale profile was blank as a cameo cut from bleached bone. Voiceless as furniture, unkempt and unnamed, her mute presence seldom drew notice as her hands accomplished the tasks too delicate for her fire-scarred mistress. Yet she was alive, and no empty husk, who once had been titled First Senior to the Prime's seat, before the disgrace that debased her.

The balked hatred behind her porcelain mask blazed livid as pressurized magma.

'Remove the top cloth. Then unlock the casket.' Selidie pawed the chain slung from her neck and bestowed a silver key on her live automaton. 'Take the knife from the table and slit the warded silk that swathes the crystal inside.' The assignment was given without concern, that an ambitious rival sentenced to perpetual punishment should have access to a lethal instrument. Answerable only to the Prime's will, the woman unveiled the melon-sized sphere couched inside the coffer with flawless subservience.

An unnatural chill flooded over the chamber. Even in darkness, the faceted amethyst radiated a charge to unsettle the nerves. Perilous power slept at its core, even after the extreme measures that enforced its quiescence since the disaster. Sequestered in total darkness throughout, the jewel had lain embedded in the Skyshiel glaciers that stayed frozen year-round above the snow-line.

Now covered by a calyx of ice, the crystal rested like a stopped heart-beat, yet embraced by the chamber's unrelieved night.

'Stand back,' the Prime directed the expendable creature whose fingers had broached the protections. No subordinate sister yet possessed the initiate experience to master the Great Waystone's attributes. Selidie must risk the treacherous trial herself, without help for her clumsy deformity. 'Be ready to act at my command. The instruments are laid out on the trestle beside the candle and brazier. Strike no light unless you are told! If I call for a sigil or a string of chained ciphers, a quartz stylus is primed for your use.'

No enchantress past third rank required a flame to locate her tools in the dark; and this one, though leashed under absolute thrall, had achieved her eighth-level initiation. Her closest rival, at seventh, was the next-strongest talent within the order. No other had strength or training to match hers, except for the woman who ruled from the Prime seat in unchallenged supremacy.

Since none but a matriarch worked the Great Waystone, Selidie thrust the clawed stubs of her hands into the opened coffer. Frigid water immersed her scarred nerves and drove a hissed breath through her teeth. She endured as she must, and laid her welted palms against the jewel's slick facets. Even quiescent, the stone's direct contact reamed needles of chill through her flesh. Selidie vised her mind into stillness. The least uncontrolled thought might waken peril. Above everything, she must do nothing to stimulate the stone's dormant focus.

She listened. Poised in rigid silence, she waited until the faint tingle of *something* stirred in the stilled depths of the stone. While the great sphere's tuned faculties stayed passively blank, this questing wisp surfaced through the jewel's matrix. Parasitically separate, it bumped against the Prime's coiled awareness, starved for light, hungry for warmth, and drained into vacuous weakness.

Selidie suppressed her wild urge to smile. *Her hour of triumph arrived at long last!* The meddlesome *iyat* that Arithon's malice had unleashed in the heart of the Waystone finally was bled helpless and denuded of charge. It had no reserve energy left to wreak havoc and no will beyond its overpowering, blind instinct to feed.

The Waystone's locked focus provided no fuel. Its lattice was bleak ice and fast darkness throughout, null except for the blood warmth that radiated from Selidie's unshielded hands. Needy for an infusion of energy, the *iyat* bounced and banged like a frustrated gnat against the panes of a lamp. Only the human presence fixed its desperate attention. No sigil could be set to bind it in place. Not yet, and never in close proximity lest the Waystone itself should be provoked to resonate. Selidie held her breath in steeled tension, while the ravenous *iyat* inside the jewel yearned to absorb sustenance from her body heat. Though it craved renewal, its insatiable drive was gripped yet by a sigil of enthrallment imposed within the Great Waystone. Since the entrained working could not be released without waking the jewel itself, the moment to unhook the sigil's engagement must be timed with utmost delicacy.

'Quickly!' the Prime commanded her servant. 'Configure a binding sigil for *iyats*, and link the constraint to the candle. Then attach a cipher to expand the illusion of fire, tenfold, and surround that construct with a ward. Use the nine sigils of confinement, but leave the closure unsealed.'

A bustle of silk in the dark bespoke the due diligence that readied the trap. The aligned spellcraft must be accomplished at speed, before the Prime's naked hands transferred warmth into the iced face of the Waystone. Should the amethyst lose its chilled state of inertia, the energized matrix would refuel the invasive *iyat* and keep it entrenched.

'Ready the striker,' Prime Selidie said. As a puppeteer to her servant's live flesh, she must prompt each critical step. 'Do nothing but wait on my signal.'

Gently, slowly, the Matriarch withdrew one ruined hand from the coffer. With the crabbed wrack of one finger and three welted stubs, she scrawled the counter-framed cipher of negation. Clumsy, but adequate, the glyph appeared, a shimmer that bordered upon ultraviolet in the stultified gloom of the chamber.

Braced for the critical moment, Selidie shouted, 'Now!'

The configured spell for the *iyat*'s release activated, precisely timed to the shear of the striker as her servant ignited the doctored wick. Light blazed, followed by crisping heat as the spellcrafted illusion attached to the candle erupted the semblance of a bonfire on top of the trestle.

The freed *iyat* shot out of the sphere and arrowed straight into the ferocious blaze.

The jewel woke, also. Selidie yanked her other limb clear. She slammed the lid of the casket. With the Waystone's malignant sparkle doused back into ice-ridden darkness, she instructed her servant, 'Close the ward ring, immediately, and seal that benighted fiend in containment!'

Power crackled. The unleashed charge lifted strands from Selidie's coiffed hair and shivered her skin into gooseflesh. Yet her goal was accomplished. The Waystone stood cleansed of its riddling parasite. Weaned separate, the *iyat* gorged itself on the lit wick, pinned down beyond further harm.

Selidie cradled her mauled hands, exultant and flushed with success. 'Light the sconces,' she ordered. 'Build up the fire and open the curtains. Then properly banish that captive fiend, clear the table, and disperse the spent warding.'

Unquestioned obedience attended each task. As her eighth-rank servant sparked the chamber's matched candelabra and kindled the logs on the hearth, the Matriarch reopened the lid of the coffer. The Great Waystone gleamed, couched in ice and wet silk, visited by her detailed inspection for the first time since the compromise of its integrity.

Selidie stroked her grotesquely wracked hands over the exposed facets, possessively eager to tally the damage inflicted by Arithon's assault.

Her anxious assessment encountered new superficial cracks, but no dreaded sign of fractures or chips. But if the stone's surface symmetry stayed flawless, the amethyst had not survived unscathed. A flash-point flare of citrine blazed a clear yellow plume through the violet matrix in the sphere's upper quadrant. Selidie measured that invasive inclusion with wary care.

As she feared, the frequency shift that bridged the interface changed the crystal's structural resonance. A visual survey could not determine how many records of initiates' vows might be compromised, or which of the order's historical archives might have become fragmented, lost to posterity. Worse than any disrupted parcel of knowledge, the jewel's core pattern stood altered beyond recognition.

Selidie tapped the chill face of the crystal, her initial exhilaration dampened to a frown as she assayed the scope of the problem. While her side-lined servant looked on, forgotten, she weighed the pernicious hurdles left to overcome.

Dispelling the troublesome fiend had been a brute matter of iron patience. But no other competent Senior enchantress could access or harness the Great Waystone's channelled power without protective oversight from an initiate prime matriarch. To activate and wield the raised focus married the spirit into the lattice of crystalline energies, the act itself a knife-edged dance fraught with consummate peril. Experience offered no surety. The amethyst's volatile properties ever had been a vicious trial to master.

Selidie sensed the warning tingle of charge spun by the cold crystal's aura. Traced barehanded, the flawed patch of citrine threw an imbalanced field through the energy web that wrung her to sweating dread. Always unpleasant, the stone's ancient malice sapped her nerve as never before.

Even inactive, the crystal's roiled depths all but wailed, stamped by the raw rage of uncounted failed aspirants and layered with the sediment of uncleared spellcraft deposited over the centuries. The cumulative forces bridled to use by untold generations of enchantresses required an untried, solo effort to be charted anew and recalibrated. This, while the jewel's fractious nature itself battled to establish dominance. Any fresh bid for the sphere's subjugation bore the harrowing risk of becoming subsumed.

Selidie sighed. Vexed beyond words, she lifted her crabbed hands and massaged her aching temples. None of her predecessors had faced such a trial: refounding the keys to access the Waystone posed her a potentially lethal endeavour.

Yet to forgo the effort would place the order's capital power forever past reach. No chance the Koriathain could break the Fellowship Sorcerers' tyranny without that signal advantage.

The seeped drip of ice melt puddled the floor and roused the Prime from disturbed contemplation. She straightened and noticed the searing regard of

145

her neglected servant. Hatred smouldered in those tawny eyes. As with the great amethyst, the suppressed spirit within yearned to seize back its plundered autonomy.

'Ah, my dear!' jabbed Selidie. 'Who recalls your name, besides me? Most are dead, who remember your inadequate tenure as my potential successor. How pitiful for you, and convenient for me, that your gall has been turned as my tool.'

No retort was possible. Leave would never be granted to unlock this subservient initiate's tongue, or permit her the free speech to disclose the grim secrets behind the Matriarch's unorthodox accession. Aware of unconscionable crimes, worse than scandal, the servant suffered her oppressor, blank-faced, except for the spark of undying rebellion a cruel term of punishment had never subdued.

Selidie smiled with supercilious relish. 'Fetch me a square of white silk. Once I have the Waystone immaculately secured, you will bind up my scars straightaway.'

While the puppet touch of her diminished rival wrapped her fire-scarred limbs with soft gauze, the Prime taunted, 'Be sure, Lirenda, you shall act as my hands through the restoration of the Great Waystone. Who else but you should I submit as my expendable proxy? Perhaps you'll survive,' the Prime mused, then laughed.

Secure in the face of the fury that seethed through the abased creature before her, the Matriarch finished, 'I will fling your balked vengeance a bone, Lirenda. For the greater good of the order, the capture and trial of a renegade initiate is my next item of business. You will fetch me the chest with the Skyron aquamarine, and also the locked jewel-box that safeguards the personal crystal attuned to Elaira.'

The trade town of Redburn perched like an unkempt eyrie above the snagged crevice, where the River Issing jetted into the deepwater narrows that let shipborne commerce from Rockbay pass southward through South Strait. On fair days in spring, snow-melt off the high peaks of the Storlains frothed the torrent that hammered and leaped rock to rock down the gorge as a seething maelstrom. The steep streets and roof-tops sparkled through veils of blown spray, and the misted air shimmered with rainbows. But when winter's gales screamed through the teeth of the ranges, snow frosted the dormers and chimneys like icing and serrated the eaves with icicles blasted into fantastical shapes. The sun and the view lay quenched under blizzard, while the throaty roar of the Issing shook floor-boards and walls with its tireless thunder.

Such a brute storm choked the harbour-side inn where Elaira mewed up to outwait the weather's delay. In the cheapest room closest to the cliff rim, the river's tumult was deafening. For her, the constant barrage posed a blessing: gale-driven flakes and lofted showers of iced spray effectively foiled the order's scryers. Which slender edge posed her only advantage against the tense set-back of a night's enforced stay past the designate bounds of Ghent's free wilds.

But no galley-man braved Rockbay's treacherous shoals in harsh weather; and with Havish's late queen on her bier, the kingdom's commerce paused for the ritual Crown's Night of Mourning.

Elaira paced, desperate. The prickle at her nape shouted in warning: she ought to be gone. Her sensitivity to Arithon's location was too volatile a liability. She needed to make her escape on salt water, and quickly, since the jumbled-up flux in the Storlains no longer gave shelter, and charter rights under town jurisdiction placed a magistrate's court between her direct access to crown-law redress. The Koriathain exploited that added disadvantage. The sharp sweep of the sisterhood's probes had tested Elaira three times within the past hour. Just barely, she escaped being pinned at the dock, when she had treated with an out-bound captain to secure a sea-passage to Shand.

The vessel would sail on the ebb-tide at dawn, provided the snowfall slackened. Yet tomorrow's hazards became a moot point if she failed to withstand the aggressive assaults sure to come through the night.

Since erratic motion made her harder to strike, she gave in to anxiety and quartered the floor-boards while flung spume from the gorge frosted the window-panes to dull white. Periodically the plastered crust shattered, cracked away as the casement rattled. Wind boxed at the rafters, and the limed walls shook to the boom as the Issing's thrashed current smashed bergs and black water through the rock channel below.

Beneath the violence of the elements, Elaira sensed another disturbance: as if the ground under the building itself flexed to a shift in the flux stream. The oddity stabbed her weathered skin into gooseflesh and zinged frissons down her cranked nerves.

She tried soothing her fraught state by tidying her hair, when the sudden, sharp rap at the door jumped her nearly out of her skin.

'Your dinner's here, traveller!' Snappish, the kitchen drudge banged again, impatient to deliver her meal.

Elaira threw her comb aside and unhooked the loop that secured the latch pin. Stressed to raced pulse, she endured the suspicious stare from the girl, who thumped the laden tray down on the armoire and fled. Elaira hoped the distrustful reaction stemmed from the tattered leathers and wind-burned squint that made her appear as uncivilized as the mountain trappers. Half-starved as well, she should have felt famished.

The inn's savoury stew and fresh bread smelled delectable after weary weeks of fire-seared game gnawed straight off the bone. But relentless anxiety spoiled her appetite. Elaira made herself scrape the bowl clean. She needed her strength against the certainty she could face an attack at any moment. Ruffled by chills yet again, she laid down the last bit of bread. This upset was not caused by hostile scryers. Somewhere, a direct surge of power stamped concussive rings through the lane flux.

Elaira pushed to her feet, afraid not to identify the anomaly. Under threat for too long, she reached for the basin on the washstand, then discarded the idea of sounding for information through the interface of stilled water. The spate in the gorge caused vibration enough to ruffle the mirror surface required to cast a clear image. An attempt at tranced vision by way of the Issing's river-course would become torn apart in the boisterous spate. Even had she been adept with air, the storm threw off too much static; and her paltry touch with fire was no use since her twopenny lodging lacked a hearth.

Earth had never been her natural element. But time spent in sanctuary with Ath's White Brotherhood had opened Elaira's awareness to Athera's land sense. More, the Paravian maker's mark cut into the inn's worn threshold bespoke a foundation set into harmonic alignment with the deep strata of the bed-rock beneath. The stone building ought to resonate to the flux strongly enough to be tapped in rapport.

Elaira abandoned the meal tray. She crossed to the casement, her soundless tread on waxed floor-boards unnaturally smooth after years spent in rugged country. The thought made her wince, that extended exile had ingrained the habitual stealth of a deep-wilds clan scout. Separation from Arithon slowly drove her mad in more ways than she cared to admit.

Desperate not to wake her empathic link to him, she flattened her hands on the chill granite window-sill. Eyes closed, she quieted her breath, then loosened her defensive boundaries and settled into the straightforward grain of the masonry under her touch. Unlike the reactive nature of quartz, which responded to each slight deflection, the sturdy calm of aggregate mineral embraced her with dauntless endurance. She sank into its calm until her inward eye opened to refined awareness. Refigured before her, the latticed structure of fitted blocks unveiled the interface of their core energy, written through by the coruscation of flux currents beyond the range of visible light. The Paravian artisans always had shaped their working in partnership with the mysteries. The old inn's alignment matched the bias of the greater lane flows that streamed through the landscape. Which resonant connection expanded Elaira's vantage across a hundred-league radius.

If the Koriathain were hunting, their assault would be channelled to focus through quartz. Any collaborate crystal would shine out of the glimmering, cool back-drop of flux like a red-heated star.

She detected four of them! Not distanced, but within Redburn, and in close proximity to her position. If the sigils wrought here did not yet burn with the brilliance of fullest engagement, the sisters behind them already moved to seal their strung net. The tavern where Elaira sheltered would become a locked trap unless she fled straightaway.

Yet before she withdrew her refined connection, another phenomenon rippled across the vast web unveiled to her Sighted vision. The building presence snagged Elaira's attention, too powerfully strong for her trained experience. Haplessly entrained, already ungrounded, she lost her solid awareness of the attic-room. Flurried like a spark snatched into an updraught, she reeled through a potent convergence of energies that rushed like a gale-wind over and through her. Drawn into concert, she shared the vision of a ceremony that occurred in another closed room, at a Second Age site also founded by ancient Paravian masons at Telmandir . . .

. . . where the Fellowship Sorcerer, Asandir, stood tall in bright candlelight, his combed hair a silver cascade over straight shoulders. He was clothed in state, his severe robe of midnight blue velvet banded at cuffs and collar with the glint of silver ribbon. A youthful figure knelt before him, dark brown hair braided clan fashion against the rich red-and-gold of a heraldic surcoat that seemed an awkward fit for his unfinished frame.

Yet there, initiate vision read power beyond the pale of surface impressions. This young man's aura revealed the same stamped gleam of the attunement Elaira knew well as handfast mate to the Prince of Rathain. She understood that sanction by Fellowship auspices connected a royal heir designate into confluence with the land. The binding here matched the template of Havish, which identified this scion as the appointed successor to the realm's queen.

More than curiosity held Elaira riveted. Arrested, all but laced into enthrallment, she witnessed the start of an elaborate construct of Asandir's making. His capable hands, poised above the stilled prince, worked the precursive shimmer of intent as the primary stage of a seamless nexus. While she watched, a ring of live fire took shape, horizontal between his spread fingers. That seamless geometry no sooner formed when a second appeared, wrought of water, crossed at right angles and linked through the first. Another, invisible, welded out of air, whirled through the twined figures and spun them into blazing motion. Opposites, still, both fire and water braided into a fluid triad of balanced formation.

Then Asandir murmured a Paravian word and conjoined his masterful figure into the flux. Power bloomed, widened, sang, a shimmering ripple that danced to the infinite song of Athera's deep mysteries.

Breath stopped, Elaira viewed the formed circlet that raised an Atheran crown prince to sovereign accession. Melded upon contact, the prior attunement to earth would flower into its rightful completion and bestow the fulfilled power of the s'Lornmein heritage upon the next High King of Havish.

Asandir cradled the crackling diadem, its interlaced forces wrought with such matchless finesse, not a hair was disturbed on the royal head bent in trust to receive the burden. All else forgotten, roped captive by wonder, Elaira braced for the climactic moment when the prince aspirant already wedded to the land became engaged with the flux stream, then bound through the consummate marriage of all four wakened elements.

As a moth pulled towards flame, she could not turn away as the force that safeguarded the realm's farthest quarters was bestowed into mortal hands.

Asandir lowered the blazing crown construct. The instant of transfer deluged the interface with a clarity harmful to witness. Elaira gasped, blinded and witlessly deafened, when a *bump* shocked her vision off balance. Her awareness of the land's confluence imploded. Shoved out, then pushed safely away, she heard the sent voice of Althain's Warden admonish her over-bold reach. *'Brave Lady! This is no time to be caught immersed in an earth-based linkage inside the bounds of Havish! Handfast to a sanctioned prince as you are, the high resonance involved in the accession ceremony could affect you. Spoken for by Rathain, you must stay well clear as High King Gestry receives coronation.'*

Elaira plunged back into herself with a shudder of shock. Collapsed to her knees beneath the window-sill, she braced to recoup her frayed nerves. The cramped attic-room was lightless and cold, enclosed as a trap as four Senior enchantresses descended, under direct orders to corner her. Aghast with fear, Elaira realized their strike was deliberately timed: as the new sovereign assumed his fresh charge of the realm's warded protections, the defenses that upheld crown justice in Havish momentarily would be under strength.

Worse, her tie to Prince Arithon disbarred any help from the Fellowship Sorcerers.

Elaira pushed erect, pressured to act before hot pursuit blocked her threshold. She snatched the last crust of uneaten bread and shoved it into the satchel she had not unpacked. Unwashed, still belted in her rugged leathers, she tossed the coin owed for her lodging onto the supper tray and flung on her damp cloak. Then she bolted from the room and careened down the darkened servants' stair to the inn's kitchen. The cook had retired, but three slatterns washed pots, immersed in salacious gossip. Elaira slipped past their turned backs, ducked behind the racked pans and chopping block, unlatched the rear door, and stepped out.

Her feet squished through the midden, while the cruel night veiled her form in the barrage of wind-driven snowfall. Icy mist seared her lungs, thrown off the rush of the flume far below. The air shook to the violent roar of white water while, sparkled in subliminal currents beneath, the event at Telmandir rippled etheric waves through the flux. She dared not tap into that excited flow to measure the proximity of her pursuit. While Asandir's act of grand conjury eclipsed mage-sight, the Prime Matriarch's pawns understood very well their quarry's resources were weakened.

Elaira edged over the steamed hummocks of garbage, pressed against the inn wall at the jagged rim of the Issing gorge. At the hazard of a break-neck fall, she reached the cobbles of the adjacent by-lane and sprinted. She banged her shin on a buried hand-cart, which startled an alley cat to yowling flight. The adroit dodge that avoided a horse-trough blundered her into the slats of a hen-coop. The upset fowl shrilled with alarm, and several wooden shutters crashed open. Chased by the vociferous complaints of roused citizens, Elaira raced onwards through the pressed welter of black air and snowfall. Oriented by the percussive falls in the gorge, she stole down the switched back street, stumbled over the frozen ruts of the caravan road, and darted between the pillowed drifts that clogged the wood frames of the water-front market stalls. The rows of capped bollards beyond marked the wharf, where the tied galley under Havish's flag promised her prearranged passage to Shand.

She must board at all costs. No matter if the gangway was run in, and the hatches dogged shut in the storm. Quartz-driven assault weakened over salt water. Better still, the order's ranked Seniors might shy from the peril of a slippery deck. Since their privileged longevity was bound through crystal, they should be loath to chance the fatality of a sea-water immersion.

But her hope to seize that slim advantage was thwarted.

A mantled figure blocked the gateway where the customs men checked the tax stamps on inbound cargo. Elaira skidded to a frantic stop, her opening to escape forestalled by two more initiates, who closed in on both sides of the lane that flanked the spiked wall at the quay-side. The fourth would be placed at her back, with the spells woven to snare her the instant she tried an evasion. No appeal to crown justice might salvage her plight, even had Redburn's delegate magistrate not been snoring in his bed. The raw weather emptied the dock side of witnesses, with even the town watch holed up in sheltered comfort.

Cornered, beyond desperate, Elaira confronted her adversaries. The least powerful of them outranked her by lengths: all wore the red bands of seniority. But the detail that hammered her pulse in her veins was their inhuman lack of expression. Past question the Koriani Matriarch wielded the sigil of mastery behind each woman's stony facade. These sisters did not act by their own will but functioned as the Prime's suborned puppets. Four ranged against her, thralled in locked synchronicity, they posed enough ruthless force to annihilate her at one stroke. Elaira still breathed the icy winter air *only* because the order's usage desired her capture, alive.

'I will not be stopped,' she defied through the ache of exhaustion. 'Through every avenue I might claim, seen or unseen, by any right power and with all my heart, I oppose you!'

Once before, the same declaration had summoned a Sorcerer's aid, and the perilous wrath of a dragon. But not tonight. Her bluff must be called, since Asandir's sworn constraint upon Arithon's fate dropped the shield of the Fellowship's protection.

'Submit now to the bonds of your sisterhood oath,' the enchantress in the gateway demanded. Her implacable command wore the steely ring of Selidie's supreme confidence as she added, 'Do so, and you may retain your right mind. Refuse, and you will be served with the lifelong penalty of witless obedience.'

'I give you nothing!' Terrified, trembling, Elaira gripped the strap of her satchel and braced for the worst.

The rage jabbed after centuries of harsh resistance, that every breath taken in agonized pain throughout Arithon's captive separation should have been endured for naught! She had not been born, nor shared such a magnificent love only to be vanquished in this desolate winter-cold alley.

'May Dharkaron Avenger stand as my witness!' she gasped, 'Whatever you try, no matter the outcome, my spirit will pass through your hands whole and unscathed.'

Yet the bravest words rang uselessly hollow: her initiate's vow, recorded in crystal, had not been sworn under duress. The Prime's minions opposed her, supremely unmoved, harnessed through the might of the Skyron focus and backed by the intimate signature linked through Elaira's abandoned spell crystal. The stone had not been cleared, or detached from her personal imprint. Selidie had only to impose her master sigil upon the closed net to claim her victim's defeat. Elaira stood erect, beyond caring how hard she would fall when the Prime's will drove her unconscious. Since nothing more could be done, she chose to step forward and meet her fate.

The whisper of her footfall raised no flash of cold force. Cruel as a false promise, the moment hung, then strung out, while the raced blood sang in Elaira's taut veins. *Why did the Prime's thralled minions not strike?* Did they push to snap her defiance beforehand? Since she refused to cave in, why *not* wrest Arithon's location from her outright, unless the small fact she refused to surrender carried a thread of significance?

Elaira drew in a shuddering breath. Between the thick snow and the bone-chilling wind, might she scent the faint trace of brimstone? Her heart surged and lifted. Dragon! Was such a reprieve even possible? Did the Sorcerer Davien in fact turn Betrayer against the unbroken honesty of his colleagues? Could he stand to her defense in direct violation of Asandir's oath without rending the terms of the compact?

'Come on!' taunted Elaira, charged to an insane burst of courage. 'Will the Koriathain dare to cross the might of Seshkrozchiel?'

The Name of the great drake hung on the storm-whipped air: could the Prime *in fact* risk a rescue from that quarter expressly to rend the Fellowship Sorcerers' inviolate integrity and break their bound service to Athera's vanished Paravians? The dread prospect screamed that such a terrible price was beyond all conscience to risk. But the outrage inflicted by Arithon's captivity cut Elaira too sharply for selfless reason.

'Invite total ruin at such stakes, if you will!' she challenged her hesitant enemy. 'I am not your bargaining chip, nor even the Fellowship's keeper!'

Another step, then two more, Elaira advanced.

Power spoke then to her overstrained senses: not the blow that fore-ran her annihilation at the hand of the Selidie Prime. Instead, the shudder that ripped through her viscera was the unmistakable threat of an immanent scorching fire: no dragon's! This emanation was not acrid but clean as a sunbeam struck through a glass lens. Elaira had been visited by Davien before. Since the drake's dire bargain had claimed his fate, she knew, well enough to raise hackles of terror, the perilous shape-shifting *presence* that coiled in the aura of a living dragon. Yet this strange force – inexplicable beyond knowing – was *other*. Perturbed by the puzzle, she leaned on bravado and questioned her foes. 'Why should you hesitate, sisters?'

No answer was given. Instead, with a hiss of stymied frustration, the enchantress who blocked the harbour gateway *stepped back*. As though hazed by poison, she raised a hand in aversion and collapsed the spelled net staged to seal a third-rank initiate's capture. Animated by the Prime's snarl of fury, she promised, 'This will not end here!' Selidie's words, on her lips, rang vicious with crystal-sent brevity. 'You will pay dearly and for far worse than your flagrant oathbreaking!'

'Choke on your failure, first!' Elaira shouldered past the Prime's sigil-turned minion and nipped through the gate to the wharf. She did not look back at the defeated sisters or question whether her stroke of fortune stood for good or ill. Later, in safety, she could pause to ponder whose might had stymied the Koriani Matriarch.

The rest of the night saw her huddled against the storm on the open deck of the docked galley. No attack ever came, and no other invasive presence disrupted her vigil of bitter misery. When solstice dawn brightened the rags of spent cloud, and the blizzard abated to the azure sky of a diamond-bright morning, the boat's crew arrived at long last to set sail at the change of the tide. They chaffed their early passenger as a land rat and a layabout, before the cook offered her shelter in sympathy and gave her the welcome of a hot breakfast.

Warmed up and fed, Elaira leaned on the rail when the ice-crusted lines were cast off the dock. She heard the bells of Redburn toll twelve times for the death of a queen, then peal the carillons to celebrate the coronation of Havish's new High King.

Her own piquant mystery remained unsolved. No speculative cogitation on her part revealed whose hand may have acted to spare her. Though the suspicion rested: quite likely the answer might lie on the far desert shore of Sanpashir.

Solstice Day

With dawn yet to break on the eastshore at Whitehold, Selidie Prime rages, stymied over the shock of an unforeseen defeat; and her bitter tirade that reviles the order's most ancient enemy concludes, 'Elaira is declared forsworn and condemned! She and the Biedar tribe must never meet! At all costs, and by any means, stop her from reaching Sanpashir alive . . . !'

Rocked by the confirmed proof of a rising of Darkness and threatened by two minions of havoc at large, the True Sect high priest at Erdane's temple decides to send a Light's Hope to Etarra out of season: and the delegate ambassador he selects to petition the apostate avatar is not the usual political embarrassment but the most aggressively astute candidate among his talent examiners . . .

While the Sunwheel dedicates redouble their patrols up and down Tysan's trade-roads, two affable farm-hands in travel-stained clothes trade several raw hare pelts for eighteen silvers; and if the fair man's face is suspiciously battered, and his dark-haired companion refuses to speak, greed seals the exchange with a southbound teamster eager to seize a quick profit from the portside jackleg who sews charms against drowning for sailhands . . .

V. Mis-step

Tarens knotted the coins into his belt pouch, uneasy under bright sun in the open, while the tinker's wagon rumbled away around the next bend in the southbound trade-road. 'That crafty dealer will sell us both out,' he warned, the jingle of silver a bad trade against his shaken confidence.

'He will.' Arin tucked up his jacket collar against the blast of wind that lashed his tangled hair against his raw cheek. 'But I think, not immediately.' The shifty carter's sidelong glances had been fearful, behind the gleam of his mercantile avarice. Arin's tuned senses suggested their betrayal would happen, but only at a safe distance.

'Then why aren't we bolting for cover?' chafed Tarens, the pink scars from his ordeal just barely knit, and still too vividly obvious.

'Run where?' Arin's gentle truthfulness always eased any sting of reproach.

Tarens cursed, that holed boots and the agonized threat of frost-bite had driven their need to bargain with the wily trader. If the man's skilled repairs had patched his torn soles and eased his traumatized feet, the respite did not change the untenable fact that the terrain ahead exposed them to greater hazard. The wood-lots opened into the inhabited flats by the river-course, where the pastures and fields were well kept. The few stands of timber had been thinned for board wood and fence-posts, and cleared of the thickets essential for shelter.

Their hunted course lay flanked on the right by the sparkling rush of the Silberne, cowled in shelves of grey ice at the verges, with the frigid current a diamond-bright race, too fast and deep for two men with no boat. By nightfall, their progress slowed down, each league stolen in covert spurts. The farther

155

they skulked down the eastern bank, the more the attentive villagers' husbandry hampered their forward course. Thorn-hedges gave way to fenced pens for livestock, and hurdles of woven withies kept browsing deer off the barley. Tilled earth left fallow for winter held tracks, and the frosted ruts bogged every footstep.

Safety beckoned in the dense scrub and thatched briar that choked the opposite shore-line. But without any viable crossing, the fugitives risked being sighted and pinned where the crook in the Silberne flanked the southbound trade-route. Nor would their prospects improve over distance. Beyond Cainford, a stonewalled tow-path with ox teams dragged the laden barges up-stream from Valenford. Caravan teamsters and rowdy rivermen thronged the thoroughfare by day, and frequent, packed inn-yards handled the constant traffic that bustled to and from the port docks at Mainmere.

Tarens wiped sweaty palms on his grimed cuffs. 'How can we slip the law's capture through there?' His desperation referred to the Sunwheel troop encamped by the road, complete with boys beating drums by the verge to muster new soldiers. The stir that meant war might resume against Havish had the provost's patrols out in force. Mounted men swept the hedgerows for deserters each night, another obstacle against the long odds the two could creep past the company's outposted sentries.

The big crofter's natural patience turned snappish, beset by constant hunger and cold, and short sleep from the ache of his injuries. 'We're going to be set upon. Hazed like vermin caught in the corn-crake with those dedicate search parties hot on our tail.'

'Not if we join the ranks,' Arin said, reasonable.

'*What?*' Tarens stopped short and stared. Had his brother ventured that frivolous crack, Efflin would know to duck the quick-tempered fist swung to flatten him.

Yet Arin's calm gaze glinted with wicked irony. 'Were you a lance captain on your high horse, decked out in flashy accoutrements, would you leap for the yap of a tinker concerning the presence of evil itself?'

Despite himself, Tarens snorted. 'I'd be more likely to collar an underling to chase down such unlikely facts.'

'Then, what if your inquiry turns up the suspicious yokels in line to enlist, nicely yanking their hayseed forelocks?' Arin broke off and laughed. 'Ath above! Or, rather, the Light's *blinding* truth, the unlikely threat we pose to temple authority should fall apart under scrutiny.'

Such insane enthusiasm proved too infectious. Tarens choked and gave in to a smile. 'Any braw farm-hand could've banged up his face caught out by a kick from a milch-cow?'

'Or better,' topped Arin, 'What ingrate son doesn't get walloped by his mother for larking off to the glory of war?'

Which forthright boldness stole Tarens's breath, until better sense unravelled the lunatic notion. 'How long, do you think, before I'm recognized? Perhaps you might get by, since nobody but Grismard caught sight of you. But I'm too well-known about Kelsing. With my name condemned and marked with a head price, any dispatch sent north to check on my origins would turn up some nosy neighbour. One honest man's word would have me back in chains to burn as a minion of Darkness!'

'We need less than two days,' said Arin, quite earnest. 'During that time, we march in the open, fed and rested among the recruits. We buy our way past the most dangerous ground without getting flushed on the run. Thirty leagues by road gets us up to the fork where the bridge crosses over to Taerlin—'

'Where we desert?' Tarens broke in, unexcited. 'We would be ridden down by trackers with hounds, and if no one told you, the country that fringes the free wilds of Caithwood is desolate!'

'Yes,' Arin agreed. 'But the clansfolk who dwell there do not love the canon that upholds the True Sect religion.'

'They would kill us on sight should we dare to trespass,' Tarens snapped, heart-sore. Each step he took led away from his family. From fire and death, he had won survival, but at such a cost, every path led to nothing. The idea of throwing himself at the brutal mercy of an insular society of barbarians seemed a blow-hard's short cut to suicide.

'Clan scouts on patrol would hear our case, first,' Arin ventured, insistent. 'Surely they might if I addressed them with due respect in Paravian.'

'Why do I feel as though an ill wind just bristled the hair at my nape?' Tarens's bitterness rang in the brittle chill. The stone he kicked in frustration startled up a scolding mob of grey-and-black chickadees. 'I might die on the point of a clan scout's javelin quicker than by the sword on a temple scaffold. Show me how I'm not a buck-naked target if your cocky idea chucks the rock in the wasps' nest.'

'This could be a wrong steer,' Arin agreed. 'If so, do you trust me to rescue you?'

Tarens found nothing further to say, since the hell-bent zeal of the Sunwheel lancers seemed likely to corner them anyway. For better or worse, he had no choice but to walk in uncanny company. After seven rootless weeks on the dodge, he resented the harsh recognition: left on his own, he would not be alive. Whatever Arin had been in the past, the courageous initiative that drove his odd loyalty knew how to thrive in adversity. This brash proposal to hide in plain sight was not made by a man who tamely accepted defeat.

The bold course prevailed, since retreat was impossible. Turn back, and they would be trapped from behind, chased to earth like starved foxes.

The Light's recruiting officer stationed himself at the centre of the armed encampment. Perched at a plank trestle braced overtop the branded crates used for supply, he cheerfully processed his line of straggling aspirants. Dressed to impress, his meaty bulk strained the thread on his gleaming gold buttons. The fleshy smile he posed to all comers dimpled his jovial features. Up close, his porcine eyes were not merry. Arrived at his pleasure, Tarens was reamed by a steel-hard stare primed to pounce upon lying discrepancy. The officer's sword was field-sharp and deadly, casually rested under a fist horn-callused by veteran service. Beside him, a spindly clerk dipped the pen to list birthplace and name, and notate the trained skills of each applicant. Four more strapping fellows flanked the makeshift post, starched to parade pomp and armed to the teeth in bedazzling gold accoutrements.

Tarens's sensible nerve should have crumbled before he stepped up with a falsified claim.

If Arin experienced any such qualms, he was busy upsetting their option of subtle retreat. Trailed after his friend at a discreet distance, he embarked on an outrageous string of lame blunders that raised consternation and ripples of outraged dismay. The rumpus included a runaway horse, then a trip snagged over a guy-rope that flattened a tent, to spectacular yells from the half-smothered occupants. Next, an overset slop bucket rolled downhill and leveled the lance sergeant's weapons rack. An equerry's obscene curses chased Arin's heels into the recruiter's fold, where two more brutes recoiled with stomped toes, to louder oaths of annoyance. As the affronted parties piled in to add fisticuffs to the chorus of injured complaints, the rash of turned heads and annoyance thickened like summer flies on hot dung.

Arin seemed oblivious. Wedged beyond reach amid the thronged hopefuls, he cloud-gazed in the midst of a loud altercation as several braw fellows fresh off the farm debated whether or not fallen acorns griped horses to colic and caused them to founder – hooked into their talk, Arin ventured a comment. The effect aroused knee slaps and laughter. With a half dozen regulars itching to strangle him, and a cohort of bystanders amused enough to cheer on his frisky mayhem, nobody noticed Tarens's bowed head, far less commented on his smashed nose. Even the recruiter's ruthless glance bent towards the magnetic diversion.

'Set your mark here!' The brusque clerk stabbed a forefinger into the log sheet next to the ink-pot and quill.

For once, Tarens welcomed the bigoted presumption that his country dress and big hands made him simple. Clammy with nerves, he scrawled an illiterate's X on the line beside the fake name written out for him.

'Move along, then!' The bark of dismissal brought little relief, with Arin left on his own to withstand the galled officer's scrutiny.

Called forward in turn, he shambled up to the trestle, shamefaced, nondescript, his frame too slight to seem fully grown in the jostle of robust company. The Light's officer surveyed him, then sneered in contempt, 'Give me one good reason why I should let a failure like you sign onto my rolls.'

Eyes downcast, Arin straightened the dirty, holed cap found as a discard in a wayside snow-bank. Brow knitted, he mumbled, 'Lordly men prefer not to clean their soiled boots. They don't peel vegetables. Or empty their jakes.'

'A servant, were you?' The answering glower of purse-lipped disgust could have curdled an egg. 'No doubt you crawled here to cadge a free meal. Were you cast off for incompetence?'

Arin stiffened, astonished. 'I swear not. My lord.'

The recruiter showed teeth through his bristled beard. 'Then, little rump-licker, what was your position?'

The dejected sigh that emerged showed affront. 'I was a musician,' Arin declared. 'But as you see, I was turned out to starve without livelihood, lacking an instrument.'

'Run out for light fingers? Hard drink? Got caught rampant and naked in the wrong bed, or were you just tiresome, warbling your soppish drivel too far out of key?' The recruiter laughed off the indignant response. 'Light's blinding glory! I don't sit through anyone's sappy excuses. If you think yourself fit to serve with this company, you'll prove what you're worth to my captain's standards!' Aside, to the clerk, came the stiff ultimatum. 'Put this daisy down for a trial review. He'll have three days to back up his limp claim that he isn't a lovesick disaster.'

The upright stick with the captain's sash ordered the recruiter's trestle packed up within the next hour. His push to march southward resumed straightaway, with most of the troop's mounted lancers at the forefront with the Light's standards. The banners beneath identified the company as Tysan's Eighteenth True Sect Mounted and Foot, its badges of valor and streamers of past victories borne by its liveried bearers. Behind came the signal flag-man, then the drum corps beating the pace, positioned alongside the horn blowers and trumpeters, whose clarion blasts told the message runners where to locate the officers during an engagement at the battle-front.

Behind tramped the stalwart veteran foot, ranked into squares ten by ten with their pennoned pikes shouldered upright in bristling formation. Breathing their inglorious dust came the new comers just attached by the muster, bullied into the semblance of a matched step by a drill-sergeant's bellowed threats. After them straggled the cook wagons and baggage train, the camp women, and the insolent draggle of by-blows chased from lagging by the rear-guard. These last were mounted career men, campaign-scarred or aged, valued for disciplined training of the fractious officers' sons. They mentored the boys not yet fit to bear arms but whose privileged birth started them out as squires in charge of the lancers' equipment and remounts.

The column's progress was grindingly slow, mired further as cloudless sun softened the road to a welter of wheel-ruts, dropped manure, and churned slush. Most of the recruits tramped in caked boots, chafed raw at the heels by the sodden leather. Soon the most unfit limped in carping exhaustion, bullied like dogs if they slowed down the ranks.

Near asleep on his feet, Tarens slogged through the morning, careful not to jostle the men nearest when the soupy footing caused him to stumble. Arin, behind him, nursed no such intent, to judge by the staccato scatter of oaths and on-going cracks of amusement.

'Light above! Keep that nuisance away from sharp objects!'

'On the contrary, why not hand him your knife? Let the idiot skewer himself straightaway and rid us of the bumbling nuisance.'

'Forgive!' Arin gasped. 'I'm sorry!' His glib appeal sounded pathetic enough to disarm the most fierce irritation. Tarens experienced a sudden chill, unsettled as Kerelie's past admonitions ruffled gooseflesh over his skin: *'Don't place undue trust in mild appearances.'* And much later, *'Either your creature's as daft as the moon, or we're watching a sorcerer work.'*

Set under the pressured scrutiny of armed men, the simplistic show of incompetence assumed a sinister aspect.

Tarens's qualm was more than the offshoot of anxiety. Unaccustomed to lies, distressed by the deception of his honest fellows, he wrestled the uncomfortable fact he knew nothing of Arin's past background. The man showed enough evidence of true talent to condemn him as a sorcerer out of hand. If yesterday's kindness was just as effortlessly feigned as today's show of bumptious stupidity, the pitfalls loomed deep beyond measure.

Which jagged concern could not be addressed on the march in a snake-pit of militant dedicates. No bald-faced ruse, however disarming, could shield him from the horror of fire and sword if a diviner's Sight unmasked signs of a renegade talent. Tarens stayed in step and withstood his frayed nerves. Pitifully as his companion might plead, the forced march carried on without let-up. The wretched toll of fatigue shortened tempers. The brutes who got bashed each time Arin tripped became less inclined to humour him. Trickled sweat itched under thick woolen clothes, and squelched steps through soft footing pressed the least hardened men to puffed breath and leaden exhaustion. When Arin's inept balance jostled two neighbours into a puddled pot-hole, the splash doused the bull-necked fellow in front. Despite the drill sergeant's annoyed reprimand, the sprayed victim swung a furious fist at his fly-weight offender.

Arin salvaged his gaffe by an opportune trip that dropped him face-down in the road. The thrown punch he escaped ripped onwards through air and clipped the jaw of the chap just behind: one whose filled boot blundered into the pot-hole. The strayed blow rocked him back in a windmill stagger that nearly flattened the men on both sides. Incensed curses acquired a poisonous edge, with Arin's hapless sprawl the ripe target for the vengeful kicks of his upset neighbours.

Prostrate, plastered to the eyebrows with mud, he foiled the mob with a clownish kiss planted on the toe of the nearest man's boot. That antic roused gut peals of laughter, broken up as the drill-sergeant's shout hazed the ragged line back to formation.

Tarens kept his head down throughout, harrowed enough to be grateful the manic display let him stay unobtrusive. At each step, he shrank under the relentless dread that his mangled nose might expose him to his enemies. At least his hunched posture no longer stood out from the greenhorns distressed by their sore feet and blisters.

The troop's trumpeter sounded the midday halt before the most tender among them limped beyond the hope of remedy. While the column paused, a red-cloaked surgeon made his brusque round to attend the afflicted. The tired recruits sat on the bare ground to rest. They wolfed down their ration of smoked meat and biscuit, while the dismounted lance troops lounged on camp stools, and the officers dined off porcelain plates, under the shelter of awnings. Least privileged of all, the ragged horse-boys, squires, and grooms snatched their meal on the run as they curried the spent destriers and transferred saddles and gear onto the string of remounts.

Tarens surveyed the activity, perched to one side on a tree-root. Separate from his friend as a prudent precaution, he listened through the flow of wise-crack remarks to the tidbits of rumour around him. Frustration ran high, after fruitless patrols had pulled this company away from its accustomed duty at the south border. Eager speculation still rehashed the stories surrounding the temple's escaped murderer.

'. . . said to have been rescued by fiends, then sprung by spellcraft out of locked shackles.'

'Disappeared clean! A huntsman in that tavern claimed not a track marked the country-side after fresh snow. No one in the Light's service has ever seen an uncanny feat to match that.'

'Do you really think the condemned was a minion in league with the Spinner of Darkness?'

'Could be. My grand uncle said he heard a Koriathain lay claim that the Master of Shadow once conjured a plague of fiends. Turned them to work his fell bidding, she said, though he argued he didn't see how such was possible.'

While a passing equerry scoffed that the priesthood at Erdane spouted too much idle wind, an adamant pikeman assured that his cousin had been an eye-witness. 'He insisted the pins on those shackles were sheared! Not by a chisel or saw, I tell you. The steel was razed clean, slick as a knife through butter. If not an act of deep spellcraft, what natural force could've done that?'

'Your cousin,' jeered someone, 'was cross-eyed with drink!'

'Not likely,' a grinning companion cut in. 'Shamsin's too pious. Born with his neb in the watch captain's backside, and a festering stickler for the Light's duty!'

'You'll be that yourself, soon,' someone else quipped, to a smatter of laughter. 'Swinging a blade in a prissy white tunic, defending the louts in the market against something bat-shaped and Dark-spawned.'

'Not amusing if we're actually faced with the next rise of evil!' somebody shouted back. 'Why else should we be dispatched through the country-side for what amounts to an off-season muster? Best take due warning. If Darkness stirs after two hundred years, the same moves that foiled the temple's diviners could be a sure sign o' the Shadow Master himself!'

Tarens managed not to choke on his biscuit. A stone's throw behind, the unlikely author of infamous deeds crouched with his forehead rested upon folded arms and propped knees. Apparently nodded off in a catnap, Arin did not appear to be either dangerous or deadly. The cluster of men seated nearest joked about milksop prandeys at his expense. As their ceaseless taunts skirted the threat of rough play, Tarens smothered the protective urge to intervene. His jangled nerves were no match for the stakes of the strategy set into motion.

If Arin deliberately angled to get himself tossed out of camp as a ham-handed nuisance, his blistering wiles at least required the staunch backing of patience from his less facile companion. Resolved to hold back for the sake of discretion, Tarens missed the disastrous evidence that none of Arin's miscued awkwardness had been staged by intent.

Nothing prepared Arin for shock of an atmosphere well worn to familiarity: some part of his past had known, *all too well*, the martial taints of winter-wet wool, sweat, and goose grease. The spiked tang of the rust etched into oiled chain-mail rocked him off balance, until he tumbled in and out of bouts of waking vision that could have been glimpsed scraps of memory, *or prescience*. Whatever the cause, reliving or foresight, his traumatized senses repeatedly reeled to the sickening reek of fresh blood.

Arin jammed his forehead against his taut wrists, unable to maintain his focus. As discipline failed, he fell back upon sound, and engaged his wits by interpreting the noisy activity about him. Turmoil at the horse pickets informed him of a messenger's arrival with urgent dispatches from the Light's temple at Erdane. Hot news from the far north, relayed to the troop captain, raised a stir among the grouped officers. Taut as a plucked wire, Arin spun to the shift as their dizzy rush of emotional charge scattered ripples into the flux. He fought to shut down, leash the hectic bursts that sparked his sensitivity into untoward stimulation. Hands clamped to mask an onslaught of trembling, he closed his eyes and fought his breath steady.

His best effort did nothing to stem the rush of his runaway faculties. Worse, he broke into a clammy sweat when someone nearby drew a sword and plied a pumice stone to scour his steel. The raw scrape savaged Arin's peeled nerves. He swayed, unravelled by yet another harsh surge of displacement.

He knew the cold thrust of a blade in his guts, and felt the agony of a man, dying. His passage or another's, he could not tell which; the taste of bile soured his throat as his muscles spasmed in extremis.

Not real; not now; what he felt was *not present*. Arin strained to anchor himself. Huddled upon the hard winter ground, arms clenched to suppress his uncontrolled shivering, he waited for the clean chill in the air to centre his unmoored perception. His unruly senses overturned anyhow. He gouged his thumbs into his temples to drive down another explosive irruption. The call to march must find him on his feet. No choice remained! He must cling to appearances and endure, since no haven lay within reach to grant him the quiet he needed for respite. Unstrung to confusion, he feared, above all, that his lapse might waken enough suspicion to drag Tarens to shared destruction. Concern for the one friend he had in the world drove his panicked need to stifle the maelstrom inside of him.

Arin held on, though surrounding noises struck him too loud, and the least small disturbance upended reason. He choked off his scream as the jingle of a bystander's mail shirt triggered the next blast of hallucination. He saw, not today's idle men paused at ease amid civilized farmland: *but another place of dank mist and jaggedly rocky terrain, sprawled with war dead; and after these, other corpses, fallen in graphic slaughter under a green canopy of summer forest.* The re-echoed torment of those fatalities drowned his identity, and much worse. He heard again the pealed cries of terrorized women and children put to death in a frenzy of massacre.

Retching and sick, Arin hauled his wits from the morass. Doubled over, distressed, he struggled to steady his volatile awareness and stay fixed on his current surroundings: a place in full sun, where horses stamped, and a freckled groom whistled a plangent air, and a living soldier slapped a comrade's back and chaffed with derisive humour.

'. . . and I say the whole business is overblown nerves and hysterical fear of the Dark! Not even sorcerers walk without tracks!'

The horse-boy's tune ceased. 'Well, they do,' he declaimed with smug conviction. The lathered courier's mount on his lead rein backed up his claim to authority. 'The messenger closeted with our captain carries urgent news from the north.' More avid bystanders quieted to hear as the boy related, 'There's a second case of a condemned sorcerer who freed himself from locked chains. The official report says he broke out of a cell, blindsided two guards and every posted dedicate sentry, then vanished from Lorn with nary a trace.'

'Hogwash!' a man scoffed. 'Two random events a hundred leagues distant? How could they be connected?'

'Could well be they are,' a companion argued.

Then the trumpeter's call to form ranks cut the chatter. Men grumbled, stood up, adjusted their belts, and shambled back into formation. Arin assumed his place with the rest. What few bites of food he had eaten did nothing to settle his light-headed queasiness. Movement would help, and the cold breeze if he lasted until the midday sun waned. He must hold out, at least until nightfall provided the opening to slip away.

The company halted at twilight and camped beside a marshy, ox-bow lake carved out by the river before the channel was dredged straight for barges.

The site was not remote, or even quiet, bounded to the west by the active trade-road and the torch-lit berm of the tow-path. If the site posed a natural deterrent to deserters, the cover of darkness eased the cranked pitch of Tarens's anxiety. Between the haphazard scatter of cookfires and the tent shelters crowded with boisterous men, the deep shadows made his bashed nose less obvious. When the temperature plunged, he pulled up his high collar and scarf and muffled his damaged features.

The confidence of anonymity let him keep a closer watch on his erratic companion. One more man's entrained interest would scarcely draw notice – not since the barrage of ungainly mishaps made Arin the butt of the drill-sergeant's animosity. The party of griped recruits swelled into a crowd, with more idle veterans strolled up to enjoy the diversion as the sting of petty annoyances dealt Arin a round of light-duty punishment.

On his knees for an hour with a bucket and rag, he was made to clean the mud from the boots of any man wanting a polish. The cold numbed his raw hands and unstrung his dexterity. Fine-boned as the musician he claimed to be, he became mocked as a pampered ornament. Then what appeared to be effete incompetence upset the bucket just refilled to rinse his clogged rag.

While the nearest onlookers jounced back from the flood, the ribald soldier seated with splashed ankles elbowed his neighbour. 'D'you suppose the git's as much of a disaster, cut loose in the sheets with his whanger?'

'Light forbid! Wrecks my digestion to think such a pathetic jape ever stood his pole up to breed offspring!'

'Let's buy him a wench!' a bystander yelled. 'We could watch. See whether he knows how to grope the right hole or unties his own drawers without tangling his equipment!'

The coarse gibes passed over Arin's bent head as he gasped his breathless apology. Hunched and shivering, with his trousers and jacket front drenched, he groped after the bucket's rope handle and stumbled erect. A squelching step reeled him towards the lake-side to recoup his sloppy mistake.

'Save us! He minces!' The outburst of laughter widened his audience, and banter erupted around him like cross-fire. 'How long do you think he'll survive without being cosseted in a rich lady's boudoir?'

'A day, perhaps,' a burly pikeman shouted back, then jingled his coin pouch in a shameless invitation to take prospective wagers.

Tarens's uneasy stance became jostled as others pushed in to enjoy the affray. More than their raucous amusement disturbed him. Those same fingers, engaged in rough labour before, had never displayed tonight's show of maladroit fumbling. As the servile round of boot cleaning gave way to the task of collecting the recruits' soiled food bowls, the stakes became piquantly raised. Arin staggered under a tipsy stack of crockery piled with chewed bones and food scraps.

'For Light's sake, stand back,' a roisterer cried, 'before he lands on some luckless fool and delivers a lapful of garbage!'

The warning did not seem an empty threat: Arin's fierce frown and intense concentration did little to steady his tottering steps. The role he played was too brilliantly close, among soldiers galled reckless by boredom. Worse, the sharp drill-sergeant welcomed the chance to keep his fractious troop in high fettle. He made no effort to curtail their sport but smirked with crossed arms while the horse-play turned cruel, and a bystander snaked out a vengeful foot to trip up the gullible victim.

Arin fell hard, sprawled over two other men's knees, while the upset bowls flew, hurling cold gobbets of gravy. The mess touched off a clamour of furious shouts. One splattered victim unsheathed his sword. Other bystanders recoiled, while Arin rammed backwards, cat-quick to evade as the angered brute lunged through the scramble to skewer him.

The flicker of fire-light lit his face and exposed a blanched fear that froze Tarens's blood. The crude sham had gone irretrievably wrong. But the chain of misfortune unreeled too fast to attempt an intervention.

'May as well spit the wretch properly,' goaded the man whose lap had received the revolting brunt. Bedecked in thrown gristle, he drew a main gauche and hurled the blade at the gutless offender.

The weapon flew point first through the dark.

Without a glance over his shoulder, never turning a hair, Arin ducked and snatched the blade from mid flight. His hand closed on the thrown grip with practiced experience: once, twice, in blinding fast form, he parried the swordsman's impetuous attack. The defensive moves damned him for speed and sheer brilliance. All question died, that he had ever been the inept musician he claimed, prone to feckless clumsiness.

To yells from the side-lines and whoops of encouragement, Arin's murderous antagonist bore in to finish the fight. A tough, career soldier with a powerful reach, he raised his heavier weapon for a classic stroke. Arin checked the blow with a high block. Blade clanged on cross-guard, a shrill ring that drilled across an abrupt, fallen quiet. Arin gasped. As though the sound opened the flood-gates to nightmare, he dropped to one knee and flung the dagger away as though burned. Crouched helpless and retching, he bent with his nape exposed to the next killing blow.

Tarens shoved forward, but not fast enough. The sergeant's rush barged him aside and curbed the aggressive scrap short of a fatality. But the turbulent charge on raised tempers stayed ugly. Denied a lethal quittance, the onlookers seethed with unspent excitement. Aghast, Tarens belatedly realized that his friend's sharp collapse was brought on by a vicious reliving.

Whatever past poison such memory contained, the rip tide drove Arin to mindless anguish. His visceral cry pealed against mob-fed outrage, primed yet to seize retribution.

Tarens elbowed to push through, cut off in the press as the troop sergeant's discipline failed, and the disaffected mob closed upon Arin. He offered no fight.

Dragged upright by a score of hostile fists, he returned not a whimper of protest. His opened eyes appeared without focus, inwardly fixed on the vista of some savage, unknown atrocity. Which limp unresistence only annoyed the dog-pack circle of his oppressors. Before the camp's senior officers took notice and bore in on the scuffle gone riot, the ringleaders wrestled off Arin's coat. The sleeves of his shirt tore under their mauling and bared the pale flesh underneath to the fire-light.

The inevitable shout of salacious discovery broke over the tumult. 'Light protect us! Looks like he's got shackle marks on his wrists.'

'Do you see? This wretch has the scars of a convicted felon!'

'Back off! Move aside!' The sergeant muscled his way to the fore and confirmed the shocking, grim evidence. 'By glory, we'll get to the bottom of this! Have yon scoundrel strung up from that tree until he gives over the truth.'

Though the weals were long since healed white, the upstaged officer seized on the evidence to appease his insubordinate troop. 'If a criminal's dared to swear into this company on false grounds, I'll make him an example you men won't forget! For lying, the wretch will be put to the lash. Then the captain decides whether his case merits a summary execution.'

Tarens was forced to observe from the side-lines. Choked silent, afraid, he wondered how long he had before someone recalled the two fugitives on the lam from the Light's justice. Alone, he could not deflect the armed might of a dedicate company. Should Arin betray the least sign of born talent, the mistake would set off a witch-hunt. Pinioned, his slight stature posed no one a threat. But the display of polished aptitude with edged weapons must open a stiff round of questions. Without solid answers backed up by hard proof, his dilemma would only get deeper.

Jostled aside, Tarens braced himself to bide until chance might present him an opening.

Cast adrift by a rampant surge of reliving, Arin strove to shut down the blind surge to unleash every faculty he owned in reflexive defense. He clung to restraint, ridden by the desperate certainty that he could destroy more than just himself if he fought the mailed hands laid upon him. While the baying pack dragged him up to the tree, he curbed breathless terror and reached for the inward discipline to shut down his inflamed sensitivity. But sapped by poor sleep and short rations, he could not recover the presence of mind to separate his stressed sensitivity from the tumultuous barrage of raw stimulus.

The chime of byrnies against tempered-steel weaponry sang a continuous blood-dirge into his bard's ear. More, the mingled scents in his nostrils raised the rampaging spectre of war, a horror renewed with untenable clarity at every traumatized breath. The immediacy of his peril undid him, too vividly powerful to withstand. His last restraint had snapped on the instant his grip closed over that fateful, thrown weapon.

The heft of a main gauche in his hand, then the jarred clash, as edged steel deflected the hostile riposte of a larger opponent tore through the veil that darkened his past and unleashed a cascade of blocked recall. Nerve and bone, his body remembered its treacherous history: the same classic move, *once before*, had ended a duel by murder. He still felt the heated spurt of fresh blood as a low, left-hand jab sank his blade in the vulnerable flank of a man who had been the most steadfast of liegemen. The cry wrung from his tortured throat, then, haunted still: *'Caolle! Ath's mercy on me, Caolle! Dharkaron strike me, it's death I have dealt for your service!'*

This night, called by Arin, he scarcely felt the blow that buffeted his exposed face. He stayed deaf to the heckling shouts of the drill-sergeant's henchmen. Ripped near to tears by the visceral fear that another man's loyalty might fall to ruin because of him, he did not resist as they noosed his wrists, then tossed the rope over a sturdy bough. Eager hands hoisted the slack till he dangled, toes scarcely in contact with the frosted ground.

'Who are you, really?' someone demanded. Without pause for answer, a blow hammered his ribs and knocked the wind from him. 'Where were you taught sword-play, and how did you earn the punishment of chain and shackles?'

Still undone by spasms, Arin could not speak. As if any bold lie could, ever again, reconstruct a false claim to innocence. The irrefutable rip tide of relapsed experience damned him too straightly to deny tonight's accusations or protest the abuse hammered into him. Arin languished, no more responsive than a rag puppet hung from a nail. The punishment to his person meant nothing. Not while, thousands upon uncounted thousands, his past toll of fallen resurged to stain his culpable hands in let blood. If he gave way, he might number their endings: by arrow and steel riven through cringing flesh, until the harrowed noise of their ghostly screams deafened him, and the horrific wreckage of split organs and smashed bone sucked the air from his lungs, and whirled him insensate . . .

Arin woke, choking, to the gritty splash of marsh water, hurled into his face.

'We should leave you strung up all night,' snapped the man who wielded the pail. 'Maybe find out how loud you can sing before cock's crow in the morning!'

Spluttering, wet to the waist and helplessly shivering, Arin groaned. Someone had strapped a rock to his ankles. Against that cruel weight, the ropes binding him were being raised until his stretched shoulders popped, and his spine blossomed to star-bursts of agony. He understood, from the bystander's shouts, that his unpleasant predicament was a stop-gap step, improvised for expedience. Once the troop's provost returned from his sweep to round up deserters, the sergeant would lay claim to the chain and cuffs to properly shackle him.

Someone spat in his face.

Arin blinked, chin tucked against his strained arm in a thwarted effort to shield his eyes. A shudder ran head to foot through his frame. Lost again to the powerful currents of memory, he whimpered, while the fierce cold that bit to the bone hurled him back into harrowing wind on a sleety mountain side. Where, once in the past, he had climbed in exhausted flight to evade a troop of Sunwheel lancers. Almost, he remembered the names of the commanders who hunted him down for capture.

But a nearby, familiar voice snapped the vision. Eyes opened again, frozen in wretched earnest, he recognized Tarens, importuning the sergeant to let down the snubbed rope and show mercy.

'You know this rogue, then?' The frustrated officer turned on the crofter, his hawk's glance whetted to suspicion. 'Who battered your face? Are you thick with this criminal miscreant?'

Before the brute sized up his new target, Arin broke silence and pealed with quick sarcasm. 'Yes, the dumb mule has claimed my acquaintance. How do you think he busted his nose? Didn't teach him a thing, since he's grovelling again, when even a girl with good sense should keep to the side-lines.'

'Took the fist for you, did he, last time someone got pissed?' Primed for amusement, the drill-sergeant tipped back his pot helm, licked gapped teeth, and bore in. 'Or is this the side-kick who saves your runt hide from the scrapes touched off by your fumbling?'

'He's saved no one,' cracked Arin, fast as a whip. Where, before this, had he turned a riposte with such cruelty, to strike *that* note of withering ridicule? With venomous ease, he hit the raw nerve guaranteed to evoke searing recoil. 'What could you expect but soft sap from a man who ducked out for the scandal of incest?'

The clubbed shock of betrayal on Tarens's open face raised hoots, then bellows of amusement from the gathered onlookers. Drawn in from the side-lines, others became riveted. The drama unfolded with such callous honesty, the sergeant broke into a guffaw. 'Light's sweet sake! You don't relish the story of your filthy act aired in public? Tell us, fellow. Did you run with your sister bunged up with child, or did she whip you off like a rut-snorting bull?'

'Oh, no,' Arin cracked. 'His older brother poked the goods first. If the line breeder who fathered the brood shot the same, I'd bet this lummox is hung like an ox, fit to stir family sauce like a champion.'

Gut laughter exploded with an ugly roar.

'Ox-wang!' The sergeant's gibe rammed through the tumult. 'Light's own, there's a name a stud greenhorn could never live down!'

'Let him try!' someone shouted. 'We'll cheer him on, since the whores hereabouts are callused with use, and bossy as crooked-horned dairy cows.'

Hazed scarlet, Tarens broke from stunned stupor. Ripped to naked rage, he bent and snatched up an iced clod of mud. His overhand throw hurled the missile full force at the prisoner's face.

Arin could not duck, slung from his numbed wrists. The impact slammed his jaw and split his upper lip. Eyes open, set swinging, he spat blood, and denounced, 'Bully for you. Now, deny that I've spoken less than the truth.'

Whitened beyond fury, Tarens glared at the captive with arctic intensity. To the sergeant, to whom he had just pleaded for blankets, he said, charged to terrible calm, 'Build a fire to warm the gleeking scum, for all I care.' Jaw clamped, he turned his broad back and walked off.

Still safe! Arin loosed his pent breath, shaken limp with relief. No one pursued his friend into the dark. A sharp prod in the ribs sped the twirl of the rope, followed fast by a taunt. 'Cat got your tongue, little weasel?'

The mocking jabs became thumping blows, which swung the line lashed to the creaking bough. The involuntary shudders set in from the chill made the victim jig like a hooked fish.

Arin set his teeth to endure. Shoved, punched, and whirled nauseously dizzy, he scarcely cared that the macabre suggestion of fire caught on. To raucous whistles and cheers, a dozen enthusiasts hurried to gather dead wood. All but driven mad by the pain of stressed ligaments, Arin suffered the gamut of goading attempts to upset his nerve and break his clammed silence. He held out, not for pride. As long as his sorry predicament lasted, he held the crowd's focused interest. If he failed, the disastrous end could be worse. The instant that sharp inquiry widened the search, the description of last month's blond runaway would call for a cursory inspection beneath Tarens's sleeve cuffs. Fresh weals from the shackles set upon the condemned would unmask the priest's misplaced criminal.

Where Arin could draw on an untapped well of resource, at risk of the horrors that occluded his identity, the kind-hearted crofter possessed no such ruthless store of experience. Tarens had strength, but no guile. Caught out, alone, he would be undone by the same strait-laced virtue that had led his family to ruin.

Let him stay heart-sore and distanced and free, Arin whispered as an inward litany. He clung to that commitment to save his frayed balance. Trained to overmaster the body's complaint, he pitched himself to withstand the harsh course and outlast the malice of his tormentors.

Yet Tarens had no such callousness in him, to witness another man's punishment. Huddled by the darkened warmth of the horse-lines to nurse the sting of betrayal, he could not shut out the mingled shouts and coarse laughter as the spurious hazing continued. He saw men stack the driftwood beneath Arin's feet. Heard the serious threat, as someone's rash eagerness kindled a torch. Thin through the noise, he heard Arin cough as a flaming billet was waved in his face, and the greasy smoke billowed off the oiled rag choked his wracked effort to breathe. Sparks showered and ignited the laid store of fuel. Since the drill-sergeant hoped to prompt a confession, his gesture forbade the man with the bucket to douse the premature blaze.

'String the wretch up! Crank that rope higher. If we toast his toes, he'll sing all the quicker! Why not make a dull evening more lively?'

Eager hands hoisted, while Arin, strapped helpless, was set swinging in ponderous arcs above the lit kindling. Night-wind fanned the flames. The logs singed and caught. Within moments, the blaze crackled in earnest.

Tarens swallowed, distressed.

If not for that little man's saving help, he would have met a hideous end on the scaffold, pierced through by cold steel until he died screaming. No matter how vile the slanderous words, despite the unforgivable mockery that heaped filth on the tender love that Efflin had cherished within the close circle of family, Tarens could not watch any wretch burn alive. Not even to vindicate the mean blow that savaged his brother's private dignity.

Big and good-natured, he was slow to enrage among strangers. His easy manner tended to be misread, and his forceful speed was underestimated, always, in those moments he did choose to move.

As a whistling horse-boy jogged past with four mounts saddled up for the messenger's relay, Tarens seized the moment and snatched the looped reins. His vaulted leap straddled the nearside gelding against the boy's stupefied protest. Without stirrups, the crofter dug his desperate heels into the chestnut beneath him. He reined around shouting, and plunged the stolen string of horseflesh back through the camp at a break-neck gallop.

Men scattered away from their trampling hooves. Kicked buckets tumbled. The cook's trestle upset. A snagged guy-line collapsed a command tent, to corrosive oaths and confusion. Darkness lent wing to the erupted chaos as the stampede caught senior officers and troops in flat-footed surprise.

Tarens snatched up a pennoned lance from a rack. He swung the tip and sliced through the picket line that secured the war-trained destriers. While the squire attending them stood and gaped, Tarens whipped the released animals into a charge. Onwards, he pelted, trailed by pandemonium as the freed horses thundered away, helter-skelter. The furious dedicates were compelled to choose: to chase their loose mounts or to murder the lout hell-bent on sowing mayhem.

Someone with a cool head in the tumult strung a long-bow and nocked an arrow. In darkness, his target was a muddled silhouette, blurred by flying manes, upflung necks, and fanned tails against the spent coals of the cookfires. The shots snapped off his bow-string flew wild, more likely to maim an innocent soldier as take down the maniac fugitive. A powerful veteran cast a lance, and one of the riderless animals went down screaming. Its agony drove the rest of the herd into a rampage of panic.

Tarens rode for his life. Wedged amid the crazed seethe of the herd, he had no level head for strategy. But his crofter's background knew all the best tricks to drive terrified livestock. A few judicious jabs with his lance-butt ran his hacks straight into the lynch mob under the tree limb.

The sergeant swore murder but could not hold his ground. While men peeled away to escape being milled under, only a few stalwart veterans regrouped and drew swords. Yet they dared not strike without risk of crippling the couriers' race-bred steeds.

Tarens shucked the spear. Jostled amid the swirl of crazed animals and partly shielded by the tree trunk, he drew rein and blocked the prisoner's pendulum swing, before the arc reversed and scythed back over the pyre. Arin's bound form crashed full length against the chestnut's shoulder. Tarens pulled the home-made knife from his boot. Reins dropped, with the remounts snagged in pin-wheeling upset around him, he snatched the rope while their rampage foiled outside intervention. Somehow, with taut heels, he steadied the gelding. Kept astride its jostling back by sheer grit, he sawed through the hemp and cut Arin free. Powerfully strong from a miserable autumn spent busting frozen sod at the plough, the crofter clawed the smaller man's limp weight astride with the singed rocks still attached.

No time remained to hack Arin's limbs free. Tarens kicked the gelding, drove it hurtling against the equine melee, and tangled the snagged wrack of lead reins. The bunched horses staggered. Dragged pell-mell with him, disgruntled and squealing, the nags chased their liberated four-legged brethren and pounded at an ear-flattened run out of camp. Furious officers howled orders to give chase. But the frantic men scrambling at their command were too hard-pressed, catching animals, to regroup for an urgent pursuit.

Tarens had sense enough not to glance back. Bent over the rescue draped on his mount's withers, he let the crazed beast tear through the night at an uncontrolled gallop. His break-neck course crashed through thickets and the pelt of low-slung twigs, then clattered in untrammelled flight onto the trade-road. Tarens hissed through his teeth and swerved the herd leftwards, then drove them over the ditch and onto the berm to hammer onwards down the tow-path. In minutes, the gelding he straddled was winded. Bred light for speed, meant to bear a slight rider, its strides laboured under the double burden. Hope to reach a safe haven was lost with the bridge south of Cainford ten leagues off, at best, and no dense forest at hand for concealment. A river-crossing stayed beyond hope. The channel remained too deep and wide, the deadly gleam of black water riffled between grey sheets of unstable ice. Worse, from behind, the camp's archers regrouped. Their ragged volleys snicked a hail of arrows through the trees at the verge. Tarens plunged the horse down the steep bank into cover, where softened ground bogged down each stride. The chestnut's hooves punched hock deep into mud, and thrashed into rattling stands of dead reeds. The crofter swore under his breath for the noise.

Best to cut his losses at once. He turned his knife and sliced Arin's bonds, then freed the lashed stones and ties at both ankles. He tried not to care, that under damp clothes, the body he handled was shivering.

'We are quits,' Tarens snarled, his throat strangled by fury too fierce for forgiveness.

But Arin rejected the hate and the severance. 'You'll be killed on your own. I can't let that happen. No matter how ugly the method I used to distance you from my crisis, I won't leave you defenseless to be ridden down.'

'Stop me!' snapped Tarens. Bright anger killed pity. He grabbed at wet shirt with both hands and pushed.

Arin slid, helpless. Numbed fingers found no purchase on the plunging horse. The tremors that shuddered his chilled body hampered his agile balance. But nothing slowed his sharp presence of mind. He snagged the bridle rein under one elbow. The yank as he fell snatched the bit up short and wrenched the horse into a scrambling stagger.

Tarens tumbled off also.

Both men landed together, trounced by the glancing blows of shod hooves as the gelding shied into its trailing fellows. The spooked horseflesh bolted away through the brush, while the locked pair of men thrashed onwards down the embankment. They fetched up in a heap on the frigid, soaked sand of a shoal where the swift current lapped at the verge.

'What gave you the right?' Tarens fought two-fisted to rise unencumbered. Act quickly, and he might catch a stray horse, perhaps fly ahead of the dogs brought to bear by the lance troop's head-hunting trackers.

'Not this way,' snarled Arin. 'I won't see you killed!' His wiry, slight form recouped with fraught speed as exertion flushed warmth through his sinews. Beyond his secretive skill with a blade, he knew how to fight barehanded. Move for move, he used all he had beyond mercy to foil Tarens's bid to break off.

Knuckles and knees thudded. Grunts hissed through shut teeth, embellished by Tarens's blistered swearing. Kerelie would have been beyond shocked, that her good-natured brother could spout ruthless language while being battered to the crazed edge of extremity. Felled at last by a blow that raised roaring rage for the ruthless denouncement of honour, Tarens dropped, sick with pain and kicked breathless. Paralyzed by discomfort, he felt icy fingers latch onto his collar.

'Don't thank me, just live!' snapped his winded nemesis.

A determined jerk heaved him onto his back.

Then a savage and soundless descent of black cold hurled him into a chill almost too intense for survival. Swallowed into that blanketing void, the shocked air screamed like a gale wind. Tarens could see nothing. His eyes burned. Even the shallowest breath seared his lungs. Lids shut tight as the freeze fused his tear-wet lashes, he reeled under a burst of galvanic fear.

The temple's diviner had not been wrong! Here was deadly proof that the

Light's sacred canon was not based on an empty threat. Tarens cried out, shamed at last by the hideous error that placed him in the clutches of a genuine minion of Darkness, perhaps even the Master of Shadow himself.

His scream went unheard. What sound reached his ears became chiselled by dread into preternatural clarity. He marked the harsh course of forced passage as his clothing scraped over the ice-crusted sand, and on through the shallows that lapped over the sand-bar. The splash of his struggles, and the hissed gusts through the bank's fringe of reeds seemed the last trace of a solid world, wrapped by oblivion. Then the shore-line's firm soil fell behind. Terrible as a nightmare beneath his hauled frame, Tarens picked up the glassine spang of rough water, snap-frozen in mid-cascade. He felt, through his skin, the rickle and groan of the raging current trapped underneath. His panic leaped to each juddering snap, as the paned ice overtop cracked like crystal beneath Arin's rushed footsteps.

'Don't try to stand,' his enemy warned. 'Struggle at all, we will both break through. Stay down! Spread your weight. The thin surface will hold. Very soon, I promise, we'll find safety on the far side and build a fire to get warm.'

Tarens failed to muster the will to resist. Cold and agony drained the fight out of him. Curled up, half-unconscious and beyond helpless, he let himself be dragged to the river's south-western bank. There, in the company of who knew what evil, he entered the proscribed free wilds: ruled under the barbaric tenets of old law, kept in force by the clan war bands of Taerlin.

Repercussions

The Warden of Althain pin-pointed the moment when Arithon Teir's'Ffalenn recovered the use of his elemental mastery of Shadow. As the blanket of dire darkness cold-struck the earth to an arctic freeze, and a river transformed on a breath to brittle ice, the tortured scream of the elements unleashed across Tysan's winter landscape pocked a dense ripple across the night flow of the flux. Sethvir's earth-sense tracked the cascade of response: as horses exploded into redoubled flight and careened between tree trunks and obstacles, and a Sunwheel war camp's aroused pursuit changed pitch to fraught terror and panic. Worse than these, the rabid rebound to excitement, as the Koriani scryers assigned to the lane watch reported the outbreak of conflict, and the Prime's shout of triumph called their best Senior talent to pin-point the cause.

The event blazed the trail to pursue their lost quarry, stripped of his birth-right and trained protections.

Sethvir's experience sorted past the flurry of resounded echoes. His split-second awareness captured the signal image that mattered: where a fire burned in the bleak patch of brush on the wild shore of the Silberne several leagues below Cainford. Two miserable fugitives huddled over the flames, drying wet clothes in a desperate bid for survival . . .

Sound carried from the far side of the river, a tangled profusion of horn-calls and shouts punched through by the thud of galloping hooves, and the whined hiss from inbound flights of arrows shot blindly from extreme range. The barrage clattered through the dead brush and thumped into the dirt several yards short of the flames that exposed the runaways' luckless position. No hounds bayed on their trail. If the brutal tradition of head-hunter trackers cut their dogs to run silent, no horse and no man could cross over the river: the tissue of ice finessed by the brief blast of Shadow already broke. Rickled into a jumbled mass, the pack parted under the shove of the current and swirled away downstream.

Clothes steaming, his shuttered hands jammed to his face, the blood prince reduced to the diminutive, Arin, battled yet to stem the uprush of visions that confounded his grasp of the present. In spurts and surges, the nightmare relivings continued to stream through his tattered control. He fought, breath to breath, to restore equilibrium and seal the torn boundary between his inflamed instincts and the reason that measured sound choices.

No lancers would die at this river, tonight. Unlike another, where a Sunwheel company ridden against him had perished almost to the last man. Under cold moonlight, those casualties had lain unmourned, limbs frozen and hearts stopped beneath the ice grip of implacable Shadow. The same crafted darkness just spun without thought shook off tonight's hunt at the riverside.

Arin reeled from self-revulsion and emotional shock, nakedly damned by the recall of his former atrocities. Ungrounded despite the support of firm land, he wrestled the spin of his unruly thoughts with the only inviolate truth he possessed: here and now, he had taken no life. His friend had not been left abandoned. That achievement *mattered,* while, moment by moment, the hectic clamour of fragmented identity threatened to break him.

Tarens had no inclination to help. Angry, betrayed, his pummelled injuries aching, the big crofter lashed out with venomous blame for the terror of his predicament. 'Who are you, really? Don't try more deceit! I saw you work Shadow with my own eyes. Past question, I'd rather die as a mortal than fall under the vile usage of Darkness.'

A shudder raked through the small, black-haired form clenched tight in distress by the fireside. 'Swim back, then. Or run. Take your own path to suicide. I won't lift a finger to stop you.'

'You just did!' Tarens argued. But self-honesty impelled the bitter acknowledgement. He would bear the brunt of an informed decision if he chose to walk away this time. Alive by the grace of a forced intervention, his bed-rock character still would not be silenced. 'Answer me honestly! Who or what did I shelter beneath my family's roof?'

The moth-wing clasp moved. Bared by entreaty, Arin's sidelong glance revealed only transparent sincerity. 'I did not recall, then. Or forgive myself now for what seems like a planned deception. But until the hour I stepped into that war camp, I did not realize that I carried such a volatile past. There is no recompense for the fact I couldn't remember. I've undone your home, and much worse, endangered you.'

Tarens spat. 'How do I know you aren't spinning more lies?'

'In my place, what would you have done?' Arin opened his hands. 'Was there any strategy I might have used to salvage the error that set you at risk?'

'Does the answer matter?' Tarens raged, flustered. 'What harm has not been said and done already? When I cut you free, that action was witnessed. I've made myself the willing collaborator of who knows what servant of evil.'

'You'd have been killed without quarter, thrown to the swords of that Sunwheel company,' Arin reminded.

'Maybe better off dead than damned on all counts,' Tarens snapped in chill misery.

'No.' Arin's level regard did not waver. 'Because you've survived, there is a next strategy. I can give myself over. As a bound captive, you could turn me in and redeem yourself. Soon enough, two days at the most, the Sunwheel patrols will cross over by way of the trade bridge and run us down.'

Which shocking suggestion undercut every righteous angle of argument. Tarens stared, speechless. He had never embraced temple doctrine, before, always had been quick to nap through the sanctimonious lectures of the Light's priests. Undermined by tormented uncertainty, he found no foothold for comfort. Arin's glib tongue and inventive cleverness gouged up the sharp echo of Kerelie's warnings. Dread rode the memory of Efflin's healing, since everywhere a strait-laced man turned, folk whispered of a fresh rising of Darkness.

As if conflicted doubt could be read, Arin spoke. 'Tarens! Take courage. Look at me straight on.'

Wordless, Tarens glared back with his jaw clamped.

He already knew he could not deny the being stripped to naked pleading before him. Arin seemed only human. He looked nothing else but sorrowfully thin, hunched in his wet clothes by the fireside. His wracked, flame-lit face still seemed that of a friend, faultlessly kind and gentle.

At due length, Tarens responded, stung enough to nurse his cold anger. 'If I tie your hands, how do I know you won't resort to sorcery? Or strike back with Shadow and move against me when the moment comes to defend yourself?'

Arin answered with delicate care. 'If I was the fell creature your temple priests claim, surely I would have killed without pause for remorse already.'

Such a massacre in cold blood would have happened had he engaged his talents with deadly intent. Grudging, the crofter conceded that point.

'Think, Tarens, before you condemn me for past acts I don't even know, yet. Tonight's only casualty, acknowledged as mine, was a loose horse run afoul of a lancer.' Arin tipped his head, wrenched by a shiver. Arms tightly clasped to his drawn-up knees, he also suffered the merciless ache of exhaustion. 'If you find out otherwise and my word proves false, you still have the dagger I gave you. Hands bound or not, as friend or foe, you have my leave to make use of it.'

'How can you trust that I won't, regardless?' Tarens snarled in cornered defeat. 'I could turn in your corpse and still clear my name with about as much credibility.'

'I believe in your goodness,' said Arin, direct. 'You need not decide, now. Get warm first. Weigh up the matter until our pursuit takes the roundabout route and comes after us.'

On that steadfast statement, the world's future hung. Back at Althain Tower, Sethvir held his breath. His hands stayed tied to noninterference, even as his earth-sense disclosed the grim repercussions to come. That one brief burst of elemental Shadow would unleash an upheaval beyond any threat the beleaguered fugitives had scope to imagine.

They had two days, perhaps less, before the thwarted Sunwheel troop overtook tonight's trail and gave chase. Already the commander's fastest courier galloped southward on the trade-road. The urgent word that Shadow itself moved abroad would shake Valenford before dawn. Terror would galvanize the town's garrison. Armed pursuit raised in force would march out to broach the free wilds of Taerlin. Against Sunwheel dedicates mustered at strength, the furtive clan presence duty-bound to hold Caithwood was too thin on the ground. The defenders in place could never withstand a determined invasion.

More and worse, the impact of tonight's unmasking upset a volatile balance long held in abeyance. Sethvir sensed the start of the ugly cascade, and prayed the frail safe-guards set into motion would withstand the opening onslaught.

For already a power awakened in back-lash: the cursed fury held in check by a thread, and the one man allotted the most fragile stay of them all . . .

Asandir's instructions had been unequivocal: '*You will attend each state function and social if your Lord Mayor decides to appear.*'

As night blackened the shut casements and winter gusts battered the glass from outside the palatial grand ball-room at Etarra, the ubiquitous servants maintained the lit ranks of candles and glass chandeliers. The expensive wax flames warmed the vaulted room paneled with curly maple. Heat soaked the overcrowded air, while Etarra's finest glittered and laughed, bedecked in their jewelled finery.

Daliana perched on a stuffed chair at the side-lines, the voluminous lace sleeve foisted on her by fashion flapped one-handed to fan her flushed face. The conversation around her droned away, beyond tiresome. She had little patience for the cutthroat politics or trade, conducted by men lean and hard with ambition under their soft words and manners. As vicious, for spite, were the gossip and innuendo exchanged by the ladies. With painted eyes and sharp tongues, they stalked the carpet like predators, plumed in brilliant gowns and layered petticoats, and regaled in a bouquet of exotic perfumes.

A languid fellow in peacock blue velvet approached with intent to engage her. Daliana arose. Adept, she side-stepped the unwanted advance and pursued the more daunting objective: the barbered blond head that gleamed like buffed gold amid a flock of fawning admirers. Etarra's Lord Mayor, Lysaer s'Ilessid, was never a man to be cornered alone. He was the male prize, sought after and coveted, and also, for time beyond living memory, the peril gloved in urbane, handsome charm that led females to folly and downfall.

'*You remind him of someone,*' the Sorcerer had mentioned. But no one Daliana had asked knew the name of the woman the cryptic comment had referenced. The paragon whose wit and beauty might once have pierced Lysaer's heart had not left any memorable trace of renown behind her. Elusive, her secret had died without record: the vital fact that might access Lysaer's guarded vulnerability had been erased from history.

Daliana gathered her elaborate, layered skirts. Trimmed with rosettes of gold-and-fuchsia silk, the style posed a stark hindrance, while steering an aggressive course through the packed social. Three rakish dandies tried to waylay her. Other sober citizens bent in pursuit of town ministers on touchy guild business turned in fuming annoyance as she brushed past.

As swiftly, their sour frowns cleared as their avaricious eyes refocused upon her. More than the insolent sexual advances, such patronizing leers made her grit her teeth. Men tended to underestimate Daliana. Petite, beautiful, perceived first as an ornament, she sometimes mined that mistaken impression for the advantage. But on the morning her mother first marched her into the Lord Mayor's presence for an introduction to Etarran society, her quickness had acknowledged a wary intelligence, unlikely to fall for the shallow bait of female entrapment. Lysaer s'Ilessid was no brash fool blinded by self-importance, or cocked up with the rife prowess to be nose-led.

Then, Daliana had been pushed forward, naive. No armour of experience could have steeled her soul for a sensuous encounter fit to wrench any tender, young heart to palpitations. Attentive charisma and unparalleled beauty were endowed, in one man, to a radiant blaze of magnificence. Lord Lysaer was a vision to sear mind and spirit. Until his arctic blue eyes had stared her through with the acuity acquired through ageless centuries of state sovereignty.

The memory still raked her. Daliana felt inwardly twisted in knots: for one breath-stopped instant, that needle stare had peeled away all that she was; then had curdled into a summary rejection of all else she might grow to become in the course of a lifetime.

From across the thronged ball-room, Daliana suppressed her reflexive flinch. But she did not run or give ground before dog-fights. Fear, she held in contempt. More, she detested the contrary feminine weakness that raced her pulse. Dread would not shake her. Tasked by a Sorcerer, she must broach the impervious wall of this powerful ruler's defenses.

Yet before she could challenge her past brusque dismissal from Lysaer's personal train, Daliana measured her tactical choice to breach his tight circle of sycophants and jealous admirers . . .

*   *   *

Back at Althain Tower, Sethvir might have rifled every strategy weighed by Daliana's alert mind. He sensed the taut tremor, strung through the lane's flux, as her stalker's footfalls skirted the pitfalls stewed up by Etarra's jockeying factions. Without effort, he tracked the acrid ambition that paraded in smiles and silks, and exchanged pleasantries with transparent aggression. Respect curbed him in her case. Daliana was a force in the world, a bright law unto herself. As Sulfin Evend's acknowledged successor, Sethvir trusted her shrewd autonomy. His refined perception confirmed her timed move. Instinct prompted by true-born talent had sensed the percussive ripple, before the night's shattering upset in Taerlin wore down Lysaer's defenses.

'In your forefather's name, my dear, pay attention!' But the Sorcerer's exhortation stayed muffled behind the hand clenched in his beard . . .

The harpy with the gilt-dusted eye paint surveyed Daliana from head to toe. 'Girl,' she dismissed with arid contempt, 'your betters are occupied, and certain to flay skin for the bumptious offence if you elbow into their company.'

'Lasted no more than a single night, did you?' Daliana cut back with scorn. 'Don't presume because I came unescorted. Not everyone aspires to stoop for a steamy roll in our Lord Mayor's sheets.' She slipped past as the woman drew herself up and ducked fast enough to evade the poisonous retort.

One snappish, court lap-dog left behind, with the jostling thick of the pack yet to go, Daliana assessed with barbed humour. The lift of her chin tossed the horse's tail of hair, spilled from a coronet of tight braid and fastened by mother-of-pearl pins. She measured the bodies next in line to displace, from the plump middle-aged and skeletally worn, to the young, done up in flounced lace and extravagant, jewel-toned eye paint. Candle-flame glowed on skin like sateen velvet, or underscored the matte gypsum and rice powder caked over aging wrinkles.

Etarran society was vainly intoxicated on the peacock display of its wealth. The dazzle of sequined fringe, the flare and glitter of sapphire, emerald and ruby as ever lay thickest around the charmed presence of Lysaer s'Ilessid.

Yet before Daliana advanced on that bastion, movement rippled the ranks. The fair, golden prince couched in their midst took his precipitous leave. His closed circle unravelled like jerked crochet as he broke away for a sudden departure.

Daliana found herself smack in his path.

The formal scarlet-and-gold blazon of his Etarran office was garish enough to overpower ethereal colouring. Lysaer posed the striking exception. Blessed with the unstudied grace of born royalty, he was tall but not massive. His poise lay in quick, precise movement. Although the harsh tabard made gilt hair look pale, the sculpted symmetry of his features prevailed. Pretentious fashion fell into his shadow. His vivid attentiveness could overturn sense and derail the most seasoned ambassador.

Yet not today. His eyes, still that piercing, chill blue, were turned inward and opaquely preoccupied.

Daliana realized he did not see her. An abnormal distress drove his hasty steps towards escape. Whether by opportune indecision, or the inspired art of pure genius, she curtseyed and let his distracted state cause a collision.

Both parties were adroit enough to salvage the silly embarrassment. Neither fell sprawling onto the carpet. Each clutched the other as athletic reflex snatched a recovery out of rocked balance.

Daliana captured the crisp impression of disciplined fitness beneath his tailored sleeve. His clothes had no scent. The flat belly, blundered briefly against her, recoiled with a tiger's self-aware reflex.

Lysaer, in turn, met youthful effrontery with nettled annoyance. As he disentangled his long legs from her skirts and withdrew the ring snagged in her hair, he identified her for the under-age *girl* that his word once had dismissed from his court.

That signal displeasure caused him to snap, 'What are you doing here?' while the gentleman's manners that were second nature clasped her waist and more graciously steadied her.

Daliana looked up. Subject to a frown that brave men could, and had, sacrificed their lives to appease, she cringed, almost cowed.

Nothing in life prepared her for the impact of him at close quarters. Nor had the women tumbled to captivation been the dizzy fools unkind gossip assumed. Before thought, all but fatally moved by attraction, Daliana clung to his arm as if loath to relinquish the beguiling contact.

His expert touch moved. Masterful at avoidance, he would smooth her mussed dress. Truesighted instinct forecast his recovery: in the breath-stopped instant while her knees weakened, he would draw her nerveless hand free, clasp her elbow, and assert seamless charge to be quit of her. Daliana forestalled him and tightened her grip. To free himself, Lysaer risked tearing his sleeve. He knew as much. The massive seal ring upon his right hand flashed to the tension of his checked gesture.

'Why should you defy me?' he demanded, annoyed.

Against the regal sting of reproof that bid for capitulation, Daliana rebuked, 'Because, picked to stand in my forefather's shoes, I've been acknowledged by a Fellowship Sorcerer.'

Lysaer lost wind as though struck in the face. For an unchoreographed instant, his eyes locked with hers. Daliana saw through his ironclad poise. For that stopped moment, she glimpsed the desolate turmoil clamped behind his controlled isolation.

How many ever saw past the mask or the beauty? Who guessed that such towering equanimity might break, or that the harsh vigilance of supreme will might be made to mis-step or falter? Behind the buttress of cool self-reliance, Lysaer was human, and fallible. Yet who lived in these times that he trusted? Or did he let no one perceive the vulnerable core underneath the fierce trappings of statesmanship?

Then the opening fled. The visceral force of his repudiation resurged like a fist in the gut.

Daliana stayed staunch.

'You should not be alone, Lord!' Low and fast, she accosted him with a forthright certainty, sprung intact across generations. 'What's more, you're aware of the danger you court. By all means don't waste my time or yours if you are too prideful to listen.'

His dismissive laugh reclothed stifled bitterness with mockery. 'Daliana sen Evend.' The hand she had not possessed with a death grip closed over hers, stroked her knuckles, then tightened down with a warning, near-cruel sensuality. 'What value do you stake on your reputation, girl? Are you so hot to become just another sweet face in the love-nest?'

Experienced, bored, Lysaer's glance assessed her, until every cover of silk and chemise felt stripped to the innocent flesh underneath. 'My taste has palled for simpering virgins. How do you think you are different?'

Mistresses, he enjoyed in abundance, but of their liaison, no warmth and no children. He possessed deadly enemies, ones too viciously unscrupulous to risk the collateral target posed by a cherished associate. The bold female who vied to be more than a trinket and the forward few who played him for ambition invited the fall that bundled them off to oblivion. No matter which woman pressed her brazen claim, or angled to snag his affection, he sent her away endowed with a pension and refused the sight of her forever after.

Some women died pining, subject to Lysaer's quittance.

Exposed to the ruinous draw of his magnetism, Daliana threw the challenge back into his teeth. 'You haven't much choice, except to trust someone. If not me, who else would stay by you? My reputation,' she added, 'will surely be measured by how well I carry the name of my forebear.'

Hard breathing, she suffered his furious glare. When he did not speak, for her gall, she dared him to bald confrontation. 'Either choose cowardice and ask me to dance. Or else pluck the rose and retire.'

The terrible truth stared him down, either way. The bane of the curse, left dormant for centuries, stirred towards an aggressive awakening: despite the harsh clasp of his hand, upon hers, he could not quite subdue his onset of trembling.

'My dear,' he cracked, smiling. 'How could I refuse?'

Between them, no secret, he did not capitulate. His grasp was the opening throw of a wrestling match as he tugged her into the curve of his arm, then advanced through the envious, riveted crowd of socialites and trumped rivals. Marched past the snake's glare of the by-passed harpy, Daliana allowed the most prominent prize in Etarra to escort her away.

Every step of that public retreat was remarked. The sensation of Lysaer's untoward new partner would fly far and wide before the evening ended. The grand doubled doors of the salon swept open with salacious deference before the Lord Mayor that history named as the Light's fallen avatar. Then the panels closed behind with an irrevocable click, with Daliana granted the perilous gift of his privacy.

Lysaer did not speak throughout the brisk walk that paraded the upstart chit down the polished corridors of Etarra's state palace. Dizzied in waves by the prick of Desh-thiere's curse, and hounded by the acute awareness that *somewhere*, an old enemy had wielded Shadow – Lysaer clung to the immediate sensation of his virile impact.

The girl who stretched to match his longer strides would smell the spiced oils his valet used to finish his immaculate shave. She would squint against the raw blaze of his jewels as he passed the crystal-paned lamps, and be exposed, if not broken, by the lewd stares of the guardsmen on vigil within the echoing chill of his marble antechamber. Lysaer felt her slight stiffness as he rushed her steps towards the carved doors that separated the palatial state chambers from his personal suite. Paired with him, she broached that intimate threshold. The door porter who tended his inner quarters and the awkward young body-servant who minded his wardrobe sprang forward to meet them.

Lysaer wrestled the spin of his unmoored senses. Fast-breathing, he gauged the effect on the decorous partner latched on his arm. Daliana appeared no more shaken than she had been throughout the rush that swept her from safe company. Her pert chin perhaps rode a notch higher. Her flush suggested a tinge of defiance, or else betrayed the healthy alarm sparked off by regretful discomfort.

He wanted the innocent idiot gone, the quicker the better. Through the bite of his wire-strung nerves, Lysaer realized his grip on her arm might in fact strangle her circulation.

'Shut the door,' he rebuked.

The poleaxed chamber steward leaped at his tone. As the panel swung closed, Lysaer released the young woman's trapped wrist.

The valet still reeled, his jaw dropped with astonishment. 'Lordship! No one mentioned—'

The shaken steward intervened, stammering, 'If you'd sent word ahead, I'd have arranged for the usual urns of fresh flowers and—'

'No one's been remiss,' Lysaer snapped. 'Carry on!'

Which made the valet jump, heels together, to resume proper service. 'Your Lordship! Lady.'

Brisk rebuff made no headway. The thunderbolt loosed by Daliana's surprise presence *still* caused the servants to miss every blatant cue.

'Do you think tonight's trollop too tenderly young?' Lysaer goaded, his polite inflection a mockery.

The boy lackey flamed pink. His shocked deportment avoided the girl, who stayed silent, as the servant's uncertain fingers scrambled to accept the linked collar of state, then the braid-edged sash and emblazoned doublet, which Lysaer impatiently ripped off his shoulders. The silk waistcoat beneath became bundled aside with the same crisp exasperation.

Measured by the frozen stillness beside him – he deigned not to look – Daliana never once moved.

Lysaer was informally stripped down to shirtsleeves and breeches, before the chamber steward bobbed the neglectful bow due upon his Lord Mayor's precipitous entry. Still shaken, the fellow tripped over his own feet to turn down the coverlet on the lavish bed. Lysaer paid the lackeys' frothed upset no mind. Ears taut for the light scrape of female slippers, retreating, and as expectantly poised to accept her plea for release through the firmly locked door, Lysaer plucked the jewelled studs from his cuffs and high collar. He jerked off the ruby seal ring with Etarra's incised cartouche, then tossed the state baubles with a contemptuous clash onto the tray by his razor and basin.

While the servants scrambled to keep pace with what looked like a conflagration of indulgent lust, Daliana side-stepped the furor surrounding the mattress. At long last, she seized the reins of autonomy.

But not to flee: she packed quite enough of her forefather's courage to touch off blistering mayhem.

'Bring tea for us both,' her cool voice instructed his flustered chamberlain. Then she breezed ahead. Uninvited, she flung wide the only interior doorway. From the intimidation of the bedchamber, all polished marble, gilt trim, and swagged curtains, she stormed, uninvited, into the sanctum of Lysaer's private study. Barged inside before anyone stopped her, she made for the hearth and installed herself on the comfortable, stuffed chair kept aside as his favourite.

Which effrontery left him the one spartan stool, the naked sill of the casement, or worse, the upright wooden seat used to keep him wakeful in the late hours when administrative business demanded his forced concentration. Tonight's stacked documents were weighted in piles by the only visible ornaments: a ghastly array of expensive jade animals, gifted by tasteless ambassadors and kept on the desk to remind him of the ugliness too often masqueraded in unctuous finery.

Lysaer strode in the wake of her female intrusion, teeth clenched as the latent seethe of the curse stirred him to mild nausea.

'I beg your pardon, girl!' Even while distraught, his caustic stare burned. 'Tea is not required for an assignation. Or other delays for society manners, that I was ever aware of.'

Daliana finished her survey of the room: a cold space, as ruthlessly bare of intimacy as his suppressed personality. She met his jab with a sparkle of mischief. 'You're going to throw something, other than me. Why not pick the piece that will smash with extravagance?'

The clay crock on the desk, nestled with quill pens, raised her impudent ante. Lysaer dumped the feathers and pitched with a vengeance.

Bracelets chinged and lace fluttered: Daliana caught the aimed missile with the reflex of a trained swordsman. 'While the Mistwraith's gall rides you, do you always indulge in petty violence?' She set the rescued flask down beside her stitched-velvet shoes. Then placed her pert chin into cupped hands with her elbows propped on her tucked knees. There, with astonishing nerve, she regarded him, tawny eyes wide and dark lashes too bold, and her extravagant tassel of hair draped across her decorative shoulder. The artless strands glinted a rich walnut brown.

Lysaer shoved back the savage sting of old pain: hateful memories resurged, too powerful to smother into forgetfulness.

'I will see you damned as my next cast-off whore,' he promised, controlled frost laid against desperation.

Daliana did not have Sulfin Evend's pale eyes. Or his martial prowess and seal-dark colouring. Yet her style, gloved in skirts, proved just as ferocious as she invited, 'You'll try.'

Only a blinkered fool disregarded such a tenacious independence. Lysaer understood he could not fence with morals. Not against the rare woman who rejected conformity. This one did not fear to be ostracized. Threat of gossip found her unflinching. With social pretence already shredded, Lysaer drew breath and addressed her again with the note of respect she had earned. 'Sulfin Evend slept across the threshold to my chamber throughout the worst of the bad times. He fought me hand to hand time and again, often to the edge of survival. Every harrowing day in the battle-field and in council, I risked his death on my conscience.'

Still, the vixen gave up no ground. 'I was well warned of the perils I'd face.'

'But I did not sanction the consensual risks!' Lysaer slammed the door. He paced as the old, dreaded restlessness quickened his blood to the drum-beat of violence. 'I was never consulted! Did you or that Sorcerer pause to imagine? This matters! I might wring your neck in the throes of the curse. Why should I shoulder the chance of a murder that undermines all self-respect? What if I tell you that such a pitfall would hasten my certain destruction?'

'The whole world stands as naked before your cursed might,' Daliana agreed in riposte.

Sweated by the fact she laid bare his worst fear, Lysaer slashed back with as brutal an honesty. 'Sulfin Evend was a trained man-at-arms. He started with the fit strength and the weight of advantage required to outface me.'

'I should blink?' She scoffed, 'Is brute male prowess the only weapon?'

Lysaer turned his back. Innuendo that struck at his manhood never scored in the way she might think. He battled against a fresh onslaught of vertigo. Those intense golden eyes, the satin sheen on that *particular* shade of brown hair – Ath forbid Daliana should ever discover that she herself was the weapon, incarnate. She embodied the most hideous of his regrets. Past reprieve the instant she first crossed his sight, her presence woke memories that pierced him too deeply. Lysaer steeled his frayed nerves. Sick inside, crushed to blood-less authority, he stared through the dark panes of the casement. 'Child, you can't have a clue what you're talking about.'

Not a rustle of cloth betrayed her uncertainty. 'We are discussing your last line of defense on the hope to outmatch Desh-thiere's curse.'

The yawning silence that followed exposed all of his horrified distress. She would hear his uneven breathing.

Kindness, not victory, tempered her calm. 'Look at me, Lysaer. Then tell me whether the stir of that geas isn't what drove you to flee from the ball in the first place.'

He did turn then. Glacial blue, his eyes turned on her were furious. 'Nobody dares to address me this way!'

He possessed a ruler's merciless poise, honed by centuries of vicious politics. Against her tender innocence, his experience knew just how to stab to intimi-date. Aware how much of her front was bravado, he watched her gather the will to defy him.

'Then go on,' she urged. Her pupils were widened and black under strain. 'Take the next step. Resort to brute handling and be rid of me.'

He felt as though kicked in the belly. Touch her now, he was lost, and to far more than the back-lash response to his half brother's Shadow. 'I have come to regret every moment of trust I was fool enough to place in a woman. Can you claim the impossible fallacy that you also won't come to betray me?'

'No one could.' Her smile was open. 'Can you rest your case? That, under the curse, you won't come to betray yourself far worse, and sooner?'

At heart, *like his*, her concern was genuine. His immaculate gold hair became jabbed into tangles as he gave way at last and raked distraught hands at his temples. 'Either you are arrogant beyond all belief or else suicidally stupid!'

'Then let dare-devil cleverness stand in the breach. You can't truly be fond of those disgusting ornaments?' Without pause for answer, Daliana seized the impetuous initiative and dragged her chair forward across the carpet.

An irreverent sweep of her arm raked the weighted stacks of state papers off his desk. 'Nothing else in your life is important as this!'

While the hideous jades bounced and cracked underfoot, she dug inside the silk purse at her waist and deployed a dog-eared pack of cards tied with string. Her deft touch dealt out two hands on the sanctimonious gloss of his furnishing. The patterned cloth backs were beer-stained from past play in shark's dives and barracks taverns. A hoyden in silk, Daliana laced into his speechless shock for the effrontery, 'We'll play Ten Jack. Five bouts should allow you the time to explain how the rise of the curse will bedevil you. Counter-measures can be strategized, later. For now, who gains the top three scores takes all. I'll bid to win any jewel worn on your person. Choose what stake you'd wrest from me in return. The door's shut, and I'm not particular.'

Lysaer sat opposite in the hard, wooden chair. He would call for strong wine, let the drink spin her head, then seal the document for her immediate banishment. Forward women had been summarily dispatched, before. His facade of amiable acquiescence should smooth even this rank embarrassment with a semblance of decency.

'I'll unveil my stake at the victory,' he agreed with suave charm. 'Promise me now you'll abide by the consequence?'

She flashed even teeth in a blood-letting grin. 'Call the first card. I will declare the matched pearls on your points as my jeopardy for the first round.'

Lysaer took up the cards. His fingers trembled as he ordered the suits. But as he indulged in her offered strategy, the dizzy aggression raised by the curse faded into retreat. The flood of relief cooled down his clammy skin. Forced to acknowledge Daliana's madcap ingenuity, he ventured his first card, then realized, as clarity settled and steadied, that he would be able to think. Perhaps, even, he might be empowered to speak with clear-mindedness while the acuity required to tally the game of numbers absorbed him. With the pull of the geas thrown into eclipse, he might safely consider whether he could risk the unthinkable shame and one day entrust his deadly weakness to another confidante.

Winter 5923

Shadow of Calumny

On the same windy night, the fishing lugger from Lorn that granted passage to the Fellowship's ousted spellbinder made a safe anchorage across Instrell Bay. Green from more than his habitual seasickness, Dakar fretted through each stroke of the oars that rowed him ashore in the boat's rocking tender. The boat's crewman let him off in the protected shallows of a wooded cove. His reluctant first step plunged him groin deep in the ghastly chill of the winter surf.

'Daelion's fell vengeance!' he cursed in falsetto. 'I've frozen my marbles and shriveled my joy at least till the end of creation.'

The crusty fisherman gave a gruff laugh. 'Suck it up, butty! Salt water won't bite. Soon as you're properly stowed into port, some saucy trollop will troll for your purse and flip yer limp fish like a porpoise.' Before the randy gibe saw him doused, the pesky oarsman back-watered his stroke and shot his dory back into deep water.

But Dakar's dicey temper stemmed from a threat far worse than the pinch of dire cold. Dread curdled his nerves as he faced ahead. Shivering with his scant belongings bundled on top of his head, he waded towards the dunes that bounded in the free wilds of Halwythwood. Too much the brash fool to turn tail, he arrived on the sand shingle, stripped his wet breeches, and quickly changed into dry clothes.

No lights burned, here. This desolate shore-line offered no building or habitation to comfort a stranded traveller. Across the trade-road that flanked the coast, the black loom of the trees showed tortured grey limbs, scrawled white where the storms rampaged off the north gulf and blasted salt spray beyond the high-tide mark. Each rattle as gusts tossed through the dead brush startled Dakar halfway out of his skin. He had broached proscribed territory.

187

Any trespasser who strayed off the marked route invited an armed challenge from Halwythwood's vigilant clan scouts.

Dakar stamped on his boots and pressed forward, regardless. He transgressed in blatant defiance of fact, that he no longer claimed the safe passage once granted by Fellowship sanction. Old business drove him to attempt a fool's errand within the heart of the forest. He must evade notice. Duck those formidable patrols for as long as possible, and not because of his driven urgency to make speed.

'Fiends should gnaw out my liver, before I try this,' Dakar grumbled through chattering teeth. After the crippling chill of immersion, his palms already were sweating.

Not only must his rushed step make no noise; the need to stay circumspect in this place also posed a masterful test of his arcane ability. Dakar skulked across the frozen expanse of the thoroughfare. He plunged past the fringe of crabbed scrub, poised motionless under the darkened loom of old growth, and laid his gloved hand against the first of the towering trees: a battered sycamore, ancient and scabrous with seasons of shredded, shed bark. Eyes shut, he plunged into rapt trance. He entrained the exacting permissions in strict form, then borrowed the pattern of the tree's aura and cloaked himself in its staid peace.

When he pressed on, the pulse of his animal presence no longer deflected the flux. Even that delicate mask might not lend the sufficient cover to hide him. Blindsiding a woodwise clan talent was always wretchedly difficult. To ease past the scouts' guarded net of tuned instinct, Dakar must project a seamless accord with the land's resonant signature. Two centuries past, the feat would have been easier. Then, the wracked conflict of Desh-thiere's cursed princes had thinned clan numbers across the breadth of Rathain. But those tense generations of stand-off had slackened after the justice of Lysaer's mayoral authority stood down the entrenched feuds, and by fiat, at the last, enforced change and restored the due process of trial at Etarra. Through mailed fist and gloved charm, his lord's grace had imposed the historic decree that curbed the payout of bounties to head-hunters under his rule.

For two centuries since, Etarra's fat treasury awarded gold only for raiders, caught outside the boundaries of proscribed lands, with those accused proved guilty by law before they were sentenced for a violation.

Where clan presence elsewhere remained suppressed under the True Sect's persecution, in the free wilds of Rathain, the old blood-lines strengthened in a recovery that rebounded with each generation. Dakar walked the more lightly, aware how he skirted the brink of edged peril. He crossed the swift creeks without careless splashes and crept under the vaulted crowns of the oaks without snapping so much as a stick. If he drew the attention of owls and deer, he took pains not to set them to flight.

The least such disturbance might earn him an arrow, shot from cover without pause for parley. He might never see the leather-clad sentry, or hear the bow-string that released its broadhead shaft to waylay him. Distrust ran fever-pitch high towards outsiders who ventured off the road. Light-blind fanatics too often dared to poach for clan scalps, rewarded at distance by the temple priests. The Light's canon promised a blessed reward in the after-life, and paid in gold coin from the head-hunters' leagues to the west, where talented heritage was damned as the ally of Shadow. Inside the secretive deeps of the greenwood, murderous deaths yet occurred on both sides with disturbing frequency.

Dakar ranged eastward. His progress stayed steady until after moonset, when the extended use of refined vision to find his way wore down his stamina. Then he found a quiet hollow out of the wind, laid down tight wardings, and rolled up in his cloak, shoulder braced to rest against the mossy bole of a beech. Sleep found him smiling with smug satisfaction. He felt he had crossed through well-guarded terrain with as much finesse as his former master.

Which complacency lasted until he jerked awake to the kiss of steel at his throat. 'Move, and you die,' an unfriendly voice warned, whetted by a deep-woods clan accent.

Dakar opened his eyes with a long-suffering sigh. 'How did you broach my defenses?'

A brief laugh from the scout, whose ruthless hand rifled the spellbinder's town clothing to confiscate his paltry collection of weapons. 'Nobody ever complained that you snore?'

Divested of dagger and eating knife, Dakar was roughly hauled to his feet. A striker snapped, leftwards, and a second hostile party shoved a lit spill into features screwed up with embarrassment. Before the fat trespasser mustered the words to explain the errand that brought him, a female scout coughed from the side-lines.

'Looks like you've bagged the Mad Prophet,' she announced with vicious scorn.

Another scout spat in his face with contempt, while the one whose hard fingers latched onto his collar jerked him backwards with brutal force. Tripped up by a root, Dakar crashed on his arse. More swords licked his throat. Someone else's vindictive kick bashed his side and robbed him of breath to defend himself.

'Traitor's patsy!' The insult accompanied the bite of a rawhide cord as someone's brusque hands lashed him up like killed game at the ankles.

'I wasn't,' Dakar gasped, indignant with injury.

But clan memory for trouble stayed rigidly fixed. The grudge festered still for the galled fact that the spellbinder had borne witness but done nothing: none of his trained power had been engaged to change fate on the terrible night of the royal betrayal. Alongside Eriegal's, Dakar's name bore the blame for Prince Arithon's captivity two hundred and forty nine years ago.

The heated resentment ran beyond reprieve despite the fine point, that the same oath of debt which enforced that inaction had been sworn, first of all, to save Rathain's threatened crown blood-line.

'Revisit your history!' Dakar protested, in vain.

The grim fellow who lashed his legs did not desist but tested the knots, then moved on to bind up the spellbinder's wrists. No one else seemed inclined to listen: that Arithon would have perished at Athir, long before Eriegal hatched the secretive plot which cast his Grace, living, into Prime Selidie's entrapment.

'Don't try to appeal based on your former status,' the woman cut in ahead of the lie he might fabricate to buy a reprieve. 'Althain's Warden sent word to us weeks ago, that Asandir declared you in disgrace. Everyone knows you've been dismissed from the Sorcerer's apprenticeship.'

'Fellowship service can't shelter you now,' someone else crowed with satisfaction. 'Cosach s'Valerient will tear out your throat to redress the stain on our clan heritage.'

'I came here to ask for his audience,' Dakar declared, justly stung.

'Frost would blight the groves at midsummer, first!' his captor denounced, then jerked the restraints unpleasantly tighter.

Dakar yowled with pain. 'Is this an amputation?' He received no relief, and no answer. Instead, his manhandled senses upended as the mob hefted his struggling bulk with intent to sling him from a pole like a hunter's dressed trophy. 'Cut me loose! I'd accept your armed escort with dignity.'

'Daft seer!' The woman's rough palm briefly cupped his flushed cheek. 'Are you panting to die like that yellow dog, Eriegal?'

'Cosach will grant me a hearing!' Dakar insisted. As a cut length of sapling was shoved through his bonds, hand and foot, he continued his rant against the barbarity. 'The news I carry at least will summon the clan chiefs to the high earl's lodge tent. Count on my word, a runner should be sent to Fallowmere for the cool-headed counsel of Laithen s'Idir.'

'Don't bet your breathing life on that, pigeon!' Stone-hearted and deaf, the patrol's ringleader signalled for an immediate departure.

The scouts fell silent and shouldered their load. They bore the Mad Prophet at a ferocious pace, his strapped body jounced through the whip-lash of branches with little allowance for mercy. Such fever-pitch haste did not bode well. Dakar gave up pleading into stopped ears. Bravado, not courage, masked the anxious dread that, in his case, the arm of the realm's justice might fail. Once before in Tysan, s'Ilessid infamy had decreed the execution of an invested *caithdein*. The sentence then had been carried through with a sword in cold blood, despite the clear verdict that the woman accused had done nothing except enact the lawful charge of her office. Worse than that shameful hour of infamy, Rathain's clans in Halwythwood bore the unforgivable shame of a liegeman's conspiracy against their blood prince.

Dakar endured the hours of cruel strain on his limbs. Eyes squeezed shut against the rake of twigs in his face, he wrestled to stem his rushed surge of panic. He had come alone against the cognizant risk that he could be tried as a scapegoat. If he was duly charged for his part in the past events that caused Arithon's downfall, he feared the vital tidings he carried to avert a fatal recurrence might die unvoiced. The fresh news of the crown prince's jeopardized escape might not spare his neck from the swift sword of s'Valerient retribution.

Stand Downs

Tarens times his move just before dawn, when Arin's tormented visions dissolve at last into helpless sleep: one sharp blow stuns his victim for long enough to bind hands and feet with ripped cloth; and as green eyes open with pained reproach, the crofter snaps his resentful apology, 'No man should be asked to shape his own demise. Taken this way, you're at least free to hate the hand that throws you to your enemies . . .'

Informed of her quarry's captive plight in Caithwood, Selidie Prime alters her plans and calls for a council of Seniors to act on changed orders: 'I want the best of our resources called off Elaira's pursuit and turned to retake the Master of Shadow. Corner that prize, and everything else will fall into place in the aftermath . . .'

Day brightens the mullioned casements when the door to Lysaer's study cracks open at last, with Daliana clothed in immaculate composure; she calls the aghast chamber servants inside, where their lord lies asleep with his head pillowed atop his cleared desk upon folded arms: 'For comfort, you might see your master to bed. Use care as you raise him since he's suffered the misery of a brutal night . . .'

Winter 5923

VI. Haunted Wood

O f the elusive clan enclaves that survived in Tysan, the armed bands
of scouts who risked life and limb to secure Caithwood's free wilds
ranked among the most secretive. Those with the keenest eyes and
ears and the most gifted trackers ran the riskiest sweeps at the verges. They
shot no arrows point-blank from the thickets. Generations of temple persecution had thinned their old blood numbers too far to waylay unsanctioned
outsiders without extreme care. When last night's rash pair lit their heedless
fire on the west river-bank, direct confrontation was deferred until the list of
their allies was known; also who might miss them, and what faction's business
led them astray from the road that gave honest traders a safe right-of-way
through the forest.

Moved in force since daylight, the scouts' furtive presence flanked the
skulkers set under scrutiny: the larger of them a fair-haired brute, likely
outlawed, and the other, less obvious, whose quieter step through the scrub
belied his bound hands as a herded prisoner. Dark-haired, begrimed in a
cut-down cloth jacket and ill-fitted breeches patched at the knees, that one
spoke tenderly, nursing harsh bruises that unquestionably made his head hurt.

'Thank me for the complaint, or I'll bash you again!' the blond fellow lashed
out in sore temper. His grousing carried a crofter's broad vowels, flattened
further by the welted scar that inflamed his crushed nose. 'Bad things befall
folk who set foot in Caithwood.'

The captive's subdued response escaped hearing.

'Oh, aye!' the farm-bred chap ranted on. 'The damned *trees* are said to be haunted! I told you I wouldn't grovel here at the mercy of a bunch of deep-woods barbarians. This way, too, you won't be thrown to your execution without the moral leave to defend yourself. Best do that, forbye! If you don't display some natural fight, I'll stay accused as a sorcerer's patsy.'

The clan scouts who lurked in the scant winter brush exchanged interested looks and raised eyebrows. A signal from their lean captain restrained the youngest, who eagerly fingered the knife strapped over the hip of his buckskins.

The flicked message came back, signed in indignant hand code: *'Who dares to haze talent is no friend to us!'*

'Patience!' the veteran leader returned. *'Watch now, and spring later.'* He leaned forward and tapped the fur-clad shoulder of the rapacious woman endowed with the hunter's gift. His wordless touch urged her to tighten the glamour her birth talent engaged to mask them. No chance must be taken. If in fact the large blow-hard's captive commanded an initiate's awareness, his mage-sense might notice their presence. More, if his source for such power was rogue, he might prove exceedingly dangerous.

The trespassers angled southward meantime, unaware of surveillance. Their course wended through the flats carved out by the floods which roiled over the river-banks when the snowpacks broke in the northern peaks. Spring's torrent would flatten these brakes, where today's grey cotton-tail rustled in hiding and deer bedded down in the dry stands of marsh reeds. Ignorant enough to thrash through the tangle, prisoner and henchman raised enough blundering racket for ten. At their flanks like a pack of shadowy wolves, the avid scouts stalked them apace.

The dark-haired man's reasonable tone drifted clearly through the laced thickets of catkins and witch hazel, torn a bit breathless as his captor bullied him onwards. 'What do you actually know of me, Tarens? Start there. I will answer for everything.'

'Keep your wretched excuses. I don't want to hear them!' The bumpkin kicked venomously at a hummock. 'What gave you the right to revile my brother's most intimate secret?'

'Your survival! Yes, exactly that!' the bound man snapped, out of patience. 'Not one of those dedicates or their uppity dedicate officers knew the names of your family. Your aunt's past the Wheel, beyond callous slurs! But what sorrow would befall Efflin, to lose you? How could I answer to your bereaved sister? Before I let you get killed out of hand, or worse, see you run back to Kelsing in chains, I would act again! Times over, if the bold choice kept you safe. A friend set free without harm is the measure by which I weigh my actions and character.'

'Charm the birds themselves,' rasped Tarens, as low spirits gouged him to bitterness. 'I'm done with your sweet-talker's poison. The croft's lost. My own kin would be mad to absolve me of murder if I defied sense and returned to them.'

Screened by the brush, the scout captain's lip curled. *'Escaped felons!'* His signalled verdict tensioned his slit-eyed companions to lethal readiness.

A stick cracked. The big townsman's angry shove prodded the smaller wretch through a deadfall. Another push overset his strapped balance, with curses against the hell winds of Darkness grunted through the savage yank that manhandled his staggered frame upright.

Untoward abusiveness offended clan mores: the scout captain waved for his squad to close in, with another baleful glance pitched sidewards to curb the blade of the bloodthirsty youngest. Arrows worked best for a swift execution, safest when faced against an unknown arcane talent, where surprise trumped the risk at close quarters. Soundless as the shade cast by the wan sunlight, the clan patrol unslung their horn bows to dispatch the invaders.

While they eased feathered shafts from their shoulder-slung quivers, the dark-haired fellow was speaking again. If he had no identifiable accent, his emphasis packed a sincerity that *almost* bloomed a flare of pure light in the flux.

'When hope dies, you breathe it back to life again! No matter how long it takes, or what time's required to heal the wound. Disappointment will not last a lifetime unless you lie down and give in. I don't know how I came by this truth. But nothing, and no one, will strip my belief that we live by free choice in this world for a reason. Don't buy the lie of futility, Tarens! No matter what comes, or how far the course of your future is changed by my influence.'

To listen invited the chance of beguilement. The clan captain shook off an uneasy chill. Against the peril of a sorcerer's wiles, he nocked a broadhead shaft to his bow-string. His closed circle of scouts backed his choice without argument. Caithwood's defenders were desperately few; a mistake on the wrong side of caution could break their last tenuous foothold, if not doom their rare family lines to destruction.

In stealthy unison, five recurve bows were bent to full draw.

But through the half breath to take steady aim, just before the signal to fire, the tension between hunted prey and poised killers exploded into pandemonium.

'Tarens!' gasped the dark-haired prisoner. 'Hold up!' Ignored, he repeated, urgently shrill, 'Stop, Tarens. Now!'

When the bull-necked crofter refused to comply, the smaller fellow pitched sideways and dropped. Twisting with his tied wrists swung as a club, he chopped the bumpkin behind the knees. Both men tumbled into a disorderly heap. The bigger chap roared and punched back in raw fury.

The lashed victim resisted, at rank disadvantage. Fractionally quicker, he jack-knifed and rolled to wrest clear of the crofter's hammering punishment. His adversary snagged a hold on his jacket; a jerk backwards flattened him beyond recourse. Through a blow to the jaw, then a knee in the groin that curled him, half-senseless, he still managed to shout across the vile insults heaped on him by his oppressor.

The phrases, cadenced in flawless Paravian, voiced an emphatic appeal: *'Ama'idan eth erathiri awen nahil kithiran! Da i'liosmariennt, tur eth fadael s'roth-itieren kiranlaer, dasil'i'laire s'i'kewiar-seyshaleng ple ei criesient lesan'ii'eng s'lesh-llieriennt!'*

The scout captain eased his bow-string and swore. No order to loose could be sanctioned, not now. Clanborn were fluent in the ancient tongue, and this stranger's words were delivered in form to invoke an inviolate tradition: *'Mercy for strangers arrived without welcome! By charter law, under the creed of guest-oath hospitality, grace us with a hearing for an honest request to seek sanctuary!'*

Constrained by strict legality, the scout captain stood tall. Covered by his armed henchmen, he strode forward, his own level shaft kept aimed at half draw on the blond man's struggling back. 'Desist!' he snapped, cold.

In seamless step, his squad of four also emerged from cover. All weapons stayed poised, with the scuffling pair pinned under the sun-caught gleam of keen arrow-points.

Their armed advance rattled Tarens back into sensible reason. Purpled with rage, he opened his hands, then glared in resentful defeat from a crouch that still ground his pinned trophy into the leaf mould. Underneath, bleeding, the surprise linguist gasped through split lips, momentarily too battered to speak.

The scout captain eyed that one with murderous calm and demanded in scornful town dialect, 'Who is he?'

The sullen crofter squared his broad shoulders. Jaw raised, his mauled nose flushed livid, he glowered at the inimical archers. 'In truth? I don't know.'

'Do you not?' A muscled lynx faced by a wounded bear, the clan captain had little tolerance for a town-bred's brute-fisted recalcitrance. His dark glance flashed, another swift stay for his hackled squad to hold their fire. Custom demanded! The mystery at hand must be answered forthwith. To the farmer, who should have been meat for the vultures, the lead scout said, impatient, 'Your nameless baggage has spoken for you! Say why I should ignore my better instincts for the word of an upstart stranger!'

'Because—' Tarens began.

The pinned victim broke in, *'Tadais ielt y'ne ei sielte, krav yadur-thal quenien.'* Despite the hacked cough that mangled his diction, a lilt of sly humour shone through: *'Because he's a good man. Just pigheaded ignorant.'*

'And you're not just as foolish, whoever you are?' The captain did not relax his weapon one inch. 'What makes you believe we'd show bootless criminals the courtesy of a safe haven?'

'The fair hearing, requested,' said the man on the ground. Constrained under difficulty, he added, 'No lie has been spoken. Our need for protection carries an urgency.'

The vengeful archers remained unappeased.

'How many enemies are belike to come after you?' the patrol captain snapped.

'A full company,' Tarens admitted, resentfully stiff, but not reckless beyond common sense. 'Sunwheel lancers.'

The woman tracker among them showed teeth. 'They'll be on the lam, since Broken-Nose, there, accused his runt fugitive as a renegade sorcerer. The chase at their heels will draw deadly heat! Our exposure increases the longer we dawdle.'

The captain eased his bow-string and signalled for silence. 'I agree, we can't sort this mess here.' To the squad whose vicious distrust kept aimed weapons, he ordered, 'Two of you only, stand down. Disarm these outsiders. Then free that one's wrists. Get him up on his feet. If he tries any tricks, take fair warning! The rest of my scouts shoot to kill.' Bleak as nails, his glance raked the crofter. '*Iyat-thos!* Tarens! I'll have the short answers, quick. What turn of misfortune makes you think you've been caught in league with a criminal sorcerer?'

Tarens swallowed. 'My family took the wretch in off the road. We thought him a penniless vagrant. What I saw at the time bears up his claim, that he may have been held for years by the Order of the Koriathain.'

That moment, the scout who bent to release the tied prisoner shot straight and hissed through his teeth.

'Ath forgive!' cried one of the bowman, alerted by his fellow's shocked discovery as the knotted bonds fell away. 'Will you look?'

Bared to view, the captive's right palm showed a whitened burn scar.

'Fire and frost!' the vexed captain swore. 'Damn well be sure, first! Cut back his sleeve.'

A competent slash of the skinning knife parted both jacket and shirt. Flattened beyond struggle as the rags were peeled back, the dark-haired man grunted a protest. His green eyes widened with acid affront as the scouts' brisk handling shoved Tarens aside, then rolled him over and straightened his arm to the detriment of the rope burns and abrasions left by the dedicate soldiers' prior rough play.

'Your custom of guest welcome has fallen to shame?' he accused in acid contempt.

No one recovered the presence to answer. All stared dumb-struck at the exposed, older weal: a mark that looked to have been seared by lighting, scored into a half twist from wrist to elbow.

The captain recoiled a stunned step back. 'Dharkaron's flaming Black Chariot and Horses! If that's what I think, we are stewed.'

While around him, unasked, the trained bows were lowered, his embarrassed regard flinched aside and encompassed the crofter's confusion. 'Iyat-thos, you luckless dupe, did you know? Likely you've tossed us the Koriathain's most infamous prisoner and flung wide Sithaer's gate to disaster!'

'Have I so?' Tarens folded his sturdy arms with unregenerate obstinacy. 'Best ask him, yourself. Then make certain he's speaking the truth when he tells you straight-faced he cannot remember.'

* * *

. . . the voices re-echoed, a shower of sound and harmonic light that ruffled through his presence as he resurfaced through glue-thick confusion, back towards wakened awareness. Adrift, his grasp of himself insubstantial, he felt the swirled buffet as tentative fingers stirred through the layers of his subtle aura. The touch raised disembodied ripples of sensation, then impact: a not-quite-comfortable *pressure* that triggered the heavier, distanced impression of his own aching, bruised flesh.

He vaguely recalled the unpleasantness of a recent bout of mishandling.

Before memory, cognizant function resurged, and the streaming music and colour of speech resolved into meaningful words.

An unfamiliar woman still spoke, her alto voice rust-grained with age. 'Living mercy! What an intricate mapwork. I've never examined the like of such layered complexity.' Her excited quaver resumed, hushed, as the bothersome source of the intrusive pressure probed upwards over his torso. '. . . there. I feel the resistance of yet another entrained working. Pure light. Most refined. Not a blockage, I think. Not like that balanced array for longevity but more of a functional affinity, or an attunement. If you tap *there* with cleared vision, what do you see?'

A second speaker, this one male, replied softly. 'Can't be doubt, this time. Your proof rests in the signature of the maker. That's the genuine seal of Asandir's sanction, the Fellowship stamp of acknowledged crown legacy, and beautiful! Though by glory, I've not witnessed this pattern, alive. Only recorded by touchstone, handed down through my teachers as a rote memory.'

Cloth rustled. After a tensioned pause, a third party clipped out with impatience, 'Then he is who we thought! You will be expected to swear formal witness since the report on that point must be verified. But why in Ath's grace does the prince not recall? How could he, or anyone, forget the feal charge of an endorsed royal legacy? Or wear the deep seal of a blood oath to a Sorcerer and not even carry the memory?'

The old woman sighed, irked. 'I don't know yet!'

'Find out!' Aggravation redoubled by bitterness drove that imperative snap. 'The answer affects our very survival. If the Koriathain have dared to subvert a crown prince's destiny—'

The male seer cut in with firm equanimity. 'He's not sent as a trap, if that's what you fear.'

'Prove it!' The steel sharp voice hedged that abyss of distrust. 'I cannot disarm the chieftains or the council with theories, no matter how certain the facts that confirm a true claim to crown blood-line.'

Through the blast of dissent, the subject set under discussion yet suffered the airy, persistent riffle of the crone's dauntless investigation. Her nettlesome fingers quested upwards and hovered over his head. That intrusion tickled an etheric eddy that tightened his jaw till his teeth clenched.

'Ah, here,' murmured the woman, oblivious. 'This stay throws off spikes. Almost like a sigil, but actually nothing like any I've ever encountered. The working in question was not meant to last. I'd say this prince has been blocked by a remnant adjustment, which now appears a bit frayed. Which explains his lapsed recall. Right here, have a look.'

A second person's touch laced into hers. Combined, the invasive tingle slapped into a star-burst of disturbance. Recoil followed and woke him to razor-edged, forceful resistance. His body arched, a reflexive shudder that savaged him to a gasped breath.

Quick hands pressed him down to restrain the convulsion. Direct, unexpected, the sudden force burned. Skin and bone, he flinched as his shocked awareness crashed back into sensitized flesh. Full cognizance returned with a brutal rush. He woke all at once, blistered by the embarrassment that he thrashed naked in blankets. Bruised and unstrung, his head wheeled, dizzied by a state of mild suffocation that muzzled his natural reflexes.

'Ath above!' swore the woman. 'Mage-trained, indeed. And with a vengeance! I've never seen anyone burn off a valerian posset this quickly!'

Helped by another, her grip tightened down on him. His struggles were pinned against a mattress of deer-hide, fragrantly stuffed with pine needles. Battened in softness, the nightmare recall resurged: of a *prison* spun like a cloud silver cocoon that once had enveloped him in cruel isolation, until he felt buried alive.

He cried out. Fury exploded through him and launched the wild urge to strike out and retaliate.

'Easy!' exhorted the testy old woman. 'Your Grace! Lie still! We gave you the drug to lay down your defenses. For the need to verify your identity, you asked if someone could sound for the cause of the damage afflicting your memory.'

But her reasonable appeal failed to pierce through the roar of his rage-driven anguish.

'Let him go! Now!' Seer-gifted as empath, only the male attendant was equipped to ease the raw gap. '*A'liessiad*, Arithon Teir's'Ffalenn!' he exhorted, enforced by the calm of emotional peace. 'You are free.'

The invasive hands that wrestled him prostrate released him and melted away.

Threat subsided before the tenuous dawn of self-recognition. Offered the true Name bestowed at his birth, Arithon opened his eyes. A breath let him ground himself back to cleared alignment. Another restored him to sharp self-command, while the reflex schooled by past initiate training swept through him again as a shimmer of heat. His skin beaded, then streamed with a purging sweat that stung his abrasions and bruises. '*Si seysha'd*,' he acknowledged, Paravian for, '*I hear*.' Flushed and fevered, he subsided through the flicker of back-lash, while his body burned off the last traces of drug-induced lassitude.

A grey shaft of daylight sectioned the gloom, hazed through an open-flap doorway. He lay under the rooftree of a cramped hide tent, hovered over by the small, wizened woman who served the clan camp as healer and herbalist. The talented seer who partnered her efforts was a much younger man, stilled in her assertive shadow. His wary, cocked stance showed a wind-burned, lean face and a scout's buckskin leathers and knives, worn to the shine of hard use.

A rigorous existence, dogged by scant supply, spoke through such rough dress. Both parties wore shirts of coarse linen, and the woman's leather leggings were layered under a threadbare cloth tunic sewn with an unfamiliar insignia. Typical of poking meddlers everywhere, she pursued her fascination with arcane infirmities as though her subject were deaf.

'Did you catch the same vision that I glimpsed,' she gushed. 'That last working's maker was a female talent, ancient with years, and white-haired.'

Several paces removed, the third onlooker appointed to satisfy the clan council cut in with rattled concern, 'He's suborned by the Koriathain?'

'Oh, certainly not!' the male seer reassured. 'This interaction was recent and forceful; no wicked Prime Matriarch's ploy, but clearly an effort aligned in direct opposition.'

Jolted to an astonished step forward, the peppery authority revealed himself as a man of middle years, with a badger's bristle of greying hair and the squint of a crafty intelligence. 'Then she was the party who set this prince free?'

'That's likely. I think so.' The seer fingered his clan braid, his brow furrowed with thought. 'She did not appear to have tribal ancestry. Yet I could sense that power alive in her. Yes, I'll stake the certainty. The lines evoked by the Biedar who work the Dark's mysteries at Sanpashir are quite unmistakable.'

'Daelion avert!' the clan healer exclaimed, shoved aside to rinse her wrinkled hands. The water in the clay ewer splashed briskly as she expounded, 'Few dare to meddle with their sacred wisdom! Even unwound by partial attrition, that seal might cause harm under an ignorant attempt to rescind it. I won't try. Desert elders guard their secrets too fiercely. No talent steps afoul of their wards without getting viciously burned.'

'Or Koriathain!' the council's spokesman insisted. 'They will be in hot pursuit of this prince. We are thrust in waters over our heads, pinched between such intractable factions.'

At which point, irritation sparked blazing impatience. 'Am I a prisoner?' Arithon broke in.

All parties suspended their discourse and stared.

'No, your Grace,' the man with position hedged carefully. 'Our own record recalls you once shared a guest cup under the formal welcome of Maenalle s'Gannley. More—'

But Arithon was no longer listening. Braced for the savage complaint of his bruises, he flipped back the blankets and, careless of cold and decorum, shoved to his feet. 'Where is my clothing?'

The empath jumped, *fast*, to appease that rankled question, while the exasperated healer continued to natter across the unveiled wrack of his contusions. 'Rest, first!' Drying her prim hands on a cloth, she bustled up to take charge. 'Those wrists need a poultice to draw down the swelling. Afterward, you may consult with our loreist. She should be more than pleased to recite the history of your ties to Caithwood's clan heritage.'

Arithon ducked her purposeful treatment. 'Is Tarens restricted?' he asked of the authority, who nodded, adroit enough to avoid the scrap as the slighted healer gave chase.

'Then if my royal status bears weight, release him at once on my surety!'

The council's man understood when to cut losses. He nipped from the tent on a blast of rushed air, while Arithon's irritation fastened back on the old woman and dared her outright to lay hands on his nakedness. 'The crofter can sit at the feet of your loreist while I take my own path to recovery.'

'The roots of your memory will lie in Rathain,' the affronted healer pushed tact to suggest.

Arithon's smile flashed back at her, edged. 'Have I gathered the events that exonerate me took place before the Koriathain seized me in captivity?' Not waiting for more, he acknowledged the seer's astute alliance and snatched on his worn breeches. Still speaking, he accepted back his defaced shirt and jacket, neatly mended by someone's contrite needle and thread. 'Tell me, good mistress, perchance were you also alive then?'

Faced down at last by his ruffled dignity, the silenced healer flushed scarlet.

The more tactful empath staunched his amusement to disarm the explosive stand-off. 'Your Grace, I'm told your last interaction with Caithwood's clans took place well over two hundred years ago. A Fellowship Sorcerer in fact bore witness. Should I apologize? Our camp doesn't have Asandir in tame residence to provide the first hand account.'

'Then I won't rely upon second hand words.' Still squared off with the healer, Arithon cracked, 'Have you a stock of dried seer's weed, instead?' Which bruising effrontery killed the one-sided discussion since none cared to broach the indelicate question of whether his mastery was versed to handle the herb's lethal after-shock. Vindictive, the healer rifled her stores and fulfilled his upstart request.

In the turbulent wake of the royal departure, the young empath straightened up the rumpled cot while the nettled herbalist tidied up her corked flasks and stacked her strewn packets of remedies. She slammed her box shut, then collapsed on the lid, limp with effusive relief. 'Ath spare me the temper of Torbrand's descent!'

Her associate chuckled. 'On that count, at least, the tales of the grandmothers weren't coloured by fancy?'

The jaundiced healer huffed, then raked back the lank hair pasted to her craggy temples. 'I'd rather wrestle an angry cobra! The drastic exploits his

Grace used to fight the oppression of Avenor's s'Ilessid pretender ought to have lent us fair warning. Convalescent, in those days, that fettlesome s'Ffalenn bastard singed everyone to murderous fits and raised hackles.'

'Best to save your sympathy for our harangued council,' the seer soothed, which summed up her black sentiment exactly.

Fair weather stiffened the fresh breeze that raked the hidden encampment where the patrol scouts took pause to survey the problem that strapped their resources. Aware they sheltered two dangerous state prisoners, now they must rise to meet the catastrophic imperative and provide sanctuary to hunted royalty. Arithon measured their limited assets: a meager handful of oiled-hide tents hidden under the loom of the older-growth forest, where Caithwood's silvery towers of beech and ancient oak rose out of the low ground expanse of the river flats. The lace-worked vault of winter's shorn branches threw mottled shade over the site, selected for fast retreat and quite useless for defensible cover.

Small children in fur caps scuffled between the pillared trunks, kicking a stitched-hide ball. Their vigorous game was played in stark silence, while the drab leathers they wore blended seamlessly against the sun-splashed drifts of the autumn leaves. Wild deer were less wary. The rumpus stopped still as Arithon appeared. Large eyes in gaunt faces surveyed his passage across the sheltered dell, where no adult guardian appeared in evidence.

The combative independence of such offspring required none. Already wise to the hunt, bred and raised under threat of fanatical slaughter, these little predators measured his size, then his hitched stride, afflicted by yesterday's bruises. Suspicious, they eyed him for weapons and weighed him up as a target.

The shattering sadness struck Arithon hard; that in Tysan, the grip of entrenched temple doctrine should stamp such fearful qualities in the hearts of the young. Dormant memory prickled. He flashed back to the recall of a knife in his hand, carving whistles for another skittish band of small admirers. The burst of remembrance faltered at once, broken off by the vicious tenor of these youngsters' mistrust. This pack would shy off from the stranger who sought to engage their delight. The tenacious impression refused to dispel, that grim as survival had been for the clans, their plight had grown immeasurably more forlorn through his years of extended captivity. Here, the marginal foothold that secured their survival could never withstand the onslaught of an armed invasion.

Arithon fingered the muslin packet just cadged from the reluctant healer. The herb leaves inside offered him powerful leverage to seek hidden answers. But he needed settled quiet and solitude, and the bold courage to try. If he scarcely had breached the blocked threshold of his prior experience, the true Name just returned, and the treacherous properties of the *tienelle* provided the explosive keys to pursue his former identity.

Beyond the dense gloom that concealed the settlement, early sun through the tree boughs striped the sere ground, patched in lace-crystal fans of rimed snow and bronze carpets of beech-leaves. That particular rich shade of auburn made him ache, for some indefinable reason. Arithon felt suddenly wrenched by a sorrow that wrung him to desolation. As ever, the reason eluded his grasp. Determined thought failed to unearth any name behind his unnerved state of emptiness.

He leaped across the glare ice of a brook, where the camp's outer sentries passed him without challenge. Their stiff nods mixed deference with formal reserve. One murmured, 'Your Grace.'

That annoyed him. Although their instant acceptance had helped to salvage the disastrous impasse of Tarens's disaffection, the title made Arithon bridle. He flicked the scouts a brusque nod in response and moved on, hunched against the breeze with his bare hands tucked inside the cuffs of his jacket. If clansfolk were raised woodwise, Arithon's trained skill owned the masterful awareness to let the land's flux currents guide his direction.

Unlike the quieter flows encountered in the tamed country-side, the tidal web of the world's subtle current resounded untrammelled within the free wilds. The delicate ripple of wind in the tree-tops, the staid calm of stone and black earth, and the industrious rustles of foraging animals: all things spoke through the tuned range of initiate senses. Tacit listening led Arithon to a small sun-drenched clearing sheltered by an angled rock ledge.

A streamlet emerged from its winter armour and trickled over a matted dam of broken sticks and snagged oak leaves. The span of open water swirled through an eddy, then plunged, burbling, back under a grey pane of ice. The playful music pleased his bard's ear. More, the brisk hour's walk had eased the complaint of sore muscles. Arithon sat on a fallen log. He snapped off the available cache of dead branches and built a neat fire out of the wind. While the frenetic blaze cooked down to red coals, he picked open the strings of the herbalist's packet and sniffed the crumble of serrated leaves tucked inside. The scent lanced his nostrils with the astringent sting of sharp potency. Seer's weed, known as *tienelle* in Paravian, was an expansive narcotic laced through with toxins.

Arithon fingered the cache, dried to brittle brown, but alive to the discernment of mage-sense: the effects would purge his body with harsh force. But while the poisons ran their due course and until they loosened their deadly grip, the mind spiraled into an uncontrolled trance. If the assault frayed his damaged identity too far, he might perish under the onset of dehydration and fever. Yet the risk must be taken. His surges of incomplete recall stirred up far too many harrowing questions. Answers of the profound depth he sought would not lie with the loreists' recounted history.

To smoke the herb straight could unhinge him headlong; an infused tea diluted the efficacy. Cautious, Arithon consigned just a single pinch to the open coals. Flame ignited a curl of blue smoke, which he fanned into a haze, then drew in on a shallow breath.

Still, the whirlwind kick upended his senses. Dizziness took him by storm as the uplifting rush magnified his perception. Sounds struck his ears with unbearable force, and the wan, winter light shocked his vision until eyesight rippled, then shattered. The raced beat of his own living pulse trip-hammered the nerves beneath his thinned skin.

He clung to the log. Distressed, drowned amid the etheric barrage, he tumbled unshielded into the reactive currents of Caithwood's live flux. Against that streamed turbulence, he imposed his birth name with the focused intent to be recognized. If he had set foot in this forest before, he would find himself in the stamped record left by his first hand experience.

Time swirled. The ice brilliance of his present surroundings melted into the warm, dappled shade of midsummer . . .

. . . and unreeled the fleeting fragment of a guarded encounter with scouts amid the wild greenwood. The solemn council convened, with himself clad in leathers and exhorting a bold plan of action with deepwater ships to spare clanblood from illegal slavery. Darkness swallowed the moment. Next, Arithon viewed a night under oak trees and stars, where he touched the teeming heart of a quartz crystal, and on the strings of a superlative lyranthe, he evoked the most plangent of sorrows as melody. Then the black shadow under the oaks melted into another impression: of a lightless, close heat as dense as the womb. There, the arms of a friend clasped his wracked frame while he shivered and wept, and voiced an appeal beyond hope of requital, 'What rightful prince ever murders his feal liegeman?'

Cold bit his lungs to the wracked draw of his breath. Winter's breeze seared his cheeks like red flame. He pinched his split lip in his teeth till the scab tore to stifle his anguished scream. For alongside the birth name he knew for his own, he recognized the volatile agony linked to another.

'*Caolle!*'

Plunged into the horror of nightmare, he knew the slick feel of steel sliding home through live flesh, while his mind thrashed, deranged by a madness of spirit beyond endurance . . .

. . . which shattered . . . !

. . . raked across by the sliced rush of air through a Raven's spread wings. The past friend whose steadfast clasp once had staved off despair in the close heat of blind darkness spoke now, softer words that quenched the fraught echoes of pain: '*This is a dream . . .*'

Wings beat again. Primaries cut from the nethermost void slashed through the cloth of perception, carving up eddies like roiled smoke as Her passage sliced open the gateway to Ath's greater mystery, where he fell, tumbling, lost . . .

. . . light exploded. A power like music arrested his plunge. Arithon felt himself lifted, then spiralled effervescently upwards. The laceration of his old grief fell away, banished to wisps that dispersed as the glorious tapestry that *was* Caithwood spread in panorama over the forested vales in his vision. The flux lines blazed incandescent with life. Their vibrant past glory wove through his being and sang, while the course of the uncharted future unfurled as a ghostly overlay shaded in phosphor. Reshaped by a thought, his sighted awareness might have shared every step once trodden by the Paravian dancers, or else unravelled the thread-fine patterns of every mage-worked construct imbued by the wise. Yet the chance to linger and admire those fleeting impressions streamed by, the wonders of the ages caught up, then surpassed in the explosive course of onrushing unfoldment.

Arithon had no self-command left to impose. His eyes knew starfields, but did not see: he was blinded, deafened, undone by the brilliant blaze of the *presence* that suddenly captured and cradled his human awareness. He had known such, before! Surrounded by what seemed a pillar of fire, enveloped by caring more tender than the blush of a new sunrise, the touch cherished all of his imperfect being as undivided and precious.

Flesh could but weep for the knowledge such beauty had once walked alive in the world.

Then, as from the velvet glimmer of spring rain, a voice with the unbounded might to shake mountains encouraged, 'It is not meet to retread what is finished.'

Wrapped in harmonic sound fit to wring his overstrung nerves unto breaking, Arithon strove to encompass the speaker, shimmering, unknowable, lost to form amid the singing barrage of pure light.

Mage-sight pierced the dazzle enough to suggest the tall silhouette of a being imbued with the weighty immensity of the earth. The creature's antlered head wore the flame of a majesty too fierce to tame. Through a tingle of joy sweet as summer sunshine and the ineffable fragrance of clover, the Ilitharis Paravian bade gently, 'Walk on. Go free.'

Once before this, those same words had sealed his forgiveness. Arithon cried out, undone by a flash-point release that pierced him with ecstasy. 'Brave Exalted, have I ever known you?'

'I once stood as guardian for Caithwood,' the centaur's sending responded. '*Teir'ii'dael,*' he added in formal address for a prince granted Fellowship sanction, 'We have not crossed paths before. The summons that called me forth out of time was raised by my brother, Kadierach, whose life's tap-root sprang from Rathain. You would know him again, since his touch steadied yours on the hour your willed choice embraced absolution.'

'I cannot remember!' Arithon lamented, his sore regret as a spear through the heart.

'*Tirient!*' Caithwood's past guardian responded. '*Abide.* Hold as truth that your steps will be guided.'

Beyond mortal reach, the vast presence let go in farewell. The sharp poignancy of separation inflicted a pang of desolate loss. Arithon shuddered. Wracked spirit and flesh, he poured out his reft protest. 'Oh, Brave! Ath's Beloved, is mercy abandoned? Why has the grace of your kind gone away? Who is left to uplift us without the Athlien dancers to quicken the mysteries?'

The passionate appeal received no answer, but only the fading echo of an admonishment, 'Teir's'Ffalenn! I must go. For Caithwood's defense, you are needed . . .'

From the drifting deeps, Arithon roused to the disruptive intrusion of somebody shaking his shoulder. 'Your Grace!'

The solitary site with its musical brook no longer cushioned his unleashed faculties. Nor had the *tienelle*'s influence waned. The cobweb awareness of augmented vision still flicked at his senses, scrambled to electrical tingles of torment as the intruder's unshielded turbulence needled his nerves.

'Your Grace? Teir's'Ffalenn!' The bothersome grip worried at him again, ignorant of the cramps that knotted him double, arms clamped to his drawn-up knees.

'Go away!' The effort of premature speech slammed the pit of Arithon's stomach to nausea: not yet the fierce spasms of toxic back-lash, but the shock inflicted by a forced reintegration.

Instead of the space to steady jarred wits, the vigorous punishment continued until he opened his eyes with a snarl of annoyance.

'Your Grace, forgive!' The diffident scout did not back off but bore in with a galvanic tension that stormed across overtuned senses.

Arithon reeled, overset by the vivid barrage of etheric detail: of the animals taken for stitched, trail-worn leathers, and the blood cry of the hunt on sheathed steel. Thunderous passion exploded, as well, from the drilled acorn worn as the gifted token of a youthful love match. Through the crescendo of unfiltered noise, the lad's spoken apology crashed like flung stone. 'The patrol captain's sent me. You're asked to come in. A dedicate force of lancers has crossed over the river for an armed invasion.'

The herb's influence sparked off precognitive vision, an unstoppable surge that immersed Arithon into the headlong cascade of unborn probabilities. Poisoned by blood and death, he became the char of a forest put to the reiver's torch. Through the crackle of fire and choked curtains of smoke, he rang to the steel clash of weapons. Traumatized by the terrified cries of small children, he died over and over, unable to separate his suffering from the clan defenders who fell to the slaughter as the Sunwheel troops penetrated the fast peace of Caithwood. His tears fell at one with the wounded earth as hobnailed boots and shod destriers chewed across wasted acres of blackened stumps and sere ashes. Where the head-hunters' dogs found no scent on charred ground, he watched True Sect diviners in glittering robes track down the routed survivors. More and worse, the Light's talent did not act alone. When zealot sinew and resource fell short, the butchery became spurred onwards by subtle sigils spun by a Senior-ranked Koriathain.

Also engaged in the stream of tranced scrying, that one lowered her violet hood. She looked up, warned aware. Through the arcane vista of *tienelle* vision, she glared into the eyes of his dreaming Sight with gut-curdling antagonism. Arithon tasted the malice behind her intent, bitter as metallic poison: *the chase to recapture him had been sealed ever since he had worked his Shadow to spare Tarens.* Clenched by dread that all but stopped his breathing, he slammed into recoil and resurfaced, gasping.

'Your Grace?' murmured the scout. 'Our clan presence must be withdrawn at speed.'

But the bracing tranquillity of the unmarred winter wood did not dispel the sullied imprint of the web the initiate sister plotted to spin. More than the after-taint of smoke and ash raced Arithon's pulse to stark terror. Disturbed by the same merciless power that once had enforced his captivity, he breathed the cold air in gasps until his lungs cleared. Regrounded enough to shove past the reach of well-meant interference, he dipped his hands in the stream and drank in shuddering gulps. More icy water splashed over his face helped to disperse the whip-lash of prescient overlays. When he glanced up to acknowledge the scout, he found the intrusive breach of his privacy trampled the last pretence of dignity.

'It's a gang-up conspiracy,' Arithon attacked. The nurse-maid healer's effrontery also dragged along the embarrassed young empath. Between them, they carried the rolled blanket and poles to fashion an invalid's litter. Which mistake met short shrift. 'No apologies. Pack up your solicitude. Leave me alone if you value goodwill.'

'Time's too short!' snapped the healer. 'We've orders to fetch you. Thank your good fortune that we came prepared for the nuisance since you're unfit to walk.'

'Your Grace, safety demands,' the empathic talent cut in, desperate. 'Word's sent for the war band. But until they can gather at strength, our scouts must move this settlement to refuge deep in the forest.'

'You're already too late!' Arithon ran roughshod across protestations. 'That inbound lance company spear-heads a zealot invasion. More will come after them! Not just from the Valenford garrison. The reserves at the border of Havish will be stripped for swift reinforcement, with men moved by ship across the narrows from Barish and Mainmere. You will face a war host whipped to a blood-frenzy by temple diviners, and abetted by Koriathain! By force of sheer numbers alone, I have foreseen Caithwood's wholescale destruction. Your stoutest defenders will be mowed to chaff. However bravely your chiefs stand their ground, you'll see the free wilds of Taerlin razed without quarter!'

'Sound reason for royal blood to leave now,' the scout interrupted, stung to alarm.

'They are coming for me!' Arithon rebutted. 'Take your children and run. Flee ahead of the storm and leave me the space I require to defang the danger!'

The scout stiffened to argue.

'You doubt my capabilities?' Arithon uncoiled from his stream-side crouch. Erect, roughly clad in town clothes, by size alone he should have seemed a larking fool before experts. Except that his eyes held the depths of a sorcerer's, and his voice rang with desperate sadness. 'People, I beg you! Consult with your loreists. Ask them to measure the consequence if I should ignore the sent guidance of Caithwood's last centaur guardian.'

The scout's awed gasp tangled with the healer's bitter contempt. 'You are unhinged with *tienelle*! Distraught, stripped of memory, and quite delusional!'

They were three to his one, fit enough to overpower his fraught state of depletion. Yet Arithon's mulish fury resisted. 'I will not abide! For the sake of your lives, I will break every sworn tie held sacred, even fight tooth and nail should you try me.'

Alone, the young empath steeled his rattled poise and measured the prince's fraught regard. What he read drained the heated flush from his face. Shocked, he placed his appeal to the others. 'Trust to history. What's left? This prince once swore guest oath to Lady Maenalle s'Gannley in the presence of Asandir.'

Like returned sunlight, Arithon smiled. '*I share fortune and sorrow as your brother, my service as steadfast as blood-kin,*' he quoted directly. 'Don't force me to fail you. The margin remaining for me to act is too dreadfully small!'

He did not wait for capitulation but turned his back and rekindled his spent fire. The instant the sticks blazed, he spilled the entire packet of herb leaves into the flames. Blue smoke plumed upwards and enveloped his head. To avoid being swept under narcotic influence, scout, healer, and empath scrambled backwards to a safe distance. Through their hasty retreat, against the savage uprush of his unleashed senses, Arithon heard a remonstrance from his past, and knew the fond edge of exasperation for Caolle's: '*Dharkaron break me for idiocy, how did I come to swear fealty to a dreaming fool?*'

Then all voices faded as the excruciate torrent of amplified sensation whirled him headlong back into rarefied cognizance.

This time, Arithon forged his purposeful way through the onslaught. Not groping blindly into the unknown, he leaned on the centaur's directive to focus the reflex of his initiate discipline. Exigent need quenched the errant flares of distraction until he re-encountered the glorious, live tapestry that unveiled the flux map of Caithwood.

Amid the unfurled nuance of flow, he found the traces imprinted by mage-craft embedded like whorls of floss silk and stitched light. The brightest patterns wrought by the wise had been evoked in alignment with the dynamics of mystery and harmony. From those, he selected which strands to awaken and amplify. Two and a half centuries of enchanted captivity spent confined to a detached awareness left his talent exquisitely practised: just as he would have settled a wraith, Arithon stretched his inner talent to sing . . .

Two days later, shafted in morning sunlight beneath the vaulted ceiling in the Koriani sisterhouse at Whitehold, the marble floor engraved by the seal of the Fellowship Sorcerer's oath should have cracked asunder.

Or so Prime Selidie fumed as she paced across the inscription with the agitation of a nettled tiger. The violet silk of her red-banded robe hissed across stone's witness to Asandir's pledge, the incised line of runes serenely cool and unshattered beneath her vexed steps.

'I stand on the sure proof! The grand oath stays true,' she snarled at the subservient Senior who witnessed the moment's bad news. 'That Sorcerer swore before my own eyes. Never imagine that I could have been so blindsidedly fooled!'

The seeress looked on in mute disbelief, hands gripped to the quartz sphere kept enabled for long-distance contact. The active crystal all but spat bursts of sparks as the Prime's declaration spiked a charge of frustration through the link to the remiss enchantress posted in Tysan: the one whose trustworthy experience manipulated the Sunwheel invasion staged for Arithon's pending recapture.

Caught as the intermediary holding the interface, the attendant seer flinched as the tasked sister's response reverberated back through the sphere. *'I have not mistaken! Asandir's personal signature taints the working that balks the temple dedicates' advance into Caithwood.'*

Selidie raged over the corrosive irony. 'Then be sure I'm informed in exacting detail! Precisely how has our effort been thwarted? Just what slippery practice has let that Sorcerer side-step the terms that discharged the protection of a crown heir?'

The seeress who wielded the quartz matrix braced her nerves and relayed the urgent demand, while the Prime's impatience suffused the high hall, with its pillars inlaid with copper sigils of guard, and its stonewalls fraught with the murderous echoes of centuries of dead-locked conflict. More than one ancient enemy resented the order's existence. The vicious implication of an allied conspiracy against the Matriarch's higher interests could not be ignored. Whatever noxious reverse stymied her played gambit in Caithwood, the source *must* be unriddled with accurate speed. The Matriarch fumed in tense wait, her coiffed blond hair stabbed by the glint of diamond pins in the knifed slice of outdoor light through the lancet windows.

Beyond the leaded panes, workaday life seethed in gaudy, oblivious colour. The brisk pulse of the shoreside commerce came measured by the thunder of dray wheels in the cobbled street and the warbled cries of the meat vendors. The chants of the muscular stevedores, unlading, snaked through the hectic shouts of the children who raced the stray cats to snatch up the fish scraps tossed off the luggers at Fishermen's Pier. Moored trade galleys lined the bay front with furled sails, crowded as tightly as wing-folded moths into shelter. A gale brewed offshore. The cold eastern sky wore the plumed, horsetail clouds that fore-ran a swift change to foul weather.

Inside, the froth of Prime Selidie's anxiety vibrated on the stilled air. If Asandir's touch had tipped her hand in Tysan, if his meddling Fellowship dared to thwart her by outright deceit, the cascade of consequence would unleash wrack and ruin!

Second to second, the Matriarch hung on the seer's painstaking response. Just this once in the order's long history, she hoped her archrivals were desperate enough to try such a fatal mistake.

'By your will,' murmured the seeress at due length, 'I've acquired the full record for your inspection.'

Selidie spun away from the day-lit window. The flint gleam on her jewels flickered as she passed yet again over Asandir's mark. The marble mocked her, smoothly unflawed by the crack that should signal a breach! Which effrontery perhaps should have raised no surprise. Sethvir's most dastardly subversive schemes *always* came gloved in bright innocence. Though, by the perpetual ache of her scars, Davien the Betrayer's did not! Enraged beyond pride, Selidie stripped the mitts that concealed her deformity by tearing them off with her teeth.

'Give me the charged quartz,' she ordered, her crippled palms outthrust towards her cowed subordinate.

The seeress complied, unable to suppress an undisciplined shudder of revulsion as the imprinted crystal changed hands.

Expressionless as glazed porcelain, but colder, the Matriarch cupped the sphere awkwardly and accessed the chronological sequence stored in the matrix. The trouble in Caithwood had started when the first company of dedicate lancers crossed over the trade bridge, and their squad of advance scouts failed to return . . .

A tracker with dogs set off with an armed escort to recover the men gone astray. The hounds circled where their fresh trail left the road, then spilled into the undergrowth and abruptly ran riot. No command and no whistle checked the pack's rampage. Under hot pursuit, the mounted man at the fore tumbled out of his saddle. He pitched to the ground, sprawled as though asleep, except that no one's rough measures could rouse him.

The tracker from Cainford was seasoned. Years spent poaching scalps for temple bounties had shown him what befell trespassers gone too far into the free wilds: Caithwood's uncanny hauntings were not fanciful tales in the glens where the heart-wood grew thickest. But no such disturbances troubled the verges. There, even the oldest trees did not whisper in waking dreams, and game did not lure unsuspecting men into circles that spiraled their minds into madness. Suspicious of an intervention by sorcery, the tracker advised the search-party to collect its stricken dedicate and retreat straightaway.

The felled victim awoke upon their return to the troop, stalled in wait along the main thoroughfare. Propped upright, he proved unable to speak, which alarmed the temple's diviners. Three sanctioned talents conferred over his case, then resolved to revisit the site and investigate. Taken there, two cowered in hysterical fear, while the third and the bravest ventured off alone and lost himself in the wood. By late afternoon, he wandered back dazed, chanting nonsense that branded him as a Shadow-touched heretic.

Caithwood emanated the language of grace, he insisted between vacuous smiles. No threat of burning made him recant. He claimed to hear music beyond the pale of all mortal experience. In his eyes burned the divine fire of conviction bestowed from the etheric realms of Athlieria.

While the disgruntled priesthood took charge of its stray, and the lance captains barked threats to quash rumour, the Koriani scryer in Tysan plumbed the affray for herself to seek evidence of dark spellcraft.

Selidie took pause, forewarned to engage her defenses before she proceeded. Yet even encountered through tight-laced protection, the pattern of causation relayed from Caithwood rocked all of her jaded experience. The unfurled glory of shimmering lines sprang from a music of such exquisite refinement, the thrill of cadence and harmony raised an irresistible state of entrancement. Selidie scrambled to shed the allure, shocked to tears and a shudder of ecstasy. Even at second hand, this relentless assault could hurl a stunned onlooker into derangement.

Prime power demanded the skills to master the weakness of human emotion. A stalking spider upon that strung web, Selidie recovered her objectivity and traced the signature threads woven through the beguilement. She encountered Asandir's tell-tale handiwork instantly: a historical remnant, snatched from a past grand conjury when Caithwood's trees purposefully had been wakened to thwart a prior invasion. The older framework, borrowed at today's need, lay entwined with others, more ancient: from song cached within stones imbued with the lilt of the flutes once played by Athlien dancers; to the touch of gilt dew on a unicorn's horn; to the grounded traces laid down by the might of the lost centaur guardians; to the deep groves yet held sacrosanct by dogged clan vigilance: mystery breathed still in the glimmer of starlight, where Athera's power coiled yet in dire force, alive where Mankind's step was forbidden to venture.

No Fellowship Sorcerer had wrought this combined edifice: none. Athera's Masterbard acted alone, inspired by the faintest of echoes left imprinted into the flux. Arithon's talent had gathered each disparate theme and braided them into symphonic alignment. Given Caithwood's history as his sounding board, his healer-based senses had not wrought for harm. Gently implacable, this trap was raised clean, until any unshielded awareness that strayed from the trade-road was bound to succumb. Initiate talent, or folk gifted under the heritage of clan blood-line might pass with a measure of impunity. But the men-at-arms and the temple diviners would fall prey, enveloped by an exalted beauty fit to unstring them to the last man.

Fury could not abide in such a presence. Despite ironclad control, the Matriarch's features eased into a smile of wonderment. 'This is purest genius,' she declared at a whisper. Thought leaped at the prospect. The sheer possibility, if Fellowship mageworks and Paravian remnants could be harnessed for pervasive use!

The musician's consummate skill framed a potential not lost on Selidie Prime. She had enabled the prodigal talent, and such radical innovation. Arithon's artistry had been perfected throughout centuries spent appeasing wraiths, while his captive spirit had been kept sealed in her spells of etheric confinement.

The rarefied heights of his current achievement inflamed the Matriarch to a fever pitch of ambition. Cold eyes agleam with excitement, she disengaged from the record retained in the crystal. She returned the blanked quartz to her attendant seeress, and avowed, 'We shall reclaim what is ours for the betterment of our sisterhood.'

No care was too great, and no patience too trying: the order's vast resource must stay positioned for the opening to bring Prince Arithon down: not to kill, but to take him alive for her use as an exclusive weapon.

Today's set-back became a short-term defeat. Though Asandir's presence had not forced the old score with the Fellowship to a final reckoning, the Prime's exquisite quarry could not stay holed up inside Caithwood's protection forever.

Late Winter 5923

Lash-Up

Dakar bit down on the hand that fed him hard enough to draw blood.

'Wretched barbarian!' The clanswoman jerked her clamped thumb from his jaws, unamused by the outburst of laughter from the trail scouts who watched from the side-lines. 'Dharkaron take your feckless malice! I should let you starve and leave the crows the ripe gift of your carcass!'

'I'd leap at the favour!' Dakar groused back. He rebuffed his portion of jerked meat and dried fruit, which tumbled down the front of his jacket and pattered into the morning's layer of fresh snowfall. He raised his lashed ankles. Stamped the food into pulp beneath his contemptuous boot-heels aware that such wanton waste in the lean season stung clansfolk beyond any insult. 'Is a fortnight of captive mistreatment your idea of civil behaviour?'

'You're still hale and breathing,' the clanswoman sniped back. 'That's more than polite, it's the kiss of kindness itself for a traitor.'

Dakar ceded the argument.

For his rough eastward passage through Halwythwood, the relays of scouts who ran messages and supply between outposts continued to pass him from hand to hand. None relished the task. Foisted off with their routine sacks of provisions and their memorized rounds of dispatches, the prisoner had been driven along without mercy, prodded at weapon-point into the trackless forest until his feet blistered inside his drenched boots. Unlike his facile escort, the Mad Prophet had not been raised woodwise. His awkward weight broke through the iced streams. Mis-steps tripped him up in thorn thickets and brush, and fetched him sprawling atop roots and sharp boulders. When his limp bogged the pace, and his piteous groans stampeded the game, the sabotaged scouts salved their frustration by strapping his dead weight astride. Travel on

213

horseback had never favoured his short legs and stout constitution. The abuse, Dakar whined, ached his bones, snapped his teeth, and pinched his bollocks to fiery perdition. Complaints only goaded his captors to make his mount trot, which thumping torment chewed his knees bloody and addled his brain. A man might go crazy jounced for days like a cargo sack, lashed by his ankles and wrists to the dastardly surcingle that clansfolk preferred over saddles.

The patrol captain shrugged without sympathy. 'Suck it up, fellow! We won't have to watch. Tomorrow, somebody else will be tasked with the effort to shift your lame carcass.'

Which trial taxed Dakar's inventiveness daily, since the change of the guard in camp every night saw him foisted onto a new batch of keepers by the next morning. Any chance to wring them for advantage was fouled by his assigned keeper: a purse-lipped, middle-aged female whose luckless ancestry landed him under her charge for the wretched duration.

While she nursed her nipped thumb, Dakar eyed her with such distilled fury, a blush finally purpled her weathered skin.

Her surly glare fixed on him: peat-coloured eyes, festered with hatred. Bedecked with knives as a weasel had claws, and bad-tempered enough to gut vipers, she remarked, 'Our craziest toddlers have better manners!'

'Oh, nicety, is it?' An awkward twitch of the Mad Prophet's shoulders denounced his bound hands, strapped behind his back with deer sinew. The urgent fact that he needed to piss laced torment through his rife aggravation. 'Since when have the tenets of charter law permitted this mockery of crown justice?'

'We should be ashamed?' Derisive, the camp cook tipped back his bearskin hat. He poked up the breakfast fire, too lazy to share the hot water, which soaked the dried winter rations into a palatable gruel. His tin spoon licked clean, and his leather jack empty, he resumed the snide sport of baiting the captive. 'We're called out by the blackened honour of one who abetted a royal betrayal? That's ripe! If you're minded to task us for immorality, stow the lecture till we're on the move.' A tall man with the natural grace of clan get, the cook rose and stretched, dumped the dregs from the tin pannikin, then kicked snow over his small fire.

'That's not what occurred!' Dakar yelled over the popping hiss of the steam roiled off the doused coals. Since the fellow's slur just as callously stained his warden's ancestral birthright, he changed tack and pitched for her sympathy. 'Do you know why your forebear was not cast out, or denied his Named inheritance as a kinless exile? Because Elaira spoke in Eriegal's behalf. She faced the wrath of the clan chiefs at his trial and begged for a pardon since Arithon wished it!'

'How did that enchantress know what his Grace would have said?' his sour keeper remarked in stiff disbelief. 'Or you either, come to that. By then our prince's fate had been abandoned to Koriani captivity.'

'Because of the truth!' Dakar snapped in her teeth. 'Be sure the Fellowship Sorcerers spoke in favour of Arithon's intercession. I was there! Made to bear witness when their effort failed, then forced to seal the ugly bargain because I was the one to enact the debt against Rathain's crown in the first place.'

'We know your hand bound his Grace over to Selidie Prime!' the woman agreed with ripe scorn. 'A loyal friend would have died, first.'

'Except that his Grace forbade me.' Dakar bore that grief, still. Nothing might ease his cankered remorse, that the deepest secret behind what transpired at Athir could never be aired to vindicate his choice of action. The icy gusts through the boughs overhead could not rival the razor-edged chill of his afflicted heart-ache. Since the desperate purpose behind today's errand also must remain veiled, he mustered what dignity could be found, lashed helpless in distrustful company. 'You might believe I complied out of cowardice. But whether or not that opinion's mistaken, kicking me hither and yon as your scapegoat can't overturn the penned archives at Althain Tower.' The Warden's irrefutable script kept the words of Prince Arithon's exoneration for Eriegal's part in his downfall.

Today's contemptuous descendant crouched, forearms crossed on her knees, and stared Dakar down, eye to eye. 'Why?'

'Because, tangled by a misguided revenge, Arithon understood the motive behind his betrayal.' Here, Dakar quoted the prince verbatim from history. *'Grief suffered in childhood broke the man's spirit. If Eriegal dies, if he's cast out, he might never outgrow his child's rage for the family reft from him. Alive to accept the result of his choice, he might heal the wound of his losses. As I have, one day he might find his forgiveness for the human short-falls which led the clans to stand their doomed ground for my sake at Tal Quorin.'*

'A prince's pardon for my forefather's perfidy? Who listened?' The pesky female shoved erect in disgust. Stamped off to girth up the horse, she fired her scathing dismissal over her shoulder. 'Naught but the wind marked the carcass tossed off for the ravens and wolves! My foremother scarcely mourned her mate's passing. Clan record says she kissed the red steel that dispatched his treacherous spirit.'

Which sad truth prevailed: an irrevocable tragedy sealed by a past chieftain's formal condemnation, and forced through by the damnable quirk, that on the fateful occasion that Earl Barach had sworn fealty to his crown prince, the rebellious immaturity of the realm's next *caithdein* had created an embarrassing vacancy. Braggen had been appointed as the stop-gap replacement, charged to bear the unsheathed sword to uphold the honour left in the breach. Awkward with the accolade, the odd, sullen loner had gripped the bared blade and pledged the ceremonial surety when Prince Arithon knelt in trust to offer his back, and Barach s'Valerient, as liegeman, bent his neck under the weapon's edge for the ritual promise of fealty. Which true steel must answer for the horrific defection arisen from inside the high earl's own war band.

Unlike these descendants who reveled in bitterness, Dakar remembered as a first hand witness. Braggen had wept to serve Eriegal's ruin. Compelled by tradition, his rigid nature had not shirked the horror of duty against a Companion, even to spare the youngest survivor of Tal Quorin's desolate massacre. The sorrowful aftermath left its ugly mark on the generations that followed. Grief had rooted the clansfolk all the more stubbornly into their insular heritage.

Dakar's unhappy reverie ended as the day's appointed muscle arrived to press the next stage of his journey. Hauled up by the armpits and dragged like strapped meat, he abandoned his struggle, for once, and forwent his colourful howls. The cold was already too ruthlessly fierce, and quite enough vicious affront had been served by the food spurned under his heel. His limp bulk was heaved onto the horse and strapped down, without anyone's bother to dust off the snow that clung to his haunches. The melt would redouble his punishment, later. Morose, the Mad Prophet groused into his beard, 'Were your crown prince present, he would surely weep.'

'Tears don't feed children,' his brisk escort snapped, 'and pitiful reasons can't undo the harm caused by fools for their wrong-headed actions.'

'Neither does murder put an end to grief, or my suffering ease yesterday's misery!' Dakar jerked at his bonds with pointed eloquence. 'A townsman's chained hound suffers less needless cruelty!'

'And does the dog bite without provocation?' The woman who favoured her mauled finger snatched up the reins and knotted them into the string with the cavalcade's pack-horse. 'Even if you hadn't been party to treason, every time we've left your legs free, you've slunk off and tried to escape.'

'Not to run,' Dakar bristled. 'Believe my warning, you rabid lynx! We serve the same cause. I don't plan to quit your pestilent forest before I've had my audience with Cosach s'Valerient.'

'Who knows for what end, if not purposeful mischief?' The clanswoman's feral smile showed teeth as she whacked her mount into line past a pack-mare with flattened ears. 'Who'd trust your word since you've refused to spill the lofty reason that's brought you?'

The Mad Prophet shut his whiskered jaws like a clam. No agonized interval jounced on a horse could make him open that subject. News of Arithon's freedom was too dangerously volatile to risk outside of the s'Valerient lodge, and without the wisdom of Rathain's high council. Nor would he engage a conjurer's arts amid the scouts' acrimonious company. The refined talents bred into clan lineages had intensified, culled as they had been by interminable wars and ruthless years of persecution. He dared not provoke their deadly distrust and risk the message he carried. The future relied on their threatened prince, lost beyond recourse if his desperate news could not outpace the breaking wave of disaster.

Too often, Dakar sensed the subliminal tingle that fore-ran his bouts of precognition. But day upon day, his precocious talent stayed quiescent. He sweated out formless fears in his dreams, then jerked awake without memory. Exhausted and irritable, he listened to *silence* until he felt stretched unto breaking.

'Hie!' called the trail boss. 'Time to be gone!' While the last-minute stragglers shambled to order, the close-knit party of outriding scouts vanished into the wood, and the pack-train struck out on the move.

The shaggy horse beneath Dakar was jerked forward into a trot. He cursed, and complained of the strain on his stomach. When his moans were ignored, he bashed head first into a low tree bough and let the bent twigs whip backwards into the black frown on his keeper's face. Act obstreperous enough, and he might speed the pace, even plague his clan escort to the point where they took the wise choice to be rid of him.

Three days later, Cosach s'Valerient, High Earl of the North and oathsworn *caithdein* to the Crown of Rathain, forded the north fork of the Arwent and rode into Halwythwood's deep, dappled shade, where the thousand-year groves of oaks towered still, bare trunks garlanded with mistletoe and snow-capped ivy. The war band he kept at vigilant heel pushed their mounts on return to the clan's east-side settlement. Amid the feral, jostling pack, Cosach was the blade on the axe at the forefront. A huge man with a beard shagged like a bear's coat, he came cold to the bone from a fortnight's patrol across the open sweep of Daon Ramon Barrens. An unsated wildness clung to his presence. The great sword in his scabbard was too recently blooded, quenching the starry-eyed greed of a Light-blinded company of bountymen; and his hunting knives, scarcely cleaned from the chase that had bagged two grey-coated bucks.

The dressed carcasses rode on a pack-horse, slabbed with the rich meat found in the remote vales where the golden grasses once grazed by unicorns kept stubborn hold in the briar. But no man had seen the fabled grace of the vanished Paravians for more than eight hundred years. If such history lived on in the mouths of the bards, Cosach did not mourn the bygone past. The late slant of pale sunlight gleamed in his hazel eyes as he laughed at his son Esfand's latest wisecrack. The lad was approaching fifteen years of age, unfinished and rash, with a temper as fitful as mercury.

'You won't cozen us to race back to the lodge,' the war band's gruff captain shouted above the young game-cock's banter. 'Rush ahead, push your horse to fresh sweat, you'll be walking him dry until nightfall. When you get to the bath, the vat will be cold, and the rest of us will be feasting.'

Then the cheerful mood died. A runner dashed up to meet them, too breathless to carry good news.

As though talk had been strangled, the inbound company reined up in sharp order, bit rings muffled and weapons gripped ready for draw in twoscore tensioned fists.

Cosach demanded with ominous force, 'What's gone amiss in our absence?'

'The Mad Prophet,' the messenger gasped, not only run to exhaustion but flummoxed beyond ready words.

Cosach's level eyebrows snarled into a frown. 'Dakar?' he snapped, mystified. He remembered the spellbinder: a whey-faced, chubby toad, always found in the shelter of Asandir's shadow.

Cosach nailed the point that the messenger's fretted distress had left dangling, 'The Sorcerer's not with the sneak coward, this time?'

'No.' The runner grimaced. 'Patrol picked the rat up skulking in the forest by way of the north-west coast. They had him held in bound custody all the way into the settlement.'

'And?' Cosach snapped. 'What happened then? Don't say that yellow slinker invoked spellcraft, unwound the scouts' knots, and broke free?'

The winded runner blushed with embarrassment, rallied his nerve, and said, terse, 'All that. And worse. Crazy prophet's tweaked the flux lines to static and afflicted the lodge with a fiend storm.'

'Toss the damned lard-sack out!' Cosach roared. 'Is the whole cringing watch parked like girls on their rumps?'

'Not a man among them has slept for two days,' the crest-fallen runner insisted.

Cosach gathered his reins, unconvinced. 'Then they're nodding off while you galloped here to sob out their woes on my shoulder? Take over that pack string and haul in the meat as a fit reward for stupidity.' The High Earl rammed his tired mount forward. The panting runner became crowded aside as the restive war band acted on signal to move on the double.

'By Dharkaron's Black Chariot, the problem had better be far out of sight before we arrive,' Cosach threatened the men assembled a brisk step behind. 'Or I'll have the settlement's duty guard spitted alongside that sniveling spellbinder's flensed carcass!'

The messenger shouted in anguished frustration above the thunder of departing hooves. 'We tried! The guard's fashed. Lord, you'll see for yourself. No one can reach the lodge, far less get inside to lay hands on the weasel.'

The *caithdein*'s frothed company drew rein at due length, with every wind-blown mount's winter coat sweated to whorled foam. Their state of exertion at journey's end rushed the horse-boys, who sprinted to snatch up the reins as the war band dismounted. Rathain's clans maintained no permanent stabling since the nearby presence of domestic animals posed a dangerous magnet for tracking hounds. Horses in use were rotated on picket lines, with the herds at rest by long habit turned loose on the barrens to graze. Once the forest camps had been as ephemeral, with dwellings tailored for instant mobility. But that rigid practice eased in the recent years under Etarra's enforced, lawful justice. Lately, the winter settlement dared to include the comfort of permanent structures.

Here, the High Earl's anxiety raised furious force, since any threat brought into the heart-wood placed innocent lives in harm's way.

'I'll stuff that fat spellbinder's head through his liver!' Cosach swore as he peeled off the encumbrance of the fur mantle best suited for blizzards in open country. He paused only to task his impetuous son with the chores required by the master of horse. Around him, the war band stripped down to bare leathers, sheathed weapons adjusted from shoulders to hips, and with javelins hefted in hand, they pressed onwards afoot at grim speed.

Not one trail-weary spirit complained of exhaustion. Hard-bitten and lean, the men jogged the last homeward leg without flagging, prepared to arrive on their mettle to fight like singed wildcats. Except that the narrow trail to the settlement was blocked by a pert woman, near term with child.

She said with an eloquent toss of her head, 'How did I expect you'd charge in like a bull with horns lowered to gore?' Wrapped head to foot in an exquisite green mantle, and her silver-blond clan braid pinned up in carved wooden combs, she stiff-armed Rathain's *caithdein* with a slender palm at chest height, and mocked gently, 'As though a rampant fiend storm could be sliced apart and dispatched by the sword!'

Rammed short in his tracks, Cosach exploded: 'If you came here to plead for a traitor's doomed neck, step aside!'

'Without my kiss for your welcome home?' Mate to his cantankerous temper for years, Jalienne stepped in, and before the grins of the abashed war band, burrowed her face into her husband's wire beard. 'You will raze off the ticklish overgrowth,' she murmured, muffled, then received the dubious solace of his chapped lips.

Cosach laughed, then succumbed and wrapped her gravid form into his massive embrace. The imminent birth was a gift come late, and a mixed blessing, burdened by worries a man handled best by addressing the crisis at present. 'No infants inside the settlement are at risk?'

Jalienne bridled within in his bear's grip. 'I'd have rolled up my sleeves, first!'

Yet even in these times of tight timber roofs, a *caithdein*'s concerns were not lightly dismissed. 'Then that runner met us in a lather for no reason?'

The war band stirred, restless, while the earl's lady paused for a heart-beat and frowned. 'You'll see soon enough when you reach the settlement. Or at least,' she amended with speedy tact, 'you might if you don't try to barrel straight in without thought and a curb on your temper.'

'I'd just perish your brisk tongue the sooner,' groused Cosach as he released her. He detailed a man to escort her back at a more sedate pace, then tossed her too-canny advice to the wind and bolted his war band ahead at a sprint. The problem could be measured, he felt, with the drive in the men kept at fever pitch.

Set inside a cordon of concealed sentries, the clans' winter quarters blended seamlessly into the surrounding forest. The round shacks had walls of vertical planks, kept dry by bark shingles bespattered with lichen and raised off the ground on stone piers. The turfed roofs wore mantles of leaf mulch and pine needles, mottled with the late season's patched snow. Since cookfires burned only in outdoor pits, banked back or extinguished in daylight, no smoke betrayed the location. The central lodge hall itself rose two stories, ringed around the pillar of a living oak. Its weathered beams peaked beneath the wide-spread canopy, whose massive moss-hoary limbs drooped like a convolute skirt and cloaked the building in neutral shadow. The structure eluded the casual eye; but not on the hour of Cosach's arrival.

Secrecy and tranquillity were heaved into a mad uproar by a manic cyclone of air-borne objects that whirled around the site. No natural wind tossed the crown of the oak, but a fiend storm of virulent ferocity. The on-going harass-ment was not random, either. The eruptive assault selectively snatched only those personal items worn or carried by the remiss day watch. Daggers, belts, boots, a treasured hip flask made of horn, and every sundry item of clothing from leathers to small-clothes tumbled and tossed in the grip of the gyre. Bystanders kept their safe distance or else risked being stripped, if not razed flat, by the murderous pelt of the maelstrom.

Cosach dropped his reprimand for the watch captain. Lips tight-set and beard bristled like a terrier's ruff, he surveyed the scene, beyond speech. His grim pause ascertained that the under-age children were bundled away out of reach. Before anyone sighted his approach, or quite realized the war band was back from Daon Ramon, he unbuckled his sword, stripped off his knives, and tossed the load of baldric and blades into the arms of his right-hand captain. 'You will stay where you are. Hold the men. No one follows, I'm clear?' Beyond argument, he shucked leathers, shirt, and laced breeches, then his linen down to pink skin.

'I'll have that prophet's neck in my barehanded grip,' he promised as he muscled forward. The oblivious gawpers caught in his path were shouldered roughly aside. Ahead of the sensible move to prevent him, the realm's *caithdein* charged stark naked towards the rim of the vortex. Neither the cold nor the shouts of alarm deterred him, or the comet-tail of hazing fiends that bedeviled his straight-line approach. Clearly, the renegade spellbinder had steered the assault with intent to repel his clan wardens. The sly trick would not spare his doomed hide. Since Cosach wore nothing the crazed sprites could seize, their rampage would scarcely waylay him.

While he bored in, they snagged at his hair, yanked his beard, and painfully tweaked at his ears. He knew well enough to smother annoyance. Excessive emotion excited the entities' penchant for mischief. The war band's cries of dismay never turned the shaggy head of their chieftain. Too busy dodging hurled objects, Cosach dared not admit the distraction, far less turn tail to attempt a retreat.

The gamut he challenged carried lethal stakes. Cosach ducked a barrage of flung blades. Yanked off a flapping shirt that noosed his neck, then stumbled as, in animate malice, the sleeves hooded his face and attempted to blind him. A ferociously fit man who disliked subtle tactics, he tore that nuisance away by main strength. While the garment's owner cursed him from the side-lines, a hail of shed boots, several baskets, and a stray pot hurtled at him with whistling force. Cosach dived flat. Crusted snow scoured his buff frame, scuffed again as he wrenched clear of a tumbled hamper that burst open and disgorged its load of dried peas. Pelted to stinging welts, he bounced to his feet and just missed being garrotted by the laces slipped out of someone's twill trousers.

As a naked sword cart-wheeled in from behind and nearly slashed his left hamstring, Cosach swore. He forgot the imperative need for constraint as a coal-pot whooshed by and showered live cinders over his head. He clapped out the caught bloom of flame in his hair. Blistered, now furious, he hopped too late and caught a whacked shin from a child's filched game stick. Then a welter of horn spoons clattered into his nape, followed up by a meat fork, which grazed him. Beleaguered, he finally questioned the wisdom of taking the headlong approach. While his sally carried him up to the door, exposure to the cold numbed his reflexes. If the lodge entrance was fiend-bound or jammed, he might perish of chill just as easily as suffer a fatal stab in the back by a friend's purloined dirk.

Cosach's evident danger held the war band riveted. No one cracked ribald jokes or laughed over his crazy predicament. The near misses as he ducked and dived through the onslaught raised a pall of stark silence, sliced by the deadly whistle of steel, and the whip-crack reports of flogged leathers that clansfolk could ill afford to replace.

The murderous rage for the offensive waste drew the fiends down on Cosach like vengeance. A knife nicked the wrist he raised to the latch. Scored to bloodshed, then clipped to a snipped hank off his braid, he bellowed and rammed against the shut panel, and wrenched at the fastening for his very life.

The latch was not jammed. The oiled pin tripped. Cosach's impetuous bulk flung the panel wide open and spilled him, rolling, across the plank floor boards inside. Splinters gouged his flesh in unmentionable places. The sting launched him back upright with a foul-tempered roar. 'Spellbinding coward! My oath says you're crow-bait!'

Yet no scuttling fugitive presented a target to satisfy his berserk outrage. Cosach surveyed the hall. Benches, and trestles, and stone fire pit loomed vacant. The wood stack and kindling bin lent the slippery prophet no haven. The tapestry hangings, the targes and javelins remained serenely mounted on the timber walls. The fire tongs and pokers, the meat spits, the antlers kept for carving, and the pegged frames to stretch the green hides rested untouched in the dusty light shafted downwards through the smoke vent.

'Show yourself,' Cosach bellowed. 'I promise your end could be made grotesquely unpleasant!'

Nothing moved. No sound arose through the din from the fracas outside, random crashes cut by the snarl of ripped cloth and outbursts of clatter as the possessed items tangled together, and hard objects banged in collision. Within the lodge, everything remained still. The chart chests, the lard barrels, the shelves with their casks of supplies and the crates of forged arrow-points, dearly bought, stayed inviolate. Although the doorway gaped open, no fiend broached the threshold. Either the storm was repulsed by design, or the stamped tin banes against infestation were not overwhelmed by the charge the spellbinder leaked as an attractant.

Which finicky trivia did not concern Cosach. He would ferret the verminous meddler out, whatever bolt-hole in the furniture sheltered his shiftless carcass. Spattered red with the droplets from his gashed wrist, chilled to gooseflesh and chattering teeth, the Earl of the North stalked towards the javelin rack, its socketed weapons kept honed for rabid wolves and forest wildcats.

A blanket unfurled into his path from above, tossed over the rail from the upstairs gallery.

'High Earl Cosach!' The Mad Prophet called downwards, his hopeful tone pitched to defang the hunt. 'You'll appreciate why I have to face you, disarmed! If you're also humiliated, that's only just. I've been handled in ways that defame charter law. Kenneled dogs have been better treated.'

'The snake who sold out Rathain's royal line should teach me the meaning of honour?' Cosach chose not to redress his nakedness but snapped up a javelin and advanced on bare feet. 'I say my border scouts were remiss! They should have knotted their rope round your neck and dispatched your misery forthwith!'

Overhead, a chair scraped. The insolent prophet leaned over the rail, his clothes rumpled enough to confirm his complaints of mistreatment. His ginger-and-white hair was screwed into rat's tails, stuck with sundry leaves and small sticks. The brown eyes that glared downwards at the realm's steward held a feverish gleam of annoyance. 'Before you leap for my throat, hear me through!'

Cosach hurled the javelin. The shaft hissed upwards, speared through Dakar's chest with a clean whisk of air, and slammed into the wall hanging behind. There it stuck, its stout ash shaft quivering.

Quite unscathed, the Mad Prophet snorted with glee from the opposite side of the gallery. While the hoodwinked high earl snarled a curse and seized the next available weapon, his missed target added with acrid sarcasm, 'When you're done skewering the heirloom tapestries, I'll explain how your crown prince came to escape from Koriani captivity.'

Cosach froze. His aimed point fixed, he snapped, 'Tell me the meat of the matter straight out!'

Given that scant second of truce, Dakar reeled off facts. 'His Grace is alive. Free, and in refuge with the last clansfolk who stand ground in Caithwood.

He's surrounded by a tissue of wardings raised through his mastery of music. The reprieve cannot last. Tysan's temples have called for a formal muster. To destroy the spawn of Darkness itself, they've pulled three thousand dedicate Sunwheel troops away from the border of Havish. Double that number have marched already from the garrisons at Cainford, Valenford, and Mainmere. More from Barish will join them. When the troops from Tysan's south-east quarter reach strength, the Koriathain will have forged the twisted alliance they've angled to secure from the True Sect priesthood for years. Expect that such combined power will launch an invasion beyond your worst night-mare.'

'Don't think to blindside me, you milk-sucking toad!' Cosach cocked back the javelin. 'I'm versed in the history of our royal lineage. Arithon Teir's'Ffalenn would leave Caithwood's protection before drawing the doom of a hostile war host down upon innocents.'

'That's what terrifies me,' Dakar confessed. Not illusion, this time, he edged out of the shadow between the bench seats lately used for concealment. His short-strided tread creaked the pegs in the risers as he stumped down the open, plank stairway. Brazenly worried, he dared the lethal threat of the chieftain's poised weapon, and pleaded, 'If you will consent to convene Rathain's council? Before you pass out from the cold, I need to know, quickly, exactly what you plan to do on behalf of your crown prince.'

Late Winter 5923

Embassy

The temple's appointed ambassador to Etarra departed in sumptuous state, by decree of the high priest enthroned at Erdane. Tasked as the Light's Hope, he set forth to mend the infamous rift with the fallen avatar. The apostate founder of the religion stayed entrenched and, the most jaded theosophists claimed, blinded by a wayward obsession with his civil office. Lord Lysaer reigned as the elected Lord Mayor of Etarra, while his dispossessed temple kept the True Sect faith throughout the centuries since the Great Schism flawed the unity of the blessed canon.

Since earnest historic efforts all failed to reconcile the grievous fracture, each embassy since embarked to the fanfares and pomp of a ritualized pageant. The figure-head office was never awarded to men on the rise: instead, the politically difficult, the dangerously ambitious, and even the obstructively incompetent became saddled with the dead-end mission.

But not this time. No less than Erdane's most adept examiner shouldered the duty to win back the Divine Prince's good graces. His task forepromised a thicket of thorns. The archives kept the record in painful detail. Lysaer s'Ilessid had packed off his predecessor with cow-horns, blatted in flatulent chorus from Etarra's gatehouse.

No such crude embarrassment could swerve the determined power of this delegation. Provoked by firm proof of Shadow's rising, and fed by the machinations of the Koriathain, the current Light's Hope set off eastward too late for travel by way of the Camris trade-road. His Radiance's train forewent the port terminus at Miralt Head, where in summer's calm, the Sunwheel priesthood ventured the sea, tucked like eggs inside their swift galleys. While the northern gales stirred Instrell Bay to a fanged hazard of ice-floes, and the sparkling fleet lay mothballed in sheds, the embassy weathered the journey in cavalcade, forced across the notched heights of the Thaldein Mountains before winter's snowpack choked off the passes.

The priest-ambassador disdained the inconvenience of camp in the open. Therefore, his servants, his bannermen, and his armed escort of Sunwheel lancers veered south from the cross-roads at Isaer and greased the hands that fed the supply lines which sustained the stalemated conflict with Havish.

Wherever it passed, the Light's Hope bolstered morale. It tightened the slackened reins of compliance with the guild-halls and soothed the cantankerous field generals stuck with locked horns at the border. From thence, it polished the rapacious gleam on its moral rectitude to squeeze tribute from the magnates, specifically those who gouged the Light's treasury over the short-falls that troubled East Bransing. The passage of dispatches meantime overtook the ambassador's sedate pace. The flow of news borne by the network of commerce kept Etarra's apostate Lord Mayor informed of the embassy's progress.

Even fallen from grace, Lysaer dared not ignore the perils stirred up by a dogma that maintained a war host.

His chess-plays as a statesman were expertly set: town ministers who owed favours stalled the high temple's train with politic invitations. While the feasts fattened their gold-belted waistlines, Lysaer's influence curbed their profligate bribes for trade favours, and diminished their bare-faced proselytizing the farther the embassy passed down the Mathorn Road. By the hour the priest-delegate's party lumbered up to Etarra's capital gate, the crisply stacked papers on Lysaer's private desk detailed the personage behind the title's wax seal. Covert reports had brought the background summaries of all his staff, even down to the menial drovers and chilblained grooms.

That list had preoccupied Daliana's young mind since her impulsive foray broached Lysaer's chambers a fortnight past. Ostracized from his court, and rebuffed by his steel-faced servants, she suffered the same treatment as every other female his lordship's fickle eye had singled out for a conquest. The contempt of Etarra's elite society also changed her circle of admirers overnight. From eager suits chasing marriage, she faced the interest of men who desired the piquant thrill of entertainment. She fended them off. First with scornful words, then by contests at knives with cutthroat wagers that fleeced their pride and their purses. The conspicuous lack of a treasury settlement lent her chastity no vindication: only low whispers that her nubile performance must have fed the mayor's ennui.

Daliana met such salacious unkindness with laughter. For displeased and astonished the man had been, surely; as well as blindsided to judge by his effort to armour himself in retreat. Awakened to daylight amid his thrashed papers and tumbled jade animals, Lysaer would have understood she could not be routed by intimidation.

By the morning Daliana braved the bitter dawn streets in her stylish mantle trimmed at the hood with red fox, the only party in Etarra more coldly received was Erdane's pampered priest-ambassador. His dedicate lancers were not quartered inside the gates, a lawful precaution to forestall needless outbreaks of armed rioting. Yet where even unfriendly accredited envoys were received in high state, the Light's Hope enjoyed no such courtesy. Since His Radiance's entrance five days ago, he and his noble train had been left cooling their heels at shameful remove in the outer town precinct.

Daliana did not hesitate to tread those brick streets, or to rub shoulders with folk in the district's mean taverns. Places frequented by common travellers and labourers, with tiny let rooms packed four stories high, and walls of squared stone, crammed at street level with tap-room warrens where master craftsmen wrangled over sour beer by day, and where their aproned artisans brawled, drunkenly boisterous, after nightfall. In contrast, the early hours were tame, the reek of yestereve's carousing chased out by the breeze through the latched-back shutters, and bright with the sunlight filtered through the panes of the street-front casements.

Flushed from the chill, tawny eyes sparkling under her dark lashes, Daliana skirted the outdoor sweepers and the sleepy drudges who shuffled at large to fill buckets. She tripped the iron latch at the Red Cockerel's front door and paused with a shiver of unease at the threshold. She checked the throwing knives tucked into her girdle. Something about the banal correspondence spilled from Lord Lysaer's desk had continued to ruffle her natural instincts. Though the temple's embassy presented its grandiose figure-head with the usual train to furnish a spectacle, Daliana shoved in to inspect the Light's Hope for herself. While Lysaer forestalled her close guard in his presence, she could scout the perimeter on her own merits.

The unlit common-room loomed empty of customers. A listless slattern with ruddy hands scrubbed the floor with a bucket and brush. Another, more alert, mopped the trestles, and recognized the distinctive fox hood. 'Come to collect on some gallant's debt on the sly?'

Daliana flashed back an edged grin. 'Don't all of them skulk from their angry fathers?'

'Shouldn't wonder, the rich idiots, played until they're milked dry. It's breakfast for you? No wonder you're slight, eat like a bird as you do.' The tavern maid bawled towards the kitchen. Presently, a puffy-eyed scullion poked out with hot tea, honey butter, and bread.

Daliana paid up as her basket arrived. To discourage chat, she perched where the boards remained wet, farthest from the warmth of the chimney wall. She ate, tucked in gloom, while eight off-duty gate guards stamped in, noisy and armed, their tread harsh with the grate of hobnailed boots. They ripped off sheep-lined gauntlets, chafed their numbed hands, and bellowed for food and a jack of mulled wine from a lass in the mood for a kiss. The baker's boys came, cheeks smeared with ash from their pre-dawn stint, stoking ovens. Then two out-bound carters clumped down the stair, cheerfully talkative, followed by four aproned lads with dye-stained hands, and a one-eyed smith flecked with cinder burns, whose broad wink thanked Daliana's flamboyant skills, the stakes for which lined his pockets.

The raunchy remarks overheard from the beer tap did not dismay the uptown young woman. Randy goats who sought an unpartnered wench were not these, rousted early for honest labour.

She kept to her corner, while the badinage and coarse laughter swelled with the size of the crowd. As the off-shift hostler trooped in, and the horse-boys emerged from the stables, she bent a keen ear to their gossip. Either the Light's embassy was as it seemed, or her qualms meant the Lord Mayor's superb network had admitted a pack of wolves in priestly trappings.

The ambassador's servants kept to themselves. Their distinctive white livery filled several trestles, at least two dozen grooms required to tend the cavalcade's equipage. Their talk remained insular, not a surprise: the True Sect branch of the Light's faith had never taken firm root beyond Tysan. Their unguarded comments sounded coarse enough to verify their lowly station.

Daliana still listened with formless unease when the east-bound relay of fast couriers burst in, voices shrill with excitement. Shadow had struck east of Valenford, they said. While comment erupted around them, she tightened her grip on her mug. At long last, the first hand news of the outbreak disclosed the cause that sourced Lysaer's struggle to quell Desh-thiere's curse.

'Save us, there'll be war!' The smith's exclamation rose over the clamour. 'Damned to Sithaer! I'll be tempering steel for guild notes at my forge, with my raw stock attached for the armourers.'

As shouts of dismay ebbed to rumbles of worry, only the stablemen in the True Sect's livery failed to share in the excitement.

Cold in the midst of the steamy common-room, Daliana studied the temple servants' calm faces and watchful eyes. A talented spy would be tucked in their train. Very likely a vested diviner, since the breaking word out of Tysan did not unsettle their poise.

As the carters dropped their napkins and bolted before the alarm upset commerce, cadres of tradesmen with furrowed brows sought the privacy of the back corner. Jostled among them, Daliana almost missed the slight, mantled courier who darted in from the street. Agile, gloved hands unslung the strap of a dispatch bag bound in unseemly haste for the trestle that seated the Light's delegation.

Chills chased over her skin, a warning raised by her ancestral instinct. Daliana whipped up her furred hood. She braced for the shock just barely in time as a burst of true vision stormed over her senses. *She saw snow sprawled with masses of battle-field dead. Where the trampled ground wore the pink stains of carnage, and the hacked flesh of the fallen still seeped, the air carried the crisped smell of burning . . .*

227

Then the partial glimpse fled.

Daliana bent forward. A swift, scalding mouthful of tea masked her choke as her gorge rose, but no quiet moment allowed her to rally. Ruffled again by the whisper of trouble, she froze: late to rise, another patron came down the inn stairway, this one ostentatiously robed in the gold-and-white silk of superior rank.

Immaculate in his Sunwheel regalia, the fellow looked discommoded. A big man, imposing, he was no puppet. The splintered gleam of light in his collar studs bespoke choice diamonds, not glass. Florid skin glowed from the use of fine soap.

Fresh from the attentions of his valet, the official dealt the noisy, packed tap-room an irritable survey down his flared nose. Which was wrong, utterly. Billeted far beneath his genteel station, he should have sent for a private meal, served upstairs in more select company.

Instead, the priestly aristocrat shouldered into the hurly-burly. He bullied one of his servants aside to gain the head seat at the trestle. Conspicuous in the morning light, his thinning brown hair, cleft chin, and thoughtful blue eyes identified him as no less than His Radiance, the Light's Hope, himself.

Daliana had no chance to steady her nausea. The road-muddied messenger who unsettled her nerves already elbowed a path to the delegate's table. This unlikely meeting seemed prearranged. Worse, observed carefully, the mantled courier displayed the suspect shimmer caused by a talisman or a spell-cast glamour. Daliana's perception was not easily fooled. Truth-sense keen as the hot blood of her ancestry noted the hip sway that revealed a woman cloaked in male dress.

Which subterfuge spurred overwhelming alarm. Daliana reeled under redoubled foreboding. The encounter before her unfolded too fast. Caught unprepared, she acknowledged the fear, that whatever occurred here involved a conspiracy beyond her depth. While Daliana's instincts raised gooseflesh, the disguised female courier pawed through her document pouch and withdrew a wrapped packet.

Like the voided charge after lightning, Daliana's gifted senses saw blankness: *nothing*. The packet contained *nothing* with such emphatic force, the contents could only be swathed under wards. Wrought spellcraft, for certain, and something else: the faintly electrical taint that suggested the work of a Koriani initiate.

Daliana muffled a gasp, bolt-struck by reflexive terror. *Again, she saw slaughtered bodies in snow. Then the trampled drifts became paper and ink. The let blood streamed scarlet through Lysaer's reports, which detailed the temple's sent embassy, scattered amid the fragments of tumbled jade ornaments.*

The vision let go. Left with the sinister certainty that death would follow if the item in that covered packet changed hands, Daliana had no chance to plan. Her distress, or her gift already betrayed her. She had flagged the courier's notice. The beardless face in its outdoor hood swung to stare, while the priest-ambassador tensed, pushed back from his seat and half-risen to stage an innocent retreat. Another rendezvous would be arranged, with the dangerous peril to Lysaer untraceable.

Impelled to act first, Daliana shot erect, whipped one of the knives from her girdle, and threw.

Steel sliced the gloom. Bystanders yelled, without time to scatter. The little blade flew on course, slit the packet, and gashed the gloved grip of the courier. A tavern wench screamed. The off-duty gate guards reacted and charged. As they closed, tumbling benches and trestles and plates, Daliana caught the brief flash of burst wards. The spelled wrapping parted and bared her marked target: a swathed object fashioned of copper thread-work and silk, barely glimpsed before the breached wardings unbound with a singeing back-lash.

The stink of burned hair wafted up in blue smoke, while the clothes of two bystanders scorched, and the Light's Hope's white sleeve flared into flame. Pandemonium erupted. The gate guards elbowed their way through the press. Their barged course upset patrons and furnishings. The two men in the lead snatched the drudge's filled buckets and sluiced wash water over the screaming afflicted. Others yanked off their cloaks and used the bundled cloth to smother the oddly persistent flames.

The other three guards split off with drawn steel to arrest Daliana. She allowed them to seize her. Nothing else could be done since the discharge thrown off the wrecked construct hurled her talent into a cognizant vision: *the thing may have seemed an innocuous amulet made from scrap cloth and oddments. But windings of hair fixed in place with wax seals, then stitched with gleaming, spelled wire had encompassed the essence of a live man. Truth-Sight beheld him: black haired, green-eyed, with sharp features and a smile that flaunted challenge. With no other prompt but ancestral awareness, Daliana recognized the active semblance of Arithon Teir's'Ffalenn, his presence wrought by vile craft to break Lysaer's will under Desh-thiere's bane.*

Then the courier's sliced palm stained the fetch and destroyed it by contamination. The thrumming howl of power snapped off, with Arithon's conjured imprint drowned out by the initiate bearer's unmasked aura: beyond all question that of a sister dispatched from the Koriathain.

Daliana recovered her distraught awareness, restrained by the grip of mailed hands. Through the panicky screams of a witness, the Light's priest cried murder. More than singed, beyond the misery of his soaked vestments, he also suffered a cut forearm from the knife's deflected momentum.

'Etarran justice will not forgive blood drawn on a temple ambassador,' he accused, shoved forward and officiously incensed enough to cover the false courier's chance to melt into the crowd without notice. 'This assassin will burn as a minion of Shadow! All here witnessed her sorcerous move to attack me!'

Amid the raw uproar, the gate guards closed ranks. 'That will be a matter for the Lord Mayor's magistrates, priest! Etarra does not acknowledge your canon's authority.'

Daliana shrank against the guardsmen's armed bulk. Without fight, she accepted their custody. Her straits offered no place to run, and quick wits under pressure instantly grasped that submission became her the best tactic.

For public assault on an accredited ambassador, she would be removed at rough speed to safe custody. The witch left at large could do nothing more here. The public uproar that surrounded His Radiance might threaten her order's dark secrets. Better, the due process of a criminal trial must bring Daliana back inside the Lord Mayor's fastidious defenses. Lysaer could not refuse to rule on a diplomatic offence except by state formality, in person.

Brought face-to-face in the prisoner's dock, granted her lawful hearing, Daliana planned to snatch the offensive and use the opportune moment to warn him.

Late Winter 5923

Ripples

The servant who bears the daily breakfast tray to Lysaer's private study encounters an unprecedented locked door; when his knock for entry raises no response, he calls out in appeal but receives no answer: he only hears a barrage of violent thuds, followed by frenzied crashes . . .

In Halwythwood's clan settlement, the Mad Prophet pleads for a fast horse to race northward at need, and when Cosach demands to know why Rathain's prince should be abandoned to languish in Tysan, Dakar shouts, 'That's your task, not mine! Forget the ugly course of the reckoning when Arithon recalls I've betrayed him. A prescient vision just ripped up my guts! If I don't ride *now*, Lysaer's cursed nature will fall to an irreversibly vile entanglement . . . !'

In a lonely tower westward of Ithish, the Reiyaj Seeress sits in her gimbaled seat with her pearl-blind gaze turned sunward and sees: an aspected raven abruptly soars north; a galley lately from South Strait rows eastward; a dark-haired prince prepares to leave Caithwood; while a crone in Sanpashir speaks a word beyond time that calls one of the oracle's silent attendants to shoulder a critical errand foreseen for millennia . . .

VII. Confrontations

The urgent summons pressed by Sethvir's news overtook Asandir in the north wilds above Penstair, amid a tense altercation with a young dragon. The creature he faced was grown to full size but not yet fleshed out to maturity. Doused under the massive loom of its shadow, the Sorcerer stood as a mouse. If his adamant presence was not to be trifled with, the dragon's perceptions were under-developed. Its cognizance had yet to evolve far enough to grasp the range of its own power.

'*Push!*'

The explorative tendril of curiosity *shocked* with a force to liquefy matter; air rippled to a shriek of recoil. But before the rock shore underfoot flew asunder, or the nearby atmosphere unravelled to dissolution, Asandir absorbed the wild energy into his aura with consummate skill, then transmuted the disordered blast into a precise word of reciprocal balance.

'*Serenity.*'

The drake whuffed a startled tendril of flame. Ebon claws flexed. It minced the ground where it poised into shreds. Agile as a cat upon horny, scaled talons, the creature gleamed a glorious green-bronze. Its barely grown coil of exuberant strength did not recognize boundaries or know enough to counter the might of its own unfledged desires. Its eye blazed a searing sun yellow with challenge. The slit pupil, dark as primordial night, loomed as tall as its human-sized adversary. Nameless, unmated, too unformed to show the traits of its destined gender, this scaled invader smoked with aggression and failed to regard the Fellowship Sorcerer as threatening.

A mistake Asandir preferred to disarm, if he could, without lethal damage. He watched in deceptive, poised calm, while the arched neck above him snaked downwards. Bared teeth like sparkling scimitars slashed at the *speck* that obstructed its path.

'Push!!!!!'

Enveloped in puffed fumes, rattled by thunderous roars, Asandir held firm. His counter-thrust whispered: *'Tranquillity.'* Clear grey, his eyes, as his monstrous adversary blazed into a sudden, mad glory of colours, its agitated auric mantle unreeled towards the cusp of explosive attack. When the Sorcerer's concepts for *nothing* and *quiet* failed to recontain that burst of impatience, Asandir braced for the next eruptive attempt to fray his shield of denouncement.

Uncanny, reactive chills ripped his skin, as the young dragon wrestled with the novel discovery that it faced an obstructive presence.

Then, *'Push!'* became *'Poke!'* followed up, hard, by *'SHOVE!'* with the sudden, erect clash of crest spikes the brisk warning that its curiosity moved beyond an idle game.

Asandir gave back unresistence, without sound or movement: *'Emptinessssss . . .'*

But the restless drake shook off his blandishment. It refused to be swerved or blindsided. Not after being drawn to Athera by the latest, strayed ripple of an adult dragon's entrancing discovery – Seshkrozchiel, who wielded her bargain with Davien, and who had not tired of the novelty.

Asandir side-stepped a spurt of raw flame, while this creature's exuberant frustration spiked yet again. Its pique flared into an active contempt, sparkled with dangerous annoyance. Any drake provoked into a full-blown rage could unravel the solid surrounds of Penstair, fast as jerked yarn from a knit.

The flesh-and-bone wisp of Asandir's planted form appeared frail as spun glass upon the vulnerable ground he defended. Which bare vista jutted against the storm-whipped breakers of the northern ocean, a place gashed across by the scars from the last outbreak of drake war, fought to a stand-off fifty-six years ago. Spume smoked over the concretion of slag, flash-lit to steam in the rippled air. Stone itself roiled like heat struck off a forge, as the drake's tempest of ignorant emotions shimmered like a flare hurled earthward. Enveloped by the tortured clash of the elements, the Sorcerer gently shaped his own suggestive whisper as, *'Boredom . . .'*

The drake's lambent eyes narrowed. The stamp of a talon jarred stone into fissures, and shuddered, quaking, through the deep layers of magma beneath. One more vicious thought, or a clap of sail wings could wrench the region's geological stability straight to mayhem. As *boredom!* netted the roil of back-lash, then crumbled away without quenching the young drake's aggression, Asandir regretfully changed tactics. In silken, soft increments, he bled off a trickle of the drake's intrusive emanation.

Which crackling, fierce currents he fed to the gale, already inbound for the headland. A savage gust ripped, seemingly out of nowhere, and bellied the drake's folded wings. It staggered, surprised, then crouched, weasel quick to regain its balance. Flame sheared from its snout and boiled the nearby shingle to fumes that stung Asandir's lungs. He coughed, a mistake.

The small noise betrayed his animal *aliveness*. As the drake struck to kill, the Sorcerer sprang sidewards. Teeth clashed, and thought roared! Asandir was not thrown off guard. Neat as a fencer, he fielded the murderous charge, then cancelled the volatile wave as it broke with a rune that shocked a thunder-clap out of clear sky.

Except for the last packet, flicked by his intent, which tweaked the world's wind again. The deflected strike sliced the crests of the waves and razed off their foam tops like a cleaver. Sheared gallons splashed over dry land like poured ice, and the dragon back-scrabbled, hissing.

Of all things, great drakes detested a dousing. This one trumpeted, startled into a crouch. Before it sprang, Asandir topped the aggressive *force!* of its distress with a gushed resonance that shouted, *'MORE WATER!'*

The dragon whirled. Knife-edged tail flukes clove the wind, whistling, while spread sail leather cracked, and clawed talons scrabbled for purchase. Hazed to awkward flight, the youngling fled from Athera and dived headlong through the oiled film web that spanned the massive stone archway of Northgate. Across the barrier, designed only for drakes, its unbridled might was banished offworld just in time to avert broadscale mayhem.

Asandir clawed back his singed hair and blinked briny spray from his eyes. Shaking, beset by the turbulent eddies that hammered the shore-line, he recouped his upset priorities. Three hours belated, he acknowledged the emergency dispatch from Althain Tower.

'I'm on my way, shortly,' he snapped off to Sethvir, 'unless greater need commands my presence soonest?'

His colleague's earth-sense must acknowledge the anvilhead tempest poised to slam into Anglefen. The gale ought to be settled before the disruption raked through the groves in Deshir, and unnatural stress wracked the mysteries there and snarled the fourth lane with lightning squalls, out of season.

'Our culpable colleague sends his regrets,' came the abstruse response, which told Asandir that his requested stay was cancelled forthwith. No cry of emergency might stem the whim of Seshkrozchiel, coupled with Davien's errant genius. The energetic allure of their paired activity involved an obscure work of invention, done for drakish fancy, and set in motion from the desolate, far continent of Kathtairr. Sethvir added, 'You couldn't determine why Chaimistarizog's not minding the watch on the drake side of Northgate?'

'Not yet.' The youngling had been too rash to test its incoherent intelligence with questions. Tall and wind-whipped, a gaunt figure as austere and grey as the storm front, Asandir hastened past the glassine fissures and slag craters pocked by drakefire, both ancient and present. A whistle summoned his horse from the sheltered vale where it grazed in safety. He replaced bridle and saddle at speed, then mounted and turned the black stallion's head towards the Second Age ruin at Penstair. The lumped towers and vine-tangled, melted stonewalls lay fifteen leagues distant, an unpleasant ride under pressure. Yet the Paravian focus there must be engaged before sundown for his transfer to Althain Tower. Sethvir's cagy reluctance to disclose the reason for speed raised concern. Asandir extended his vitality to augment his mount's stamina and galloped with reck-less disregard for reserves.

He arrived in fraught state, met by no helping hand at the third lane focus circle set within the tower's guarded foundation. Alone, the field Sorcerer passed through the grand warding. He saw his tired horse rubbed down, stabled, and fed. Cloaked, and still clad in leathers ingrained with the sulphurous reek of drakefire, he raced up the narrow dungeon stair to the ground-floor trap, lifted by counterweights. The nine flights that spiralled above the first level were ascended as fast. His rapid step echoed past the closed doors of the storage vaults that housed the world's treasured antiquities. Sethvir's quarters loomed empty, with no fire laid against the on-coming night. Above, the King's Chamber was deserted and cold. Asandir climbed upwards, silted in shadow, the wall sconces unlit to greet his return. Other rooms, higher up, bound in iron locks and wardings wore their grim silences, undisturbed. Without pause to recover his breath on the landings, Asandir strode into the library housed on the tower's top floor.

Afterglow spilled through the western sills and chased fading glints off the rows of leather-bound record books. The haphazard jumble of chairs remained vacant, as well as the threadbare tapestry cushions in the single uncluttered window-seat.

Icy air past the threshold replaced the cozy fust of parchment and wax. Except for weighted papers and a quill pen frozen upright in an uncorked horn ink-well, the table-top's obsidian polish reflected the wan silver glaze of first starlight, sky-studded, from the eastern casement. The carved dragon pillar that supported its base cast a sinuous shadow across the carpet, with the looped silhouette of the candelabrum snaked against the glass panes, shut and latched against the bitter gusts.

Cued by Sethvir's absence, and led onwards by the influx of draught, Asandir turned towards the left-hand rank of shelves and pressed a brass stud that looked like a fastener. He stood back as a click released a hidden catch. The shelving swung away on an oiled pivot. A recessed ladder hidden behind led upwards to a trap-door that nestled between the overhead rafters. The small balcony under the outside eaves above had been built for Ciladis, who once had enjoyed the dizzying vantage on summer evenings to encourage thought.

Tonight, the wide-open trap let in the black sky of winter. Unlike Ciladis in peaceful repose, Sethvir communed with the heavens when he was inconsolably troubled. Asandir set his bare hands to the rungs. Hungry and tired, already bone cold, he outfaced his dread and shouldered the climb.

Acute distress never made Sethvir thoughtless. He tended a small flame to brew cinnamon tea, tucked into the niche where the sheltered observatory caught the last rosy tint of the afterglow. His cache also included fresh bread and warm stew in a cauldron, a waxed wheel of cheese, two raisin puddings soaked in cream, and almonds crusted in molasses from Southshire: enough sweetmeats to sate the ravenous appetite of the colleague returned from the field.

Asandir surveyed the spread, then folded long limbs and seated himself. 'Where will the next crisis take me?' he asked outright, since Sethvir's sly tact had not troubled to mask the spell-clad restoratives laced into the readied meal.

The huddled Sorcerer painted in fire-light stirred out of earth-sensed entrancement. His locked fingers stayed clasped to his tea-mug, and threadbare maroon robes flapped in the stiffening breeze. A moment passed. Then the question's cryptic response emerged, muffled, through snagged strands of hair and white beard. 'Havish.'

Asandir all but lost his grip on the ladle as he scooped the lamb savoury over a wedge of brown bread. 'Havish!' Which outburst fell away without echo into the deepening cobalt sky.

Sethvir qualified through a shared fragment of vision: *of an argument in bitten clan accents over the fate of a blond man with a broken, scarred nose, just loaded comatose into a horse litter.* 'This afternoon,' the Warden added, morose.

'That's Tarens!' Asandir exclaimed, appalled.

The misery behind Sethvir's nod left his colleague to assemble the logic: that the brilliant defense wrought by Arithon's talent, which deflected the march of the True Sect's armed zealots, also had provoked an unforeseen back-lash. The ancient lineages were bred to withstand the sharp rise in resonance that now rendered Caithwood's reactive flux currents a dire hazard to hapless outsiders. Town-born, and brought far inside the forest as a guest of the clans, the crofter possessed no such protection. Afflicted by dreams, then stunned to raving madness as the shock unhinged changed perceptions, the beset mind would shut down. Left unattended, the false haven of unconsciousness could progress into wasting decline. Tarens risked death without an initiate's know-ledge to seek restored balance.

'My oath prevents aid if the man should succumb,' Asandir snapped with gruff bitterness. 'Unless, of course, someone overrules Arithon's headstrong loyalty. Can the chieftain's enclave shake him to his senses, or press him against his grain to abandon a friendship?'

'Not yet,' Sethvir whispered. 'Rather, the clan healers have drugged Tarens senseless with possets. They acted by Arithon's request, hoping to buy enough time to carry the stricken crofter past range of Caithwood's uncanny influence.' With his Grace's active involvement, no Fellowship Sorcerer might intervene.

237

Asandir railed in bitter exasperation, 'Ath forfend! Such adamant heart will drive us straight to ruin. Our prince might break outright for the loss of another man bound under his protection.'

'His Grace doesn't recall that history, yet,' Sethvir admitted. 'He's barely encountered the sorry fact his own hand caused Caolle's death.'

Even so, the instinctive contour of yesteryear's horrors shadowed Arithon's determined choices. The cruel roll-call of names, and the grief impressed by more than one steadfast friend's fatal stand had firmed a character that would not forsake another comrade to die. No argument might swerve the foolish departure shouldered in Tarens's behalf. Sethvir allowed, not resigned, 'The fellow does have a chance to survive, perhaps even recover his wits without harm.'

'If he escapes the reach of Caithwood's raised mysteries in time,' Asandir cracked in frustration. 'And at an unconscionable risk to Rathain's irreplaceable blood-line!' Helpless to defang that intractable thorn, the field Sorcerer ploughed into his meal, and chased the suspiciously side-tracked purpose for his destination. 'Then I'm bound back to Havish to hasten the High King's unfinished training? That doesn't explain the rush on my recall.'

Sethvir sighed, and admitted, 'The throne may require the might of its crown jewels in defense.'

Asandir grunted, strong jaws busy. The bind in that political chess game was clear. If Arithon's ill-advised effort succeeded, if he slipped past the armed blockade at Tysan's border and brought Tarens to sanctuary under the charter law that ruled Havish, the by-play could ignite war. Reviled as the infamous Spinner of Darkness, he very well could draw the militant might of the True Sect religion.

Sethvir said with crisp delicacy, 'You've a handful of days, and not weeks, to complete your task at Telmandir and withdraw, lest our Fellowship should become forsworn.'

'But that would mean Arithon—' Which brute gist put the torch to Asandir's patience. 'Dharkaron Avenge! Who's tipped the black hand of the priests to spark a concerted invasion?'

'The Prime herself. We granted her opening. Since Arithon's escape, she's used fear and suggestion, aligned with false writ to manipulate canon policy from the high temple at Erdane. She's turned the Light's muster to further her own ends.' Into the snap-frozen stillness of shock, Sethvir temporized, 'Well, we knew she was only biding her time to unseat the throne and break the compact in Havish!'

The sorry conclusion granted no quarter: for in fact the odds had been stacked for centuries, that someone's invasive arcane manoeuvring might rekindle Lysaer's false cause. Arithon's fate offered the convenient linch-pin, with the poisonous plot pervasively shielded by Asandir's stay of noninterference. Sethvir's conclusion fell like a thunder-clap. 'We cannot back the high king's defense, should Arithon's presence breach Havish's border! You must agree that our line of intent would be clouded.'

'I'll have King Gestry prepared to wield the crown jewels.' Such innocuous words, against the flash-point rage that flickered in Asandir's eyes.

Sethvir tried and failed to recoup shattered calm amid the sharp current of tension. 'I've known your heart, friend, too long and too well. It's scarcely your nature to sit still and take this.'

Yet Asandir's anger did not unleash. Ruggedly outlined in stars, he demanded, 'Don't side-step! You haven't disclosed the worst, yet. Best give the rest, quickly. What other disastrous development must be left to run amok at my back?'

Beyond bearing now, the weighted pause stretched, filled by the delicate tingle as hoar-frost etched patterns across the slate roof.

'You'd have the fraught list?' Sethvir's sideward glance of naked appeal met the chiselled rock of his colleague's rapt focus. 'I would prefer to slit open my veins first!'

Asandir applied himself to his meal. Overhead, silent, the silver stars turned. An owl's plangent hoot haunted the dark, while a bloated, late moon notched the barren hills to the east and limned the stone tower in eldritch light.

Merciless, the field Sorcerer's quiet impatience cut deep as a surgeon's blade.

Even Sethvir's ironclad reluctance gave way. 'If the cascade begins, we'll face the torrent, regardless.' Resigned, he unburdened the damning scope of Prime Selidie's covert plan. 'Her insidious prompts angled for the certainty that the Light's Hope dispatched to Etarra included a trained diviner, as well as the most influential of Erdane's temple examiners.'

Asandir's glance turned baleful. He grasped the design: when word broke, and the witnessed proof of Shadow's re-emergence in Tysan reached Lysaer, the inflammatory news would incite an unguarded moment of vulnerability. 'And the catalyst?'

Sethvir disclosed the recipe with distaste. 'A Koriani initiate was bidden to transfer an enabled fetch into the corrupted grasp of the temple's delegate.' Seed for deadly mayhem, that cloth figure had been charged by a stolen lock of Prince Arithon's hair, and the infused record of his aura, taken under the influence of Desh-thiere's curse. Handed off to the ambitious priest, the ugly construct aimed to plunge *Lysaer* into the throes of the Mistwraith's geas.

Asandir's shove to arise met Sethvir's cry of anguish. 'The subversive entrainment's already in play!'

'When?' Asandir shouted.

The Warden's sent images fleshed out his cold-cast recap of the crux that unfolded at sunrise, in public, inside of a crowded tavern. Prime Selidie's bold thrust had been thwarted when the young woman sworn to stand guard for Lysaer stepped forward into the breach at Etarra. Her accurate knife throw had destroyed the fetch on the fly without wisdom's thought for the consequence.

Asandir flinched. 'Daliana?'

'Alive!' Sethvir stated, but with the drawn sorrow that warned of events still in flux and poised to turn for the worse. He raised open hands, barely able to stem the recoil of Asandir's anguish. 'She's in jeopardy, not lost. Share her straits for yourself . . .'

The Lord Mayor's justice was ironclad law at Etarra, enforced by tyranny and the sword until Lysaer's adamant rule forged the constancy of due process. Yet on the day Daliana stood accused of felony, sunset came and went without the established hearing and formal arraignment. The long hours spent behind bars without summons wore her to shredded nerves. She paced the tight confines of a locked cell, steps multiplied by the echoes bounced off the vaulted brick dungeon built beneath the magistrate's ward-room. Shivering from the dank chill, Daliana fumed without recourse.

'Damn all to the thorns of disgruntled male pride! State cause ought to trump the pitfall of embarrassment.' Again, she shouted down the vacated corridor outside the grille. 'Roust up your officers and bring on the temple's stuck pig! Make the man show his cowardly face in complaint or else let me go without charges!'

But no guards arrived to conduct her upstairs. Nightfall doused the light through the sunken window well and plunged the cold air into oppressive darkness. Blindly, she counted her steps to and fro: click, click, plonk, as her fashionable winter boots rang against the metal drain cover set in the floor. Etarran justice did not endorse misery. The stone underfoot was swept bare, scrubbed often enough not to soil the pert mantle that swished at her ankles. If her fox-fur hood lay rumpled from rough handling, the town guard had not rifled her jasper clasp pin when they confiscated her weapons. Brusque efficiency had not led to incivility: jeering comments had not become threats. No one's lewd fingers had harassed her modesty, and plain fare was provided at meal-times.

Daliana refused to be rattled by the contemptuous slangs of her gaolers. Rough men, honest about an infraction made in the presence of witnesses, they had every reason to think her conviction would be wrapped up in short order. But as the hours crawled past, the pressured anxiety over her hearing cranked Daliana near to the breaking point.

Someone's scraped tread approached from the stairwell. Daliana whirled, incandescent with hope. Summoned before Lysaer's overdue presence, she could deliver her warning of danger at last.

But no relief came. Not a palace official in the elite colours of the Lord Mayor's livery. Instead, the magistrate's garrulous warden arrived on his rounds to collect the supper tray.

If his cheerless duties did not cosset the guilty, his ornery nature softened with females. He unclenched the toothpick from his bearded jaws and chattered through the noise as his gaunt turnkey unlocked the door and removed the used crockery. 'Can't take your parole, sweet. It's the bars, till your trial, and belike the same until you've been served with your sentence. Though our Lord Mayor's scarcely on back-scratching terms with yon priests, I'll admit. There's some might applaud your raw cheek for pinking that pompous temple ambassador.'

'My knives hit on target when I choose to throw,' Daliana retorted.

'Spelled blades would do that,' the turnkey avowed, then spat at her feet in contempt. He scuttled backwards, juggling the tray, resecured the door, and with smug finality, hooked the key-ring back onto his studded belt. 'Should've realized, maybe, that the Light's ambassador would be righteously protected before you tried murder by sorcery.'

'Yon wee vixen's no witch,' the warden scoffed.

'Is she not?' The turnkey gave Daliana his wall-eyed inspection, and uneasily licked yellowed teeth. 'True Sect says otherwise.' Roughshod over her outrage for the delay that forestalled her fair hearing, he added, 'Shouldn't take foolish chances, myself. Or leave a chit on a black-sorcery charge down here without chains after midnight.'

'She's Etarran born and from a good family,' the plump warden protested. But his beefy fingers nervously fumbled to kindle the wall sconce in the dimmed corridor. 'And taking the mayor's pay as we do? It's disloyal to repeat the Light's claptrap, that his Lordship's their downfallen avatar.'

The turnkey shuffled ahead, immersed in his dour argument. 'You'd risk an after-life with the damned, swayed by the cant of a heretic?'

The warden's bass tone rumbled back through the tramp of his staid retreat. 'I'd have to swallow the false canon, first off. Which I don't. Lord Lysaer himself gives that nonsense no credence.'

'But your knife-throwing snip's a direct sen Evend descendant! Did that vicious fact slip your notice?' The turnkey's jutted chin swivelled under the caught flicker of flame light. His jaundiced stare raked the suspect's locked cell with naked malevolence. 'Besides the blood taint passed down through that lineage, I don't trust the pretty ones. Never did. Shied from their wickedness, so I have, just. My blessed mother warned me to steer clear since I was a brat in the cradle.'

Daliana called after him, 'That's a lame-brained excuse for the more truthful slight, that generous women won't have you!'

But no retort came as her gaolers retired to the snug comfort of the upstairs ward-room.

Alone behind bars, and left the lit torch out of fear that Darkness itself was her ally, Daliana fretted, beyond desperate to pass on her urgent message. Lysaer himself must conduct her arraignment or risk a state insult against Erdane's titled ambassador. Yet night deepened around her. The hour grew late.

By the midnight change in the guard, even the warden's apple-cheeked optimism could not dismiss the upset as routine. Daliana overheard his querulous uncertainty, badgered by the windy turnkey's fanaticism and other snatches of unsettled gossip that filtered down to her cell as men idled through their turn of duty. Time passed. Anxiety chewed her shaken nerves ragged. Then, from outside, eruptions of shouting drifted in on the drought through the window well. Rushed footsteps warned of unrest in the street. When the marched tramp of hobnailed boots indicated a forceful muster of soldiers, Daliana broke into a cold sweat.

Nothing was right. Trouble developed, disturbingly fast, ominous as the rip at the tide's change. Whatever Lysaer's situation, since morning, his governance at Etarra had veered off its steadfast course. Daliana slumped against the brick wall. Forehead cradled in trembling hands, she realized her desperate effort at dawn might not have averted the plunge towards disaster. Though the threatening spelled construct had been discharged, the secretive enchantress in courier's clothes had escaped. Dark craftwork done once could be repeated. Lysaer's downfall might have been deferred by no more than a brief inconvenience.

'Spare the worst,' Daliana pleaded at a whisper. She missed the gentle advice of her father, whose reasoned calm during earliest childhood always had quelled her worst nightmares. But his past reassurance that most worries were phantoms did not avail her, or ease her brooding distress. Instead, she encountered her bleakest fears when a dozen Etarran guardsmen arrived to reinforce the watch assigned to the dungeon.

Their tumultuous news reached the prisoner's cell as their sergeant supplanted the magistrate's warden. 'She's to stay under more than lock and key. Condemned for assault on the temple's ambassador, yes. And blamed for malign practice, too. Sorcery, aye! Why else would she turn in murderous malice against the Light's sanctioned delegate, who bears the rank of a temple examiner?'

'This verdict is called before an arraignment?' the warden pealed back, incredulous. 'Whose authority has upset the process of law? No Etarran case proceeds without a hearing. Not in anyone's memory! Lord Mayor Lysaer will never endorse the reverse.'

'Under seal and signature, he already has,' another party rebutted. 'Oh, yes! The sentence will be aired in public. Since Etarra's governance has been granted to the Light's Hope, the trial for sorcery is already scheduled.'

'What?' The warden's electrified shock drilled the air.

'You hadn't been told?' the watch officer snapped. 'Well, here's the straight line. His Radiance petitioned Lord Lysaer behind the shut doors of a private council. His case claimed the backing of decisive evidence, that the Master of Shadow broke from cover and attacked a dedicate troop back in Tysan.'

'Warned as much, didn't I?' the turnkey sniped, gratified. 'Repent, better had, while you're still alive to embrace faith and follow the holy canon.'

While Daliana paled, paralyzed by dread, the relief guardsman gushed on with enthusiasm, 'Already, the whirlwind muster's been called. The town barracks are thrown into an uproar, there's truth. By dawn, orders say, they'll march east alongside the Light's dedicate lancers. The decree was announced from the central square. Our Lord Mayor leaves for Tysan as the divine avatar for the True Sect followers. He will raise the Sunwheel banner and spear-head the war against Darkness.'

The turnkey said, smug. 'You heard from me, first, that the righteous cause would find triumph. Believers will hunt Shadow to final destruction, then strike down the sorcerous grip of the Fellowship's compact.'

While the excited stew in the guard-room swung from argument to speculation, several men in formal Etarran scarlet and two more clad in pristine Sunwheel surcoats secured the downstairs corridor. Temple orders posted them by the cell to contain the criminal sorceress.

Daliana stood and gripped the steel bars, beyond terrified. 'What upstart writ has overturned justice? I have not faced a tribunal for any hearing to answer the charges against me!'

'Your sentence will stand,' the nearest Sunwheel dedicate corrected with stony rebuke. 'The ceremonial trial will take place in a fortnight, with the gravity of state panoply to impress a warning on the unsanctified populace.'

'This is Etarra!' Daliana shot back. 'True Sect doctrine's unlikely to overthrow reason through brainless dogma.'

The soldier regarded her, ablaze with importance behind his gold badges and burnished mail. 'Word is being sent through the outlying country-side that folk must attend to bear witness. Light's justice decrees that black minions shall burn to put an end to such wickedness. Your example will be staged to turn other heretics towards their redemption.'

Daliana retreated, face masked in cold hands to hide her tears of despair. Trapped by the earthquake shift in town policy, she admitted the disastrous set-back: that a second fetch surely must have replaced the foul construct discharged by her throw in the tavern. In fact, the Light's embassy would have garnered their access to Lysaer when His Radiance presented the formal complaint. The opportune process caused by her assault played straight into the priest's scheming hands. For only a spell-cast illusion of Arithon's live presence could have triggered Desh-thiere's curse with the force to drive a whirlwind campaign to scourge Darkness from Tysan.

Lost to corrupt influence, Lysaer now supplied the volatile spark for the zealot expansion. Stripped of natural reason, and pressured by geas-born hatred, he would further the temple's false cause. His twisted drive to underwrite justice would wed him to the True Sect expansion.

Helpless in confinement, Daliana could do nothing to jolt his warped mind back to sanity. The pain cut, glass-edged, that she had sworn the same oath as her ancestor, Sulfin Evend, and when called, had hastened the course of her liege's destruction and left him abandoned to dishonour . . .

*   *   *

A harsh grip on Asandir's wrist smashed the vision and checked his agitated surge to arise. Regrounded, his outraged awareness snapped back into cold air and night stars, and the stone silence of Ciladis's niche at Althain Tower.

At his side, rough as gravel, Sethvir declared, 'I've sent Traithe.'

'Ath's mercy!' That news propelled Asandir to tug free and launch all the way to his feet. 'Pitted against the political might of an invested temple examiner? A straw hope!'

'Not just yet!' Sethvir qualified, rushed, 'Traithe's defense will extend the mockery of Daliana's trial, if only to buy precious time. Enough, perhaps, for the wild-card player our own hand has tossed in the breach.'

'Dakar!' Asandir's eyebrows rose with such outraged mixed feeling, the Warden of Althain chuckled aloud. Not dissembling, for once, he coughed into his beard. 'Don't fear for your oath to Prime Selidie, yet! I sent no veiled prompt. The ripple of pending event by itself roused the Mad Prophet's spontaneous prescience. He left Halwythwood yesterday. Rathain's *caithdein*'s been entrusted, and rightly, as the realm's conscience. Cosach will decide what, if anything, can salvage the gift of Prince Arithon's escape.'

Asandir glared. 'Dakar had forewarning that s'Ilessid would become swayed through dark spellcraft? Your earth-sense unveiled this *yesterday*?'

'That Etarra would fall under the thumb of the True Sect priesthood?' Althain's Warden clawed back a tendril of hair. 'Yes.' Like a faithful dog hunched to ward off a blow, he snugged his empty mug between his draped knees, then poked up the embers to brew more tea. As the water boiled with unnatural speed, he spiked the steeped leaves with peach brandy, then said, 'Your prophet's bound northward, sped on his way by the scout's relay through Halwythwood.'

'To stare down the teeth of Lysaer's spear-head muster, dispatched under influence of Desh-thiere's curse! I should be appalled.' Cold iron before his colleague's frayed optimism, Asandir declined the filled mug and paced the tight space like caged lightning. 'You've read the grim odds? We could lose them. All three!'

'I see no better path.' Sethvir looked up, owlish, tucked hands with white knuckles the sure sign he also was inwardly bleeding. 'Sit down,' he pleaded. 'Sweet tea will soothe very little, but the dawn that commands your departure won't wait, and Rathain's wild fire must be left to burn.'

'While my hands stay tied for the outside chance I might bolster the safety of Havish?' Asandir fumed. The life of the young woman abandoned as sacrifice stung as deeply – no, more – than the brutal necessity that also tossed Traithe's crippled faculties into the hotbed of jeopardy. At length, the nettled field Sorcerer relented. 'I can't fault the priority. Though never pretend I enjoy the stacked odds, with our staunch allies pitched against the trap-jaws of temple justice. There are days,' he railed on, face tipped back beneath the starred sky of Atainia, 'when I would wring the serpentine necks of the dragons whose dream claimed our deathless service.'

'The razor's edge must be walked, and by friends,' Sethvir admitted, aggrieved. 'Above everything else, save that Arithon lives, the spellbinder you trained must not fail.'

Asandir said nothing at all, but accepted his drink from Sethvir's unsteady hand. The two Sorcerers sipped, while the night fled away, and strained quiet drowned their conversation. For the weal of the world, more than Dakar's endeavour hung in the reeling balance. The fate of another, as brave, was bound to face trial before him. Sethvir chose not to burden his colleague with the awareness, even as his earth-sense disclosed that the enchantress Elaira sailed towards a danger past reach of the Fellowship's purview.

On the black, pre-dawn hour, before Asandir saddled his horse to begin his rushed passage to Havish, farther east, by the southcoast of Vastmark, the pale glow of daybreak already etched the winter-bare foothills under the rim of the Kelhorn Peaks. There, in the trackless wilds, the isolate stone tower of the Reiyaj Seeress raised a thin silhouette against the bronze glow of the morning sky. The post she inherited numbered among the oldest of the Third Age powers extant in the world. Daylong, she perched in her high, gimbaled seat, blind eyes like pearl turned sunward. Immersed in deep trance, she followed the light and saw whatever the solar rays touched directly, or reflected off the night face of the moon. Born in her remote eyrie of stone, she never descended. Few knew she existed, and next to none understood her dedicate purpose.

At times, throughout ninety years of stern service, she viewed events that the Fellowship Sorcerers were wise to avoid. Her Paravian title, in fact, meant *'to touch the forbidden.'*

Life showed her squalling births and the bleeding death of heroes, the outbreaks of wars, and the fevers whose grievous cruelties broke minds and hearts. She knew secrets and perceived beyond sight. The golden flares where dragons dreamed were clear as language to her perception. Also the music, untamed, where Athera's most unfathomable mysteries still walked the green earth.

Where the light went, the oracle's sight followed, never with more unswerving persistence than in the dark places where secrets stayed hidden for reasons most fair, and graspingly foul. The moon's subtle rays, turned back in reflection, had lent her the keyhole's view through the warded shutters, behind which Selidie Prime wove her plots to upend the power of nations.

Dawn that morning, the Seeress's keen awareness watched the Matriarch's shadowy nexus.

Unblinking, with her seamed eyelids cupped to desiccate orbs like milkstone, the Reiyaj Seeress traced down the source of that pattern. She beheld a galley streaming the banners of a Havish registry run in her oars for a landfall at Ithish. There, the ship's ready crew cast the docklines ashore to tie up and off-load her cargo. On deck, braced at the rail through the jerk as the longshoremen's heave snubbed the vessel, the Reiyaj crone received her clear view of the woman about to be tested: the extraordinarily gifted, rebellious initiate the Koriani Order desired for the sole purpose of baiting a trap.

Elaira's inestimable worth as the tool to stalk Arithon's movements brought a circle of five ranked enchantresses to Ithish, pitched for ambush in the waterfront streets. The moment the oath breaker set foot ashore, she would forfeit the protection of Havish's crown justice. Which shift to town law made her fair game to be snatched back into the sisterhood's custody.

As the eyes that served the Biedar eldest, the Reiyaj Seeress surveyed the moment of reckoning poised to unfold. Her insight a lens of infallible clarity, she saw a woman driven to fierce independence by the scope of her natural gifts. Bound like the jessed falcon under the constraints that crushed most child conscripts to obedient subjugation, Elaira bore the survivor's scar of unquenchable determination. She was still self-possessed, whole and vital in spirit. But the tenets of choice remained to be seen, sprung from the deepest tap-root of her character. Just as a balance, soon to be rocked, might heal or destroy the exalted mystery that sourced Ath's sacred gift to the world, this woman's fate was the candle that could illuminate, or the torch that would spark mass destruction.

The threads of bound energies, touched by the sun, stripped the truth from all masks of concealment. The fey sight of the Reiyaj Seeress read into the forged lines of Elaira's purpose and unveiled no tangle of murk; no dishonesty clouded the enchantress's presence. Handfast as Arithon's beloved, she had completed this rough winter passage to seek guest asylum of the Biedar tribe in Sanpashir. For that quest, and for the grand tapestry of a future yet to be written, the Reiyaj Seeress kept vigil. Appointed as visioner for the eldest of Mother Dark's guardian hands, she launched her bid to determine which of two strands would prove to be strongest: the hatred or the merciful instinct that nurtured the heart of the healer.

Testing

Elaira snugged her salt-fusty mantle against the chill wind, blown off the snow-fields of Vastmark. The brisk work of the deck-crew, laying out fenders, ended with a thump as the side strakes of the galley jarred into the bollards. The gangway was rigged and run out, while the first gulls climbed, weaving against a sky pebbled with gilt cloud and notched by the steep roofs of Ithish. Elaira adjusted the satchel strapped under her mantle, a precaution that foiled the quick knives of the cutpurses, and saved her bottled remedies from freezing. While the quartermaster debarked in a puff of fogged breath, ship's papers in hand for the customs shack, the enchantress lingered aboard. Her careful survey measured the seaport and the certain prospect of danger before her.

The witch-hunt deferred on departure from Redburn would resume, sharp-ened by the tactical advantage lent by weeks of advance preparation. She expected no quarter. The extended delay, spent sheltered in the Cascains while the galley rode out the fury of South Sea's black storms, would have spurred the Matriarch's temper.

Yet daylight revealed nothing sinister awaiting her at the wharf-side. The weathered planks glistened, blotched with damp where the wool-capped men off the luggers landed their iced barrels of cod. The reek of fish-oil mingled with smoke from the salting shacks, and the shipboard taint of tar, oakum caulk, and mildewed sail canvas. First port on the east-bound passage around the twin spurs that flanked South Strait, Ithish was the plainest of the southern anchorages, a battered jumble of timbered sheds hard-worn as a supply stop and ship's chandlery. Wealth did not settle here, coddled by the tropical current that warmed the coast farther east, where the flow of riches and jewels moved with the silk trade from Atchaz.

This rough-cut landing was not exotic with the fragrance of orange crates, or perfumed by the pitch tang of lumber. Instead, the docks sagged under the rancid weight of the wool bales, shorn raw off the Vastmark flocks. The brittle alpine cold rippled under the fumes of the smelters' flues, where mined tin from the mountains was refined and cast into ingots. Instead of artful stained glass, tropic spices and marble statuary, the exported bounty of salt cod and goat cheese was packed in straw and sealed in stacked barrels. Burly stevedores in fleece jackets muscled the flow of goods between ship's hold and wagon. They did not flaunt bare torsos or wear nosegays of jasmine twined into their headscarves by the teasing wiles of belled harlots. Here, the list-bearing factors went bundled in fur, not satin brocade.

Amid the patched leathers of the high-country drovers, the frayed slops of bronzed sailhands, and the coarse garb of the labourers, the order's cosseted Senior talent would stand out like trinkets dropped into a nail keg. Hardened locals were apt to flip talent the sign for the Evil Eye, or flash temple talismans to avert wickedness. The order's sisters were not loved at Ithish. Not since the bitter, lean times, when Vastmark's shepherds once had been forced to sell out their talented daughters to save themselves from starvation.

Arithon's influence had ended that past trade in flesh, a fact fallen to obscurity through ten generations of book-thumping Sunwheel advocates. But for the Koriathain stationed in Shand, the grievance stayed raw as their aged ranks thinned, deprived of that source of young talent. The sisters staked out to waylay the Prime's renegade held bones aplenty to pick, and a revenge hell-bound to fall without mercy on the best beloved of Rathain's crown prince.

Wooden shutters clattered as the dock-side shops opened for business beneath the painted swing of chained sign-boards. Any window might hide unfriendly eyes, while the shaded mouths of the alleys offered the ready cover for a hostile ambush. Elaira shivered under her mantle, hesitant as the early foot traffic thickened. More folk abroad lent no safety in numbers, with the increased bustle as likely to mask the movement of enemies.

Her foreboding became cut short as the galley's first mate arrived with a token payment dispatched from his captain. 'Here's silver, with thanks for your salves to ease the oarsmen's salt-water sores.' Above the yaps of a stray dog from the street and the cry of the slop-taker's boy, he apologized, 'I'm asked to direct you ashore, if you please. We need the deck cleared to winch up the hatch for unlading.'

Elaira accepted the coins with good grace. Moved on, she considered stalling to warm her numb toes in the customs shack. But as she picked her way past the stacked crates and baled wool, and the clucked complaint of fluffed poultry in wicker baskets, she skirted a beggar, curled up in the fish-nets heaped on the wharf. If any man napped in such miserable straits, likely the Ithish officials gave the discomfort of vagrants short shrift.

Shivering beneath her wool cloak, Elaira scanned the approach to the street, obstructed by a fishwife's parked hand-cart, and several stevedores burdened with cargo sacks. Attack would overtake her beyond the dock: Koriathain reliant on the use of charged quartz shunned the counteractive effects of salt water. They must not risk the chance she might bolt, or delay them with wards of protection.

Cautious, lest the town housed a temple diviner, Elaira opened to mage-sight and assessed the mixed swirl of life energy emanated by the passing traffic. Her healer's eye could discern the male aura from female; differentiate the blotched taint of the hung-over sailhand from the tired grey of the blowsy whore. She could sort the red jangle of ire let off by a cheated craftsman, or the vital orange of the labourer who unloaded kegs from the brewer's.

The joyful vitality of the children who chased the mangy dog sparkled a scintillant flare across a recessed alley, where a more sinister skein of hazed brilliance shimmered from a hidden cleft, entrained by the matrix of an active crystal.

A Koriani initiate lurked there, poised to spring. Patient, Elaira engaged in light trance. Her refined senses might sort past the back-drop patterns of brick, board, and mortar, and neatly unveil the conscious connections to expose the covert pack set against her.

Except the chased dog skidded around the baled cargo and plunged in a scrabble of claws down the dock. Its manic vitality excited the chiaroscuro tapestry of auras and lane-ripples into a cross chop of chaos. Elaira dampened her heightened faculties before the upset wracked her to nausea. She surfaced to a sharp breath of air, just as the stray bolted past her. A smiling longshoreman snatched for its scruff, but the wily animal skittered sidewards, tongue lolling. One hind paw hooked through the dumped fish-nets. Wrenched up short, the dog yelped. Its panicked struggle tugged the leg free, but the drag of the mesh also dislodged the sandbag that wedged the stacked casks. The unstabilized pile collapsed, layers tumbled apart with a deafening boom that scattered bystanders, swept over the wharf, and caromed off the bollards and crates. One barrel burst to a white puff of flour. Several others splashed into the harbour, to screams of dismay from the customs shack.

Elaira dodged clear, while two alert workers grabbed the pelting children and whisked them out of harm's way. The only casualty was the beggar, wakened too late to respond. As the last of the casks bounced and rolled to a stop, or bobbed like corks in the tide's race, the struck victim lay still as caught wrack amid the yanked snarl of twine.

Elaira looked on in silenced distress as the distraught dock crews gathered in sympathy. Fresh blood snaked over the man's brow, bright against the heaped wrack of fish-net. Too well, she knew that head injuries were dangerous. Without skilled help, the luckless fellow might perish. Perhaps worse, he might suffer permanent damage, left to the ignorant handling of even such well-meaning bystanders.

Torn, she knew if she paused to assist, her Koriani enemies would refine their strategy for her capture. Wisest to move on for Prince Arithon's sake. No one would condemn her for selfishness, with her remedy bag tucked underneath her thick mantle and no recognizable badge to mark her profession. She could slip on past with none the wiser. The stricken oldster was a penniless layabout, without a spare button to reward her services.

But impulse outpaced the clamour of reason. 'Don't shift him!' Elaira blurted to restrain the well-meant concern of the dock crew. She ran, cloak flung back to access her remedies. 'I'm healer-trained. Please, let me have a look! That person may need critical care. His condition might require a board litter before he can be moved with safety.'

The nearest longshoreman pushed back his knit cap. 'Mistress,' he acknowledged, then backed the oblivious gawkers aside to make way for her. 'Bless your generosity. Tell us anything else you might need.'

She nodded. Dropped to her knees in the welter of nets, she traced light fingers over the flaccid body bundled into its noisome layers of frayed clothes. She parted the grease-shiny rags and explored the ripe flesh beneath without pause. As a child, she had known such misfortunate misery, when homeless poverty forced her to scrounge for life's needs on the streets. Then, a canny destitute man she named Uncle had shared the poor-quarter squalor and watched over her. Had he not shaped her earliest years by his kindness, she could have been seized as a toddler, then sold by the ruthless to service the vice in the back-door brothels of Morvain.

Elaira could no more have passed this wretch by than will her own flesh to stop breathing.

'No broken bones, no damaged spine or cracked skull,' she declared as she fastened the mangle of mismatched buttons to restore the man's dignity. Surrounded by curious labourers, she perched on her heels and appealed for assistance. 'The gash from the bang on the head requires stitching. For that, I could use a pail of hot water, and another with packed ice, and a towel from one of the taverns. Best to begin straightaway, before this poor fellow wakes up.' Unflinching, she cradled the beggar's bloodied head. A practiced lift of each eyelid confirmed the matched reflex of his pupils, a favourable sign. The blow may not have caused a concussion.

Elaira concluded, 'Does Ithish maintain a charity ward? Good. This man ought to be taken there and held through the night under observation.'

The requested items arrived, hauled by a flushed, cheerful barmaid who also assured that the dock-master heard of the accident. 'None will disturb your good work. Today, divine Light's blessed the needy, that's certain.'

'Human caring, in fact,' Elaira snapped, tart. 'I give succour for joy, before duty or dogma.' On the open wharf, shielded inside the huddle of gawkers, she cleaned the victim's cut forehead, then applied black-root oil to numb his nerves before she set the gut stitches. The advanced techniques learned from

Ath's adepts let her soothe the man's traumatized aura and infuse the calmed energies with the harmonic frequencies to encourage mending.

'By Fate's Wheel, did you see that?' a longshoreman marveled. 'Treats that nameless bloke just as gently as if he was family!'

'Wish my carping shrew had such heart. Seven years married, she's sore in the tits as a crooked-horned milch-cow.'

'Beats on you, does she? That's a proper comeuppance for planting her belly with too many weans.'

Through laughter, the complaint from the hen-pecked husband ran on with rueful amusement, 'Rails, rather, the old bag. Froths at the mouth from morning to dusk with a tongue like a rusted razor.'

'Try bringing her flowers just once, or forgo your taste for the drink,' Elaira suggested.

The afflicted spouse shoved a thumb under his shirt and scratched at his navel. 'Tide and tempest,' he marveled. 'Not drink! And how could a silly bundle of daisies do aught to shut the brass trap on that harridan?'

'Dumbfound her, maybe,' a comrade chipped in, to grins and more wisecrack advice.

Elaira finished the cleaned wound with tansy salve and firm bandages, then administered a dosed infusion to ease the pain of stiffness and bruises. She stayed on while the fellow regained his senses and ascertained he suffered no dire complications. A few minutes more saw him settled from shaken confusion. The moment he was back on his feet, the bored longshoremen broke up to resume their day's tasks. Elaira chose not to leave before she satisfied herself that two silvers paid to the dock crew's foreman would see her head injury escorted to a bed in the Ithish infirmary.

The scruffy dog and the children were long since gone when she cleaned her steel needles and packed up her satchel. Pallid sunlight had shortened the shadows, with the water-front dives immersed in midmorning's brisk business. Koriathain still lurked amid the thickened crowd, strengthened by reinforcements: to Sighted vision, the nearer side alleys now crackled with the crystal-tinged blaze of their presence. Disconsolate, Elaira hunched into her cloak. Too late for regret, she faced the misfortunate penalty, that the shimmering blaze of the healer's techniques learned from the wise at Ath's hostelry had marked her out like a beacon.

Exposed beyond salvage, measured by enemies as if she had stripped all protection, Elaira abandoned the marginal haven lent by the open wharf. She edged into the teeming street braced for trouble. The first strike might come in straightforward assault, launched by what seemed like a commonplace ruffian. Or she could be waylaid by insidious means, her active shields breached by a spell of compulsion. Prepared for both tactics, Elaira clasped a sweaty grip on the belt knife under her mantle. With the quartz shaft of a natural Atheran crystal palmed, left-handed, she skirted a dray-load of Sanshevas

JANNY WURTS

molasses, ducked a matron hawking meat-pies with leeks, and side-stepped
the rank splash as a shaggy cart-horse balked in its traces to urinate. Alert
senses poised between subtle perception, she strained to winnow the nuance
of threat from the seethe of dock-side activity. Her facile experience was
hard-pressed to sort, since the taint of the charm maker's talismans to ward
drowning, and the spiced aphrodisiacs worn by the whores might also mask
darker workings.

Noise always rattled her heightened focus. The clangour of a wheelwright's
mallet shaping an iron rim, and the chatter of a vacuous girl paraded on the
arm of a sweetheart rang in her ears, underscored by the bass grind of
the brewer's emptied hogsheads being rolled from a cobble-stone tavern
yard. At least Ithish austerity did not lend her predators the opulent southcoast
convenience of pierced grilles and lush courtyards, with balconies and shaded
lovers' nooks.

Hungry, and pressured to a tension headache, Elaira fought the fear that
threatened an onset of trembling. Buffeted by the crowd, she encountered the
drenching tingle that bespoke a warded boundary. She tried to stop short. Jostled
ahead despite planted feet, she stiffened her defenses, to no avail. The seamless,
enchained sigils outmatched her strength and netted her on all sides. While she
struggled to strike down the web, a second assault speared into her mind, honed
with the master sigil the Prime used to subjugate oath-bound initiates.

That measure alone should have finished the contest. No subordinate
enchantress might withstand the bond that committed her autonomous will to
the order.

Elaira fought anyway. No matter how futile the effort, she resisted the ugly,
imperative noose with all the ferocity of her free spirit. She met the searing
agony that fashioned the sigil's imperative with the woman's steel of her fierce
loyalty that would defend Arithon's interests, even above her own life. Knocked
to her knees, suffocated to the black edge of collapse, she focused her frantic
need through the crystal aligned to her use by the precepts taught by Ath's
adepts. Healer-schooled to redress harmful influence, she mapped the patterns
bent to enslave her, then matched their measure with balance and wrestled to
disarm the wrapped coil of forces through entropy.

The red-hot wires that strapped her lungs gave and loosened. She gasped
hoarsely for breath. Through wheeling dizziness, she heard a bystander ask if
she needed help. Too stressed to answer, scarcely able to move, Elaira wiped
tears from her eyes, shoved off the cold cobbles, and staggered back upright.

The ringing in her ears did not subside, or the queasy wave of faintness
that rippled her vision. Elaira could not catch sight of her adversaries or determine where in the crowd they might be hidden. But through pins and needles,
she sensed the fierce gather: a heaviness like heated bronze choked the air as
the hostile circle of Senior enchantresses refashioned their defrayed intent.
Before their prey rallied, they hurled their renewed assault against her.

Inflamed to pure fury, Elaira unsheathed her belt knife. As she must, she would stab her own flesh to foil the vile incursion. No limit existed, before desperation. She would not fall to Prime Selidie's hand or risk being turned as the mindless tool to drive Arithon back to captivity.

But her adversaries changed tactics to compensate. Their thrust passed her by. Instead, a man's strength pinned her arms from behind. Elaira twisted like a bagged wildcat. She glimpsed the baffled, bearded features of one of the dock crew's longshoremen. Horror met her discovery, that her enemies' dark working had fixed an unconscionable spell upon him to hold her at bay. The burly man hoisted her off her feet. Suborned as their string puppet, he had no training to resist, or protest an act of abduction prompted without his conscious volition. Elaira had no time to choose which arena to forfeit before her defeat.

She could let go, loosen her stubborn resistance to the Prime's master sigil, and buy the moment she needed to snap the longshoreman free of beguilement. Or she could sustain her last resource to shield, and stab the thralled man in the shoulder. Her surgeon's knowledge could sever the artery with a deft stroke. His hold would loosen as he bled out. The murder would be almost painless, and fast, while the shocked uproar as he went down lent the turmoil to hide her escape.

A split instant to act and no chance to reason, or weigh the grief of remorse. Her gut reaction sprang from the innate emotional truth in the heat of the moment.

Elaira responded to what *was*, and not the projected concern for what *might be*. The live man who pinned her commanded need, *first*, before Arithon's distant predicament. Her pealed cry of anguish split the cold air as she shredded her self-protection and answered the healer's call to intercede for the sake of the labourer's violated integrity.

Her practised unbinding severed the sigil that enslaved the hapless man's mind. Horror followed on the recoil. She braced to reap the hideous consequence, keenly aware how her action might recoil and jeopardize her beloved. Yet no master sigil flayed her awareness. Instead, the brutal assault suddenly melted away. Confounded, still reeling, Elaira fought to regroup her battered composure.

Breathing too fast and dizzied by her electrified pulse, she encountered no triumphant sisters. Only the ruddy face of the longshoreman, who crouched over her in perplexed concern. No longer coerced, he cradled her shuddering weight, his weathered forehead creased with apology. 'Lady, are you ailing?' Embarrassed, he added, 'I was on my way past with your charity case, headed for the infirmary. Should I take you there also?'

Ridden by panic, Elaira shook free. 'I'm not sick, thank you.' The man evidently did not recall his exposure to hostile spellcraft. Though the order's dark work had been banished clean, nothing rational suggested why the Prime

Matriarch's tasked circle also should withdraw before they clinched their sure victory.

The stevedore was nothing more than he seemed. A generous fellow, born without talent, Elaira saw naught about him to explain the sisterhood's abrupt retreat.

She disentangled herself, repeated her distressed murmur of thanks, then sheathed her blade and arose. Around her, several curbed wagon teams sidled, to shouted oaths from their drivers. A street urchin sucked dirty fingers and stared, while a muffled girl with a goose crate irritably shouldered her way through the crush of stopped traffic.

But one step away stood the beggar, whose gashed forehead she had just bandaged. Angular, thin, still filthy in his tatterdemalion rags, he planted himself squarely in the path of the Seniors dispatched to waylay her. Not by chance, Elaira discovered, caught aback. In fact, *he* was the power that thwarted them. A badge raised in his gaunt hand cast a ward of protection that blazed blindingly bright to the nuance of her mage-sight.

Shielded by forces beyond recognition, and rattled by sheer disbelief, Elaira asked, 'Should I know you?'

The peculiar man faced her. Poised with unshakeable serenity, and quite unconcerned that his vagrant stance snarled the thoroughfare, he bowed and acknowledged her. That frivolous gesture incensed the stalled carters, who cried murder for the obstruction. Manners made him seem no less disreputable. The fresh swathe of bandage across his stitched injury remained the only clean rag on his person. The wrinkled skin weathered by fierce, southland sun was oiled with dirt like worn teak.

'Don't mind the deception posed by appearances,' he declared in bemused apology. 'The Koriathain set after you by their Prime dare not cross the one who sent this.' Palm upraised, he extended his unearthly talisman with a smile of invitation.

The metallic disk was nothing Elaira recognized, marked on its face with a sun and moon, encircled by stars and incised foreign characters.

'Whose servant are you?' she inquired, adrift.

The awkward pause lengthened. While the puzzled longshoreman withdrew his offer of escort and sauntered back towards the dock, the flow of inconvenienced pedestrians brushed past an encounter that rippled like the mirage in a fever-dream. Elaira swayed. An annoyance, after all, that she might faint as her weakened knees turned to jelly.

The ragged man offered a thin, vital hand and supported her elbow. 'On all counts, you've established your worth. As you are the mate, and she, the guardian of Mother Dark's chosen, the Biedar eldest has consented to grant the audience you desire.'

Which specious pronouncement stunned Elaira beyond speech.

'Food and rest, first.' With infectious kindness, her strange ally drew her aside before she collapsed in the street. Through the grind of wheels and the jingle of harness as the congested way cleared, he said, 'You'll have the grace to recover while I visit the bath and change into respectable clothing.'

'You're no mere beggar!' Rebounded to guarded suspicion, Elaira eyed the fresh blood-stains leaked through her neat bandage. 'But that cut, all those bruises. Your injuries were real!'

Her odd savior nodded. 'I was tasked to be there when the barrel stack fell. And I was beside you for rescue since your charity also saw fit to arrange for a destitute stranger's care at an infirmary.'

'You're precognizant, also?' Elaira exclaimed, a bit shrill. Several alarmed bystanders turned their heads to stare. Remanded to caution, she lowered her voice. 'These events were all staged? You got hurt for the sake of some meddling party's sadistic amusement?'

'Not the attack!' Indignant at last, the bronzed stranger summed up, 'That plan was Prime Selidie's doing, executed by a master circle of twelve with the fullest intent to accomplish your downfall.' A tender touch to his blotched bandage became dismissed with a fatalist's shrug. 'You earned your right to rescue, sweet lady. Rest assured, my discomfort has served a true cause.'

Elaira balked outright, dismayed, while a boy who shouldered a bundle of kindling cursed her for a Dark-sent nuisance, and barely missed mowing her down. 'Explain!' she demanded. 'Right now! Who are you? Who sent you, and what perverse whim draws your unforeseen stake in my destiny?'

'A keen tongue, as well as a mind devoted to unswerving honesty.' The lean stranger raised quizzical eyebrows and laughed. 'My dear, you can drop the death grip on your knife! By the will of the Reiyaj Seeress, and after such proof of your sterling character, I have orders to safeguard each step of your journey the rest of the way to Sanpashir.'

Late Winter 5923

Mission

The last time that Dakar rode at break-neck speed out of Halwythwood to address a white-hot crisis down the Mathorn Road, the breathless pace over wild terrain took a fortnight, with his sluggard's bulk in the saddle pounding horses to foamed sweat under the brass heat of summer. Then, his urgent rush had backed Arithon's effort to destroy a cabal of dark necromancers, dangerously entrenched at Etarra. Never brave in the face of consummate evil, that past day's dire necessity had terrified Dakar to yanked hair, already streaked white at his temples.

Now, his head bleached more silver than chestnut, the Mad Prophet shouldered the arduous journey again. This time, he faced the same passage under the cruel freeze of winter, with the distance to be crossed to salvage disaster allotted less than six days.

On the first leg, the scouts' relay rushed him northward through Halwythwood with cracking efficiency. He changed mounts each half hour and crammed his meals of jerky, nuts, and raisins, eaten still astride. Dakar should have crowed over the piquant reverse, with his former smug captors forced to jump at Earl Cosach's command to support his case. But their crashing speed whipped him through low-slung branches and chafed his tender skin raw. The relentless gallops on fresh horses without saddles made him sore in the back and too breathlessly cross to speak.

The River Aiyenne was shoaled enough to risk the ford in cold weather. His competent clan escort cut him loose on the bank to finish the distance alone. Sunwheel lancers were ever a peril to their kind beyond the wood. All the more, with their clanbred nerves cranked to painful dread that the threat of Lysaer's instability might corrupt the Mayor's justice at Etarra, subject to renewed pressure from Desh-thiere's curse.

'Fare well, ride hard,' urged the grizzled scout, then slapped the rump of the handsome bay gelding lent to hasten the spellbinder's errand.

The horse leaped into the sandy shallows, then splashed chest-deep into the black swirl of iced current. Dakar clung astride. His shrill curse became swallowed by the vast blue sky as the water flooded up to his calves. Knees raised to keep his boot-tops from filling, and both fists locked in coarse mane, he weathered the lurch as the hardy beast under him stumbled through a pot-hole and breasted the bore of the rapids.

Across with soaked toes, paused at the verge to re-centre his tipped seat as the dripping horse lashed its soaked tail, the spellbinder regarded with trepidation the frost-scoured vales and whipped broom that unrolled ahead of him. No chance at all that sensible action would see him through in time to matter. Asandir's instruction had shown him how to apply his longevity training to extend a horse's stamina. Though such transference of life-force was recklessly dangerous, need demanded: Dakar must cross thirty leagues and reach the nearest post-station through the night. If burning his reserves did not wring him unconscious, to perish of chill in the desolate wind whipped off Daon Ramon, at the end, he confronted the test of his life: a feat grave enough not to countenance failure and a grueling trial to outstrip the scope of a master spellbinder's faculties.

For a spirit best suited to lie with a strumpet, Dakar shouldered the course with the humor of a rankled bear. Starved himself, he attracted, then dispelled two packs of ravenous *iyats*. He had not a stray wisp of energy to spare, stressed beyond sense since the outset. As the soft, excess weight melted off his short bones, he punched new holes to tighten his belt and cursed every moment that his fatigue forced a catnap, curled in misery amid the thorn brakes. Altogether too much like his past mentor's style, Dakar avoided the wayside taverns. Withdrawn to dour silence, he fretted through each harried pause to change mounts. The bustle of grooms and the noise made him wince, while the harsh use of magecraft inflamed his senses.

Dawn on the third day, he left the exposed downs of the barrens and began the climb through the Mathorn foothills. Farther on, the trade-road crooked upwards between rock-clad scarps, which steepened into the switched-back approach to Etarra. The slopes acquired petticoat ruffles of fir, broken by vistas of clumped rock and snow. Where the steepened grade wrung the winded draught teams to lather, the wayside coach-houses and stables to service town-bred travellers became more frequent. Apple-cheeked boys by open hearths in the yards sold roasted nuts and mulled wine for a penny. But the fee for fit hacks came dear, since the fodder and grain stores hauled in by cart were reserved for the couriers' mounts. Dakar lost more flesh as his horses tired under him. He napped on cold ground and barren ledges, and once, in the ditch where he rolled when he tumbled senseless out of the saddle.

He woke gimping stiff. Ringing ears and light-headed exhaustion still dogged him, worsened by hunger pangs that wrung him faint. Since his strayed mount was nowhere to be found, he persisted on foot, aching and bruised and jolted through each abused joint as he tripped over the bristle of snow-capped, stunt saplings. Under the pewter flood of new daylight, he counted four nights, since his journey began. Unless he intercepted Lysaer's cavalcade before sundown, his star-crossed endeavour was a lost cause.

The hills beneath stretched away like crimped burlap, napped dark green where evergreen flounced the bare scree, and the runged ice of the frozen springs bearded the vertical scarps. Above, rumpled foil snagged in black rock, the peaks pierced the tatters of cloud that lidded the scoured crests of the ridges. The trade-road gleamed with iced puddles where the seamed wash-outs were patched with shored slate. Except for the whine of the gusts, the sole sounds were the clatter of an out-bound messenger, underlain by the bass grind of wheels from the ox-train that snaked up the slope at his heels. Nothing else moved but the cinnamon dart of a fox and the lazy spirals of hunting hawks. The drab vista held no west-bound state cavalcade with liveried outriders. No flash of gold from white banners or Etarran scarlet rounded the switched-back curves in descent.

Dakar shivered. Grumbling, cold, his leathers like board and his mantle caked grey with horse sweat, he scraped at the itch of his beard and shook off low spirits. His saddle-sores stung. Last night's fall had sprained his left knee. He gimped off the thoroughfare, sought a sheltered hollow, and hunkered down under a stony outcrop chiselled by frost fractures. There, he engaged his worn faculties with intent to ascertain that his quarry had not passed him by as he snoozed by the verge.

No sooner had he settled in trance when a chill point of steel poked his nape. He surfaced, stung by someone's triumphant shout, called back to a titled superior. 'Eminence! Here. He's holed up where you said we would find him. Yes, send up the shackles. He's captive at sword-point. That doesn't mean he's not dangerous.'

Dakar grumbled a filthy word through his teeth. Wits clogged by the harrowing effort to reach this drear pass in the first place, he added, 'It's a criminal act to nap in the open?'

Mailed hands hooked his armpits and jerked him upright. 'Reeking of lawless talent, as you do? Our diviner's sensed your filthy practice! He's tracked you for leagues. Light blast the effrontery of your lying tongue, you'll not blind us through a false claim of innocence!'

Dakar swivelled his head. Brown eyes rolled to the whites, with his neck placed at risk, he blinked against the dazzle of the gold-on-white Sunwheel worn on the puffed chest of his accuser. 'You don't know turkey turds, chick,' he declared. 'I came to have words with your Blessed Prince, anyway. Don't bother to dally for shackles and chain. If the True Sect requires boot-licking prostration, just sheathe your weapons and lead me to your avatar's stirrup. I'll kiss the ground in his sanctified presence, the sooner to have the mummery over with.'

The predictable happened: the muscular *chick* in his glittering armour raised his mailed fist and belted the jaw of the insolent heretic. Then, before shock dropped him prostrate, Dakar was dragged through the brush upon jellied knees.

At length, spitting blood, Dakar found himself hurled face-down in the gravel road-bed, where he lay moaning in outraged complaint for loose teeth. No one listened. While his rumpled cloak wicked up mud, he stayed prone, unable to move for the prick of more weapons in the twitchy grip of three dedicate lancers.

'Insult the Light's grace, and we'll skewer your heart! There's enough stunt fir here to build a hot pyre, and sure cause for a quick burning.'

If Dakar possessed the arcane means to resist, he was canny enough not to test the riled aggression of his oppressors. Mewling, he languished as the buffoon, an act better practised than the lofty use of high conjury or subtle patience.

Hooves clattered up, presently. Several sets, shod in steel, attached to well-bred fetlocks, which circled his form until a drill captain's bark ordered the milling encroachment into disciplined formation. A stopped interval passed, filled by restive equine stamping, and the swish of cord tassels and wind-snapped pennons. Through the jingle of curb chains and bits, someone cracked a sly joke, while another man's deferent voice reported to his griped officer. 'We've brought down the slinking sorcerer whose filthy practice was detected by our diviner.'

But the polished authority that broke in and took charge was a voice Dakar recognized, even to the bitten inflection that screamed danger. 'Get him up!'

'Blessed Lord,' someone else objected, alarmed, 'that's unwise! He could be a spy or a Dark-sent assassin.' Anxious, exasperated, and strangled by tact, the speaker qualified, urgently reasonable, 'Our lancers are capable. This matter's beneath you. Let the temple's prerogative handle this.'

Instead, the sovereign order was repeated with searing impatience. 'Get him up!'

Spurs chinked. A lone horseman shouldered through the closed cordon and threw Dakar's shivering frame into shadow.

The prick of the lance points withdrew with cowed haste as two sets of mailed hands seized Dakar's rumpled clothing, and bundled him onto his feet.

The harsh move spun his balance. He swayed, dizzied to nausea because he dared not shut down, or dampen, the emotional tumult that hammered against his wide-opened mage-sense. Assaulted further by the rough handling, and subject to the lancers' coarse jests, he also withstood the merciless inspection as the temple diviner's crude talent raked into him. Dakar bore the inflamed interface of his unshielded nerves. While the temple-trained probes stabbed like wasp-stings to his viscera, he curbed every scandalized instinct. Survival demanded: he must stay immersed to the utmost degree of his attuned awareness without flinching.

For the straits, now engaged, hung his life by a thread. A wrong breath, a mis-step, or the least careless choice would see him dead in an instant.

With every alert faculty pitched to the razor's edge, the browbeaten spell-binder looked up. Shot through by the watermark sheen of refined energies, his regard travelled over prime horseflesh, first: an animal radiant with the gloss of good health, superbly bred to reflect the quality of its rider. Its caparisons glittered with gold, stitched onto scarlet trappings, not white. The rider's boot in the nearside stirrup was waxed calfskin, buckled with engraved gilt spurs. Dakar's close survey combed over a sculptured knee in knit hose, then the polished gleam of chain-mail, and the shimmered light spattered off rubies. Sword-belt and accoutrements, no less than royal, adorned the confident frame, strapped over a surcoat emblazoned with the device of the Lord Mayor of Etarra. Beauty and stylish flair set off the gloved hand lightly clasped on the reins.

Dakar sucked in a breath as most did as he measured the face of the aristocrat reined in before him. Yet the cameo-fair skin and blond hair remained exactly as he recalled, steeped in the scents of leather and greased steel, not the effete perfume of temple incense. The living man had once been a friend, whom Dakar had not met for over two and a half centuries. Which shared past was unlikely to help this critical moment's reunion. Tainted by the change of allegiance that once had attached Dakar to a Fellowship Sorcerer sent as Prince Arithon's envoy, he had been the harbinger of a bitter affront: Lysaer s'Ilessid would have no cause to forgive the dicey exchange for a ransom coerced for the safe return of a cherished first wife.

While Talith's unspoken name burned like fire amid the wire-stretched tension, the Mad Prophet endured the pinned grasp of the lancers, not fearless. Curd white with dread, he weathered the encounter as, wide open to vision, he let Lysaer s'Ilessid take the bare-faced measure of him in return.

What looked out of those gemstone blue eyes was not sane. Fury paled, and obsession fell short. Under Desh-thiere's curse, the man's magisterial command raised an aura of glory that defied description. Human poise sat the saddle with godlike stature, enlivened by an upright conviction that poised on a breath to mow down opposition.

'Are you Fellowship-sent?' Lysaer inquired, crisp as chipped ice.

'No.' This truth arose, not from Dakar's lips, but from the Sighted diviner. 'He bears no trace of the signature mark, stamped on those advocates who come under the Sorcerers' sanction. This creature is a minion of Darkness, arrived to dissuade your purposeful Light from the sanctified course of divine service.'

'Prince Arithon's cat's-paw,' Lysaer agreed, softly as the first patter of rain, before thunder-clap.

'Not this time.' Dakar gauged the steely flame in those eyes, and the rage that blazed through a geas-turned madman. He had but one line, perhaps less, to reach through before the Mistwraith's curse triggered the order for his execution. Of two drives that swayed the s'Ilessid before him, he angled to waken the compromised character Desh-thiere's warped directive cast into eclipse.

'Do you truly want another innocent killed for the grasping ambition of factions who have played your hand, and worse, employed vile spellcraft to arrange a state murder, whitewashed under the guise of religious morality?'

The diviner vented his incensed outrage. 'This accusation is specious!'

But against the ear tuned to birth-gifted justice, the denial rang falsely shrill. Lysaer wavered.

Dakar sucked a tight breath. Not ready to die, he lacked Asandir's courage; had never been heroic, quick-witted, or glib, caught in the pinch of a crisis. But his Sighted vision was accurate to a fault. Already reeling under the overload that frayed his seer's talent, he finally tagged the dissonant pitch his frantic need had been seeking. The fetch carried the deadly, spelled shimmer of Arithon's presence. Activated by a clipped lock of hair, and wrapped under three Koriani-made sigils stamped under the dark rune of chaos, the warped construct that triggered the Mistwraith's directive rested in Lysaer's saddle-bag. Worse, someone's diabolical inspiration had jammed the monstrosity into the slip-case for his flask. More than a direct prod, its fiendish imprint would taint each sip of water its targeted victim drank to quench thirst on the road.

Dakar had just one second to act, and no option for self-preservation. The least use of conjury would see him condemned. Eyes shut, a hung rabbit in the armoured grasp of the lancers, he unfurled a *thought*, shaped from a crystalline memory. With select clarity, he projected the corrected pattern of Arithon Teir's'Ffalenn's aura, taken after the triumph snatched in the King's Grove in Selkwood, when his Grace's bold appeal to the Athlien Paravians had risked everything to lift the afflicted curse. Lysaer's bastard half brother had claimed his right to heal, sealed by the might of such presence.

One projected burst was all Dakar possessed to negate the fetch's crude influence. But a concept could move worlds, spun by intent from an initiate awareness. The spellbinder brought to bear centuries of trained experience, learned under the most exacting of Fellowship taskmasters. At the crux, he dared not waver from his entrained focus. No matter whether the Light's lancers moved against him, or struck to kill at the priest's dismayed orders.

Dakar said, strained, 'In Talith's name, Lysaer! By the sorrow inflicted by her assassins, hear my appeal for Daliana sen Evend, who faces the sword and the pyre if you should forgo reason and falter!' Through shouts, as he wrestled the lancers, and beset by their blows that slammed him to his knees, Dakar cried, 'Examine the flask case cached in your saddle-bag! Then let s'Ilessid character review a wronged woman's case. Rise to my challenge, or be less than a man. On my life, dare to expose the truth.'

Fractures

In the wake of the unforeseen defeat that secures Elaira's journey to Sanpashir, just one enchantress in the Koriani Order gloats on the Prime's failure with triumph: yet under duress to serve as her Matriarch's hands, Lirenda lives for the mis-step that may bring Selidie's downfall, and deliver her from anonymous slavery to the restored status of her stolen rank . . .

Far southward in Kathtairr, rippled under the glare as noon blazes the parched rock beside the sterile waves of a mineral lake, a lean Sorcerer meets the gold eye of the dragon Seshkrozchiel, then ventures his considered opinion: 'Undo the harm here? Ath wept! Try that, and you realize the shock wave you cause must upshift the resonance of the entire planet . . . !'

Acrimoniously parted from Caithwood's clan encampment, Arithon regards a battered lyranthe, locked into terrified silence, while the empath who bestows the gift pleads in earnest, 'Your loyalty to that comatose townsman is what gave our clan council offence. But you should not leave us empty-handed. You don't recall? Ath's sweet grace, man, you've held the claimed title as Athera's Masterbard. Legend says your talent's unmatched anywhere in the wide world . . .'

VIII. Trial

D aliana was slinging invective to redden the ears of the obstreperous turnkey when Etarra's enraged populace began to hurl rocks from behind the magistrate's hall. As the first vicious missiles clattered down the barred window well and smashed against the cell floor, the pepper-shot pelt of chipped masonry cut her spate of curses to a chopped yelp.

'Serves your foul tongue right if you sting!' her tormentor jeered. While her outcry encouraged the spiteful crowd outside, he added with ripe satisfaction, 'I'd lob stones myself. A damnable shame, that I'm stuck with the chore of keeping your carcass unscathed.'

The retort from a woman versed at throwing knives was a shied fragment of rock, pitched with vengeful marksmanship. The routed turnkey scuttled to safety, hands protectively clutched to his groin.

But his brief discomfort came at high cost. The Light's dedicates on duty by the cell door did nothing to curb the mob's hateful assault. They flipped her snide gestures to ward against Shadow, even taunted her to save herself through a feat of dark spellcraft. The rest watched, amused, while their sharp-tongued charge huddled in the far corner to escape the bounce and crack of the ricochets. They laughed, then placed bets over each strike that scored as the malicious barrages redoubled.

Daliana shielded her face and endured, tucked in her crumpled mantle. She made no other sound. But that staunch pride only prompted the most rabid fanatics to try forcing the window grille from the street. Before the mob's viciousness tore her apart ahead of the Light's public trial, a belated squad of

265

Etarra's town guardsmen deployed to clear out the alley and block access from the main thoroughfare.

Yet no vigilant cordon might quell the mass chants incited by the thwarted rioters. Their ugly revilement roared on day and night, with chilling demands for redress against evil and shrilled threats to be visited upon the witch's close relatives. If Daliana's widowed mother and young brothers had not yet been run out of town, they dared not chance a brief visit to lift her morale, at the risk of their very lives.

As nothing else, that bitter abandonment wore her down as time crawled past. No other friend came to ease her condition. Branded an outcast, Daliana was despised by relentless strangers and named as a minion of evil past any redemption by the True Sect sacrament. She lost count of the long, lonely days, while time fed her formless dread. The keep guards no longer shot dice in the warden's absence. Instead, they poked weapons at her through the bars, or amused themselves by describing lewd acts to bedevil her from sound sleep.

When the turnkey came late with her supper, whining over a headache caused by the noise, Daliana spat in his teeth. 'Serves you right for your tight, upright morals! Why not go bleat with rest of the flock or beat yourself off in a frenzy?'

But her cheek only spurred on the cruel man's wickedness: next morning, the dish on her breakfast tray arrived piled with dog scat.

She might have hurled the mess through the bars, to the ruin of one temple zealot's white surcoat. Yet better sense curbed her. Safest not to flaunt herself as a target before the humourless might of the Sunwheel dedicates.

Empty and dispirited, Daliana stretched out to seek rest on the barren stone floor. She had no blanket. Her creased winter mantle served as her bedding and offered inadequate warmth. Despair made the chill seep down to her bones that much faster. The moon rose at length. Flooded by pallid light through the grille, too ground down in spirit to weep, she watched the sliced, oblate square creep across the cell. Hopeless as the hours slid past, and too soon plunged in jet darkness, she had nothing left but regrets, branded by the shame of her failure.

And her final dawn came. The first seep of grey through the bars brought the temple's dispatched escort under brisk orders to fetch her. The six select men were life-pledged, and agleam in parade arms and full-dress surcoats. Their proud young faces displayed no expression. None would meet her eyes, as though a mere female in rumpled finery posed their righteous souls an endangerment.

'Shine for the Light so brainlessly bright, be careful you haven't blinded yourselves,' Daliana snapped, irked enough to challenge their superior mask while the smirking turnkey unfastened her cell door.

But the True Sect's unnatural creatures did not rise to her baiting comment. Silent, they pinioned her with mailed gauntlets and locked heavy cuffs on her ankles and wrists.

Chained like a felon, she lost her balance when they prodded her forward. Her stumble was yanked up short by brute strength before she crashed to her knees. She asked for a comb, pleaded at least for a moment's respite to tidy her hair.

Ignored, she was shoved onwards down the corridor, in step with the stone-faced escort.

'The Light's judgement won't bide for your vanity,' the superior captain denounced.

Daliana planted her feet. 'Heartless pawn!' She jangled her shackles in brazen contempt. 'Is your emasculate priesthood so driven to fear, you can't stop for one act of kindness?'

The man coloured. His subordinates dealt her a yank towards the stairwell. Since each upward step posed a trial, in fetters, the soldier who reached out to steady her elbow caught her incensed glare, before thanks.

'Do you think I might swoon if I was unbound and permitted the grace to walk upright?' Fright gave her humiliated snarl sharp teeth. 'Tell me, does the temple also chain butterflies? Do you pin down the innocent, night-flying moths, lest some lunatic granny should stir the poor flits into a poisonous potion?'

Her spouted sarcasm was given short shrift, and no answer, as the polished procession hustled her upstairs. She passed by the warden's office and the gouged trestles in the emptied armoury. More guardsmen stationed by the outside entry fell into step as she was thrust through the stone arch at the threshold.

The plunge into daylight was dazzling, after days spent in unrelieved gloom. Gold braid on white surcoats and the flares of reflection thrown off polished armour watered her eyes. As she blinked to compensate, Daliana sighted the open, flat wagon parked in front of the magistrate's hall. The cargo bed had been rigged with a cross-bar on a post, and fitted with bolts for her shackles.

'You will be paraded on public display,' the captain confirmed, beyond sympathy. 'All of Etarra will witness your shame before the priest's judgement condemns you.'

Mortified, haggard, with disheveled hair and the hem of her jaunty, fox mantle frayed into tatters by the dragged chains, Daliana retorted, 'I pity your mother. May you wonder lifelong what base coin she was paid! Surely desperation brought her to breed with a lout too crass to be worthy of fatherhood.'

His slap, gloved in steel, laid open her lip.

'Violence, but no manners?' Daliana observed, and spat blood. 'If the apple hasn't rolled far from the tree, doubtless the sad woman was raped.'

Metal clashed, as her verbal jab goaded the brute to draw steel, which move became waylaid fast by a sensible colleague. 'No, brother. Not here! A premature death is too good for her.'

Daliana showed the dangerous conduct her back and brazened her way forward in clanking steps to the head of the stairway.

A wall of sound slammed her. Shrieked curses and catcalls, obscenities and vilification: the sheer volume of noise made her weak at the knees. Vivacious, endearing, quick-witted in scrapes, Daliana had never imagined such horrendous spite existed in the wide world. Debased as an icon, she dared not give way. While the sky overhead seemed to spin, and the icy cuffs gouged her flesh, she shut her eyes to the howling mob and wrestled the drag of the chain in descent. Someone hurled a rotten onion. It splattered the carved lion atop the left balustrade, while tossed stones rapped and belled off the plumed helms of her immaculate escort.

The harassed captain bellowed, 'Close ranks!'

Armoured guardsmen eclipsed her from hostile view and shielded her awkward course down the stair to the street. When the high step into the wagon defeated her, Daliana sustained the rough grasp that hoisted her, then fastened her upright against the cross-bar. Throughout, the restless crowd chanted abuse.

'Shadow's whore!'

'Servant of Darkness!'

'Burn for your crimes! Seethe in flames for eternity!'

She endured, while her quilted mantle was yanked away from her shoulders. A sword sliced the laced ties of her girdle. After the stiffened green velvet dropped from her waist, her embroidered silk over-dress was as ruthlessly ripped from her body. Left to shiver in her thin linen shift, she watched, horrified, as the temple dedicates tossed her rifled clothing to the ravening crowd. The few decorative seed pearls did not explain the explosive, mad scramble, or the feral hunger that shredded the fabric like jackals set on a carcass.

Veiled as the wind caught her snarled brown hair, Daliana heard the crack as the reinsman whipped up the harness team. The felon's cart jerked and rolled her ahead, the rumble of the iron-rimmed wheels lost into the howl of the crowd. Daliana fixed her gaze upwards. Dawn stained the sky overhead like a bruise. A raucous flock of scavenging crows wheeled above the slate rooftops, notched by Etarra's peaked gables and carved cornices, and smeared by hazed smoke from the chimney-pots.

Across the teeming throng in the plaza loomed the timber frame of a newly built scaffold. The corner posts snapped with the temple's white streamers, and the True Sect's Sunwheel banner replaced the mayor's device on the flag-staff. More snowy bunting streamed where the plank stair on the platform led upwards to the stacked pyre. Laid across a gold-cloth on a ceremonial altar, the silver sword of the Light's executioner waited to pierce her through. Daliana shuddered, chin turned to escape the nauseating reek of poured oil that thickened the breeze. She prayed the ordeal ahead would end quick, before horror unravelled her dignity.

But the ghastly procession dragged on without mercy. Down the main thoroughfare, lined on both sides, gleaming rows of horse-lancers braced back the excitable spectators, while Shadow's captured minion was paraded past as a trophy. If her loosened shift spared Daliana's modesty, the brisk wind cut through the thin cloth with relentless cruelty. She shivered as much from pure gall, that her steadfast effort should be so reviled, then used as the visceral ploy to engage the masses. The Light's priesthood would reap today's raw fascination, a palpable force fanned incandescent by the barbaric prospect of a blood-sacrifice. Lord Lysaer's integrity was already lost. Hounded to war by Desh-thiere's raised curse, he ceded the mayor's seat to a temple usurper. No Etarran possessed the authority to resist. The faithful would riot if anyone tried. The mounted company that backed the Light's Hope held their ironclad files, splendid as heroes, the polished threat of their sharpened arms more than a ceremonial display.

Compelled to bear up, Daliana refused to acknowledge the crowd. The dashing male partners who once had shared her exploits in the taverns or taken her dancing under the lanterns at midsummer, all too likely stood alongside her accusers today. She would give such betrayal no satisfaction. Drama would only fuel the cause of the Light's opportunistic recruiters. More potent than coin or a jack of strong whiskey, the intoxicate promise of glory swayed the town's impressionable bravos. Appalling, how many signed up to bear arms, swept away by the temple's pageantry.

Daliana watched the new day unfold, the sky egg-shell blue and shell pink as the clouds ignited with brightening sunlight. Flocks of birds soared like gilt flecks on the breeze. Life endured, despite her harsh misery. The Sorcerer who had requested her service never promised her a safe outcome.

She must cling to what strength still remained, while the cart rolled her onwards past the smithies, the confectioner's shop, and the vintners, the bakeries, and the threshing mills, the weaver's and the cooper's, tucked chock-a-block in the side streets, familiar ever since birth. Each filled her nose with its distinctive scent: from the acrid reek of the tanners, to the floral bouquet of the perfumer's wares, soaked into brilliant silk scarves that fluttered in the breeze for display.

Daliana wept then, unstrung by the sweetness of roses and mint, of patchouli, gardenia, and lavender. She ached to experience the gladness of spring and acknowledged the loss of her future. Nothing remained but to hold her head up until the sword's point forced her silent.

A shadow swept over her, the sun's stingy warmth eclipsed by the high, tiled roof of the magistrate's hall. A lone raven perched on the spire, a sinister harbinger in most of the tales remembered from childhood. Daliana shuddered. The wagon came full circle too soon, with the hour of judgement upon her. Too swiftly, the crowd's gaudy tumult fell back, dimmed as the temple officer's orders cleared the staircase before the entry. The prisoner's cart rocked to a stop. Men-at-arms with chipped-marble faces stepped up to the cross-post and unpinned her shackles. When Daliana's numbed sinews failed to carry her weight, the impersonal grasp of golden-scaled gauntlets bore her up, colder than ice. Daliana reeled, near helpless, as the Sunwheel dedicates hefted her down.

The sullen beat of the crowd's animosity hammered away at her back, dulled to an ominous growl as she passed beyond public view through the arch at the stair-head. The nervous guardsmen bullied her onwards. Despite her black-out faintness and the onerous weight of her chains, she mastered the clanking drag at her ankles and walked through the carved, double doors. The matched tramp of her escort punched echoes the full length of the grandiose passage beyond. Enveloped in the surreal tang of citrus oil and wax polish, Daliana received only a jumbled impression of tessellated floors, the gleam of fine marble like a closed tomb. The corridor's end swam to her over-stressed senses, and the indoor warmth clogged her tight throat like wet wool.

A herald's trumpet silenced the buzz in the magistrate's hall as she passed the threshold. The hush left her painfully isolate. Her march between the packed rows of seating funnelled her to the forefront, where an overhead dome with costly, paned glass illumined the chamber of state. The solemn ranks of Etarra's town council-men lined the circular wall. Centred upon the half-round dais, the magistrate's panel perched at their bench, gowned like vultures in judicial black. If their robed severity failed to unnerve the criminal supplicant, the crescent array set the centremost stage for the mayor's chair, carved from a block of stygian marble.

Lord Lysaer's absence for the True Sect cause left the white-and-gold pageantry of the temple's robed examiner atop that sovereign throne. Light juxtaposed against dark, aflame in the scintillance of gold braid and diamonds, His Radiance carried the bolt-lightning presence to command subservient awe.

The cry of the herald splintered across the expectant quiet. 'All rise! Honour the truth and defend the meek innocent, let the day's trial commence!'

The dedicates shoved Daliana into the railed enclosure beneath the examiner's feet. Other guardsmen bolted her shackles. With no stool for relief, she stood in isolation, as though she were deadly, or dangerous. The escort secured the gate latch behind her and stayed posted on dutiful watch.

Then the herald banged his mace on the floor, aglitter in his ceremonial tabard. 'May justice prevail, and divine Light defend the path of the righteous!'

The rustle of silk and stirred brocades breathed a mélange of expensive perfumes as the onlookers settled their finery and sat. Several coughs pocked the expectant murmuring. Daliana braced herself to endure. Dizzied and frightened past reason, she suffered the dissecting gaze of the High Priest Examiner, who pressed his charges of dark craft and murder against her.

As nothing before, his venomous survey crippled her courage with dread. Couched in waxy lids, those pale, granite eyes denounced doubt, until pity was absent. His statuesque posture and ringed fingers appeared bloodless as chiselled stone. For the Light's glory alone, he existed. His creed wrote the world's only script for salvation. His upright gold mace and the lot of the damned seemed as righteously unassailable.

'We are gathered today to destroy a grand threat to well-being, goodness, and innocence,' the examiner opened. 'The accused, you may think, wears a harmless appearance. Small, a mere snip of a woman, she may not appear likely to wield any subversive power as a minion of Shadow. That lie will be stripped before witnesses, here. The masquerade of such girlish meekness harbours an evil so monstrous, no upright citizen dares to speak as her advocate.'

'Let me correct you,' denounced an unruffled voice from the commoner's ranks. A lean man arose, clad in plain scholar's black, and limped down the central aisle. Outflanked by his mildness, the dedicate cordon had no cause to stop his advance. He tipped up a wide-brimmed felt hat and declared, 'Let the magistrate's record restate that Daliana sen Evend does have an advocate. More, the folk gathered here may prefer not to be swayed by unfounded rhetoric. Let us hear forthright questions. If this court is honest, and not a staged drama to heighten the thrill of an execution, I charge the panel to weigh the events that have called this tribunal in session.'

A livid pinch clamped the examiner's lips. Inconvenienced, and cornered by the rote tissue of ceremony, he barked at the clerk's sallow servant. 'Fetch a chair for the prisoner's advocate and let the proceedings resume!'

The intellect behind his needled impatience broke Daliana into a quivering sweat. Snared game before the scrapping of wolves, she feared for her volunteer ally.

'Don't do this,' she implored him under her breath.

Her distress met eyes of limpid, warm brown, creased at the corners by laughter, and genteel silver hair, worn shoulder length, and tied with a velvet cord. A matching band of filigree adorned his dark hat, tipped back from clean-shaven features. The dome's frosty light only reinforced the sincerity written into the weathered face underneath. The stranger's scarred grip accepted the chair brought by the flustered chamberlain. Leaned on the back to relieve his game leg, the fellow refused to be hurried.

'Daliana sen Evend, you are not alone,' he declared, pitched only for her. 'Never believe that hope has deserted you.' The burled grain that roughened his voice was as water in drought, and lightened her heart like the glimmer of starshine.

Then the gavel banged on the magistrate's bench. The Lord Examiner's reprimand splintered across reassurance. 'Silence, before the assembly!'

Unperturbed, the advocate turned the chair to face forward, and sat. 'Please call me by Trey.'

Daliana's breath caught. The name well might be the short-form for another, attached to a Fellowship Sorcerer: Traithe, whose dauntless work had cut off the Mistwraith's lethal invasion through South Gate. The cost left him crippled, and scars from the trauma yet impaired his faculties. To show himself here posed a terrible risk. The limp posed a red flag to anyone versant in the particulars of Third Age history. Traithe had played no small part in the failed effort to restore s'Ffalenn rule at Etarra three centuries past. And Erdane's older archive, sequestered with the temple, held the fullest account of his greater renown. The Sorcerer's attributes were infamous there, with the Sunwheel priesthood aligned as the Fellowship's inveterate enemies.

The intensity of the Lord Examiner's glare suggested the advocate's identity had been exposed. The man would close his trap on bigger quarry if he could, aware of the delicate vulnerability that had kept Traithe sequestered in long-term obscurity.

Though wise beyond measure, this was not Asandir, fit and able to outface a high priest's tribunal without mortal risk.

'Faith, brave one!' Trey whispered. His sly wink brushed off Daliana's dismay, that he walked naked into the snake's den. 'I do have a plan for redemption at hand.'

But the unspoken truth lurked behind the fact he had guaranteed no deliverance.

The cat-and-mouse gambit unavoidably thrust his life into jeopardy alongside hers. Daliana saw little chance of reprieve. From the buzzard's row on the bench, Etarra's magistrate called the first witness against her.

The apple-cheeked barmaid from the Red Cockerel minced forward. She curtseyed nervously before the dais, her holiday skirt clutched between work-chapped hands, and her lank, mousy hair tidied up with shell combs. 'Your worthiness,' she declared, 'by the holy Light, hear the truth.'

Daliana all but collapsed with relief. Hattsey had been her fellow conspirator through more than one high-jinks scrape. Her reliable kindness had unbarred the back-alley door many times to lend shelter from hot-footed pursuit.

'As I live and breathe,' the barmaid declared, 'what took place on that morning was witchcraft.'

The earnest betrayal denounced every vestige of former loyalty. Daliana stared in stark disbelief at a friend changed into stranger.

Hattsey wrung beefy hands and avoided the prisoner's shocked face. 'I've known Daliana sen Evend for years. Never took her for a pawn of the Dark. But I can't say otherwise, your worships. Not now. I had a clear view when she threw her knife that day in the tap-room. By my own life, I swear the unnatural flash was a spell meant to murder the temple's ambassador. More, I can vouch for the years Shadow's evil required to refine her intent. Half the young men in Etarra have lost their purses to her deadly prowess.'

Simple, unpolished, the damning phrase hung.

While Daliana reeled with hurt, the magnanimous examiner blessed

Hattsey's courageous honesty, then invited rebuttal from the defender. 'Will the advocate speak for the prisoner?'

'Not at this time,' Trey stated, crisp. His walnut brown eyes regarded the Light's prosecutor with quiet interest. He had noted the subtlety: the barmaid received the Light's leave to retire, a high-handed assumption of judicial authority.

While the scraping pens of the clerks filled the pause, and Hattsey tramped back to her seat, Etarra's upstaged magistrate cleared his throat and intoned, 'May the second witness for the case come forward!'

The Red Cockerel's lanky bar-keeper stood up, wooden in his formal jacket. Steps pinched in stiff shoes with buckles, he stalked to the fore with his chin out-thrust and his beak nose pink with embarrassment. 'I could not settle my conscience, your worships. Since our Lord Mayor Lysaer's gone to war against Shadow, my part's to come clean and speak for what's decent.'

Daliana realized, horrified, that he, too, believed she connived hand in glove with the forces of Darkness. Of those turned out for the summons against her, the front rows were packed with people she knew. All avoided her glance. Even strangers turned from her, lest the sight of her face should spread the taint of corruption. One by one, from tradesmen to shop-girls, workaday folk stepped up and condemned her. Many were loath to risk their own necks, or seem involved by association. Others assumed she was guilty out of persistent ignorance. Confusion or malice, the difference was moot. Hatred and fear forged their devout sincerity into an adamant chorus.

As each statement finished, the examiner kept form and offered the advocate's right to rebuttal; and each time, brief in courtesy, Trey waived the chance to argue for the accused. Disheartened and wrung by nervous exhaustion, Daliana wrestled her strangling doubt, afraid her Sighted instinct had been mistaken.

The scholarly fellow could not be Traithe come at risk, but a man: brave enough for a token gesture of comfort but too spineless to challenge the temple. He listened in silence, while the packed throng grumbled and squirmed in their seats. As morning wore on, their restlessness chafed through the stream of repetitive statements.

'Get on!' a heckler burst out from the rear. 'Heard enough claptrap to know right from wrong! Let's have the sentence and watch the witch burn!'

'Bring on the torch! We're tired of waiting!' a matron agreed from the side-lines.

More clamour arose. While the magistrate rapped his gavel for order, and the dedicate guardsmen broke ranks to quell the offenders, the examiner sat motionless, jowls pouched over his gilded collar and his fleshy hand firm on his mace. A viper might lurk with such coiled stillness. If he appeared content to bear through the laborious detail, his chilly quiet acknowledged the tactic spun by his disarming adversary.

The case dragged to tedium without an enlivened spark of dispute. As the grind of procedure back-lashed, and the swell of high feeling edged towards rebellion, the examiner cracked out in reprimand, 'Advocate Trey! If you make no appeal, I suggest your defense is a mockery that squanders the court's precious time!'

'You would stoop to a premature settlement?' Trey stood, unassuming, more than a bit awkward as he favoured his crippled leg. Yet somehow his soft rebuttal shamed the fretful listeners for their impatience. 'Should your verdict carry the least spark of doubt? A young woman's life is at stake! Condemn her outright, or pass sentence on her before the last witness is heard, and what justice is served? Before stakes so final, I suggest that lost time is a trifling nuisance! Since when has an officious seat on a hard chair become so absurdly unbearable?' Through titters and several muffled guffaws, Trey pursued with adamant gentleness, 'For Daliana sen Evend, the outcome today weighs the sum of her living days. Is authority gone soft before the gravity of a charge of dark practice, or worse, does the temple's creed bend its morals for mere mortal frailty?'

The examiner raised long-suffering eyebrows. 'How many damning testimonials do you deem sufficient before the accused receives judgement?' Scorn became sarcasm, with the restive crowd played for a deft riposte. 'Must we exhaust the truth unto tedium when all the accounts have converged? The honour of principle matters by all means, had dispute been raised by even one voice.'

'I have heard the same evidence.' Trey smiled at his glittering adversary with delighted complacence. 'Certain facts align, this is true: that a knife was thrown; that harm resulted. Also, that an arcane flash was observed, caused by a discharge of rogue spellcraft. But are the bystanders we've heard thus far equipped to discern the origins of such power? Let me demonstrate the uncertainty of an eyewitness presumption!' A raised hand forestalled the examiner's bristle, as Trey pressured back, firmly reasonable, 'I choose to speak now in Daliana's behalf!' Against rising protest, he framed an appeal that rang echoes off the vaulted dome. 'A just law will defend that hearing!'

Uproar swept the audience. The magistrate banged his gavel repeatedly, while the examiner's officious, jerked nod was compelled to acknowledge due process.

Trey beckoned towards the cluster of latecomers packed against the rear wall. A mantled figure answered his summons and strode down the central aisle. While heads turned, and seated folk craned their necks in curiosity, expensive silk rustled to each dainty stride, distinctively trimmed with fine burgundy ribbon. The diaphanous hood laced and beaded with pearls raised murmurs of shocked recognition. Hats were swept off with astonished respect. Appalled murmurs of *'milady,'* pocked the silence that settled over the chamber.

Except for the magistrate on the justiciar's bench, who shot erect, and blurted,

'What are you doing here?' Crimson with embarrassment, he cried, 'Who has coerced my wife to stand for a crass charge and appear in a common assembly?'

'She hasn't!' Trey gestured for the demure arrival to lower the jewelled hood.

Revealed beneath, shamefaced and shy, was the drudge who mopped floors at the Red Cockerel Tavern.

Through the explosion of talk and rough laughter, the magistrate shouted, more outraged, 'Then who stole that mantle from my lady's wardrobe? I will not bear the insult! Or see my wife made the butt of vulgarity, or have my court turned into a charlatan's puppet show!'

Trey added nothing, but waited, while another fashionably attired figure arose from the public seating. Also unveiled, and quite unabashed, the magistrate's pretty wife came forward and retrieved her aristocrat's mantle from the tavernmaid's awkward grasp. 'I lent the clothes,' she announced, crisp enough to pierce through the bedlam. 'Since the advocate asked, lest an innocent burn, I agreed to assist the defense.'

The official beside the deflated magistrate snatched the gavel and pounded for quiet while a dutiful clerk on his opposite side grasped the upset husband's sleeve and urged him back into his seat.

Trey held the floor as the uproar subsided. His sweet-natured courtesy dismissed the tavern girl, then thanked the magistrate's admirable lady. To the gathering at large, and the bench, he pronounced, 'Have I not demonstrated the difference between informed truth and impressionable opinion? All testimony must be weighed to the end to eliminate prejudice.'

The Light's Examiner fielded the unforeseen set-back with narrowed eyes. Masked displeasure soured his suave refutation. 'You are wasting our time and for what, if not sleight of hand presented for dishonest subterfuge? The woman accused was bare-faced through her crime! Daliana sen Evend wore her own raiment when she unleashed her act of dark sorcery against me!'

Not feinting now, Trey was earnestly swift to agree. 'Daliana sen Evend threw a knife in a public tap-room, which drew the blood of a temple ambassador. A subsequent eruption of wildfire ignited some clothing and, afterward, blistered a few patches of skin. But whether such bodily harm was intended, or if you, as Erdane's delegate, were the intended target, we are not here today to dispute your claim for a personal injury! Rather, this court must determine the party responsible for the unwholesome craft discharged in the course of the incident. Guilt on that count has yet to be proven! Though I do concur: to seal the writ for an execution, culpability or innocence must be established beyond question.'

The Lord Examiner smiled, all teeth. 'You confirm, as the advocate of the accused, that the testimony of each single witness must rest, or be clearly refuted?'

'Yes, of course.' Trey inclined his hatted head, grave. 'All accounts must concur. To eliminate the least shade of doubt, do resume straightaway.'

That promise the bait to silence contention, the temple's examiner accepted the challenge, convinced of his inevitable victory.

Trey reclaimed his seat, diminished again to a scholarly stoop. More witnesses came. The inexhaustible stream droned through the same repetitive story. Before the advocate's rapt neutrality, and the examiner's stifled impatience, every testimony insisted the minion should burn for liaison with Shadow. Noon's glare waxed and faded, replaced by the cerulean light of late day. From outside, the increasingly rambunctious mob protested the undue delay. An officer's horn-call raised shouted retorts. Tension mounted as the dedicate lancers outside re-formed ranks to curb the crowd's shiftless ferocity. Tempers shortened on both sides as True Sect faith clashed headlong with the restless dissent of Etarra's populace. Denied the blood thrill of their promised spectacle, the volatile multitude boiled towards riot.

And still, the onerous trial ground on without a crisp end or conviction.

The examiner clenched his jewelled mace, well aware he must finish debate. If the straightforward verdict dangled much longer, he risked being made the advocate's puppet-strung fool.

Meantime, a smith's boy stumbled through his painfully earnest statement, while questions from Trey prompted what seemed a useless review of detail. 'You say this temple official received a wrapped packet brought to the Red Cockerel by a female courier? And that the thrown knife sliced open the wrapped object which changed hands? That instant, you swear, the flash of released spellcraft ignited the ambassador's sleeve. Tell us about the item itself. Can you recall its appearance?'

The smith's boy screwed up his florid face. "Twere cloth scraps, mister. Covered in silk, and twisted with copper wire and hair. The thing reeked when it caught. Know this much from working the forge, hair stinks like that when it burns.'

'Good,' Trey encouraged. 'What of the courier? Was she unusual in any way?'

'I didn't see,' the smith's boy apologized. 'She was cloaked. But the street child who blacks boots for the merchants noticed she had a strange scent about her, not like anything natural.'

The prisoner's advocate pounced with asperity. 'I insist on a statement from that same street child. More, another witness at hand observed the questionable packet. The boy who cleans ash from the tavern's hearth stated the item was silk-wrapped, and still tied when Daliana's knife sliced open the covering. When the noisome contents became exposed,' Trey added, and smiled at the fidgety smith's boy, 'that was the moment when you saw the flash?'

'Enough!' The Light's examiner swept erect with a rap of his ceremonial stave. 'This sham ends! By the sacred Light, I demand solid evidence.'

'One attested item, wrought of cloth scraps and hair, wrapped in silk, and brought to the scene by a woman disguised as a courier? We have a significant break in this case,' Trey contradicted. 'The boy here has just described a fetch wrought by craft, which your defendant's knife disarmed prematurely within public view. I insist the conclusion has been misinterpreted! Daliana sen Evend in fact thwarted a vile plot, and much more. The guilty party who engaged that rogue practice would be the anonymous messenger.'

The examiner snapped. 'Your spurious tale is designed to thwart justice!'

Trey scraped back his chair and stood also. Above the unsettled growl of disturbance, and more muffled noise from the outside corridor, he pealed, 'If you think this young lady has not suffered the worse for delay, you are pitiless. Look at her!'

Pale and trembling, Daliana clung to the rail at the strained edge of collapse. Before the picture of her mortal frailty swayed the crowd into sympathy, the Lord Examiner leveled his mace towards the advocate.

'This is a meddling effrontery!' Well aware whom he faced, secure in his power, he lashed back in formal accusation, 'Who is this man, bent to obfuscate truth with pathos and trivia? I'll not have the Light's sanctified cause swerved and twisted! Only a collaborate servant of Darkness or a sorcerer would hinder this clear-cut case!'

However Trey might have pleaded, the dedicates poised by the dais moved to order, unsheathed weapons, and surrounded him. He made no resistance. Pinned under arrest by a dozen bared swords, he seemed doomed beyond all reprieve.

Daliana buckled, wrung faint under pressure and barely aware of the second commotion, erupted at the back of the hall. One leaf of the double doors barreled open. The report as the panel banged the far wall shattered echoes through the assembly. Inbound, determined, someone's irreverent bass slurred a drunken verse of snide doggerel.

While the dedicates seethed in a steely pack to quash the abrasive intrusion, the stout intruder bashed through their midst, caroling loudly off key:

> 'We don't kiss the hind cheeks of the hog on the seat,
>   sucking up to his pig-turd religion!
> Roust up, bust his bollocks, kick arse with a wallop,
>   and pluck the Light's game-cocks like pigeons.'

Incensed to bulged eyes, the temple examiner lost his decorum. 'Arrest that sot! Now!'

The two Sunwheel dedicates in closest pursuit snagged the singer's stout wrists and planted their feet. Their manhandled quarry checked short in midstagger, folded abruptly, and sat.

His rump hit the floor with a smack. The almighty yank transferred to the braced guardsmen, whose hobnailed boots found no purchase on the slick marble. Before sliding, they bowed, cracked helms with a clangour, and dropped in a heap overtop the roisterer.

The squashed fellow heaved off their dazed bulk, his tuneless meter broken to insults. 'Tin-plate pansies! Learn to walk, can't you? I resent the damnfool whack on the head. As if my soused brain wasn't already sore from the lies spouted off by your tinsel-sham priest!'

Provoked to a roar, every Sunwheel dedicate charged to defend the temple's maligned honour. They converged. The drunk scrambled. The concerted lunge to capture him missed, as the entangled ranks tripped over the dazed sprawl of their own fallen. The tangle threshed in an oath-riddled effort to sort itself out. While men hampered like turtles with plate steel whacked elbows to free their hooked gear from their fellows, the miscreant squirted out of the heap. Panting in a frantic hands-and-knees scuttle, he shot down the centre aisle.

Someone's yell alerted the soldiers still upright. Their quarry dived left and wriggled between the packed seats, progress marked down the rows by the flustered spectators, who raised startled feet to avoid him. Others shrieked in outrage for yanked buckles and crushed toes, while the furious soldiers in hot pursuit funnelled into a jam with a din like a smithy attacked by a fiend storm.

'Don't trash the parade-ground shine on your gear,' the victim mocked through his alcohol fumes and choked laughter.

Hornet mad, the hazed dedicates unsheathed their swords. They shoved in with points brandished to skewer the rat, who rolled sidewards and eeled underneath the low benches occupied by the commoners. Commotion erupted, tracked by feminine squeals as his burrowing progress snagged skirts. Heaved furniture upset, topsy-turvy, with several citizens dumped into the laps of the disgruntled spectators behind them. Annoyed bellows changed pitch to snarled oaths as order unravelled like snags in jerked knit, and more armoured dedicates sallied down the aisles to flank the juggernaut course of the fugitive.

But their chased prey doubled back like a mole and headed for the front rows. The Light's defenders waded in after him, bashing the hapless bystanders aside in the course of their red-faced pursuit.

Hysterical raps of the magistrate's gavel failed to mend the court-room's fractured decorum. The onslaught of pandemonium crested, with more alarmed shouts from the rear of the hall, where a disproportionate number of dedicates were still down, and a captain's dismayed expletives swore by the Light that stray *iyats* kept the stricken from rising. Worse, the fierce chase in progress amid the packed chairs lost its cohesive forward momentum. The balked pack of dedicates circled and split, confused when the path of their quarry erupted in several directions at once.

'Sorcery!' shrieked the distraught examiner. 'This is an invasion, provoked by rogue magecraft allied with Shadow!'

The rumpled head of the perpetrator emerged at floor level, bracketed by two chair struts and bonneted over forehead and ears with the ruffles of a woman's petticoat. 'Sorcery? No. That would be the pearls,' he confessed. 'Big as marbles,' he added, 'broken loose from a rich lady's necklace. A dastardly mess, beyond question.'

Which sabotage explained why several braw guardsmen sharply windmilled their arms and crashed flat. More were obstructed, shoved aside, even tripped by the greed-driven scrimmage to salvage the glittering contraband.

The insurgent drunk became pummelled, as well, since the female whose skirt indecently sheltered him screamed and clipped him on the ear with a patten.

The hen-pecked fugitive wormed backwards and vanished before her jealous husband booted him senseless.

Abetted by a weasel's agility, the offender's inventive course of sown havoc threatened to stall the proceedings indefinitely. While the elite cordon who safeguarded His Radiance deployed at their captain's crisp order, the suspicious temple examiner turned his thwarted fury upon the advocate held at his mercy.

'Have that man searched for a sorcerer's evidence,' he snapped to the dedicates who seized Trey. 'Disarm him if he carries even a penknife.'

Pinned down by unsheathed steel, Trey was brutally searched, his clothes rifled, then torn, until beyond question his person was proven to be weaponless.

That semblance of harmlessness galled the examiner's patience. 'Shackle him, now! We can't risk an escape. No, don't wait for the warden. Instead, share out the woman's restraints. Take the cuffs from her ankles and bind up his wrists.'

The gate to the criminal's stall was unfastened, with Trey bustled inside between four armoured stalwarts. While two bent to handle the short-fall of fetters, their vigilant comrades pressed Trey's back at weapons' point. Still, his underhand whisper reached Daliana, masked by the on-going, urgent commotion stirred by the errant drunk. 'If this rescue goes wrong, your chains will be struck. Run for your life. Snatch a civilian's mantle and hide. Should we fail, here, the peace will be broken past recourse. Your chance for escape will be narrow.'

'What about you?' Daliana gripped the rail, transparently frightened. If a Fellowship Sorcerer offered himself as a sacrifice in her behalf, the bitter stakes must lie beyond imagining. 'What will become of your foolhardy henchman?'

'He's not what he seems.' Traithe winced, pained by his infirmities as the mailed hands of the dedicates pinioned his shoulders. They laid bare his spider-web array of scars and locked his wrists into shackles.

By then, the stout clown under siege in the crowd lost his luck, cornered at last as the elite reinforcements bashed through the last barrier of vacated seats and collared him like a loose mongrel. Yanked up short by the scruff, then manhandled through the riveted onlookers to a salvo of howled epithets, he fought his captors tooth and nail down the aisle and up to the base of the dais.

There, a gruff dedicate with a bloodied nose levered him with an arm-lock that flung him belly down at the feet of the temple examiner.

Expectancy quieted the moiled gathering, underscored by the ominous noise still boiling in the outside street. If that brew of roused fury sparked into a riot, no dedicate lancers' stern prowess could stem the mob poised to storm the assembly.

The examiner stood. Pressured to appease the riled crowd's discontent, he leveled his shining mace at the prostrate heckler. 'Since your gross disruption of these proceedings has delayed an execution for dark sorcery, I declare your life forfeit for abetting the forces of Shadow! By sword and by fire, I will see you dead! Let your carcass share the scaffold and burn alongside your two confederates.'

The condemned miscreant lifted his chin from the floor, brown eyes widened with mirthful astonishment. 'You'd see a man damned for a lark's binge on *beer*?'

While half the disgruntled audience laughed, and the flushed magistrate pounded his gavel, the Light's examiner towered full height and glared until the righteous force of his office choked the unruly guffaws into a scorched silence. 'Drunken or sober, the charge is rogue practice! Or how else did this scapegrace side-step the Light's guard and crash through the closed doors of this chamber?'

A befuddled blink, a loud belch, and a pinched frown filled the pause as the accused buffoon twisted his head, eyes slewed upwards to rake the high dais. Through his disordered mop of grey-streaked chestnut hair, his pouched features showed jilted surprise 'Ath!' he blasphemed with heretical nerve. 'You accuse *me* of corrupting your Sunwheel dedicates? *This* through some dab trick of spellcraft on my part?' Abashed to a squirm that sketched a sheepish shrug, the sot added, 'Here's a ripe True Sect fallacy, spoken in cast-iron form! Surely you never meant to admit that your lily-white troops might be hoodwinked? Why not confess they've bowed to a godhead who, frankly, spat in the eyes of your priesthood at Erdane two centuries ago and walked out!'

The goaded examiner smothered his fury. Resplendent in his gemmed dazzle of vestments, he contrived to sit down with aplomb, his haughty regard flat with boredom. 'No one's deceived by your pathetic diversions. Mockery is the sure mark of the cynic, unredeemed and cut off from salvation. But then, Dakar, your name's already blackened as the affiliate prophet of Sorcerers. Hand in glove with Fellowship interests, and in cahoots with this false advocate, *Trey*, accept that your effort to free a practitioner in league with Shadow has failed.'

'Your canon's outdated,' Dakar retorted. 'You haven't heard?' He broke off and smiled, all teeth, then let fly. 'I was booted from the Fellowship's good graces for upstart behaviour. Correct your holy records on that point, at least! As for the spurious charges just cited, what hard proof do you have to condemn any one of the three of us?' Still distastefully pinned by two muscular guards,

Dakar waggled his hips with obscene invitation. 'Go on, you egg-sucking albino parasites! Strip me to the skin like you did the old man! You'll find nothing interesting tucked in my rump cheeks. Not a splinter of bone, or a plucked wisp of hair tied in cloth and infused as a fetch to bend anyone to my purpose.'

The examiner sniffed. 'The dangerous fact that you mock such rare knowledge refutes your pat claim of innocence.'

'Does it?' Dakar stiffened, awkward as a gaffed trout beneath the crush of hobnailed boots. 'I've been Fellowship-taught to discern the nuance between right workings and wrong. Tell me, what arcane study makes you an expert? *Prayer?* If Trey could be summarily searched at your whim, then bound in chains without cause, shouldn't we watch while you turn out your own sanctimonious pockets, first?' Forced to shout, the Mad Prophet hurled down his gauntlet. 'Or how does the court know you aren't twisting my will? Or anyone else's, for that matter?'

Outrage exploded into a shocked uproar that plunged Daliana's plight into eclipse. Even as the dedicate captain raised his sword to impale the lout heretic, Dakar turned his cheek and shrieked over the noise, 'I demand a formal review of this case by an accredited temple diviner!'

More concerned for decorum, the Lord Examiner curbed his aggressive officer with a rebuke. 'The Light's blood retribution will take place in public.' Then, unsmiling, he dismissed Dakar's pestering plea. 'Pity your case! The diviner attached to my train left for Tysan at the right hand of the avatar, Lysaer s'Ilessid.' Against the barrage of unrest from the street, his remonstrance pressed yet again for swift closure. 'Sadly for you, Etarra does not maintain a staffed True Sect temple. With no resident diviner to serve your appeal, my office determines your fate. Let the record be sealed. Have the guilty removed for immediate execution.'

That peremptory sentence unleashed the guard, who moved at once to drag the condemned to the scaffold. Since Trey offered no fight, and no fetters were struck, which dashed her last hope of escape, Daliana shivered, too parched to speak through her terror as the white-armoured dedicates closed in to take her.

No such set-back quelled Dakar's ripe tongue. While his bucking contortions sweated his swearing guardsmen to grunts of effort, he raged, 'Who are you pimping for?' Mulishly kicking at armoured shins, he pealed at the officious examiner, 'Why rush for the sword and the pyres? Or does your false doctrine fear a change of verdict if you waited for the word of a vested diviner?'

'But I am here!' a clear voice declaimed through the turmoil. 'More, I'm bound by my office to declare this session a mistrial!' Mud-stained from hard travel, the out-of-turn speaker barged through the already breached doorway. While the dedicates at the threshold gave way, the newcomer added, 'No act of sorcery has befouled these proceedings!'

Swept down the aisle like a scud of storm-cloud, the temple diviner raked back his hood. 'Free the prisoners at once,' he commanded the captain.

'On what authority?' the examiner shrilled. 'This is a flagrant breach of High Temple order!'

A thin man with a sensitive face and a shock of disordered, red hair, the diviner looked pithlessly trapped as he tugged off his glove. Unveiled, the ruby seal ring he wore gleamed with the mayor's cartouche, bestowed as Lord Lysaer's token. 'I carry fair warning. Disobey at your peril!'

'Corruption! Conspiracy!' the flustered examiner howled. Through the restive roar of the crowd, he snapped contrary orders to the ranked dedicate. 'Captain! Seize that forsworn diviner. He has been suborned by Darkness itself if he thinks to commute a criminal sentence with a counterfeit claim to be the spokesman for divine will!'

'This is not temple ground,' yet another arrival declaimed, whiplash curt from beyond the broached portal.

'Seal off that entrance!' the examiner fumed. 'Is every free-booting protester allowed the fool's chance to disrupt this tribunal?'

While the chastised dedicates swarmed to bar the doors, a flash-point barrage from the outer hallway crisped the wood panels to cinders and smoke. Shouting, astonished, the guardsmen reeled backwards, several beating live flames from singed surcoats. Then, as if clubbed, they sank onto their knees.

Lysaer s'Ilessid emerged through the flurry of sparks. Haloed from blond head to spurred boots in pure light, he breezed past the smelted wreck of the hinges and kicked through the last smouldering, charcoal debris. Fresh from the saddle, his scarlet mantle wafted the scent of foamed horse as he whipped back the folds and exposed the emblazoned seal of Etarra. Down the aisle he came in clipped strides, ablaze with a corona of power not raised in public sight for over two hundred years. The view shattered objective credibility. For doubters who had smirked over a myth, or scoffed at the embellished fancy of legend, denial smashed at one stroke.

The examiner blanched. His impervious poise blasted to disbelief, he darted a furtive hand beneath the breast of his Sunwheel robe.

Whatever he sought with brazen desperation prompted a shudder of dread. Prickled by a surge of blood instinct, Daliana screamed. Still chained, all but felled in the paralyzed grasp of the dumbfounded dedicates, she wrenched at her bonds, pressured by the raw need to take to her heels for survival. In concert with her terrified struggle, Dakar bellowed in warning.

Trey moved, shed his poleaxed guards by stark force and smashed shoulder down through the rungs of the prisoner's dock railing. His forward surge ducked the belated guard. He straightened as fast and swung his cuffed forearms in a sweeping stroke that slammed into the examiner's propped mace. The metal-shod tip skidded backwards and hooked between the official's robed legs. Trey caught the jewelled tip. His adroit wrench torqued the examiner's balance and tumbled him down the carpeted stair.

The object just surreptitiously palmed was flung clear. A small packet cast loose from an untied silk wrapping bounced to the floor near the Mad Prophet's feet.

Dakar pinned the item under his heel, then yelled bloody murder until the temple's diviner dashed forward and retrieved the crushed morsel of evidence.

Etarra's town council beheld the construct just unveiled: a wad of scrap linen torn from a man's shirt, twined about with a stamped copper band and fastened by a lead sigil. The spelled mark, quite deformed by Dakar's apt weight, still clamped a hank of black hair. More than the item's sinister appearance, its aura of *wrongness* pitched Daliana to clammy distress.

The mere touch stung the temple's diviner to recoil. 'Light Avert! That thing reeks of dark sorcery wrought with vile intent to seed ruin!'

'Well it should,' declared Dakar, bitterly crisp and no longer afflicted by drunk affectation. 'The sigil configured into that seal is a bane ward wrought by a Koriani grand circle! Your priestly delegation has spear-headed a conspiracy. Behold the proof of a plot launched to usurp the mayor's seat and ensnare Lord Lysaer as the order's string-puppet to extend the True Sect's influence.'

Trey shrugged free of the dedicates' hold, shed his locked chains, and tipped back his bent hat. 'There's danger yet active. Let me dispose of that.' Commanding despite the tattered wreck of his clothes, he took firm charge of the construct before Etarra's stunned magistrate murmured a protest. Past the outflanked guards in a purposeful stride, Trey ducked down the side aisle, limped past the gawping crowd, and left through the open door.

Colder than sword steel sheathed in ice, Lysaer did not turn a hair, or remark on the irregularity of a Fellowship presence. He spared no glance at the awe-struck onlookers. Swathed yet in a blaze of adamant light, he confronted the examiner, collapsed in prostration amid his crumpled regalia.

'Who carries the key to the prisoners' shackles?'

Movement, to his right, as a trembling dedicate owned up to that responsibility.

Lysaer cracked, 'Withdraw your men! Dakar is not guilty, and Daliana sen Evend is reprieved from this baseless charge of dark practice. Release her at once. Then answer my call to account for the harm done by this court's ruthless case of mishandling!'

With scarcely a pause, the searing rebuke laced into the disgraced examiner. 'How dare you sully my law by disrupting due process, then seeking to lay wrongful blame on an innocent?' Arctic blue, the Lord Mayor's eyes did not waver. Tangled hair and aristocratic, pale skin lost no majesty for the grime ingrained by hard travel. In whip-crack consonants, Lysaer raged onwards through a hush that gripped the air like sheared diamond. 'That woman's heroic stand with a knife has exposed your criminal ambition! All present have witnessed that your temple works hand in glove with the Koriathain. What blandishment did their Prime Matriarch offer your high priesthood at Erdane?

Did you truly think to parade me as the front to incite the followers of your false doctrine?'

The diviner grovelled on in fraught shock, then gushed on in supplication, 'Blessed Lord, forgive! Most of us knew nothing. Nothing! I swear by the Light. Our examiner's grotesque corruption was enacted under tight secrecy! Let His Radiance carry the blame for his guilt, and show divine mercy to those of us in his train who have stayed righteously faithful to your god-sent cause.'

'Faithful? To what!' Lysaer returned a glare that smoked with fury. 'I reject any claim to become the figure-head avatar of your religion. Your creed is hollow and nothing of mine, but a sham to entice weaker minds into slavery!'

Before the shamed diviner drew his next breath, Lysaer dismissed his plea with a roughshod demand that brooked no appeal. 'Tell me how your priest-hood would punish the act of wielding a charged construct fashioned by forbidden practice?'

The distressed diviner pressed his damp forehead to the floor and recited by rote from the temple canon. 'The penalty for malign sorcery is death by a sword through the heart, with the body consumed to ashes by fire.'

'Then stand erect and take charge of your own!' Blistered past patience, Lysaer declared the verdict forthwith. 'By your own covenant, see justice done in my town square before sundown. Make use of the readied scaffold and pyre. Then withdraw your discredited embassy. Get out of my sight, to the last mindless hypocrite, and be far beyond Etarra's walls before your apostate's remains have cooled. Or else forfeit the delegate's grant of safe conduct as I challenge your Light-sotted dedicates to take arms upon my field of war!'

After-shock

Daliana returned to the hazy awareness of close warmth and the intoxicating softness of linen bed-clothes, pressed and sweetened with herbals. A bliss lately encountered only in dreams did not shatter upon reawakening, transformed back into oppressive, dank stone, and the stiffened aches of a body beset by relentless exposure to chill.

Instead, she basked in the sweet kiss of sun spilled through sparkling glass, which bathed her shut lids in carmine. Memory recognized the spice blend of sandalwood, overlaid by the scent of the bees-wax polish that infused the Lord Mayor's private suite. The creamy linens and fine coverlet that cosseted her smelled of the patchouli a rich man's valet used to soothe fair skin after shaving.

Astonishment followed. She was in Lysaer's bed: a circumstance ripely deplored by her ancestor, Sulfin Evend, when his two-fisted heroics had snatched his liege from the past jaws of disaster.

Reprieved from the scaffold, Daliana sheltered under the tenacious protection that Lysaer s'Ilessid awarded to those who defended his weakness at mortal hazard. Therefore, truth backed the legend: loyal persistence in fact could destroy his regal shell of reserve. A terrible hurdle, that few friendships crossed, since the hazardous service that guarded his back held no guarantee of survival.

Daliana smothered her vixen's smile before that spontaneous reaction spoiled everything. She was in Lysaer's bed! Not the outcome she had imagined, or wished, though at present, his imperious motive seemed chaste. Though the nicety of her feminine privacy did not receive the same degree of respect. Daliana noticed that someone's gentle fingers stroked her hair, while two heated male voices clashed in debate, immediately overhead.

285

'I will not rescind that order! The muster proceeds. Don't argue! This ugly development requires an armed stand to confirm my active resistance.'

'That's madness!' Gruffly pitched, less controlled, the denouncement packed sting. 'Lysaer, you cannot ignore the dire influence you must withstand—'

Contradiction came, smoking. 'Yes! I do know. The pressures of risk must be faced! Compromise at this pass is unthinkable.' Movement provoked the slide of a silk sleeve, as a gesture forestalled interruption. 'The True Sect temple's aggressive crusade now seeks conquest by outright invasion! The priests are not allied with the Koriathain through shared interest. Their temple aims to consolidate power, a drive the Prime Matriarch steers for her own ends to recapture my half brother—' The breathless, strained pause stretched into harsh tension before Lysaer curbed his besieged will and resumed. 'Believe this, Dakar. I knew when the Master of Shadow was freed. Did you truly think the onslaught of the Mistwraith's curse would escape me? Heaven's grace! Ever seen a fox caught in a leg trap? This horror is unimaginably worse. Defy that at your peril! You can't grapple the nightmare. Nor will I allow you. My trials won't stand your mage-sighted conscience stumbling about underfoot.'

The clipped rejection rang with a chill most would have mistaken for enmity.

Daliana's inborn talent for truth-sense perceived only deeply armoured defensiveness. Lysaer, afraid, retreated behind the unimpeachable facade of the statesman. Even in private, he dared not give ground. Weakness only fed the malign forces he grappled. His sharp evasion desperately sought to vent deadly pressure before the frothed pot boiled over. 'The Mistwraith's geas resumed on the instant my mother's bastard recovered his liberty. Since then, the coal of irrational hatred burns in me, waking and sleeping.'

Silverware chinked against porcelain as Dakar broke off his pursuit of a meal. 'You know you can't hope to stand in the breach!' he bristled in anger. 'Don't fool yourself, twice. That lie led to slaughter. Front a war host again, and you doom yourself to far more than your half sibling's murder.'

The hand paused amid Daliana's warm hair. Its trembling contact betrayed the stark struggle as her liege beat back the next surge of unnatural hatred. He dared not speak. Even the thought of his half brother's name might tear the first breach and unleash disaster.

Lysaer drew a firm breath. Then another. His stopped fingers stirred, then combed once again through the chocolate tresses fanned over the pillow. Whether the activity lent comfort or distraction, or forced him to plumb some deep, hidden strength in the presence of female helplessness, he managed to leash the levin-bolt storm of cursed madness. Flushed to cold sweat, a bit laboured, he clarified: 'Prime Selidie burns to reclaim her chess piece to check the Fellowship's interests. I don't favour magecraft. Never have. Never will. That stance sets me up as the order's best tool, if only to pitch this world's civilized peace into chaos. Are you listening?' His brisk pause underscored the dull throb of unrest, where dissenting fanatics still mobbed the outside streets.

'Against such odds, I will stand or fall! Whether or not I can rise to surmount the trials before me, I plan to step forward and fight.'

Dakar's repressive quiet caused a tense hitch. Lysaer's fingers bunched into a fist, then uncurled. His determined caress resumed like a litany, wedded to vigilant tenderness.

Unlike his whiplash of imperious authority. 'Don't expect me to turn a blind eye on the Koriani Order's unscrupulous meddling! I will not become the Prime's icon to spur on the priesthood's agenda or raise my sword to unleash the temple's dedicate legions against Havish. My enmity has been declared in public against the True Sect religion. I must back that position with emphatic force, or else the just integrity of my word is reduced to posturing calumny.'

'We agree,' Dakar said, seemingly rattled frantic. His chair creaked to the sigh of squashed upholstery as he shifted his stocky frame. 'At all costs, and on all counts! That's why I must challenge your choice to march at the forefront of conflict. You cannot defang the Light's canon, Lysaer! The false creed is a juggernaut, long since spun out of control. The masses who cling to such figure-head worship won't bear restraint, or be led through your better intentions. The myth that glorifies their blind faith will defend itself against reason. Never mind kindness, or upstanding morals! If cornered, the temple priesthood will shed blood to secure the web that feeds its survival!'

'This should stop me?' Lysaer's laugh followed, vulnerable with all the caring warmth of his unselfconscious humanity. 'Such execrable power already *has* underwritten the execution of innocents! We've exposed a plot that shields itself under ambassadorial credentials for the actionable purpose of treason. The canon's debased cause does not blush at suborning the law! More, its wickedness has conspired with tools of dark sorcery in a covert assault to break my free will! Tell me again that I have no cause to destroy the edifice of this false doctrine? These hypocrite priests do not serve mankind but manipulate secrets to fuel their ambition. Who is left to oppose that violation? I must turn this insidious tide of abuse and stand up for humanity's born right to freedom.'

'Such arrogance started this mess in the first place,' Dakar rebuked with bald viciousness.

Lysaer rejected debate. 'I will excise the rot, which was, we agree, my own shameful creation in the first place. Responsibility rests in my hands. I claim the redress, without question.'

Sunlight itself should have cracked before the cold censure in Dakar's silence. 'You would drag Daliana on your campaign against the True Sect's dedicate war host?'

A bridled catch of intaken breath, then Lysaer's palm cupped her cheek on the swift reflex of instinct. Afterward, the self-contained fury erupted. 'No! I cannot bear to expose her to risk! She reminds me too much of—'

'Yes!' Dakar bulled through. 'That's half of the reason why Daliana sen

Evend was chosen to stand as your shadow! And also precisely why you can't afford to banish her from your presence.'

'I will brook no such orders!' Lysaer said, his goaded ire beyond dangerous.

'Well, you cannot protect her alone!' Dakar objected. 'Don't deny the undercurrent behind what *almost* took place in the heart of your personal jurisdiction.'

Amid brittle silence, subject to shatter, Daliana parted her lashes. Lysaer sat beside her, his stamped features in profile. He still wore his soiled dress from the road, the heraldic doublet peeled off to expose a creased shirt and shoulders rammed too stiff for the light-weight cloth. His cheeks were unfamiliarly hollow, and more remarkably, still unshaven. Dakar slouched in a stuffed chair nearby, a ravaged food tray perched on his lap. His mud-splashed breeches were tucked in wool stockings that showed frayed holes at the toes, without boots. Spaniel brown eyes displayed the bruised circles of a man bludgeoned sleepless for days, kept astride despite cruel fatigue.

Both combatants locked stares with clamped jaws.

Before one or the other destroyed the veneer of civil restraint, Daliana ventured from her silken pillow, 'I daresay you need us both.'

The galvanic discovery she was awake jerked Lysaer into recoil as though struck in the palm by a viper.

Thrown the advantage, Daliana scooped up her spread hair and elbowed erect. Two-handed, she combed and released the cascade down her back; which artful move let the coverlet slip. The clean shift that draped her scarcely masked the youthful, curved flesh underneath.

Atop frank embarrassment, the sight was sufficient to stagger male nerves like a thunderbolt. Amid the impelled shift in focus, and over Lysaer's stopped breath, she announced, straightly reasonable, 'You look kicked to exhaustion, my Lord Mayor. How long have you been in the saddle, and when was the last time you snatched proper rest? Since you've tired yourself to secure my release, I shall thankfully cede you my place in your bed.'

Lysaer back-stepped. 'I have political fires to quench. Affairs that can't wait. A maid will be sent to assist you.'

Before Daliana enacted her threat and tossed off the blankets in bold provocation, Lysaer spun on his heel and made a singed retreat that carried him through the doorway. Safely past the threshold, he summoned his chamber steward. 'Have the kitchen bring a fresh tray. Since,' he concluded, 'the Mad Prophet's already demolished the meal brought to ease the privation of my guest's unjust incarceration.'

Daliana slouched back into the pillows, then met and matched Dakar's smitten stare, unabashed. 'Tell me what happened,' she said.

'Just now?' Dakar blinked, beyond smug. 'I won't say. If you don't yet know whose remembrance torments him, I won't be the one to whet the killing edge on that knife. Asandir should have left warning. You're an exquisite weapon. Just what kind, and how sharp, might bestow too much leverage.'

But the fixed focus of her tawny eyes was like staring down a crouched tigress. Daliana repeated, 'What happened? No games! I will not be bandied about like skinned meat for the sake of masculine innuendo.'

Dakar cleared his throat. Glanced down. 'You should meet Elaira,' he said, then flushed pink and plunged into the pitfall his maladroit side-step had failed to avoid. 'If you ask what took place on the Mathorn Road, I escaped getting fricasseed. Barely.'

Daliana pushed back. 'Barely's a victory dance, in this case. That temple diviner was truly an unaware innocent?'

'His equerry wasn't.' Dakar cut to the chase. 'That's who tucked the active fetch in the saddle-bag underneath Lysaer's water-flask. And the one who admitted, when pressed, that he had planted the construct at his Lord Examiner's orders. The diviner was forced to expose his superior, or else face Lysaer's punitive wrath. Which fate would you choose?'

'As part and party to a vile assault, aimed to overthrow more than Etarran sovereignty? I'd be terrified.' Daliana shoved back the sheets and stood up. 'Sulfin Evend's old notes make one point dead clear. Lysaer's not likely to drop his enmity towards the Koriathain.'

'A miscalculation the True Sect high priesthood at Erdane may rue, set in flames at the forefront of war.' Dakar hunched like a turtle and dug in to clean the last crumbs off the tray. One hand, exposed, showed a welted bruise. The other, nursed in his lap, appeared singed, untidily bound up in bandaging. Chewing, Dakar peered sidewards and caught Daliana's morbid interest. 'I got stepped on,' he said. 'Temple dedicate's boots have hobnails and heel caps, very painful.' He swallowed, sweating beneath her regard, since the fabric that covered her breasts was too sheer. 'Before you ask, yes. Three charged fetches existed to manipulate Lysaer. They burn when disarmed. You were wise to have done for the first with a throwing knife.'

'That wasn't my question. I won't be put off.' But the servant's tread that approached from the corridor threatened to disrupt their privacy. Daliana stabbed for the crux straightaway. 'You've been Arithon's ally. Lysaer's not wont to trust you again. I haven't the right to rely on your training, or ask you to stay at the risk of your life. Not if you long to be elsewhere.'

Dakar grunted, caught at odds, since nothing remained on the plate to consume. He toyed with the silverware, his moon-calf face veiled and his thick lids obstinately lowered. 'Lysaer might throw me out on my ear,' he admitted, too canny to bare his feelings.

Daliana pressured him, traumatized yet by her narrow escape from the murderous temple examiner. 'The True Sect and the sisterhood will not back down. You'll still help?'

'You'll need more than help!' Dakar looked up, flushed and deeply offended.

'Because if Lysaer falls to Desh-thiere's geas, the Master of Shadow is next to helpless.'

'My concern is not for Arithon Teir's'Ffalenn.' Daliana hurled that name like a thrown gauntlet, then watched the stout spellbinder for his reaction. 'Where does your primary interest lie, Dakar? I have to know, before I'm tripped again by my green inexperience. I don't have the background to be the sole shield against the wiles of the Koriathain.'

The latch lifted. A flustered maidservant burst through the entry, bearing an armload of clothes. Another followed hard at her heels with a laden tray from the kitchen. Curiosity made them fall over themselves in their eager rush to cosset the Lord Mayor's new favourite.

Daliana shoved away from the bed, in no mood to be fodder for gossip. She sent both women packing. She would tend herself, and not let the Mad Prophet slide by without an honest answer defining his loyalty. 'Better say which half brother you'll move to protect.'

'I don't know!' Dakar discarded the fork in his hand, pushed aside the picked bones of his meal, and glared back. 'Girl, I've lived for too many years, with far too much unassuaged heart-ache.'

Daliana said nothing. She also refused to ease the pressure lent by her piquant state of undress.

Granted no quarter, Dakar's explosion was the more fearsome for being silent. 'Since you've never encountered his Grace of Rathain, believe me! You're too fresh to weigh the distinction, or measure the dicey strengths of the one man set against the other. Besides, the problem's already come to roost for Lysaer, right here.' He gestured with impatience and, grumbling over the trials inflicted by hard saddles and horseflesh, stirred his bulk and arose. Adroit when it counted, he side-stepped the hazard of female temptation, gimped to the window, and widened the dagged velvet curtains.

More than crystalline sunlight sliced through the uncovered glass. Raw noise slammed like storm surf from the street below: the unruly crowd gathered to witness the trial now milled against the brick wing of the palace. The bestial sound surged to a deafening crescendo when Dakar unlatched the frame and flung open the casement.

'Just one of the snags in Lysaer's grandiose plan,' he shouted over the full-throated roar of acclaim, surely kindled by the recent dramatic display in the court-room. 'What will your liege do to wean these people from their fixated worship? Better think on how you'll disarm that problem! Or the starry-eyed flock will be knocked to their knees every time dire straits press his nibs to raise light to enforce his inborn drive to seek justice.'

'The awed masses don't worry me,' Daliana admitted, the source of her personal terror ripped naked instead, as she sorted the clothing left for her use: Lysaer, *or someone*, had shown the presence to send to her mother's town house. The garments were hers, taken from her own wardrobe. Throat tight, she battled an uprush of tears for the grace of perception behind that small kindness.

'Lysaer won't fail these people,' she managed at length. 'Not unless the temple's armed posturing leads to bloodshed on the field of war. I must seize every narrow advantage, meantime, since my liege will try to shoulder the impossible load of everyone's responsible care. He can't salvage this harrowing mess on his own. Not beset by a Light-struck multitude of fools who can't think or stand on their own merits. Fanatics don't choose to stop blinding themselves. His Lordship's more at risk of becoming the figure-head steered by the needs of the mob.'

'What man who leads a pack of followers isn't?' Dakar challenged back. 'Above everything, Arithon's brisk handling taught me the wary wisdom of true independence.' Turned away from the window to add something more, the stout prophet lost wind as though kicked in the groin.

Daliana regarded his poleaxed shock, her slender hands busy threading silk cord through the eyelets of her brocade bodice. 'Were you planning to stay on and gawp while I dress?' Her sweet smile had teeth. 'I think not. This discussion is ended.'

Caper

Since High Earl Cosach s'Valerient could not barge his armed war band head-long into Tysan's sovereign territory, the explosive risks to salvage a crown prince left at hazard hung up in thorny debate for a fortnight. Still, Rathain's closed council thrashed at sharp odds, even after the need for cool wits summoned Laithen s'Idir south from Deshir. By then, the chafed tempers and unresolved argument tensioned all of the Halwythwood settlement.

Not only adults aired their snappish frustration over the threatened fate of Rathain's royal blood-line.

Forbidden outright to sit with his father, and indignant to be shut out of the affray as the *caithdein*'s heir designate, Esfand seized the resourceful initiative. Currently, he shivered in the outside cold, belly down on the lodge hall's roof. Vivaciously quick to share any prank, his cousin Khadrien stretched at his side, a knobby assemblage of elbows and knees flopped into a lanky sprawl. The pair had been eavesdropping on their rankled elders on and off for a week. Both were old enough to start shaving. Shamelessly brash at fifteen years of age, they possessed enough discipline to endure the misery of hours spent in motionless silence. Stealthy as scouts on enemy turf, they pressed their attentive ears against the shagged moss that crusted the weathered shingles.

The tempest beneath them showed no such restraint. Another thunderous bang on the map trestle pocked the clamour, as Cosach roared in retort, 'You'd have our best talent mince in there, unarmed and under strength, across borders defended by two entrenched war hosts? Just suppose your tiptoeing foray stalks through without getting slaughtered! What then?'

A cool bath of water, Laithen's logical calm supported her High Earl's ferocity. 'Taerlin is crawling with temple diviners!' Which obstacle was unlikely to change, with the True Sect stirred into an uproar by the Koriathain, and the outbreak of the first true use of Shadow witnessed in living memory. 'Worse, the word of Caithwood's haunted glens is hell-bound to spike town-born nerves. The mayors need no other excuse to be frightened to rife paranoia.' Any talent not clothed in a Sunwheel robe would be suspect, if not hounded and marked for death by the zealot examiners. 'Tell me,' Laithen snapped, 'how would you mask our true-seer's aura, thrown into that seething school of sharks to search for our crown prince? May as well drop an oil-primed torch in a drought, just to spot the chance gleam of a needle!'

None could refute the risk. Isolated for two hundred years by relentless persecution, until graced with the haven of Lysaer's justice, Rathain's clan blood bred a concentration of gifted talent. Outside the free wilds, their kind would shine like lit beacons, obvious to the Matriarch's scryers, or the temple-trained Sight of the True Sect's diviners.

'Ath wept!' Cosach snorted. 'With Tysan at the boil to capture rogue talent, any experienced band we might send would find themselves hunted for bounty. They'd be chained on the scaffold and burned for religion before our scout trackers could blink!'

Shouts erupted. Steel clanged, as someone rapped a knife blade against an unsheathed sword in a vain effort to restore order. 'We should languish for cowardice?' somebody cried. But the clan chief's bellowed denouncement stood down the furious outcry. 'I forbid the attempt!'

The blast of that ultimatum raised hackles, even outside in fresh air. Esfand rolled his eyes and traced a circle with a raised forefinger, the covert stalker's signal for hazed game that spun and trampled its own trail in confusion.

Khadrien's freckled features returned an infectious grin. All beaky nose and carroty hair, he mimed the chopped blow to the wrist for the brainless ineptitude that led a fool to hack off his own limb.

Esfand did not laugh.

Inclined to snap choices and mercuric moods, Cosach's heir hated slanging with words as much as his short-tempered sire. Shamed by his father's unnatural post-sitting, Esfand bottled his desperate fury as the striped shade cast by the overhead boughs lengthened towards another sunset. The meeting below would drag on into nightfall with the same propositions chased to a standstill. Esfand clenched his fists in frustrated agony. How much more precious time would slip past, while Rathain's crown prince languished, endangered? Why did his father enforce the delay? For Arithon's need, Cosach should have rammed a plan through by fiat long since. His leadership had quelled his detractors at sword-point before, to quash a split council's dithering.

From inside, the endless debate nattered on as someone else rose to deliberate. '. . . how many to venture! By what devious route? How do we locate our hunted prince to make contact, to start with?'

'We pick someone to journey to Tysan, first off. Sure as frost, his Grace stays at risk while we're parked on our arses, chewing the fat!'

The back-lash of shouting made that point moot as an accurate, tossed pebble stung Khadrien's forearm in warning. Stout third in conspiracy, a northern-bred daughter to s'Idir, Siantra posted their alert watch from the ground. Serious, quiet, and lately grown to a willowy height that topped the s'Valerient heir by three fingers, she could move like a wraith. If she avoided a bird's call to alert him, then the threat of discovery was imminent. Khadrien nudged his cousin and rapidly hand-signalled. Already, the tramp of footsteps approached, mingled with conversational voices. Foragers, likely, just back from the hunt, and a problem, since they would be endowed with game-sense. Even dead still under camouflaged cloaks, the young lurkers could be detected by an adult tracker's skilled awareness.

Both miscreants ducked. Scout-trained to be agile, they scuttled over the far side of the roof, then scrambled down a drooping oak branch. The instant they dropped to the ground, Siantra snagged their shoulders in steely fists. She shoved them ahead before they tumbled into the snow for their usual tussle. 'Run!' she breathed.

'What, from a foraging party?' Esfand mimed a cough of disgust.

'No, infant!' Siantra flipped back her deep brown braid and smothered a giggle. 'Khadri's grandmother's one step behind. She's angry.' Eyes the clear grey of her ancestral lineage pinned down her friend's darting glance, which shone a limpid, too-innocent blue. 'You were expected back at the home lodge,' Siantra guessed. 'Something about splitting fire-wood for the oven?'

Khadrien flushed to the tips of his ears, which stuck through his unkempt, curly hair. 'Dharkaron Avenger's Black Spear! I traded off that chore to my little brother for my best stag-handled knife. If the whelp ditched the bargain, I'll be chewed meat!'

'Bloody shreds, thrown out for the head-hunter's dogs!' Esfand teased. 'Your grandame's got a butcher's arm with a cleaver.'

The three took to their heels, unwilling to test the beldame's fierce temper. High spirits took them out of the settlement by way of the narrow cleft that plunged downhill towards the river. The more sensitive perimeter scouts likely sensed the flicker as their wild run crossed the guarded lines set against an outside intrusion. They were not stopped for their truant exuberance since their flight made no careless noise. Clan young were encouraged to think for themselves. Guile was not only needed, but prized. For the skills the old blood-lines required to survive, such youthful high jinks received tolerance: provided the rascals were not clumsy or foolish enough to get caught.

The riverside terrain at the edge of spring thaw posed a challenge to anyone hurried. The three friends avoided the south-facing mud-banks, heaved by frost, where the lightest of steps would leave footprints. Likewise, they skirted the black clots of leaves, choked in the caved slush heaped after the last blizzard. They trod instead on the jutted dry rocks, racing each other at break-neck speed beneath the bare oaks and marsh maples that knotted the steepening bank. Like wind, they slipped past the springs where the yellow fronds of the willows trailed in flounced curtains down to the ground. The exultant clouds of their puffed breaths joined the gilt notes of bird-song, jarred here and there by the scolds of disturbed jays and chickadees.

The ravine tightened down, roofed over by deadfalls capped in glaze ice that plunged into gloom. Here, the branch streamlet they followed lay frozen, buckled to rills that tumbled over the log-jams and boulders. With Khadrien leading, Esfand and Siantra dodged through, bundled tight in their cloaks to avoid snagging the furs. Shared grins acknowledged their scatheless escape, with the settlement fallen behind them.

Khadrien dared a low whoop, as the steepened pitch of the gulch dipped sharply towards the main river-course. Reckless enough to savour rough thrills, he barreled ahead onto the crusted ice, then flopped on his back and tucked up his feet. Momentum hurtled him into the bowl, where the falls splashed in summer and swirled the green depths of a trout pool.

The snow-drift at the base was spring-soft. Khadrien crunched, laughing, into the granular mass, and just missed overshooting the verge of the creek. The basin beyond was iron-hard still, rimmed with lace frost, except where the open sluice tumbled, roiled to froth and skeins of black ripples.

Since the iced surface was too unstable to cross, the pranksters dropped panting on the stony shore.

'Why swap a fine dagger to duck the few minutes needed to split a few logs?' Esfand remarked, dogged as a terrier in his pursuit of loose ends. 'That's daft!'

Khadrien's lips curled, pink and smug as a clam. 'Had secret business.'

Esfand rolled onto an elbow, dark brows gathered above the glint in his pale hazel eyes. 'What business?'

But his cousin's evasive grin vanished fast. Khadrien shifted the subject. 'What do you think Prince Arithon is like, really?' When no response came, he poked Esfand's ribs, exposed as the s'Valerient heir leaned forward to toss a loose pebble downstream. The throw splashed where the current rushed, gurgling, under the next shelf of ice.

'Who knows. Why wonder?' Esfand's challenge bared teeth. 'The accounts all agree his Grace shows Torbrand's blood. Which means royal-born to be difficult.'

'Yes, but difficult, *how*?' Khadrien persisted, steered by some circuitous point behind his evasion. 'You ought to be curious.'

Since, after all, the prince was alive, the encounter with crown rank seemed likely to happen. Siantra listened, obliquely absorbed with picking out the snagged sticks from her clan braid.

Khadrien's impetuous prod would not rest, with his cousin in line for the title as Rathain's *caithdein*. 'Esfand, come clean! If you must stand shadow for your sanctioned liege, you had better grapple some sense of the man who'll hold your pledge of life service.'

For the loreist's archives contained a disparate collection of stark contradictions. Where Esfand admired the dauntless courage recounted in the ballad of *Braggen's Stand at Leynsgap*, the ferocity there did not mesh with the tenderly vulnerable spirit that Siantra imagined, sung with passionate sorrow in *Jieret's Lament*. Nor, to Khadrien's undisciplined buoyancy, did the steel-clad will described in the meticulous record of Sidir's difficult service match the pithless weakling reviled in the *Lives of the Fourteen Companions*. The three comrades pictured their crown prince quite differently, reflected within a shared moment.

'Can't outsmart the trained mind of a sorcerer, anyhow,' Esfand concluded, impatient. 'What good should I try? No question, that weaselly spellbinder Dakar seemed terrified of his Grace!'

'Surely the Mad Prophet has reason to fear,' Siantra broke in, disgusted. 'I would, too, had I been the one to bind our liege over to the Koriathain after Eriegal's gutless treachery.'

Esfand flicked a snow-crusted twig and shivered beneath his tucked cloak. His slump suggested resistant dismissal, except for the frown, which spoke volumes.

'You do want to know!' Khadrien wagged a roguish finger. 'As I breathe, show me wrong? You've probably thought about nothing else since we heard that Prince Arithon was set free in Tysan.'

But the steadier insight of Siantra's truth-gift made her drop her mussed braid in anxiety. 'The council's decision is taking too long.'

Even Khadrien's thoughtless tongue stilled when the s'Valerient heir matched her glance with piercing acuity. 'You, too, Sian?' Rail thin, an immature scarecrow where his turbulent father wore tigerish muscle, Esfand inherited the same chill hazel eyes and seal hair, glinted red, where the sun kissed. 'I've felt gnawed to my nerve ends, if not eaten alive for more than a sennight!'

'You've approached the camp seer,' Siantra prompted, the sober remark not phrased as a question.

'Didn't listen!' Esfand shot upright, his anger uncorked. 'In fact, the damned hag turned her back! She brushed me off though I've dreamed for nine *nights* something bad's going to happen to Arithon!'

Surprise spurred Khadrien onto his feet with a haste that dropped one careless toe through the sugary ice. But the splash that wet his boot went unnoticed. 'That doesn't make sense!' An embarrassed flush rose beneath his scatter of freckles, that his heedless shout may have threatened their pact to evade the outlying patrols.

But his companions reproached that impulsive carelessness with dead-pan silence. S'Valerient carried the talent for Sight. That famous endowment – possessed by an ancient, long lineage bred for the courage to stand behind kings – should have stopped talk, even called the stubbornest minds in the council to rapt account.

Siantra asked, thoughtful, 'What did you dream?'

'It changes,' Esfand admitted, then unburdened the rest in an explosive rush. 'Always, the prince has appeared as a hidden shadow, pursued. His step in flight on the land seemed almost insubstantial. I watched his Grace sought by Koriathain, tracked by a circle of seers using crystals. Next, he was running from Sunwheel diviners, and another time, he fled across a battle-field soaked in fresh blood. That vision showed me a wide-open vista scattered with war dead. Fallen horses lay snagged in the wreckage of chariots.'

'Which banners?' Siantra probed gently.

But Khadrien broke in, excitably awed, 'Ath wept! You think the True Sect might break the hundred-year stand-off with Havish?'

But Siantra's self-contained urgency struck the more strident note. 'What else? Go on.'

'Last night.' Esfand paused, shut his eyes, then resumed in distress, 'Last night, I saw the prince shelter a man in his arms. The fellow was fair-haired, strong as an ox, and dressed like a ploughman. His nose had been crushed by a blow to the face. The recent scar had healed without sepsis, and yet, he appeared to be dying.'

'What was the season?' Siantra stood also, her grace distinctly feminine though she wore the same scout's leathers and hide cloak. 'Were the trees leafed, yet? Did the dream show green grass? If so, you're precognate. The dreadful events you perceived may not have occurred, yet.'

Esfand unbent enough to rub his damp palms on his sleeves. 'I just have this feeling! Every day, our war band's inaction is driving the prince into deadlier danger. And, no, before you ask, Khadri, I can't think of a reason between sky and earth why my father's dug in his heels. Never before this has he blathered on, hell-bent upon useless stalling!'

Khadrien heatedly opened his mouth, cut off by Siantra, who argued, 'Esfand, your foreboding matters! Yes, I'm sure, since you've chosen to speak. *What changed?*'

The High Earl's son shuddered, arms clasped to his ribs. Desolate over the thrash of the falls, he admitted, 'The prince glanced upwards in my latest vision. His eyes focused, directly. *He saw me!* Somehow he sensed my aware-ness, I swear! The contact felt downright uncanny.'

The inflection of horror sobered Khadrien finally, as Esfand's hoarse recount continued. 'His Grace seemed lost. No, *confused*. As if in his heart, he believed himself wholly alone, trapped in dread of both past and future. A man might have that look if he had endured a whole lifetime, cast adrift with no know-ledge of family. This morning when I awoke, I just knew! We can't wait. Someone must shoulder the miserable odds and go after him.'

Siantra paled with dismay. 'You think your inexperience will prevail? Esfand! That's crazy as leaping head first off a cliff!'

But this time, Khadrien's flighty impulse interpreted his cousin's crest-fallen hurt, first. 'Not you, alone, friend. If you try this yourself, we'll be there to back you.'

Siantra gasped, horrified. 'Are you both suicidal? Lord Cosach was right. Any clan presence sent abroad in Tysan will draw True Sect diviners like flies. More, a move in defiance of the chieftains' council is no childish adventure. If not outright treason, you toy with a choice more than likely to get yourselves killed!'

'We have to go! Us,' Khadrien insisted. He planted himself, squelching with one ankle drenched, and confronted Siantra with the feckless humour stripped from him.

Which forced the reluctant acknowledgment: he shared the matrilineal legacy of s'Valerient, one generation removed.

'Oh?' Siantra folded her arms. 'If this bent of madness is rooted in Sight, then show me something more than a hunch. Explain how you plan to blind talent diviners, not to mention deflect the Senior seeresses engaged by the Koriathain.'

'We don't have to,' Khadrien admitted, his manic features no longer animated by impish laughter. His wild mood banished, he confessed the unthinkable. 'I had this prompt to break into the hidden armoury.' Burned scarlet again, mulishly determined before the appalled stares of his companions, he shrugged off the criminal feat. 'At the time, I believed we'd be pulling a prank—'

'*What?*' Siantra's shock overran his speech, roughshod. 'You dishonoured your father's life pledge as a *caper*?'

Khadrien bridled. 'I had no idea the affray would turn serious! Trust me, the move just might save our lives—'

'*You've dared to steal the black sword, Alithiel?*' Esfand pealed, unaware he had struck the bass tone of authority his father used to curb the fractious war band. 'Cousin! Don't try the rash claim, that the family heritage brought you to this insanity.'

'No.' Impulsive, but never dishonest, Khadrien came clean. 'But I woke in the night gripped by the most horrible precognition. I knew we'd be leaving the settlement. Now. We won't be going back. I've already cached the provisions we'll need, and the weapons to hunt on the trail, though this morning, I didn't know why.'

The breeze through the branches suddenly chilled, with spring's song in the brook a lost memory. Iced drifts and stripped trees appeared stark under the failing light. The bite of evening's frost braced the air, each drawn breath cruel as a knife in the lungs at the prospect of night, without fire.

Nailed by his best friends' stunned incredulity, Khadrien lifted his chin. 'Why else did you think I staked my forebears' knife to bait my young brother to cover my absence? Esfand, trust me, under seal of Dharkaron's Black Vengeance! Your vision was real. By fate, it's my duty to back you. We have to rely on ourselves, or Prince Arithon may die in the breach. What else do we have for right guidance if we don't heed the prompt of our ancestry? Please bear the black sword in your liege's behalf. If you don't, I believe that the last of Rathain's clan honour will become forfeit.'

'For the true cause of a prince's survival, the great blade is bound to awaken,' Siantra allowed with shaken reluctance.

'I love a good scrape, sometimes to my folly,' Khadrien agonized in appeal. 'But on matters that threaten the roots of our heritage, we cannot stay safe and live up to the names of our forefathers.'

While Siantra weighed over the desperate measures behind Khadrien's shaky defense, a glance at the iron behind Esfand's frown ripped down her cobweb rebuttal. His uncanny dreams had convinced him already. No coward, the *caithdein's* heir designate: he would act before the council's delay abandoned their crown prince to jeopardy.

With little more than the clothes on their backs, two boys sealed their choice to leave the free wilds in Halwythwood. Ill-equipped for the lethal dangers, they faced a perilous journey of six hundred leagues into strange and unfriendly territory if they sought to brave the True Sect's guarded turf within Tysan.

Siantra swallowed, much more than afraid. Between Esfand and Khadrien, she was the cool head that restrained them to natural balance. If she stayed behind, their brash effort very well might become doomed to fail.

The tears welled, too fast. Siantra s'Idir dashed the moisture away. Her trembling uncertainty hidden, and her sweet alto voice drawn to steel, she engaged her cunning to help map the steps to cross the scouts' lines, undetected. None of them dared to take leave of their families. They would be stopped if anyone in the settlement caught wind of their intent. The prospect was frightening, that every covert skill they possessed would come to be bitterly tested. Overfaced against the unknown, cast as pawns before powers beyond imagining, they hung their young lives upon legend and hope: that the Paravian star spells laid into the sword of Rathain's ancient high kings held the potency to disrupt hostile scrying and defy the might of Arithon's fatal enemies.

Long after sunset, the Halwythwood clan council's dead-locked debate over the fate of their stranded crown prince suffered an untoward interruption. Under the blaze of the wall sconces, close air soaked into fever-pitch tension almost sparked bloodshed when the infraction involving two boys and a dagger was presented before High Earl Cosach.

The knife in question rested on the board trestle, a stag-handled heirloom laid down in agitation by Khadrien's grandmother. The pert woman looked as quaintly hard-used, red-cheeked, and cocky as a spring robin in a traditional hide skirt with split panels. Her spare manner garnered widespread respect, and her lively, dark eyes, missed very little.

Yet she was not smiling when she snapped her closed fist to her heart in formal salute.

'Speak!' Cosach cracked, sharpened gruff since the wrangle deferred his evening meal.

The old woman never flinched from his temper, despite her unpleasant news. 'I'm here to report one of my own, who failed to come home after sundown. Sadly, a point of clan honour's been breached.'

Cosach raised bristled eyebrows. 'That's a grave offence. Which lad? Do you carry proof?'

Lips pursed, the old woman inclined her white head towards the blade on display. 'Khadrien left that dagger in the hands of my youngest grandson to seal a promise not to speak out. Here is evidence enough, since bequest of this knife is bound to our family name. Had the lad not been bent upon untoward mischief, he would never have gone without such a gift sheathed against need at his belt.'

Cosach stood. Broad-shouldered, severe, his clan braid draped down his taut back, he addressed the scout on guard at the hall door. 'Find the captain in charge of the watch. Ask if anyone else has gone missing.'

While talk broke out, and a clan elder's irritable inquiry demanded why the misdeeds of children should disrupt more important affairs, another arrival in female dress slipped into the lodge and braved the clamour to address her husband.

Cosach confronted his wife, wrapped in a robe of white ermine and pinched to a pallor that stopped his heart. Hit gut deep by a qualm worse than any endured amid an armed charge at the battle-front, he said, 'Jalienne? Esfand hasn't come in.'

'No.' Up to the board trestle, her pregnant step firm, his lady came on unswerving. Her anguished eyes searched his rough-cut features. 'Our whelp's gone with Khadrien. Did you ever doubt?' A harried glance sidewards acknowledged the anxious brown eyes of Laithen s'Idir. 'Siantra, too, near as we can gather. No one in the settlement has seen the three of them since early afternoon.'

Laithen said nothing, but shuttered her eyes with her tapered fingers. Known to be whipcord tough, she quailed under a distress that shattered her famous composure.

'You expected this!' an elder from Fallowmere accused in aghast discovery. 'Or something like it?'

'There is more, High Earl Cosach,' the granddame snapped, grim. 'The black sword is gone. Alithiel's been taken from the hidden armoury.'

Cosach heard, stone-faced. His shout of quittance disbanded the rest of the council from session. 'Debate here is finished!'

Against the torrent of explosive surprise, suddenly deaf to all urgency, he abandoned the chieftain's place at the central board and swept his distraught wife into his arms. She buried her grief into his warm shoulder. He held her, his cheek pressed against her fair hair, breathing in the evergreen-scented warmth of her. While the uproar around them mounted towards frenzy, he lifted one arm and drew the slight form of Laithen s'Idir inside the comfort of his massive embrace.

'They are away,' Cosach murmured to both mother and wife. 'At long last, and in time. Ath bless their young strength. I may die with regret. But let us be grateful, together. We were never forced at need to lay this dread duty upon them.'

'You knew?' screeched the granddame, obstinately planted outside of the parents' closed circle.

Cosach lifted his head, his iron beard bristled over his clamped jaw, and his surly glance gone defensive. For a terrible moment unable to speak, he nodded, then managed, 'Not everything. The prophecy given said three would go. But we weren't sure who.' Now the moment had come, wrung deathly white, Cosach realized he must nerve himself to confide in his flustered council.

A push at his arm, and Laithen ducked free. 'I'll tell them,' she offered. 'Let me do this in your stead.' Dauntless before Khadrien's outraged grandmother, she addressed the gathering at large, 'Ath wept! By now a deaf post should have guessed an unnatural delay was afoot. No one's seen such a display of arse-sitting obstinacy for as long as Cosach's served as Teir's'Valerient. Always before, we've been forced to knock down his bullheaded plunge to take impetuous action.'

'Damned well, I'm not sanguine!' Cosach exploded, his helpless fury enough to stun the clamour to silence. 'Bad enough, that we're pushed to the crux, before I should live to set trust in the prescient word of a traitor.'

The shocked quiet deepened, while Laithen's clear voice recounted the forecast delivered by Dakar's infamous talent: that three of their young must take on the perils in Tysan. 'In free will, dedicated to duty, Esfand, Khadrien, and Siantra have just shouldered the desperate journey to relieve Prince Arithon's straits.'

In the blunt wake of Laithen's announcement, Jalienne also relinquished the supportive arms of her husband. Proud enough to stand in adversity, she added, 'They left Elshian's lyranthe in the armoury. I wonder if that oversight was a mistake?'

Cosach shook his head. Still too choked up for speech, he strode forward to belt on the great sword of s'Valerient. 'I think not,' he managed, as his grip fumbled with the hang of sheathed steel and baldric. 'The Paravian blade was the wiser choice.' How could three youngsters journey across half the continent, into who knew what hostile danger, saddled with the world's most irreplaceable heirloom lyranthe? 'That fragile treasure would place them at risk should they be set to flight for their safety.'

Jalienne reached across her husband's chapped hands and helped adjust his buckles and belts. She could arm her man, had done so many times, while too numbed and heartsick to think. 'And you'll set off after them?'

'To guard their backs as far as our border,' Cosach promised, his throat painfully tight. 'I'll take our six most talented scouts. The children won't ever know that we're there.' He likely would miss the birth of their child, another regret he had no breath to voice as he fought his hard words to the finish. 'Dakar's prophecy must be kept to the letter for the weal of the kingdom. Though mercy on us! I'd rather have lost adult lives to a failure than see the day I must leave this harsh task in the untried hands of our offspring!'

Shock Wave

A split second ahead of the breaking event, the Warden of Althain bolts to his feet with snap-focused alertness; while far off in Kathtairr, a great dragon dreams, and the Sorcerer bound to her service shapes the fiery interface between inchoate inspiration and solidified form: and in barren soil where nothing has grown since the dawn of the Age of Dragons, a seed materializes and germinates, and throws out a pale green shoot . . .

A spreading, simultaneous ripple of *movement* shocks through the fabric of the world: which impact throws the High Priest of the Light at Erdane's True Sect temple onto his knees; five diviners drop, comatose; while the Koriani Prime Matriarch shouts aloud as every crystal in the order's possession rings like a bell in resounded sympathy . . .

In flight through Halwythwood, hidden to avoid the scouts likely sent on their trail, three clan children sense the vast shift shear across the subtle web that sustains the mysteries; deluged by an ephemeral flicker of light, then gripped by the note struck in resonance from a sheathed black sword, two gasp dumbstruck, while the other exclaims, 'Fire and frost! *What in Ath's Creation just changed . . . ?'*

IX. Throes

The dragon's dreaming on the continent of Kathtairr unleashed a vast shock wave that crossed the face of Athera. Disruptive, the ripple of raised resonance shifted the harmonic balance that underpinned everything in the world. No place and no living being escaped the surge of causation untouched. Change coursed outward, a sudden, momentous recalibration of energy that struck without a second's warning. The unwary inhabitants caught in the web had no chance to brace for the onslaught. Every lane that channelled the planet's electromagnetics pulsed in reverberation, excited to tones never sounded before, in the registers past human hearing.

Through sites where the mysteries flourished, and across the free wilds where the flux ran untrammelled, the urgent burst passed as a lifting tonic, sped through the land's natural conduits. The mighty surge unreeled through Caithwood, its fierce glory heightened where sensitized ground resounded yet from the Masterbard's song of reawakening. There, no longer nameless, the musician who also bore title as Arithon Teir's'Ffalenn collapsed to his knees, overset. As the grand chord that founded all earthly existence flowered into an elevated intonation, the bell tone struck his mage-trained sensitivity and ignited a fragment of memory. He *felt* the haunting strains that anchored Kathtairr's scarred ruin drop out, revitalized by the etheric flare of a massive, spontaneous renewal.

The majestic scope of that healing riffled his skin, and ran, quivering, through his viscera. Hurled into the throes of a flash-point gestalt, Arithon glimpsed the distant, sun-baked barrens where a seedling plant took wondrous root. *He recognized that terrain; knew that once, he had sailed across distant seas and explored its strange, blighted shore-line.* But the chance to pursue his fragmented impression became trampled under the back-lash of refined stimulation.

Morning wind struck his exposed flesh like a knife thrust. His ears rang. The echoes thrown off by his forest surroundings struck a flourish of ephemeral notes, until the responses of rocks and bare trees made the winter air quiver with harmonic overtones. Rocked breathless while all of Athera's life matrix became reforged on the flare of the moment, Arithon expertly damped down the preternatural reach of his talent. Yet as he grounded himself out of mage-sight, a nearby thread of dissonance in the weave prickled his nape in sharp warning. The tingle fore-ran an auric imbalance: not his own, but a threat to the unconscious friend, nestled within the horse-drawn litter beside him. The spike of overload caused by the peak onslaught battered into a spirit already frayed under crisis.

Spurred by concern, Arithon examined Tarens's wrapped form. Stressed energies met his anxious touch. Like a cold bath on his nerves, ragged fissures torn through the crofter's aura raised currents that lifted his hackles. Worse, through the man's panicked onslaught of fear, subtle hearing detected the dissonance of fatal despair. Years spent mending the afflictions of stranded wraiths drove Arithon to frantic worry. The explosion of inchoate confusion assumed the torment of an unconscious nightmare. Tarens's frame arched. Seared from within as though set aflame, he had no reference point to grapple what must seem a horrific state of separation.

'Tarens!' Arithon caught the big man's convulsed shoulder. 'Tarens, be easy. You're never alone. Someone who cares walks beside you.'

Yet words of encouragement and his warm contact failed to bridge the morass.

'I won't let you go, Tarens!' Opened to mage-sense, Arithon gently probed for the foothold to stem the rank flood of disorientation.

But the sudden maelstrom that altered the flux had sped the cascade of cause to effect. Arithon's urgent effort to stabilize Tarens plunged his empathic sensitivity too far. The overfaced healer encountered disaster: the torrential burst of raised resonance had stripped the boundary that defined his friend's human identity.

With every familiar marker erased, Arithon battled to anchor his embodied presence, too late. The storm upended his gifted faculties. He became swept headlong into harrowing chaos, drilled through by Tarens's shrill panic. As the spiral bled his upended awareness into the mineral bones of the earth, Arithon might have seized his own recovery from there. Except the upheaval transmitted from Kathtairr also had stressed the strata of bed-rock itself. Instead of stone's trusty stablility, Arithon reeled to the violent jolt as the earth's pressured fault-lines juddered and quaked in release. After-shock rolled him, as ocean waves peaked to unnatural crests, and the crocheted whitecaps exploded to froth on the salty face of the deep. His bone marrow sang to the crackling *snap!* where the dormant channels of Athera's slack flux lines became reamed by impetuous force. Freed, the dammed energies flushed through and loosed still more showers of primordial harmony.

The life matrix of a man was never fashioned to withstand the naked fusion of the elements, far less an event evoked on a planetary scale. The reverberation shredded human vitality and scoured the fragments to spider-web wisps. Tarens's self-awareness dissolved at a speed that spun Arithon's equilibrium into the moil through the uncontrolled gateway of sympathy. His royal lineage alone spared him from flash-point immolation. Bred to withstand exposure to the mysteries upon quickened ground, and lent the reflex of experience, he had been immersed in the perilous seethe of Athera's wild lane currents before.

Once caught barehanded in a prior crisis alongside a Fellowship Sorcerer, Arithon had tamed the tumultuous tides of an explosive lane surge through the interface of his music. The instincts retained from that earlier breakthrough salvaged his unravelled poise. He recouped his flayed bearings, pulled back, and re-centred himself on the innate strength of his greater Name. Distraught, left on his knees panting with vertigo, he breathed until his distress quieted. Then, tightly guarded, he sounded Tarens's condition again and let the flood speak to his masterbard's insight.

Even so slight a delay had cost dearly. The unravelled knit that was *Tarens* rapidly lost cohesion. Worse, the thundering spate of the lane currents also resounded to countless other individuals, stricken elsewhere. Arithon's tuned senses deafened under the blast, as the teeming mass of collective humanity became caught aback by the world's broad-scale shift. Beyond Caithwood, where the land's reactive electromagnetics were not kept cleared by the rigorous oversight of clan guardians, the trammelled flux web recoiled in standing waves of reverberation.

True Sect power in Tysan had disregarded the old boundaries laid down by Paravian wisdom, and worse, altered the great nexus at Erdane, where the ancient Second Age foundations transferred the lane current. The snarl there piled up into unforeseen havoc as the powerful surge to peak resonance whipped the jammed flow into kinks. Slammed against the heedless placements of temples, and bridges, and mill dams, the adamant backlash raised trauma. Thousands of ignorant, unwary townsfolk became buffeted in the wrack.

And Tarens reeled with them, as a struck tuning-fork hammered by the discharge of reactive distress. The recurrent concussions of etheric forces whiplashed in shock-wave bursts. Each impact tormented his unshielded nerves and pitched him into convulsions.

Arithon wrestled to quiet the larger man's thrashing, outmatched in strength, and beleaguered as well as his subtle awareness breasted the overload. Amid Tarens's agony, he also suffered the turmoil sown far and wide through the compromised landscape. Distance damped nothing, as the cross chop elsewhere ignited spontaneous fires and caved roofs to cascades of spilled shingles. He jerked with the jolts, as cracked masonry walls crumbled in sudden collapse, with screaming bystanders crushed in the choked streets. Mankind's fixed structures tumbled down into rubble wherever the banked pulse of the mysteries had lain muted or dormant. Change shuddered the firmament like a stung beast, with every imbalance caught in its path whipped into contortions and broken. Wind squalls kicked up apocalyptic towers of cloud, which spat lightning and hail out of season. Farm-steads suffered livestock stampedes, and shop-stalls became flattened, while the merchants' mansions and poor-quarter tenements were winnowed like chaff, until the deranged pressure carved out a cleared channel.

The toll exceded the horrors of cataclysm. Through the eyes of initiate mastery, Arithon viewed the grievous scope of causation as the ripples of unshed charge laced through an unguarded citizenry. The result would stop hearts, sow back-lash fevers, and inflict widespread outbreaks of madness, as townsfolk born to a mage-blind existence found their latent perceptions torn open at one brutal stroke. Some fell into fits of Sighted vision as the bore of the flux rushed over and through them. Others fainted, wracked senseless or killed by the heightened shock of a spontaneous healing. Still more gibbered, lost amid the shadowy quagmire of their unconscious fears. Some would find natural recovery in sleep. But many broke outright, snapped by rage-driven malice to undertake acts of ungoverned savagery.

The loud crescendo of human anguish broke Arithon into a shivering sweat. Again overset by the painful barrage, he wrestled for poise and reined in his runaway faculties before he exhausted himself. Back in hand, grounded into his natural senses, he found the alarming, first flickers of overextension already shot heat lightning shimmers through his peripheral eyesight.

Worse, Tarens lay slack, too fordone to surmount the rip currents that streamed through his uncontained aura. The big crofter's heart labored, with each shuddered breath more erratic and thin. The disrupted vitality that sustained his body verged upon irreversible damage. Another convulsion might finish him.

Tried at the brink of that fatal threshold, Arithon struggled to focus. Discipline warned him: further effort on his part surpassed folly. The grand event unleashed from Kathtairr spurred talent and frayed even his schooled awareness, until the brush of mere wind scalded his naked skin. The fecund life in the soil underfoot hammered his soles to distraction, while the forest above shuddered with ephemeral light, set ablaze by the sheen of the flux tide. Alive to the half-world inflamed into turbulence by the course of excited electromagnetics, Arithon struggled to slow his sped pulse and damp his rampant sensitivity.

Since Tarens's plight could not wait, Arithon shivered and crouched. He plunged his hands to the wrists into wet leaves, hopeful that the cold might wrench his overstrung senses back into alignment. But the quiver that wrung his shocked nerves failed to settle. The pressured clamour that wailed through the flux stream still threatened to drown his autonomy. To exert his sighted faculties again in this state would be unimaginably dangerous.

Prudence that argued for self-preservation said Tarens was best off abandoned to die. The man's abraded life-force had scattered too far. Left a body emptied as a beached shell, this near to final passage across the veil, the healer ought to entrust Daelion Fatemaster's wisdom to recoup the lost threads of a friend's deranged consciousness.

Yet Arithon refused to abandon the fight. He had one last, untried avenue left to shoulder the improbable challenge. Doubt had no place. Pitched against failure that courted the abyss, and reliant on naked instinct, Arithon shoved erect and goaded the pack pony harnessed to Tarens's litter.

'Hup, fellow! Move.' He urged the shaggy beast to a trot. Crossed the hill's crest, and found a secluded hollow that cut the raw bite of the wind. There he unhitched the traces at speed, then removed the animal's tack and rope headstall, and freed it to find its own way.

With his stricken friend settled upon sheltered ground, Arithon tucked in the blankets. Tarens's extreme pallor tinged towards grey. His slack skin felt alarmingly clammy. The passing seconds lost more precious ground at a price too dreadful to contemplate. Yet caution demanded. Arithon unstrapped the supply packs. He cached some provisions, and took up the lyranthe gifted by the clan empath's forethought. Aware that his effort must draw hostile notice, he slung the wrapped instrument over his back and sprinted down-slope to seek solitude.

The forested cover thinned and gave way to tangles of salt-marsh, where tasseled reed-beds girdled the flat stretch of shore-line. Arithon waded across silted skeins of small streamlets and ploughed through shoals of muck like black glue. Ducks exploded ahead of him. Past their flurried wings, the gulls cried, startled upwards in raucous white flocks. When the scudded foam swirled ankle deep, he stripped off leathers, breeches, and boots, and forged through the hummocks. Deep inside the maze of inlets and tide-pools, he selected an isolate patch of dry ground, hidden amid last season's straw thickets of sea oats and sedge. He replaced his shed clothing and trusted to luck, that the flood-tide would erase his footprints.

With Tarens's survival his only concern, nothing else mattered but time. Arithon unsheathed his belt knife. He slashed the ties on the lyranthe's fleece covering and nestled the instrument into the cradle of hip and raised knee. His hands settled knowingly into position against the fretboard and strings. Yet the ease that confirmed his bard's skill did nothing to lessen his danger. He would be taunting fate: a gamble made against desperate odds to salvage a friend, laid against an unknown array of ill consequence.

'Dharkaron avert!' Arithon swore to distance his hag-ridden dread. Tucked into his cloak, he attended the peg heads, where his accurate ear did not fail under pressure. He tuned fourteen silver-wound strings to true pitch, aware that Tarens had no chance at all unless he forsook every layer of protection and stripped his most guarded boundaries.

Arithon tilted his head to one side. Recklessly brave, he engaged his rare gift. The first note speared through him, a sweet pang that woke joy and a longing akin to agony. He sounded another, then struck a full chord that declared the golden heat of high summer. His melody moved, deepened into black earth, enriched with the heady, blanketing fragrance of cut clover and sun-cured hay. There, amid boyish laughter, he found Tarens, immersed in bare-chested labour, pitchforking fodder into the oxcart.

Inspired by trout pools mantled in shade, and by the night chirp of crickets beneath the silver-foil gleam of the moonlight, Arithon's composition took soaring flight. He played *Tarens,* again, with the key changed to autumn, replete with the bounty of harvest, and brilliant as fire with the turned leaves that ripened in the wood-lots and hedgerows. He spun the comforts of winter's snug kitchen, while Kerelie sewed by the hearth, and Efflin's patient strength mended rope-handled buckets and worn harness. The bard did not rest there, but stitched the descant themes of a beloved aunt and uncle into his weave. Deeper, he drew in the tender memories of parents, deftly recaptured against the wonders of spring buttercups and the chased flit of jewel-toned butterflies. From the care-free exuberance of earliest childhood, he built theme upon theme, with today's loyal tenacity wrapped, warp through weft, through the honest heart that framed adult character. The bard played *Tarens* with masterful force. He shaped the primal chord that spoke Name, then built his call to an imperative shout of individual unity. Even still, the exquisite cry failed. The fragmented spirit stayed swept at a loss on the electromagnetic roil of Athera's flux currents. Since Tarens lay scattered beyond all recognizable sense of himself, perforce, the music's reach had to follow.

Alone in the marsh, honed to singular purpose, Arithon tapped into his mage-tuned awareness. He thrust his song downwards, flung its clarion registers into the stream of the free wilds' lane flow. Lent wings by his gift, he released the blast of his music for *Tarens!* to resound throughout the life pulse of the world . . .

Far off at Althain Tower, Sethvir shot erect as the poured light of the Masterbard's summons tingled through his earth-gifted awareness. Distinct as a stamped signature, the harmonic melody rang the full length of the second lane, exactingly phrased to shear through the planet-wide muddle of human affliction. The Warden's dipped quill dropped from his stunned grasp. Ink splotched the meticulous lines just penned in his miniature script. The flung spatters splashed, ebon on obsidian black, across the library's stone table. Which small spill passed unnoticed as the Sorcerer's turquoise eyes lost his dreamer's reverie and kindled to flame.

'Dharkaron avert!' he gasped, swept by the chill of a pending catastrophe.

Infallible compass, his earth-sense aligned, with all other events in the unsettled world fused into a flash-point gestalt. Sethvir's provenance sequenced the stream, still unfolding, and plucked out the electrified points of convergency: *a True Sect diviner crowed with discovery, handed the signal location of the murderer, escaped from the Light's justice . . .*

. . . while elsewhere, a scarred veteran in dedicate's armour took maudlin pause, and mourned the family that forced duty had made him abandon. Then, overcome, he broke into tears of lament for his second born son, last seen as a fair-haired toddler . . .

. . . a sibling who polished brass in the True Sect temple at Kelsing gasped under an onslaught of melancholy, suddenly wrung by the loss of a brother condemned by canon law . . .

The scar-faced sister who stitched the tapestry for a Sunwheel altar-screen shivered, ruffled as though fondly brushed by a beloved, but unseen hand . . .

Sethvir jammed gnarled fingers through his white hair. At present, the flux ripple exposed only Tarens. The signal inflection that also marked the bard had not *yet* snagged the voracious interest of the Koriathain's lane-watching scryers. Sethvir braced on his elbows, momentarily stilled in the etched fall of sunlight through the east casement.

'Cry mercy,' he murmured, heart-sore for the fact the musician's brave effort to spare his comatose friend was predestined to fail.

The flux stream was no place for an unsheltered awareness to wander. Its powerful cascade stretched too far past the reach of tactile sensation. First disoriented, then battered to fragmentation, the untrained mind could not cope. Tarens was utterly lost to himself. No matter how skilled the bard's summons, the stricken man would never awake upon this side of Fate's Wheel.

Forewarned of that sorrow, Sethvir ached. He yearned for the moment of blessed relief, when the musician abandoned his sorrowful venture and restored the safe anonymity of silence.

Yet the sweet, liquid spill of sound did not lapse. The hand in command of those silver-wound strings never flinched in the face of defeat. Arithon's passion contested this loss, against which no risk seemed too reckless to contemplate.

Far southward, exposed upon Mainmere's wild shore-line, Arithon reached into himself, stared down ruin, and plumbed his own grace to seize fresh inspiration.

Time itself seemed to pause, as Sethvir stopped breathing. The bookish miasma of paper and ink made the hush in the tower library closer than a sealed tomb. Suspended in dread, the Warden plumbed the moment's appalling set-back and mapped the driven change designed to wrest hope back into the bard's doomed endeavour. Anguish wrenched a groan of despair from the Sorcerer as he grasped where the desperate measure was leading.

Still, Arithon played *Tarens,* the reactive flux used as his sounding-board. Clean as struck crystal, he sustained the resonant imprint to fuse his friend's consciousness back into wholeness. Yet where sympathetic vibration alone could not mend the man's tattered awareness, a deft shift in key, delicately followed by an expanded intonation unfolded an ingenious pattern, spurred by necessity. To secure Tarens's essence, then reknit the breached boundary and seat his mortal consciousness back into his slackened flesh, the bard now extended *himself.*

Sethvir jammed his fists to his temples, distraught. He could do nothing but watch while, without thought for the penalty, Arithon wove his own patterns of mastery into the skein of his harmony. He offered the bridge across the abyss: blazed the safe path back to human identity by translating the core of his personal knowledge as a bastion against the unknown. He held to that beacon. In clarion song, he presented the initiate's template to restructure the morass of unbounded existence.

The effect shot a lighting-flare through the flux. Any talented seer might recognize Arithon's broadcast signature. The first would be enemies, avid to track him. Arithon understood and rejected the danger. He would not back down, but blindly trusted his own clever resource to cope when adversity forced him to run.

With the shelter bestowed by a cruel anonymity destroyed at one heedless stroke, Sethvir cried out in anguish. Chained helpless by the bonds of Asandir's oath, he wept as the Fellowship's deadliest adversary detected the intimate presence of Rathain's last crown prince.

Three hundred and forty-one leagues due eastward across the Paravian continent, the Prime Matriarch of the Koriathain also perched motionless in the slant fall of the late-morning light. Amidst the jangled cascade of changed resonance when the shift at Kathtairr raked the face of Athera, she displayed no sign of discomposure. The pearl pins that fastened her pale coil of hair lay doused in shadow beneath her violet hood. The table before her raised seat was draped under a square of featureless velvet. On its black nap, etched white in the sun, rested two shards of quartz: the wand accidentally snapped when the abrupt surge had startled a third-ranked healer, now put on trial for her careless mistake.

Damage to a crystal brought harsh charges, even under the onset of a worldwide crisis. The stream of disaster tracked by the lane watch stayed shut outside, while the Prime sat in closed session to hear out the case.

The miserable girl trembled, tearful and shamed, on her knees before supreme authority. 'Prime Matriarch, I plead your forbearance. The unforeseen spike in the lane forces made the enabled wand vibrate in sympathy. Who wouldn't have been unprepared for the shock when the excess charge shed a burst of electrical static?'

'No lenience is due, here!' countermanded the peeress, whose vigilance governed the sisterhouse. 'Not when our basic practice to safeguard the use of a crystal was flouted! This wand was dropped, unprotected, above a stone floor!'

Selidie listened, cold as painted porcelain, her perfect cream features expressionless. Which impersonal serenity took on a disquieting aspect of horror with the linen wraps stripped off her crippled hands. The raw glare emphasized the grotesque, claw fingers, and the welted palms, cupped beside the broken crystal. Quiet reigned throughout the Prime's assay to sound whether the fragments should be recut, or, the worse for the terrified miscreant, decreed for the arduous process of mending.

The chill room stayed fireless, the air choked still. A life hung upon the Matriarch's choice, ruled by the fate of the crystal. Initiates were replaceable, as the original set of mineral tools brought to Athera when the order took sanctuary were not. Sealed under the law of the Fellowship's compact, the precious legacy of imported matrix preserved what remained of the sisterhood's autonomous might.

More, the full reach of Koriani knowledge stayed proscribed for as long as the Sorcerers' ironclad tyranny bound the terms of Mankind's resettlement. Hobbled, the order must hoard its pure heritage, passed down across generations. Among the ranked Seniors born after the great exodus that had stranded humanity on Athera, none was more raptly aware than the Prime of the burden her office defended. The gravity of her predecessors' directive now rested on her mantled shoulders. She alone comprehended the scope of the secrets locked down by the Fellowship's interdict. Only she held the guarded keys to ensure the sisterhood's future revival.

The steely edge of her sovereign command also gripped the twelve attendant Seniors, arrayed in subordinate silence behind the abased initiate. Hooded also, severe in demeanour, they fenced the accused like statuesque pillars, gloved in lavender silk with red ribbon. Sole sound amid the unbearable tension, the back-drop rustle off to the side, where the Prime's enslaved puppet, Lirenda, tidied the stripped wad of bandages back into pristine rolls.

Which task filled the pause, when the intrusive disturbance of footsteps from the outside corridor broke across the assembly's glass quiet.

Selidie glanced up. Her blue eyes flashed with warning displeasure, and her final settlement fell sharp as a cleaver. 'The snapped wand shall not be recut, but turned over for healing. Remand this initiate into custody. Let her sacrifice serve as a lesson to others, that negligence will not be excused under the privilege to wield an heirloom matrix.'

The condemned sobbed aloud. Her plight found no pity. Two fifth-ranked sisters dragged her upright. Their brisk grasp braced her stumbling retreat, while another with scarlet bands on her sleeves curtseyed to the Matriarch, then moved forward to secure the damaged crystal. The fragments were wrapped under warded silk by the time the inbound petitioner breached the closed door.

'I bear urgent news, relayed here from the second lane's watchers, in Tysan!' the newcomer pealed. 'Let me through!' Her untoward haste did not pause for leave, but rammed past the escorted prisoner in bald-faced need to cross the threshold first.

The Prime's scalded annoyance shifted to expectancy. Only one topic, ever, forgave such an intrusion.

A presence unnoticed as furniture, Lirenda observed from her menial seat at the end of the table. Like the caged tiger, she itched to bloody the keeper beyond lethal reach. Her hungry intelligence never slept as, fingers busy, she tracked the breathless messenger from the lane watch who sank in obeisance before the Prime's chair.

Breathless amid her fanned crumple of skirts, the sister blurted, 'Matriarch, by your supreme will! I bring confirmed word of your royal prisoner, escaped from containment in Taerlin.'

'Ah! At last.' Selidie's exclamation held more than pleased triumph. 'Stand. Give me the report.'

The sister dispatched by the day watch arose, head bowed with fearless respect. She unclipped a small bag from the sash at her waist, reverent as she laid the offering upon the draped square of black velvet. A nod from the Matriarch summoned Lirenda, whose dutiful service loosened the draw-string and bared the small quartz sphere, buffered inside.

'Pass the crystal to me!' commanded the Prime, lashed to snappish impatience.

Suborned though Lirenda might be to dumb misery, her faculties stayed unimpaired. The brief contact as she transferred the seer's crystal to Selidie exposed her to the lane watch's momentous discovery. Her eavesdropping awareness snatched the fleeting impression of a bold phrase of music: song transmitted through the lane flux, clear as light. The brilliant pattern unveiled an artistry that promised more – *oh, far more* – than the urgent news just rushed to the Matriarch's notice.

The voracious spark kindled in Lirenda's eyes stayed masked behind downcast lashes. Her predator's snarl, locked silent inside, sped her pulse to exquisite excitement: *that her nemesis, and likewise, Prime Selidie's bane, at last disclosed the signature of his presence!* Lirenda's nerves quivered with anticipation. The weal of the order demanded Arithon's pursuit, destined as he was to become the instrument to break the course of the prime succession. Selidie could not risk her position to fate, or allow any threat to the ancient knowledge guarded by her intact heritage.

The Prince of Rathain must be brought to heel. Lirenda savoured that sweet rush of conjecture as her oppressor clutched the quartz sphere in crabbed claws and plumbed the imprint netted in the matrix.

'Sweet glory!' Selidie crowed at due length. 'We have the s'Ffalenn bastard at last!'

The spokeswoman sent from the lane watch clasped parchment hands and ventured out of turn, 'Matriarch, I regret, not yet, not precisely. The Senior seeress in Tysan insists that your quarry still shelters in Caithwood. Though we've divined the fact that his royal significator flows through the second lane, more help is required to fix his location precisely. I'll need three other sisters sited at a distance, strong enough to remain immersed in deep trance to triangulate his position.'

'You shall have the resource,' Selidie reassured, not in the least bit distempered. Entranced by the inducted record, she inclined her mantled head inclined towards the top-ranked sister at her beck and call. 'You are assigned! Induct twenty-four of our most gifted initiates. They will convene a grand circle, directed as the lane watch in Tysan sees fit.'

'By your leave, Matriarch!' Impressed by the prodigious allotment of talent, the appointed Senior excused herself and bustled off to bear out the instructions.

'This work will take time,' the lane seeress warned, prepared to risk bracing displeasure. 'We may be cut short, or get thrown off the trail well before our trace can achieve a finished alignment.'

'Rush nothing!' Selidie glanced up from the quartz crystal nestled within her covetous grasp. Chiselled in silhouette against the sun lit casement, her face remained shadowed. Yet the hooded gaze beneath her mantle's stiff headband chilled like an arctic blast. 'Arithon plays to redeem a friend who's become mazed in the thrash of the flux. His Grace won't forsake his interest. I know his mettle. Even under assault, his loyal sentiment will keep him engaged past the point where better sense should bow to defeat. I assure you, this prince will not relent short of death, or until his pet crofter recovers sound wits.'

Remanded to duty, the seeress curteyed. 'The watch serves your will, Matriarch,' she said, and departed to execute the Prime's command.

No other attendant Senior was excused. None dared to breathe, while the record quartz remained couched in the Matriarch's ravaged grip. Hush seized the closed room as their mistress savoured the crystal's imprinted message. Few guessed the stress behind her fascination. None living recalled the old prophecy which forecast her doom at the s'Ffalenn bastard's hand: except for Lirenda, whose long fall to ruin ferociously welcomed the tang of endangerment. For the rancorous shame that condemned her to suffering, she also wished Arithon crushed! But only after his vicious cunning toppled Selidie from the lofty seat usurped through malign practice.

Hungry with ambition, Lirenda burned to survive the tiresome yoke of her servile punishment. Perilous, patient, she stalked for her chance to upset the Prime's corrupt grip. Yet until the reins of the Koriani Order could be snatched from the dust of defeat, the course of blind service commanded. Selidie's buried froth of anxiety provoked a fresh set of instructions. 'Fourth rank! Yes, Helda, stand forward! Gather to me a circle of six. I want a seeress endowed with the talent and reach to sweep the far coast-lines of Lanshire and plumb the salt waters of Mainmere Bay. This effort calls for the Skyron aquamarine. Fetch the crystal's locked coffer, and enable the matrix for my immediate use. By the time Arithon's location is traced, I will have the True Sect priesthood engaged as our puppet-string allies. If need warrants, we'll use every measure required to reclaim our custody of Rathain's prince.'

The shocked quiet deepened. None dared to speak. A Prime's purpose ruled, beyond question. Yet the Senior-ranked sisters still present stifled stunned gasps at the scope of the stakes. Such draconian measures incurred an untoward risk since Asandir's stay bound the Sorcerers' reach only in behalf of Prince Arithon. A working that called for compulsion of innocents too likely might force Sethvir's hand. If the Warden's earth-linked vision caught wind of Prime Selidie's proposed violation, such flagrant activity might provoke an enforcement of the compact. Push the Seven to respond, and no living power on Atheran soil could withstand the punitive consequence.

'Such an insolent silence!' Selidie lashed in contempt. 'Do my faint-hearted sisters believe I should fear the whip-hand of the Fellowship's tyranny?' Bared teeth flashed beneath the hood's velvet shadow. 'I intend to take adequate steps for protection. Measures that will drain lives in the breach! Four newly sworn novices must stand as my proxy for all that occurs in my circle. The invocation to fuse their vitality against an outside interference will be fashioned by my attached servant.'

The Sorcerers' precepts did not sanction murder. Under their Law of the Major Balance, the Prime's brazen coercion might be left to stand.

As the linch-pin called forward to seal such defenses, Lirenda well knew her life-force might be tapped to uphold the forbidden construct. Once, she had raged against such a fate, as helpless as any oath-bound initiate called forward to be risked as a thoughtless sacrifice.

But two centuries spent crushed under Selidie's chokehold piqued the moment's suicidal thrill. Perish, and Lirenda would win her release from the trial of a living death. Stay alive, and the outcome might yield her the pinnacle of great reward.

Prime Selidie would cross Arithon Teir's'Ffalenn at her peril, while Lirenda lurked, bloodlessly poised for the mis-step that could wrest power from bitter oppression.

Immersed in his effort to draw Tarens back, Arithon measured the resonant pulse through the flux as his wrought summons pealed outward. The inert signature for his comatose friend showed no change. Clearly, his crafted measures failed to close the bleeding breach torn through the crofter's vitality. The fatal fragmentation of spirit had yet to reverse towards cohesion.

Disheartened, Arithon chose to persist. Hope gleamed unextinguished, for as long as his flawless expression of talent sustained the bright coils of raised power. Obstacles beset him. The penetrating cold first of all, since his oiled-wool mantle with its caped hood did not shield his bare hands. Worse, the goose grease that sealed his scout's leathers from damp succumbed to the seep of the boggy soil.

If his fingering stumbled, or if his frayed concentration mangled an unfinished passage, he would unravel his painstaking effort. The natural intervals for respite were short. He snatched what brief moments he might, to stand, stamp his feet, and restore circulation. He dared build no fire lest the blaze should draw hostile notice from the Light's sea-borne patrol in the strait. Since the music shouted his personal signature, such fraught concern for the movement of enemies must not mar his tempo and pitch. Measure by measure, layer upon layer, he shaped a master-work, each chiselled note spring-wound towards crescendo, until the matched resonance to recall Tarens became reinforced to the least nuance. Arithon reached farther, extended his faculties and engaged the ringing harmonics to quicken the registers above hearing. His work unfurled like a ribbon cast into the void, sound magnified to complex skeins of light, while for daunting hours, intense concentration wore down his reserves without let-up.

Unsheltered, alone in the open, Arithon built his appeal through the morning. As he entwined the painstaking frequencies to knot an etheric boundary, noon passed. The tide changed. The ebb swirled black waters through Mainmere cut and stranded the sprawling reed-beds. Raucously squalling, flocked gulls mobbed the shallows to feed.

Their dissonant cries jangled the musician's peeled nerves. The stiffened sea-breeze buffeted his ears to distraction. Arithon shut his eyes. Head bowed, he played, while the sun shifted angle into afternoon, then late day, and the tangles of marsh grass around him acquired backlit gilt rims. Persistent against the thinnest of odds, he shaped his adamant art like etched crystal. Moment to moment, nothing else mattered. Patience rooted him like set granite as each precise phrase unreeled after the next: until the precursor to change stole over his work with the delicacy of a pent breath.

Filament fragile, the balance point trembled. His friend hovered between life and death, volatile as a feather wafted aloft by a vagrant breeze. The back-turn towards recovery might never happen. But for a minute, an hour, or a day, the remorseless bleedout had ceased. Tarens poised at the cusp. As the candle hand-shielded amid a black gale, he flickered, suspended just shy of extinction.

The hard pressed musician lifted his head. Around him, the bay shore lay stippled with the ultramarine shadows of sundown. Gusts slapped off the water, brisk enough to dampen the moment's hard-won encouragement. Arithon knew he must anchor firm stays before nightfall. In the deeps after midnight when the veil thinned, the ties between spirit and flesh were most wont to loosen. By then, his initiate mastery must strengthen and seal the ephemeral pathways through mystery. If such translated guidance could steer the lost crofter across the known threshold to heightened wisdom, every struck note must ring to perfection. If not, this tenuous passage for Tarens surely was destined to fail.

More than mulish confidence steadied the bard's hands. The echo persisted, that once before, somewhere, he had accomplished a similar feat. Remembrance whispered of a fire-lit cave, carved in carmine stone by a river-course. There, he had faced such a crisis at need, and sung another friend's talents awake. Arithon recognized the stark discipline, firmed then, to withstand tonight's brutal course. Ingrained training warned of the multiple perils should he slide too far into trance. Heedless, he could suffer crippling frost-bite, or perish of thirst, burned out by the fevers of back-lash. A man might forget hunger, though his tissues starved. His breathing might flag, or his heart stop, unnoticed, if the unearthly frequencies known to mage-sight beguiled his human perception.

Skilled enchanter, Arithon fixed his art by the sun and the turn of the stars. He marked the time as nightfall unwound, and the hours of nadir yielded to dawn.

By sunrise, he faced the edge of the abyss. The shimmers that rippled his peripheral vision and the hollow warning of nausea told of the strain on his faculties. Relief must come later. The ripple he raised in the flux must be lifted to resonate as a standing wave. Else if he stopped, his grand pattern would unravel when the lane tide reversed at next twilight. He dared not snatch any rest before then, even to stretch his cramped limbs.

The set-back he dreaded struck as he tired, pressed near to over-extension. Arithon felt the burn of a hostile influence *seeking him.* Yet the invasive probe did not bear the taint of the diviner's search he expected. Bone and blood, Arithon recognized the horrific sting of spelled sigils run through an enabled quartz matrix: ugly enough to wrench his beating heart, the dissonant pitch of the powers that once had spellbound his cruel captivity.

Recoil disrupted his seamless engagement.

Shaken, Arithon faltered. The harmonic weave of his composition distorted like light crumpled through rain-streaked glass. He steadied his strength, recaptured the thread, and forged onwards despite an onset of blind terror.

Retreat was unthinkable. Failure to rally would cost Tarens's life! Recognition followed: *that this horrid quandary had faced him before!* Koriathain had no scruples. They could, and had, destroyed those he cared for to leverage a past bid to break him.

Arithon took grim charge of his talent. Fury hardened his focus. He acknowledged the risks, that the personal mastery unfurled to spare Tarens ignited the flux like a torch. Past question, the witches would pin him down. But the natural brine in the marsh where he sheltered diffused their crystal-based craftings. After they ferreted out his location, they must invade this remote shore, drive him at bay, then exert the muscle to collect him. He had a brief hour, or a handful of days, before the Prime's hunters could touch him.

Until then, he would stand off this assault. Win or lose, his friend's fate must resolve. Then woe betide the ruthless enemy who threatened an innocent life to subdue him!

Arithon dropped the tissue of subtlety. He hammered his music into the flux, warned that the reverberation he shaped must withstand far more than the bore's shift, at sundown. The empowered guidance he fashioned for Tarens must ring true through the course of calamity, a harmony shaped to outlast his defeat should his lyranthe come to be silenced.

Night arrived once more. The moon shone, a nicked crescent that spangled reflections off the ruffled sheen of the tide-pools. The cold settled in, and hoar-frost whiskered the mud of the verges. Hunched against the relentless chill, Arithon laid his lyranthe aside only to cat nap. Wakened again to a pearlescent fog sifted in off Mainmere narrows, he snacked on jerked meat, and the sour, dry fruit and hard biscuit the clan scouts packed on extended patrol. Then he unwrapped the lyranthe, retuned, and resumed. For each measure unreeled, the order's seeresses circled him closer, like vultures.

Tarens breathed, yet. The flow of his life-force had not shifted towards healing. But at this pass, Arithon's sounding touch met the barest whisper of brightening change. He played that slight difference to clarion strength, though he streamed clammy sweat to the fever of over-extension. Hope could hurt too much, while the flare in the flux currents also informed that his adversaries stepped up their search.

Arithon flexed his cramped fingers. He danced chord upon chord, raised tensile melody into a shout of pure light in defiance, then welded his resilient harmony into an unstoppable force to illumine, resolve, and bind into cohesion. Through midnight, then into another cold dawn, as the pewter mist of an overcast day mantled the reed-banks and marshes, his desperate cry went unanswered. Tarens did not find his way back to consciousness before the Koriathain ran their elusive quarry to earth.

One moment, Arithon breathed the free air, while the poisonous touch of the seekers plumbed the flux stream, beckoned on by his music. Braced and aware of their immanent closure, he did not let his hands falter. He thought himself prepared. But when the seeresses snapped their spell closed, he encountered the scope of that miscalculation.

The trauma inflicted by his long captivity almost spelled his defeat. Arithon cringed, unable to stifle the terror that lanced like iced glass through his viscera. Through the recoil that squeezed at his gut, only firm choice and discipline rallied him. He kept his head, with eyes opened to mage-sight. Just as the enemy beheld him, stripped naked, as a trained master so also could he steal his insightful knowledge of them in return.

But that reverse twist yielded him no advantage. Instead, he uncovered the shocked revelation *that his lost memory had been no long-term impairment, but in fact an impenetrable veil of protection imposed by the clever crone who arranged his escape.* The damage wrought by his blindside disclosure was done, the consequences irreversible. The Prime Matriarch and her circle of witches grasped how severely his innate defenses were compromised.

Their counter-move struck.

Maliciously sure, the Prime offered Arithon the seductive temptation, *to know himself as he had been before the enspelled term of her imprisonment had stripped away his greater faculties.*

Shoved against the noose that would seal his doom, Arithon shut his eyes. He did not succumb. For Tarens only, he plied his strings, steadfast and true, while his enemies lashed back in redoubled retort and tried uglier means to unseat him. The wisped faces of his past ghosts were brought forward to sting him to aggrieved defeat. He saw others like Tarens, struck down in cold blood for the singular fact they had cherished him. From the brash, blond woman who had been a superlative blue-water navigator, to the surly grey war-captain spoken for by a centaur guardian's wisdom, to the redheaded *caithdein* who had perished alone under enemy torture, to others cut down by the sword in defense: Arithon suffered the gamut. He mourned the cruelty. Their brave spirits must stay unbearably nameless for the sake of today's harrowed crofter, still living. Masterbard, he surmounted the fierce upwell of his personal tears. Unconsoled, surely damned, he endured the punishing roll-call of his fallen, turned upon him as a weapon.

No matter the toll of yesterday's grief, his fight in the present had yet to be lost. Still, Arithon's call to raise Tarens pealed outward, etched light sourced by sound, and quite bold enough to quicken the trained instincts of a temple diviner.

Which peril had cause to destroy him, already. Rocked by a bolt of rogue far-sight, Arithon captured the posited tangle of interests that shadowed his movements. In horrific fact, he discovered that the Koriathain had been the covert hand that unleashed the True Sect's armed fervour against him. Once his gifted perception knew where to look, the manipulative strings of coercive spellcraft sprang stark to his eye in the flux. *There,* and *there,* he discerned the entrained sigils that twined the Light's faithful on puppet strings to see him run down and killed. He saw worse: *that the Prime's malignant meddling also heaped the false blame for the lane shift's explosive catastrophes at his feet.*

The wave of overheated reaction already spurred the muster of dedicate troops in retaliation. First response to the Light's call for action against the Spinner of Darkness, the temple fleet that patrolled the blockade over Mainmere Narrows changed course for the marsh that fringed Caithwood.

Against an invasive landing by troops, Arithon stood quite defenceless. His hands were tied: a move at that pass would kill Tarens. Unable to flee from the True Sect hunt, Arithon gave rein to his rage. He cast off every restraint and sang out! Unfurled his vindictive passion with the actinic charge to raise the dire stakes and seed tempest. The whipped flux responded like fire and storm, and heightened the Prime's stealthy measures to havoc. Let the manipulative thrust aimed against him spin wildly out of control! The effect would draw in all comers, and worse, inflame their desires to indiscriminate savagery. The Prime's Circle could chew nails till they choked on that suicidal, volte-face reverse.

Arithon's shout leveraged the enemy's own game, until the vicious greed of every blockade runner and bountyman aligned like weathercocks onto his trail.

Let the wrong party set hands on him, first! Against plain steel and muscle, he might have a chance. Therefore, as day brightened, he plied voice and strings, till the thunder-clap fugue of fierce harmony seemed all he lived for within the wide world.

Shot through that mad theme, he still played for Tarens, a delicate pattern of caring that rang on in the sheltered eye of the hurricane. Arithon's silver notes sounded yet, when the splash of intrusive footsteps smashed through his thin cover of reeds. Wrapped in mage-sighted glory, he scarcely heard the shrill shouts of discovery, peppered in salty vernacular. But the fish-taint of oilskins stained the dawn breeze, and lifted his head, when the first, hostile party arrived to lay claim to his head price.

Though his blistering courage still had wrought no victory, Arithon burned his last chord into the streamed flux like a brand. Notes pitched in closure to honour the life of his comatose friend described *Tarens!* until the brute prick of a knife at his throat drew blood and forced him to silence.

Early Spring 5923

Transition

The planetary flux tides waxed and waned, each cycle a high-pitched emission that crested like an intense burst of fireworks, then subsided as keening static. Human nerves were never designed to withstand the electromagnetic maelstrom. Thrust beyond range of his natural boundaries, Tarens languished, awash in an ocean of chaotic pain. Name and identity had abraded away, until his entire existence became the sussurant stream emanated by the naked elements.

His wracked mind did not think. *Being* became an extended torment, played through a forgotten burden of flesh, and denied any concept of ending. Had he been able to access the natural ties to warm-blooded awareness, Tarens could have remembered the gateway to death and sought surcease through mortal release.

Instead, benighted, he hovered at the threshold, shackled to inertia by hopeless despair.

Then out of nowhere, a note pierced the void. That clear, ranging sweetness melted his misery and inscribed a bubble of fragile stability. Another tone followed. Then another, sustained, which framed a melodic triplet. The harmonic resonant lifted, then soared, striking an aligned sequence that shattered the vise grip of his insensate existence. A rainbow of blinding light was unleashed, followed by a thunder-clap shock wave that toppled disorder and rearranged *everything*.

Featureless noise broke out into bird-song, and meaning returned, lifted free of the inchoate continuum of discordant sound. Hearing recognized the sigh of the wind through a forest's bare branches. Awareness recaptured the salt-wet pound of blood in warm veins, then like echo, picked up the rolling, back-drop refrain of splashed ocean foam, where the hissed surge of breakers rolled against a firm shore-line. The purl of the lane flux, vast beyond conscious thought, re-formed under shifted perception. Patterns emerged, jolted into formation out of abstract bewilderment. Life spoke of itself. As a being reborn, he encountered the rich texture of frost-browned earth and the nacreous glow of daylight through morning mist. Memories returned and meshed into cohesion, and the refounded sense of a solid existence rushed back with a roar like flood-waters burst through a breached dam.

He was still cast adrift. But at least in suspension, the raw static pulse of the elements spoke in language his beleaguered spirit could translate.

The simple triplet progressed to a chord, the tensioned transition from major to minor tones an exquisitely wrought, complex tapestry. Touched, then gently haltered, he felt the clock-work impact of each measure's adamant clarity. Then a shift in tempo and a tingle that *pulled* drew his scattered frame of awareness inward through a hard spiral. He crossed a threshold scribed in florid light. Hurtled past, momentarily dazzled again, he plunged through a sharp drop, akin to the scarcely remembered sensation of *falling*.

Breath swooped into lungs he had forgotten he possessed, keen as the plunge of cold steel. Shock hammered a whimper from his parted lips. Tarens recovered the weighted awareness of *self* like a bird netted down on the wing. He might have screamed, harrowed by the sudden trauma. But the peal of the music surrounded and steadied him. Eyes closed, he dreamed, tenderly married back into his flesh, but not roused enough to awaken. Minutes passed, while his restored consciousness realigned and adjusted, propelled past the crucible of flash-point change. *He was not who he had been!* The shift just embraced was not going to be revocable, should he resume his existence, incarnate.

The lens of his innate awareness had become melted down and recast. *Peace.* The music whispered of patience and care, while he reclaimed the courage to choose.

Wrapped in protective measures, Tarens was shown the Name of his being, one indelible thread woven into the timeless fabric of Ath's creation. Supported by a ribbon of melody that reinforced his unique awareness, he recognized the musician whose shining talent extended the posited gift of renewal. Step forward, embrace life, and Tarens understood that his faculties would be altered: the gateways through the mysteries of initiation were Arithon's own, offered to suspend the fatal onset of entropic disorientation.

Such constant love held nothing of Shadow, no whisper of evil purpose. Just as Kerelie had, and Efflin before him, Tarens embraced the Masterbard's intimate welcome, sung for him only, without reservation.

Response flooded back, an immediate reassurance that should have been flawless, had nothing gone wrong.

But a discordant whisper rippled the weave, slight, but enough to disturb Tarens's augmented awareness, still twined into the skein of the lane's flux. His sympathetic alignment with the Masterbard unfurled into Sighted, first hand immersion. Hurled outside of himself, he *became* Arithon, shoved by rough hands to his knees in the reeds of a salt marsh nearby.

While one weathered fisherman nagged his exposed ribs with a knife, others clad in sea-boots and redolent oilcloth bound him at ankles and wrists. They knotted the lashings cruelly tight. Tarens tasted their triumphant greed, spurred by the ferocious thrill of the hunt, and blind with the Light's creed of righteous belief.

These brash adventurers intended to claim the temple bounty for minions of Darkness.

Like a spark dropped to tinder, that concept kindled the fire of prescient dread. Many more ambitious parties than this one scrambled to seize the same prize. Bountymen, smugglers, and the blockade fleet's warships joined the chase like moths drawn to flame.

The flux exposed every last vicious twist of motivation with transparency. Also the desperate cost in self-sacrifice that Arithon had paid on the chance he might rescue a jeopardized friend.

Tarens gasped.

Ripped awake by horrified grief and the echo of the musician's despair, he opened his eyes to the sight of bare tree limbs, etched against an overcast sky. He felt flayed. The brush of the wind scoured over his stripped nerves, each sensation unbearably amplified. The least breath barraged his nostrils with scents of last year's rotted leaves, and wet mud, and the keen chill of salt and snow-melt.

Nearby, the disturbance of another creature burned him to jagged alarm. That presence included outbursts of snuffling that savaged his ears like a spike through the brain. Tarens turned his head, scraped almost past bearing by the abrasive wool-blankets that covered his body.

Nothing monstrous threatened him. Only a rough-coated brown pony stood hip-shot, rooting its whiskered muzzle through the unlaced canvas of a supply pack to rifle the grain cakes.

'You little fiend!' Tarens exclaimed, his voice hoarse from disuse. Beside the thrifty need to rescue the rations, such rich forage risked the foolish creature to colic.

But his instinctive thrust to sit upright whirled Tarens to violent dizziness. He lapsed back, distressed. Cradled within an invalid's litter, he raged to find himself weak as a newborn kitten. The clamorous flow of the lane's flux continued to flood him with urgent alarm. He could not shake the unpleasant conviction his surrounds would shortly be *crawling* with enemies. Already branded as a red-handed murderer, Tarens acknowledged the perilous turn, that he could no longer be overlooked as an innocent under the Light's charge of dark sorcery. Initiate, wakened, now immersed in communion with faculties shared by the mageborn, he carried the auric stamp as a talent, irrevocably, and for life.

In fact, Shadow's minion had invoked the rogue gift, though not as the instrument of corruption: the signature writ in the flux *could not lie*. Light and song spoke instead with a shining clarity to shred the deception of the True Sect doctrine. Shown a working arisen from selfless love, Tarens wept for sorrow, ever to have fallen prey to misguided distrust.

The motive behind his forced flight into Caithwood had not been a cruel betrayal.

Small use to regret the harsh words exchanged then, or lament over misunderstanding. Tarens ached for the venomous irony, that neither would the Light's entrenched faithful take pause to seek after the truth. Placed at trial before the Sunwheel examiners, he and Arithon would burn, condemned by the temple canon.

Worse, Efflin and Kerelie might suffer fresh scrutiny, even be put to the question again with lethal stakes set on the outcome.

'Not while I breathe,' Tarens swore through clenched teeth.

Since he could not stand up, the loose pony posed his last chance for salvation.

Tarens rolled off the litter and landed, sprawled atop the supply sack. The startled equine shied off with a snort. It stood with wary, pricked ears ten yards off, while Tarens curled, helplessly retching. Flashes of spurious light marred his vision. Whirled adrift, he had no certain anchor beyond the phrased song left embedded into the lane's flux. The pattern retained the cohesion to ground him, though latent surges of vision continued to upset his rational thoughts. Doggedly, Tarens clung to the present.

Despite his turned senses and parching thirst, he wormed himself off the pack and pawed through the rifled contents. The reek of food hit his sensitized faculties and wrenched cramps in his hollow gut. He persisted, frantic. If the unsettled pony lost interest and wandered to browse, his last prospect was finished. Small use, to think upon Arithon's plight, too likely already foredoomed.

The scout's fare Tarens salvaged consisted of honeyed hard-tack, forest nuts, and pounded raisins, mixed with salted strips of deer jerky. The ripe smell distressed him. Miserable, all but gagging with dry heaves, he broke a dense biscuit and offered the crumbs on a trembling palm.

The pony peered through its tumbled forelock. A nicker whuffled its nostrils. Enticed, it pawed once, then ventured forward, its neck extended to nibble.

A round-braided head-stall lay inside arm's reach. Tarens snagged the heaped leather. He placed another hard cake on the ground and coaxed the pony another stride closer. When it lowered its nose and lipped up the treat, the crofter flipped a loop over its crest and held on. Luck stayed in his favour. The beast did not yank free but crunched on the treat and butted for more.

While the clan pony lipped at his leathers and chased the strayed crumbs, Tarens eased its greedy muzzle through the cord nose-band and slipped the crown strap over its ears. Then he knotted the lead and muscled the supply sack over the short-legged animal's withers. A harder struggle saw his flaccid weight hoisted upright to lean, wobbling, against the pony's slab shoulder. Tarens flopped forward, heaved a leg over its rump, and clumsily dragged himself astride.

He gasped and clung, dizzied by terrible cramps. His furred tongue tasted like unwashed socks. Awkwardly perched and too drained to sit upright, he let his dangled toes drag on the ground while the pony meandered, snatching willow sprigs off the thickets. Clawed by branches and vines, Tarens lay in a draped heap, with the pack clinched under his belly. He tugged on the head-stall until the bedeviled animal shambled downhill.

Exhausted, he fought to stay lucid, while spontaneous surges of flux-borne stimulus flared through him in tingling waves. He saw double, then gasped as his forest surrounds wrenched into split image, overlaid by the silvery veil of other terrain sited elsewhere in Mainmere. Each wheeling onset confounded his senses, already set under vivid barrage. The sea air clogged in his laboured lungs, thick with the marsh taint wafted off the exposed mud-flats. But such queer starts and flashes of arcane perception also steered Tarens's course. Distinct as a fire's heat on his skin, he detected the flux ripples stamped by a disagreement between Arithon's captors.

The rough men had little use for frivolity. Uneasy with handling a servant of Shadow, they clashed like bulls over whether to smash the lyranthe just forcefully pried from their prisoner's arms. The pungent fear behind their clipped oaths whiplashed through the lane's subtle currents. Tarens's over-reactive flinch flushed a squirrel, which pelted and startled the pony. He slid as it shied. Half-unseated, spun dizzy, the crofter clung like a tick and stayed astride through brute obstinacy. He was practised enough. Survivor of many a drunken ride homeward, he stung yet from the remembered jolts of rejection: hurt feelings seethed still from the courtships gone sour under his family's indebtedness. Which virulent eruption of past resentment momentarily trampled his grasp on the present day.

'Damn all to the greedy bitches, the lot!' Tarens groused, his cheek crushed into rank strands of horsehair. 'Fat Ennie, and Onion-breath Onya, and don't forget Urmala, the farting cow! Broad in the arse as a hay-barn, and worse, a man would need to be pissed on jack cider to smooch that moustache on her upper lip!'

Since fury helped to steady his focus, Tarens damned each jilting female, one after the next. Then he let fly at the ones who spurned Efflin, and joyfully added the louts who had humiliated Kerelie, with extra revilement heaped upon Grismard, whose ratted word to the temple authorities had caused his cruel straits in the first place.

At least Taren's rage trampled the outbreaks of fugue, which pushed his raced mind to seek futile meaning in the rustle of leafless branches. Each second, he battled the listless urge to take shelter in the profound silence of stones and chill earth.

Tarens hugged the pony's jostling warmth, whiplashed into poignant melancholy. He could never go home, or return to his straightforward lot as a crofter. The youthful, male itch to rut in the hay now seemed dwindled and strange as desire from another lifetime. He endured that displacement, while the uncanny pulse of the flux twined itself through the thundering pound of his heart-beat, and the clipped thud of the pony's hooves topped the next rise and broke into the open.

Distracted by the wind in his face, then jounced to the animal's braked strides in descent, Tarens snatched the reeling impression of tide-flats, bare and glistening under the ebb. A fishing lugger with battered white strakes floated in mirror image upon the slack water, her snubbed bow rust-stained at the hawse from the sloppy trim of her anchor. A limp bundle of streamers hung from her mizzenmast. The entangled splash of bright colours contrasted the patched crumple of her downed sails, draped over worn spars without furling. Her empty deck showed no life. Only dipping gulls snatched scraps from the nets, gathered in like flounced scrim at her counter.

As raucous as the cries of the flock, human voices carried on the inland breeze where tuned instinct drew Tarens's attention. The desolate strand showed him stippled brown hummocks, wrapped about by dun stands of bog and the sheet-silver ripples where the stilled channels skeined through the jumble of brush-covered islets.

Then the overlook view dropped behind the dense scrub as the pony ploughed downwards. If eyesight was obscured, the static swirl of the flux unreeled its raw stream of etheric deflections, unslackened. Tarens perceived those other layers underlaid, as the resonance of the unseen registers augmented his surface impressions. *There*, the musician's erstwhile music had set down subtle roots. The shimmer of that stark beauty lingered, laced through the chaotic shock of brutality where subsequently, the bickering invaders dragged the captive bard off by the heels. Clear, as well, the precognate shadow of violence, distinct as a wave unfurled under pressure.

Tarens gasped, his cohesive thoughts trampled. Again, consciousness wavered like water-drowned light. The sting to his stripped nerves rocked him dizzy. He sucked a fast breath, overwhelmed, while the pony skidded, still headed down-slope. He lacked the strength to force it to turn, far less face down six – perhaps eight? – brawny brutes, aggressively angry and toughened by their lifetime's toil, hauling filled fish-nets.

Instead, Tarens targeted the unguarded dory, left beached at the verge of the bay. Since the pony plunged in that direction already, he planned to row out to the anchored lugger. If he boarded, unseen, before the disgruntled shore party returned, he might contrive to release their trussed prize.

Yet thought of the future unveiled a freshened riffle of urgency embroiled into the flux currents. Tarens fretted, aware that unknown forces elsewhere gouged up a redoubled blast of raw charge. Which change swept down like an inbound storm front: *and pending ripples of on-coming death loomed into convergence, motivated without thought of mercy, blood and steel to determine the outcome.*

The pony's pace felt disastrously slow.

'Git up!' Tarens kicked the beast's ribs with his heels, made it stop snatching mouthfuls of fodder. Shouldered ahead at a choppy trot, slapped upon face and shoulders by low-slung branches, he broke through the scrub to an overgrown game trail, and winced to the panic of flushed birds and rabbits. Briars raked his bare hands. Tarens hung on, overwhelmed by the reek of the marsh and stabbed by the piped cries of plovers. Sounds pierced his magnified hearing like knives, and each movement wrung him to nausea. The pony balked. He forced it ahead, wrestling the slide of the unsecured pack as the land leveled off, and his mount's unshod hooves chopped through the soggy silt of last season's shed leaves. The rumpled row of punched tracks flagged his presence, all the worse when he ploughed into the reed flats, and left a furrow of bent stems in his wake.

Soon, his hardy mount sank knee deep in the muck, propped its front legs, and refused to move. Tarens bullied another brave stride, forestalled as the animal mired. Dumped off as it rebelled and floundered to safety, he landed in a stranded heap atop the supply pack. Too fevered and weak to give chase, he wormed onwards. The salt-wet ground soaked his elbows and knees, and the cut of the wind set him shivering. He arrived at the dory, panting and spent to the verge of black-out unconsciousness. Rested prone with his cheek pillowed on his squashed rations, he weathered the spasms that raked his huge frame and chattered his teeth.

When he moved, as he must, his effort to launch the small craft met with failure. The grip of the mud glued the dory's keel fast. A stout vessel fitted with doubled benches and rowlocks, she required a hale man to shove her afloat. Outfaced, Tarens collapsed across the bow, heaped with damp fish-nets and a jumbled stack of slat crab-traps. He heaved his sack of provisions inside, then flopped awkwardly over the thwart and burrowed under the forward seat. There, he pulled the stinking, weed-coated mesh with its clinking glass floats overtop, and chanced to fate that his stowaway presence might stay overlooked.

Since hunger fed weakness, he made himself choke down the crumbled remains of the honey-cakes. The piled nets broke the wind, which meager respite let him dry out and get warm. But without the purpose of active exertion, Tarens drifted into a half-world of waking dreams. The heightened perception of overset senses bled unchecked through the interface, with chisel-punched fragments of vision sprung from a masterbard's song to redeem him . . .

The veil thinned, and the past saturated the present. Again, Tarens was a child with skinned knees, howling in a fit of furious tears. Only his mother's iron grip stopped him from hurling himself at the white soldiers. They burst in with drawn swords in sparkling gold surcoats, and boots that shook the floor-boards like thunder. The small boy hated the bearded one whose helmet was hackled with plumes. That man gave gruff orders, while the rest seized Tarens's father's arms and dragged him out of the kitchen, still shouting. They claimed he went for glory and salvation to grace the temple's divine service. That did not explain why his mother was weeping. Or why Efflin had snuck out the back window and run off to warn Uncle Fiath to hide in the haystack.

'Tarens!' The plea sounded as the last soldiers clomped out, and the company formed up into columns to leave. 'Tarens! Be strong! Look after your sister and mother!'

'Father . . . ?' Aggrieved still by cruel abandonment, the child's forlorn whisper resounded, unanswered.

The grown man shuddered behind the noisome screen of lead weights and moldering fish-net, then wept afresh as his wounded heart tore where embedded pain left him broken. As his desolation deflected the flux, the intimate linkage offered by the bard sparked off a spontaneous glimpse of shared vision. Wracked sobs mingled with a different sea-breeze, while the musician's lost, dark-haired father spoke to lend healing comfort. *'They say that Ath's ocean holds all the tears in creation. Man need shed no more . . .'*

Soothed by that tender, paternal wisdom, Tarens accepted the balm, unresisting. Wide open, unmoored, and melded seamlessly into the weave of Arithon's personal experience, he unwittingly wakened the parallel imprint, when the bard's mastery had forged a similar, mystical linkage to recall a strayed spirit, once before. *Then, as well, a bared blade at the throat had drawn blood under threat to the singer.*

In fiercest passion, adamant for the care of a different friend, the bard's art re-echoed against itself. The consonant patterns of past and present collided and triggered a flash-point gestalt. Tarens's dreaming slid into the seared memory of the crisis lived by Arithon, two hundred and forty-three years before . . .

Night dimmed the striated-sandstone cavern carved out by the flood of a free-wilds river. There, a red-bearded clansman blood-pledged as a brother huddled against the seeped influx of winter draughts. He was a large man, sturdy as the upright oak, repeatedly battered by tempests. A scout's leathers, scuffed with hard use, and the gleam on his weapons belonged to a fighting man. Tonight, run to earth and surrounded by the advance guard of three Sunwheel war hosts, he faced despair. The battle rage in him ran glass-edged with fear, for the challenge before him outmatched the skilled limit of his experience.

The rite of initiation he faced was never the tactic of choice, but a bleak necessity forced by survival. Underlit by the ruddy gleam of a fire, the clansman lifted grey-hazel eyes and asked in tight trepidation, *'Do you have any sureties to offer me?'*

Strained by unflinching truth, Arithon's grave reply: *'None at all.'* A fragmented echo, come later, the vision delivered his gentled assurance, '*I'd give you my music to guide you . . .*'

For Tarens, the musician had sung again, his matchless art lifted into command by the bold course of this previous hour's endeavour. An authority that *twice* transcended the veil fused time with a tingling *jolt*. Hurled past the pallid dimensions of dream, Tarens felt the pungent bite of the herb smoke drawn into another man's lungs. In graphic sympathy, he became immersed in the plight of the free-wilds liegemen in Daon Ramon, two and a half centuries ago. Anxiety pounded his heart-beat, linked through him by the resonance forged, then, to salvage the doomed lives of the cornered war band.

Without further warning, the dream's fabric tore. Tarens separated and fell back into his present-day self-awareness.

Nestled securely inside the beached dory, he breathed nothing more than the taint of damp fish-nets. He knew the earth's pull, and the tug of the moon that riffled the tide through the narrows. No burned herb, but the lane's flux lashed him as raw catalyst, now that the bard's strings were silenced. Scared, Tarens realized that the ruled lines of melody steering his course through the morass were fading away.

But the initiate changes firmly laid down by the bard's gifted influence remained entrenched in his being. Buffeted by the flux stream's unfiltered cross chop, Tarens's new-found awareness tumbled into the turbulence of random events . . .

He scented honed steel where True Sect dedicates billeted at Barish broke camp and marched towards Tysan's border. Their ranked columns tramped south for invasion of Havish . . . while the exhortations of a Sunwheel priest decried the outbreak of terror unleashed by the Spinner of Darkness . . . while townsfolk deranged by the lane shift cowered and shrieked in crazed fits, and temple diviners backed by armed troops forced a house-to-house search to purge those corrupted. The traumatized faithful left unafflicted gathered fire-wood to burn their condemned. Others unwilling to help earned the stigma of Shadow's collaborators, and were put to the question for untoward influence . . .

Nearer at hand, etched against the mercury eddies that roiled by salt water, the Light's patrol fleet carved an inbound course down Mainmere's deepwater estuary. Packs of determined head-hunters came also, bold or foolish enough to prowl the forbidden verges of Caithwood. Opportunists descended in crab skiffs and punts, eager to snatch a rich bounty. Ahead of them all, rife to seize the prize first, sailed the contraband runners in their narrow grey sloop, cleaving a swift course through the inlet.

They were coming for Arithon . . .

Shattered by the flicker of runaway Sight, Tarens reeled to the volatile burst of intent that lured every two-legged predator caught within range. From gifted diviners, to temple high priests, to the hapless fishermen beguiled from their nets and now holding their luckless captive – every mind tuned by greed or the stamp of blind faith descended like wolves on the marsh flats.

Tarens shuddered, aghast. Caught in the path of a fire-storm hell-bent to reap death and destruction, he realized he would be smashed by the rival contention of Arithon's enemies. Lost to futility, unstrung by failure, the crofter saw the last hope he might save himself trampled. Ahead of him, beckoning, he beheld the lost shades of two nephews, untouched and radiant with joy. With them, his uncle Fiath and aunt Saff smiled and raised welcoming arms to gather him in.

Tarens yearned towards that peaceful promise of respite. Death would free the fierce shackles of grief and release his burdensome exhaustion. But as his spirit's cry for surrender impacted the flux stream, the song of the Masterbard's making resurged, doubly amplified by the ethereal pulse of parallel resonance: the red-bearded clansman from Arithon's past also had mourned for lost family. He, too, had reached for the ghostly comfort of kinsfolk departed untimely. When the acute shock of initiate passage had unstrung his magnified faculties, he had languished in the same black-out coma at the threshold between life and death.

Heart-broken past sense for that long-ago friend, the Masterbard's cry of denouncement had challenged the turn of Fate's Wheel. His vehement song, *then and now*, raised raw power that beseeched the elements for a redemption. The shock wave unleashed. Past and present shimmered into an alignment that sheared across space and time.

Tarens, unwitting, became rocked by that force. Where the bias of history matched the resonant stamp of his personal experience, he became milled under by the same exultant rainbows of harmony. His awareness was seized by Prince Arithon's singing, then upended and whirled into the rift.

Fusion

Tarens did not lose consciousness. Only his senses were darkened, the void itself just another gateway of passage. Before he spun through, an ephemeral grip drew him in, then gently restrained his wandering spirit.

'Not yet, friend!' said a voice. 'Hold on. I beg you to bide. Think carefully first, since a crossing made here becomes permanent.'

As though restored to his natural body, Tarens blinked. Rattled to find he no longer nestled within the beached dory, he viewed instead the rough sandstone cavern taken from Arithon's imprinted past. The draughts here wore the diamond-hard chill of the gusts whipped in off the winter Barrens. But no fire burned, as it had in the original vision. Not a glimmer seeped through the cleft to show whether the world outside lay under night stars or daylight. The eerie, half gloom that Tarens experienced was suffused by a silvery cast, apparently shed by the water-worn walls, though the layered striations seemed otherwise ordinary.

'Where am I?' he asked where he stood, still clad in the muddy leathers outfitted by Caithwood's clan scouts. 'How on earth did I get here?'

'You are not on the earth,' the same voice replied, its timbre emerged from the shadows. 'What you call *here* is nowhere, and everywhere, a reflected vibration seen only when the disembodied spirit explores the half-world opened through first-level mage-sight.'

The speaker sat across from Tarens's vantage, with his large, scarred hands laced over the scraped buckskin breeches that covered his knees. Red-bearded, brought living from Arithon's past, the clansman surveyed the crofter with tender expectancy.

'You!' Tarens gestured towards the mineral walls, unknown to his personal experience. 'This is not my own time and place. Who are you? Why have you brought me?'

The grey-hazel eyes fixed on him were a hunter's, seared into lines by the glare of high summer and seasons of blizzards that whipped cruel cold across Rathain's wild heartland. On a face like a map carved lean by hardship, the skin crinkled with latent laughter. 'This is not the past.' The correction included a gesture too graceful to fit a man of such powerful stature. 'You are poised between life and death, my friend, beyond the range of familiar perceptions. Your history knew me as Rathain's Teir's'Valerient, and we are brought together because my oath as *caithdein* has tied both our fates to Prince Arithon's need.'

Tarens flushed, unsettled to find that his mettle was being weighed up as a defender. Before such acute scrutiny exposed his short-falls, he blurted, 'I am scarcely fit! My brother was better at slaughtering stock. Said I bungled the job. Too kind-hearted.'

The tall clansman raised dark, level eyebrows, amused. 'Do go on.'

Tarens bridled, fists clenched. 'I am nobody's killer!'

The clan chieftain returned an infectious grin. 'The war-captain who trained me would've said, of your whining, that you only dig the pit deeper by protest. Look at you, fellow! Tell me straight, with that frame, you don't fight like an ox!'

Frustration sparked temper: the same accusation from Efflin would have launched Tarens to fisticuffs. Since this needling barbarian was hung with a broadsword and a ruthless array of sheathed knives, prudence suggested the impasse was more wisely defanged with contempt. 'You realize I meant to deliver your prince into the hands of his enemies.'

'He sang for you anyway,' the old blood lordling declared, turned humourless as the crouched tiger. 'The love in his music has not denied you. My liege and my sworn brother risked life to redeem you. Yours, now, the charge not to abandon him.'

'Are you real at all?' Tarens taunted, afraid. 'This may be nothing more than a dream.'

But the denial only evoked melting sorrow. 'The moment is real,' the s'Valerient said. 'You and I stand at the verge of the veil where the boundaries between etheric perception and substance are thinnest. What we decide here will affect what happens, not just to your destiny, but Arithon's. Yet not mine. I returned from this place and completed my given fate. Transcendent, at death, my loyalty answers your crisis only because your choice now might help Arithon's survival.'

'Who were you, to him?' Tarens asked, despite himself piqued to curiosity.

The tension dissolved to rich laughter from the apparition. 'My liege knew me as Jieret. Hasn't he cursed my bull-stubborn nature, or laughed over my feckless sea-voyage to Innish when he's fallen into his cups?'

Tarens swallowed, abashed by the overtones of an intimacy that left him stranded like a blindfolded trespasser. 'He may not remember. You don't know your liege suffered the loss of his past after being held captive by the Koriathain?'

'Aye, the frigid, murderous parasites!' Jieret snapped, brows pinched to a spine-chilling frown. 'Sithaer take their meddling sigils, you won't notice the evidence under your nose? They seek his Grace still through their filthy use of coercive spellcraft.'

Tarens stared, blank. 'I saw no witches. Only opportunists, faith-driven or pressured by greed, since the temple's posted a bounty in gold as a head price.'

'Don't say you were hoodwinked!' The clansman unfolded his rangy frame and shot off his rock perch in distress. 'How could you miss the poisonous storm of compulsion polluting the flow of the lane flux?'

'You think such overpowering urgency is suspect,' Tarens mocked, head turned to follow the clansman. The large man paced like a predator, muscled arms crossed as if chilled. 'Why?' Tarens pressed. 'You say the sisterhood's wiles stir the pot? It seems excessive to rock the stalemate with Havish over a hunt to trap one escaped prisoner.'

'Oh, the witches claim to have cause, beyond question!' Jieret insisted, his sideward glance baleful as his ferocious strides quartered the narrow cave. 'My liege was named the Spinner of Darkness as the author of wholesale slaughter. Truth lent the bitterest seed for the lies that have whitewashed a cursed war in religious trappings. Though, by Ath, my prince never walked the role given him. He has not embraced the ways of black practice, no matter how viciously he's been hounded, or how bloody the field as his enemies raised their unscrupulous wars to seek his downfall, again and again. Your move might stop the next round of innocent pawns being put to the sword, as they move to provoke him!'

'Arithon?' Tarens stared back, astounded. 'We speak of the same man? He's the most unassuming, compassionate healer I've ever met!'

'Ah!' Jieret chuckled and jabbed an admonishing finger. 'Don't be fooled by his kindly heart! Or worse, be disarmed by his runt appearance. Arithon s'Ffalenn is more dangerous than anyone you will ever live to encounter.' Jieret glanced at his hands, perhaps wrenched to naked regret, as he added, 'You've noticed he's also daft over sentiment. Few are privileged to witness the frightening depth of his vulnerability. He does need a vigilant sword at his back. Since I cannot serve, would you stand at his shoulder and guard a safe return to his feal clans, in Rathain?'

'I'm a steader who ploughs, scarcely qualified as your successor,' Tarens declaimed.

'You are fit,' Jieret argued. 'Or will you rebut the genuine loyalty that also spared your close kin? Can you claim that you killed a temple diviner by accident?'

There, Tarens could not deny his own courage. But neither could he disown his honesty before this skilled warrior's rapt eyes. His own hands were strong, but not those of the swordsman, scarred through hardened experience. He was not schooled to arms; could not stalk and hunt game through the life pulse of the mysteries. He was ill suited as a royal defender, far less to shoulder the role of the steadfast liegeman that Jieret implied. Tarens knew that his capable nature sprang from mulish persistence, heroic only through berserk temper in the rare moment when he was goaded.

Jieret laughed. 'Ath wept, man! You've undervalued yourself! Don't commit to that foolish mistake. Such pigheaded modesty will see you cut dead before you can father your heirs.'

Tarens protested, stung. 'I can mend harness straps well enough. Swing the scythe from dawn to dusk, and even manhandle rampaging oxen. But those skills can't shelter your liege against sorceries, or turn the armed strength that's committed against him.'

'Aye, well enough.' Jieret grinned. 'There's the sore point that I've come to remedy. My liege and I were once blood-sworn under the auspices of his mastery. Due to the gift he also bestowed to uplift both of our latent faculties, a bridge of connection has opened between you and me. Just for this moment, that gives me the chance to bequeath you the sum of my knowledge.'

At Tarens's blank look, the barbarian qualified. '*This* deep in the mysteries my hands are not tied! The initiate awareness Arithon wove for you has fused with a part of my being. We can tap that connection. Forged through the lines of his Grace's past oath, I could cede you all of my faculties. You won't be the same man, ever again. But since you made the bold choice and fled Kelsing, what else might you dare to become?'

Already hurtled beyond the familiar, Tarens weighed up the proposal, uneasy. He had *Seen* the ships, and the armies; tasted the bitter scorch of the power set in motion by the Koriathain. He sensed the measure of Arithon's enemies, and worse, feared the flames and the scaffold he might face himself. Already condemned as a fugitive and sentenced to die as a minion of Shadow, he knew that he lacked the means to thwart the arcane pursuit of the temple diviners. And yet, hesitation still clawed him to ribbons.

'You must decide quickly,' warned Jieret, fretted to sudden impatience. 'Once you've crossed the gateway towards life or death, I can no longer help you.'

The clan chieftain was too prideful to plead. War-scarred and stern, he towered with such human presence, Tarens found the prospect of an intimate exchange with him all the more keenly disturbing. 'You are asking me for a liegeman's true service. Blind trust in your cause for the sake of your prince when you've just cautioned that I barely know him.'

'I could share my deep ties of commitment to him,' Jieret answered. Not lightly offered, such a private exposure would lay bare his heart's very core in the flux: the grace that sustained greater mystery could not falsely glorify petty motives. 'I won't hide the blood on Prince Arithon's hands,' Jieret stated without apology. 'But if you understood why I survived my past trial of awakening only to suffer and die for him, you might find the footing to ease your decision.'

'No.' Tarens ducked the personal embarrassment. His own upright character demanded that he stand or fall by his own merits. 'Arithon risked all that he had to give selflessly, for both of us. And Caithwood's folk showed me the fibre of clan honour. I believe you speak with integrity. For those reasons, I'll shoulder your task, and do what I may, though I can't promise your liege can be steered anyplace he refuses to go.'

'Ath wept! That's the way of him. I've cause to know.' Rueful with relief, Jieret stepped forward and gripped Tarens's forearm in his people's traditional clasp to seal amity. 'Fare you well, town-born, whatever befalls. Fight bravely, heart of my heart.'

Words were finished, between them. The chieftain's firm touch melted away, lost into a blast of white light and a peal of exquisite, grand harmony. Blinded in the deluge, deafened by ecstatic joy, Tarens became overset. Hurled momentarily beyond reach of all sorrow, he gave way to the elemental shout of celebration. Both cavern and clansman vanished; or not: *somewhere in time, the cry of a master singer had awakened the exalted power made manifest by a Paravian enchantment laid into an ancient, black sword. For a sanctioned crown prince's naked appeal to call Jieret back to himself, the bright chord that once had Named the winter stars rang through the weave of Ath's creation. Or not; perhaps the tone woke instead to the blast of a dragon-spine horn, winded by a centaur guardian . . .*

The majestic note stripped away human reason. Its shattering fullness peeled Tarens's being and laid siege to his mortal essence. The hammer-blow smashed all frames of experience. His human awareness scattered into shards, then split again, ripped down to particles of singing energy. Then whole cognizance reassembled with a gut-wrenching swoop. Poured back into the clay flesh left behind in the dory, Tarens curled helpless behind the heaped fish-nets. While time streamered like ribbon through the closed gaps, he shivered and wept as the molten core of his being reshaped and emerged from the white-heated crucible of sweeping change.

Plain as daylight, he grasped that his last request had been disregarded. *Closer than a brother, he knew how Jieret had died. And more: too much more to assimilate.* Whiplashed by the rebound of stressed senses, and pierced by the unbearable, fading echoes of beauty and hope, Tarens wept for the unconsoled sorrow. The grand chord had passed its thundering crest. *Nothing* in life prepared him for the overwhelming loss of separation. Grief tore through the breach with a shock of agony that nearly stopped heart-beat and breathing.

'How can I survive this?' Tarens gasped in extremis.

As the final thread of rapport diminished, he received Jieret's last exhortation.

'I offer the advice my Teir's'Ffalenn gave, as master, when he guided me through the final stage of initiation.' The wistful farewell the shade offered was bitter-sweet, piquant with humour and boundless affection. 'The gifts you've inherited will settle with sleep.'

'I don't think I can,' Tarens mumbled back from the cod-tainted reek of the dory. Scarcely conscious, he repeated the selfsame protest once used by the shaken clansman, centuries before him.

As the glimmer of the grand chord dispersed into the background scatter of lane flux, Tarens's raw confusion was eased by last words, which might have been Jieret's, or Arithon's. 'You will. You must. I can help, if I have your permission.'

Since that kindly plea could not be refused, Tarens let go. Profound silence embraced him, dense as black felt and peaceful as final oblivion.

He woke to the clash of irritable voices, immersed in hot argument over his head. Tarens could not guess how long he had rested, crammed under the fish dory's bow seat. Filtered through the stinking cover of nets, the latest contender sawed on, '. . . pains my bollocks something worse than wicked to be robbed by a pack of cod-seiners!'

'Terrified of them, are you?' another man mocked, gruff as the grate of chewed gravel. 'Captain should forfeit your pay share for whining, then toss you off for the sharks if you can't come to grips.'

'Blight, man!' a laconic chap intervened. 'Yon fish-slitters aren't mincing daisies, or harmless. Remember that drunken blow-hard who was killed on the public wharf? Got himself reamed by some clam-stinky bloke with a shark gaff. Anyone's moon-sozzled, who thinks to knock down the buggers who've nabbed our mark, first. Best to take their measure and make a plan.'

Pinned down throughout the singeing exchange, Tarens tallied the separate voices to number the sea-wolves hell-bent to take Arithon.

The fourth on his list groused in clipped sibilants, 'We've got no leeway to pussyfoot, Cayte! Not with hardened bountymen hot on our tail! More, we can't hope to dodge those war galleys peeled off from the Sunwheel blockade.'

Gravel-tongue gave his opinion, again. 'What if yon fishing blokes posted a lookout? If someone's holed up on that anchored lugger, one whistle in warning will flush their slinking shore party like stoats. The brush here could hide them for hours.'

'I'm not beating the reeds in this bog to flush anyone,' a smug fifth fellow agreed. 'That's begging to get us pegged by clan archers. I say we make straightaway for the spoils. Square off with that rival crew, then bolt with their prisoner. Leave here, before this place gets choked with bully-boys frothed up to kill for religion.'

'Should scuttle this cockle-shell first,' drawled the thoughtful tactician among them. 'At least stop the nabs on that lugger from chasing our wake through the gauntlet.'

'A scavenging rat could do better!' This voice female and piercing with scorn. 'Given the weather's too frigid to swim? Just shove off their dory and let the ebb-tide sweep her away down the channel.'

Another male circled with an objection. 'But that leaves any louses left on their fishing smack—'

The woman's abrasive contempt cut him off. 'Not if we pounce on the prize opportunity! Let's raid their wallowing fisher's tub now! Snag off her mast pennants and escape under her official grant of safe passage, ourselves.'

'No,' said a more measured authority. 'We'll board that lugger and sail her intact. Shut the bound criminal inside the hold, gagged and bagged up in a crab sack. Then we cross Mainmere channel dragging her fish-nets. Meanwhile, the rest of our crew takes the sloop. Let them run ahead through the Sunwheel fleet, innocent as a decoy.'

'She gets flagged down, inspected for nothing, and let go slick as spit!' The observer whistled in admiration, through back-slaps and brays of laughter.

'No bother, then, boys. Let's hop and flense ourselves a few mackerel men.'

'Daft nitwit!' the woman pealed in rife scorn. 'You thugs will have us branded for murder. No killing! We ambush the fishermen, snatch the temple's fugitive, and go on our merry way. If yon dory's cut adrift on the tide, the blokes will be stranded here, helpless. They might fashion a raft and snag their loose boat. But not before we've made our landfall at Barish and cashed out the temple's bounty.'

'You and you!' the commander snapped, then gave his decisive orders. 'Quit nodding off and launch this bath toy of a tender!'

The contraband runners grasped the dory's rope thwarts and shouldered her from the strand. She lurched ahead, splashed into the shallows, and yawed in the swirl of the rip current that riffled past the mud-shoals. As the boat bobbed out-bound down the estuary, the hidden crofter hunkered within fretted in helpless frustration. The shade of Arithon's past liegeman implied that the highest of stakes rode upon today's outcome.

Yet until the loosed dory drifted to a safe distance, the sly marauders stayed free to pursue their bold plan unobstructed.

The sea-wolves did their dire work quickly and slipped out unscathed, reviled from the beach by the furious shouts of the plundered fishermen. While the narrow, swift sloop that had brought the marauders spread her pallid canvas and sailed to decoy the patrol fleet, their robbed victims cursed them: first, for the theft of the valuable prisoner, and again, with more murderous injury, for the ruthlessness that had jacked the lugger needed for their livelihood.

'Unnatural, blood-sucking lampreys!' the stranded captain frothed in contempt. A wiry man with bleached whiskers and a suffused, dumpling face, he ranted away as he stumped down the shore with his disgruntled mates.

His dock-side expletives suffered a hitch. 'Look there! The blind nerve!' In fact, one of the pirates was caught in the act, trying to lift their boat's dory. The incensed captain hefted the cut sapling, carved to a point, that had failed to defend the snatched prisoner. He charged into the shallows waist deep, pitched to skewer the raffish blond lubber, caught trying to escape through the shallows. The captain's baggy slops ballooned in the current. Worse, sucking mud mired his ankles. Which ungainly grace alone spared the thief. The loon was not gaffed because the stumpy fisherman overreached as he lunged to attack.

His jab missed. The stick dropped as he windmilled his arms to avoid sitting down in the channel. Nobody laughed. If he toppled, his canvas breeches would fill, and the tide's pull would quite likely drown him.

The bungler chose not to snatch the rude advantage. Instead, he leaned sidewards and grasped the wet rope tied in farmer's knots to the mooring cleat. He tugged. The dory glided ahead through brown water, not aground after all, but staked to the bottom by dint of a bashed-in crab-trap. Which folly was not only stupid but blind, with the boat's proper tackle left in plain view in the bow.

Never mind that the dory had not washed into the Westland Sea, and that a destructive brute's use of his trap-line heaved the jacked tender back into reach. The beached captain grabbed hold. He straddled the thwart, hot to strangle the stowaway before he lit after the pilfering rats on the sloop.

Until what the stranger was telling him pierced the blind haze of his rampage.

'I amn't your enemy?' The luggerman's bristle of whiskers deflated as he sucked in his puffed cheeks.

'No,' the liar replied in town accents, his smile raggedly nervous.

Eyes black and suspicious as a nest-robbed wren's resurveyed the blond hulk, who in fact was no sailor. Rumpled in a snagged cloth jacket thrown overtop the buckskin preferred by the free-wilds barbarians, the fellow was dirt-scuffed and raffish. The captain said, cautious, 'You claim to know where yon skulkers are bound?'

Even teeth flashed again through the glint of gold stubble. 'I do. But not if you threaten me.'

The fisherman harrumphed. His muscular yank and a glottal protest from the mud saw him into the rocking dory. 'Say on, lad. Make your case. Mayhap my boys might decide not to dice up your liver for crab bait.'

'I secured your loose tender,' the wretch pointed out. 'Politely, you might call me Tarens.'

'Ah, laddie, I'm thinking you did that to save your own skin.' The inimical survey measured his length, then abruptly dismissed the hopeful thought of drafting him for the oars. 'Yer peaked at the gills. Get seasick, do ye?' Without pause for answer, the captain laughed, deep-chested as an emptied beer keg. 'Shift your arse, then. Ach, no! To the stern seat. Damn you for a brainless, overgrown puppy who thinks we keep a mud-hook to play strong man's hurley!'

Tarens flushed, embarrassed. In fact, he had wrestled with the anchor until the dead weight of the iron defeated him. Although his brief nap had begun to restore him, he preferred seeming ignorant to the admission of puling weakness.

'Well, speak up!' barked the captain, his beefy hands busy slotting the oars in the rowlocks. He chopped the left blade, torqued the dory about, then put his back into a shoreward stroke to pick up his marooned crewmen. 'Slack tide's in an hour. Need to row like Dharkaron's almighty Chariot to overhaul that vile sloop. Not to mention clobber the rogues who've cast loose my blowsy bitch of a lugger. Best hope she's run hard aground on a mud-bank, and not torn apart on a reef!'

'The sloop's away, clean,' Tarens rebutted. 'Chase her down, you'll get no satisfaction. She'll shelter under the law since you don't bear hard proof that her sailhands have done you an injury.' Which impertinent statement earned him the end of an oar, jammed into his larynx. Bowed backwards, Tarens gasped through his crimped throat. 'S'truth.'

But the burly fisherman stayed unimpressed. 'In cahoots are ye, laddie?'

'Not!' Alarmed as the tilt of the dory scooped up a slosh of cold water, Tarens twisted his chin and tried pleading, 'Listen, at least, before you crush my neck! That sloop's running empty to mislead the chase. Your lugger's not drifting at large, she's been stolen! Sailed by intent with your prisoner aboard, she's lending those brigands the cover to slip the blockade.'

The stout captain exploded. 'They're faking innocent, *using my nets*?'

Knuckles clenched to avoid being rammed overboard, Tarens wheezed, 'I overheard them say they'll dock at Barish, smug as fed ticks, acting ordinary.'

'Well, that won't work! We're a Torwent tub, above-board by the custom-house registry.' The oar's pressure relented. The listed dory righted herself, while the disgruntled captain reset his looms. He carved a mighty stroke, still complaining, 'We're licensed to fish here only if we sell our catch to the bursars who supply the temple's war host.'

Hurled ahead by the jerk that vented balked rage, Tarens massaged his bruised neck, his silence mistaken for disapproval.

'Don't like being forced to feed the realm's enemies!' Baleful, the captain spat into the sea. 'But boats get sunk, or our fish-shacks and houses burn down each time we've bid to shake off the Light's requisitioners.'

Inclined towards sympathy, Tarens inquired, 'That's why you sought the head price for the fugitive? You needed the coin to rebuild?'

The captain huffed, his tousled head cocked askance to guide his craft towards the shingle. 'Oh, for gain, right enough. We're taxed something brutal for the official pennants that grant our free passage through the blockade.'

Which subject's bleak frown implied desperation, should that rightful waiver be lost to the hands of the contraband runners. The next vengeful pull shot the dory ahead, while the gulls screamed and dipped, and the bow sliced through the low breakers and doused spray that left Tarens stung blind and frigidly streaming.

The captain braced his oars, without comment. The moment his furious crewmen arrived and splashed into the shallows, he bared his stained teeth, and announced, 'Bag this one, boys! He won't bring the same price in gold as the first. But the temple's decree named a tidy fee for the capture of the blond accomplice.'

Tarens shouted in protest, while two men caught the boat, and the others pinned him in rough custody. 'You don't have any idea what you're risking!'

'Do we not?' The captain belted out another coarse laugh. 'Tie yon wretch with the painter. We don't need the line for cleating the tender till after we chase down our lugger.'

While the disgruntled crewmen piled in like wet dogs and doubled up on the benches, the captain bellowed, 'Stroke, you laggards! Those jackers handling a gaff rig aren't apt to make prize-winning headway. Hands used to a sloop will pinch her sails. She'll lose way like a hog when they tack. Even if they mend their mistakes, the tide will shift in our favor within the hour. Keep our stroke nippy, and we should be able to overhaul their position!'

'Take back the black-haired singer, as well,' snarled the skinny man, bent to lash the fair captive's wrists.

'You have no idea,' Tarens warned in a frantic attempt to be heard. 'The fellow might seem to be mild and small. You probably found him well-spoken. But the contraband runners won't have their way. Believe me, that mettlesome prisoner's more dangerous than you imagine.'

'Are you joking, or daft?' The dory's burly coxswain glared back, irritated.

'I'm telling you straight,' Tarens insisted. 'Your enemies have taken on deadly trouble.'

'Hell's glory!' cracked the coxswain, impatient. 'We already know that! The little criminal fought like a hooked shark from the very moment we grappled him! Sliced two of us bloody with Hammon's filched knife. And see, Bish's arm that's strapped up in a sling? His wrist's swollen purple and probably broken!'

While Tarens gaped speechless, the lugger's captain grumbled in sour corroboration. 'We'd gotten the bloke roped. Wouldn't have lost him, forbye, if the contraband crew hadn't snuck up behind, with us caught licking our wounds from your henchman's dastardly round of rough punishment!'

Early Spring 5923

Causes

Having lost her bid for Elaira, the Prime Matriarch exhorts her stymied Seniors in Tysan: 'If that lugger can't be seized in the estuary, or in case our live prize isn't landed for bounty at Barish, we'll spur the surprise invasion of Havish and harrow the coast-line southward to Torwent. Arithon won't slip through that net. Not since yesterday's massive stir in the flux galvanized the Light's faithful against him . . .'

'Don't make the fatal mistake!' Dakar shouts, raked by the prescient sight of red war and frantic to stop Lysaer, who mounts his fresh horse with an insistent resolve beyond reason, 'I must ride at speed ahead of my troops! Who else alive can spare the Light's followers from wholesale slaughter on the Prime's game-board? Chase my heels, as you wish. But nothing you say can shift my moral charge to try for an intervention . . . !'

Rushed into a premature departure by his oath of Fellowship constraint, Asandir warns the young High King of Havish: 'You'll face dire events. Expect vicious purges of clanblood, and wide-scale burnings of newly fledged talent. Koriathain are putting the spurs to your enemies, and worse, they have baited Lysaer s'Ilessid to pledge a disastrous return to the field . . .'

X. Reversals

The contraband runners who held the creature suspected for acts of rogue practice were canny enough not to trust the restraint of a dangerous prisoner to kindness. They crammed the minion of Shadow forthwith into a draw-string crab sack.

Stiffened by salt, the hemp mesh chafed like wire against skin pummeled raw from mishandling. Bagged and slung up from an overhead beam, Arithon's contorted weight cut off circulation to his cramped limbs. Eyes shut in distress, he tried and failed to ease his position. Despite miserable discomfort, his straits were not dire. The drubbing dealt by his captors left him battered and grazed, with kicked ribs that ached until every breath hurt. But his bones were not broken. As his bruises subsided to a dull throb, he determined that his joints were not damaged. Surely, left enough time to himself, he should manage a clever tactic to free himself.

Except that the trauma left ingrained by his prior imprisonment would not let him stop trembling. The visceral kick of stark terror refused to bend under the trained discipline of his faculties. He dared not give in, or dismiss the grave set-back. If his emotion could not be quelled or harnessed to constructive purpose, he must restore control before the crisis undid him.

Yet the inchoate desperation that rode him only tightened its grip. He was not in fit state. This had to be recognized. The unwise, hard use wrung from overstrained faculties throughout his attempt to spare Tarens left him pressed to the brink of delirium. Or so he presumed, beaten limp at the rough end of a wildcat fight. But after an hour alone in the dark, he still shuddered under the after-shock. Unease raised the unpleasant possibility that he suffered far more than the straightforward abuse of injury and over-extension.

In cold fact, the struggle in him had gone berserk long before the first bite of the ropes. Beyond the sickness brought on by prolonged immersion in the flux stream, Arithon traced his persistent, crazed fear to the *taint* of an arcane compulsion, still fastened onto his captors. He acknowledged his part in that ground-swell of chaos: his own back-handed move to upset the darker intent of the puppeteer powers against him should have raised every ship on Mainmere's seaboard against him.

Now, as he languished, Arithon grappled the recoil unleashed by his inflammatory stroke. *Indeed, he would reap the whirlwind to come.* Just how deadly the match, he dreaded to think, as the dissonant *wrongness* cranked his nerves beyond sense at close quarters. Which persistence did not add up, after the incendiary measures driven by his music faded to quiescence. Apparently his captive state had not satisfied the Koriathain's perverse purpose. Rather than retire their black net of sigils and pluck their snared prize from his keepers, the sisterhood maintained their compulsive influence in force. Why they should burn power at such reckless strength that hapless folk stayed afflicted bespoke wider stakes, for who knew what unfathomable end game. Arithon reeled through fitful waves of rogue far-sight, forewarned that their provocation inflamed the True Sect doctrine towards broad-scale war. He could not react, entrapped as he was, dangled as the hot lure for a crafting that flicked his tuned instincts to light-headedness.

The roll of the hull swung the crab sack in ponderous arcs over the silvery gleam of the cod catch. Inside the shut, reeking gloom of the hold, the stink and the working creak of ship's timbers should have unstrung his frayed nerves. Instead, the noise and rough motion put Arithon at ease. The splash carved up by the bow and the slap of the wavelets against weedy strakes seemed familiar. The distinctive, sharp lurch confirmed that impression, when the inbound current through the narrows tugged the crosswise course of the vessel's keel. His instinct chafed at the blatant mishandling, as pinched canvas riffled a plaintive warning, then slatted into a jarring clatter of spars.

Rushed footsteps banged, above decks, while a scathing shout cut across the crew's dismayed outcries. 'Steer small, damn you!'

'How can I?' the disgruntled helmsman snarled back through the thunder of slackened sails. 'Persnickety bitch has no way left to her. Whipstaff under my fist's gone as limp as a lubber's prick in a whore-house!'

'Mind your course and shut yer gob, butty!' bellowed the man in authority. 'Want a stiff sword rammed up yer tucked arse? Lose our lead, and the Sunwheel armada will have us carved up for their admiral's trophy.'

The pintles squealed sternwards. Someone's almighty shove threw down the strapped rudder to a lugubrious slosh of pressed water. The lugger yawed, wallowed amid the cross chop and nearly in irons. Her dumpling bow battered the wave crests to splashed spray through her ponderous swing, until the rampaging flog of her head-sails backed wind with a whump that shuddered her length.

'Jibe, ho!' screeched the captain, then changed target to singe his first mate. 'Move those louses amidships, you star-gazing lummox!' The tirade suffered a pause, likely because he ducked the main spar, which scythed across to a rattle of blocks and threatened the heads of the men on the wheel deck. 'Like it or not,' his rant resumed, 'we're hardening sail on port tack!'

Booted feet thumped. Taut hemp thrummed and squeaked, as the harried hands sweated the sheets to make fast. Still, the prevailing breeze blew too light for the full-bellied hull to gain steerage. After the current turned back in her favour, she might be dragged northward on course to reach Barish. But not quickly. Cast out of sorts, she spun at the whim of the eddies, equally likely to fetch hard up against the bluffs of the Lanshire shore-line.

As the lugger wallowed into a heel and her heavy, patched sails riffled taut, the cantankerous captain rode herd on his helmsman again. 'Head her up! Three more points. Idiot! Because I said so! We have to maintain appearances.'

'That's serious, truly?' the mate fumed, still riled from some bent of foolishness just sorted out on the foredeck. 'You're hell-bound to haul that forsaken mass of fish-tackle astern? Blight that daft notion! Already, we're ploughing our nose in the bath like an egg-laying turtle.'

'In a waffling tub, under safe-passage pennants?' The captain bridled. 'I don't give a fish's tit! We act like douce fishermen whether we have to hump down this channel, arse backwards. If we don't make the effort to trawl, Light forsake us, we're a suspect target. So toss off those damned nets and wag to the Light like a virgin, before we get hailed by a Sunwheel patrol with some fettlesome doggo aloft with a ship's glass!'

To the laggard crew, doubtless caught gawping, 'You heard! Free those booms and cast out the nets!'

Feet shuffled, underrun by a whiner's complaint.

'Blight take a ninny!' the stressed captain snarled. 'We're bobbing along in a hull that a jettisoned beer cask could overhaul! Luff you for a mooner if you think that blockade's patrols won't try us inside of the hour.'

The mate's gravel tones rumbled through the splash of weighted twine, plunged over the stern-rail.

'Worried? Surely I am,' the captain responded, still surly. 'But not over quibbling dark sorcery. That underfed mageling attacked with his fists when those fishermen cornered him. Shut up with the reek of dead cod, in a sack? When we haul the wretch out for the bailiffs at Barish, he's sure to be green and heaving.'

But except for sick air in the dark of the hold, the crab-netted prisoner suffered no landlubber's set-backs. His adaptive ease suggested, instead, that he knew lines and sails with the intimacy of past experience.

Canvas slatted, again. The captain's bellow bristled the helmsman to retort, 'Already, your orders've pinched her too tight!'

While the lugger bucked into an ungainly roll, first head-sails, then main and mizzen revolted. Canvas riffled in protest, then thrashed. Blocks clashed and disordered spars rattled as the stout hull shook herself like a dog. Flogged across the eye of the wind, gripped in the spin of an eddy, she drifted backwards over her nets. Whence her iron-strapped rudder became snarled, wreathed, then wrapped, and finally roped fast by her ponderous coils of twine.

'Dolts! Now we're roasted!' The captain's orders shrilled beyond fury. 'Hop to! Clear that fouled steering before I have you lot wading. Hard up in a clinch, you'll be kedging this hulk off the mud, bereft of a tender!'

Even afloat, dampened out by salt water, the discordant tension deflected the flux.

Arithon mapped the on-going disturbance from the hold below. Eyes half-lidded, lapsed back into mage-sense, he followed the shimmer as the cascade rippled outwards. Here and there, he detected the odd, dimpled whorls where other inquisitive beings took pause. Lured away from their feeding upon the energies stoked by the tide, those primitive motes tasted the ripe charge of dissonant emotions. Excited into sudden alignment, these abandoned their random grazing to gorge.

Always, the flare of human distemper became the hot magnet for *iyats*.

A well-maintained vessel carried a fiend bane to ward off such an invasion. The lugger possessed one: an exemplary work of wrought ciphers, stamped into a green strip of copper and tacked to the midships hatch. Arithon traced its faint emanation as light, which enveloped the lugger with a subtle boundary from both mastheads through the full length of her hull. His refined awareness observed the effect as the defensive halo unravelled the *iyats*' cohesion. The ward's influence drained them, the closer they came. Any too recklessly thralled to shy off became sucked down to a state of null charge, which unravelled their penchant for mischief.

The quelled fiends drifted aimlessly as limpid wisps, stunned inert until the ship's passage moved the active ward out of range.

The dim hold, the pestilent slosh of the bilges, and the creaked of complaint of caulked timbers, ringed about by the tang of prowling *iyats* – the ambience sparked a sharp breath of epiphany. Arithon stifled a manic laugh. In piquant fact, he might strike back at will. The tiniest flick of cast shadow might stop off the ciphers stamped into the vessel's protective talisman. Douse the ward, and the mettlesome *iyats* would milk the crew's rage and seize their free rein to wreak havoc.

More, and far better, Arithon *also* recalled a past crisis, shut in another ship's hold under threat of a fiend storm. He clearly remembered: a host of tiny lights, drifted air-borne like stars, shaded pale blue and bright indigo, to scarcely visible tints of deep violet . . .

When Tarens's affable temperament broke, his brow knotted first with a thunder-cloud frown, followed up by the lightning clout of his fists. But not this time. The latest, most bitter reverse saw him trussed in wet rope and thrown face-down, with his crooked nose spluttering bilge in the fisherman's dory. The puddle sloshed to the stroke of four oarsmen, pressured at speed, a nuisance too shallow to drown him in earnest. But his miserable coughs as the salt stung his nostrils wracked him to dizzy prostration.

Flung spray off the oar-blades spattered his back. Yet more than soaked clothes set him shivering: the awakened thrust of intuitive instinct also blew chill through his bones. Though he was not gagged, his husked warnings failed to convince his fixated captors to pause and listen to reason. Hell-bent, they pursued their crazed chase up the estuary.

Their burdened craft wallowed dangerously low. Her nicked thwarts all but sheared the lapped wave-crests. Ninth man in a dory built to hold six, Tarens was kicked by rough boots each time the tired oarsmen spelled themselves in relief. Plots hatched, bandied in bursts overhead, concerned about bearings, and light wind, and shoals, betwixt fierce debate over vindictive strategies, aimed to retake their jacked lugger and reclaim sole custody of the bound prisoner.

That the man they discussed was a minion of Shadow never dampened their rampant enthusiasm. Wedded to the pursuit of stark madness, they argued whether their effort to board should be launched under cover of darkness.

'Nip in close, wedge the rudder with one of the oars, then clamber on deck with a noise to scare the daylights out of their livers,' urged the current contender.

'Wait for nightfall, we'll lose her. You think those animals are going to show lanterns to welcome us in?'

The captain's stubborn opinion prevailed, for a headlong assault at the rail amidships. 'The first time those rats bested us, we were ambushed. Matched eye to eye, we'll give them a rumpus to shred us fresh bait for our crab-traps!'

None thought to weigh in the captive presence of the black-haired fugitive.

Tarens alone fretted over that score. His attempt to speak out earned a kick in the ribs that knocked the wind out of him. At risk of worse injury, he lay flat and gagged, until the savage cold shortly made the drubbing seem merciful.

The clan liegeman's apparition had cautioned from the shadowy half-world of dreams. *'Don't be fooled by his Grace's mild appearance.'* Yet even that counselled warning fell short at late day when the errant lugger was overtaken.

The men rowed through the scald of the westerly sun, gadded on by their game-cock captain, who perched with bristled hackles on the stern seat. Since his dory fetched in through the shimmered reflection, the bedazzled watch on the lugger posed little concern. More than the weather lay in his favour, since the negligent slop to the rig meant his stolen vessel lay dead in the water. Her tan-bark sails were down, but not furled. The starboard anchor still hung at her cat-head. Not underway, or gripped by the tide, she presented the round-bellied swell of her side, nudged by a white rill of current.

'The useless louses have run her aground.' The captain spat leeward in rank disgust. 'Row, you buckos! Let's have her back in our hands while she's helpless.'

Tarens could see nothing, while the gap closed to the pull from the benches. Still tied on his side, his cheek pressed against the dory's soaked floor-boards, he heard only the captain's colourful comments as the details spurred shock and astonishment.

'Merciful Light! Will you look at her *rig*? Blast all to the damnable meddling of Shadow! She's been trounced! Looks like a gale with a half dozen water-spouts swept her from stem to stern.'

The stroke faltered, as the oarsmen swivelled to assess the grim picture. Then their speechless, awed rage begat curses.

'Quit slacking!' barked the captain, ripe to spit nails. The gawping pause broke to the bite of the oars, and a furious thrust hurled the dory ahead.

'I'll stake their gizzards to the last man,' one brute husked, as though strangled. 'That wasn't a gale, boys. No natural happenstance. Spars thrown down like that! All her rigging unravelled? That's no salvager's work. Boat looks like a wrecker's been at her!'

The chap crammed in the bow seat groaned through his hands. 'Don't want to think what's befallen our nets. Merciful grace! We'll be sunk, and our families, too, if we don't claim that Sunwheel bounty.'

'Stuff your miserable yaps. Just haul for your lives!' snapped the captain. 'We don't hop quick, there'll be nothing to save!'

The chopped bite of the looms increased rhythm, to taxed grunts from weary men who now were galled beyond desperate.

The violent slew as the dory fetched up alongside rolled Tarens face-up against the tender's worn ribs. Gulls launched overhead, screaming from their chock-a-block perches on the lugger's bowsprit. The dory thumped and sloshed in the waves, rocked sharply enough to take on water as the men surged erect and seized the trailed ends of their vessel's slacked stays. Yelling, they swarmed up the craft's lapstrake planking. Tarens braced for the fight as they boarded, helpless to see past a sky-caught impression of bare masts, jumbled spars, and a wracked snarl of unfastened lines. No shouts erupted. Not a clamour of steel broke the stifled silence. Blocks and sheaves, the boat's dismantled rigging streamed in abandoned disarray from her stripped masts.

But the lugger's deck was not deserted. Silhouetted against that rat's nest of ropes, a stilled, black-haired figure with tied wrists: haltered to starboard, the contested prisoner braced his elbows against the gouged railing.

'Your best twine is intact,' said the insolent creature, hunted for acts of dire sorcery. Against outraged ownership frostily pitched to seize upon murderous vengeance, he qualified, 'The standing rigging's down, but not severed. If a few blocks went overboard, you will have spares. Once you've calmed down enough to inspect, you'll find nothing worse than the splices holding the stays have unravelled.'

With both fists cocked like battering rams, the captain swore back from the dory. 'Here's blight on your grave in the deep, and torment to chase you in the after-life! I see no reason my crew shouldn't gut you.'

'Your craft is hard aground,' the pert stranger agreed. A curtailed gesture displayed his lashed wrists, made fast to the pin-rail. The knots were a mariner's, expertly laid, while the breeze off his person belted the nose with the shocking stink of dead fish. Under full sunlight, the fellow sparkled, dusted all over with cod scales. 'I was dunked in the catch,' he apologized, glib. None the worse for the noisome abuse, he added, 'Had your dastardly jackers allowed me the helm, your seaworthy dear would be floating.'

''Twon't spare you, wretch!' While the fishermen mobbed the open deck, the near-vacated tender bobbed like a cork as the captain launched from the stern and snagged the first line within his reach. 'By chance are you claiming our fiend bane has failed? There's a rash fancy for an excuse! I've lived long enough to hear better ones!'

While his angry crew closed with punitive hands, the serene reply underwent a strained hitch. 'Not precisely.' A sharp break, as the mate's punch clouted the speaker's ribs. His protest resumed, a touch breathless. 'The louts you actually ought to have beaten are strapped at your mercy already. Look for them. They're laid out like stringers up on the foredeck.'

'He's truthful,' a red-faced crewman yelled back. 'I've seen. All eight, safely hog-tied and gagged. How in the black name of Shadow could a blighter hitched to the railing do that?'

'Sorcery, surely,' the bound heckler suggested, his expression wide-lashed as an owl's through tangled hair flicked by the wind. His added complaint to the rightful captain smouldered with fettlesome irony. 'By all means, welcome back aboard your command. I presume I'm still worth the bounty offered by the high temple? Or do you plan to hatch crabs in that boat, while your other bagged felon turns blue at your feet and slowly dies of exposure?'

The stupefied quiet split into an uproar that echoed off the grey bluffs of the Lanshire shore-line. Gulls wheeled. Wading birds in the marshes took squawking flight to the taunted captain's shrilled orders. While his pinched lugger groaned to the thrash of the tide, shoved harder into the mud, two subordinates jumped like singed stoats and hauled the stupefied landlubber out of the dory. 'Get that brute warm and dry and be quick about it! Dead, he'll pay less, since the public won't have the spectacle of a live burning.'

The stout captain dispatched the rest of his own to mend the disastrous mess of kinked rope and spilled tackle draped over his free-board. In the scramble to rove in the requisite stays and brace up the tilt in the lugger's masts, then to secure her canted spars from sliding overboard, the precious prisoners were herded into the maw of the aft lazarette.

'That sorcerer claimed he escaped from the hold,' a deck-hand observed, eyeballs rolled to the whites. His plaintive fear saw a fisherman's luck charm woven of hemp and hen feathers tossed into the locker after the pair, followed fast by a burlap bag filled with rock salt, pinched from the stores used to pickle the catch. The sack thumped into Tarens, to a man's muttered prayer, earnest in the belief that such simples and faith in the Light might deflect ugly practice.

Then the hatch banged shut. The hasp clanged, and the snap of a lock punctuated another fool's soft-hearted protest.

'Shouldn't we leave water and something to eat, if not a warm blanket? We'll be at least a day making repairs before we're back underway.'

'Going nowhere at all, we don't kedge off this sand-bar!' the captain rebuked in disgust. Securely in charge of his vessel at last, he subsided to grumbling bluster. 'Won't risk my neck or my soul, feeding sorcerers. As for those blighted jackers? They'll keep in the hold. They can gnaw the raw fish if they're hungry.'

Cramped in squalor atop mildewed bights of spare rope, Tarens heaved off the crushing weight of the salt sack. Sheltered from the wind, his chills eased enough that his teeth slowed their incessant chattering. Bound hand and foot, he squirmed and resettled, a hissed breath for each bruise rammed against the spare tackle, and another as his battered frame gouged the stiff rolls of hide, stowed for use against chafing. Above decks, the crew settled to their thankless work. The bump of their boots came and went through one perverse man's cheery whistle, and a back-drop of disgruntled carping.

Tarens resigned himself to discomfort. Stuck with his wrists knotted behind his back, he peered through the darkness at his companion.

Arithon sat tucked like a ruffled cat, his roped limbs poised on his drawn-up knees, since his forearms stayed strapped in front. A haze of what seemed filtered light faintly picked out his angular face, blurred at cheek and jaw-line with swelling contusions. The lazarette's vent holes, cut through to the hold, wafted the fragrance of cod from the black depths of the bilges. The overhead deck seams were oakum caulked, and the hatch cover sealed to be watertight. Which meant the locker should have doused sight in pitch-darkness and shown Tarens nothing at all.

Clammy with nerves, the crofter wondered whether he discerned through mage-sight until a more careful inspection traced the source of the eerie glow to Arithon's left hand. Thin bands of some uncanny working wrapped his smallest finger to the first knuckle. The rings glimmered with subtle tints that ranged from lightest blue through dark indigo, to the deepest ephemeral violet.

The man had never worn arcane jewellery before. Uneasy, Tarens noted the fixated green eyes, immersed in a survey that tallied the embarrassing toll of his weaknesses.

'Welcome back,' stated Arithon softly. 'For too long, I thought you lost to this world. Thanks to Ath's grace, you have chosen to stay.'

'Might come to regret that,' Tarens rumbled back, 'if we're taken from here to the pyre and faced with a Sunwheel executioner's sword through my heart.' A bit hoarse, he might have run on, had a *bang!* from above not warned him silent.

Arithon returned the distinctive, edged smile that his liegeman, Earl Jieret, once had viewed with alarm. 'I might regret, yes,' said the Prince of Rathain. 'But only if we sail to Barish.'

Which murmured admission met blistering threat from the frazzled crew of the lugger. 'Still yer yapping tongues! Or the captain will have you gagged in a trice, strung up by the heels in the fish locker.'

'That's already been tried,' Arithon shouted back. 'Or hasn't anyone gone down below yet and measured the hole in the mesh of your crab sack?'

'So that's how you came to dive into the catch?' Shut in, the poisonous stench was appalling. Nose offended, Tarens surveyed the unkempt person before him, with the shared evidence of recent manhandling livid enough on marked skin. The jolt of incongruity dawned as the crofter sized up the other's unnatural, complacent composure. Befouled by the dried glister of fish slime, Arithon's fox features almost seemed amused. In fact, he appeared to be biding his time, relaxed in reserved, alert interest. Which detachment suggested that the lugger's condition, aground on the reef, may have been a deliberate strategy.

Tarens grappled to guess how the feat with the unravelled lines had been accomplished.

The crew above decks were not reassured, either. As they tackled their morass of needful repairs, they soon found an uncanny finesse that outstripped all credibility. No lines were destroyed. Not a plank had been sprung. The downed spars had not cracked in the violent crash when the stays and topping lifts parted.

In fact, the vessel's sail rig lay dismantled with dreadfully expert precision. The hull languished without any crippling damage, a selective run of sabotage fit to freeze the blood of any blue-water sailor. Morale turned brittle when someone remarked that no living person aboard had commanded free hands when the owners arrived for the reckoning.

With the mood above decks cranked into fraught tension, Tarens's frown deepened until his head ached. He threshed through the contrary facts for a plan and found naught but the manic design for a suicide.

'Light's blinding glory!' a distraught hand shrilled topside, apparently sent to haul in the snarled nets. 'Not a mesh is unravelled. That means witch's luck, or else a fell trap to swallow us whole for a certainty.'

Then the mate unburdened his rattled report. 'Every shred of gear needed for sailing's been messed useless, with nothing burst. That's not canny! Forbye, a rope doesn't strap a man's wrists by itself. Whose dance script to hell are we following?'

'Best be underway before we find out!' rapped the captain, then amended his standing orders. The man gone below to sound the bilges for leaks was told instead to remove the gag from one of the jackers. 'Question the wretch! Find out how a sorcerer's wiles could make such peculiar things happen.'

When the subsequent blame was pinned upon *iyats*, the strained oaths from the men assumed a cracked note of hysteria.

Thought clicked into place. Tarens whispered, appalled, 'You intended to keep us set up as bait?'

Arithon stirred. 'Bigger fish. Are you frightened?' Belated confession, or the cryptic apology that he was undone by exhaustion, his response evoked a drawn silence until his avid gaze doused at a blink. Reclined on the cordage, eyes shut, he resumed, 'No one's cowed enough to ditch us ashore, as I'd hoped at the outset. We'll see, very soon, which destiny springs from my sorry effort at meddling. I'd rest, while we can.' At which point, he bowed to his own sage advice and earnestly settled to sleep.

Asandir sensed the time growing urgently short, his ride to vacate the Kingdom of Havish deferred until the bitter, last moment. Dismounted again to ease his winded mount, he greeted another morning on foot, the sharp wind in his face, blowing northerly. Winter's persistence yet seized the sere ground where the buckled seam of the steppe west of Scarpdale sheared into the blunt, limestone bluffs that hemmed Mainmere Bay. Here, the lingering grip of the cold belied the thrum of the lane's flux, agitated to dissonance beneath his steps.

The Sorcerer did not require his colleague's earth-sense to interpret that drum-beat of war. The limestone ground under him all but rang aloud to the ripples of turbulence. As the risen sun laced the dun landscape dull gold, and spangled the glitter of dusted frost, the wave of energetic convergence that marked the invasion resounded through the subtle web. No moment remained to lament, with its onrushing crest now unstoppable. Asandir's oath compelled Fellowship interests to cede the field.

Stared in the eye by that bleak course of destiny, constrained to be gone before Rathain's captured prince came ashore, the Sorcerer abandoned his ninth-hour tutelage and left the inexperienced hands of Havish's freshly crowned High King with the crushing responsibility of defending the threatened north border. Alone, that serious young man amassed his guard and his clan war bands, a day's march at the Sorcerer's heels.

Everything to be done lay in motion. Asandir threaded his adamant course through the cusp as the peace came unravelled. Last night's brutal ride sped him towards the border by way of the ancient Paravian footpath worn by the past guardian centaurs, whose steadfast tread once hallowed the seasonal Paravian migration along the coast. The shadows of present-day sorrow weighed on the Sorcerer's shoulders as heavily as the loss of such consummate beauty. His mount's hooves traversed unmarked turf that might soon bear the wrack of a battleground.

But not yet.

The cloudless sky wore the pale tint of aquamarine, while plump robins hopped over the newly thawed swales, and the melt puddles splashed scatters of liquid diamonds under his black stallion's hooves. Like secrets, the sheltered hollows lay velvet-clad, tender green and crowned with the budded stars of the snow drops. Life quickened, despite the shadows of violence that streamed through the lane's flux: and where emphatic human beliefs snapped and sparked, collided to strident contention, without question the cauldron was stirred. Rampant chaos abetted Prime Selidie's meddling hand as the impetuous shift dealt the world by the drake's dream in Kathtairr torched mass fear into wildfire crisis.

Sunwheel fanaticism reached fever pitch, with countless innocents snagged in the throes of back-lash paranoia. If crown law in Havish did not persecute talent, Asandir sensed the ranging probes of the True Sect diviners unleashed to purge what they viewed as an outbreak of heretic practice. Past the border at Barish, his attuned awareness traced the rank terror incited by their summary executions and mass burnings. The smoke taint unsettled him, though the gusts that riffled his bare, silver head in Havish blew clean.

'Avert,' Asandir murmured. He refused to take stock, or measure the horror, or count how many blameless lives stood at risk if the temple's false doctrine seized these lands in misguided conquest.

Near Torwent, as nowhere else, the outlying crofters bore the mixed descent of clan blood-lines, exiled in a long-past wave of exodus, or linked by generations of fishing folk whose rooted tradition of amity had forged kin ties with the chieftains in Caithwood. Asandir remounted his rested horse. Agonized, as one of the world's greater powers, he could do naught but fare through the threatened district unobtrusively.

The free-wilds trail became a dirt lane between stone-fenced pastures. Hedgerows squared the fallow earth of the barley fields, yet to be turned by the plough. Asandir rode plain-dressed. His sturdy leathers matched those the king's couriers wore, topped by a laced wool jerkin as rough as a mendicant tinker's. Despite his innocuous, felted grey cloak, his passage raised surly stares from the steaders out tending livestock. None gathered to shout inquisitive questions, or ask him for recent news. Boisterous children did not mob the traveller who might pay honest coin for a farm-wife's meal. Instead, they bolted inside the thatched cottages or ducked behind distrustful parents. The village mill and the smithy lay silenced. Even the elderly idlers clustered at the brewer's sat close-mouthed under a pall of unease.

A dread not groundless, to Asandir's eye, as he drew rein before the pale, rocking figure hunched in the brambles beside the road. The woman's distress personified the upset unleashed by the afflicted lane currents. Out barefoot in her soiled night-rail, with mousy hair fallen over her contorted face, she shivered under the blanket draped over her huddled shoulders. Bursts of sing-song gibberish muttered to herself dissolved into spine-chilling screams, provoked by nothing apparent. A relative had left her a basket of food, ignored, while a rib-thin stray cur anxiously wolfed down the contents.

Asandir swung out of the saddle. He secured the loose reins on his stallion's black neck and freed it to graze by the wayside. Then, quietly calm, he approached the traumatized woman.

The cur jerked its head up and bolted: not fearful of him, but startled away by the flanking charge of a heavy-set man with a leveled pitchfork.

'Keep your distance, stranger! She's got nothing to rob, and a kinsman's roof provides her with food and shelter!'

Asandir stopped in place. Empty hands raised, unthreatening, he said, 'She's your dead brother's goodwife.'

The distraught relative ploughed in without hearing. 'Leave her be! Don't disturb her!'

Asandir agreed, disarming, 'When approached, she gets violent.' He arrested the pitchfork poked at his neck with the feather touch of one finger. 'Be still. I might help, if you'll let me.'

The farmer blinked puffy eyes, red from weeping. His bristled aggression ebbed, as he fully acknowledged the *presence* his thoughtless rage threatened. 'Ath's glory! I'm sorry.' The raised pitchfork dropped from his nerveless grasp and thumped flat at the Sorcerer's feet. 'Do you know what ails her?' He doffed his knit hat in distraught respect. 'Several more in the village have suddenly turned as piteously deranged as she.'

'This one's only seeing her ghosts,' Asandir corrected, but softly. 'Stand aside, if you would. She's been much too sharply awakened to talent. Rest assured, she's not sick, just severely disoriented.' He knelt, unmindful of puddles and filth, and cupped the woman's smeared chin. 'Talla, daughter of s'Criadien?' he asked, and with tenderness, surveyed her features. 'You are present and living, not lost in the half-world.' Through the rope tangles of her tumbled hair, the Sorcerer regarded her eyes. He waited, motionless in the chill wind, till her darting glance steadied to meet him. '*Anient*, Talla. Be as you are.'

She shuddered. Cried out, then collapsed in a heap in the Sorcerer's arms, which dismayed her fraught kinsman.

'Fear nothing, she's sleeping, just as she should.' Asandir rearranged the blanket, then lifted her raw-boned frame from the frozen verge.

Patient, without censure, he watched the goodman wring his forgotten hat between worried fingers. 'You would be something of a sorcerer, mayhap?'

Before the fellow bolted in panic, Asandir said, 'Here. Take her home.' Still speaking, he transferred the woman's limp weight to the man's anxious care. 'Tuck Talla in bed. Let her rest undisturbed. Her opened awareness will settle, I promise. Three days from now, she'll sit up and be hungry. She'll remember her family and friends, and be rational, though I expect her past values will shift. New perception has sensitized her awareness. She may see things you cannot share. Don't tell her she's crazy, or isolate her out of ignorant disbelief.'

The countryman's brow furrowed. 'Then a Sighted awakening has caused this?'

Asandir sighed, without time to explain. 'Ask the gifted among the clans. They have the trained background to help, and by charter law, they're obliged to share their understanding.' The old blood-lines would realize the markers had moved: that one sweeping peak moment seeded from Kathtairr had reforged the subtle currents that laced the firm ground underfoot. Altered forever, the flux pulsed to a different harmonic register, which revised the staid fabric by which most of humanity mapped its existence.

'Our village has others in desperate need,' the crofter ventured, transparently hopeful. 'Let me show you, once I've settle Talla.'

'I'm aware of which cottages house the afflicted.' Hurried past courtesy, Asandir pressed his point. 'I can find my own way. No, I won't take your coin. Just find a measure of grain for my horse if such stores can be spared without hardship.'

The Sorcerer strode off, nonetheless braced to meet the next round of distrust with sympathy. Rare were the gifted, able to discern the delicately volatile interface between human senses and the world's energy web. Rarest were the wise healers, who could settle an inflamed awakening of dormant sensitives. Asandir would do all he might to balance and mend the afflicted, even at the high cost of delay. For relief would be scarce, amid a widespread onslaught of epidemic proportions. The lane currents were roiled enough to rattle the deafest of instincts. Even the blinded with no gifted faculties must feel the looming anxiety seeded by cataclysmic upheaval.

'Cry mercy against the Light's zealot priests!' Asandir snarled under his breath. Even as his trained vision assessed the brightened shimmers that marked the prevalance of innate talent, the overlaid stain of the probable future outlined the villagers' fate. The sight should have raised tears, given room for indulgence. For if Havish's northern border was breached, the frenzied cleanse by Tysan's temple examiners must condemn every innocent inhabitant. These people here, interbred with clan lineage, would be haplessly slaughtered by fire and sword. Altogether too little could be done at short term to wrest these folk clear of the blood-bath.

For the critical future Asandir dreaded was sealed well before he completed his business, remounted his horse, and set off on his way. Out of pity, Sethvir's contact withheld the bleak news after the field Sorcerer remounted and set off alone down the road.

By then, the last daylight faded with sunset, the deep shadows metallic with frost. The Lanshire winds blew bitter and brisk, and rattled the bracken that speared through the patches of granular snow-drifts. Asandir pressed the black horse at speed over the iron-hard ground. His inward eye beheld the turned course at twilight when the lane tide crested, and the darkened train of event became manifest: a spate flushed into crimson and fire, inflamed by the onset of bloodshed and war.

'You have seen?' Sethvir's thought, framed as words, touched his mind with pained clarity. *'The landfall will happen south of the border.'*

'Torwent,' Asandir acknowledged, gruff and breathlessly bitter.

'By Arithon's doing, yes.' Sethvir's fractional pause held sheared steel. *'The recoil might have gone worse for us.'*

'How, exactly?' Asandir reined in his restive stallion, not sanguine. He listened, his formidable, cragged features intent, while Althain's Warden delivered the cryptic summary. The sequenced flow of images showed Arithon and Tarens summarily bullied from the deck of a grounded lugger into the armed custody of the blockade fleet's flagship. The robbed fishermen's protests were roundly ignored, until the wracked state of the vessel's rigging breached the arrogant crust of higher authority. The appalling damage was assigned to an unnatural infestation by *iyats*, with a witnessed claim that the smaller prisoner's dark practice had befouled a temple-blessed fiend bane. Appalled by the risk, the armada's captain dispatched a message by courier sloop. Then he made haste to raise sail and shed the knotty problem of sorcery into the hands of the Sunwheel campaign commander.

Which hair-raising twist would bring the captive pair under the interim custody of the True Sect's dedicate field-troop: perhaps safest in the short-haul for Tarens. But beyond the custody of Tysan's established priesthood, the precipitate course only galvanized the swift assault upon Havish. With the Spinner of Darkness headed for Torwent, the True Sect's forces marched over the border and attacked to stem the fell threat that evil itself might claim shelter under crown sanctuary.

'I'm far behind schedule,' Asandir cracked in summary. 'How long before Arithon sets foot ashore?'

'Dawn, latest.' Sethvir's assessment ached with regret. *'If you run northward, your objective is lost. The site of the marker stone at the border is already in the midst of the battle-field. You'll turn for the focus circle at Fiaduwynne?'*

Asandir's oath acknowledged the crux: he must leave the kingdom forthwith or break his vow, set in stone, to relinquish involvement in Arithon's embroiled fate. Sethvir's tacit query implied that the tired horse under him should be reined around and sent at a thundering gallop back towards Carithwyr. A grim expedient, since the Sorcerer's life-force must be shared to sustain the brutal pace without flagging. The course would bring Asandir to his knees, reliant upon the confluence of lane forces at the Second Age monument to restore himself. The sure choice, that route could enable his direct transfer out of Havish by daybreak.

Asandir drew in a harsh breath, iron-nerved. 'I am not going south.' He stroked his mount's neck, precocious successor of a long equine lineage kept in his service by selfless free will. Then he touched the rein gently and turned the stallion's starred head towards the east, by the grace of sweet trust, asking everything. 'I will ride for Athili.'

'*And blaze such a trail as to curdle the moonlight to hammered silver?*' Far off in the library at Althain Tower, Sethvir shut tortured eyes. Distraught, rendered speechless, he ached for the awareness: his colleague's bold decision risked the life of an irreplaceable equine companion. Just as tautly unspoken, he sensed Asandir's curse, which damned the feckless name of Davien.

Which vicious sharpness drove Sethvir's response. '*You know why, if he prompted Seshkrozchiel's dreamed action with reasoned deliberation.*'

Asandir's snarled thought blazed with bottled anguish: his grand oath, of course, sworn under stone's witness before Koriathain surely could tip the balance and plunge the continent's life web towards entropy. Davien's unconscionable move had bought time, given the terms that dictated Mankind's precarious leave to inhabit Athera. Asandir did not have to like the raw taste: the close anger that tore him through stemmed instead from the salvage, *now useless*, of eight gifted villagers, *three of them children*!

Words lacked any power to soothe. Nor did Sethvir claim the moral high ground, or argue the bald-faced necessity: that through healing the aberrant flux rifts in Kathtairr, the resonance of the planet was lifted *perhaps* just enough to secure the threshold of Paravian survival. If the disastrous turn of affairs wracked Havish into violence beyond salvage, where no prior slack had existed, now a slight margin buffered the long-term stability of the planet. A pretentious grace, if the peace upset by the Koriathain deranged the flux lines, or worse, engendered an ebb fit to damage the flows which sustained the deep mysteries in the free wilds.

The hollow stillness behind Sethvir's quiet, more than everything else, pierced Asandir's armoured regret. Above the drum-roll of hooves as the stallion began the break-neck race over distance, the field Sorcerer gasped, 'Ath wept! There is more? Are we pitched to the very brink of defeat, that we face such a desperate stop-gap?'

'No,' Sethvir temporized. '*The act at Kathtairr may have been as much the dragon's caprice, with the day's human casualties never granted a second's consideration.*'

'Kharadmon won't accept that,' Asandir warned. 'Be sure his forbearance won't forgive the outcome, or believe Davien's partnership was ambiguous.'

'Well, the pot and the kettle are equally black!' Sethvir snapped, his beard all but ripped to the roots in frustration. Afraid for the chance that such courage could snap the Fellowship's most dauntless spirit, he added, 'Tell me you don't tread a desperately fine line for a hope that might yield our case nothing but heart-break!'

Asandir returned a humourless laugh; brittle mask for a grief past expression. 'Ath forefend and woe to humanity's fate if my effort tonight meets with failure.'

But his statement dangled against a stark silence. If Sethvir's earth-linked faculties grasped such foreknowledge, his tacit contact withdrew.

Deadlock

The jolt as Dakar's toppled bulk struck cold mud sprawled him face-down in a melt puddle carved by a wheel-rut. Slush and gritty water splashed up his nose. Bludgeoned awake with a spluttering grunt, then savaged by the ache of chilled sinuses, he cursed the fall that had pitched him headlong from an inopportune catnap in the saddle. Clawed onto his knees to arise, he discovered he had not succumbed to exhausted sleep, after all. Suddenly overset, he doubled and hurled up the dregs of his dinner.

The night's drizzle clung like a drenched cocoon, punched through by the fading drum of shod hooves as his riderless horse bolted off in the darkness. Too wrecked to give chase, Dakar spat bile and oaths, flecked with the odd bit of gravel. He was wringing out his soaked gloves when Daliana circled back to redress his delay.

'What happened?' she snapped, sharpened by the awareness that Lord Lysaer spurred onwards, alone. No one's wise argument salvaged the fact that his sensible retinue from Etarra had been abandoned to make better speed.

She drew rein too close, her unskilled seat astride only kept by ferocious determination. Dakar cringed, showered by icy spray churned up by shod hooves. He was not seeing double: more than one sidling horse threatened to stomp him to mincemeat. Daliana had his skittish mount gripped in tow, eyes rolled white and resentfully snorting.

'I did not fall asleep!' Dakar said in stung injury before she attacked him for moronic clumsiness.

'Well, we've fallen disastrously far behind. Had I not witnessed your meal at that post-house, I'd swear for a magistrate's fine you were drunk.' Daliana dismounted. Undaunted by her girlish frame and slight strength, she snagged his collar to haul him erect.

The loud squelch of her boots, and her touch seared away another layer from his peeled nerves. Dakar's finicky stomach revolted, again. Seized helpless with dry heaves, he gripped his cramped gut, distressed beyond coherent speech.

Daliana braced him with sudden concern. 'Was the mutton bad, truly?'

The paroxysm eased. Before she bent down, or worse, tried to lay her palm against his flushed forehead, Dakar jerked free and forced a clamped breath. 'No.' He scrubbed his face with a handful of snow, then coughed to clear his sour throat. 'This is only the damnable back-lash caused by a prophetic fit.' He staggered erect and finished up, hopeful, 'Maybe I shouted loudly enough? Did you catch the gist of my raving?'

'I heard filthy swearing,' Daliana allowed bravely.

Dakar swayed, rocked afresh as her other fist seized his rucked jacket and steadied him.

'You're not in fit state,' she ventured, fearful he might collapse like a drenched sack of rags in the ditch.

Dakar shoved her off before his trembling melted her to obstructive sympathy. 'Forget my dignity.' He floundered ahead. Grasped his mount's dangling stirrup for balance, instincts stung to foreboding by the muffled quiet. The Lord Mayor's horse had passed far beyond earshot. 'Just help me astride. If the post stable equipped your nag with a lead-rope, please use it. Tie me into the saddle. We've got to spur hard and overtake Lysaer! Stop for nothing unless I should pass out again. If that happens, take heed and recall what I say.'

'And if you start spouting nonsense in tongues?' Daliana sniped back, likely galled by the sores of a novice equestrian.

Dakar stifled pity. 'Should I speak in an older Paravian dialect, memorize what you can. Yes, the service is vital! Restored to my senses, I'll take your best effort and try to translate.'

'You should be tucked in bed!' Daliana protested, strained as she shouldered his clambering effort to heave himself back astride.

'Just do as I say!' Dakar snarled, past tact. 'More than the life of your liege may depend on this!' Faint and wobbly atop the restive mare, he fretted over his bout of spurious prescience. No use to decry the loss of the prophecy just delivered, or to lament the damnable quirk that those forecasts he made amid a blind trance were destined to happen, regardless. On-coming trouble shadowed the flux lines. Overset by grim pressure, the spellbinder swore in steamed language under his breath. He need not consult with Sethvir to imagine the perilous wake of the recoil unfurled by the tumultuous lane shift.

The sensory reach of human senses had been elevated within the span of a moment, with all the known boundaries shattered. Anywhere initiate wisdom was absent, error and ignorance must rule in the breach. The True Sect's priests would be quick to inflame their mass following amid the windfall storm of chaos. Past question, fanatical turmoil already festered the dangerous crux, with Lysaer s'Ilessid poised on the razor's edge, at gravest risk of entanglement with Desh-thiere's curse. Dakar dared not discount the insidious web spun in secret by the Koriathain. Too easily, Lysaer's flawed character might be twisted to front the ideological blood-bath, prosecuted by a ruthless war.

Which unpleasant snare in the thickets of consequence rammed anxiety against the flood-gates of panic. Dakar adjusted his reins, streaming clammy sweat. The latent tug of his precocious talent suggested his worst fear, already tipped into cascade towards ruin.

'Just ride!' he shouted, while Daliana fumbled her way back into the saddle. 'Rest on my word, we are racing to stem a disaster.'

In earnest, the Mad Prophet stabbed in his heels. His flighty horse surged away with flat ears, Daliana in precarious pursuit without a breath of complaint. Like a burr, she clung to her mount with locked teeth. She managed well enough to keep pace, while the pall of night fog wrapped dank as grave-cloths about them.

The going stayed miserable. Cold off the high Mathorn summits threatened fresh sleet, dense with a damp that bit to the bone and muffled the thud and splash of rushed hooves on the puddled roadway. Quick passage demanded a jolting, fast trot, interspersed with brief walks that wore sinew to a leaden ache. When the spurred pace failed to overtake Lysaer, the riders' tired spirits sank too low for shared conversation.

At grim length, the fuzzed glow of lanterns pricked the scrim of the grey fog. The peaked gables of the next post-house loomed in silhouette. Rest became a necessity. The horses were spent. Daliana bounced awkwardly in her irons, reins loose as she clutched double handfuls of mane to stay mounted. Dakar nursed his raw calves, rubbed to blisters that watered his eyesight to sparkles of pain.

Yet where a snug roof promised haven, and thoughts of roasted meat off the spit should have comforted the beaten travellers, the wafted smoke from the inn tap-room's chimney also brought the clash of hysterical voices.

'I thought so!' snapped Dakar. At wit's end, annoyed, he rousted a final burst from his lathered horse. Sharply reined in at the stable-yard gate, with Daliana straggling behind, he slithered gracelessly to the ground. The dazed groom, a step late to receive his blown mount, was forced to snatch the freed horse's trailed reins while Dakar charged on ahead. Short-tempered and broad, he hammered his way into the packed mass of bystanders clustered under the bull's-eye lanterns that brightened the carriage yard.

A wraith in his wake in a travel-stained cloak, her drawn features hooded, Daliana broached softly, 'You expected what?'

Dakar turned his head, his jutted beard stiff as a badger's ruff. 'Stay well clear!'

Warned off, but not daunted, Daliana took stock. She would not have missed the piled kindling stacked in readiness for the fresh load of logs: pitch pine, cut still green, and hastily hauled to the yard in the bed of a brewer's dray. Past the volatile mob that besieged the inn-door, her eye snag next on the glitter of jewels, worn with casual ease on a too-familiar male frame. The hatless, bright hair, agleam like found gold, outshone the flicker of flame-light: Lysaer was backed against the tavern wall.

At first glance, his hag-ridden tension stayed masked. But to any who knew him, the adamant set of trim shoulders raised a red flag of alarm.

Stripped of his armed retinue, the True Sect's fallen avatar faced a rough crowd, accosted by catcalls. Bristling drivers brandished coach-whips and cudgels, while the irate tradesmen and travellers in town dress cornered him, shaking raised fists.

'The unwitting fools!' Dakar gasped. Blind to the pressures of Lysaer's cursed nature, this backwater crowd had no way to measure their consummate danger. A half breath from horror, they stood in the path of wanton annihilation: no one crossed a man compromised by Desh-thiere! To try was to pose an impediment. Resistance against the drive of the curse sparked off an attack reflex past sane volition.

A ribbon of sweat streamed down Lysaer's temple. The pounding, fast pulse in the vein at his neck bespoke naked will set under explosive strain.

Dakar knew those dire signs. Too often, he had witnessed the dreadful descent when Arithon fell sway to the Mistwraith's cruel influence. In this night's cold dark, squeezed onto the fringes, he watched Lysaer fight and lose ground while the remorseless drive sapped his equilibrium. The geas degraded the stoutest intent. The least move might trigger a drastic response, before which no safe-guard existed. In the glow of the lamps, the liquid shimmer of Lysaer's collar studs betrayed a sharp onset of trembling. Under hot provocation, a wrong breath might transform the inn-yard into an abattoir.

'How can you behold evil's work and do nothing?' a country beldame shrilled from the forefront. Her indignant thrust forward swung the wool ties of her lappet hat as she accused, 'There are children afflicted by malicious practice in there! Innocent people turned minion through witchcraft. Don't claim that Shadow's not risen to plague us! Or spout the bald lie, that Darkness itself's not abroad, sowing mayhem!'

Lysaer's minute jerk in recoil screamed warning: he looked like a wretch pushed at bay with a murderer's knife at his throat.

Dakar elbowed ahead. Swearing fit to sting a drover's ears pink, he plunged into the breach. Around him, the cries of shocked outrage swelled louder. Murderous glares swung his way, almost welcome: safer that the crowd's hatred should fix on him to give Lysaer a measure of quarter. Dakar blistered insults back at all comers, inspired to bid for the prize as a public nuisance. If he earned the lynching, he would field that nuisance in step. Better the small crisis he could contain than see this mob fried alive as Lysaer's besieged restraint came unravelled. Buffeted in the press of rank animosity, aware every second became borrowed time, Dakar broke through and launched into his s'Ilessid target, unblinking.

'The upset at large is no act of Darkness but due to a sharp change in Athera's electromagnetics. Despite groundless claims made against acts of Shadow, endorse the bare truth! Step back and move on. These problems rest outside of your sovereign charge. You can't save every person afflicted.'

Drowned out by the fire-brand storm of retorts, Dakar shrugged off someone's aggressive grip. He shouted, frantic, 'Return to your palace. As a seated town mayor, your duty lies there. If you're justly moved, use your rightful authority to quiet the unsettled populace at home!'

No one rebuked Etarra's elected lord with such peremptory autocracy. While the agitators jostled at Dakar's back and bellowed their disapproval, before him, more fearsome, Lysaer's hauteur resharpened. Terrified to encounter the spark of stark madness as those blue eyes lifted to meet him, Dakar attacked first as the crowd's living shield. 'Don't play the rank idiot. You can't make your stand here or assume the false mantle of saviour.'

Thus, the mouse taunted the teeth of the tiger. Dakar held the line as the lightning-rod, braced for the punishing strike. Or, save his hide, he might grant the space Lysaer needed to mend the last threads of frayed reason.

As the split second dangled, no levin bolt razed an insolent buffoon for meddling.

Lysaer's famously arrogant, gemstone blue eyes kept their downcast glaze. Pushed to the brink of curse-borne compulsion, his expression appeared inexplicably ripped to naked pity. Staggered again by the restive crowd, Dakar caught his first glimpse of what Etarra's Lord Mayor defended.

The infant he cradled was scarcely a month old, a worn-out scrap of pallid flesh, folded into a tattered blanket. The mite gasped in the throes of extremity, its traumatized cries devolved to a broken wheeze.

No matter the depth of a spellbinder's experience, the awkward thrust of the foot in the mouth still sandbagged him to humiliation. Dakar wrestled to salvage his callous gaffe, barged sidewards by someone else's untimely arrival.

'Get back,' he snapped. 'For your life's sake, let me handle this!' Sight locked forward, breath stopped, he had no attention to spare.

'Who is that child's mother?' The proprietary demand was Daliana's, hurled into the volatile crux.

Which interruption froze Dakar's blood.

Lysaer answered, false calm welded over a strain that could, if he slipped, destroy lives the breadth of two kingdoms. 'She's locked in the root-cellar, condemned to burn along with a dozen others. Folks here insist they're corrupted by Shadow. Some have fallen to madness. Others are raving from fever. For days, they have suffered from violent purges brought on by an unknown affliction.'

'I know why they're ill.' Dakar rammed in, persistent. He moved in time, stoutly blocked Daliana, whose rash desperation to swerve Lysaer's focus invited an outright disaster. The Mad Prophet drove on: 'Foul practice and misplaced beliefs have nothing to do with the onset.'

Daliana plucked at Dakar's sleeve. Still ignored, she urgently shook his forearm as the ugly atmosphere simmered towards riot. Hostile mutters became threats as the balked fanatics insisted the evils of Darkness should be purged straightaway by sword and fire.

'You stand in the way of the Light's Divine Grace!' a whiskered drover accused.

A stringy chap in a miller's apron shoved to the centre, and shouted, 'Truth will be served! Behold the false avatar who turned apostate to the faith! Should we let his strayed wisdom sway us? I say better to take a righteous stand and send for the judgement of a True Sect examiner!'

Hedged on all sides by volatile hysteria, Daliana accosted Lysaer headlong. 'Debate on the cause of distress doesn't matter! My liege, you must act. Grant the families of the afflicted every power of mercy at hand. Promise them hope of deliverance before any innocents are put to the torch.' Then, heedless of her own peril, she dodged Dakar's bulk and barged past.

Under the lamps, Lysaer's fair-skinned features glistened with sweat. Hard up against the taut signs of his conflict, Daliana dared the unthinkable: she reached out at speed in direct intervention and snatched the suffering babe out of Lysaer's defensive clasp.

His hold upon human restraint snapped at once. While Dakar gasped, frozen, Daliana turned her back on the presence of certain death. Visibly terrified, she thrust the fevered, wailing mite and its blankets into the spellbinder's stupefied grasp.

'Inside!' she snapped. 'You have work to do, Dakar!'

The rise of the whirlwind storm she defied was anything else but disarmed. Against the recoil of Lysaer's cursed reaction, she stood her brave ground: a slender, cloaked form poised in saving distraction; or else the sacrificed target in line to be torched as a rank provocation.

'*She is not Talith!*' Dakar cried, appalled, into an atmosphere shocked like tapped glass.

Lysaer shuddered. Tormented, he pulled in a searing, hissed breath. As though he stared down his final undoing, his heart seemed to stop through a dreadful, hung moment. Then he forced a smile. Eyes rinsed blank with an incomprehensible effort, he bent his head in a courtly, ironic salute.

Someone's movement responded. The packed crowd stirred as the innkeeper, or a patron preternaturally astute, seized authority and cleared the inn's blockaded doorway. 'My Lord, step inside,' he urged with a quaver. 'Can you help, there are kin who'd be grateful.'

The mob surged as the studded oak panel swung wide. Dakar and Daliana resisted the press. If Lysaer refused this chance to seek respite, all would go for naught: the inn-yard would stage the seed of a holocaust.

'For the sake of the child,' Daliana exhorted.

Her plea moved him. Spurred by the humane need to shelter the infant, Lysaer escaped the jammed yard with its lynch-mob stew of charged rage and stepped into shelter.

Dakar pushed Daliana over the threshold and reeled after her, jostled as the plump man with the keys slammed the door on the turmoil outside. Cut off, the unruly throng milled and shouted, unaware yet how narrowly close they had come to outright immolation. A stark, worried glance through the tap-room's warm gloom showed the statesman's steel poise, knit back over a spirit still set under siege. Dakar expelled a sharp breath in relief. Against terrible pressure, the hair-trigger reflex of Desh-thiere's active geas appeared to be stalled, momentarily.

There, Daliana's insightful courage quite humbled the spellbinder's greater experience. She had grasped immediately that Lysaer would seize on the child's plight as his sheet-anchor.

Thrown her fragile life-line to sanity, he sounded calm as he addressed the barmaid who cowered in the shadows. 'Please show us where you've secured the condemned. Let me intercede for their case. No one burns for the Light! My coin will pay to feed them. If kinsfolk are present, invite them inside. If they'll agree to sit down and wait quietly, we shall see what, if anything, can be done to restore the afflicted.'

The tavern cellar was chilly and dank, the grimed beams overhead strung with cobwebs. Despite mortared walls of whitewashed fieldstone, the wan shaft of light cast by the innkeeper's candle-lamp scarcely pierced the oppressive gloom. Jumbled stacks of dry casks and dusty junk cluttered the dirt floor between trestle shelving, with the fusty atmosphere loud with the haunting moans of the benighted. A young man chanted in sing-song riddles, huddled up with clasped knees in a corner. Two older children languished with fever. A grand-father sprawled on the floor as though comatose, and a woman with tangled hair rocked without sound, muffled in the rags of a shawl worried threadbare by her plucking fingers.

Dakar attended the noisy ones first, if only to give himself peace. After the infant, two shrill screamers were silenced by sleeping-draughts, then the most desolate of the moaners. Several wretches beat their heads with their fists, a thin teen and a tear-stained toddler among them. Again and again, Daliana climbed upstairs to the pantry to fetch the spellbinder's sundry requests, which ranged from buckets of well-water, to clean glass flasks and cheap gin, to blankets and linen for compresses.

The nerve-wracked spellbinder had not paused to eat, against his hedonist's nature. He kept Lysaer pinned beneath his watchful eye, and rejected the helpful offer of lending him illumination. As much as the man's gifted touch with the elements might brighten his work, Dakar refused to encourage the misguided awe of the Sunwheel fanatics.

'Clear space and find something to bed these folks down,' he ordered instead, too aware that the chafe of Desh-thiere's curse tended to feed upon idleness.

His survey to assay the blockages that disrupted the victims' auras commenced by mage-sight in the dark. Soon enough, the brutal demand on his faculties overtaxed his tight concentration. Dizziness sucked at him in black waves, atop travel-sore weariness already sufficient to flatten him. He slouched like a lump, while the two beefy fellows who bounced the inn's drunks rolled the supine bulk of his latest case onto the pallet that Lysaer fashioned from flour-sacks. They hovered in wait after that with glazed boredom, while the spellbinder knuckled his gritted eyes and pushed back his leaden exhaustion.

'I'll take the girl with the bitten nails, next.'

'Litter's upstairs, have to fetch it back,' the more talkative brute admitted, then stumped after his clamp-jawed, liverish companion and mounted the rickety stairway.

Dakar scrubbed the soaked hair off his temples and started the meticulous task of spell-charging a measure of water to ease the distress of the woman his subtle skills had just sounded. Each chosen cipher infused the neat energy required, an exacting match that must counteract her imbalances, precisely. A misjudgement begged failure by coma, or death. While Dakar gripped the filled flask in slick hands, attuned to the delicate flow of ephemeral frequencies, the stricken folk who were yet to be treated whispered restively as stirred leaves. The musk of their stale clothing winnowed with the draughts, thickened by the scent of hot wax, as Lysaer opened the pane of the lamp and softened the seal for the flask to bottle the completed antidote.

Since paper for written instructions ran short, Daliana tramped upstairs again to plead for supplies from the landlord's clerk.

Dakar stabilized his effort with the rune of ending, and blotted his forehead against his rolled sleeve cuff. He was not Asandir, to ease the traumas of fifteen deranged spirits at an instant's notice. He passed the tin cup with a trembling hand, rescued from a spill by Lysaer, whose grasp was just as unsteady. Dakar noticed, and argued again for sound sense. 'At least permit me to lay basic wards of protection over your person.'

Jewels glinted against the rich sheen of silk, a show of state splendour that jarred amid squalor as Lysaer tipped the infused water into the flask, plugged the neck, then pinched off the flickering wick of the wax stick. Princely features plunged into ominous shadow, he said, 'You might as well bay at the moon, I suggest. If you'll notice? Your deft touch is failing.'

Truth bit with a vengeance, more since an enspelled boundary could scarcely defang an interference that sprang from within. Dakar dried his aching, wet palms on a towel filched from the tap-room, and argued, 'No game plan is fool-proof, given your plight. But I might stall the speed of reaction, a bit. Perhaps shield your person from a manipulative interference. Outside interests have ever provoked your affliction as a ready spring-board for their private agendas.'

More to the point, Dakar itched for a circle of guard to alert him in time to field a defensive response. But to voice the need behind his suggestion might spur a counter-reaction. The curse defended against outside meddling. If a crafted line of suppression risked piling tinder atop smouldering embers, no safe-guards at all left Lysaer's weakness wide open to usage by enemies.

Caught nodding again, Dakar feared he must ask Daliana to transcribe the caregiver's instructions for the sick woman's family. He cradled his forehead. Plagued by the pangs of a searing headache, he hoped he was not too foredone to dictate.

'Why are you sure I'm predestined to fail?' Lysaer pushed, as yet dauntlessly nettled.

'Because the Koriathain were jerking your strings!' Dakar lowered his hands, swore over their shaking, and flared to annoyance. 'One foul trap with a fetch nearly drove you insane. Prime Selidie won't give up her chance to seize further leverage through your warped straits. While you cling to pride, she will plot again.'

Sudden gooseflesh riffled over the Mad Prophet's moist skin, perhaps the nascent prelude to a fit of prescience. He stifled the surge, obliged to stay watchful. Upstairs, plied with drink, folk were actively hostile. Any more arcane portents would fan the chaotic fears sown in the wake of the lane shift. Untoward delay also hurt the critical cases that languished, untreated. Someone's mindful care must stay the course, with no other initiate-trained healer at hand to ease their fraught torment.

Another worrisome snag in the maelstrom, Lysaer toyed with ideas that might easily slide into another evasion. Dakar gave the man's vulnerable morals short shrift. 'Don't let Desh-thiere's pernicious influence lure you into false confidence!'

A ringed hand reached across, snatched the near-empty bucket from the spent spellbinder's fumbling grasp. Lysaer took over, poured the dregs into the next readied flask without spills, then admitted, reluctant, 'Of course, you are right. But if I don't fight, the geas reacts as though I've relinquished my choice and surrendered.'

Which might be truth, or another barbed coil. The Mistwraith's vile working applied its directive with relentless ingenuity. While Dakar groped for the wits to respond, Lysaer slammed down the bucket, and added, 'If you cannot trust in my flawed integrity, address the bald fact: does this True Sect crusade launched in Tysan stand any chance of being disarmed? How many will die on the borders of Havish if I hang back and cower and never venture the ethical effort? Should Prime Selidie trigger the curse with a fetch, I'm no safer holed up in Etarra, past question!'

Dakar lost his breath. He could not gainsay the blistering courage behind that bold cry for justice. Nor could he outmatch an honesty backed by the punch of ingenuous humility. *The brave claim was not new.* When Desh-thiere once held sway, Arithon, too, had tried the same line: an insidious plea surely tainted beneath the false colours of human entreaty.

Dakar picked his weapon, then smashed the pretty glass-sculpture dream like a criminal. 'Will you recognize the moment you must ask for help?' Braced to deal the crude blow to keep a torn spirit on the harsh path of redemption, he followed that knife thrust and twisted. 'By the grace of Sulfin Evend's supreme dedication, Asandir has given you hope, through Daliana. Do you shrink to ask her to stand by your side and share the grave risk of your short-falls?'

A shocked silence ensued. Lysaer went still.

'Or will you turn your back? Disdain the fallible shield granted by her human love in trade for the arrogant deception that your ego ought to protect her?' Dakar could not watch. He knew well his barb struck where a man's private wounds remained all too nakedly vulnerable.

The tormented moans of the wretch in the corner did not mask the sawed rip of Lysaer's next breath. Whether he suppressed rage, or tears of regret for his most irremediable losses, none knew.

The taut moment snapped as Daliana's thumped steps traipsed downstairs and wrecked privacy. 'They're chanting up there, do you hear?' Her brim-full pail sloshed, plonked down by the litter. She flipped her jaunty braid over her shoulder, then freed the dog-eared sheaves of paper clamped beneath her left elbow. Her glance at Dakar softened to apology. 'The noise drowned me out when I asked for quiet for the sake of your convalescents.'

By now, rhythmic stamping against the floor-boards sifted loose dust through the lamp-light. Dakar guessed the rallying cry extolled the merits of true faith in the Light. His healing labours would be declared divine miracles, no doubt dispensed by the beneficence of the temple's recanted avatar.

Which unvoiced exasperation did not escape Lysaer, who pointedly dipped the dried pen and took up a blank sheet.

Dakar recited. Through the misguided salvo above, he listed the dosage aimed to restore the oblivious matron to her right mind. The rolled paper, tied to the flask with a string, would be handed off to the woman's hysterical kinsfolk once the inn's borrowed muscle reappeared for duty. The spellbinder also tasked them to haul the next wailing fellow from his wedged nook between the slat shelving.

While the heavies restrained the man's witless terror, Dakar steeled fraught nerves, then invoked his trained faculties. Immersed into deep trance, he heard and saw nothing beyond the etheric eddies his overtaxed talent laboured to map. He resurfaced at length, ears ringing with strain. Through vision marred by pin-wheel flashes and the syrupy haze of stretched cognizance, he sensed the haggard, close-quarters flame of someone else's anxiety beside him.

Not Lysaer: Daliana offered the filled flask, readied for him to imprint, a staunch support sweet as grounded iron against his head-splitting tension. Since his spent vision showed no other presence, Dakar broached the unspeakable subject.

'Sleep across your liege's threshold,' he advised. 'A *caithdein*'s oath gives you the obligation. First to stand guard as his voice of true conscience, then to act if he should breach integrity.'

But that earnest entreaty crashed into silence.

'Ath save us!' gasped Dakar. 'What's already happened?'

'Lord Lysaer's gone,' Daliana admitted, snapped terse. 'He went upstairs to eat. Didn't lie. He was hungry. When he failed to return, the innkeeper told me he left for the stables and made the grooms saddle him a fast horse.'

'Then we'll have to follow. Catch up with him, now!' But Dakar's distraught effort to rise floundered against wheeling dizziness. 'Help me up.'

'No use, we're too late,' Daliana confessed. 'You were tranced for an hour! I'm sorry. You're dead right. I should not have let Lysaer slip past me.'

'No failure of yours!' Dakar snapped. 'He had help.'

'Beyond question.' Daliana's accusation broke through, pitched with a fury to lacerate. 'What did you say to him in my absence?'

'No driven man hears unwanted counsel,' Dakar dismissed with a shrug.

'Oh?' Daliana smiled with all of her teeth, tawny eyes wide in the flame-light. 'Then explain to me: who is Talith?'

Dakar clammed up. There were limits. The intimate grief from a man's private past had the born right to stay sacrosanct. Forget the fact that his inept silence damned him: glib words and suave wisdom eluded him, still. He could cozen pleasure from the most jaded whore, while the tact to misdirect one honest woman slipped his grasp like a panicked trout. 'You won't hear from me,' he stonewalled, then flinched, braced to field what his threadbare evasion deserved.

Daliana struck, fit to trounce any male caught out in shrinking retreat. 'Then you broached whatever Asandir implied, that lends me the unfair advantage? Of course, you wielded that ruthless leverage and *stupidly* challenged Lysaer's masculine ethics.'

Dakar clamped his jaws, guilty.

'Ath forfend!' Daliana cried, exasperated. 'What madness possessed you? *Don't you see?* You've driven my liege straight from the crucible into the enemy's web!'

Contrite as a kicked mongrel, Dakar smothered his bleakest suspicion. Just as likely, Selidie Prime had tipped the scales against Lysaer's sound sense through some act of vile practice. Her order's mission was ruthless: Desh-thiere's curse run amok and a border war turned against Havish applied the strategic pressure to upset the Fellowship's compact.

'The stakes we confront are dreadful enough, without your punishment, added in hindsight.' Dakar quailed to shoulder the urgent necessity of a deep scrying. Drained to the pith of his bones by exhaustion and rattled queasy with worry, he doubted his fitness to sound a safe course through the thicket of hostile interests. The cruel irony stung. After quashing repeated prescient surges, he dared not rely on his natural instincts. If he tapped into his precocious wild talent in such ragged state, he might pass out and spout raving nonsense for days.

'We have to pursue,' he insisted. 'Support for Lysaer is far more important than the hung fate of these stricken townsfolk.'

Daliana said nothing.

She lent no kindly hand in support as Dakar reeled upright, swearing. He careened across the disorganized cellar, his course marked by hollow clunks as he ricocheted off the dry kegs and tapped-out wine tuns. First mired in heaps of used flour-sacks, then whacked on both shins to a ghastly clatter of tin pitchers, he tackled the narrow stair without mishap, only to bang head first against the shut wooden trap at the top.

Some idiot outside had bolted the panel.

Dakar's yelp of pain raised gruff laughter from an alert vigilante, parked in the pantry. 'No one gets out! Might as well stuff your noise. If you're all that you claim and no minion of Shadow, we'll have our proof! When the touched ones clapped down there along with you emerge, restored to their wits, you'll go free. But not until then. That's my orders.'

'Upon whose authority?' Dakar howled.

'Light's own glory, himself,' word returned, adamant as stuck nails.

Dakar damned the faith in blasphemous epithets, then plunked on his haunches in outfaced defeat. 'May Dharkaron's Five Horses trample the honey tongue of yon trumped-up s'Ilessid statesman!'

For Lysaer's sly subversion had foiled the devoted escort of friends he had wished to shed from the start. No protest might shift such fanatical obstinacy, fixated on a divine mission. A forceful escape would only deliver the cellar's hapless souls to the sword and the pyre, forthwith.

'Come down and get busy,' Daliana admonished, backed by the stir-crazy rustle of loonies not yet reprieved from the lynch mob. 'Unless you prefer to be put to the question by the Light's Hope delegation you just ousted in shame from Etarra?'

For inevitably, the temple's ambassadorial train must pass this wayside inn on its plodding retreat to seek outbound passage from Narms.

'Mercy on us,' gasped Dakar. 'Whose rash guarantee backed the groundless claim that I could salvage every case of derangement down here?'

The failing wick in the candle-lamp flickered through Daliana's disgusted reply. 'Best pray for the time that we never had to waste on the road in the first place.'

Dakar buried his face in his hands, crushed to dejected, bowed shoulders.

Whichever case ruled a curse-based motivation, the gallant's instinct to shield a young woman, or the more sinister ploys of the Koriathain, Lysaer s'Ilessid was hell-bound for Tysan. Dakar confronted his worst fear. He had failed to thwart fate. Nor had he ducked the cankered poison sown by his scapegrace past. The threatened spirit he most shrank to encounter already stood at lethal risk, with the life that carried the Fellowship's destiny poised to go up in flames should Lysaer's resolve come to falter.

By the grey tinge of dawn, only hours away, Arithon Teir's'Ffalenn would arrive in Torwent, bound over in chains to the adder's nest of his enemies.

Three Questions

Nowhere else on Athera did the deep-night stars burn with such splendour. Above the black sand of Sanpashir, the sky was an indigo bowl, mote-dusted in glory that flickered and danced with the glitter of chipped opal and diamond. After seven days' travel on foot due north-eastward on the Innish trade-road, Elaira encountered the view from the deep desert, guided yet by the Reiyaj Seeress's mystic escort. The dunes ranged before her in overlapped folds, a jet velvet vista stabbed with the flash-caught sparkles thrown off by loose quartz grains and mica. The cold wind and stark beauty stole her very breath. Unlike most who sought an encounter with the country's insular tribal inhabitants, she was not brought under hostile captivity, disarmed and blindfolded.

Instead, she was guided in frightening solitude, where the old roadway sliced a transient groove, pocked by the tread of the silk caravans' mules and kept aligned by the compass. Time and wind had buried the cap-stones of the ancient stelae that once marked the way. Others were broken or bowed to the fury of centuries of weather. People died here. Strays who wandered off the known route, or the foolish who witlessly trespassed where desert folk held their inscrutable rituals: all perished of darts, shot by unseen sentinels, or else vanished without a trace.

Elaira arrived, no better informed. Written archives recorded nothing about the tribes' history, or their secret practices. Such knowledge was *old* and most fiercely guarded, an oral tradition not shared with outsiders. Whatever their tie to the blinded oracle in the sealed tower at Reiyaj, the protector sent by the Seeress's auspices answered none of the enchantress's respectful questions. Their travel together had passed unremarkably until, without explanation, the accustomed camp had not been pitched amid the rose glow at sundown.

The moonless night was three-quarters gone when the cloaked figure bearing his unadorned quarterstaff stopped short without any warning. He touched his crossed palms at his breast and formally bowed to her, then smiled too briefly to soften his abrupt farewell. 'Elaira, the duty my mistress laid on me is finished. Your destination is nigh. Wait here until someone comes for you.'

Elaira thanked him. Her shock strained the basic fabric of courtesy and left her with nothing to say. Distraught, she watched her enigmatic guardian turn face about and depart due westward towards Forthmark. As his cloaked figure vanished from sight, she stifled the urge to chase after his heels. The coward's choice to give way and plead for the comfort of human company was not a safe option. Elaira hardened herself to surmount the clamour of her insecurity.

She had reached a cross-roads, with no place to go. Forward, she chose to bear Arithon's legacy, his ring on her hand no false token but a commitment deep as life itself. Behind, stalked the order and Prime Selidie's tyranny: death or much worse, if her sisterhood's oath called down the punitive force to destroy everything she held dear.

Alone by the roadway, Elaira shivered, a live speck amid the wild vista. No clue arose to suggest how long her solitary vigil might last. Gusts whistled around her. Snaking wind devils of sand stung her eyes and erased the last, shallow smears of her inbound footsteps.

The waning crescent arose, a poised ivory sickle low in the east. Shortly, its pallid yellow glow became notched by a silhouette that suggested movement. Then the breeze brought a quavering fragment of song. Heralded by a clear voice without gender, nine forms crested the dune in the moon's path, graceful as wraiths and veiled featureless.

Elaira was met. Not by the male dartmen swathed in the black robes and the stern dignity of desert-caste warriors, but by young women, the feather-light tread of their bare feet gracefully dancing. Colourful yarn shawls swirled from their slim shoulders. Fringed hems and layered skirts jingled with trinkets that shimmered like chiming bells. Delicate hands adorned with glass bracelets thumped the hide drums of small tambourines, whose brass cymbals clashed with a timbre sweetly piercing as crystalline chimes. The odd rhythms and eerie tonalities prickled Elaira's nape.

As the dancers flowed towards her, then ringed her around, the singer they also had circled stepped forward. He pushed back his hood. Elaira faced a weathered, ancient man, time-worn to an ebony polish, with features as used as creased leather. Long and lean and whittled as bone, he took her chilled fingers in hot, slender hands. His speech rolled in the thickened gutturals stamped by his desert dialect. 'Are you to be the first of your order to come here with seamless integrity? None has tried, since Jessian Oathkeeper, who gave over her life for the virtue of silence.'

'Forgive me,' Elaira admitted, uneasily warned that she had missed a critical fact. 'Who was Jessian? Should I know her? If so, I don't recognize her by that name.'

The old man stood, crowned in his back-drop of stars, while the wind tossed the wool hems of his layered garments. He wore no bells, not a fetish or trinket. His surrounding wheel of dancers had stopped. They now faced him, motionless. The musical clash of their charms dangled, mute, the silence woven through the presence about them thick as an invisible mantle.

Spear-straight, perhaps thoughtful, the aged tribesman accepted her stranger's ignorance. 'The records of your Koriathain condemned Jessian for treason because she swore three oaths, later to find them in irreconcilable conflict. She broke the two that would have brought harm before keeping the one least convenient.' His sharp black eyes surveyed Elaira. A harsh moment passed, perhaps as he sounded her being for the same measure of courage. Then he added, not as an afterthought, 'This happened before our kind and yours set foot on this world, Athera.'

Which historical reckoning spanned thousands of years. The course of the ancient events his lore referenced could not be imagined.

When Elaira did not speak but stayed attentive instead, the old man seemed pleased to omit further conversation. 'Follow. She awaits, our most revered Eldest. Your coming has been expected among us for far longer than anyone but the Fellowship Sorcerers have been alive.'

The bells shivered to life as the dancers resumed their gyrations. Surrounded by that watershed of splashed sound, given nothing to assuage her raw dread, Elaira let the desert folk draw her away, into the dunescape beyond the trodden path.

The brisk walk through the trackless, soft sand did not take her far. A few hundred yards to the east, a rough rectangle of pitted foundation-stones marked the site of a tumble-down inn. The ruin had burned, once. Though the signs of the fire were long since scoured clean, and countless seasons of wind and rot had demolished the broken, charred timbers, the subtle signature imprinted by flame stayed embedded within the range of initiate vision. Plain sight showed a tombstone of chimney-stack, drilled thumb deep with the sockets where the iron spit once turned the roasts that fed hungry travellers.

A short distance removed, a crumbled stone ring rimmed the shaft of a derelict well. If the depths retained water, no bucket and crank-shaft remained. Abandoned, perhaps, the site was not deserted: melted into the landscape, an ancient woman perched cross-legged within the sheltered hollow.

Her form was swathed in unrelieved black. No feature showed. Only her seamed, mahogany hands, folded motionless in her broad lap. The escort of dancers had melted away, their departure so seamless that Elaira felt dizzied by the sudden silence. She froze between steps, dismayed as the old man broke her reluctance with a gentle push forward.

'There. She waits. Your spirit name is well-known to her.' His grainy speech ruffled her flesh like a ripple beyond word or sound, that rearranged thought and impelled the uncanny remembrance: *once before,* she had been addressed by an adept as *Affi'enia,* and by an Araethurian seer as *Fferedon'li.*

Which peculiar lapse into reverie rushed through and filled her with a ray of warmth. Elaira aroused like a sleep-walker, shaken. She found herself come before the wizened crone, whose piercing regard and obsidian eyes saw down to the core of her being.

She whom the tribal man had named Eldest did not arise. Instead, she leaned forward and sifted loose sand grains between the clean joints of seamed fingers. When she spoke, her voice was the whisper of wind, fluted over edged granite. 'Here in this place past, Meiglin s'Dieneval gave over her fate to Mother Dark's workings, and conceived the girl child your Sorcerers' records call Dari s'Ahelas.'

Elaira caught her breath. These familiar names held widespread renown. Meiglin's issue had been the ancestral cross which linked the old *caithdein's* lineage of s'Dieneval with the royal heritage that endowed the High Kings of Shand. The princess, sanctioned as the surviving crown heir, had been born gifted with Sight and rogue prophecy. Dari's willful bequest yet remained, woven into the heritage of her descendants. Most often passed down as a latent talent, in Arithon s'Ffalenn, the legacy had wakened in force in the aftermath of his passage through Davien's maze at Kewar. Lysaer also displayed signs of the trait; who knew to what depths the errant talent exerted an influence.

As though such mindful facts were broached aloud, the crone peered upwards, eyes crinkled to her wheezed laughter. 'Not a rogue gift at all! The legacy bestowed upon Dari also was ours, danced into manifest focus and made flesh and blood for the purpose of Mother Dark's service.'

Elaira stifled her torrent of questions. Never more acutely warned before this, nor shown with such frightful precision, she grasped how the thread of Prince Arithon's fate ran like stranded light through Biedar fingers. What part Lysaer might play in the weave, she lacked the bold wisdom to speculate.

The old woman nodded. Privilege granted to an astute listener, she continued to speak. 'The coupling I speak of occurred in this place almost nine hundred years ago, as your way of measure counts time. But for Biedar folk, understand, the light of the Anslien'ya's hope shines before and afterward. The moment is *now,* where Meiglin's youthful joy found fertility in the arms of Shand's last-sanctioned crown prince. The sand here' – gestured by the sweep of an arm – 'the stars and the air are electrically brilliant, for us yet alive to the spirit-making that shaped this event. Your beloved, Arithon, does comprehend this, although he does not acknowledge the meaning, yet.'

'He wouldn't,' Elaira said, carefully poised as a footstep set down upon glass-thin ice. 'He's surely told you he has enough strident factions demanding a piece of him.'

The desert matriarch's regard became discomfortably acute. 'Then have you come to plead this man's case, that Biedar Tribe should release what you view as an unfair hold on him?'

'No.' Despite herself, Elaira suppressed the inward chuckle startled by her certain awareness of Arithon's fiercely indignant reaction. 'The man, as you call him, would speak for himself and strike down such an act of presumption.'

The old woman's deep, direct stare stayed relentless, though perhaps her seamed lips twitched a fraction. Her suggested amusement never broke through. Instead, she broached her next inquiry. 'Say why you've journeyed through hardship to come to us.'

Such aware Sight perceived with pure honesty, through all layers of willful pride and self-deception. Elaira hesitated. She weighed her response, altogether too conscious she skated the razor's edge: of countless thousands of words she might use, the least shade of meaning must perfectly match the authenticity of her intent.

Less had to be more, she decided, and plunged. 'Gratitude brought me.'

The crone's pause stayed adamant; she demanded the whole.

Trembling, finally, Elaira admitted, 'Kharadmon told me the Biedar had bent time and space to accomplish the feat that allowed Prince Arithon's release.' The tears she'd dammed back spilled over, regardless. Forced to a wracked whisper, she finished, 'Thank you for breaking the merciless sigils wrought by my order to keep him caged.'

Now the ancient smiled in fact, radiant as sudden moonrise. 'Oh, my dear! Your Sorcerer did not disclose all of the truth. In fact, your own mindful action at Athir spun the first thread for Prince Arithon's bid to regain his freedom.'

Elaira's breath shuddered to a shocked stop.

'You might ask for that story,' the crone invited, eyes gleaming beneath her sable mantle. 'You possess the right to know, *not just as yourself,* but also by claim of the seal ring you carry.'

Discipline could be made to impose a recovery. Elaira clung to an effortful calm while more volatile feelings she could not suppress drained her white, then unstrung every effort to rein back her weeping. Her terror spoke foremost. 'If the clan woman, Glendien, conceived on that night, I must plead for the sake of Arithon's quietude, and your kindness, let me never hear!'

When no granted promise of silence was given, Elaira sank to her knees. Beneath the sharp stars that burned nearly as brilliant as others, above frigid white sand on the fated beachhead where the ritual just referenced had called Arithon's life back into incarnate existence over two centuries ago, she attempted to bow as the supplicant. But the Biedar's most revered Eldest refused to leave any spirit so stranded. Dry, withered hands clasped her younger fingers and firmly arrested the move to abase herself.

'Oh, bravest!' declared the most wise of the tribe. 'You are not so bereft! Our own male singers also helped to loom the exalted pattern begun by your spinning. For this, you are blessed! Share with me, now. Partake of the essence that your bold weaving bestowed upon this troubled world.'

Touch alone could never unleash such a flood of harmonic brilliance. The crone's gift of augmented sensation showered through Elaira's awareness, then thundered into a roaring cascade. The overwhelming rip tide of bliss all but hurled her spirit out of her warm flesh. Torn wide open, then ravaged by pure experience, she cried aloud for a joy like wild fire and storm, magnificent beyond the limited scope of any mortal imagining.

Then the peak moment ebbed. Quietly as a sigh, Elaira was spiralled back down, where a strength tough as wire supported her tremulous balance. 'Be comforted,' the crone said, and no more. Nothing threatened the tissue of buried secrets as she gently finished. 'Rest at ease. Further grieving is groundless. Your act kept right covenant. Proof resides, as you saw, in the resonant purity wrought by the imprinted echo. The weave stands complete, since the free will of *all* parties concerned has stayed inviolate.'

Elaira wrestled her overset equilibrium. A tactful quiet ensued until the crone loosened, and then freed her supportive clasp. The little pause finished, and her voice resumed, raspy as the sough of blown sand. 'Against odds, your beloved was born. Beyond odds, he survives. What favour does your need ask of us?'

'No favour,' Elaira gasped, wiping her eyes.

Swift reprimand answered. 'We could shear away every claim imposed by your childhood vow! Do you wish to renounce your burdensome service, sworn to the Koriathain?'

Nothing apparent had changed. But the depths to the old woman's stare held a spark, and the solid, bleak space where she sat of a sudden felt storm-charged with danger.

Elaira had no time to weigh her response, far less measure the yawning pitfalls. She could read only nuance. Loud as a shout, in all ways that mattered, she recognized this offer was not fashioned as a reward. Still, she was being tested. 'I have never served the Prime Matriarch,' she denounced. 'Not once. Though I have done her bidding.' Slammed through by the raced thud of her pulse, she repeated the gist, once affirmed many years ago before a Fellowship Sorcerer, while a drift-wood fire blazed in the rain on the shingle at Narms. Another moment, as tensioned as this, when dire temptation *almost* impelled the choice to breach her bound loyalty to the sisterhood: *'My Prime may command my obedience. She does not, and never will own me in spirit!'*

The crone brushed the air with a dismissive hand. 'Autonomy is yours to claim at a price. Defiance under the grip of the Koriathain did come to cost Jessian Oathkeeper her life. Would you beg a reprieve for the sake of your safety?'

Elaira closed her eyes. Trembling, she clenched her fists, torn to conflict. For by the past counsel of Ath's adepts, she did not stand alone to enact such a choice. Her voice was not steady, conscience saw clearly the fork in the path at her feet. 'If I were to pose that request of your tribe, what would become of a quartz crystal joined into my personal partnership, left behind in Prime Selidie's possession?'

The hawk-nosed features of the Biedar ancient might as well have been carved of seamed stone. 'The mineral structure that houses the spirit being of that steadfast friend would shatter. A light loyal to you would depart from this world, no more to shine as a beacon in darkness.'

Elaira bent her head, torn to anguish. 'Then, with respect, Lady Elder, in this world, I'm not free to indulge my desire. Not through the sacrificial destruction of another.' The words carved a pit as final as doom, wide as a chasm, uncrossable. But the destined outcome was yet to be. She must live out her fate, enforced by an ethic stern enough to break the unbearably tormented spirit.

Before Elaira, the crone sat rock still, mantled in a neutral silence that shouted of power past knowing. The dreadful pressure did not bend for her comfort. Neither was the dread interview carried to bring about release or closure. The old woman's gaze continued to measure, black as dipped ink. 'Your heart's tie to Arithon is not addressed. Handfast to Rathain, what path will you take concerning your care for him? You have been told that his best protection relies on your absence. Now you tread the path of thorns with acceptance, that his trials are not yours to shoulder.'

Elaira shivered, run through by bleak cold to make spring's tender promise seem void. Empty-handed, she could but temporize. 'I have trusted Arithon to survive by the strength of his own merits before. He has surmounted straits close to dire as anything he now faces.'

The crone acknowledged. Almost as an accolade, her head dipped to a glint of the silver-white hair, netted under the night-dark hood of her mantle. 'By that tenet, you must count his weaknesses, too, and rely on his bent towards goodness as never before. He must do the same through this passage. Will you let him? Aware of what he has become *now*, do you have the strength in yourself to keep faith even as he crosses under the shadow of failure? Or will you break before holding the risk, that the overwhelming mistakes from his past might yet destroy him through self-condemnation?'

Fear itself lay unmasked by the ancient's soft words. Elaira's unrestrained tears fell and fell, her pallid cheeks striped with glistening ribbons, each one vivid with sting as a whip-lash. 'What are you asking of me?' she gasped, hoarse.

Her plea brought no quarter.

'Can you let Arithon go beyond your control?' the crone questioned. 'Do you love enough to keep faith in him, even afflicted by your own loss? For he will seek his fate. If he can invent a fresh course by his wits, he will try to resolve his own happiness. Stand or fall, his life's path shall be forged in this world. The gifts of his birthright will claim their full due. He will find himself, with or without you.'

'I will not let him down,' Elaira insisted, stripped to the steel of stark character. 'I must back his claim to contentment first, whatever becomes of our union, which as his sworn mate, he has left in my protected keeping.'

'That could cost you dearly,' the eldest warned with a snap. 'Would you find yourself left aged and alone, forgotten by him in obscurity?'

'I might die unrequited.' Elaira swallowed, huddled against the cruel chill that speared her through bone and viscera. 'That is why Arithon trusted me to guard the one vulnerable flaw he knew he lacked the stern fibre to shield.'

The ancient Biedar woman cupped her seamed palms. She might have raised an ephemeral flame that burned beyond the range of visible eyesight, or perhaps she awaited an offering with bare hands that might never be filled. 'Your beloved would surrender himself to your Prime before letting any harm come to you.'

Wrung past words, Elaira managed the nod for that insufferable affirmation. 'If he should fail me, or I fail in him, the Warden of Althain assured the result would call down a disaster. I would break in two,' she admitted, sapped dry. 'But the hurtful stakes if I fall are not malleable. I'm not callous enough to withstand such a course. *All the wrong parties would triumph.*'

The crone clapped, to a clash of the glass and copper bracelets that weighted her stick-thin wrists. For a split second, the black sands seemed rinsed white by a deluge of illumination: *where the inn stood intact, a young woman emerged, bearing a laden supper tray. Her face was turned towards the hollow where a young man glistened, naked and wet from a wash at the well, his dusty clothing slung over one shoulder . . .* then the echo raised out of sound died away. The night was the same: darkened and ordinary under the blaze of the wheeling stars. The crone pronounced, 'You will stand the course.'

'Ath wept!' Stripped beyond subterfuge, Elaira exclaimed, 'I shall try. At best, I am human. No less subject than any to mortal limits and fallible resource.'

'Mother Dark's mercy walks even where no light appears to be found. The grace of the heart is not subject to boundaries, and witness is made and sealed by the moment.' The crone's sudden smile appeared as a balm. Her touch cupped Elaira's salt-wet chin and lifted her tormented face. 'Biedar do not exclude other folk as outsiders. But we hear them only by the awareness they carry directly from spirit. You are not known to abandon a friend. Or wont to leave a stranger in need out of self-absorbed callousness. Actions colour your purpose more clearly than even the most honest talk. Arrogance does not admit to its weaknesses. But love does, respectful for fear of love's absence. You are true, by our measure. Therefore, you are destined to blaze the way as our emissary.'

The statement took a leaden moment to penetrate. 'What?' Elaira blinked. 'Emissary to whom?'

Spry fingers brushed away her last tear. The ancient reached into her loosely layered robes and drew forth a wrapped object, fringed with decorative shells and glass beads, and hung with esoteric small talismans. 'I speak for my people, whose stolen covenant was sworn to be satisfied in the breach. You are tasked to put right the consequence of Jessian's unintentional legacy.' Upraised again, the seamed palms offered what starlight revealed to be a stone knife, beautifully wrapped and sheathed in laced deerskin.

'Is this a burden or a signal honour?' Elaira asked, shaken and wary of accepting a hallowed item, freighted with an unknown consequence. 'I did not know Jessian. You'll need to explain.'

'Once, your Koriathain but trifled with power,' the Biedar eldest revealed, her uncanny gift not withdrawn. 'Persecuted, then imprisoned for sharing our ways as a witness, Jessian died with the secret behind an enigma. Her victory over an unsatisfied Prime Matriarch drove the Koriathain to pursue a reckless policy of acquisition. The order's ranked Seniors grasped after power without any thought for their impact. They abandoned scruple, struck bargains even with factions they deemed moral enemies to seize more and more dire means of extracting domination through forceful control. When they gained what they wished, they turned false on their allies. Acts they claimed as necessity were justified to enforce their own mission, declared for the greater good. All of the significant arcane knowledge in the sisterhood's annals stems from a pack-rat cache of suborned sacred writings, and theft.'

Sorrow bled through, as the matriarch finished. 'Biedar were never their willing participants. We do not broker initiate knowledge. For that, our kind suffered abuse without conscience. Koriathain made use of drugs, by extortion. They entrapped innocents and applied twisted means to rifle the sacred ancestral lore of our tribe.'

'I haven't the background to understand all of this,' Elaira protested, dismayed. Cut so far adrift, never made privy to her order's vast store of closed records, she felt bereft of informed guidance, and helpless.

'The hidden past shall be exposed in due time,' the old woman declared with complacency. 'Some of the historical detail you seek will be found with the Warden of Althain. Search there, first. Bide in patience. Take our knife with my blessing. Know that the purpose behind the blade's shaping one day will make itself known to you.'

Further avoidance somehow seemed uncouth. Elaira accepted the weight of the offering, braced. But no shock of encounter met her anxious touch. The deerhide stayed cool. The beaded patterns glittered, at present just ornamental embroidery fashioned of shell and plain glass. The stone blade inside stayed inert in her grasp as she took possession. Since thanks seemed displaced for a duty laid on her, Elaira settled for humour. 'Just how much blood, or which finger must I offer in sacrifice?'

The crone chuckled, brim-full of amusement. 'You hold a Biedar artifact made long before our people arrived on Athera.' Beneath the brow-band of her mantle, the crone's jet eyes caught the reflections of the overhead constellations as she tipped her head to the sky. 'I will tell you this much. The blade is a talisman, made ages ago for one purpose only: to end the defiled practice your Fellowship Sorcerers decry as the abomination of necromancy.'

Elaira sank onto her heels, jolted spineless. 'Grey Kralovir perished. Their remnants were cleansed.'

'Two offshoot forms of the vile discipline remain,' the First Eldest corrected with sorrow. 'Affi'enia, for our sake and your own, trust that your steps will be protected. Have you not guessed? Your Prime Matriarch fears that blade above all things, except perhaps the Named life of the one whose forepromised task is to wield it.'

'*Arithon?*' blurted Elaira, appalled.

The crone would not confirm, but said only, 'Our charges are these, laid on you as bearer. You will carry the knife and deliver it into the living hand of Arithon Teir's'Ffalenn at a time of your choosing. Until then, you may use its virtues but once to take action on your own behalf. Decide wisely and well by the love in your heart. For Prince Arithon's fate is entwined with your life-course. Mother Dark's mystery walks in his tracks. But you, Affi'enia, are the shining Light on the path come before him.'

Before trepidation found voice for protest, the ancient ended the audience. 'Accept your role for the sake of my people, that the wrongness done with our blameless heritage may be ended, put right, and reconciled.'

'I will agree to consult with Sethvir,' Elaira allowed, which was far as she dared to promise.

The crone bowed her head. Behind her, the black sands remained empty of dancers. The melodic clash of their brass cymbals stayed gone, replaced by the moan of the wind across the stone ring that rimmed the ancient well-shaft. Where the young women had been, a ring of male elders now stood, robed from head to feet in dark silk. Whether they sang, or dreamed, or chanted in whispers, Elaira was not permitted the licence to know. A wave like a ripple passed over the scene, clouding her arcane awareness. The strange disturbance passed in an eyeblink. When full clarity surged back, the surrounding dunes were swept clean of tribesfolk.

Not a footprint remained, and no impression showed where their cherished Eldest had sat to pose her stern questions. The breeze riffled over the old inn's forlorn foundation, where the scoured stones trapped the shifted sand like bunched felt, as they had for centuries beneath twinkling starlight.

Dawn paled the eastern horizon. Alone as the early glimmer of day burned into a mercury haze, Elaira regarded the primitive knife, laced into its barbaric sheath. The talisman was all that had stayed, nothing more, as a worldly power beyond her ken set her hand to pursue a frightening task by her merits.

Elaira slipped the knotted loop over her neck. She tucked the wrapped heirloom beneath her travel-stained blouse, aware she was horseless, and hungry, and tired, and shivering from the chill. In these times, no inns relieved the trade-road between Atchaz and Innish. Where the route sliced across the westernmost rim of Sanpashir's arid waste, travellers preferred not to linger amid the wilds claimed as the tribe's sovereign territory.

The site was as far removed as might be from Althain Tower in distant Atainia. Elaira hiked back towards the marked route, resigned. The next passing caravan would determine whether she fared northward by land or turned left to seek an extended passage by way of the galleys that moved silk bales and spices and Southshire's famed oranges by sea.

But unlike every other dawn before this, a spark of renewed hope lightened her weary steps. Whether the knife's possession brought fortune or bane, its legacy promised a future encounter with her heart's most beloved.

Scourges

'But our long-term interests are served by the upsurge that Sorcerer's dragon wrenched through the flux!' Prime Selidie declaims, anxious to counter the dangerous threat posed by Elaira's meeting with the Biedar Eldest. 'The families of the afflicted must look to us to spare their stricken kin. Our debt lists will swell under their obligation and better, our shelter can spare their threatened daughters from the Sunwheel purges and bolster our aging ranks with youthful new talent . . .'

The watch runner's breathless news shatters the precarious peace at the Camris outpost: that the black-market exchange of raw pelts for supply has ended with a massacre by Sunwheel soldiers. 'They march on the clans to purge what they name a lethal outbreak of black sorcery. We're blamed, they say, for the madness provoked by the lane surge. The war band assumes the rear-guard in attempt to buy time to empty our low-country settlements . . .'

Althain's Warden bows his head on clenched fists, beset by the whip-lash of recoil set-backs: while traumatized fear wracks Etarra with riots that reinstate the Light's canon against Lysaer's edict, elsewhere in Havish, the Sunwheel dedicates drive their whirlwind attack to seize Torwent; by temple directive, they cordon the harbour to secure their flag galley inbound with the Spinner of Darkness . . .

XI. Upheaval

A
t Althain Tower, Sethvir paced the library floor. Too swiftly, the convergent speed of events unfolded the moment that fueled his darkest foreboding. The war galley entrusted to bear the temple's ill-omened freight of bound prisoners nosed against the stout wharf, locked down by armed conquest at Torwent.

By then, the quay seethed with threat great enough to wreck any hope of reprieve. The town's bewildered faithful had not been restrained by the Light's imposed curfew. Shaken by the recent outbreaks of madness, too many welcomed the Sunwheel presence with bewildered relief. Hecklers stirred by the fraught threat of Shadow jeered from the water-front lanes, fractiously jammed against the armed muscle charged to safeguard the newly raised scaffold. Those grim tripled ranks were not complacent regulars drawn from garrison posts, but life-term veterans hand-picked from the precipitous thrust that had burst the defensive lines at the border of Havish. If their blooded weapons were oiled and cleaned, the lethal edge was scarcely restored from the whirlwind attack. Their buffeted stance sealed the fishers' wharf as the day inexorably brightened.

Where Mainmere's fleet should have tied up to unlade, the clay-tiled roofs notched a scrim of sea-mist. Girdled by pyramids of stacked barrels, the bait seller's shacks wore a tarnish of dew, board shutters barred against commerce. The cod-oil reek of the idle presses stained the sea air, thickened to redolence by the vacated chopping blocks where, today, the shawled circle of women did not gossip to the flicker of knives, dicing raw fillets for market. Instead, the cobbled apron at the water-front heaved, the drab wool of its seafaring residents splashed with gaudy colour where the Light's true believers unfurled Sunwheel pennants. More flags marked a second phalanx of foot-troops, which guarded the dais that seated the war host's attached priests, and a high temple examiner. Before them, the massive log pyre with its raised post to shackle the prisoners and the yellow timbers of the executioner's platform, still pocked by salvoes of hammering and the saw-cuts of last-minute carpentry.

More pennons streamed from the parade rows of socketed spears, where a light horse division reined into place to forestall the botched handling that had shamed Kelsing. Also present to ensure the minions' demise, the Light's Supreme Commander of Armies fumed in ceremonial dress, couched in an armoured war-chariot drawn by four white geldings. The glittering wedge of his entourage crammed the harbour-master's handkerchief lawn, gilt-trimmed by his herald, his standard-bearers and trumpeters, and above these, deployed like ruffled steel lace on the overhead widow's walk, a reserve squad of archers on station in case the spectacle started a riot.

But the True Sect conquest that choked Torwent in pageantry went unseen by the prisoners locked below deck on the galley.

While the brawny stevedores warped the flagship to a readied berth, Tarens and Arithon languished in darkness. The impotent yells and catcalls shrilled from the landing carried faintly through the thumped bangs of the hull, and the squeal of taut hawsers worked in frantic haste to end what the vessel's officers named a cursed passage. Odd, sweating nightmares plagued half of the crew. Two maniacs raved in the surgeon's care, roped harmlessly into hammocks. Rumour laid blame on the small, dark-haired prisoner, with no credence given to fact: that the plague of such ills had started before his incarceration aboard. More, the condemned had done little else but sleep off profound exhaustion. But too many fearful eyes had beheld the fisherman's lugger said to be thrashed by his infestation of fiends.

'Can't be quit of yer hell-spawned hides fast enough!' swore the burly armed guard assigned watch on the ship's brig.

The partner too jumpy to risk shooting dice also vented his spiteful boredom. 'Half the Sunwheel brass in creation's out there, sworn to cleanse the wickedness of yer dark arts!'

'The sooner the sword's pierced your black hearts the better,' the ship's mate agreed, a spidery fellow with a skewed eye, who waited to a fidgety jingle of keys. 'Burn quick and bedamned before others get moonstruck by such as your tricksy foul practice.'

'Our dock rats at Barish aren't this tar slow,' the nervous guard fumed, impatient.

Amid the industrious scrambles above decks, an officer blistered, 'Stow that line, damn you! I'll flay living skin before risking the captain's vile temper!'

The gangplank rattled out to a priest's chanted prayer and the restive growl of a populace primed to witness brutal justice. Wracked by the aftermath of the lane shift, folk demanded redress for the unhinged kinsmen recently put to the torch. They would seize retribution, with or without the law blessed by the temple canon.

Confined in expectation of their barbaric fate, the doomed minions did not pass their last moments of penury lightless. The eerie bands stacked upon Arithon's finger cast a subtle glow amid gloom. Tarens's scarred profile loomed a cold azure, sweat-burnished and tinged to corpse pallor.

'You'd best have a plan,' the big crofter ventured against the ominous uproar topside. 'At least, don't pretend the role of the scapegoat hasn't turned upside down while you slept.' When his jagged dread received no reassurance, he lashed out, 'The numbers won't give! If we're going to escape from this mess alive, you must wield your talent to kill.'

Chain chinked in sour protest.

Ripped to frayed nerves, Tarens blurted, 'Man, this isn't the place to be hobbled by the tender guts of the healer!' He added, bidden by uncanny instinct, 'I was told to remind you, if you thought to cringe: *once, you swore a blood oath to a Sorcerer that you would do all in your power to survive!*'

The brazen moment of recoil hung, followed by a ripped catch of breath. Then a convulsive movement doused the faint glimmer on Arithon's left hand. '*Who told you this?*' Under darkness, his tone was sheared ice, surely stressed from an unveiled memory.

Too late for regret, that the cruel admonishment blindsided a man's inner privacy. Tarens reeled also, defenseless to soften the prompts of an arcane perception too fresh to assimilate. Past question, he *knew*: the cut of a blade upon Arithon's wrist once had set ruthless terms on a binding to live, no matter the means or the cost.

Belatedly, he sought to soften the wound. 'High Earl Jieret s'Valerient informed me. He claimed to have been your sworn friend and the voice of your royal conscience.'

'The shade of my former *caithdein* appeared to you?' Arithon shuddered, beyond distraught. 'When did this happen? How? The man passed the Wheel in vile duress. His crown service finished long since in Rathain, several centuries before you were born!'

'The visitation occurred in a persuasive vision while I was unconscious.' Tarens steeled himself against pity. 'And you're wrong. Your liegeman's commitment transcended the veil. For love, the debt the High Earl left on you has been passed down to me.'

The pained stillness extended, loud with the outraged barrage of hatred racketed from the shore-side spectators.

Then the docked galley rocked to the tread of armed boarders. The metallic rasp of the key in the lock put an end to the awkward discourse. When the narrow hatch cracked, speared through by lamp-light, the scald of reflections off polished armour bespoke temple dedicates come in force to take Shadow's minions in custody.

The bark of their Sunwheel officer quashed the issue of upstaged authority. 'Don't bother! The escort's equipped with a cage and a cart! Just release the chains from the overhead bolt. They're to mount the scaffold in shackles.'

The ship's turnkey welcomed the change with relief. 'Have the sail crew rig the staysail boom as a hoist. We'll sling the wretches on deck through the cargo hatch and set them back down on the wharf.'

While the prisoners blinked in the dazzle of light, hard men caught and pinioned their arms. Their restraints were unfastened. Shoved forward, they stumbled over the threshold into the central hold. There, eager sailhands lashed their cuffed wrists to the line, then yelled topside, 'Haul away!'

The rope whumped taut to a squealed block and lifted them, dangled limp, upwards into fresh air, rabid noise, and cold daylight. The salt-wet scents of tide wrack and fish and ship's tar filled their nostrils, while stretched skin and bone drummed to the throaty roar, erupted from the quayside to meet them. A spun glimpse showed the pebbled vista of faces, packed like storm wrack against the bulwark of Sunwheel soldiers.

Then the view jerked away, as vindictive fists caught the prisoners' ankles and hauled them like gaffed meat onto the open dock. Bundled upright again to a rattle of chain, they were pushed headlong towards the tail-gate of a cart. The bolted, plank sides designed to pen livestock had been topped by a cage of wrought iron. Tarens glimpsed Arithon's face in the shuffle as the temple's escort closed ranks. Beneath tousled hair, his pinched expression and shut eyelids displayed the pulped agony of a man seemingly stabbed through the vitals.

'You have to fight back!' Tarens yanked the men clutching his arms off their feet. Others grabbed hold. Someone's back-handed blow knocked him dizzy. The shackle cuffs bit and drew blood as he struggled. Dragged like a maddened bull towards his doom, he barged into Arithon's shoulder.

To the bowed head crushed against his split lips, Tarens threatened, 'Come what may, coward, don't you dare falter now!'

The green eyes flicked open. 'I can't!' The plea came silent, mouthed through the gasp as Arithon recouped the breath knocked from his lungs. 'Not again!' Recovered enough to speak, he pealed, 'Tarens! These are, every one of them, innocents!'

But the adamant iron in the crofter's glare met that humane protest with censure. Another vulnerable memory resurged: of a past, chilly daybreak at sea-side, when Jieret's pitiless stance had forced through the finish of an intolerable strategy. Then, a fleet of ships chartered to transport a war host had been torched into flame in a northern harbour.

Horror drained Arithon's skin to milk glass. 'Please! For mercy, don't ask this!'

No reprieve came. Only the punch of insistent mailed gauntlets that clubbed helpless flesh until the captives reeled separate. While the howl ashore swelled to a crescendo, armoured fingers pried open their jaws and inserted the rough, twisted cloths of gags. No use, Tarens's half-strangled shouts of indignity. The temple's wardens battened both of their heads into coarse draw-string sacks, and sent them onward to meet their due fate, served up blind on the oil-soaked scaffold.

The onlookers screamed their atavistic frenzy as the condemned were shoved into the waiting, barred transport. Tarens crashed into urine-soaked straw, lately used to dispatch swine to the slaughter-house. He thrashed to sit upright, unlike Arithon, tumbled limp in the mouldered dung alongside. Rusty hinges squealed to a shudder of boards as the cage door clanged shut behind them.

Tarens wheezed through the gag, galvanized by stark fear, then seared by the unexpected assault that rattled his augmented awareness. His heightened instincts screamed warning that something was very far wrong. Ferocious chills shuddered over his skin. The discomfort built into an agonized sting, worse than salt rubbed into flayed nerves. He felt faint, half-smothered by the cloth sack. Masked eyesight dissolved into star-burst sparkles of pain. He gasped, while his gut-punched faculties spun, jangled in fiery waves. However he cowered, he found no escape. Teeth sunk in the gag could not stifle the agonized whimper wrung from him.

'There's a proper taste of unpleasantness, boys!' A taunting clout raked the bars where he curled, cramped double with nausea. 'May you suffer for every one of the sorry ills you've inflicted on others!'

Laughter followed, clipped by more obscene jeers. Collapsed on his side, Tarens dimly sensed that the quivering recoil also flattened his mage-wise companion. Trained talent afforded no measure of relief. The outside hope died, that a working of sorcery might ease the appalling onslaught.

'Feelin' the jab of yon sigils, my lads? The temple's seen fit to bless your last journey under a string of grade talismans. Your muckle spells won't do aught to save you. I'll crow as you scream, denied any mercy throughout your overdue reckoning.'

A whip snapped nearby. The cart rumbled forward, bearing its wretched occupants towards their doom with all gifted access rendered incapable. Tarens's hazed fury blossomed to panic. He had chased a fool's dream. The compassionate empathy that had composed music to reel him back from the void never owned the aggressive, harsh core to rise to this moment's necessity. Neither had the dutiful charge raised by Earl Jieret's shade broken through Prince Arithon's aversion to bloodshed.

Naught remained but endurance against the hounding dread, that the Light's executioner might fumble his stroke; that frail courage would break before the end came, debased by animal terror. Tarens shivered, afraid, that his last aware moment might hold spineless tears and futile pleading.

The wagon lurched. The cage-bed suddenly tilted, then slewed sidewards to oaths from the discomposed escort. No one had seen the linch-pin work loose. Therefore, the commotion raised shouts of surprise as the right front wheel slid off the hub. The bare end of the axle banged into the dock to a shrieked grind of splintered wood. Someone's apt handling halted the horse. But the leading ranks became socked from behind as the drunken wobble of the errant rim scythed through their neat files and splashed into the harbour. An unbalanced man fell. The comrade he jostled as he crashed flat rocked into a stagger and tumbled headlong off the wharf.

Immersed in full armour, he plunged straight down. Amid yelling dedicates who shucked off their gear in the scramble to shoulder a rescue, the temple officer ordered a hands-and-knees search for the lost bit of hardware. Failure coloured the frantic pitch of his oaths.

The cart's mournful driver remarked with disgust, 'Don't matter anyhow. Not with the wheel lost in the drink!'

'Keep looking!' the officer snarled, regardless. 'The water's not deep. Once that clod-hopping wretch gets pulled out, I'll strip down another and send him in with a salvager's grapple and line.'

'No use.' The insolent driver heaved a resigned sigh. 'The pin's slid through a crack. She'll be sunk in the silt, more's the pity.'

'Then contrive something else!' The impasse sparked fury, that the True Sect priesthood's exhaustive precautions had seen the talisman seals to block mage-craft welded onto the cage, to thwart tampering. 'We cannot move any sorcerer safely without the use of this secured cart!'

'Aye, shout till you're purple!' the driver flared back. 'Won't be going anywhere, quick. Prayers won't fetch a wheelwright here any faster. Go on, damn Shadow's feckless ills all you like! There's no fixing the problem. Best to unload your criminals now and march them to the pyre on foot.'

Through the raucous confusion caused by the drenched casualty, hauled onto the dock and vomiting sea-water, the stout lock on the cage door was unfastened. Two disgruntled, armoured brutes crawled inside and collared the prisoners. Tarens resisted, brutalized to whacked elbows, a banged head, and skinned knees. But the passive slide of Arithon's body beside him suggested a limp state of unconsciousness. He had to be lifted onto the wharf, where he sprawled, while more shouting men endeavoured to prod him upright.

'He's out cold, you say?' The exasperated officer swore. 'Shadow's Breath! No help, then. You'll just have to carry him.'

Wagon abandoned, the armed company re-formed and marched out. Three steps, and their progress jerked short: the dragged slither of Arithon's leg iron chains had caught fast in the crack between the gapped planks. The stout links stayed wedged, despite two stalwarts, who yanked with clenched teeth, then knelt with drawn steel and lathered themselves to fruitless frustration.

'Keep at this with blades, someone's sword's going to snap,' observed a disgusted subordinate. 'The brute job calls for a pry bar.'

'That, or those irons have to be struck,' another suggested. 'Anyway, the little wretch looks done in. Struck flat by those ward seals for sure. Since he's not fit to stand, should I take half the company and march the blond brute on ahead?'

'No!' The officer sounded fit to tear hair. 'I can't split our forces, we'll be spread too thin.'

'Diabolical, these mishaps!' a gruff dedicate said. 'Not natural, one bit, but surely the evil set on us by Darkness!' His spiteful punch knocked Tarens down. 'Stay still, you! Don't move!' Through the violent edge of his apprehension, another's shrill shout laced into a by-standing dedicate. 'You, there! Secure those chains while we wait. Don't let that headstrong ox take a dive and drown himself to balk justice.'

While a man secured the slack links to a bollard, the abusive scorn of the frustrated spectators swelled to a vicious crescendo.

Tarens hunched, his breath short and his clouted ear ringing under the draw-string bag. The taste of run blood wicked through his gag and compounded his queasy sickness. But the ghastly distress imposed by the sigils lost its terrible force outside of the cart. His knifing cramps eased, which partial recovery did not restore his familiar frame of perception.

Instead, the back-lash recoil of jabbed nerves and adrenaline splintered him to a rarefied state of alertness. The arcane instincts endowed by Earl Jieret led him to recognize that the odd flares of disturbance he sensed nearby were caused by the men-at-arms. Distinctly as individual signatures, he could track their movements. This turn of skilled Sight was not his birthright, but the uncanny art left imprinted by a clan hunter's legacy. Forest-bred liegemen used such refined talent to stalk prey, and to stand alert guard to patrol the free wilds.

More, Tarens detected other minute flows not seeded by human activity. Attentive to his subliminal faculties, he noted another curious tendril of energy. Purposeful, strange, the peculiar disturbance nipped through the ebb and swirl of activity like a little void pocked into the flux. The concept dawned, that Arithon's distraught collapse might be feigned. His elemental ability to bid shadow and fiends may not have been fully suppressed. Perhaps those fractious eddies of *otherness* marked the evidence of an opening gambit.

Tarens braced himself in foreboding. With their suspicious escort already cranked to a state of jangled ferocity, another ill turn in the pile-up of set-backs might provoke a straight thrust of bare steel in the gut.

'Have to strip off the leg shackles!' the troop captain snapped. 'Go on! Make it brisk.'

'Shadow's blight on us!' a man groaned, at wit's end. 'We don't have the confounded key to the irons.'

Which sent a runner back up the wharf to roust up the galley's bosun. While the soldiers fidgeted, and the muscular tumult ashore surged against the Light's dedicate cordon, the troop officer yelled in hot temper, 'If we don't get these miserable criminals moving, the delay will incite a riot!'

The Light's Supreme Commander of Armies raked a cold glance over the unforeseen snarl on the wharf. 'Damn all incompetents to the pit!' His foot-to-foot stance rocked his armoured chariot to the blast of his irascible impatience. Dwarfishly broad-shouldered, his bull dog frame and his fidgeting at first sight made him seem childish.

But mature bristles of iron hair poked beneath the dazzling gold rim of his helm. The brace of poised spearmen beside him did not snigger in condescension. Nor did his charioteer's leather mask ever crack, while the senior staff at the fore with the banner bearers showed their superior's pinched nerves only strait-laced deference.

They had called him The Hatchet for so long, few remembered his birth name. If barracks rumour remarked that the brass in his wake bowed and scraped to nuzzle his backside, the man's reputation was brilliant and the brutal justice behind his quick temper a quality no fool crossed twice.

He flicked out a mailed palm. 'I'll have my glass to see what's befouled this ninny's assignment.'

The telescope was slapped into his hand by an equerry drilled onto the hair-trigger tips of his toes. Such electric response was no sycophant's currying of higher rank.

A genius strategist whose crackling respect had been earned by hard knocks rightfully should be smoked to displeasure. A buffoon's jape brought him here: the temple's prerogative yanked him off the battle-front to shepherd a damnfool execution. Insulted by turmoil that smacked of mismanagement, The Hatchet snugged the eyepiece under his furrowed brows.

'Light blast!' he swore. 'That brainless escort's abandoned the cart.'

Dried blood rimmed the nails on the fingers that fussed the lens into tight focus. Since he only donned his parade armour to bedazzle the crowd for religion, his white-and-gold surcoat and blazoned Sunwheel breastplate had been buckled on overtop of his befouled fleece hauberk.

The grim steel of his war armour, caked yet with gore, lay in a shucked heap underfoot. Since the advance thrust underway in the field could not stall for the sake of display, The Hatchet planned to shed his figure-head accoutrements and return to the fray once the sword's thrust dispatched the condemned. Few things galled him more, that his staged invasion should be left in the hands of his inept rivals and underlings.

'Might be worse trouble here,' his ranked captain ventured, uneasy.

The Hatchet removed the glass for a brief, peeling stare, then turned his raking survey back to the wharf. The evils of sorcery did not merit a blink.

Sunwheel believers and Shadows alike made him scoff, with the recent affray that raised shambles at Cainford waved aside as a gutless ineptitude. Excuses were cheap. Light help the whoresons who mis-stepped today, with the hand-wringing flap of True Sect hysteria tossed into The Hatchet's lap. He planned to seize the dog's bone from the mess: the louder the outcry whipped up against Shadow, the more gold he could wring to supply his ravenous troops. With funds drawn skin-tight since the past summer's fevers cut into the temple's tithes, at least a righteous scare of the Dark would replenish the bursar's drained coffers.

The Hatchet drummed vexed fingers on the chariot rail, while the fumblers on the dock waited upon a runner dispatched to the ship. 'They're tail-circling over some damnfool errand!' Annoyance curled his stiff upper lip as he cracked to his spearmen, 'Find out what's amiss!'

The men under orders vaulted from the chariot and sprinted away.

Against the snarling mob that pressured his triple-strength cordon, The Hatchet bellowed downhill to his acting captain, 'Whatever the hitch, get those men on the march. Heads will roll if we're faced with a riot.'

Fenced in by the chariot's steel-clad sides, The Hatchet kicked his shed wrack of armour aside to allow his impatience more leg-room. He knew he looked like a fool ape in parade rig. He endured the ridiculous. Unlucky at wit, a puny laughing-stock at love, he held his command post in dedicate service to prosecute the arts of war. In that arena, his matchless ability raised his faults beyond all reproach. Daily, and never more than this moment, he bristled under the pious chokehold that owned the power to muzzle him.

'Light forsake the blistering nuisance!' For the entanglement on the wharf still struggled to sort itself out. 'The cart's a dead loss, either broken or stuck,' he rapped in disgust. More, with his spearmen bogged in the press that challenged the overstrained cordon, The Hatchet seethed, 'If those dimwits try marching those prisoners through here on foot, this mob will rip them to pieces before they ever get to the scaffold.'

The deferent captain of horse tipped his helm. 'You'll want us to wade in with lancers?'

'No!' Galled to a snap decision, The Hatchet commandeered two replacement spearmen, then barked at his veteran reinsman: 'Drive down to the dock. I'll shift the criminal bastards myself and be shut of this gross waste of time!'

The mounted captain's stiff protest became trampled.

'Bedamned to my dignity!' Battle-axe jaw jutted under the gleaming, link strap of his helm, The Hatchet laughed. 'Let's see who dares to flout my personal pennant.'

He braced his short-legged frame on propped arms and bellowed for haste. A whip snap advanced his four-in-hand rig, harnessed in gilt to white horses. Equipped for turf and with spiked hubs for battle, the steel wheels scored gouges into the street cobbles. Over the vehicle's rumbling noise, The Light's

Hatchet spouted his bale-fire displeasure to the breathless spearmen crammed in behind him.

'You'll kill any scum who gets in my way! I won't have my conquest blunted for nitwits, or piss away the chance to stage our assault past the Darkshiel River before Havish can bolster its routed defense.'

At least one alert officer at the dock-front grasped what his pension was worth: he spotted The Hatchet's streamered blazon as the armoured chariot cleaved into the moil. His orders shellacked the reserve troop in time to muscle the unruly populace from the path of the team's studded shoes and the razor-edged slice of spun wheels.

By then, the squad on the wharf had prodded their charges halfway to the landing. Both captives stumbled, their muffled eyes blind. The husky one thrashed in sullen resistance. His smaller henchman dragged heels and swayed, while two hassled dedicates wrestled him upright, forced to bear him on as his legs buckled.

'Bootless cravens!' The Hatchet's sneer grew pronounced as his charioteer fought the horses and rig to a standstill beside the slap of green chop at the breakwater.

Subject to their commander's rapacious regard, the tried dedicates scrambled and miserably failed to redress their untidy files. They could scarcely remedy the misfortune, that prisoners dragged towards their last gasp at the pyre rejected co-operation.

Scorched past tolerance, The Hatchet ordered both spearmen to prod the sorry business along. 'I want those clowns roped inside this chariot without any further delay.'

While the reinsman struggled to hold the aggressive team with no groom's assistance from the ground, the sensible captain assigned to the cordon ventured an impertinent protest.

'Lordship, is that wise? Those men are said to bid fiends through dark practice. Surely given the risk, you might send for another transport.'

'Nonsense!' snapped The Hatchet. 'This vehicle has seals against fiend bane, aplenty. Or is your faith misplaced? Does the ordained craftwork of a temple-blessed ward not frame an adequate protection?'

The cornered subordinate cleared his throat, red-faced under the implied blasphemy.

Since The Hatchet viewed sacrilege with contempt, his rankled frown softened to irony. 'Your worry is groundless.' His scorn denounced the pathetic display as the smaller fellow in chains was pried away from his crimped grip on a dockline. 'If that mawkish pair possessed uncanny powers, do you think they'd be cringing in fear for their lives? Were they Shadow's sorcerers, and not sniveling wrecks, they'd have done for their keepers and dismembered the ship that delivered them!'

The jackass parade reached the end of the dock, at which point the two spearmen became obliged to use weapons to curb the crowd's rabid surge against the bowed line of the cordon. Peeled raw by The Hatchet's signal displeasure, and against the roaring back-drop of noise, the dedicate escort on foot manhandled the summarily damned up to the armoured chariot. They heaved the slighter man over the rail first. Flailing in chains, he landed sprawled atop the discarded armour. The stained plate upset, which fetched him, head first in his sack, against the stumpy shin of the Light's supreme commander. Agile, imploring, his cuffed hands latched their limpet's grip onto the first bandy ankle in reach. The Hatchet vented his temper on his reinsman.

'Roll us out!' he cracked, repelled by a plea that the gag reduced to whined gibberish.

The chariot lurched forward, rushed into motion as the bigger miscreant was dumped in a heap at the commander's feet. But that brute roared and rose. Chains gripped in skinned fists, he rammed the hapless charioteer against the crescent front of the vehicle.

The Hatchet snatched for his dirk, wrist hampered by the little wretch, who grabbed hold and attempted to claw himself upright. A brief, savage struggle failed to dislodge the burr cling of the craven's panic. Worse, a dull crack and an agonized scream meant his reinsman's crushed arm had just broken. By dint of a kick and a left-handed draw, the Light's commander unsheathed his sword. Again, he was twisted off balance: the cowardly knave still weighted his knee. Caught up in close quarters that foiled his swung blade, he raised his leg for a kick fit to bash the clinched felon to his final judgement.

His boot never connected. Beneath his shifted foot, the small fellow launched upwards. One shoulder rammed under The Hatchet's squat crotch. Lifted sharply, unbalanced by the top-heavy drag of his chased breastplate and helm, he toppled head over heels. Crest plumes whooshed through the air. Flipped over the chariot's rail, The Hatchet crashed head first onto the cobbles under the stamping hind hooves of his driverless horses. Dedicates from the escort snatched the hem of his surcoat and dragged him clear before he got pulped by the clattering team.

'Catch the bridles!' he pealed, curled over his groin in shuddering agony.

But the torqued roll of the sharpened wheels drove back the spearman who leaped to respond. Then the horses reared. Another man's hand dragged them hard by their bits: somehow the smaller prisoner had yanked off the sack and snagged their dropped reins.

The Hatchet swore murder, overwhelmed by the close-up view as the matched team of four in their gleaming war harness changed their coat, stainless white rendered black as poured ink. Before his wide eyes, from proud heads to streamed tails, all four living horses transformed into an ebony apparition.

Then the ejected body of his charioteer crash-landed, screaming, on top of him. He lost his wind for an instant, crushed under the mangle as the injured man passed out and hampered him. Though his crack cordon charged to recoup the disaster, hooves shod for war and the bladed hubs drove their belated sally to shambles.

The Hatchet scrabbled out from under the scrimmage and shrieked to his poleaxed archers. 'Fire! Take that rogue down!' More choice words pinked his flustered lance captain. 'Get your head out of your arse and launch your light horse in pursuit!'

He reached to his feet finally, served the nightmare view as his own chariot was pivoted in place by the coal-blackened team. The sky-lit toss of their heads became hauled around with a skill that pitched them down off their hind legs. Sparks shot off the grind of edged wheels as the chariot skidded through an expert turn and rumbled uphill at a gallop. Then Darkness itself opened a fathomless maw and doused sight under nightfall as dense as the abyss.

The Hatchet ground his teeth. Arrogant reputation in shreds, he sank to his knees and recanted his unbelief. By heaven's Light, he vowed to repay the hour and serve Shadow's minions their overdue reckoning.

After Tarens was thrown flat in the racketing vehicle, his berserk surge to escape rammed against a back-handed shove. He crashed onto his shoulder, entangled in chains, and howled through the jammed cloth of the gag. The sack blinded his sight. None of which impaired Arithon s'Ffalenn, who shouted, frantic, 'Stay down!'

An inbound shaft creased the air overhead. The war-arrow thunked into the chariot's side where the crofter lately had clung. Sobered by that near-fatal miss, Tarens lowered his head. As the unstable vehicle careered in mad flight, he clawed at the sack with ineffective, cuffed wrists until his struggle attracted the tweak of an uncanny working. Tarens shivered, tickled as a grue of cold brushed his neck. *Iyats,* he realized in dismay, surely dispatched at Arithon's bidding. With an eerie stir, the draw-strings untied themselves. Underneath the loosened cloth, the knotted gag slithered undone as well. Then the ranging whistle Tarens recalled drilled through steel and sprang the pins on his locked shackles. The chains dropped away with a clank that left bruises, sweetly welcome as music.

Tarens spat out the soggy rag and shucked off the sack, which kited away, still possessed. Through the dreadful, black maelstrom abruptly unveiled, he snarled, 'About time, damn you!'

Arithon withheld answer. Crouched low as he leaned through a hair-raising curve, he teased the reins. The racing team swerved. The chariot whiplashed and nearly hurled his agile stance off balance. Yet method followed his ferocious recklessness. The right wheel rim clipped a stacked pile of barrels in passing.

The pyramid toppled and cascaded downhill with a throaty boom and a force fit to macerate. Warned in the dark by the on-coming thunder, the dedicates pelting in armed pursuit hopped desperately fast in avoidance. They flattened bystanders caught in crazed flight, stuck their unsheathed weapons into buildings, or each other, or else became rammed in midstride and crushed flat. Where the casks struck at speed, their split staves disgorged, gurgling, a rank gush of fish-oil over the cobbles. The stalwart man ordered to light the street lanterns slid on the greased footing and fell. The lit spill clutched in his hand shed a flurry of sparks, which winnowed and caught. A blue gout of flame whooshed downhill and scattered the belaboured lancers tasked to restore civil order. Others afoot hopped aside with scorched ankles. Obliging none, the runaway spill sluiced into the gutter and dashed into the harbour as a lighted slick.

Ships and tarred bollards fell prey to the flame, torched off like so much primed tinder.

Through the crescendo of screams from behind as the singed cordon stampeded to safety, Arithon voiced curt instructions. 'Snag the fish-net hung off that drying-rack, could you?'

Tarens grabbed the rail, almost thrown off his feet while the chariot rocked through another violent swerve. More arrows clattered and hissed overhead. The archers still fired despite blinded aim. Amid the ink darkness that smothered the harbourfront, the constant wasp hum of their wild shots sliced through the plumed smoke, more than likely to strike confused innocents. Tarens leaned outward, hooked the hung net, and braced hard as the stout twine snapped taut. The recoil nearly yanked him from the rig before the nailed mooring tore free. A shaft snicked against the vehicle's armour and rebounded, skittering. Tarens ducked and held fast as another gouged up splinters inches from his white-knuckled grip.

His trailed net snaked and flounced in the chariot's wake to a shattered glass spray of smashed floats. The few lancers who breasted the barrage of live fire flailed into the weave, mounts noosed by the fetlocks in flat-out pursuit. Their horses pitched off balance, then wrenched, belly down, mangled as the net frayed and tore loose.

'Rot in Sithaer!' Tarens shouted, flushed to crazed elation.

More bow fire shrieked overhead, close enough to pose an endangerment. The archers now shot in organized volleys, aim guided with better accuracy by the crack of shod hooves on the cobbles. Arithon loosed fiends to counter the threat. Deep indigo, and purple, and pale turquoise, the energy sprites shredded off his raised finger and tightened into a whirlwind that flung the launched shafts on mad tangents. War points smacked into Torwent's brick dormers and clattered across the slate roofs. Others bashed through the town's street-front windows to splashes of fragmented glass.

'Hah!' Tarens grinned, rocked to manic hysteria. 'That should kink a few priestly necks and ruffle some self-righteous petticoats!' Inspired by rage, he bent and sorted through The Hatchet's discarded armour. The sword he retrieved was a superb weapon, honed to a murderous edge. A sweet gift of convenience, with the dais and scaffold ringed by desperate guardsmen obstructing their passage ahead. 'Just steer a straight course!'

'You're primed for a blood-bath?' jabbed Arithon, both hands busy. The fractious team steadied and kept running abreast.

'Just get me in reach of that dog-faced examiner,' Tarens insisted, sword at the ready. 'He should be cut down. If you don't agree, how long before his diviners come ravening after us? No matter how carefully you hide our tracks, whatever you're doing to direct those *iyats* stamps the flux with a red flag of warning.'

'Whose expertise have you borrowed from, now?' Arithon snapped in whetted irony. 'Mine? Or is this a death's gift from Jieret, served up to hound me in the present?'

But underneath that glass-edged attack, disclosed by the fresh instincts bequeathed to him, Tarens heard only sorrow shielded behind vicious defense. The deep anguish, that survival commanded a punishing cost: the wheel spinning beside his gripped fist flicked a fine spray of blood from the rim.

Not every terrorized bystander had been quick, or able enough to jump clear of harm's way.

'No one's died, yet,' Tarens said, that bleak truth affirmed by a hunter's instinct. No residual streamers of spirit light lingered, ripped adrift by the shock of violent dissolution.

'No human casualties,' snarled Arithon. 'Just a few horses, broken for the knife. Never mind that the butcher's bill here will work the bone-setters like teeming lice. Every quack who sells tinctures will be up through the night, plying a gut thread and needle.' He tweaked the reins. The chariot veered. Nearly unseen in the flame-wracked dark, a young mother who carried a shrieking child just missed being trampled by the maddened horses. Arithon's nipped glance sidewards seared Tarens's blanched face. 'You've called on my oath! Don't you dare to pretend you're not squeamish!'

But the gut-punch rejoinder delivered no sting, disarmed by sore understanding. Tarens perceived today's crux in the bitter light of Jieret's experience: *for how long could a masterbard's sensitivity stave off despair against odds that demanded the ruthlessness of a killer?*

'Never mind my straits!' Tarens crouched to absorb the bucked jolts as the chariot charged the armed cordon at speed. He groped, found the commander's leather-lined helmet, and urged the protection on Arithon. 'Look after yourself!'

Arithon spurned the offering. 'In *fact*, I should skulk in my enemy's skin?'

'No,' Tarens rebuked. 'But if you fail here, you won't die alone. How many more helpless lives must be thrown into jeopardy after you?'

'You tell me, friend!' Arithon soothed the runaway team against the crazed shriek of wind, sucked into a vortex as he tightened down his cover of darkness. 'I'm stymied, since you claim to know the past measure of my mistakes better than I do.'

Faced by a dead liegeman's dauntless commitment, Tarens rammed The Hatchet's helmet headlong against Arithon's complacency. 'Put this on, fool! You're too tempting a target!'

Through the head-splitting thunder of hooves and steel-clad wheels, Arithon spoke with the horror of foresight, 'The Light's priests won't relent. How many hapless talents will burn for their thwarted fury today?'

Tarens struck back with unfair leverage. 'Never before have you suffered your wounded to fall on the field in vain sacrifice!'

'That grants me licence, in Jieret's name?' Arithon's combative venom sliced through panicked cries as the four-in-hand team slammed across the first line of steadfast dedicates.

Tarens was obliged to bloody the sword: a fanatical guardsman caught hold of the rail and vaulted to clamber aboard. The hero wore armour. A thrust in the neck bashed him into the wheel. The chariot bounced, and surged forward. The lancer who thrust to skewer a harness horse missed when Arithon's quicker reflex wheeled the team. A string of white bunting snagged on their bridles. Torn loose, the streamered silk crepe lashed them onwards in lathered stampede. Somewhere through the dark, a priest screamed for the Light. His shrill invocation received an ill-starred intercession: Arithon's inspired mayhem with the fiends overset the fire-pan that held the socketed torch.

The stacked pyre went up with a whoosh of red flame. Gusts scattered the explosive burst of winnowed cinders, which also ignited the white-and-gold canopy over the dais. Priests pelted wailing, with robes set aflame, trampled in panicked flight by their singed executioner.

'Them or me,' snapped Arithon into the breach as he barreled the chariot recklessly past the wreckage. His wrestled hold on the bits snaked the skittish team around the inferno that consumed the scaffold. Breathless, he added, 'Who sings the paean for a flagrant suicide?' But amid the rained sparks, the gale wind and the dark, the defiant gesture that clapped on The Hatchet's helm held a flourish that wept for necessity.

Tarens stifled his poisoned regret for the ruin of a once-innocent trust. The changed dynamic that now altered a friendship already ran beyond salvage. He could not denounce the day's ruthless awareness or erase the acuity that bequeathed him the whip-hand to drive Arithon from the dangerous shoals of forgetfulness. Healing the emotional wounds became moot against stakes that brooked no sane compromise. Too clearly, the hell-bent course of their escape forged a fate beyond mere survival.

Arithon said with keen desolation, 'Not only Jieret threatened to haunt me, if I should ever fall short.' He coughed, perhaps hoarse from the fumes billowed off his fiend-kindled holocaust. The contorted blaze stitched across Torwent's water-front dropped behind. The chariot climbed with the roadway, that switched back repeatedly on itself as the rise of the headland steepened above the cove harbour. Past the outlying houses, shuttered and locked against fear, he minded naught else but his dexterous play on the reins. For an interval, only the pound of shod hooves and the slap of war harness spoke through the frigid blanket of darkness. Arithon steered briskly through the emptied streets. He kept his own counsel, while the team clattered up the narrow side lanes, then breasted the crest of the shoreside bluff.

The pace had to be slackened once the land leveled off, and the cobbled road ended. Ahead stretched the flat, wind-raked heath that opened the way towards Lanshire's interior. Arithon maintained his pitch pall of shadow but curbed the blown horses before they foundered. His unimpaired gentleness eased them back to a trot, then soothed their skittery terror and coaxed them down to a nervous walk. Wedged heads shook to a jingle of bit rings. Blowing nostrils flared red and snorted. The right-wheel horse sidled, sharply restrained, while the dense veil of shadow not yet released gripped the air like cold iron and sprouted whiskers of frost off the dimpled mud left by the thaw.

Tarens found himself holding his breath.

With sound reason: Arithon's remark broke the desolate quiet with an unvarnished warning. 'I should rather humiliate a pack of false priests than confront the bravest of my stubborn shades, turned forsworn.'

He tied off the reins. Still crowned by The Hatchet's plundered helm, he stepped out of the chariot. His careful hands checked the exhausted team, looking for wounds or stress injuries. The inspection stroked down each sweat-streaked leg, then picked up hooves and tested the shoes for loose clenches. Shown no sign of bruised soles or strained tendons, Arithon pushed erect. Worn-out or ravaged, he stayed expressionless as he took pause, one fist locked in restraint on the lead horse's bridle.

'You know we're not safe to stop here,' ventured Tarens, then prodded, 'What are you doing?'

Arithon's whiplash retort forgave nothing. 'The fires in Torwent. I'm putting them out before the whole water-front burns to the ground.'

Tarens sucked in a delicate breath. 'The conquered town's fate is a luxury neither of us can afford.'

The rebuttal snapped back. 'Three boats are already sunk at the dock. Enough honest livelihoods have been ravaged!'

'Worse will befall hapless folk if you tarry.' Against even tears, urgency forced Tarens to shoulder the dead liegeman's honour passed into his keeping. 'The brunt of the tragedy can't be undone. Your gift of Shadow has just put the torch to a war that must waken disaster.'

Nothing remained but the dauntless task thrown to a man sorely unfit: to safeguard a prince through the gamut of enemies who sought his destruction, no matter the cost. Braced to mete out the most brutal reawakening of all, Tarens said, 'Time's come to recall the fact Desh-thiere's geas still grips the son of your mother, named Lysaer s'Ilessid.'

No sound emerged as that wrenching blow fell.

But Sethvir also cringed for the scope of the impact, frozen between anguished steps in the distanced isolation of Althain Tower. Not blind in the dark, he also wept, while the bleak cascade of probability laid bare as the day's events begat the bleak future. He could not intervene: even as prescient earth-sense unveiled the blood-soaked ground of the battle to come.

Two men alone must thread the gamut as two war hosts clashed, and Havish's untested young sovereign rose to engage the grinding axe of a war host fueled by fear and false doctrine. No Sorcerer might seize the initiative to salvage whole nations from chaos. Not while Asandir's desperate oath stayed the Fellowship's rightful authority. Unless Arithon s'Ffalenn could be restored to Rathain's clans alive, and until he accepted the grace of the crown's protection in Halwythwood, the fragile thread of his future might rest in the hands of three errant children.

Early Spring 5923

First Deflections

Esfand s'Valerient pressed grubby fists to his temples to ease the throb of a flash-fire headache. Ever since the markers had moved, the surged pulse of the lane flux pushed his pressured instincts with ever-more-insistent clarity. The heritage of a *caithdein*'s heir apparent prickled his nape with the nascent awareness of war. No matter how often he breathed the stilled air or steadied his disrupted focus, he failed to dispel the waves of distress that rippled through his attuned senses. Repeatedly his ordered thoughts scattered, until the urgency of pending upheaval pressured him towards the threshold of gifted Sight. Grounded, determined to stave off the painful distraction, Esfand locked his teeth. But the queasy slip-stream continued to ride him, a half-sensed invisible tumble of *motion* that riffled the depths beneath self-aware cognizance. He felt primed to leap out of his skin as the quicksilver seethe of dire events jinked his thoughts like the dart of shoaled fish.

At Rathain's western border where the youngest clan wayfarers camped, the storm's edge was ephemeral, still. Bird-song in the brush heralded only the spring-tide vigour of nesting, while dawn's pall of mist dispersed to a dull pewter overcast. The open terrain at the rim of the foothills rolled away in soft folds, with cross-hatched thickets of leafless scrub tossed under brisk gusts, cotton-damp with the promise of rain. The spare fire made to roast the winter-thin hare bagged by Siantra's bow had gone cold, with the ashes unburied.

Which careless behaviour, born of delay, spiked Esfand's already gouged nerves. The north spur of the Storlains was no safe place to be caught laggard with indecision, skulking as they were at the hostile verge of the True Sect's defended territory.

But daybreak shed no better light on their current fence-sitting debate. The brave trio who journeyed in search of their prince dead-locked over the least perilous route to broach Tysan's sealed border.

Always, Khadrien's hot-headed opinion drowned everyone else in the breach. 'That's lame-brained!'

Lounged on one elbow and stubbled as a mountebank in buckskins left ragged where fringes had been nipped off for tie-strings, he stabbed his dagger into the map Siantra had scratched in the dirt. His point skewered the crux where the trade-road to East Bransing threaded the narrows between the north scarp, and the cove inlet whose sandy shallows scalloped the south-coast of Instrell Bay. 'If we cross an armed patrol, where could we duck?' He puffed a persimmon strand of hair from his eyes, the better to glower.

Esfand agreed with his volatile cousin. 'The season's too chilly to cower in a marsh. There's no natural cover for leagues in this blighted country.'

'Well, your crackpot plan to try the trade-road is worse.' Grave and self-possessed, her knees tucked up behind firmly crossed arms, Siantra whetted her retort with cool female logic. 'No, don't tell me I'm chicken!' she upbraided Khadrien. 'To sneak a ride in a wagon is barking madness. Forget finding a stone-blind, ignorant driver, nobody born inside of a town travels through these hills alone. What about the gauntlet of temple fanatics? If they've got a diviner, their search at the border sees us cut dead at the check-point.'

Khadrien grinned, minded to give cheek.

Siantra pounced first. 'No, you go suck donkey's eggs!' Then she trampled his tirade forthwith. 'Don't dream the Sunwheel dedicates won't exercise their suspicions, jumpy as they'll be over Shadow. Better we take the longer path, south. Araethura won't leave us wrong side of Fate's Wheel, pleading forgiveness at Daelion's reckoning.'

Khadrien's insolence dared to object. 'We'd need a boat to by-pass Backwater's town garrison.'

'No threat.' Siantra squared off in earnest. 'What townsman risks the old way to Lithmarin, scared as they are of the world's greater mysteries?'

'But we don't have a season to waste on a roundabout route,' Esfand said with intent to quench further squabble.

But as usual, his tactless cousin stayed bereft of all sense of self-preservation. 'Siantra's a bird-brained female, what else?'

Tucked feline poise uncoiled at speed and hurled the stick lately used for a stylus.

Her spiteful aim met Khadrien's cobra-quick catch. He brushed off the loam showered over his leathers, smirked with flushed challenge, and continued ranting. 'Anyway, the shift in the flux surely has altered the ground. A dire proximity could be the more dangerous. Need I repeat the ugly dreams I've had lately, of purges by temple examiners? They're hunting down wakened talent in force! If we get pushed west, the flux effervescence at Athili's rim might as easily turn us at bay or maze us to confusion rather than hide us.'

'And you say I'm the sissy?' Siantra laughed.

Esfand risked his neck and thrust between. 'For sure that's a peril we dare not ignore.' Not under the heightened tide of the lane flux, which had not subsided. The *caithdein*'s heir scrapped his own daft idea, to float out by night and stow away on an anchored fishing smack. The rocky shore-line lacked timber to fashion a raft. Worse, the tidal currents that churned Instrell Bay were ferociously swift. Disgruntled himself by their foolhardy options, he could not fault his companions' derision.

Yet their vital mission surely would fail if caution led them to falter.

'Certain as frost, we cannot linger here.' Esfand shouldered the onus, as Cosach's appointed successor. 'Since we have no clue where to look for his Grace, and every proposal looks like a suicide, might as well flip a knife and spare guess-work.' He fingered the dirk at his belt for the toss.

But before the blade in his grasp cleared the sheath, sudden nausea folded him double. Esfand collapsed under the unbalanced swoop as his spun senses took leave of his body. Dizziness felled him across the crude map: *no longer a pattern scored in the dirt, but unreeled instead as spontaneous vision that unfolded the Sighted vista of Lanshire's terrain . . .*

Siantra's cry of alarm reached his ears, thinned away into distance. Then Khadrien's rough-house grip shook his arm, a heart-beat too late to matter. Esfand's unleashed spirit already took wing, catapulted too far beyond reach to respond.

'He's likely driven himself faint from hunger.' Practical even while shocked to distress, Siantra asked Khadrien to untie a bedroll. When her brisk slap raised a flush on Esfand's pale cheek, but no reflexive flutter of lashes, she sorely regretted her feckless decision to set off alone. In trouble and past reach of adult wisdom, she swallowed regret and took action. 'Khadrien, hurry. Help me get him wrapped up.'

Her tone all but shouted with censure: that on the uncanny night when they sensed the momentous change in the world's flux, they should have given up and headed for home. 'Earl Cosach will flay us alive if harm comes to his only grown son!'

'Are you light-headed, too? Or only faint-hearted?' Khadrien let fly, scared enough to fall back upon vicious bravado. 'This is not starvation. I haven't cadged bigger shares on the sly. Esfand's eaten the same rations we all have.'

'Are you certain?' Siantra's severe grey eyes never wavered. 'He's done things before to give friends the advantage. And you steal like a crow. The time we filched the stored nuts from the root-cellar, you ate more than anyone.'

'Not this time.' Stung red, Khadrien unfurled the moth-eaten blanket. 'Our purpose here is no prank. More, we've come too far to go back.' He lent his strength to arrange their companion in comfort. 'This is not weakness,' he added, insistent. 'More likely Esfand's been overcome by his ancestral talent.'

Siantra conceded this might be the case. S'Valerient Sight had been known to provoke an unconscious state. Esfand's skin was not sweated with sickness. His pulse stayed regular, his breathing, relaxed. If his spirit had withdrawn in trance, without the benefit of skilled knowledge, little else might be done. They must keep him warm, wait, and hope the pervasive visions would release him safely back into waking awareness.

'You'll stand the vigil, then.' Siantra gathered her strung bow and quiver and sprang up with the grace of a lioness. 'I'm off to hunt game and set snares. Just in case!' Her arch glance silenced Khadrien's wisecrack. 'If Esfand is caught in true dreaming, or not, we still need more jerky if we're to cross over the notch. Are you reckless enough to claim that a cookfire in the borderlands won't draw the enemy down on us?'

To blink was to miss Siantra's departure, adept as she was at concealment. Khadrien found himself solitary, with the whisk of the wind storm-scented and dense. A wedge of geese honked overhead, northbound harbingers of the turned season. Khadrien tugged the marmalade tendril of hair whipped loose from his untidy clan braid. He cursed the benighted ties of blood-kinship that saddled him with the watch. Too restless for patience and, for once, too careful to whittle where wood shavings might tip off a league tracker, he settled on the stony, chill ground and pillowed Esfand's head in his lap.

The gesture eased nothing. Khadrien possessed no healer's discipline. Untrained, he might recognize breaking danger, but only if something went terribly wrong. Without the herb-lore to brew exact stimulants, or the grace of an empathic attunement, he could offer no recourse. His best friend's stupor might spiral unchecked into a fatal coma.

The tentative palm laid on Esfand's brow encountered no fever. Not yet, the fine tremors that warned of an imbalanced back-lash. Anxiety mounted, regardless. Change had thinned the veil. The deep pulse of the mysteries unsettled human awareness as never before. Since clanborn heritage heightened such sensitivity, Khadrien fretted that Esfand's blood talent might pose a threat beyond precedent.

'Just steer clear of entanglement with the halo of light that bounds Athili,' Khadrien begged his friend's inert form.

Cosach's heir designate remained unresponsive. His dark braid with its burled glint of red draped one slack shoulder, while the hardened palm once scarred by foolish knife play lay artlessly open. His face, with his mother's triangular chin, seemed erased of all animate character. If today's earnest placement of weapons bespoke his keen will to survive, the mouth, robbed of its mischievous curl, showed no twitch of boisterous laughter.

Burdened with adult cares beyond measure, Khadrien ached for the carefree boyhood irrevocably left behind.

Time crept. The morning advanced to the cry of a circling hawk and the rustled flit of the song-birds through the scrub. Then their wing-beats vanished with the changeable gusts, and a silvered veil of rainfall dimmed the clouds bellied in from the west. Khadrien fashioned a makeshift shelter, while Esfand sprawled, yet unstirring. His pallid forehead stayed warm, but not flushed. Chills did not lace him with clammy sweat.

'Where are you, friend?' Khadrien pleaded. Prolonged delay compounded their danger, and even Siantra's stealthy touch at foraging increased the risk of exposure. 'Ath's grace, Esfand! What's drawn your spirit away from us?'

No answer arose. Only the uneasy prickle of gooseflesh stirred up by latent s'Valerient talent. Khadrien shivered, drawn in unaware as the Sighted gift shared through common blood heritage pulled him into a sympathetic reverie . . .

Somewhere at a distance, a lone blond rider puts the lash to a horse that flags underneath him . . . while elsewhere, amid the gravel-stark sweep of a wasteland, a magnificent black stallion staggers in limping exhaustion, abandoned by his rider's desperate urgency. Stripped of tack, his coat lathered, the gallant creature blows foam flecked with blood from flared nostrils, gaunt ribs heaving in fatal extremity . . .

Khadrien startled alert, shocked to terror. 'Almighty mother of storms!' Yanked back from the surge of a waking vision, he wept, grieved by the sense that one of the world's greater powers had gone irretrievably wrong. He had never been overcome by dire dreams! Always before, his ancestral gift manifested through natural sleep. Scared pithless, Khadrien could not read the sun's angle through the slate sheets of banked cloud to know how much time had slid past. Through the tap and trickle of rainfall, he heard no sign of Siantra's return. The hawk's cry was absent, the game long since fled to ground ahead of the storm front. Icy wind hissed through the thickets, and the mercury veil of drizzle drummed into a steady downpour.

Run-off already beaded the oiled wool of Esfand's blanket. He lay still in the throes of deep trance, not cold, but violently shuddering. The clench to his jaw suggested the Sight he witnessed bordered on nightmare.

Khadrien strove to recoup his rattled poise. Worse for them both, that his volatile faculties proved to be susceptible to rapport. The concern that sapped his courage was not groundless if the powerful visions that gripped Cosach's heir charged the flux with the potency to sweep a by-standing talent into hapless empathy.

Khadrien understood he must stand his watch at a safer distance. He marshalled his stiffened muscles to stand when dizziness upended his senses. The whelming surge caused by the outbreak of war rent his prudent intention to tatters . . .

* * *

To the west, where the rainfall had rinsed nothing clean, the wreckage of flesh sprawled on the killing field was too fresh to attract the large scavengers. Only pilfering crows cruised the site, chased to raucous, indignant flight by the rumble of an armoured chariot's passage. Flocked five or six to the cluster, the birds launched almost from under hooves of the lathered team. Tossed scraps of black crepe amid pearly mist, they fluttered in gyres and resettled to their grisly industry, gorging on the eyes and the tender, gored flesh of the rag-bundle corpses. Few wore mail or armour. Most of the fallen were weaponless males, clothed in the wool plaid and homespun of field-hands. Cut down with their scythes still in hand, with no more than the muscle used to shear wheat, they had fought the Light's dedicate pikemen.

Their futile stand had been brutally short. The air reeked yet of their desperate, quick agony, ended in the hour past daybreak.

None moaned or twitched, though the wounds that had killed steamed yet in the cold, and the bitter fog coiled above the drab ground still sparkled with the ephemeral, shed streamers of undispersed spirit light.

To the eye without mage-sight, the low, flattened ground spread dull brown as napped burlap, blued to a sullen cast by the damp. Mud sucked at the wheels that gouged the chopped earth, milled to clods by the lancers' destriers. The more delicate hooves of the white horses in harness jogged across the same ground, legs ribboned with spatters, tinged pink. They had been hard-run. Their soaked flanks heaved with advanced exhaustion. The war rig jolted to their laboured strides, the sole movement amid the vista of savaged landscape.

Ahead, a smear of smoke marred a view not soothed by the liquid splash of the puddles. Piercing, the distanced, terrified screams wrung from trauma-tized human throats. That shrilled note caused the slightly built man of the pair conveyed in the chariot to stiffen.

Leather showered its fringe of hung droplets as he firmed his wet grip on the reins. The spoked wheels squeaked on the axle as the tired team swerved in response. Their ragged pivot turned towards the site where the Light's dedicates slaughtered still in the course of their ordained invasion.

The fair man hunched in misery at the driver's side protested the change in direction. 'Arithon! No.' Bull-shouldered, his tall frame braced by his nervous clutch on the rail, he sawed on in a crofter's broad vowels. 'No way on this side of Sithaer's ninth gate are we fit to challenge a war host! Have you addled your brains? We're still hunted men under hot chase from the scaffold.'

'Watch me.' The fierce creature revealed as his Grace of Rathain twitched the lines and brought the blown team to a halt. He snapped, 'Steady the horses,' and passed over the reins, which were fumbled, then dropped by the other's ham-fisted startlement. 'By Ath's witness, you've shown you can kill like a soldier. Surely a four-abreast rig's not beyond you?'

The sarcasm floundered into an inimical silence. While the spraddled harness team stood with drooped heads, the royal scion sprang from the chariot, which granted the distant clan dreamer's vision a clear view of Rathain's sanctioned prince.

Small and neat as a cat on his feet, his Grace had expressively angular features, stubbled by raffish neglect. A light step that suggested superbly drilled skills advanced him to the hind leg of the left-side-wheel horse. There he bent with decision, lifted a hoof, and used a short dagger to raise the nail clenches and pry off a shoe.

The blond fellow shouted in stupefied shock, 'Sweet name of creation! You've scrapped us, right here! What if we need to bolt? This harness team's crippled, with one of them gimping and barefoot.'

'They're no use to anyone, poor beasts. That's my point.' The prince straightened up from his deft bit of sabotage, hurled away the stripped shoe, and reboarded the chariot. 'No matter what happens, this splendid foursome won't be run to their deaths.'

'One beast cannot,' came the sour contradiction.

Arithon trumped that. 'Chariot horses are schooled in matched teams. To mix them is lethally dangerous.'

'As though we could limp into a Sunwheel engagement and command the picket groom for a relief set!' The bumpkin took pause for a thunderbolt frown. Then the brosy flush drained from his cheeks. 'Dharkaron's bollocks! You daren't!' Moved to renewed fury, he dug in his heels. 'Forget your loonie addiction to mayhem! This time, I won't play along!'

A dismissive shrug waived the protest, that fast. 'Step down, then.' Rathain's prince crouched, undaunted, to the sour clank of steel as he rummaged amid the soiled plate armour piled underfoot. 'A reinsman's absence can be passed off as a casualty.' On one knee, absorbed, Arithon measured his wrist to a bracer, then resumed while he fastened a buckle. 'You could lie up here. Maybe dodge our pursuit in the guise of a corpse. Though if you try, I advise you to pillage yourself a dedicate's surcoat. These field-hands were worse than hacked down to a man.'

Arithon locked the tightened strap leather through the crusted tang. 'Have you looked?' His jade eyes flicked up, bleak. 'Every wretch who went down with a wound has been finished off with a slit throat. Don't presume any burial detail from the temple will show mercy to you as another civilian survivor.'

The blond farmer rejected the grisly prod. 'I'll not leave your back unguarded.'

The ferret-quick salvage of the breastplate and gorget took pause, through a lightning spark of antagonism. Then Arithon said, 'Not with a blade.' He glanced upwards again. 'Don't repeat the mistake! I have sanctioned no bloodshed.'

Adamant, the crofter stood fast. 'I've been charged by the spirit of your closest friend to stay at your shoulder.'

'Crown law states otherwise.' Formidably royal, that chilly locked glare, fit to raise frost on hot iron. 'Your birth in Tysan, Tarens, does not grant you a standing upon my crown oath. A dead man's appeal cannot bestow your lawful rights as my liegeman.'

But courage insisted. 'You cannot stay my hand for a forthright defense. Not if our lives rely on a sword's edge.' Though a swung fist might have flattened the prince, Tarens back-stepped as if snake-bitten. 'I've accepted the burden! You can't change my mind.'

'I won't try.' Arithon stood up. 'Own up to the truth. I knew the song of Jieret's Name. I also witnessed his passing. Whatever befell you in that dreamed encounter, you are not he, but still Tarens.'

The tang of sudden peril raised chills. Deliberate as a bear, the huge crofter rubbed at his mangled nose. 'Jieret gave me his memories of you. He also imprinted the best of his fighting skills for your defense.'

'Keep them and be damned.' Arithon's repudiation showed teeth. 'My will kept no part of your bargain.'

'How much of an ungrateful bastard are you?' Outmatched, Tarens stung back, 'Your past High Earl knows what you once sacrificed to salvage the life of his daughter. Is the posthumous gift of his gratitude not worth my charge to shoulder your needful protection?'

The recoil ceded an unfair advantage as Arithon reeled into the gap opened up by lost memory. Pity trumped the harsh play: Tarens pulled the cruel stroke that should have crushed argument. The dead clansman's benighted Sight unveiled that sordid history. He knew the fateful day of Jeynsa's wedding also had brought the back-stab of betrayal: that Arithon Teir's'Ffalenn fell to Koriani captivity on the hour he set foot in Halwythwood to play his lyranthe for the nuptial celebration.

Determined to spare that bitterest blow, Tarens almost missed the flicker of agony, banished a breath before the whiplashed response. 'I will cut the strings,' Prince Arithon threatened. 'Abjure every trusted loyalty I've honoured, if *ever again*, you try to use love as the puppet's binding to stay me.'

The kindly heart could not try that shield. Tarens watched, helpless, while Arithon donned The Hatchet's set of grieves. The scale kilt followed next, short enough to pass muster, belted tight for his narrower frame. Distaste curved Arithon's mouth, when at last he thrust on the crusted war gauntlets. 'Your cause is not mine, Tarens. But if you tag at my shirttails, regardless, you'll act as the general's charioteer and drive where I bid with your mouth shut.'

Honest to the bone, Tarens took up the whip. As the tipsy vehicle jolted and rolled, he braced himself and inexpertly managed the team's tired pace in the volatile, four-abreast harness. 'Any day, give me a cross-grained mule. Or a pair of donkeys in heat for a test of my patience.'

His ploughman's grip trembled on the oiled reins, while the nerveless masquerade at his side adjusted The Hatchet's armour.

'You'll never pass for an unprincipled killer.' Tarens coughed through the sting of blown smoke. The chorus of victimized screams from ahead frayed the shreds of his determination. 'Forget the basic difference in colouring, you're not ugly enough for the butcher you plan to impersonate.'

The war helmet just donned by Rathain's threatened prince tipped askance, to a waggle of crest plumes. His face lacked the hawkish jut to the chin. Worse, his musician's fingers did not suit the blunt fit of scale gauntlets. The broad cuffs exposed a bare patch of wrist, too fine-drawn to wield the brute weapons preferred by the figure he meant to supplant.

Pushed to a smothered, hysterical laugh, Tarens scorned, 'A masterbard clad in steel plate? A bad jest! Further, I don't look like the egg-sucking spider who serves that brute dwarf as a reinsman.'

'Do you think?' Teeth flashed again sidelong, as Arithon fastened the crested helm's chin-strap.

When he snapped down the slit visor, an uncanny riffle of chill fleeted past. The black moment lifted, and for a second a snap-frozen rattle of sleet pinged off of hoar-frosted metal. Then clean rain returned to the colourless morning. Tarens beheld the surreal astonishment and quailed, along with the distanced dreamer: the few who bore witness seldom foresaw the diabolical subtlety by which use of Shadow might craft an illusion.

For where Arithon stood, the haughty image of the Light's prime commander glared back, form remade to his enemy's measure. His mouth wore The Hatchet's ferocious, clamped sneer. The same glacial stare glinted grey beneath stubbled lashes. Neither was Tarens the hefty crofter he had been but aged to leathery skin and lank hair, and pared down to the wiry build of the charioteer.

'Spit on my own grave!' he swore in gruff shock.

Behind the grimed steel, perhaps Arithon grinned with baleful amusement. 'Dharkaron Avenger's aimed Spear avert, I hope not! Instead, let's see whether a parcel of lies might lessen today's toll of damages.'

But instead, Tarens hauled the worn team to a head-shaking halt. Nape bristled, he turned his obstinate back and retrieved from the floor-boards The Hatchet's noisome short-sword. 'This could be the world's most stupid mistake! Should your bald-faced folly turn wrong, I don't mean to watch you get spitted.'

Steel brandished, he braced to be struck aside.

Yet the uncanny semblance of the Light's Hatchet did not fall to hell-bent aggression. 'As you will,' stated Arithon in the other man's rasped voice. 'You're not mine to command. But the choice to kill always means closing the mind to the chance of a living alternative.'

'A philosophy of convenience,' Tarens challenged. 'Had I not murdered a temple diviner, I'd have seen the last of my family condemned.'

'I am not your kin,' Prince Arithon corrected.

'Argue that with the shade of your High Earl,' Tarens said.

'Then I warn, by my royal word there will come a reckoning.' Emphatic, reverted to his own inflection, the prince gave his orders. 'Roll this rig out. Or by Dharkaron's vengeance, I will throw you off for the buzzards.'

'Now, who won't hear reason? I will not back down.' Defensively cross, Tarens brandished the whip. The thin snap of leather that roused the team cracked across a shocked silence. And dread turned to horror as he grasped the change, no part of their headlong clash after all: the back-drop of screams from the fired village had stilled to an ominous quiet.

The dreamer awoke to the pound of a fist, hammered into his shoulder. He surfaced, confused. As if thrust through fractured water into a world buffeted by too-vivid sensation, he blinked dazzled eyes.

'Wake up, Khadrien!' The whispered entreaty was Esfand's, delivered with a jangled urgency. 'Fell fires of Sithaer, Khadrien, *move*! No one can waste strength to drag you.'

'Wait,' Khadrien protested. 'Listen! A vision has shown me our prince.' Morose for the discovery, he grumbled, 'Though his Grace will likely be murdered by enemies long before we can reach him.'

'If you don't run now, we'll die ourselves sooner.' Esfand's grip badgered Khadrien to his feet.

Which blunt force seemed unfair. 'Weren't you the one who blacked out on us, first?' grumbled Khadrien. 'Did you hear? I *said* that I knew where—'

'Run, cousin. Hurry!' Esfand interrupted. 'Yes, I already know that Arithon's skating the razor's edge!'

Discomposed, and towed stumbling into the scrub against the slap of iced branches, Khadrien swore, indignant, 'Daelion's bollocks! Running's no use. His Grace is a hundred leagues distant, caught amidst the invasion by Sunwheel troops near Torwent!'

But Esfand pushed roughshod across plaintive argument. 'Siantra's flushed head-hunters. We have to flee! No way we'll throw them off track, they've been sent. A damned True Sect diviner's already caught wind of us.'

'That's impossible!' Khadrien slipped on a rock, bit his tongue, and denounced, 'We should be too far out of range for a temple-trained talent!'

'Shut it, Khadrien! Buck up and take charge! If the lane shift has heightened our clanborn talent, every other natural sensitive also will be affected. Are you hot to martyr yourself on the scaffold?'

Khadrien coughed out a mouthful of twigs. 'May the great drakes seed ruin, and rain scorching piss on the upstart religion.' He added, plaintive, 'We're going the wrong way!'

Esfand grinned over his shoulder, then slithered into the icy freshet that frothed down the nearest gulch. 'Wet your laggard feet. Or the league's dogs will track us. Siantra's ahead. She hauled the packs while I kicked you awake. And we're going the right way. My Sight was explicit. Our only clear path takes us southward.'

JANNY WURTS

'But Prince Arithon –'

'Yes!' Esfand agreed, at last ripped to anguish. 'My visions showed me his Grace's straits, too.'

Which desperation bespoke a sorrow fit to crush their adventuresome spirits to heart-break: for the last living scion of Rathain's royal line was pitched into the killing field of the enemy war host marching on Havish.

'We'll find him,' snapped Esfand. 'But for now, his Grace's plight must abide! Little good we'll do anyone, if we don't fly like the wind and survive.'

Second Deflections

The courageous crofters who dared to resist the pre-emptive shock of Light's armed invasion lay dead to a man on the acres their spring labour shortly should have ploughed and sown. Only scavenger crows yet descended to pillage. Still warm in death, the knots of the fallen steamed on the fallow fields by the settlement, where the timbers of their neat, clapboard cottages already blazed beyond salvage. The last of the women and children were being scorched out of the root-cellars as the flames roared through the torched thatch and the fumes hazed them to near suffocation. They bolted out, doubled with coughing, to be run down by the mounted lancers.

Rounded up squawking like panicked hens, they were penned with the others inside a stout hay-barn, left intact by the temple diviner's decree. The banked stone foundation muffled their cries. Amid fallen calm, under billowed smoke and sullen flurries of embers, a methodical foot squad cleaned up. The jab of their weapons through wood bins and corn-cribs dispatched any errant survivors. Other dedicates sorted the spoils ransacked from larders and pantries, the milled flour, the rice, the millet, the waxed cheeses and joints of smoked meat claimed to bolster the provision for Havish's conquest.

In charge of their grim industry, the ranked captain sat astride his war-horse, nostrils singed and his throat rasped hoarse. The pursed set to his mouth and his tensed grip on the rein showed his disgust for the filthy business.

The flames that gutted the cottages never masked the pervasive stench. Or the oily, black pall, which veiled and revealed the toll of stilled flesh sprawled amid the scattered wrack of rifled possessions. Colourless through the grisaille fall of rain, the foot ranks tramped through the sputtering hiss as the drizzle plumed steam off the embers.

Only the muted wails of the infants sawed through the shocked aftermath when the temple diviner in his stainless robe stepped forth and demanded full closure. 'Fire the barn.'

'Kill them *all*?' The captain's aghast protest turned too many heads. Regrouped in formation, his idle men listened, their once-polished trappings befouled with gore and their weapons too clotted to sheathe. A boastful few with strong stomachs wiped their slicked steel on their grimy surcoats. The glued blood left behind a filmed smear, while the smatter of macabre jokes floundered into appalled silence. Rain pinged off plate steel. Behind a fired house, someone's choked scream cut off.

The dedicate captain released a tense breath, misted with condensation. 'I can't sanction the butchery of young babes,' he said in discomfort. 'We have fathers among us. Men with wives and sisters.' He tussled with the ornery sidle of his hammer-head mount. 'Murder's no task to lay on my soldiers. Don't ask me to rip the heart from this troop for your gutless atrocity.'

The diviner's uncanny regard remained placid. 'These heretic families are, none of them, innocent. Be sure I have read them, each one.' He flicked his clean fingers, sparkled with the hellish reflections off several topaz rings. 'Each of the condemned bears the quickened taint of clan birthright and a heritage of wild talent. By the True Sect Canon, under righteous law, none must be left living to breed.'

'I command fighting men, not paid executioners!' the sickened captain objected.

Inside the locked barn, a scared mother started a tremulous lullaby. More voices joined in, wracked sour by fear and the sobs of female bereavement. Which brave effort did little to soothe the howls of traumatized infants; or the plaintive child whose tearful demand pleaded to know when her father would get up and free them. Unsettled mutters swept through the Light's ranks: more than the malcontent grumble of wisecracks, the growl held primal unrest.

The men were glutted on death, weary and dispirited enough from the horrific dispatch of the settlement's wounded. They had shouldered that action for tactical necessity, since the invasion could not afford to march onwards, overburdened with hostile prisoners. Even the veterans chafed with unease, thrust deep into enemy territory. Cannier than the recruits, they knew today's slaughter must unleash a ferocious redress when the High King's enraged reinforcements arrived to defend the realm's savaged border.

'We do not kill children,' the captain insisted.

'Are you a hypocrite or just cravenly soft?' The haughty diviner curled his lip. 'Where is your vow to serve the Light on this day, that once pledged the will to uphold hallowed principles?'

More smoke winnowed past. The rank destrier pawed, while the officer's glower sparked daggers. The priesthood's precocious talent stared back fearless, his shaved chin and finicky grooming still fresh. The gold ribbon that trimmed his white vestments stayed unsullied though he trod the same mucky ground that splattered the foot-troops' boots and leathers dull scarlet.

The power behind his reproof carried threat wrapped in righteous silk. 'Shirk your duty, Captain, and I promise this. These heretic spirits will die on the scaffold. A closed barn offers them the more dignified pyre. Someone with fibre must shoulder the torch.' With venomed conviction, the priesthood's hound added, 'If not, your troop gets cashiered to a man. For their ruin, the Light's high examiner puts you to the question in turn. You'll face the sword as a traitorous minion found in wicked liaison with Shadow!'

The captain stiffened his bull neck. 'Find your own volunteer, then! I don't buckle to threats.'

A ruddy staff sergeant stepped up and kindled the torch, although no command had been issued. While the captain's bold stand-off crumbled, for naught, an intrusive, gruff shout from behind the rear-guard burst through the caught crackle of oiled lint.

Fresh commotion unravelled the square of reserves posted on alert watch by the trade-road. Formation disrupted, they pelted like boys scattered by a smacked wasps' nest.

'Light's glory! You're deaf as a post *and* stone blind?' The inbound barrage of insults gained force, vicious enough to haze the most stalwart dedicates to scarlet embarrassment.

Then the chaos that seeded the whirlwind burst through, drawn by four white horses harnessed abreast, streaming rank lather and hitched to an armoured war-chariot. The escutcheon embossed on the sides sowed stupefied shock, and even the troop captain lost the hardened poise to stem the surge of pandemonium.

Sharp as forged nails, The Hatchet leaped from his platform perch before his wheeled vehicle ceased rolling. Dwarfed by the socketed pole of his own banner, he brushed past the flurry of belated salutes and pursued his hammering tirade. 'I said harness me a fresh team. Straightaway!'

The troop's flabbergasted horse-boy apparently failed to move fast enough. Caught clutching the string of officer's remounts kept close at hand for emergencies, he had nowhere to jump as the Sunwheel host's Supreme Commander of Armies uncorked his vile temper.

'Feed your eyes to the buzzards, they're good for naught else!' The Hatchet snatched the ribbons from his charioteer. Angry, he whipped the freed ends through the terrets and lashed the wet straps in the face of the master of horse, just puffed up at a flustered sprint. 'Have me back on the road with your best team on a ten count. Then strip your insignia. You're demoted!'

The Hatchet barreled onwards. Above the excuses gabbled in his wake, his bellow laced into the foot-troop, abrasively pitched to split heads.

'Prepare to march! Are you simpering girls?' Through the petrified rush to form lines, his gravel tongue flayed a lummox for sloppy deportment. 'Refasten that helm, you!' Elbowed through the nearest standing row, The Hatchet lambasted another misfortunate. 'What's this? A shambles? Yes, your trum-peter's neglected to announce me by fanfare. Milk-suckers! You're unfit to be nose-led. This is my battle-field, not a parade ground! Yet I don't see a proper dressed weapon among the sorry lot of you!'

Bow-legged and broad as a bristled mastiff, The Hatchet spiked his way past the front ranks. He wrenched the lit torch from the cringing staff sergeant and whipped the flame in a contentious arc. Herded backwards, the diviner scuttled in an arm-waving flap that nearly toppled him on his rump.

'Move aside. Where's my captain? Ah, there, you lame wretch! Get this troop on the move. March them north at the double!'

'North!' yelped the diviner, snatched back from a fall, and self-righteous enough to swerve granite. 'Lordship, you're possessed. The True Sect will never revoke the Light's call to advance against Shadow!'

'Your fussy talent's unfit?' The Hatchet's contempt rang through his slit helm, tilted upwards in withering survey. 'I've more use for a hog's sack of rotten potatoes than your sanctimonious whining.'

The diviner stiffened in mortal affront.

The Hatchet laughed. 'Piss yourself. Here's the real news: the Master of Shadow's slipped past your puling priests.' A scale gauntlet jabbed coastward, where more billowed smoke smudged the horizon. 'The clever bastard set Torwent in flames, then bolted off like a jack-rabbit. If your misbegotten dedi-cates hop quick, we may pin the devil-spawn down before he reaches the river. To stop that disaster, I'll chew holy hide! Can't risk letting the search get bogged down if that quarry holes up in the marsh at the inlet.'

Recoiled, slit-eyed, the diviner engaged his intuitive faculties. His adroit probe raked into The Hatchet's subtle aura, seeking for traces of coercive spells or the suspect pattern of insanity.

But the frothed-up commander refused to keep still. A lightning pivot chased his frocked antagonist backwards again, then forced a drastic, stumbling retreat from an aggressive stride pitched to pulp flesh. 'Report to the head-hunters,' The Hatchet snapped. 'Double quick! If your gift's not useless, then steer their first sweep. Show them which direction their dogs should sniff to quarter this forsaken country.'

To the by-standing captain, The Hatchet barked, 'Are you soused? *I said, move!* Get these slackers away on the jump!'

The jutted helm swivelled back like a wind-vane, slot sockets trained on the diviner. 'Your task, from my mouth: this invasion gets turned face about.' The Hatchet strode off forthwith, still abrasively howling, 'Drop other priorities. The high priests demand that the border gets sealed! Every resource we have regroups to defend Tysan. Woe betide us if you lot fail today since our quarry's the Spinner of Darkness himself!'

To the captain, last words flung off in scorched haste, 'If this dandified ninny gets in your way? Here's my direct order. Tramp over him!'

The by-passed diviner took umbrage. Robes hiked to his skinny knees, he sprang in fixated pursuit. His path crossed four head of fractious horseflesh as the relief team just harnessed swept down at a jog, hitched to the general's war-chariot. The diviner swerved and missed their milling hooves. But not their panting groom, who cannoned into him. Both tripped, entangled. Flung from his desperate grip on the lead, the horse-boy went down, his upset too loud for the flattened diviner to exercise his refined talent.

Meantime, the horse-drawn vehicle rolled past to a deafening clatter of wheels. The honed rims were lethal. Nobody died since the general's daft reinsman sprinted after, at risk of life and limb as he vaulted aboard. Eyes ringed white, braced against the careening sway of the platform, he freed the hitched reins and curbed the runaway vehicle.

'Nice to see one good man on his toes.' The Hatchet sprang within as the rig rumbled past. Above the commotion, through the stamp and plunge as the fresh horses fought the clamped hold on their bits, his ferocity climbed a bilious notch higher. 'That barn's to be fired, your worship? Yes? Shut your yap. I'll do that myself! But not before I see your Sunwheel rump chase the dust kicked up by my troops' brisk withdrawal!'

The diviner shoved off the bothersome groom, whose obsequious apology included limp efforts to blot the splotched muck off his vestments. 'You'll pay for this! I will see such blatant insolence leashed. You'll bow to your true master, brought to your knees before Erdane's high priest!'

But the indignant threat raised no impact, lost in the back-drop of tumult. While the assembled foot ranks marched past, their jangled agitation effectively foiled the diviner's empathic Sight. No temple-trained talent could pierce through that morass, even to target a suspected heretic. The diviner tried anyway. Purpled with effort, he stretched his focus to survey his antagonist, distanced as a toy on the fast-moving chariot. Yet his probe embroiled in yet another outbreak of humiliation and turmoil as The Hatchet upbraided the miserable men detailed to round up the villagers' livestock.

'Leave them *loose*?' a scarlet-faced wrangler howled, shocked. 'But these animals will only strengthen the enemy. Better they're moved on the hoof and corralled to feed our own troops!'

'Not on my watch!' The Hatchet redirected his reinsman, who responded and veered the fresh team through the unwieldy, mixed herd at a gallop.

Bawling cattle stampeded. Startled plough horses bolted. Goats and sheep bleated and scattered. Their terrorized flight battered through the out-bound files of troops, who pelted lest they become trampled. Above the pound of hooves, through shouts of dismay as crazed animals also routed the lancers' neat ranks helter-skelter, the Light's Supreme Commander yelled over the sensible protest of his hag-ridden captain. 'You suggest my supply lines are as ineptly managed as this?'

Under scrutiny again, the chewed officer blanched.

Reassured at speed that *everything* elsewhere remained in smart order, The Hatchet snatched up the team's reins himself. He muscled the splendid four-some onto their hocks and wrung them to a sliding stop. A second spectacular move made them rear. For a hung moment, his whip poised over their quivering backs as they wheeled on their hind legs. Then they settled without mishap.

While the fraught bystanders stared with pent breaths, poised to dodge the next irruptive rampage, The Hatchet bored back into the crest-fallen hostler. 'I'm told our provisions are not under threat. Let those blighted beasts go! This troop's on quick march without use for stragglers. I'll put the next yapping fool to the sword who crosses me with a hindrance.'

Blistered under The Hatchet's evil regard, the disarrayed pack of steel helms coalesced with the speed of clumped mercury. The Light's dedicates vacated the riven village in a whirlwind retreat and left the charred ruins and the slaughtered corpses for the dismal rain to rinse clean.

Only the balked diviner seethed enough to risk a brazen glance backwards. He distrusted the runt officer whose tin-clad abuse had overstepped the arm of temple authority. The diviner maintained his stubborn watch as the Light's sanctified observer. He would not cede his post before he verified the execution canon law had decreed for the tainted captives.

Therefore, he watched the arc of the thrown torch, then the spurt of the flame that ignited the hay-barn's thatched roof. Though the act made The Hatchet's faith seem above question, righteous doubt would not rest. Never, before his sanctified talent divined that the screams of Shadow's condemned minions were genuine. He listened, intent, until the galvanic surge of raw human terror beat the air, ripped into the primal patterns of panic.

'Light's will be done,' he murmured, devout. Then he shielded himself, before the agony of multiple deaths distressed his sensitive faculties. Infallible talent discerned the clear truth: abrasive, insufferable, The Hatchet had not flinched from his honour-bound duty. Shown nothing to prove a liaison with Darkness, the Sunwheel diviner abandoned the pyre, bristled to fury, but satisfied.

No dedicate eyes remained on the scene to bear final witness. For the villagers trapped inside the blazing barn, the inferno that roared through thatch overhead promised death without hope of reprieve. The desiccate air shrieked, roofed over in fire. Smoke billowed. Each thickened breath hurt, until their laboured lungs felt stuffed with hot flannel. Wafted flurries of cinders scorched their nostrils and throats. Their horrified screams shredded reason. Children wailed, while the desperate mothers pried and pounded their fists bloody on the fastened doors.

The nailed planks held firm. Long before the stout timbers succumbed to the fire, living flesh would blister and scorch. Suffocation already threatened survival. Lit crimson and ruby and sulpuhrous orange, the pall deadened the piteous cries of the victims. Poison fumes folded the weakest ones, coughing, when a frigid blanket of darkness clapped down.

Like a nightmare apparition, the phenomenon swathed the rampage of the conflagration. Its arctic breath inflamed skin with a chill to bring frost-bite, and cracked stones in the dry-wall foundation. The shot slivers exploded with whip-crack reports and pings like glass tapped under pressure.

Galvanized beyond panic, the hoarse shrieks of the women and children shrilled to their redoubled terror. None realized the worked veil of shadow descended with intent to spare them. In harrowed dread, nails torn to the quick, they battered and clawed to escape in a bestial frenzy. Few noticed the persistent male voice that exhorted them to stand down. Arrived in the pitch-dark as though sent by an arcane miracle, a stranger caught their hands and touched shoulders, and gentled their hysterical children. His shout pierced through the clamour at last. 'The sorcery that suppresses the heat of the fire was wrought by the hand of a friend!'

'Who are you?' an outspoken woman inquired. 'A True Sect deserter reformed by regret?'

'No,' he responded, stung to offence. 'I'm no temple believer!' He had entered the barn through an overhead window, too high to access with safety. 'You are going to be saved, but not that way!' He added quickly, to forestall a stampede to scale the burning wall, 'We haven't the time! Besides which, the loft tackle's burned through.'

His urgency rallied the desperate mothers, who gathered their hacking children.

'We have to move, quickly.' Choking himself, set at risk alongside them, the valiant stranger ran on, 'Wrought shadow can't clear the smoke, or keep the blazing roof from collapse. I will lead you out! But you must cling to each other. Keep quiet and stay close. If you scatter and run in thoughtless disorder, your escape will draw enemy notice.'

Amid the blind dark, the man gathered the women and their hysterical children. Huddled with them, he urged their groping steps towards the back wall of the barn. The paralyzed and the recalcitrant received his steady encouragement. The easy strength of a farm-hand helped the tottering elders to stand. Punished equally by the unnatural cold, the earnest fellow commanded their trust.

'Rest assured, I won't leave anyone.' He stripped off his cloak, tore the fabric in strips to cover the noses of any who struggled to breathe, then wrapped a shivering child in his jerkin. He steadied the infirm, and chased the last stragglers to the rear entry. There, against the ravenous crackle of flame, and beneath the snap of frost in the black air overhead, the industrious creak of a pry bar disclosed another's fierce effort to break through the nailed panels from the outside.

Then the wide door burst free. Fresh air swirled in, needled with sleet where the dark shroud of sorcery snap-froze the curtain of rainfall. Doubled with coughing, the blistered survivors burst over the threshold and surged towards safety. The fire they fled burgeoned all the faster, fed by the draw of the draught. Live cinders flurried, quenched harmless by shadow. But the groan as tortured wood settled above gave warning the roof timbers already buckled.

'Hurry!' cried the man still inside, held back with the brave who shouldered the need to carry those fallen unconscious. In the hellish scamble to rescue the laggards, no one noticed the fate of the fellow who had broken through the sealed door.

But grey daylight at last unveiled the soot-streaked, tall stranger who defied temple justice to spare the condemned: a muscular crofter with a family man's kindness, and a recent, pink scar on his disfigured nose. 'Keep close,' he instructed. 'The fired barn must mask you until the troop's rear-guard scouts have passed from view down the road.'

'Your friend's gone to make certain?' somebody asked, while a disheveled maid with torn sleeves and freckles stepped up to offer a blanket.

Her loan was refused. The blond stranger tipped his head back and stared upwards: saw, in fact, that the retardant barrier of shadow had parted to nothing and vanished. Carmine flames towered skywards unchecked, a searing inferno that roared in sheets through the skeletal remains of the timbers.

Around the forlorn group, the thick smoke swirled, teased apart by the rush of the updraught. The outlander looked on in haggard dismay, then exclaimed in shocked hurt and betrayal.

For a distinctive armoured chariot had gone, along with all sign of the clever companion left in sole charge of the reins.

Surrounded by refugees distraught with tears, and burdened with clinging children, the stranded stranger stood speechless. Soaked through his shirt by cold rainfall, he watched the fire's frenetic destruction until the hay loft whoosed into collapse and the massive beams tumbled like jackstraws.

'Whose sorcery crafted the darkness that saved us?' a woman with red eyes and singed hair asked at length. 'Was your companion Fellowship-sent? If so, take my word, if you don't know already. An initiate power comes and goes in this world for no man's idea of convenience.'

The blond fellow's distanced stare stayed disconsolate. 'In this case,' he said gruff, 'I provided a reason.' In fact, the galled surety haunted: that the sword in his hand pledged in stubborn defense surely had provoked this brusque quittance. 'But safest for all if I hold my tongue. The person who spared you stays nameless.'

That secret was going to be kept though they pleaded. Beyond doubt, Tarens knew: the prince whose heroics had spared these villagers did not intend to return. One understood why, beyond personal scores. The inherited prompt of a clan chieftain's instincts suggested this parting also arose out of sacrifice. For the sake of a friend beloved like a brother, dead by enemy hands in Daon

Ramon Barrens, Arithon would suffer no other spirit to shoulder the same fatal risk. Neither would an upstart crofter be sanctioned to kill, even in loyal protection to guard the last scion of Rathain's royal lineage.

'Damn your finicky morals,' Tarens swore to himself, chilled to the bone despite the heat billowed off the wrecked barn. The charge laid on him became acidly plain as the drizzle doused the band of dispirited women who mustered to abandon their broken homesteads. Battered, they left their beloved slain where they lay without pause for burial rites. The remnant clan custom died hardest of all, to survive for the sake of the living.

A stout matron bundled in a plaid scarf touched Tarens's arm and returned the jerkin lately stripped to succour her little one. 'For grace, might I ask for your name?'

'Iyat-thos,' he answered on impulse. 'Iyat-thos Tarens.' Town-born, but no longer the dirt-simple crofter, he embraced the fated heritage bestowed by Arithon's former clan liegeman. 'I will be going with you to help.'

Gratitude eased the pinch of grief on the woman's capable features. 'I thank you. But we will not lack for male strength. The Fellowship Sorcerer left us a warning. We sent one strong man from each family away. The rest stayed for blind cover to hide the escape of the most able among us.'

Tarens lost his breath. 'You *knew* those who remained here were going to die?'

Tears fell then, to streak through the soot smudged on the woman's pale cheeks. 'No, though we realized some would be lost. The men and the boys who resisted the war host chose to place themselves in jeopardy. They hoped a quick victory might leave us the village, stripped of provender and livestock. But that plan to cut losses saved nothing at all. No one imagined a temple diviner demanding the murder of innocents.' She gathered up her stained skirt with bruised dignity, then reached fast enough to scoop up a small girl who cried over a sodden, ripped carcass. 'We owe you, Iyat-thos. And your talented friend, whoever he was, since we live by the courage of his worked sorcery. He dared the forbidden against the Light's canon. When you find him, please grant him the honour of thankfulness in our stead.'

Tarens knew where his foremost loyalty lay. But a weeping toddler clung to his leg, tousled and trembling for lack of a father to comfort her. A boy Paolin's age, with the same dimpled chin, flicked stones angrily through the mud-puddles. Hate sustained that one, before sorrow, while other young mothers clutched wailing infants, too overwhelmed to absorb their fresh losses. Small children straggled at their muddied skirts, without shelter or food to sustain them. A girl, perhaps twelve, nursed a bruised cheek, sequined with scabs from the punch of a chain-mail gauntlet. Nearby, a dairymaid nursed her new-born, while another riddled with cinder burns knelt keening, with two toddlers clutched in her bloodied hands. Tarens's heart twisted. On this hour, etched in fire and smoke, human need forced his decision. 'I will stay at hand anyway. Until I'm not needed.'

The upright woman accepted his offer. 'Then help me pull these people together. I'll settle the children. You might number the sick and the injured, and catch what loose stock you can halter to bear them. We must leave this place and flee southward at speed. Our picked men are away to seek Havish's war host and beg for the High King's protection. We dare not rest until we've caught up. No survivor will ever be safe, here.'

The hay-barn would burn to the ground before sundown. Once the coals cooled, the temple would send head-hunters to tally the charred skulls under the ashes. No bones would be found: only tumble-down stones, streaked soot black as the shadow that had spared the wives and the offspring of Torwent's old blood-lines.

Iyat-thos Tarens shouldered the cheerless task of shepherding stragglers through the hardship of a forced march. He comforted youngsters, helped catch scattered horses, and spoke to encourage the elderly and the desolate. He understood the loss of close family too well. His severance from Kerelie cut him to the quick as he grieved for the suffering of the bereaved.

The more unbearable burden stayed silenced, for the friend left alone in the path of two opposed war hosts. Arithon fled with no other protection than The Hatchet's stolen armour and chariot. Tarens wrestled the anguish. He had mishandled the charge bestowed by the shade of a steadfast liegeman. Hag-ridden remorse did not ease the mistake. When Rathain's prince cast off the one stalwart man pledged to stand fast at his back, far more than a defender's true sword had been lost. The summary dismissal had banished the gift of Earl Jieret's memories, as well. Unknowingly, his Grace had cut the vital tie to a past that might cost his life if he failed to remember.

Falls

'I'll wind that meddling sorcerer's guts on a post!' The Hatchet cracks, upright with a blacked eye and contusions, but too late to redress the tumultuous sabotage that upends his battle plan; and the poisonous irony stings, that naught else but his rigorous standard of discipline led his captains to take an imposter's orders without question . . .

Nursed by the kindness of a passing merchant after the spill that collapsed his exhausted horse under him, Lysaer s'Ilessid awakes to a cracked collar-bone, a bashed head, and the far uglier reckoning: that only luck and a timely bout of unconsciousness broke the madness engendered by Desh-thiere's curse . . .

Hours after the blinding, sheet-flash of light that crosses Asandir into Athili, the distressed black stallion his departure leaves masterless buckles into collapse amid the diamond-dust sparkle of bone, once the past site of a grimward; while on the far side of the world, the event makes a dragon at rest open sun yellow eyes, her crest bristled as she rears rampant . . .

XII. Bind

W hile Asandir's relentless passage traversed the proscribed ground at Athili, the convergent events that steered Athera's future also swung the Fellowship's fate in the balance. The flux lines thrummed, strained into excited suspension like a breath withheld past the breaking point. Alone in the world, the Warden at Althain Tower owned the broadscale power to track every subtle connection.

The vast spate of images sparked and flared through Sethvir's earth-linked awareness, parsed into continuous, myriad currents, sourced from the grand chord of the infinite. The onslaught streamed in unabated, although he stood with preoccupied hands, mixing ink at the work trestle inside the scriptorium stores closet. The narrow cranny with its board shelves and limed walls serviced the top-floor library. No lamp burned there, where an errant spark might threaten the trove of artifacts preserved since First Age Year One. The unshuttered arrow-slit overhead pierced the gloom with a blade of ice light, dusty with the exotic mélange of the dried plants and insect wings ground to create the luminous pigments beloved by Paravian archivists. The burnished strength of the wards in that place spared the aged dyestuffs in their muslin sacks from time's pillage of rot.

Human enough to have tucked his large feet into cozy fur buskins, Sethvir rubbed his nose, senses steeped in the ancient perfume of dried flowers and the bite of grain alcohol; *and also* the rimed sweat of a stallion, black coat gritted diamantine white by the bone-shard sand where it lay in the wasteland of Scarpdale.

Asandir's imperative need had left the proud creature in collapse at the site of a banished grimward: where, once, the field Sorcerer had stood fast himself for a loyalty that risked total sacrifice. His unflinching fortitude then had granted the leverage to settle the terrible fury of a drake's unquiet shade. Deadly tumult no longer haunted the site, close by the River Darkshiel's head-waters. The beloved stud suffered without pain in extremis. Soothed into spelled sleep, it dreamed of green meadows under the grace of the Sorcerer's protection.

But no such calm infused the sealed runes of appeal left imprinted like a water-mark in the faltering animal's aura. The obligation invoked the might of a living dragon, whose victory over the past's deranged ghost had been won through the Sorcerer's influence. To draw a drake's notice, quickened or dead, was a desperate measure that invoked chaotic uncertainty.

Sethvir listened for change, while the bellows heave of the stallion's taxed lungs threaded through the thump of his mortar and pestle. The counterpoint rhythm echoed bloodshed and rage, as he powdered the blend of charcoal and oak-galls used for his archival ink.

Sorrow spoke too, as the percussive beat against the granite bowl matched the laboured pulse of the great horse's heart; *and also* entrained to the clack of the looms in the craft shops of Morvain, which fronted the wayside apothecary's shop where Lysaer s'Ilessid winced under the ministration of the bone-setter who strapped up his cracked clavicle. The grind of stone upon stone rang as well for the sorry destruction of trees farther east: there, a woodman's axe split pitch pine for yet another pyre decreed by the temple canon. Sethvir's industry *also* re-echoed contentment in the creak of a cradle, rocked elsewhere to a young mother's lullaby.

The crunch as the Warden pulverized charcoal whispered over the demise of seeds, gnawed with relish by pilfering mice; *and also* rang to the carnage, where men's bones were milled under the wheels of the Light's southbound war-chariots: in Lanshire, The Hatchet's troops wheeled volte-face from their misled retreat. The invasion to rout the Spinner of Darkness from Havish resumed to the dolorous boom of the drums, while priests in costly bullion regalia demanded redress for the Light. Eyes pinched shut, Sethvir mourned: for the horror inflicted on the seasonal landscape, and for the downtrodden bud of spring's growth as more companies of foot spanned the melt-swollen Darkshiel with log bridges and breached the heath on the farther shore. Proscribed ground that Asandir might have defended, had the Teir's'Ffalenn not been the proclaimed cause for the war upon turf demarked as a free-wilds sanctuary.

The day's violent trespass *would* incur a Fellowship reckoning; but not for as long as Arithon's fate stayed entangled.

Sethvir turned the mortar and added more galls. His smudged sleeve cuffs rustled to each purposeful move, while his spidery fingers with short nails rimmed in black resumed the grind of stone upon stone, surly as the growl of thunder in the pause before the summoned storm. Incited by the turmoil of war, or called by the fate of a stallion, the irreversible vortex began, that *also* cried *hope* and *rage!* and *explosive peril!* Sethvir sensed the distanced crack of sail membranes where a dragon's wings and spiked tail vanes sheared through the ice-crystal winds of high altitude. The great drake Seshkrozchiel came, a shot arrow of gold that plumed flame like damascened silk across the indigo zenith. Her swift approach spiked ripples of warning through the weave of unborn probability.

A moment already pregnant with stress seemed unfit to bear the fresh onslaught. Sethvir was not fooled, or complacent, but poised with ferocious expectancy when the enemy play he most dreaded stole through his awareness.

The Koriathain were active, again. Timed for the opportune Fellowship weakness, whatever bold feint they planned this time came drenched in the reek of raw violence.

Sethvir froze, wreathed in a disturbed haze of dust. In the pause that measured what might become the last breath of a dying horse, and on the instant a dragon's wings lifted in flight, the sonorous cry of Athera herself struck a dissonant note through his earth-linked awareness.

The Warden's rapt focus pounced on the source with predatory precision. 'Like wound rot draws jackals, of course!' The vengeful witches sought to refound the mastery of their Great Waystone.

Sethvir braced to pay the reckoning for the long-standing flaw run through his former stay of protection: a troublesome change to the amethyst's matrix imposed by Davien's brilliant, but impulsive, cleverness. Unnoticed for centuries, the small breach posed the loop-hole to strike at the crux of Fellowship interests. The Warden shut his misted turquoise eyes, anguished by the murderous timing.

He made himself breathe; while elsewhere the dragon's outstretched wings descended; an expiring horse sawed through another inhale. Immersed in the stream of the world's flux, unerring, the Warden of Althain plucked the most disagreeable thread from the world's tapestry of causation.

He was armed for the challenge when a blaze of destructive wards obstructed his passage. Though the Koriathain crafted their most rigorous defenses to blind his inbound perception, Sethvir never blinked. Two glaring weaknesses faulted the sisterhood's guarded perimeter. He gained first access through the plume of citrine burned like gold flame into the amethyst Waystone, then anchored his eavesdropping probe through an old fragment of song once spun by the Masterbard: the wrought promise of love, rendered matchless by Arithon to prompt the downfall of Lirenda. Sethvir seized on her active resentment and infiltrated the prison of her indiscriminate hatred.

Fuel for his purpose, he tested the enchantress's implacable passion. Mad as a beast pinned under duress, Lirenda ached to disrupt the entrenched rule of the Matriarch. Her mute desperation welcomed in Sethvir's spying, eager to seize upon any advantage that might disrupt the sigil that shackled her.

Undetectably subtle, her eyes and ears became the Sorcerer's tools by her malicious consent . . .

. . . which perception unveiled the ward-sealed chamber at Highscarp, muffled behind velvet curtains. The miasma of suffering clogged the close air. Shattered wisps of spirit light coiled through the dense odor of expelled excrement. Except for the pallid glow of the lamp that lit the scribed circle consecrated for Selidie's craftwork, no other flame blunted the unnatural cold that emanated from the unveiled Great Waystone. The depths beneath its faceted surface spiked by a glint of dark purple, the amethyst sphere lay cradled in a gold-wire rim on a tripod. The crystal's matrix reverberated yet with the terrified cries of the lately departed: a young girl whose sheeted corpse was being lifted onto a litter by two deaf-mute male servants. Her flesh shuddered still with the seizures that stormed the nerves after violent death.

A third mute in neat livery unbarred the door. Brief daylight sliced in from the outside corridor as her body was removed for disposal.

The bright influx glanced across gold-ribboned, lace cuffs, stitched with beads, where Prime Selidie sat enthroned between two poised female attendants. Her wheat hair was coifed in an elaborate knot, the pins studded with ruby and amethyst. More stony than these, her half-lidded eyes remained fixed on the hooped sphere before her. Devoid of regret, she addressed her right-hand underling. 'Send a replacement. This time, select from the best of our third-rank initiates. Record the names of the candidates below her and have them ready as needed.'

The appointed messenger stepped forward and curtseyed. 'Your will, Matriarch.' Bound to unquestioned obedience, she rose and swept out on her errand.

Lirenda observed every move as a puppet presence. Stifled to a thought, her elated crow packed enough venom to sear even the listening presence of Althain's Warden.

Sethvir repressed his eavesdropper's qualms, while, black-on black silhouettes in their dark robes, a duty-bound ring of Senior enchantresses steadied the Matriarch's secretive conjury. These upheld their duty in absolute quiet.

Except for one fifth-rank, short-sighted enough to voice reservations, or else brave beyond measure to challenge a seated Prime's judgement. 'Dare I suggest that our order cannot benefit from the destruction of more young initiates?'

'We can, and we must,' a crone interjected to derail the foolish impertinence. Carved to skeletal bone by her years of enspelled longevity, only the Eldest Senior held standing to salvage the gaffe without punishment. 'Before your time, my dear, our tradition was different. Koriathain were not forced to scour the gutters for the cast-off remnants of outbred clan talent. Once, parents freely offered their daughters to us for training. We expect to restore this felicitous custom. Thanks to the lane shift induced by Davien's partnership with the dragon, fresh purges decreed by the temple's examiners will condemn those unfortunates opened to their latent gifts. Mothers will send us their threatened children to shelter them from the burnings.'

Prime Selidie added with clipped impatience. 'And Havish, besides, holds the scattered offspring of ten generations of exiled clansfolk. War creates orphans. We'll also glean the green prospects we need in the wake of the True Sect's invasion.'

The door opened. The mute servants returned with the emptied litter, followed by the dispatched Senior and her chosen, a slender, middle-aged woman with eyes as clear grey as her robes. The silver ribbons sewn on her sleeves denoted the third rank in charitable service. Summoned without warning, she shivered in the dire cold thrown off the Waystone. Training alone kept her white face expressionless as she bent in supplication before her superior. 'Your will, Matriarch.'

Selidie wasted no breath on acknowledgement. She extended the horrific, crabbed stub of a finger, touched the subordinate initiate's forehead, and invoked the Prime's master sigil. Without sound, beyond hope of resistance, the woman buckled, dropped into black-out unconsciousness.

'Prepare her as the others!' The Prime tucked her deformed hand in her lap, a vanity that seemed monstrously displaced as her attendant Seniors collected the senseless victim sprawled on the carpet.

They laid her comatose weight on the trestle, and tied her slack limbs with her head aligned underneath the tripod that suspended the cut-crystal sphere. The plume of citrine left by Davien's past trickery glimmered above her closed eyes, while the unspoiled, amethyst facets cast lavender stains across her pale features.

Detached as a porcelain statue, the Prime decreed, 'Proceed with the sacrifice.' Only the Sorcerer's acute awareness detected the masked thrill as she admonished Lirenda. 'No carelessness, this time! A third-rank initiate ought to withstand the strain. Don't let the husk's bodily functions shut down prematurely again.'

No objection was possible although the command involved a cold-blooded murder. Lirenda seethed without recourse. She perched on the wooden stool next to the trestle and laid her ringless, aristocrat's fingers on the strapped victim's solar plexus. Settled into deep trance, she opened an advanced initiate's cross-linked awareness. One by one, she invoked the imperative sigils that reduced the strapped sister to a live shell.

The resentment that flared from the doomed initiate burst into explosive panic. Helpless to withstand the intimate contact, Lirenda endured the ghastly process at first hand as the Prime's imposed will compelled her to violate another woman's most private self. Through memories unfolded like a painted fan, she knew a cosseted childhood with doting parents and lavish comforts. Yet where Lirenda had traded her family ties for power and boundless ambition, this tender child had eloped for the dream of innocent love. Too pampered and pretty, she had been lured from her father's roof by pink pearls, rich clothes, and silk ribbons, an easy mark for the lust of a faithless suitor. When the jilted girl faced the shame of her social ruin, the promise of shelter for charitable service had cozened her into the Koriani order.

Vows of selfless obedience brought her to life's end, pierced through by the Waystone's cruel cold. Implacably shredded by Lirenda's ministrations, but not yet consigned to oblivion, the oppressed spirit struggled to shield the last spark of rebellious will. But an eighth-rank talent outmatched her strength. Slowly, she smothered. The nuances that illumined her character were crushed out, while the Seniors posted beside the Prime's chair watched expressionless and unmoved.

They presumed her personality perished, unremarked in sealed isolation. Except that a Fellowship Sorcerer bore hidden witness to all that transpired . . .

. . . distanced in the closet at Althain Tower, the rhythmic thump of Sethvir's pestle ceased. Charcoal and gall dust plumed like acrid smoke as he met the woman's agonized fate with a shout of purest rage. 'Ath's bright mercy!'

Pacing, the hem of his robe flapping against his fur buskins, he swore with a fury that snarled through the tower's fast silence. Above all things, Sethvir hated the hideous practice of necromancy! The wicked working beneath the Prime's aegis steamed his blood to a boil.

'Of course, the witch has ensconced herself like a blood-sucking spider at Highscarp!'

Town-governed beneath charter-law jurisdiction, there Mankind's acts of free will fell under the purview of crown justice, authority which devolved in this case to the sanctioned Prince of Rathain. Though Fellowship power ever enforced the eradication of necromancy, this woman's sad plight could not be redressed: not without Arithon's direct complicity, and never against her conscious consent, sworn under the sisterhood's oath.

Unless the initiate asked for direct help, Sethvir could do nothing! Only weep, as the vile progression of sigils ripped her vibrant awareness to a mindless husk. The Sorcerer recognized the destructive construct. This twisted variant sprang from a ritual stolen by force from the Biedar. He had seen Elaira shape the same invocation in its undefiled form once before, when, by free consent, Glendien's form had conceived a doomed daughter to Arithon s'Ffalenn.

Yet this moment's forged ciphers created no act of free partnership. Instead, flesh became an animate glove for Lirenda to use as a surrogate. Prime Selidie distanced herself from the weave until the last ripple of trauma was silenced.

Sethvir blotted sweat from his furrowed brow, beyond troubled as the bent of Selidie's dark practice resumed. While the Waystone's citrine inclusion provided a secure foothold for entry, the Matriarch guided the procedure from outside, shielded behind Lirenda's trained knowledge, and secure from hazard should aught go amiss.

Lirenda threaded a cautious tendril of awareness through the initiate's body. Slowly, her cautious probe unreeled into the altered Waystone. Deeper, where the citrine plume thinned, the chorus of demented voices inside stirred awake to the stealthy intrusion.

Sethvir shivered, arms crossed at his breast. Even the nerve of a Fellowship Sorcerer shrank from the malice that lurked in the great crystal's lattice. But coerced under Selidie's intemperate need, Lirenda had no other choice. Now engaged, her own spirit stood at grave risk of becoming devoured. Her taut face dripped sweat as the jewel's morass of hostile consciousness jockeyed to seize control. Jabbed in vicious assault, the inert initiate set up as proxy whimpered and jerked. Her twitches built into raked shudders until her back arched against the restraints. Tasked by Selidie's prompt, Lirenda laid down protective ciphers to deflect the incessant barrage. Since the amethyst's fractured alignment presented an unrecognizable pattern, she trod the razor's edge of dire peril. A circle of ranked Seniors stayed poised for intervention should the effort to remaster the fractious focus stone go irretrievably wrong.

No groundless fear, Sethvir knew, prickled to foreboding while the tissue-thin veils of unbirthed possibility spun off the shadows of sinister futures. Always, the Waystone's restive nature posed danger, even when wielded under the hand of a fully initiate Prime. Too many millennia of subjugate service had clogged the matrix with ancient records. Beside the uncleared detritus of old spells and the imprinted memories of former Primes, the jewel's bleak depths also seethed with the wrack of failed candidates for the Matriarch's seat. Broken under the vicious trial to subdue the amethyst's attributes, most of them lingered, consumed by ferocious hatred. Offered an opening after exhaustive centuries of insane confinement, their trapped spirits mobbed the body of the subsumed woman, until her possessed flesh writhed and moaned to their tormented cries. As their grisly gambit, she existed only to waylay their unleashed malevolence.

Sethvir distanced his vision. He need not remain: already the smoke haze of probabilities coalesced to reveal the outcome. The Prime would seize her dauntless triumph with time, her victory reliant upon the doomed strengths of the culls she selected to serve. Until death, one by one, they would absorb the toxic dross from the Waystone's turbulent core. The map of the stone's altered matrix would be reconfigured in innocent blood.

The moment Selidie tamed the jewel's skewed focus, she would discover the change long since noted by Sethvir's earth-sense: that the disastrous shift in the jewel's main axis also altered the innate signature of the crystal's identity. The former pattern, once evoked by the Fellowship, no longer enabled Athera's resistance to dire spellcraft spun through the Waystone's matrix. The vital stay would no longer be recognized, which forepromised the Prime's fullest use of her power as an unbridled force in the world, once again.

'Davien's ghastly turn of invention had to backfire into our laps!' Sethvir groused. The pitfall unreeled, pitched to yawn underfoot.

Selidie's crippling strike at Fellowship interests loomed from possible, to probable, ever nearer to headlong collision, until the interstices shone like fixed nails snagged through the unwritten future. If Arithon's inventive use of wrought shadow had balked the Prime's bid at Torwent, Sethvir's prescience measured the on-coming crisis that darkened Arithon's destiny. Peril gathered with each step he took, until the grim nexus contorted through Lanshire acquired the ink-and-lightning lour of a thunder-cloud.

For the critical breach had smashed the weave of Teylia's stop-gap protection: Rathain's threatened prince recalled too much to blind his identity from the Prime's scryers. Fatally, Arithon knew too little yet to fight back in aware self-defense. His flight would stay harried by vicious pursuit, caught as he was between the poised jaws of two hostile war hosts.

Armed with the enabled Great Waystone, in a week, or a fortnight, or a month, the Koriani Matriarch would renew the bid to take down her choice prey.

'Like flies to a dung-heap, we're plagued!' Sethvir snarled.

He whirled, wrenched open the store-closet door, and charged through the ink-powder puffed from his robes in his haste to mount the narrow stair. Emerged into daylight in the top-floor library, the Sorcerer stalked to the stone table. He removed the piled books. A sweep of his forearm raked aside the detritus of frayed ribbon markers and quill pens. Stray manuscript pages fluttered to the floor as he cleared the wrought-iron brazier that centred the obsidian slab. His Warden's permission focused the flux lines that crossed in convergency through Althain Tower and ignited the fire-pan. Pure light without fuel shone like a star, blue-white and piercingly blinding . . .

. . . while through his earth-linked awareness, Sethvir sensed the distanced thrum on the world's winds, as the webbed sails of a dragon's wings drove its sleek body in hurtling flight; while the beat of a black stallion's heart clenched and faltered; to the raced tattoo, elsewhere, as a deer's cloven hooves crossed the trail of three young clan-born fugitives. Which spontaneous event caused a head-hunter's hounds to swerve from their course and run riot. More hooves drummed the ground: horses this time, as the pack's outriders spurred ahead to whip the dogs off and recover the abandoned scent: a precious lead gained for the audacious children who carried the black sword, Alithiel . . .

. . . as Sethvir shaped his singular will and snagged the stream of the flux. The summons he fashioned at Althain Tower arced outward and vaulted the lightless, bleak void between stars . . .

* * *

The urgent call rang all the way through to Marak. There, two discorporate colleagues took pause from the labour of healing the fissures that damaged a distant planet's etheric web.

An inveterate prankster, Kharadmon was quickest with a tart remonstrance. 'Didn't I say that Prime Selidie has the persistence of a rooting tapeworm? I'd forfeit my staked prize straightaway if your wind-bag shade could be gagged into permanent silence.'

'You'd ruin your days,' Luhaine snapped back, 'or fade moping from boredom with no by-play for your livid insults.'

'Dharkaron Avenge! A dolt might agree.' Kharadmon's snort whirled a dust-devil out of a stony, dry gulch as his disengaged essence coalesced for return to Athera. 'Forbearance on my part has lulled your wits to complacent senility.'

Luhaine deferred the ripe gambit. Single-minded perfectionist, he double-capped the last ciphers, which fussy precaution as ever allowed his mercurial colleague the lead. But the point was contested with bull-dog persistence the instant he moved to catch up. 'Your wager's not honestly won, yet, besides. The Prime has not harnessed the Waystone's might, fully. Before you gloat like a fox prematurely, I posit she'll stage her catastrophe to lay us low after the solstice.'

'Pessimist!' The dust gyre unravelled, fanned to a hazed cloud upon Kharadmon's abrupt departure.

Luhaine's more staid exit bored through and left a punched smoke-ring adrift above the baked earth. 'Arrogant flit!' he huffed in grumpy pursuit. 'When I claim the victory, be sure I'll embrace the boulder's staid wisdom and blunt the knife's edge from your insolence.'

Sethvir resigned himself to withstand the tumultuous disruption of his solitude at Althain Tower. The fretful fingers that massaged his temples snagged in white tangles of hair. Nudged to redress his neglected grooming, he uttered a charged word to loosen old knots, then considered his frayed, ink-stained sleeves, and dismissed the pointless bother of changing to formal dress.

While the tramp of the True Sect invasion pounded the spring earth to mud in pursuit of the Spinner of Darkness, and Havish's clan war bands plotted their High King's line of defense at Carithwyr, the dragon's flight crossed the meridian between Athera's east and west hemispheres . . .

Sethvir wrested his grim consolation from the battery of future threats: the great drake bound at speed to the wastes of Scarpdale would not *yet* encounter the fatal glory of Arithon's aura, intact.

Since that sore point posed a back-handed blessing, Althain's Warden muttered an expletive and boxed up his better quill pens. He cursed again for the corks mislaid from his ink-wells, then stacked his loose parchment sheets under weights and whisked off the litter of shavings strewn by his compulsive habit of resharpening nibs. Everything must be tidied. Not just to spread the black cloth for the casting of strands for a long-sighted augury: on good days, Kharadmon's tempestuous arrivals wrought chaos and worse, drove Luhaine's obsession for neatness to dithering fits.

'The spat between shades will curl both my ears anyhow.' Sethvir clapped a clay jar overtop the wheat paste, frazzled enough to rip hair from his beard as *another* hitch rocked the world's befouled affairs from a dingy inn cellar by the Mathorn Road . . .

The last nameless madman could not be salvaged despite Dakar's heroic effort. The stricken fellow screamed and frothed at the mouth, then lapsed into a rigid silence. Daliana wrapped his contorted frame in dry blankets. Nothing more could be done for the lunatic except keep him comfortable until he passed over Fate's Wheel. Since the depleted spellbinder slept off his exhaustion as though he had been kicked unconscious, Daliana weathered that vigil alone. While the tormented stranger's crazed eyes stared at nothing, she talked soothing nonsense. Whether or not the old man found ease, her voice at least masked the rustles and squeaks of the inn's brazen rats.

Miserable and gritty in her unwashed clothes, with her braided hair snarled for want of a comb, she counted two days since Lysaer had abandoned them. Held yet in duress, she and the Mad Prophet had been without food since the past morning. The slop pail left by the stair for disposal also remained uncollected. Which pervasive reek stained the cellar's already noisome miasma, the flint smell of damp masonry mouldered to decay by the soured hops breathed from the tapped-out beer kegs.

Daliana checked the comatose grandfather's limp wrist, found his weak pulse, and caught herself nodding off. Unable to finish the death-watch, she rousted Dakar to spell her.

His sawn-off snore transformed to a grunt. 'Go away. No more can be done.'

'Best think of something before the loon croaks,' Daliana insisted. 'Else we'll be condemned for dark practice.'

'I'm no substitute for a Fellowship Sorcerer,' the Mad Prophet objected, distempered as a hazed walrus. 'Quite likely the old coot has chosen his time. I can't hold any spirit that's wearied of life. Such a working would invoke the vile arts of necromancy, an offence that would justifiably see us staked out for the sword and the fire.'

But despite his complaint, the spellbinder sat up. He knuckled the sand from his pouched eyes and relented enough to arise. Wasted to dough pallor from grueling days spent in trance for the stricken, he grumbled, 'No more water's left?'

Daliana sighed. 'You drank the dregs yesterday.'

'No matter. We won't have the chance to perish of thirst.' Dakar parked his rump upon the sagged bench that cradled the pumice wheel for sharpening knives. 'I'd bet my last copper that our poxy gaolers have swanked off to stack oiled kindling.'

'Well, curse them with crotch rot if you have the means.' Daliana yawned and curled up in the nest of stale straw begrudgingly sent from the stables to succour the stricken. She slept through the victim's last fit of convulsions, and missed his collapse when he finally expired in the nadir of night.

The slam of the hatch at the stair-head awoke her at dawn on their third day of incarceration. She pushed herself upright, made aware of the tormented creature's demise by the shouted argument between Dakar and the innkeeper's burly oafs. Offered no pay for the filthy service, they refused to collect the stiff corpse.

'Yon Shadow-touched body rots where it lies. As for you heretic maggots, you can sup on dead flesh if you're hungry!'

The board stair creaked under Dakar's weighty tread. 'What loutish seed quickened the wombs of your mothers? Even worm spawn has brighter intelligence!' Through the outraged roars provoked by his insult, Dakar rolled off a curse in actualized Paravian, guttural as thunder and brimstone.

A blinding flash flared off the trap-door, to yelps of dismay from above.

Daliana blinked, dazzled, her snarled hair ruffled by the blast of hot air unleashed in recoil. 'What have you done?'

'Set a boundary ward that's seized up the hinge pins with just enough sting to raise blisters,' Dakar said with self-satisfied spite. 'I have a more difficult working to do. Can't let some bungler waving a knife venture down here to mince us to collops.'

'We were certain to burn without evidence, anyway,' Daliana agreed, irked to sarcasm.

Unmoved by the subsequent thudded barrage as the inn's pair of clods bludgeoned the planks and failed to achieve a forced entry, Dakar laced pudgy hands on his gut and reseated himself on the bottom step. 'No way those arse-kissing temple fanatics intended to let us go free. We're condemned for criminal sorcery, no matter whether I produced miracles and salvaged everyone stricken.'

As the banging assault on the hatch overhead showered down gauze shreds of cobweb, Dakar laughed. 'Go ahead! Belt yourself full of splinters, you fools.'

'Light torment your dismal shade for eternity!' came the incensed rejoinder. 'I'll see the chit you brought forced till she squeals, and dump her cursed ashes with yours in the hog wallow!'

'May your innkeeper waken with asps in his bed!' Dakar howled in cheerful rejoinder. 'You can hatch eggs on your piles of fire-wood and grovel in prayer to the Light till your knees hurt! But no mumbling piety will lift the blight that sours the beer as it crosses this threshold. No priestly blessing can salvage the roasts that char black as Sithaer's ninth hell on the kitchen spit.'

Daliana raised her eyebrows. 'You wouldn't!'

'Saddle this sty with a curse of misfortune?' The spellbinder's raffish beard split to show teeth. 'In case you slept through the interesting news, these gutless yappers decided to toss our fates to the temple delegation just banished for fraud at Etarra.' Dakar routed a spider that dropped onto his scalp and flipped an obscene gesture towards the task squad assaulting the cellar. 'What's to lose? You heard what they've left us for breakfast.'

Daliana arose, goaded by frustration. 'I won't sit on my backside waiting to burn. If you plan to spring us, how can I help?' Afoot in the cold dark, she salvaged the snapped broom-handle, discarded since she had chafed her hands raw in failed effort to wrest open the root-cellar's outside entrance. 'I could bash a few heads with this.'

Dakar clamped her shoulder, arrived from behind, and nearly startled her out of her skin.

Despite the semblance of a fat buffoon, he moved with uncanny stealth if need warranted. 'Instead, pulverize some mortar for me, and be sure to make plenty of racket.'

'For false cover?' Daliana sought to read his expression by the filtered light through the floor cracks.

Dakar ducked her regard in shameless retreat. 'I am planning to spiritwalk. Any such use of my talent is hell-bound to excite every Sunwheel diviner in range. The clamour will bring the Light's priest at a gallop. We could face resistance at dangerous strength, since the temple's false cause is now covertly backed by a gamut of enemy interests.'

'What enemies?' Daliana slapped the broomstick against her raw palm. 'Like a skin rash, you pick the most awkward moment to spring your surprises.'

Dakar's clipped head-shake cut off further inquiry. 'Ath on earth, it's bad business. I was hoping for luck, that events might not push me to take extreme action.'

Daliana narrowed shrewd eyes. 'Does this suggest I should worry more for those simpletons above stairs?'

'They're not threatened, yet,' the spellbinder evaded, scarcely audible over the clamour to stave in the warded trap-door.

'What happens when those bullies start tearing up floor planks?' Daliana inquired. 'I could break up a cask. Ding a few heads with the staves, even trip the first sally by rolling the barrel hoops. That won't stop a mob. Every whoreson's bruised friend will be hot to tear us apart without the formality of a ceremony.'

When Dakar clamped his jaws and stumped off through the dark, Daliana pursued with more questions. 'You realize if you harm these yokels through spellcraft, you'll spur on the witch-hunt to burn us?'

'These people are more likely to drop like flies from eating a plate of bad shellfish!' Dakar snapped. 'Daelion Fatemaster revels in the irony. Nobody survives. We all die at life's end from something.'

But Daliana chased her stubborn point all the same. 'Do you still plan to stand guard for Lysaer? Then your tactical choice is fatally flawed. If anyone's hurt by your arcane works, you know his royal justice won't rest! My lord will not only repudiate us, he'll be moved to defend your wronged victims. You've said Desh-thiere's curse will align to exploit even the traits of good character. If you force the virtue of Lysaer's blood gift, that surely would twist his strengths to embrace the True Sect's agenda.'

Dakar hesitated under the speared shaft of light, struck down through an overhead knot-hole. 'You're quite right, of course.' His anxious glance backwards showed eyes ringed with white. 'But don't jump to conclusions. I've never seen the straightforward scrying that ruffled a hair upon anyone's head.'

A loud, grating slide from above, and a puffed fall of dust suggested a heavier ram being dragged towards the cellar stair-head.

The Mad Prophet sneezed. Finally exasperated, he denounced, 'I would send out a probe seeking a safe course to run, before broaching the need to defend ourselves.'

Which pat claim raised Daliana's jaundiced distrust. While Dakar retrieved his crumpled cloak and cocooned himself beside the worn frame of a linen press, she grumbled, 'Why don't I believe you're telling the whole truth?'

But the Mad Prophet had already sunk into deep trance, unkempt as a discarded rag pile. Scapegrace though he seemed, and artlessly prone to clownish histrionics, the milksop had trained under Fellowship Sorcerers. Since her best revenge was a noisy diversion, Daliana vented her blaze of annoyance on the mortar that clenched the cellar's foundation-stones.

An indeterminate interval later, Dakar grunted, jabbed awake by a poke in the ribs. 'Fall over and die of the pestilent pox,' he muttered, thick-tongued and muzzy.

But the ignoramus who disrupted him only assaulted his midsection harder. 'Wake up!'

He coughed, wiped a trickle of drool from his lips, and peered upwards, disoriented. Vision wrenched double by mage-wakened faculties noted the elfin face that loomed over him: Daliana angled her stubbed length of broomstick for the next dig at his person.

'Put that down,' he suggested. 'Leave me in peace. If you won't back off, don't brain me for the mess when I throw up on your ankles.'

Not threatened one bit, Daliana reached down and grappled his wrist, then tugged until he sat upright. 'What's just happened?'

Dakar swallowed back nausea. Hunched in wait for his jolted senses to settle, he became aware of a yelling disturbance outside. The cause, spelled out in shrill screams and hysteria, inspired a vengeful, smug grin. 'Listen. You'll hear.'

Daliana dropped the broom-handle. 'Ath's glory! Don't tell me. A *dragon* has lit on the tavern roof?'

Dakar coughed, apprehensive. 'Oh, yes.' Uncertain just how his dispatched marker had managed to draw such stupendous notice, he chewed his lip and queasily welcomed the outrageous turn of events. 'We should make our break now while the innkeeper's louts are too terrified to give chase.'

Yet the opportune chance fell into eclipse. Opposite the besieged stairway, the barred planks of the root-cellar's outside door rippled like sheet-cloth and vanished. An aggressive form strode through the astonishing breach. Etched against the blinding influx of daylight, the tall male figure had wind-tousled reddish grey locks, tumbled over trim shoulders. His jet-black cloak glittered with thread-silver embroidery that flickered like discharged static. Then the opaque wooden door reappeared and quenched his arrival in gloom.

Quick footsteps approached through the cellar's cached junk, surely graced by a Sorcerer's faculties. Attentive as a raptor besides, the stranger spoke quickly to disarm Daliana's stupefied panic.

'Dragons can dream past material boundaries. The trait is unsafe, and volatile to any expressive emotion. Take my fair warning and curb your dismay.'

Dakar shivered, wrung to trepidation by the bold visitation's identity. 'Davien! Motherless chaos and Dharkaron's bollocks! What ruinous misplay brings you here?'

'Seshkrozchiel was famished,' the Sorcerer declared without guile.

From outside, a sudden, shattering *crunch!* suggested a roof-beam mightily crushed to flinders. The king-post likely suffered such damage as well, since a hundredweight fall of slate shingles clattered like flung knives into the root-cellar stairwell.

Dakar said, alarmed, 'That racket would be the dragon, shredding the innkeeper's property in search of fresh meat?'

Davien laughed. 'Didn't Sethvir hear you swear aloud that you wished this tavern razed flat? I did my part with the pointed suggestion that two relief draught teams for the coach route to Narms are sure to be stabled on the premises.'

'Ath wept!' Dakar seized a double handful of his ginger beard and tugged in distraught trepidation. 'I hope you can stem the rip tide of disaster.'

'Bid the free will of an ancient drake?' Davien's insouciant shrug was a whisper of velvet and wool in the darkness. 'Might as well strive to leash the wild lightning, and your soured opinion does not even signify. Seshkrozchiel's taken a dislike to this inn. Since it reeks of imprisonment, she's inclined to burn the place to the ground. Need I add that we haven't much time?'

Dakar said, thinly stretched, 'We were coping without interference on quite *this* order of magnitude.'

The gleam through the knot-hole lit Davien's raised brows. 'Sethvir thought

438

as much, also, until he cast strands and found the worst probabilities already convergent. I came to inform you. Lysaer's case is hopeless.'

'You can't mean he's predestined to fail!' Daliana cried out in anguish.

The Sorcerer's night-shade black eyes pinned her under his nerveless survey, from the brown hair wisped from her neglected braid to the dust smears that marred her smooth cheek. 'The unflinching truth? My dear, your s'Ilessid liege is accursed by the Mistwraith. Against the best of his noble intentions, his natural will is impaired. He cannot do other than crumple once the speed of events overtakes him.'

Dakar broke in more gently, 'The pressure of the geas is cumulative. Each time Lysaer's half brother invokes Shadow, the redoubled effect plays against him.'

Davien quashed the outside hope of reprieve. 'On a battle-field fashioned as a baited trap, Arithon shall be relentlessly driven to wield his born talent just to survive. Lysaer's been pressured into pursuit. Reason won't turn him, it's useless to try. He'll destroy whatever obstructs him.'

'Then you've come to bestow the short list of bad options?' Beyond testy, Dakar winced to acknowledge the full price of his bitter mistake. No Sorcerer's power under charter law could rout the True Sect's invasion. Asandir's oath of nonintervention bound Fellowship hands for as long as Prince Arithon's presence incited the Lanshire campaign.

'Does the irony sting?' Davien goaded, clipped to restlessness as the spellbinder's lagged reason slogged through the trajectory of current events. 'That's why the battle-line to defend Havish must be drawn farther south.'

'At the verge of the free wilds of Carithwyr?' Dakar grasped the appalling dilemma at last. 'Then this is not about Arithon's fate, but concern that the Fellowship might have to take Lysaer's life to salvage the compact?'

'A triumph for the Koriathain,' Davien agreed, snide enough to derail the backlash of histrionic dismay. 'Seshkrozchiel's bound on to Scarpdale to answer her gratitude to Asandir. She will burn this tavern and feed upon any scorched carcasses snagged in the rubble. You can flee now and risk the stacked odds of recapture. Or you could take the more perilous dare and step into the dragon's true dreaming.'

Dakar gaped, shocked beyond speech.

'She will absorb your being,' the Sorcerer warned. Without pause to describe the dread scope of that peril, he qualified, 'But replete with six horses, Seshkrozchiel will drowse. A filled belly often quiets the speed of her faculties.'

This time, pure panic spurred Dakar's conclusion. 'You gamble with fate, that we'd emerge aligned to the destiny nearest to our true desire?'

'Chance favours that outcome,' Davien agreed. 'But, of course, my conjecture holds no guarantee.'

Dakar's nape bristled. He drew breath to refuse.

Except Daliana chose first. 'I'll go.' She pushed past the spellbinder's prudent restraint, ignorant that this Sorcerer's sly provocations were not to be trusted. 'No way else can I reach Lysaer's side in time to make any difference.'

Perhaps Davien regretted her brash courage since he added a strict admonishment. 'How well can you hold your intent in clear focus?'

'Don't let him cozen you!' Dakar shouted. Savage anger raised his gorge and near choked him, that once such feckless wiles had inveigled Arithon s'Ffalenn to attempt a near-ruinous ploy against a cult of black necromancers.

'I believe in myself,' Daliana corrected, stubbornly deaf to sound counsel. 'What have I to lose? As things stand, I'm most likely to get charred to a crisp. Done by Lysaer's hand, the outcome might scar him enough to check Desh-thiere's curse through remorse. But a death on the scaffold to sate True Sect fanatics would make my whole life an act of futility.'

By then any further debate became moot. Seshkrozchiel's roar of challenge hammered the air. A swipe of her armoured tail peeled away what remained of the tavern roof, timber splintered from stone like tossed jackstraws. As her baleful fire sheared into the rubble upstairs, the floor-boards overhead smouldered and smoked. The whoosh of live cinders forced in on the downdraught threatened the stacks of dry ale casks.

'I did caution you against excessive emotion,' Davien chided. His sardonic amusement struck too suave a note as tongues of bright flame licked the length of the beams, and a clay jar of lamp oil exploded above them. 'Take my hands,' he invited, 'or burn where you stand.'

Dakar suspected the ruthless crux stemmed from a wily plot engineered from the outset. 'Don't imagine that goading me into a corner can haze me to stand to Prince Arithon's defense!' Death itself could not make him shoulder *that* dreaded confrontation.

The Sorcerer also renowned for betrayal laughed in the teeth of the spellbinder's cowardice. 'On that count, you might buy a desperate reprieve. Unless you prefer the Fatemaster's applause past the Wheel for bullheaded stubbornness?'

Yet where Daliana accepted Davien's offered clasp without blinking, Dakar dug in his heels.

His shirt and jerkin were starting to singe before he bowed to necessity and unfolded his arms to take Davien's poisoned offer. Both mage-trained and Sighted, the spellbinder perceived the moment through split awareness as his destined fate parted from Daliana's. She placed herself under Davien's purview, then buckled at the knees, dropped unconscious into the trickster Sorcerer's embrace; while in doubled vision, *at the same moment*, Dakar also grasped the Sorcerer's empty, lean fingers, extended only for him. Reluctant, he clamped hold with sweaty palms and gave over his human survival.

Before immolation by fire boiled the blood in his veins, the rainbow shimmer of the dragon's dream drew all that he was, and ever would be, into terrifying dissolution. He drifted without substance. Then nameless forces beyond his control hooked the mote of his being into a gyre. He tumbled, spinning, then plummeted through a golden, slit eye that blazed like the core of the sun.

He burned then, thought and spirit torched into a flash-point explosion that seared with the endless cold of primordial night.

Starless dark became a stallion's jet coat, sweat-caked and salted with the pulverized bone that remained of a drake skull. Swept into the storm of Seshkrozchiel's dreaming, the unmoored fleck of selfhood that bore the Name *Dakar* exulted to the wild, whiplash crackle as the dragon's auric field flared into a scintillant blaze of azure flame. He knew the thunder of wind in her wings and the ecstatic roar that shook earth and sky at the glory of her last mating. He sensed time wrenched still and thrilled to the unknowable song of infinite creation. Then in the wracked flesh of the dying, black horse, he became a heart-beat that stopped, paused, then resumed, hurled into explosive rebirth as the warp thread of the stallion's true being laced through the bright weft of Seshkrozchiel's making. In the diamantine dust that marked a past grimward, the stud did not breathe his last, but raised its proud crest, shook out its mane, extended strong forelegs, and stood.

No longer the same animal, foaled out of a drifter's best mare, by a sire with a silver, ghost eye: the refigured equine that snorted with joyous life wore the stamped likeness of his distant forebear, Isfarenn. Restored by drake magic, that *also* had forged seven human men into the mages who comprised the Fellowship, what rose and galloped on four legs in Scarpdale was a fit Sorcerer's mount, flesh and blood, but no longer mortal.

Then the drum-roll of the horse's hooves faded. *Nothing* became *something* with a dizzying rush that wrung every jangled nerve end. Dakar came back to himself and struck solid ground with a painful thump. Retching, he beheld the focal pattern of a great circle, still ablaze with the fountained sparks of an activated, dawn flux tide.

Without breakfast, his wracked gut contained nothing to heave.

But his upended senses still captured the distanced mockery of Davien's last words. 'Your cold fury, as usual, is badly misplaced. For this trump, try blaming Sethvir.'

Once Dakar recouped his scrambled faculties, he recognized the eerie, patterned spirals salted into the pillars of upright marble that marked the four cardinal points at Fiaduwynne. The Paravian site lay on the north bank of the river that flowed westward out of Lithmarin at the northern verge of Carithwyr. Apparently his adamant avoidance of Arithon's plight had delivered the chance to defuse Desh-thiere's curse at the front line of the High King of Havish's defense.

Derogation

Abed and dosed on valerian to sleep through the ache of his broken collar-bone, Lysaer s'Ilessid missed the commotion arisen downstairs in the wayside inn's common-room when the forward young woman tramped in from the road before dawn. Arrived unkempt and cold, and apparently starving, she carried no coin. Since she had no possessions worth selling, she issued a challenge to the loud-mouthed detractors who jeered at her claim to respectability.

The greasy, spaniel-faced man at the beer tap was disinclined to bestow charity. 'Don't know your way whoring, fat Rosie upstairs might let you wrestle her for a mattress!'

'I'd pay to see that!' a coarse fellow in a driver's cape roared, to interested hoots from the roisterers on the side-lines.

'Eight silvers on Rosie, pot winner tups all!' someone ventured, to sniggers and laughter.

Through the catcalls, the obscene gestures, and noisy encouragement, the young woman marched straight on through the randy crowd. She jabbed anyone who snatched for a pinch with sharp elbows, then cracked her gloved palm flat on the bar top and confronted the sly winks and the leers, quite fearless. 'My stakes, at darts. The high point winner names the prize of choice.'

'For your tiger's eyes on me? Anything, sweet!' A beefy road master swaggered to the forefront, eager to seize the advantage. 'Darts it is, girl, and we'll see in a trice which pretty target gets pricked!' Amid rowdy applause, he bowed to the men, then invited their salacious bets. 'Let's lay coin on how fast I'll claim the chit's favour between the blankets!'

He lost instead, a fat purse of coin far beyond the night price of a trollop. When the minx took a seat with her crafty gains, she ordered a hot meal. The injured demand for a rematch earned the plaintiff an eating fork, snatched from the trestle and thrown past his ear. The prongs skewered the target behind him dead centre.

'Did you think my prowess was an accident, then?' the woman demanded between ravenous bites. All but overmatched by the yells from the pack of sour losers, she understood when to stage a hurried retreat. That quickly, she claimed an outrider's horse to clinch her ill-gotten take from the deflated road master. His loose change bought the second-best cloak and spare clothing from one of the stableman's moping boy grooms. Then the chit retired upstairs straightaway, which left her avid admirers in the tap-room abandoned to grumbling boredom.

By the hour past daybreak the fleeced road master left, along with his raucous cronies and most of the dispatch couriers. Rosie's wenches retired. The innkeeper's goodwife took over the beer tap, backed by her huge arm and a massive iron skillet. She had her drudges scrubbing the trestles and the mullioned casements cracked open to air when Lysaer at last rose and clumsily dressed himself. While he sat down to a tray of crisp bacon and warm buttered bread, and tackled his breakfast one-handed, the female sensation upstairs spent three more coppers for a hot bath, a bone comb, and a boot-lace to tie her wet braid. She slipped out the back way through the servants' door. Therefore when his Lordship of Etarra emerged, brisk, and accosted the stableman for a post-horse to resume his urgent ride southward, he failed to recognize the pert fellow who steadied his nag's bridle to help him astride. Not until that sensible person announced the intent to stay on as his volunteer retinue.

His irritable rejection met with rebuff. 'Who will fetch and carry for you on the road? And tend to your mount since you're injured?'

The rough cloak did not obscure the fact that the form underneath was no boy's. 'I know you,' warned Lysaer, prelude to a lecture fit to curl toes for the gall of unwanted female presumption.

'You don't,' Daliana contradicted. Over the grind of coach-wheels and the chatter of the red-cheeked boys dispatched to harness the draught team, she added, 'You knew someone called Talith. Not me.' Face upturned, her rushed breath a puffed cloud in the chill air between them, she stood her ground upon cobbles slurried with early-spring mud. 'The moment we're private, I'll ask why Dakar invoked that name to unbalance you.'

The bustle as the morning passengers debarked in the yard magnified Lysaer's stark embarrassment. He withstood the shock, beyond astonished, though as ever his suave statesman's reflex masked the visceral depth of his upset. 'You don't know the half of this!'

Beneath the tatty hood of the groom's cloak, Daliana's pink lips curled into a piquant smile. 'Then tell me the rest.'

Lysaer's manner hardened. 'Now, you trespass. My answer's not free for the asking.' Whiplashed to anger, he set his caked boot-sole into Daliana's laced hands and transferred his weight without mercy. Once in the saddle, he gathered his reins left-handed and dug in his spurs with a vengeance. His roan mare clattered across the crowded yard, with barn cats and grooms and luggage boys scattered helter-skelter to avoid being mown down.

Daliana scrambled onto the commandeered outrider's horse and gave chase. The fit animal exploded forward before she thought to adjust the tack's leathers to suit her feminine frame. No horsewoman, she grabbed a fistful of mane, one awkward leg barely hooked over the saddle-bow. As the fresh animal thundered down the road at a reckless gallop, she held on with a death grip, swearing.

The fettlesome horse overtook Lysaer's lead. Daliana's snatched glimpse of his fair, reddened face verified his stormy suspicion: that her back-handed bribe on the sly to the stableman had assigned him a pig-lazy mare. That request had been met with earnest propriety, since the gentleman whose high fettle needed to be curbed carried one arm in a sling. Though hard-pressed by his spurs, the roan flattened her mulish ears, shook her head, and refused to extend her lumbering stride. The outrider's bay proved her ferocious opposite. It seized the bit, quickened pace, and snaked past a trundling wagon. The swerve shot Daliana's foot through the stirrup. The dangling iron wedged fast on her ankle.

'Dharkaron Avenger's Black Nuisance!' she cursed, sliding another precarious notch towards disaster. She clung, white-knuckled. If she fell, Lysaer would seize the unfair advantage. She had not bested the louts in the tap-room only to get ditched off a horse by her fumbling ineptitude. The worse for her hair-rising predicament, the brute tried a buck to dislodge her unseated weight.

'Ath wept! Not again!' Daliana howled through gritted teeth. She would *not* strand herself on the road in a flea-bitten groom's noxious clothing.

Engrossed in her struggle, she failed to hear the crack of the rein ends Lysaer used to whip on the indolent roan at her back. His sheer determination belaboured the beast through a prodigious dash to overtake her.

'Damnfool woman,' he yelled. Arrogant, he leaned out to intercept her at risk of imbalance with his strapped arm. The deft cut of his knife when he sliced her stirrup strap dropped her head over heels in a crusted snow-drift.

Dazed, scraped and bleeding, Daliana picked herself up and kicked off the entangled iron. 'Ungallant scum!' Helplessly furious, she shouted after him. 'Why'd you do that?' Chilled by the trickle of ice down her neck, and stung by more than contusions, she did not expect a civil response. Tears of frustration blurred her view as both horses pounded headlong down the open highway without her.

'This isn't over, you jumped-up rooster!' Daliana spat gravel through a split lip. She turned her back. Refused to watch as the bright, blurred fleck of Lysaer's red doublet diminished amid the mottled browns of the drab landscape.

His choice to return found her walking, forlorn, soaked shoes splashing through the puddled wheel-ruts. She did not lift her head or beg for help. In fact, she presumed the approach belonged to an indifferent, wayfaring stranger. Lysaer's presence went unrecognized until he jogged up beside her, settled astride the fettlesome bay with the slab-sided roan hauled behind, hitched in tow by a lead rein. His hat was gone. Tousled by wind, his artless hair gleamed ingot gold amid the bleak morning.

'Such a grim lack of faith,' he observed in dry sarcasm when she failed to speak or acknowledge him.

In fact, speechless with astonishment, she accepted the uglier horse from his hand. As he wrestled the restive bay to a halt, she surveyed his demeanour with critical interest. The glacial pallor she presumed was high fury in fact was caused by the pain of his injury. Forced to switch mounts, he now handled the more fractious horse, unassisted.

Therefore he braced for her temper, amused.

Her damnfool pluck stole his breath nonetheless when she failed to reward him for gallantry.

'You'd be wanting the faster mount to escape me at your convenience?'

'No.' Lysaer's smile faded as the angsty bay hauled at the bit and grated his broken collar-bone. 'Had the jumped-up rooster in question not slashed your stirrup, you'd have been dragged until you broke your neck. I haven't changed horses to put you in your place. The roan's better suited to your inexperience.' His turn, to glower at her in assessment. 'Are you fit to ride on?'

Past choice on the matter, Daliana set her jaw and scrambled into the mare's empty saddle. Game enough not to whine over bruises, she answered with spirited lack of apology, 'Crow instead to those travellers you nearly trampled. No pleas for credit where none is due. You saved nothing. I didn't fall off.'

But she did not demand back the outrider's horse. The pokey roan suffered her inept equitation until it relented to her vigorous heels and reluctantly trotted.

The next hour passed in stilted silence, pocked by the suck and splash of the horses' hooves through the thawed mud. Daliana's various aches stiffened into a persistent chorus. Sunk in isolate misery, she noticed the veiled glances Lysaer threw askance at her once her bashed eye stopped tearing up. She ventured no comment, wise enough to outlast him.

And at length, he accosted her out of pique. 'Did you actually think me callous enough to abandon you by the roadside?'

She hurt just enough not to soften her answer. 'In your right mind? Perhaps not. But the footing for trust has worn thin, don't you think, since you threw Dakar and me to the mercy of that pack of fanatics.'

The flinch behind his brief pause derived from the accusation that impinged on his honour, she presumed, until he admitted with blistered reluctance: 'You call my most unforgivable mistakes home to roost. Forgive me if I don't care to risk putting your name on the offensive list.'

'How long do you think you can bury the cankers?' Daliana attacked without sympathy. 'I'm here as Sulfin Evend's picked heir to help you resist Desh-thiere's curse. Since I'm not going to quit to salve your prideful conscience, you can guard my blind side by sharing your confidence.'

The winter's lingering chill cut less deep than the frost fallen on Lysaer's reticence. The crisp line of his profile might have been marble, except where the raw weather nipped his nose pink. Such an armour of magisterial dignity deflated guildsmen and diplomats but failed to swerve Daliana. She shouldered her mount alongside and peered upwards to measure the steel in the taciturn stare he fixed straight ahead.

No obvious cue upset her blood instincts. Neither had she been the Sorcerer's choice for female timidity. 'Say what you're thinking!' she snapped into his teeth. 'Tell me now. Before I'm obliged to throw my small knife into your strapped shoulder to drop you!'

That snapped his head around to confront her. The cruel spark in his eyes glittered, beyond frightening. A creature not human might rake her that way, except that his rigid, gloved grip on the reins trembled visibly as he corrected her. 'Somewhere, I can say with precision, a little, dark man wields the power of Shadow to hide himself from his enemies. Cross me at all, you might well be killed!'

'By your hand, yes, I know,' Daliana dismissed. 'Tell me, is that how your Talith met her demise?'

He sucked a stiff breath, singed to offence, though in fact her spiteful strike had succeeded: momentarily the hounding force of the geas seemed shaken into retreat.

'What's to lose?' Wind-flushed in the groom's tatty clothes, Daliana looked as disreputably fierce. 'You might as well serve me the truth as fair warning.'

Lysaer's gemstone blue eyes acquired a differently dangerous edge.

'You're not better off should you fall to the curse,' Daliana pressured him, adamant. She snatched the near-side rein of his horse, bold as brass, before he resorted to spurs and outstripped her. 'Speak to me for your sanity's sake, liege. Draw strength from your pain. Or else throw away your natural mind over bullheaded masculine pride.'

'This is a ruthless assault, and no kindness,' Lysaer protested, incensed by the ignominious flaw in his moral integrity. 'Since you ask, Talith died. I did not kill her. She perished of a crossbolt shot by an assassin, the murder arranged by self-serving political factions. They viewed her upcoming charge of state treason as a stain on my name as the Light's declared avatar.'

'You cherished her beyond measure,' Daliana surmised.

'Fate wept!' Lysaer let her drag his head-shaking bay to a precipitous halt in the roadway. 'She was the first woman I took to wife. Like a demonic plague on my spirit, you have the same tawny eyes. Since your naive presumptions dig for the viscera, you should know how bitterly she betrayed me.'

'Tell me the worst.' Made aware by his sudden grey pallor that the restively circling horses sawed his strapped shoulder past mercy, Daliana yanked the bay's reins from his grip. 'Dismount. Now. We are both going to walk. Then you will start speaking without reservation. I do not plan to let you fall to ruin without a fight. Since you won't abandon this rash trip to Tysan, your hag-ridden wounds are my best weapon to bind you to your better nature. Give me that willing sacrifice, liege. Or else forfeit clear sight to the twisted impulses ruled by the Mistwraith's design.'

'Sulfin Evend had the more tender heart!' snapped Lysaer, at a loss for the conscionable argument that would let him cling to his regal reserve.

'I don't have his brute fists,' Daliana corrected. 'Or was it his patent touch, hurling chain-mail?'

Lysaer failed to choke down a spontaneous outburst of laughter. 'Who told you those choice bits of history?' he asked in capitulation as he dismounted.

'He left a written memoir for his descendants,' she said, chilled breathless as she joined him, ankle deep in the rutted slush. 'The journal mentions your wedding to Ellaine. But none of the pages described Talith.'

'That's because—' Lysaer paused. A dozen squelching steps passed, filled by wind and the startled flit of small birds set to flight from the brush by the roadside. The breaking clouds let in patches of blue, less brooding than the distanced reflection behind the torment in his eyes.

Daliana gathered the reins of both horses and flanked his unsanguine pace without comment.

Lysaer shivered as though someone's offensive tread had trampled his grave-site, then broke his defended silence. 'Talith was a vicious bitch of an embarrassment, and a beauty fit to blind any man to the grace of his purpose. I lost my heart to her. She became the cause to rifle the treasury of a kingdom, then to drive a war host to horrific ruin. Unblinded by the light of religion, history would not be remiss to claim that my infatuation with her cost the lives of thirty-five thousand good men.'

Whatever Daliana expected, nothing touched the unvarnished scope of this confession. Afraid that the Mistwraith's poisonous havoc might undermine char-acter with poisonous self-condemnation, she drew a deep breath, brittle with the scent of the glaciers swept off the snow-capped peaks. As dispassionately cruel, she attacked, 'How many times in the dark of the night have you damned your-self for the indulgent weakness that once, you loved beyond all restraint?'

'But I did overstep,' Lysaer said, bald-faced. The admission still haunted. 'You have no idea how close I came to destroying the regency only for her sake.' His jaw flexed in response to his extreme discomfort, that he bared his heart's core before anyone.

Daliana sensed the force of his helpless despair. Even worse, the excoriating depths of his shame: the vulnerable secrets of a man born to rule should never become aired in public. Desh-thiere's curse compelled the breach of a privacy he might have gone to the grave before sharing.

The sunlight that lit the early green shoots poked up through the crust at the verges seemed a world removed to the gentleman stalked by his unseen peril. Lysaer checked between steps, his skin streamed to sweat on a sudden, tormented breath.

Daliana's heart wrenched for the ugly necessity: without asking, she knew her liege battled in recoil, hooked by the activity of the nemesis in Shadow-bent flight across Scarpdale.

Yet this pass, ahead of her desperate prompt, Lysaer engaged the unflinching choice, well aware her brutal tactic provided the best weapon to anchor his sanity.

Daliana listened, while he laid himself open. The story emerged in broken, terse phrasing, an astonishment from a statesman renowned for his eloquence under pressure. The ferocious emotion masked beneath such relentless reserve stayed undimmed, though the woman who left such tempestuous memories had passed Fate's Wheel over two centuries ago.

Lysaer described his early years in Etarra, when hot-blooded packs of pedigree suitors had goaded each other to feats of mad gallantry vying for his beloved's favour. 'Their idiot capers earned her contempt. She toyed with the fools who persisted.'

'You must have felt the same way as a prince,' Daliana surmised. 'Always beleaguered by fawning courtiers who saw only your jewels, your power, or the blinding display of suave manners and royal charisma.'

He stared, astonished. 'You have no idea.'

'Don't I?' Daliana grinned. 'I recall the political jungle I crossed to get close enough for a word with you. Nobody sees you for what you are through the brilliance of your notoriety. Perhaps you were the only one who respected your lady enough not to fall at her feet.'

Lysaer shrugged. But the colour arisen beneath his fair skin undermined his quiet denouncement. 'Talith had piquant spirit and wit, and the brass to wreck a man's natural complacency.' He faltered, caught unaware as his boot splashed calf deep in a flooded pot-hole. Then he finished, 'She challenged weakness in such a way that admirers broke themselves trying to impress her. But her deep affection came without reserve. She had no defense for sincerity. I have burned with regret since the hour I had to relinquish her.'

A mounted courier passed at a gallop, to a pelted barrage of flung mud clods. The afternoon coach to Narms ground by with its liveried outriders and blaring horn, then an ox-wain with wool-bales and a laden brewer's cart. Lysaer's costly calf-leather boots soaked through. His fine mantle wore the same spatters as any other commonplace foot traveller's, except when the return of fair sky and sun burnished his uncovered head. Then his fair coloring shone like gold leaf amid the drab hills and the leaden patches of snow that tarnished the gulches.

Daliana watched drivers and grooms turn to stare, and the female faces admiring him through the lozenged glass of their carriage windows. Even in anonymity, his elegant bearing drew notice. The unconscious majesty behind his charm became an irresistible force when he focused his undivided attention. The perfection of such extreme good looks all too readily eclipsed the innate flaws of his humanity.

Which quandary had plagued him ever since birth, magnified by the social walls raised by his ruling caste isolation.

Throughout his torn recitation, Daliana sensed the harsh, sweating intervals when he battled the draw of the curse. She watched him buy two sacks of dried jerky and nuts, his unselfish goodwill aimed to lighten a matron's basket. He set her sulky toddler back upright, then hoisted the balky mite onto his shoulders to the detriment of his injury. Eventually, the tired mother and child found a seat in a passing wagon. The day wore endlessly through afternoon. The westering light exposed the relentless strain stamped into his features. Daliana measured the frown that accompanied his agonized speech. Her perception exposed the straight-laced young prince who had not shared the gift of true friendship.

Today's man wore his pride like the preening falcon leashed to the block. He knew service, not freedom. Iron will, but not the playful thrill of unconstrained spontaneity. Between the buried pain of lost love and the insatiable shackle of Desh-thiere's geas, Daliana cracked the cold mask of formality. She sensed the benighted emptiness no one had broached, perhaps since the time of her forebear Sulfin Evend.

Sunset painted the western sky in tints of mauve and citrine, then faded. The first stars burned against a cobalt zenith, and the puddles wore crimped panes of ice. The hour grew late when the stable lamps of the next post-station inn glimmered distantly through the gloaming. Lysaer stopped to massage his temples, then offered Daliana a leg up into the saddle. 'You've blistered your heels for some time,' he apologized, then tucked her toe in the near-side stirrup before she could phrase an objection.

She surveyed the gaunt line of his cheek, brushed by the faint afterglow that bronzed the iced peaks of the Mathorns, due northward. 'How many assaults have you weathered today?'

'I didn't know they came separately,' he said, which effectively crushed conversation.

He mounted, his usual fluid style astride marred by the wear of his injury. They made their way after that side by side, while night deepened, and the wind's bite reversed into winter. By the time they pulled up in the torch-lit inn-yard, Daliana had received Lysaer's first hand account of the founding of his former capital, rebuilt on the Paravian foundations of old Avenor. He described the court dances held in Sunwheel Square, the laughter and the gaiety enjoyed before Talith's untimely death. Then the decades of grief, with the site unbearably haunted by her memory until the assault by the dragon had leveled the golden brick of the regent's palace and slagged both wings of the domed hall of state.

'Who else recalls that place filled with beauty, lit candles and life? The ruin's choked under a tangle of vines, except where the monument to the slain is still maintained by the priests,' Lysaer reminisced as he paid the stableman for the horses. 'Once they burned a lamp in perpetual memory. But I have not been back there to know whether the shrine is maintained.' His tossed penny eased the baggage boy's disappointment that he chose to shoulder his saddle pack without assistance despite his strapped arm.

Inside, the stewed noise in the over-packed tap-room beat against his raw nerves. He wore the pinched look that suggested a headache. Muffled into his cloak despite the close heat, he threaded his way past the contests at darts and the circles of drunken singers. He side-stepped the argumentative cart-drivers, the loose women, and the idlers talking of war. A tighter pack crowded two abutted trestles, where a gaudy troupe of traveling players staged a madcap juggling act. Their ringleader tossed a playful bean-bag and knocked the mantle off Lysaer's head.

Faces turned. First his bright hair, then his noble bearing marked him out in the press. Bad luck, that someone with over-sharp wits recognized his renowned profile.

'Light's own grace! That's the s'Ilessid avatar!'

Which awe-struck outcry raised three other True Sect fanatics to screaming revilement for his apostasy. Other folk reverenced him on their knees in his path, whining pleas for healing or gainful employment, while a swaggering cluster of adventurers begged to sign on with the officer's ranks. 'Lead us into the fight against Shadow in Lanshire!'

Jostled by their eagerness, Daliana kicked shins and stepped on toes to defend her place at her liege's side. When a matron with a squalling infant importuned him for the Light's blessing, the smutted gleam of the tavern's lamps exposed the sweat that sheened Lysaer's brow. The desperate brilliance in his eyes stemmed from black pupils distended with strain. As he fought for the presence to distance himself from the crowding sycophants, Daliana confronted the pushy young mother and attacked like a shrew.

'You idiot! Why do you daft people fall over yourselves, fawning over any blond stranger you meet? My cousin can't bless the arse end of an ox!' Amid laughter and outrage, she flaunted her groom's cloak, and pealed, 'We're sick of the bother of starry-eyed fanatics. Do I wear shiny buttons and silk? Since when did anyone ever see Etarra's Lord Mayor fare abroad without a lance escort and an aristocrat's liveried retinue?'

Lysaer observed her histrionics, bemused, until the swell of raucous noise brought the flustered landlord to quell the disturbance.

'We only stopped for a room and a meal,' Daliana shrilled on in exasperation. 'Who's to blame if the outbreak of evil unrest has put folks in a froth to mob fair-haired travellers in the name of religion?'

'Here, now, calm down. I want no trouble.' The accosted innkeeper wiped moist red hands on his apron and nervously strove to accommodate. 'Private quarters cost eight silvers a night. You can pay?'

Lysaer produced his purse, counted the coins, and added two silvers to cover their meal. Then he backed Daliana's impatient lead and shoved ahead towards the battered, beam staircase.

The landlord tucked the fee into his scrip and bellowed to one of his wenches. 'Show this pair to a room and serve them a tray with drink of their choice and hot supper!'

Behind a latched door, the chamber provided a sagged bed, a washstand with a chipped porcelain ewer, and creaky floor-boards gouged with fresh scars from the hobnailed boots of billeted officers. Lysaer stayed shod to avoid the splinters since his caged restlessness drove him to pace.

'One more day should see us to the harbour at Narms,' Daliana reminded in a lame effort to quench his impatience.

Lysaer's distemper found no relief. 'We'd be there by now if my strapped arm could withstand the jouncing ride on the night-coach.' His flicked glare pleaded to be left alone.

But Daliana dared not serve him the faint-hearted kindness of solitude. Her bald-faced efforts to forestall dire trouble must not cater to his raw tension. When supper arrived, she made the inn servant cut up his meat, then sent the fork and knife back to the kitchen to limit the convenient weapons. Since the window was built to discourage thieves, too narrow to permit egress, she filched one of the blankets and settled herself for a guarded night, stretched across the room's threshold. When he snarled over that stringent precaution, she blistered him for self-pity, then killed his argument with her demand to know about Talith's ransom by the Master of Shadow.

'One day,' warned Lysaer, 'you'll get burned by such cheek.'

Daliana fixed him with her galling, gold eyes, unaware yet that the unbound mahogany hair she brushed out and rebraided triggered other personal memories for him. Ones just as provocative and woundingly powerful, which led her to gall him the worse as she underestimated her own impact. 'The day you are freed of the curse, I'll retire.' Since his plea to snuff the wall sconce was too dangerous, she braced her back against the plank door and tucked the coarse blanket up to her chin. 'You can't imagine that I enjoy this.'

Lysaer perched on the fusty quilt thrown over the bed. He regarded the tremulous sparkle of rings that, thankfully, his gloves had kept masked in the tap-room. 'Forgive me, that I do not thank you.'

She coughed behind her wrist, sculpted with delicate bone and lean muscle where Talith's had flashed, adorned with exquisite jewellery. 'Humility wouldn't suit you,' she said.

'I was thoroughly taught, very young, to eschew any form of abasement.' Lysaer shifted his legs and leaned against the slat head-board, boots crossed at the ankle and his good arm folded behind the tousled hair licked over his fitted collar. 'The quality might signal weakness in a prince.'

Beneath heavy lids, his eyes blazed too frenetic. Stacked against the merciless wear of exhaustion, Daliana had one sharpened weapon. 'Speak instead as the more fallible man, and reclaim your right to forgiveness.'

Lysaer's features twisted with vicious bitterness. 'You are nothing if not youthfully naive. Let the truth destroy your footing for tenderness.' He proceeded with the excoriating clarity to outline the blow he had suffered at Ostermere: when the Master of Shadow had ransomed his wife and returned her chastely untouched, but with her steadfast faith in his s'Ilessid integrity debased beyond hope of reconciliation.

Cankered yet by the wounds of a love that once seized such a frightening power over him, Lysaer recounted the campaign waged at Vastmark: a madman's advance into hostile terrain, forced into the teeth of delay and brought to ruin by trickery and betrayal, then clouted into ignominious defeat by the pressures of the winter season.

'I was hot-bloodedly proud, and too cock-sure to handle the fact a bold play by my adversary had undermined everything.' Lysaer's unfocused gaze was not blank with distance, but fixed wide-lashed upon horrors no other perceived. 'I charged the troops forward, over the massacre caused by a shale slide, surely wishing I would die in the carnage. To go home without victory was to admit that the wreck of my marriage had left my life meaningless.'

A long pause ensued, while the candle-flame flickered, and Lysaer stared sightless at the frayed cobweb that streamed from the rafters. 'What words did I have to console thirty-five thousand widows whose husbands' lives had been squandered?'

Daliana watched him swallow and stir, fretted pale as he jostled his injured collar-bone. His recitation ground on, rough with condemnation as he finished with candid sorrow, 'As Tysan's head of state, I could not run or hide. There was no grace for anonymity. The curse offered my only refuge. I became its willing accomplice when I styled myself as the avatar of the Light to dodge the infamy of the unadorned public record.'

Daliana felt her breath unreel and stop, then restart to the well of her tears. Whatever she expected, *nothing* prepared her for a confession as cutting as this one. To the man who just threw her the knife to twist in the bleeding heart of his self-laceration, she had nothing to give but the steady presence of her acceptance. 'You are not the same person who was broken in the cold rain on the field after Vastmark. The future's still yours. Sulfin Evend helped you finish the siege of Alestron without a repeat of the horrific debacle. When we set sail for Tysan, I'll be at your side to back every choice and right action.'

Lysaer regarded her with what appeared to be a burning contempt. 'Women are so readily blinded. I should respect you more if you could admit that you hated me.'

Daliana regarded him, splendid in beauty and complex enough to confound a straightforward analysis. Granted a wisdom beyond her tender years, she ventured, carefully quiet, 'You don't trust any of us. If I had to guess, I'd suggest that your faith in the fair sex was undone far and long before Talith first dared to broach the fact you were curse-haunted. Sulfin Evend succeeded because he was male. I am alive now only thanks to the debt of honour you bear his memory.'

Lysaer sucked a harsh breath. Yet before he lashed back in injured defense, she trampled him roughshod.

'Don't speak! We have been fighting a last-ditch defense, not each other! The pressure of the geas has calmed somewhat, hasn't it?'

He shivered violently from head to toe, then guardedly nodded. 'A few minutes ago. I'm not anything near fit to sleep.'

'I know.' Daliana struck to keep his anxiety defused, before he buried the subject. 'If you *have* to wallow in your nettled pain, I'd like to know how you plan to reverse the Sunwheel advance into Havish alone.'

His movement disclosed his suppressed disquiet as he stood up, made his way to the ewer and one-handedly splashed his flushed face. Muffled by the towel, he barked a short laugh, then delivered the last of the day's exhaustively brutal admissions. 'I haven't designed any elaborate tactic. But surely if I raise my Light and start burning Tysan's high temples in public, the priests should be forced to recall their forces from the battle-line to confront me.'

'Count me in.' Daliana tucked into her blanket to seek what rest she could snatch before dawn-light. 'At least fire serves them a taste of the pyres they've torched in pursuit of their unholy purges.'

Rift

The head-hunter trackers' trained pack of hounds pursued the three young clanborn travellers through five brutal days on the run before Siantra's wiles threw them off the hot trail. Foot-sore and gaunt with exhaustion, they had to rest, whether or not they had outdistanced the range of the temple diviner. Khadrien finished the first watch after nightfall. No overt danger threatened. The narrow glade that sheltered his sleeping companions lay still, a spangled carpet of frost and felt shadow drenched in preternatural silence. Disgruntled and cold, he shook Esfand awake. Then he waited shivering, while his rousted friend shook off the numb oblivion of sleep and recovered his wits.

'Midnight's come, or fresh trouble?' Esfand rubbed gritted eyes and sat up, alert to the current of stifled concern that wracked his impetuous companion. 'Khadrien?'

The tight shrug returned was a rustle of movement amid the wool murk of the darkness. 'You sense something, too?'

Esfand gathered his blanket, winced over the outraged twinge of sore muscles, and stiffly shoved to his feet. 'Maybe.'

The site where they sheltered was much too exposed, a hollow beneath a ragged crack of sky, choked by ancient beeches and oak. The cabled boles were shagged with hoary moss, repeatedly scarred by seasonal storms, with split trunks assaulted by centuries of lightning. The encroachment of the battered forest felt the more ominous as a scud of cloud tarnished the moon. Dimmed stars gleamed through, reduced to fuzzed haloes, while a moist, restless gust creaked the ingrown boughs and clattered the naked, crabbed twigs. Trunks as massive as siege towers plunged the clearing into oppressive, deep gloom. Such king trees likely had been aged with years when Athera's

Paravians walked a land yet untouched by mankind's Third Age grant of settlement.

The lore-keepers revered the magnificent patriarchs that had seeded the free-wilds forest of Halwythwood. But this grove made every other seem tame. The cobweb veil of lost history lurked here, not unlike the haunted awareness that permeated the forsaken stones of Paravian ruins.

'This place gives me the creeps.' Prickled to wary gooseflesh, Khadrien folded his arms, sharp chin jutted as he glanced sidewards. 'Do you believe the Paravians might have come here to abandon Athera?'

'Siantra says not.' On historical facts, she was probably right. At least she had not joined the rambunctious truants and slipped off to hunt game when the bards' circle sang their long-winded traditional sagas. Esfand checked the hang of his weapons and nervously blew on numbed hands. 'Perhaps the lane's tidal shift has upset you. The strong currents here are quite likely to flow the more vividly.'

But logic failed to quell the jangling swell of unease. Unlike the quickened glens on their home ground, this remote hollow wore no settled aura of peace. As if these progenitor trees streamed the forces of their primordial origins, their contorted roots and crabbed crowns defied the mind's instinctive search for comfort and symmetry.

'We might've been driven too close to Athili,' Khadrien ventured. 'Did you notice? The west-facing branches have changed into summer foliage.'

Esfand's stifled laughter emerged as a snort. 'That's rich!'

'Listen up!' Khadrien threw a punch in offensive distress. 'See for yourself. I'm not joking!'

Esfand ducked the jab, startled, prepared to retort that short rations surely encouraged the delusional fancy. Yet if his cousin had dreamed the impossible, the problem became shared between them. The thick scent of living greenery filled his nostrils, sweetened by the exotic fragrance of flowering vines. When the moon overhead sliced out of the clouds, the white flood of light stamped the glimpse of an understory, dense with matured leaves and brambles.

Except towards the east, where the brooding wood stayed in accord with the natural season. Twig and branch and grooved bark gleamed as nakedly grey as any other wood before equinox. The frosty air breathed winter's mix of wood rot and mouldering fungus, and *also,* uncannily, the elusive ambrosial sweetness of wild beehives, dripping with honey.

'This is all wrong,' Esfand whispered, afraid. Danger arrested his reach for his knife, counter to reflexive instinct. Even the mere thought of edged steel drawn here lifted the hair at his nape.

A dozen strides distant, tall grass in the glade rustled with bearded seed-heads and snowy, lace clumps of asters. Crickets sang, there. Yet the ground near at hand remained rumpled from the recent snow-melt, the flattened brown mat of killed vegetation littered with a bone-yard wrack of fallen sticks.

'We've probably strayed too close to the rim,' Khadrien fretted.

'Hush!' Esfand snapped. 'Let me think.'

For the terrible fear was not groundless. The old glades here were known to be steeped in the vestigial shimmer of divine fire. Mighty beyond any mortal's imagining, the direct touch of Ath Creator at Athili had seeded the world with the three Paravian races. The gifted glory of their sacred presence had been sent to heal the afflictions unleashed by the Age of Dragons. But those mysteries were never fashioned for Mankind's mantle of plain flesh and bone.

No mortal survived, who crossed Athili's rim. To venture too near was to risk being ripped apart by its titanic forces and surreal visions.

Esfand's voice shook as he weighed up priorities. 'Did Siantra engage her hunter's instincts?' Common sense should have prompted the need for a sounding ward against the recurrent threat posed by the hounds. When protection mattered, hers was the most sensitive talent among them.

'No.' Scared beyond subterfuge, Khadrien plucked his snagged jacket cuff clear of his quilloned dagger. 'I couldn't even bear to suggest, she was run that far beyond tired.'

Esfand forgave no such soft scruple. 'Get her up.'

'You waken her, friend.' The flash of Khadrien's teeth in rife challenge disappeared, as a soot drift of cloud dimmed the moon. 'Last time I got her fist in my jaw, and a kick that just missed my bollocks.'

The *caithdein*'s heir designate snorted without sympathy and crouched by Siantra, furled as if dead in her blanket. 'Idiot sneak,' he sniped at his male peer. 'What did you grope when you shook her?'

No more compliant for him, the feminine form in the bedroll recoiled beyond easy reach. 'The goat knows enough to have called me by name,' Siantra accused, wide-awake and brisk-tempered. 'What else is amiss? I thought we'd shaken the diviner's brutes off.'

Esfand dared her bite with an offered hand. 'Your hunter's gift's needed to scry a safe course. The dogs pose the least of our danger.'

Siantra rebuffed his presumption with a fond clip on the cheek, dealt by the hem of her blanket. 'We're moving already?' She shivered. 'My braid's a damned rat's nest.'

With no complaint for the puffed ankle twisted yesterday in a ditch, Siantra hobbled erect. She started to stow her bedroll at speed, until a fallen stick hooked a tear in the wool and unstrung her stoic silence. 'Dharkaron Avenge! I'm fed up with charging through hostile country. Must we risk threading the trackers' gamut, again?'

Khadrien explained, anxious to restore himself to her better graces. 'Both of us think we've strayed too close to Athili.'

'We didn't.' Siantra glanced sharply up from knotting hide laces. 'Not being a fool, I shared your concern! But I checked this campsite for safety at sunset. I'm not deaf to the current that's set you on edge. The flux here is alive and crackling. If that means what I think, the rim's moved. Athili's vortex has encroached on us, not the other way round.'

That unsettling concept hastened their need to leave. Since everything but the essential supplies had been jettisoned under pursuit, departure involved a swift check to secure weapons, then a moment to lash their tied blanket rolls onto a cross-belt. The black sword Alithiel rode in a scabbard slung across Esfand's back. Since no one lit fires at Athili's verge, and errant smoke could flag the enemy, the campsite had no live embers to douse.

The oppressive quiet quashed Khadrien's prankster comments and pressured Siantra's sober outlook to acidity. No one discussed the eerie fact that the leafed boughs now harboured the dotted yellow flash of fire-flies. The fitful wind had turned wayward as well, from breezes that veered summer-warm from the south to icy blasts that gusted northerly. The fickle moonlight resurged to brilliance and doused to the flit of frayed clouds.

'Keep a tight watch while I'm in trance.' Siantra knelt amid the stems of dead bracken, her peaked face obscured as she bowed her head.

Khadrien chose not to mock her unease or vent his raw tension by chaffing. Siantra possessed the more delicate touch. She would be quickest. Also the most able to shield the ripple of disturbance that might ruffle the instincts of the True Sect diviner. Since the temple's talent would not have abandoned the hunt, Esfand stepped forward and claimed due position to guard her back.

'May there be a safe path farther east,' he murmured. 'Bright guidance help you to find it.'

The pause hung, while Siantra gathered her strained concentration and aligned her subtle senses to access the flux currents. Trained as a hunter to recognize the stamped patterns of all nearby animate life, her reflexive skills should have answered her seamlessly. Instead, thrown into sluggish confusion, she groped, then pushed on in the foolish belief that her tired faculties missed the connection. The mistake overtook her, beyond help to remedy. Too recklessly open, she blundered as the potency of direct contact roared through. She gasped. Inwardly wrenched as though punched in the viscera, she tried and failed to break free. Already the flux surge poured down her stripped nerves, beyond her experience to curb. The tingling jolt shuddered her from head to foot. She cried aloud in stark terror. Never before had her skills overridden her flesh or threatened to wreak untold damage.

This time the flare that savaged her awareness erupted into a blaze of visible light. She lost the wits to anchor herself. The wild intensity sizzled and snapped, an electrical burst that seared her damp palms with the branding heat of live flame.

The discharge laced golden static through her aura, then whirled into a vortex that fountained skywards. Khadrien shouted, stupefied, 'Ath wept, what has taken her?'

'Siantra!' Esfand blistered the hand he flung out to support her slack shoulder as she collapsed.

The raised nimbus flushed needles of light up her spine and over the back of her neck. The flesh beneath her leathers felt flash-point hot, the skin under his touch as he cradled her cheek paper dry as though parched by a furnace. Dread unmanned him. Afraid that her clothing and hair might ignite, he called upon Khadrien. 'Pour your water-skin over her. Now!'

But the shrill command passed unheeded. Amid the desperation of crisis, Khadrien's attention stayed fixed on the forest. 'Look!' He pointed, aghast.

The black wall of trees that surrounded the glen flickered and gleamed with the bale- fire dance of electro-luminescence. The galvanized air reeked of ozone. More, the dormant vegetation underfoot spontaneously quickened. Brown stems rustled, invigorated to tender leaf, while the grass speared up pastel shoots, scattered like stars with the tiny white blossoms of snowdrops.

'Ground yourself!' Esfand shouted. 'Hurry, Siantra!' Dropped onto his knees at her side, he risked immolation and shook her wracked frame.

Khadrien joined him. Clumsy with terror, he beat out the sparks that singed her cloak, then belatedly fumbled the flask from his belt and yanked the cork with his teeth. 'I don't have enough water to douse a hemp slow match.'

But just ahead of that desperate remedy, Siantra wrenched out of trance. She jerked erect with a grunt, swore, and rammed her singed palms flat against the moist earth. As the uncanny phosphor charge in her aura streamed down her wrists and quenched into the soil, she hauled in a chattering, shaken breath, then leaned with a whimper into Esfand's arms.

'Greater powers protect us, we're too close to Athili!' Khadrien cried. 'Is she hurt?'

'Shhh. I don't know.' Esfand stroked a tic from Siantra's damp cheek, not wet with tears but streaming with feverish sweat. Afraid to find her soaked to the skin and clammy from head to foot, he pleaded. 'Are you with us, s'Idir? Can you speak?'

'Give me a moment.' Siantra huddled against him and trembled. After a moment of tensioned distress, she admitted, 'My hands have blistered. That's not a huge problem. But unless the residual flash-blindness clears, I can't see a thing.'

The moment was cruel, for the invasive hurtle of movement that catapulted out of the undergrowth at the north edge of the wood. Cut to run silent, the trackers' pack of mastiffs barreled across the glen. Khadrien whirled, knife drawn in time to impale the lead male in mid-spring. Its slavering fangs clashed just shy of his throat. Terrified, he shouted, 'Get Siantra into a hollow tree!' Another dog fastened blunt jaws on his calf. More yet surged behind, a concerted assault of juggernaut muscle, mottled hides, lambent eyes, and bared teeth.

Khadrien stabbed the tussling hound in the kidney. Harried by the rest, too swiftly surrounded, he elbowed off animals as they leaped in a desperate fight to keep balance. Another brute clamped onto his wrist. The bloody knife dropped from his paralyzed grip. He tasted the coppery taint of blind fear as his horrible strait became hopeless. Cruel death stared him down, while somewhere behind, he sensed Esfand haul Siantra upright. Stumbling, sightless, hampered by her wrenched ankle, she could not take flight without help. Cosach's heir wrestled the ghastly hesitation, torn by the need to guard a friend's back or stay burdened by the lethal disadvantage of a helpless woman's defense.

'Leave me!' Khadrien screamed. 'Get her safely away. If you don't, none of us will escape with our lives!'

But any such sacrifice came much too late. A pack bred and trained to mangle armed men closed in and pursued its grim purpose.

Esfand kicked off the hound that snarled and snapped at Siantra's leathers. A second one fell to the thrust of his long knife. Another rammed into its place. The protective arm tucked around Siantra became viciously worried as another dog clawed up her chest and bored in to slash at her neck.

Worse, very likely frantic with fear, she struggled to break away from his embrace.

Alone and still upright, Khadrien staggered, dogs latched to both ankles. He shouted them down to the pits of Sithaer and cursed the vile trackers who trained them.

Esfand punched and stabbed, yelling also in a vain effort to beat back the marauding pack. Then Siantra ripped her pinioned arm free and reached for the last choice available.

Weeping and sightless, she fumbled by touch and seized the black hilt of the sword strapped at Esfand's shoulder.

'Siantra, no!' he cried in panic. 'We are too near Athili.'

A dog snapped at her nape. Teeth worried her braid. She screamed in bleak rage. 'If I don't, we are lost, or delivered alive to the hands of a True Sect examiner.' She kept her fierce grip despite her blistered palm. The fierce wrench as the mastiff tussled her backwards pulled Alithiel clear of the scabbard.

Light woke like a paean. The rune inlays in the dark steel shimmered and roused to an opalescent whirlwind that roared upwards and unleashed a chord of pure harmony. Ringing sound impacted flesh and bone like a hammer. The ravening hounds broke off their attack. What became of the beasts, no one knew. The clanborn companions buckled at the knees. Dazzled and unstrung, they sank to the ground, riven by speechless ecstasy. Through the splendour of brilliance and the adamant song, the upright sword clenched in Siantra's fist lit the glade in silver far brighter than midday. The trees on all sides wore emerald ivy and leaves, and the grass soaked the air with the fragrance of summer, potent enough to ravage the senses.

Then from the east, like a bloom of live fire, light scribed on the searing essence of *light,* a gold shower of illumination etched the trees into razor-edged silhouette. Then their sharpened form shimmered, first broken to shards, which dissolved into beams of ephemeral energy. The permeable border of Athili moved. The surge rampaged in, relentless as tide, as if Alithiel's pealed cry itself charged and lifted the resonant frequency of the glade's solid existence. The confluent speed of event was extreme, far too radical to assimilate. Overwhelmed by the burgeoning crest of the mysteries, the three stricken companions pitched into that whirlwind of change. Imperative urgency insisted that they must rise and run or become consumed, lost into unknowable oblivion.

No mortal broached Athili's rim and survived.

But stunned human sinew failed to respond. Will and reason unravelled. Vertigo ripped through and upended the world. All coherent thought and sensation sheared off, blasted out by the naked glory of forces past reach of earthly experience.

. . . darkness gripped the first breath of emergent awareness amid a quiet as dense as jet velvet.

Khadrien's scatter-brained insolence as always leaped fastest to dare the unknown. 'Where are we?'

The unbroken black surrounds yielded a pin-point red spark, from which a spurt of yellow flame blossomed. Quite ordinary, the spill lit a man's sturdy fingers, tough with callus as any stonemason's. The face glimpsed above conveyed no such assurance. Beaten to leather by time-worn exposure to wind and rain and strong sun, features fierce as a raptor's emerged out of shadow, nose and eyes defined by the cragged jut of bone, then frosted-steel eyes, keen enough to strip spirit from flesh.

'Are you Daelion Fatemaster, come to list our debts?' Khadrien challenged, frightened spitless and sure he had died, despite the sting of mauled limbs and the gore-sticky grip clenched on his knife.

A deep, careful voice bestowed an amused reprimand, 'You are alive still, and lucky to be so.'

The illumination steadied, a plain wax light in fact, spent to a stub and grimed with rough usage. Its jonquil halo unveiled the speaker, imposingly tall and clean-shaven, with straight silver hair clipped to collar length. For a presence that shouted initiate power with such disconcerting intensity, his scuffed leathers could have belonged to a clan scout. His dark wool cloak showed snags from hard use, redolent of wood smoke and horse sweat.

Siantra matched that patent restraint with better courtesy. 'Since your help pulled us clear before we trespassed into forbidden country, might I know your name?'

'That wasn't the question you most wanted to ask of me.' The hint of a curve flexed the mage's taut mouth. 'You did not escape Athili, Siantra s'Idir. The blade you drew sings the chord of creation that ignited the winter stars.

Such a mighty cry of pure light and sound would ignite the flux, while the lane tides ripple the boundaries. The living current of joy here responded, surely as a magnet attracts iron. You are within Athili, and held without harm, since my warding shields the frailty of your being from immolation. The bright torrent of Ath's touch has hallowed this place and unsealed a dimensional rift. Even the most celebrated Paravians cannot tread this gateway incarnate.'

'Has the heirloom weapon been lost through my ignorance, or did I drop the hilt when I fell unconscious?' The distressed question tremulous, Siantra begged, 'Tell me, please, whoever you are. If I should know you, my eyesight is darkened.'

Wool and leather rustled. The capable hand that did not hold the candle produced the Paravian sword, gripped point downwards, its black steel a polished gleam against darkness and its exquisite rune inlay quiescent. 'Alithiel's call led me to you, a perilous grace whose purpose has been kindly met. Esfand s'Valerient, Teir's'Caithdein to Rathain, will you come forward?'

Cosach's son rallied the wits to respond to the formal address. Aware whom he faced through his father's heritage, he knelt at the booted feet of the being whose summons commanded him. 'Asandir of the Fellowship?' Aghast, and mauled bloody from the tracker's dog pack, he surmounted his awe and returned the traditional greeting. 'How may we serve the land?'

The Sorcerer extended the sword towards the youthful heir designate, bent with bowed head before him. 'Stand upright, young man. My Fellowship never imposes the loss of your dignity. Nor do we accept even symbolic obeisance from anyone! Take charge of this blade. Sheltered under my auspices or not, in this place she is safest kept sheathed.'

Esfand's awkward embarrassment received short shrift as the cold weight of Alithiel was restored to him. Asandir's attentive perception promptly moved on to reassure Siantra. 'My dear, your sight was disrupted by a nervous back-lash. You suffered an overexposure to the high range flux without tight protection, too close to Athili. Time and rest will right the imbalance. Blisters mend. Your senses will stabilize without damage as well, though I warn, your innate sensitivity must resurge, strengthened by the contact.'

'Are you sending us home?' Khadrien blurted, unable to douse the simmer of his apprehension.

'For your insolence? No.' The Sorcerer's interest gained a whetted edge. 'Do you wish for my direct help to return to the care of your parents?'

Khadrien's gasp of crest-fallen dismay tangled with Esfand's snapped refusal and Siantra's emphatic entreaty to stay with the task they had shouldered.

'Free choice is yours, within limits.' Asandir's dead-pan regard yielded nothing, though his curt gesture fluttered the held candle-flame. 'The question of what to do with the lot of you does, however, fall under my lawful discretion.' Iron brows raised, he measured the abashed miscreants through a dreadful, nerve-wracked pause.

461

Esfand withstood that peeling regard, chin just barely in need of a shave raised for a heated rebellion. 'You cannot fault us for our resolve to bear Alithiel to our royal liege's defense.'

Asandir brightened the tremulous flame. Rinsed by the light against stygian dark, his stark stance seemed ruthless as Dharkaron Avenger's last judgement.

'We were arrogant, maybe,' Khadrien confessed. Scarlet with shame to his carroty hair, but with brass to back Esfand's bravado, he dared the twitch of a sheepish grin, then pushed winsome luck and gushed onwards. 'But someone had to step up and take action. The clan council wouldn't stop dithering. You'll help us along? We cannot have travelled this far for nothing, and we know that Prince Arithon's in flight from the True Sect's invasion of Lanshire.'

Asandir's severe glance remained chill enough to freeze rash effrontery at twenty paces.

The only one spared by her impaired sight, Siantra broke the repressive silence. 'Khadrien!' she scoffed to quash mettlesome idiocy. 'Our elders would stripe your backside for cheek!' Unflinching, she groped to frame an apology to mollify a Fellowship Sorcerer's stretched patience.

Asandir spoke first, impervious to diplomacy. 'Don't give me a word that's not drawn from the heart! If you find the way to the side of your prince, you will do so with no help from me.' Fleeting sorrow deepened the map work of creases that bracketed his mouth and eyes, a nuance that failed to match his brusque tone. 'No working of mine can dispatch you onwards to any direct course into Lanshire.'

His raised finger forestalled unwise pleas as a caution that their decision would stay irreversible. While the three young companions fought shaking knees, justifiably rattled to dread for their theft of Alithiel, the Sorcerer made his disposition.

'Your appeal can be honoured, not to return home. But under the compact, by your consent, you might be appointed to serve the land's greater need at a time and place determined by my discretion. If you refuse my calling, then Prince Arithon's sword cannot be left in trust under your immature stewardship.'

Esfand frowned, disturbed. Siantra's straight brows knit with furious thought. While both strove to plumb the weighty implications behind the Sorcerer's state language, Khadrien announced, 'I'll take any road gladly before I tuck tail and slink back to Halwythwood.'

Asandir's smile emerged, bright with teeth. 'Your word, as given.' His piercing glance shifted and measured the others, volatile with expectancy.

'All right. Count me in.' Esfand added, contrite, 'No way I'd face Cosach or the clan council without my cousin beside me.'

Siantra's pledge followed, rushed by honest discomfort but steadfast. No matter the stakes, she would not abandon her hare-brained companions.

The Sorcerer acknowledged with a clipped nod. 'Said is done, sealed by my auspices.' His deft pinch snuffed the candle and let in the dark with a roar that swept the adventurous trio back through the throes of oblivion.

That fast, without any gesture of ceremony, he released his three errant charges upon the rambunctious course of their fate. Straight-faced, his lower lip clamped in his teeth, Asandir stowed the candle stub in the saddle pack slung across his broad shoulder. He tipped his head back for an instant, bemused. Then all restraint burst. He laughed aloud with unbridled amusement.

'There's a devilish packet of courage!' he mused after he recovered decorum. 'That bunch will provide a rowdy match, even for High King Gestry. May the throne of Havish trump the pesky annoyance of unscheduled, back-handed gifts.' Which, in cold-sober fact, could wreck natural order or salvage the evil day.

For such wild-card gambits of tinder and flame became the tossed straws to upset the pernicious disaster painted by Sethvir's late augury. Only once in Athera's history had a strand casting unveiled such a desperate range of bleak futures. Under the nexus forged by Desh-thiere's curse, the trend mapped the onset of a full-scale war with relentless ferocity.

Too quickly, the True Sect's massed troops in the west had surmounted the thaw and breasted the flood-waters swollen by snow-melt. The rear-guard and the heavily burdened supply wagons already crossed the white torrent of the River Darkshiel. With the southern bank occupied and the open heath between Torwent and Scarpdale arrayed with enemy encampments, nothing ahead might impede the Light's determined sweep across Lanshire. The Hatchet drove the best of his dedicates to prosecute the attack. Within twoscore days, perhaps less, the fury of the Light's armoured lance and foot would be unleashed to storm Carithwyr.

Whether Arithon survived the flash-point carnage of the High King's defense almost became a moot point. Let the Kingdom of Havish suffer defeat, and the old law that upheld the compact would be broken.

'May this day's work bring confusion to the enemy!' Asandir muttered in hag-ridden aggravation.

The last throw had been cast into play. Now, the friable choices made by five human ciphers must steer the dark course towards an inscrutable outcome. To the dragon's spontaneous dispatch of Dakar and Daliana to their convergent hour of destiny, the array of unconstrained catalysts now included the intemperate loyalty of three clan children, rash with spirited inexperience.

Spurred onwards by jagged concern, Asandir reset his priorities. He thinned the bounds of his wards and let his being blur and shift into harmony with the fountain-head flare of Athili's vortex. One breath to the next, his tall frame sublimated from solid form. Upstepped to an entity wrought of song and light, Asandir focused the rift's shattering power to the singular bent of his will.

Mighty past measure, beyond vexed to be hand-tied while the Fellowship's primary interests tumbled into the quivering balance, the field Sorcerer engaged the Creator's sublime portal and vanished.

Spring 5923

Tipping Points

Triumphant after her reclaimed command of the order's Great Waystone, the Koriani Matriarch sends for the captive sliver of crystal still dedicate to Elaira: 'The time's ripe to bait Arithon to his destruction. We must strike while he's alone on the run, without friendly guidance to access the memories that hold the full range of his heritage . . .'

Alarmed by the first flicker of drakish impulse to assimilate and reflect while dissociated from the rapt power to reshape creation, Althain's Warden cautions Davien, bound in the flesh to Seshkrozchiel, whose languid bask in a fumarole fore-runs her creation of a sealed rock chamber for hibernation: *Your concern is not groundless! The renewal she wrought at Kathtairr exhausted her. The strand casting has confirmed your grim fate if her dreamless torpor extends for millennia . . .'*

In a closed counsel with Havish's war-captain, the Mad Prophet is immersed in scrying the strategies for the most effective deployment when a royal herald announces that three clan youngsters from Halwythwood come to the king's court via the Paravian Focus; Dakar shoves too quickly erect and falls into a spontaneous trance, then delivers an errant forecast that shocks the realm's defenders to helpless rage and unspeakable grief . . .

XIII. Double Bind

ince the outbreak of Shadow that disabled The Hatchet, rumour swept the length of the front lines as the Sunwheel host marched across Lanshire. The stiff debates sown by the dedicate captains became argued down through the ranks, until even the equerries who polished the courier's spurs and oiled the wet boots of superiors felt entitled to an opinion. Talk thickened in the silken tents of the brothels and livened the raucous tongues of the women who muscled the war camp's laundry. Even the snotty grooms at the horse-lines spoke their minds. Disputes bred as swiftly as dice games and lice, with no agreement beyond proven fact: that the Spinner of Darkness sought refuge under the heretic law that made Havish the entrenched haven for blood-lines with renegade talent. Crown rule used the pernicious force of arcane knowledge and allowed malign sorcery the freedom to flourish.

The True Sect priesthood assigned to the vanguard were too lofty to specu-late. They crushed curiosity and inquisitive supposition with platitudes to uphold the wisdom of the Light's doctrine. Staunch principle insisted the High King's heretical nest must be purged. For the grace of salvation, the morally faithful must destroy the grand minion of evil, the Master of Shadow himself.

The troop surgeons complained differently as they stitched up the horrific injuries only encountered on the field of war. As healers beset with rife cases of flux and the broken bones caused by brangles over the whores, supply concerned them, and the dearth of dry quarters, camped for days on end in spring's chill, windy rains. Diseases broke out where the men huddled in griped knots, coughing from the smoky fires fueled by dampened peat. The officers fretted, chapped red from their rounds, while the sergeants on the night rosters strode splashing through the morning's dense fog to make their reports at division headquarters.

'Damned swamp, this place, all blighted furze and soaked bracken,' carped the day's subordinate to the ascetic officer appointed the second in command under The Hatchet. 'It's hellish unnatural that nothing here ever dries out.'

'Don't think to whine, donsie!' the superior snapped, gold braid clothed over ill temper. 'Priests think hell's black minion's holed up like a fox. Just finish the job. Else we'll be stuck on these forsaken downs chasing yon sorcerer's trail until summer-time breeds stinging flies. There's a rife misery you won't soon forget.'

'Tell you this,' a field captain warned, ducked in to thaw his numbed hands at the brazier. 'We'll have deserters if the men are pushed harder, skin-wet and dripping.'

'You'll lose them to fever, first,' the master healer corrected. A dolorous man with a blade nose and eyes pouched from decades of worry, he poked up the coals, and lamented, 'Infection, too, from poisoned wounds since our last linen bandages have spoiled with mildew.'

But his formal protest to the high command was brushed off, replaced by the next complaint: of a surgeon's corps cloak of red wool, stupidly misplaced by a scatter-brained assistant.

'Dock pay from the negligent fellow for carelessness,' The Hatchet's quartermaster snapped. 'His lost uniform's probably turned inside out, warming another man's back to the profit of some furtive black marketeer.'

'The cold nights are brutal enough to show lenience,' said the crusty supply deputy who issued the replacement. 'That garment may save us a treatment for chilblains, or spare some poor bloke from an untimely grave.'

The petty infraction seemed beneath remark, overshadowed by action as a clever sequence of feints drove the mounted messengers to lathered horses. Outbreaks of Darkness shuttered full daylight in several locales, an upheaval that rattled routine for a week before pooled information raised the suspect fact that the strikes all occurred the same day. While more urgent dispatches criss-crossed the heath, the searches earned nothing but tangles with Havish's skirmishers, who struck with the cunning of forest-bred scouts, caused havoc, and melted past reach. If such gadfly bites culled the unwary recruits, the damage compounded when vengeful pursuit bogged down amid trappy country. Chase patrols blundered through grottos and seams, where arrows from cover left more littered dead, or burdened their squads with the prostrate wounded.

The losses mounted with each savage foray, until the harried troops received The Hatchet's orders to stand down under provocation. Slap-dash sallies that wasted sound men were suspended. The stung companies regrouped, their tattered morale whipped back into resolve by the Light's priests, who tempered fresh grief into fury with claims that the Spinner of Darkness abetted the High King's defenders.

The western line rested, while the east flank licked its wounds. Mauled worst by Elkforest's clansmen, whose relentless ferocity hammered against the on-coming threat of the Sunwheel encroachment, the outlying camps struggled hardest to cope. Too many critical casualties stressed the shortage of healers. The overworked surgeons' corps foundered in despair on the day the outriding patrol encountered the stray, afoot in the open country and clad in the red cloak of service. Set under question, the fellow explained he had wandered for days, unhorsed by a fall in a gulch.

'My unlucky mare broke her neck.' Sorrowfully soft-spoken, he lamented the precious remedies lost with his saddle pack.

The troop captain's rigorous interrogation became disrupted by the harassed surgeon, who barged in blood-spattered, and pounced on the dubious find like a terrier. 'Mercy's gift to us, don't waste opportunity! Attach the laggard to my corps immediately!'

The east flank's slit-eyed captain lounged his laconic bulk in a camp chair, legs outthrust and boots crossed at the ankle. 'You'd ignore the risk? The wretch could be a spy. Or a cutthroat deserter with a lying tongue. At least wait for my trackers to find his dropped horse, and to make sure the message sent back from that pigeon doesn't turn up a stolen mount.'

'In this benighted country, hard up by the wastes?' The frazzled surgeon flung up gaunt hands and rooted at his tufted hair. 'Are you blind? I've got too many septic gut punctures from those barbaric willow-stick traps. The horrific screams from the pain should inform you. If you send that trained healer back to whatever troop's negligence lost him, or waste his skill over fool questions, you'll have five dead who could have been saved by the grace of this one, kept idle.'

The captain brandished the witch-hazel toothpick just unclenched from his nut-cracker jaw. 'Very well. He's all yours. I'll still run my cross-checks. If your cripples expire because he's inept, or if he slinks off after nightfall, I'll hold you to blame, with your malingerer tagged and bagged through a bountymen's vermin hunt.'

The head surgeon proffered no thanks but snagged his unkempt conscript by the shirt front and hustled him off. The pair left the tent to a rattle of jargon, with volleyed references to the griped fevers and wound rot that ravaged the terminal case-load.

An hour installed with a needle and gut thread disclosed that rare man whose calm expertise was indispensable.

'Pox on our field captain's rabid distrust,' the head surgeon gushed, all but fit to swoon as he watched a neat closure expertly wrapped in gauze dressing. 'You say you extracted a splinter of bark? How did my probe come to miss that?' Then, astonished, he sucked a breath in epiphany. 'Truth, man! You're

Sight-gifted? Praise to the Light if we haven't snagged us a fancy temple-trained talent!'

The newcomer grunted, perhaps an affirmative as he bent to the lamp and passed his knife blade through the flame.

'Versed in hygiene, too.' The surgeon sighed with rapture. 'Well! That patrol better find themselves a dead horse.' He laughed, sarcastic enough to threaten in jest, 'If they don't, I'll have to clap you in irons to secure your work for the duration. Your soldier's not screaming, how not? We're flat out of poppy for painless sleep, and I see that he hasn't passed out.'

The narrow, neat hands sheathed the cleaned blade through a methodical recitation.

Which list of herbals plucked wild on the heath dropped the head surgeon's jaw. He clicked his teeth shut and clapped the stranger's thin shoulder. 'Damn the captain's suspicions, I'm grateful for the outright miracle. You're a bit starved for rations, I think?' Beak face swivelled, he bellowed to an assistant, 'Run to the cook tent and fetch a hot meal.' Turned back, incandescent, he hauled his new recruit erect. 'We have another at death's door down here. Shag the benighted division you hailed from! Consider yourself reassigned.'

The provost's patrollers back-tracked, meantime, and found the neck-broken hack crumpled in a gulch too steep to be scaled without rope. As townsmen, they never questioned the oddity that in spring, the carcass was not mobbed by vultures. When the second inquiry's response came days later, the dispatch reported no theft from the horse pickets at Barish or from the temple reserves kept stabled behind the lines at East Bransing.

By then, the raffish outsider was shaved, his tattered clothes mended and cleaned. Merit had earned his colleagues' respect, though his quiet nature eschewed gregarious company. The arduous days dropped him with the rest for exhausted sleep on the fusty cots in the corps tent. He showed no furtive intention to bolt though others who shared his billet complained that he cried out from tormented nightmares.

'Who doesn't dream badly?' the chief surgeon dismissed. 'Everyone screams from the horrors we treat, and no thanks at all to the ghastly traps set by barbarians to murder our faithful.'

The grinding routine erased lingering doubt as the hard cases died, and the fight to save the drastically injured demanded relentless attention. The new man shared the butt of the same gruesome jokes, deemed as honestly luckless as the next wretch tossed the short straw for war-time service.

And the day arrived in the first, cloudless heat before the hardwood trees budded: another critical messenger bird winged across Lanshire on a homing flight to the west . . .

. . . this pigeon alighted in its birth cote at Barish, no temple-fledged creature, but dispatched from Whitehold through the secretive relay run by Koriathain.

The unkempt crone who serviced the birds creaked up the ladder in the cobbled yard, crooned fondly, and coaxed the pigeon onto her palm with cracked corn. The packet removed from its leg held a scroll and two wrapped slivers of crystal, promptly passed on to the highest-ranked Senior in residence. The commands inscribed by the Matriarch's pen saw out-bound birds sent, bearing orders: these flew east to Bransing, and southeastward to the sisterhouse at Backwater. Another pair was released to wing south, one for the covert enclave at Ostermere. The other bore one of the imprinted quartz fragments designate for an initiate sequestered at Deal.

More than pigeons set the Prime's will into motion. The fastest horse in the stable sped a mounted enchantress to Lanshire. She carried the second duplicate quartz, refashioned with volatile spells. Dressed in a courier's leathers and cloak, this one travelled without baggage, her purse lined with gold to bribe temple remounts. As bearer of urgent news for The Hatchet, she rode fifty leagues in two days.

Her arrival at the Light's stationed garrison in Torwent did not find the Supreme Commander of Armies snugged into the officers' residence. Astride again, saddle-sore, the sister left before dawn with the dedicate relay bound for the front lines. Two more days pounding astride through rough country, with breathless pauses every few leagues to exchange mounts overtook The Hatchet's personal staff, encamped amid the taupe straggle of war tents pitched on the open heath.

Fresh from the horse-lines, and damp to the skin, the Prime's emissary found the field's command post deserted. Mud-splashed and weary, she slapped her lathered crop on her boot and cursed in the snarling teeth of the bobcat that glared, stuffed and collared, to discomfit visitors at the entry. Trained to analyze detail, the sister sized up the belligerent personality that her Matriarch tasked her to influence. Advanced into a gloom spiked with raw astringent and cinnamon, her step scraped on a rush mat, its striped chevrons frayed by the aggressive gouge of countless hobnailed boots. The Hatchet mapped his tactics on a stout sand-table, moulded topography affixed with trim lines of plug counters, carved horses and flags. The studded camp chairs were leather, empty and shoved in acute disarray as if their last occupants had been flushed like game-cocks from the thickets of conference. The weapons racks at the walls showed rifled pegs, the vacancies for swords and cross-bows and maces over-shadowed by more preserved specimens: a falcon, transfixed by an arrow; two facing hares frozen with legs in steel traps. Above these hung a flayed pit viper, nailed to a board. The triangular head had been mounted intact, with the venomous fangs extended.

A cough from a callow equerry challenged the sister's invasive survey. Peevishly correct in The Hatchet's cream livery, except for skinny knuckles sooted with boot-black, he informed, 'You must wait for a summons. The Light's Supreme Commander is engaged in the supply tent.'

'Taking a routine inventory?' The sister gathered her spattered cloak, eyebrows raised in contempt. 'Stand aside, please. I will seek his lordship directly.'

The equerry broke into a macabre smile, quite at odds with the polishing cloth worried between nervous fingers. 'Not an inventory. His Lordship's ranked captains are in forced attendance.'

The Koriani sister side-stepped the warning. On determined course, she braced to barge into a punitive reprimand for theft or a whipping for some worse infraction.

'The Hatchet is shooting rats,' the equerry called in her wake. 'Do take extreme care if you interrupt him.'

The Hatchet sighted down his cocked cross-bow, elbows clad in an immaculate white jacket braced atop an upended ale cask. The same barrel also supported the trophy row of his morning's carcasses. Careless of stains from leaked blood and urine, he took aim on his next quarry: another rodent, ferociously tracked by the rustle as it crossed the tent's floor and scurried behind a bulwark of oat sacks and crates.

Nary a twitch marred the commander's nailed focus, or his cracked smile of anticipation. One eye squeezed shut and the other bright grey as buffed armour, The Hatchet mused, 'So, then. The black little sorcerer nipped to the left, cut east, and abandoned my chariot. He'll pay for the sabotaged spokes he left broken.'

The furtive rat ducked to the right, masked yet by the stockpiles.

'Better,' The Hatchet chortled. 'Our tracker's report confirmed his next dodge. The slinker nipped south. Since the diviners sniffed out a sly use of talent, that places the fugitive Master of Shadow midway between Torwent and Scarpdale.'

The rat paused to gnaw. Fixed on the hackling scritch of its teeth, The Hatchet detailed his seniormost officer, 'Centre guard's captain! Stage your line into a three-sided square. Form up an anvil wedge, faced inside to engage and distract before capture. Both wings, on my mark! First advance, the right flank. Drive and close in, men! Let's choose which direction this varmint jumps. Ready, the rear-guard! Move at quick march and charge. Clap the lid on my trap, while the left skirts in fast to cut off a northward escape.'

Movement converged from several directions: the odd flicker of gold braid pocked the sepia gloom, encased under mildewed canvas. Lit by smoke-hazed, paned lamps with tallow dips, the jumbled sacks and baled goods cast sprawled shadows and muffled the clipped strings of orders to the poised men. Wrapped in stalker's silence, pale surcoats flitted between the odd gaps. Then an unseen signal raised a vigorous clangour of tin spoons against mess bowls and cups as the the appointed beaters advanced.

The rat bolted. It jinked and doubled back. A manic dart threaded the gap between the centre line officer's boots. Panicked and squeaking, it darted for the crannies beneath the pyramid stack of ale casks.

'Hah!' The Hatchet squeezed the trigger. 'Let that sly bender of Shadows eat this if he tries to flee through our middle!' The cross-bow whapped in triumphant release.

The loosed quarrel nipped between the supplies, creased a dangling hide to a wisp of shaved hair, and skewered the rat in mid-flight. Impetus pinned its last throes in puffed dust to a burlap flour-sack.

The Hatchet crowed. 'Nailed the slinking bastard, straight on!'

To the clatter of flat-ware and scattered applause, the martinet bounced from his sniper's crouch and laid down his discharged weapon. He strutted past the ranks of his straight-faced men, who watched his progress riveted. Several turned apprehensively green as The Hatchet laid claim to the twitching carcass. He spun, absorbed by his grisly prize, and his juggernaut stride rammed him up short, nose to chest with the sisterhood's messenger.

The tin-pot fanfare faltered abruptly. Which fallen hush stranded a blindsided officer, caught swearing in anxious dismay from behind the baled hides.

'Who let in the skirt?' The Hatchet snapped, chin tipped upwards, the better to strop his steely glare over the female intruder.

Revolted to censure in turn, she raked her cowled gaze over the limp victims impaled on the barrel top. 'This is your puerile excuse for amusement?' As the storehouse tent echoed with stifled gasps, the frosty female appended, 'Your cowed underlings don't challenge your pathetic tactics, I see.'

The Hatchet rocked on his toes and tossed the shafted corpse off to his left hand, that his bloodied right might capture her glove for the flourished mockery of a kiss. 'Not a frivolous play, that's your girlish presumption.'

The woman snatched back her clamped wrist in affront.

'Are you bruised, then?' The shark's grin widened. While seamed, wind-burned skin crimped the glint of hard eyes, The Hatchet declared, 'I am hunting a rat with the temple's war host, and you've poked your nose into my field drill. A fighting man's game. Therefore, don't try me with a lame story. You're not my routine courier, snip. Let me hazard a guess. Koriathain?'

Collected except for an angry flush, the sisterhood's messenger raked off her hood. 'Canny man.' Since his strained tension was not due to the remnant headache caused by his knocks at Arithon's hand, she analyzed the searing humiliation inflicted by wounded pride. The Hatchet nursed the volcanic seethe of his fury, pent for a flash-point eruption.

Cold stalker herself, the Prime's emissary pricked him to measure that vulnerability. 'Can you say where your rat has run to ground?'

'I have theories.' The Hatchet disengaged her, surged towards the barrel, and upended the bolt with his kill. Violence implied what his bland words did not, as he nailed the rodent's gasping carcass next to its expired fellows. He was not sanguine since his crack patrols beat the forsaken brush and flushed nothing. 'A few scraps of evidence suggest the direction to guide my armed hunt.' But the furtive glance he shot her sidelong showed frustration ignited to interest.

'I offer your coveted quarry's location.' A temptress's honey masked over poison, the dangerous woman declared, 'More, I've a talisman precisely tuned to hasten your epic requital.'

'And the price?' Not so easily bought despite his galled shame, The Hatchet folded short arms and stonewalled the gambit. 'What oath of debt must be sworn for this gift? Do you think I'm a fool? I'll nail my varmint without owing your Prime an unsavoury future service.'

'No price, except what you already crave.' Her gloved gesture encompassed the idle captains, equally strained as they sought to eavesdrop through the piled provisions. 'Have these dedicate men enact the Light's glory. Take your rightful conquest of Havish and destroy the Master of Shadow my order also wants dead.'

'That grants you the chance for a private discussion.' Fast as a ricochet, The Hatchet barked to his by-standing officers, 'Stage a field exercise. Collapse the camp, form columns and have the men ready to march. Then wait on my word to advance or stand down.' A viper's move reclaimed the cross-bow, followed by the snapped epithet his kennel-men used to present a bitch in heat to the hound.

The insulted messenger tightened her lips and gave chase as The Hatchet stumped out of the supply tent.

Moments later, installed in discomfort on a leather seat inside his pavilion, she looked on while the snobbish equerry brought a filled basin and rinsed the stains of slaughter from his master's hands.

'Say your piece, woman.' Booted feet propped on the adjacent seat, The Hatchet stewed away with snap-frozen impatience. 'Spit out what's needful. Be quick. Save your breath with regard to that talisman.'

'Consider, before you dismiss my advantage.' Young of face and form beneath her rider's dress, the Koriani sister stared back with cool equanimity. 'If the sorcerer moves on before you spring your trap, your browbeaten captains can't help. Which way will you scramble them to press the chase?'

'Waste my time brangling, I'll toss you out.' The Hatchet grabbed the proffered towel, whip-snapped the folds open, then shot upright and blotted his fingers. 'I've no stomach for pandering or the idle moment to sit here being wooed by a whore's pleas.'

Taller, her slenderness frail before his contentious, broad shoulders, the enchantress rose also. She seized the basin before the servant whisked past. Just as provocative in her contempt, she nestled the filled vessel amid the markers arrayed on the map table. While The Hatchet stiffened to that brazen challenge, she attacked, 'Pay close attention. I won't demonstrate twice. You're familiar with a primitive compass fashioned from a charged needle and cork?'

The Hatchet's annoyance mirrored the cobra, reared up with hood flared to strike.

Koriathain, and arrogant, the sister unbuckled her message case. The sheaf of dispatches inside were blank, carried to mask the false bottom she removed to produce a silk packet. 'This construct works on a similar principle but activates a bit differently.'

Intrigued, never placated, The Hatchet eyed the bait she unwrapped with care taken to shield her bare touch: a round wafer of cork, affixed to a spiral of copper wire that caged a sliver of crystal. 'I've not seen the fragment of common quartz that could be magnetized to seek a fugitive,' he said in disgust.

'Tuned, rather, and more.' Hands masked from view, the Prime's messenger set her little construct afloat. 'This piece has been fashioned into a lure with an inducted emotional imprint that will draw your bastard sorcerer like a tame hawk to your wrist.'

'You mentioned your scryers have unveiled his refuge?' The Hatchet barged ahead for the gist. 'Start there, before you defile this place with the heresy of unclean practice.'

Her smile stayed hidden. His protest came too late. Her hook already had snagged his obsession. 'The Spinner of Darkness hides in plain sight, did you know? He's attached himself as an honest man in one of your dedicate war camps.'

The natural rage that suffused The Hatchet's jowled face served the sisterhood better than spellcraft. Before the cork whirled still with the pointed end quivering due east, the Light's Lord Commander succumbed, wedded to the Prime's purpose as a weapon to corner her quarry. 'You will flush the Master of Shadow from the healer's corps assigned to your eastern flank.' By the close of the brief demonstration, the specialized shard of crystal changed hands, secured in a twist of silk.

Lost to his bitter need for reprisal, The Hatchet snatched for the last straw of due caution. 'What drives your Matriarch's motivation? Why risk the punitive might of the temple to play my armed dedicates for her cause?'

No answer arose from the vacated furniture. The secretive sister's uncanny departure briefly darkened the command-tent door. She was a shadow, then a blurred memory, there and gone in the blink of an eye.

The Hatchet shivered. He snapped impatient fingers, which brought his equerry running with his cleaned cloak. While his gold braid and polished accoutrements were fussed into place by the servant, he regrouped his intrepid poise. A task force quick-marched to investigate healers could do the campaign no harm. He would stash the cork and its damnable sliver of crystal on his person with no one the wiser. Best to seize the preemptive course of bold action, that the vile use of magic should never be necessary.

A cold blast that fore-ran another black storm, the gust shrilled through the casement at Althain Tower. Its force riffled the pages of the opened books and lashed every unbound parchment into air-borne mayhem. Sethvir dropped his dipped pen and snatched after the fly-away leaf of his current manuscript.

'The Hatchet will succumb to the Koriani overture!' huffed the discorporate colleague just breezed in to rant. 'Since the Light's thrust is now the Prime's jockeyed game-piece, her lair should be watched, mark my words.'

Sethvir scrubbed spattered ink from his wrist with a sleeve cuff already spotted. 'Too dangerous.' His misty glance lifted. 'Selidie's latest design will see Arithon flushed into flight or cut down. We can't stop this.' Braced for explosive umbrage, and quicker to snuff out a windy lecture, Sethvir added, 'I can't sanction the risk. Our straits worsen if you became compromised, Luhaine.'

More pages flapped. The winnowed quill spiralled upwards, and a leather-bound volume on mushrooms slapped shut to a miffed puff of dust. 'Don't claim Kharadmon hasn't broached the nasty matter ahead of me!'

'Neither has he.' Sethvir laid his forearm across his salvaged sheet, which distractedly smeared the wet ink. 'The Waystone's been invoked. Selidie's bound a choice circle of Seniors under her sole directive.' Strategically placed at Torwent, Ostermere, Backwater, Barish, and East Bransing, those engaged talents were welded into one force through the great amethyst's matrix. The Matriarch already worked to seal the elaborate ring of her construct to wreak the Teir's'Ffalenn's downfall in Lanshire.

'I've seen the gist of her spider's weaving!' Luhaine raged in tempestuous retort. 'The entanglement's ugly. You've noticed the gambit that fashioned the bait?' A manic whirlwind, he trampled on, streaming ribbon bookmarks and candle-flames with uncharacteristic carelessness. 'Damn the black hour that Ath's adepts sent Elaira's personal quartz back into the Prime's ruthless hands!'

'Grace would back their reason.' Sethvir blinked, his dreamer's gaze vapid as he bent to retrieve his strayed pen. 'The wisdom that moved the White Brotherhood's choice must unveil in due time.'

Luhaine dismissed future vagaries, pitched to quibble over the tangible present. 'The Prime surely knows I've upset the longevity binding she laid to secure her leash on Elaira.'

Sethvir's lips twitched amid the fleece beard overdue for a trim. 'There was swearing,' he allowed, brightened to wistful mirth. 'Even a curse with your name on it.'

Luhaine's chill pause imparted disdain. 'Do stop wasting time over trifles!'

The Warden of Althain combed the spun-glass shock of hair from his temples. 'You came to ask how the Prime intends to make use of the crystal's contents?'

'I should worry!' Enfleshed, Luhaine would have wagged an admonishing finger. 'That quartz holds the imprint of everything Elaira said or did until the hour it left her presence.'

'Emotionally, yes,' Sethvir agreed, deft enough to cap the conclusion. 'The matrix still harbours the record. But at that point, Elaira's love for Arithon was repressed by her oath, and yet unrequited.'

'No less powerful for that!' Luhaine said, gloomy. 'Don't pretend his Grace will not risk life itself to recover that vital memory. The sad fact he's blocked his own recall on that count won't stop his relentless pursuit.'

'Best pray his own seal of protection stays intact!' Sethvir warned, anguished for the cruel straits that yet forced that intimate record into Elaira's safekeeping. A mate bonded through the primary attunement of his crown sanction made their union an unmalleable match. 'If Arithon should wrest back his former awareness, we can't prevent the Prime's use of her as the matchless weapon to cripple his will.'

'Worse,' Luhaine barraged, undeterred, 'don't deny the filthy transgression! Even I felt the ripple that darkened the flux! Don't pretend that yon meddling witch sent to Lanshire didn't spin secretive wards to mask The Hatchet's heretical talisman from the True Sect diviners.'

'Quite.' Sethvir sighed. 'Since we can't intervene, naught's left but to wait for Prince Arithon's fate to unfold.'

'And everyone's swallowed that passive approach?' Luhaine's shrill tirade breezed onwards, incensed. 'Lysaer's cursed balance hangs on by a thread. Surely Asandir's damnable oath should have made Kharadmon quarrelsome!'

Sethvir glanced away. 'I've kept him too busy. He doesn't yet know,' he confessed with evasive reluctance. 'We have more than Arithon's plight in distress. Traithe required help to evade an examiner, and Kharadmon's intervention was fastest. Asandir's on the crisis with Verrain at Meth Isle, and you might better serve the Fellowship's need by sorting the tangle that threatens Davien.'

That desperate appeal gave Luhaine pause. 'The dragon who's bound him has settled to hibernate? Ath above, he's incarnate!' Once Seshkrozchiel cocooned herself into stone, her dreamless sleep might span centuries. 'Davien cannot survive locked in stasis so long!'

'He won't unless he repeats his transition as a discorporate.' Sethvir's doleful regard surveyed his mussed sheet of manuscript. 'You've noted the problem. We haven't much time. Your careful diplomacy is Davien's best hope. Please lend your skilled effort? Convince the dragon it's needful to release him, or contrive him a living alternative.'

'I'll treat with Seshkrozchiel. Just don't feed me the pretentious pap you're not worried,' Luhaine huffed in parting. 'I saw your last line before you smeared the ink. The words you had written to archive this mess were hopelessly incoherent.'

Sethvir blinked. Caught red-handed, he wiped his damp palms, sanded out the marred text, and dipped his mussed quill. He restored his distraught lines, moved to grim relief. He had not been browbeaten to reveal the grand upset Prime Selidie held in reserve: that her bid to shatter the compact also hounded Lysaer's cursed weakness. Once in a millennium, Althain's Warden managed to blindside Asandir's eagle eye. Yet to outfox Luhaine's lugubrious nature *this once* posed no victory at all, but instead gave rise to further alarm in the slip-stream rush towards calamity.

The morning The Hatchet's surprise patrol descended to flush the Spinner of Darkness began no differently in the east-flank camp. Through daybreak's slant shadows and pallid spring sun, the roar from the drill field slammed the rancid air trapped beneath the cook tent's greased canvas. The hungry men eating scarcely looked up, inured to the rough exercises staged daily to curb the excesses of idle troops.

The Light's outlying companies were bored, marched weeks on end through the desolate barrens that bounded the Scarpdale waste. Supply wagons mired in the slurry of mud, where melt-water puddled the treacherous gullies masked under clumped brush, and the hidden quagmires lay quilted over in virid mosses. The snail's pace bred fractious discontent and crapulous fights.

Blunt contusions replaced injuries from enemy snares, just as damaging to flesh and bone and as hard on the troop's corps of healers. Overworked as the rest by the relentless grind, the small, dark-haired fellow with the sensitive hands broke his bread, astraddle a bench to one side of the group seated at the main trestle. He ate in silence, while the blowsy trollop who served plates swished her skirt past his leg in saucy invitation.

Too shy to glance up, he murmured a friendly rebuff. She grinned and flounced off through the boisterous talk from the past night's patrol, mingled with the swirled smoke from the bread ovens.

'We flushed that black horse that runs free on the heath.' The comment hung while the stout sergeant shoveled a link of hard sausage into his mouth.

The cook's boy's eager soprano chimed in. 'The stallion the master of horse staked his bollocks that no one can catch?'

'He's lost pay on the matter,' filled in a wolfish scout, paused between picking his teeth. 'Excused his flat wallet and salved his pride with a curse on the brute's wild spirit.'

While the cook's bellow maligned someone's squire for a pumice filched to sharpen an officer's sword, a lanky dedicate with a lantern jaw sidled up to cadge the warm dish-water for his neglected shave.

'Likely escaped from some rich bloke's paddock,' he dismissed, head rolled sidewards to lather his neck. 'Even matted with burrs, can't deny the fine breeding.'

An idle bone-setter lent wicked spin to the gossip. 'The groom who got kicked swears it's got a ghost eye. Claimed the uncanny creature stole mares from the picket line without leaving a track.'

A detractor scoffed outright. Through the distanced blare of an officer's horn, another scout ventured, 'Perhaps it's the shape-shifted minion of Shadow we're wasting ourselves trying to chase. Why not stake out archers? An arrow from cover would prove whether or not the fell creature's an apparition.'

The sharp-eyed man shaving wiped his scummed knife and prodded the silent bench-sitter, frowning. 'What do you think, fellow? Is that horse a Shadow-sent demon?'

'No.' The dark-haired healer finished his buttered crust, then ventured in mild reproach, 'The animal's feral, and simply hungry.'

'What?' said the tracker's scout, startled to sarcasm. 'You've bested my calling and crept close enough to count the beast's staring ribs?'

'Likely he has.' The gaunt surgeon wiped his mouth, and defended, 'Past question that one spends enough time out foraging in the deep thickets.'

'The best root-stock for remedies grows in the shade.' A touch red in the face as the butt of rough laughter, the little man rose to his feet. He glanced in apology to the chap shaving and dropped his soiled plate in the wash-pan.

To the scout, who still stared, the chief surgeon suggested, 'For the sake of your health, watch your step, not that horse, while you're out on patrol.'

The wisecrack dismissal of that sound advice was cut short by a grizzled veteran. 'Haven't yet seen a spring trap rip up a man's guts? Then don't slang the blighter stuck with the needle, stitching you up as a casualty.'

The chaffed scout retorted. Through jocular noise and the screen of blown smoke, the evasive eye-witness slipped from the cook tent.

Grown accustomed to the solitary rambles that replenished the healer's herb stores, the camp sentries passed Arithon through their lines without question. Cued by his shoulder-slung satchel and the spiked mattock for harvesting plant stock, they waved him on his way without care that he wore no Sunwheel insignia. His issue scarlet cloak stayed behind, too likely to fray on the briar.

The drab leathers and dun wool jacket he favored blended into the scrub. Arithon required no furtive play of Shadow to vanish from casual sight. Scarpdale's gravel soil resisted tracks, except in the gullies, bogged with black mud, where the game trails ran tangled through thickets of thorn and dense, greening willows mottled in sunlight.

The other hoofed fugitive lurked in the same cover, too sly to be overtaken. But the plight of the errant black horse could be read from the prints left pocked in the puddles. Arithon encountered the ripped shoots of grass uprooted by voracious grazing. The filched caches of oats he sometimes laid out for the animal were always accepted.

He carried no such token kindness today, having drawn unwelcome eyes and a tracker's meddlesome interest.

Nor did this secluded gulch shelter the elusive runaway. No flicker of night black hide drank the sun: only the flit of small birds and two crows, raucously vexed by a ruffled hawk, perched a stone's throw from their nest site. Arithon stripped off his boots, hung the slip-knotted laces over his neck, and wended his way through the marshy pools. He parted the streamered fronds, newly stitched with their delicate peridot leaves. The sapling trunks yielded medicinal bark valued for drawing down fever. If the routine patrol detected his activity inbound from their sweep, any veteran dedicate knew at first hand: sound leather would crack, soaked too often.

Though in fact, Arithon walked barefoot to open his subtle faculties and sound the flux tides to the extent of his sensitivity.

Vivid, immediate, the robust activity closest at hand surged through his awareness. The chaotic, shuddering pound of iron hooves gouging turf told where the lancers charged at straw targets. A shrill, ringing overtone spoke of red-heated steel being shaped by the armourer's mallets. Arithon knew the flamed lust in the tents of the harlots and the brittle rage of rambunctious men kept leashed under martial discipline. Deeper, he picked up the dissonance fused by violent death in the metal of multiple blooded weapons. His stripped nerves twinged in revolt as clear-sighted talent shrank from that remnant horror.

Shocked dizzy, Arithon flattened taut hands against a gnarled tree trunk. The exuberant flow of quickened sap soothed and grounded his jangled balance. A deep breath and a poised moment let him resettle his tuned senses. Again, he extended his initiate awareness. Past the brute roil of the Sunwheel encampment, the flux currents rippled outward across the sere brush, which thinned eastward into the glass-chime harmonics of mineral across the lava stacks that rimmed Scarpdale. Westward, the signature energy bloomed to the rich, fecund chord of the free-wilds heath.

There, the melodic symphony of renewal unreeled like painted silk before heightened awareness: the land's teem of divergent life showered through him, preternatural details gilded in splendour. From the explosive burst of seeds out of dormancy, to the musical swell of the melt streams and the purposeful doings of insects, the majestic tapestry's intricacy outmatched the fullest reach of his stretched senses.

Arithon drank in the mystical symphony, thrilled to ecstatic enchantment.

When had his bereft spirit revelled in this wonder, before? Blocked recall stirred up an echo of the exquisite epiphany. Once another initiate mage had lent greater wisdom to show him the way. *Almost,* that dimensional encounter resurfaced: an expert touch of such immense scope, the charged moment of guidance had gentled the shock of a thunder-clap down to a whisper. Solid, the presence that had shielded his raw inexperience: tender enough to wring him to tears, the hand of the master whose care had protected him from destructive beguilement. A man might go mad, caught staring into the unbridled expanse of the infinite.

Arithon threw off his bitter grief for the knowledge his flawed mind denied him. Caution demanded tight focus to cross-check his surrounds for hostile pursuit.

Hoof-beats splashed through the back-drop swell of motion. This time no feral stallion's frisky display but a group in formation, ridden inbound at a workmanlike trot. Steered without haste, their rhythm matched that of the daily patrol under orders to sweep for enemy clansmen. Yet none moved abroad. Days since, the last war bands had withdrawn to the south, their efforts regrouped to defend the crown's lines and the sacrosanct borders of Elkforest.

But today, the flux currents transmitted the pattern of a second band of armed horsemen. Another party approached from the west, the drummed pace of their mounts spurred to urgency. Arithon froze, pricked to warning unease. The nuanced impression disclosed a company pushed at speed in full armour, collectively stamped by the pride of a mission entrusted to the elite. And yet, by strict count, two of the saddled mounts carried intangible riders.

Amid the volatile surge of the flux, even a corpse wore an imprint. Yet the animal sense of *weight* slung in one set of stirrups stayed *blank*. Patience tagged the halo of a temple talisman, wrought to shield a questing diviner.

Reflexively, Arithon softened his step. He doused his feet into the chilly freshet that snaked through the covert that sheltered him. Running water dispersed the star-burst of emotion shocked from his rattled nerves. A diviner in camp posed a dangerous set-back, perhaps even suggested a Sunwheel talent could have come actively seeking him. Worked song or cast Shadow wrought to hide him now would only confirm his exposure. Until he saw proof, he must stay as he seemed: a healer abroad in rough country to restock the camp's store of remedies. Pressed to cautious stealth, Arithon extended his senses again to explore the other, evasive void: one that demarked the being astride the horse at the head of the column.

Darkness met him, impenetrable. *Nothing* leaked through the flux from that source, not a quiver of emanation. Warded, a person might be cloaked that way. But such a dense shielding demanded adept mastery and more than exceptional skill. Flashback fear raised the spectre of the seamless walls once woven to seal his imprisonment. Arithon recoiled, his visceral shudder barely dispelled by the rush of the streamlet.

The mere prospect of meddling by the Koriathain kicked every gut instinct within him to screaming.

Traumatized, Arithon leaned into a tree, bowed head cradled against his forearm. Though he shivered with chills that chattered his teeth, he dared not forsake the water's protection. His straits must be endured. At least until the reception that greeted the irregular cavalcade disclosed the business that brought them.

Bright-edged, the electrical shift swept the flux web once the sentries sighted the riders. Arithon required no second glance to know when the mounted arrivals reined in. The initial crackle of consternation swelled to a galvanic burst of alarm: the same heightened nerves had rattled the underlings caught in the breach when his ruse with the chariot impersonated The Hatchet.

Only one reason could draw the Light's Supreme Commander of Armies backed in force by a talent diviner. Somehow, somewhere, a busy informant had unmasked Arithon's presence. That fast, the stir of excitement swirled towards the wicker kennels. Dedicates ran to roust up their dogs and trackers in pursuit of the Master of Shadow.

Caught too close to run, cornered without supplies and dressed in unsuitable clothing, their tagged quarry had little recourse. Only dim hope, that the thorny thicket that sheltered him might discourage the first wave of searchers.

Against the diviner's alert sensitivity, initiate knowledge could bleed the spark of his live signature into his natural surrounds. Not as the gifted clan hunters would bend the flux lines into blanketing mimicry: that working at close range risked flagging the temple's fanatic. Arithon chose the more difficult feat. Skills honed through the desperate handling of free wraiths and lately refined under need to save Tarens let him slacken every barrier he possessed. He sank into blank stillness. Rinsed of identity, he let his auric field subside into transparency, then resonate to the background surge of the flux.

The tactic seemed sound enough under principle. As midday sun dried the ground, the scent thinned, which hampered the coursing hounds. Deep shade obscured the muddy prints on his back trail, with all trace of his recent presence erased by running water. Unless diligent squads of beaters on foot quartered every last covert, he should stay overlooked; if not, the clamour induced in the flux would forewarn him of an encroachment.

Chill became his first adversary, and erosive anxiety, that challenged resolve with impatience. Arithon steeled himself to hold out, even as his drastic state of inertia unbearably fueled his subtle senses. That drawback also expanded his range, until the seethe of the disrupted encampment scalded across his naked nerves. The intimate dread of scared men, and the whiplash scourge of humiliation as The Hatchet grilled his flustered officers spiked crackling ripples of livid frustration. Pinned down, and defensively passive to thwart the diviner's keen Sight, Arithon dared not raise the resistance of sensible boundaries. Too fast, beyond his rushed wits to stem, the barrage of unfiltered sensation hurled him into the throes of rogue far-sight. His balanced awareness tumbled and fell, haplessly pulled as a magnet to iron into the scene at the east-flank command tent . . .

The Hatchet's stumpy legs propelled him up to the trestle top hastily draped with an unreeled map. His frenetic gait was more choppy than usual, crimped by the nuisance of a dwarfish frame, bounced astride since the uncouth terrain forestalled the use of his chariot. The sting to his saddle-sore flesh chafed his pride, already raw from his foe's wily cleverness and now galled the worse by the stammered excuses just thrown into his teeth by the east flank's captain.

Savage, he vented, 'You've lost him! By the Light, we're too late. The slick bastard's flown this miserable coop and bolted flat out for the mountains.'

'Surely not!' Summoned from drill in his mud-spattered armour, the remiss officer protested, 'You've heard the reports from my sentries.'

The Hatchet kicked a straw hassock aside. 'That an innocent herbalist left, whistling, to gather wild posies, lightly dressed and without packed provisions?' He stopped his juggernaut tirade and spat into the brazier. Through the sizzle as the cherry coals wisped up steam, he snarled, 'We are chasing a lethal master at subterfuge!'

'My Lord, beyond question.' But the hasty agreement sounded unconvinced. Even the rank-and-file men in the camp smirked in complacent amusement. Few believed that a black-haired runt who dressed pustules and dispensed oil of camphor for lice could be the dread Master of Shadow.

Only the mousy temple diviner viewed the threat of the living Dark seriously. Sweating and pinched to a miserable headache from the arduous use of his talent, he pledged to redeem his late failure. 'I will seek the fell creature again after sunset. If he doesn't walk back into camp unsuspecting, he'll be cold, weak from hunger, and tired. My search will find him. Amid the night's quiet, I assure you, he cannot evade me.'

The Hatchet's expression twitched into a sneer. 'I should stall for your puling, ninny's excuses? Suck milk!' He stopped short and yanked off his lathered cloak. The *ping!* as a dislodged gold button bounced off the map stand punctuated his staccato bark. 'Get me a task squad. Veteran lancers, fully equipped! I'll have this rat flushed in an hour!'

'Your Lordship! The men will assemble, directly.' The east flank's captain snapped off a crisp bow. The breeze from his brisk exit fanned the sprawled charts and disgruntled the upstaged diviner.

'My great lord,' the temple's sent talent began.

'Get out!' cracked The Hatchet. 'Take your prayers and sealed sanctions! So far as I've seen, your thrice-hallowed canon would make a more useful napkin for wiping my arse.' His glare as stark as the shine on a dagger, he dismissed the priest's lackey, then expelled the command tent's cowed pack of servants. The last of them sprinted, sent packing with curses, except for The Hatchet's fresh-faced equerry.

'Secure my privacy, little man. Then fetch me a filled wash-basin.'

The jumpy servant untied the tent flap, which unfurled with a slap, leaving darkness. Clumsy with nerves, he bumped past the strewn furniture on course for the resident master's quarters.

The Hatchet rooted under his breastplate and gambeson meantime and retrieved a grimy silk bag. He freed the purse draw-string as the terrified boy returned with the porcelain ewer.

'Set that on the trestle. Yes! On top of the map.' The taciturn flare of temper provoked a slopped spill as the equerry quailed. Excused with a brusque wave, the boy snatched his exit, gone before The Hatchet bared the unwrapped the talisman bestowed by the Koriathain.

Alone, without witness, he brandished the uncanny object in his gloved hand. The white glint of spellcrafted sigils glanced through the sliver of crystal, energized by the coiled copper wire when he set the cork wafer afloat. Enabled, the construct roiled a disturbance like smoke through the flux. As its charged purpose ignited, it swung like the magnetized point of a compass.

The Hatchet hissed with satisfaction as the frail marker steadied into alignment. 'Straight and sweet as the flight of a crow, I have the sly bastard's location!'

No warning arose, and no grace lent its targeted victim a second's delay. The chain of inducted spellcraft unfurled, tailor made for its hapless prey. An eruptive bolt of pure emotion torched the lane flow into conflagration.

Branded heart and mind by the adamant scald of love's boundless longing, Arithon reeled. The instant awoke a cherished joy past imagining, then sheared him with loss stark enough to unravel him, life and breath. The impact pitched him onto his knees in the icy streamlet. Wrung to a gasp, he could not grapple the shock of the terrible need that stormed through him. He knew nothing, felt nothing else but the intimate agony, diabolically magnified by tuned crystal, that spoke of a woman bonded to his spirit so deeply, he ached beyond tears for her absence. The scream torn from his throat shredded the stilled air, though his flawed memory held only raw yearning. Arithon did not know the name she had borne, or what cruel stroke of fate had robbed him of her matchless presence.

Shattered by passion that upended sense, he could do naught else except own the fact that he loved her. The excited flux pulsed to his naked reaction: for her, sweetly nameless, whoever she was, the bale fire flare struck the temple diviner's poised talent like a weathercock raked by a gale. Arithon's flimsy cover was stripped. The hunt would be after him, fever-pitch hot, while his wits were unstrung past recovery.

Shuddering, Arithon shoved to his feet. The ruthlessness of the set barb defied sanity, that Koriathain had rifled the clarified imprint of *her* private feelings to abet his enemies. That such beauty as *this* had been twisted as weapon to wreak his destruction tore him to rage beyond measure.

'Beloved!' The visceral jab of his pain trampled even the reflex of mage-taught restraint. Rock and stone, plant and animal, water and air – all resounded to his torment. Hope did not speak in such tones of despair. He never expected an answer.

Except that another lone spirit in range was just as bereft as he, aching for the absent call of another cherished companion. The abandoned black stallion flung up its head, nostrils flared and ears pricked for the voice that, long since, should have sent summons.

Arithon sensed the horse's stark longing. Empathic sympathy entrained his awareness, and surfaced a fragment of memory in recognition: *'Isfarenn?'*

Not the precise Name, but another that bestirred the ancestral imprint laced into the horse's live being through the rainbow change of a dragon's dreamed recall.

The black stallion answered. Moved by greatness of heart that burned like a torch, the horse gathered powerful hindquarters and galloped, its tangled tail streaming. It hurtled into the gulch, smashed through the dense thickets, and splashed headlong down the streamlet where Arithon huddled.

He vaulted astride. Without saddle or bridle, bereft of provisions, and shivering in his soaked clothes, he had only his satchel of harvested willow bark, and a forager's knife and spiked mattock. He spoke a melodic appeal in Paravian. The horse underneath him bolted flat out, barely seconds ahead of the dedicates' pursuit. A trumpet's pealed warning flagged his break into the open. Angry, Arithon gritted his teeth. Driven, he did as he must.

His crackling, hard burst of Shadow clapped down like a pall cut from the dread cloth of oblivion. Inside, kindly darkness cocooned him like nightfall and deadened the pound of the stallion's hooves. What ringed the periphery was not gentle or safe, a bitter cold not quite fatal at first encounter. Those lancers caught at the forefront cried out, slammed as the arctic vortex struck them with the thunderous blast of a gale wind. The blanketing chill bit their frail, exposed flesh. Dire enough to blight fingers with frost-bite and flash-freeze the spring shoots underfoot to blown glass, the pressed, brittle air scoured feathers of iced condensation on helms and breastplates. Hoar-frost bursts of precipitate snow whipped men back like a madman's breath in white chiaroscuro. The uncanny phenomenon balked their dogs and their destriers, and unmanned the bravest among them. Blinded, the trackers abandoned the chase. The devout lancers turned tail and ran, convinced more than their lives lay in jeopardy. Doubters mouthed prayers as faith destroyed reason, replaced by Light of the canon. Confirmed by six thousand eyewitness accounts, the Spinner of Darkness had risen.

Far worse than the temple diviner tracked the meteoric deflection the Master of Shadow slashed through the flux. Kept informed over distance by her seeress at Whitehold, the Koriani Matriarch exclaimed, ecstatic. 'He's flushed at last! Panicked and running! Praise be, we'll take him, despite the advantage posed by that loose horse.' To the Senior stationed in wait for her dispatch, the Prime said, 'The time's ripe. Knot the noose! Then engage the pitfall arranged to break Lysaer and carry my plan to fruition.'

Spring 5923

Onset

When a run of freak gales thrashed against the ferocious cauldron of rip currents brewed up by Instrell Bay's vernal tides, the out-bound trade fleet snugged down, berthed in the safe harbour at Narms. No galleys ventured into rough waters before the rough weather subsided. Lysaer s'Ilessid fumed throughout a fortnight's delay, until corrosive impatience drove him to pursue his journey southward by land. Daliana acquiesced to his plan without protest. Though the choice made no logistical sense, she dared not broach the subject, or her suspicion, that Desh-thiere's curse inflamed his irrational restlessness. Her guarded watch on his changeable moods tightened. While the anvilhead squall lines spat lightning and lashed them with white-out downpours, the ride down the coast mired them in the misery of soupy mud and soaked garments.

They arrived at Morvain, forced to detour past the gates where the crumbled rubble from tumble-down buildings stopped drays and clogged the main thoroughfare. The aftermath left by the frequency shift opened gaps in the cobbled road. Such wrack and ruin followed the course where adverse construction had impaired the mighty flux torrent that fed the Paravian focus at Isaer.

Through the palpable after-shock of unrest, knots of Sunwheel fanatics chanted religious slogans. Lysaer and Daliana located the livery stable through their noise and left off the borrowed horses. Afoot past the timber-and-lath guild-halls, with their gingerbread eaves and the open dye yards, festooned in rainbow yarns and reeking of urine, the undercurrents of paranoid fear tensioned the bustle of industry.

'I feel like the goose crated up for the butcher,' Daliana said under her breath. 'How many converts do you suppose have sworn to the canon in the past few weeks?'

'Enough to brand either one of us heretics if we don't spout the right slogans.' Lysaer skirted the midden in the back alley just taken to by-pass the mob at a shop-front sermon.

At least the sea quarter suffered less damage where the quaint taverns and older stone boarding-houses were built under the precepts of charter law. Beneath broken clouds and wan sunlight, the sign-boards creaked in the wind off the wharf, drenched to the gloss of dipped lacquer. Cargo, baled and boxed and in barrels, lined the harbourfront breastwork, also crammed chock-a-block with oared ships, and laced through the press by the soprano horns blared for right of way by the lightermen. The congested activity showed little concern for the perils of seasonal storms.

The duty officer at the excise house shrugged as he listed the vessels prepared to cast off with the tide. 'This far south of the narrows off Blackshear Isle, the shoals pose less hazard for westbound mariners.'

Yet a morning spent in determined wrangling failed to buy a quick passage to Tysan. The hard-bitten galley-men tied up in port might be undaunted by nature's fury, but the back-lash lately evoked by the intensive outbreaks of visions and madness pinned them under the thumb of the True Sect religion. War-bond requisition ruled those captains with flags under Tysan's registry. Everywhere, the wharves were stacked up with delayed supply bound for the campaign to eradicate Darkness.

'It's a lash-up stampede to cleanse the corruption sheltered by the Crown of Havish,' admitted the last galley's master they interviewed. 'We're taking on recruits to fight for the cause ahead of civilian passengers.'

At the end, an exchange of hard coin moved the flash-fire blaze of devout fervour. Passage was secured for unfavourable terms, with no likelihood of improvement. 'No berths for the night before sailing,' the captain insisted. He wished the dock cleared and the hold's lading finished, before any landlubbers boarded.

Lysaer paid the extortionate rate without haggling. He could do little else. Even the roughest dock-side dives displayed the seal talismans blessed by the priests. White rosettes fashioned from petticoat ribbons fluttered over the brothel doorways, and crackpots sold gimcrack amulets against sorcery alongside their stock of aphrodisiacs. Vigilantes prowled the streets. Worse, the charred taint on the landward breeze lingered from the latest Sunwheel purge.

Daliana shivered, in close step at her liege's heels. This racketing trade town was swayed by its guild-halls, and not ruled as Etarra, tempered by law to just tolerance. What talent walked here wore white for the canon. An outbred clan heritage surely might see her condemned by a mob frenzied by self-righteous redemption.

'I'd feel better if you covered your hair,' she urged Lysaer, who breasted the bustle bare-headed.

Her remark met deaf ears, or else went unheard as a rowdy pack of dyers shoved past. Sunwheel tokens on blessing chains glinted through the unlaced collars above their splotched leather aprons. Sloshed on cheap beer to piss in the vats, they bellowed obscene snatches of doggerel. A merchant in lace cuffs cursed their loud impudence and jostled the comely blond traveller.

'Light bless you, I'm sorry,' he apologized without the least flicker of awe.

Lysaer's chapped features no longer displayed the courtier's immaculate polish. Stripped of his liveried escort, and with tailored finery exchanged for a commonplace wayfarer's oiled wool, he cut through the workaday clamour without recognition.

Daliana stretched to match his brisk pace, forced to dart in front of a loaded dray bound for the joiner's. The crossed carter's invective shrilled through the mallet strokes from the forge, where sweaty men pounded out barrel hoops.

The deafening clangour failed to dampen the rival charms of two trollops, who cut her off in an obstructive attempt to snag Lysaer's attention. Daliana pushed through them, propositioned in turn as an idle sailhand whistled at her with raised eyebrows.

She jerked up the hood of her mantle and ran, while her liege lengthened stride, surely quite as unnerved as she at the prospect of lodging ashore. The sailhands' hostel that sheltered their baggage was dingy and cramped, each of its narrow rooms filled past capacity without a premium charge to stay private. If the galley's sly master slipped his hawsers without them, Lysaer's vented threat to torch her with all hands carried the ring of hard warning.

'Slow down, will you?' Daliana dodged a boy with a hand-cart of oak billets. Ducked breathlessly under a weaver's rate board, she clawed sample streamers of silk from her eyes just as Lysaer pitched to his knees in her path.

The arm she flung out to brake her collision barely avoided his injured shoulder.

'Forgive me,' she gasped. He would fling off her touch. At every turn, he enforced his cool distance, no doubt in the adamant hope she might one day recover her senses and leave him.

Except the hard shudder under her palm destroyed any pretence of clumsiness. Desh-thiere's curse had engaged him in force. Stricken speechless, he battled for sanity.

Daliana knelt at his side, beyond frightened. Every alley held eager temple informants, alert for the least sign of malign behaviour. 'Lysaer, can you stand if I lend my help?'

The strangled snarl wrenched from his throat raised the hair at her nape. Too many inquisitive heads turned to stare, hardened to slit-eyed suspicion.

Daliana sprang for the jugular, first. 'Get up!' she railed like a hussy. 'I don't care how much you drank! Rise and walk like a man. If you flop in the gutter, by Light, you'll stay down, because I'll kick your bollocks clear through your front teeth.'

Relieved laughter broke out. Workmen's mallet strokes faltered.

'Lass!' an aproned journeyman called. 'Want the loan of a rope? I've got several feisty apprentices who'd help dunk your sot in the brine till he sobers.'

'Has he paid?' jibed a chandler, to knee slaps and guffaws. 'Leave him lie, sweetheart. Pick a livelier stud for your bounce in the sheets.'

Fury blistered Lysaer erect. 'You have no limits,' he snapped to Daliana, ablaze with humiliation.

'Quite the contrary!' She tugged at his sound wrist until his testy weight stumbled into her. Bent to his ear, she capped her rejoinder through the bystanders' jeering. 'How much credible dignity would you have left if the Mistwraith's compulsion takes you in public?'

Which steadfast truth stung his pride beyond bearing. His statesman's charisma resurged as he bridled.

But her shrewish tirade trampled his rebuff. 'Fiends take you! Go on then. Wallow here in the mud. Snore through your stupor. I'd bless the relief, since in bed, you've got nothing to show me.'

The insult seared through the pull of the curse as Lysaer flamed with embarrassment. A born prince, well armed against flattery, he was peerless at disarming female attention: but not scorn. Only Talith had dared to challenge his male integrity by insinuation. Since that ill-advised love nearly brought him to ruin, no woman *ever* addressed him like this, far less mocked his prowess before the amusement of gawking craftsmen.

Daliana stared down his wild anger and laughed. 'Stand tall. Take your licks.'

Genteel protest would skewer him with derisive hoots. Should he force her silent, dozens of burly, cock-sure admirers would defend her coarse tongue with their fists. Which left Lysaer no recourse except to retreat to the tavern in tongue-lashed ignominy.

The greasy tap-room at the Gull and Anchor languished in the lull at midmorning. Two crapulous idlers smoked over dice, while a slatternly drudge with hiked-up skirts and a bucket rasped a scrub brush over the trestles. The Mistwraith's assault had not abated. Lysaer careened straight for the stairway without the intended pause to arrange for separate quarters. Trembling beneath Daliana's braced hand, pale and clammy with sweat, he had little choice but to lean on her strength to stay upright. He felt her gaze on him. Knew the sconce that illumined the dingy upper landing disclosed pupils distended with shock. The rigid clench to his jaw barely bit back the harrowed screams he suppressed. Warned that this onslaught outstripped every prior encounter on the Mathorn Road, he let her steer his tortuous steps into the dubious haven of the rented room.

He lunged free, once inside. Daliana slammed and barred the oak door, then braced her back against the stout panel: not for the explosive retaliation her cruel tactics deserved but against the feral current of danger that undoubtedly savaged her ancestral instincts.

'I want you to leave,' Lysaer said, straightaway.

'How bad is it?' Daliana demanded instead, and surveyed him with head-strong acuity.

Lost to civil argument, he met her presumption with a steely glare. The tactic proved a vicious mistake. The rich walnut hair wind-blown to tumbled tangles recalled his *other* lost wife. Ellaine, whose wrongs were as far past his reach to redress as Talith's untenable murder. The sucker punch of old guilt, crushed but never assuaged, hurled him onto the defensive. 'Get out, Daliana!'

She remained planted. 'How bad, my liege?'

The room was abruptly, *unbearably* cramped: scarcely more than a closet with one narrow bed and a mildewed blanket. The battered side-table held a dented lamp, its wick and reservoire left dry of oil to wring extra recompense for the bothered chambermaid. The gentleman's close stool was no longer padded, what forlorn wisps remained of the frayed leather seat torn away from tarnished copper tacks. But the chipped washstand supported a freshly filled basin, and the board floor was swept clean. The warmth from the stone chimney did just as little to relieve his feverish vertigo.

He unlocked his fists, edged backwards and sat to a twinge from his mending collar-bone, and a ripe squeal from the slats that suspended the tired straw mattress. 'How bad is what?' He would not make this easy. She accosted Desh-thiere's *curse*, and not him. But her weapon of choice was his private conscience, an attack too perniciously savage for banal forgiveness.

Daliana wiped anxious palms on the outdoor mantle tossed over her rider's leathers. 'I can't help you fight with polite finesse if you shut me out of your confidence.'

'I would shut you out,' Lysaer blazed back, 'if there were a single personal barrier that your crass tactics respected.'

'Oh?' Daliana bent and unlaced her damp boots, redolent of the harbour-side puddles. 'I should bow to ethics? How, when the curse compromises free will and lays claim to your mind and your person? Let's not cloud the issue of which is your bane!'

Had she been a man, he would have sprung, goaded to violence by curse-fanned annoyance. Readily, he might have struck another female of hardened experience. But not this one. Her tender innocence stymied his bleak rage. Lysaer could not lay hands on her. Not without raising the ghost of the shame from his second bride's ill-fated wedding night. No penance on his part could ever redress the raw wound wreaked upon her, bedded by force at seventeen years of age.

His harsh self-revulsion had curdled with years. Safest to answer this girl's meddling question than reopen that abhorrent canker. No matter whether the geas had held sway: some despicable acts would haunt him forever. Always, evasive revolt made him deflect all threat to his unconscionable vulnerability.

'I can tell you the bastard's in flight for his life on the run by the wastes of Scarpdale.' Lysaer sat erect as a sword sheathed in ice. He fought the pull as the geas burned in him, its drive an unquenchable fire. Its wakened, coiled power flickered charge down his nerves like bolt lightning, relentlessly fanned by the straits that pressed Arithon, until speech by itself posed a reckless endangerment. 'He's using hard Shadow against close pursuit. The presence of him never leaves my awareness but flares ever more sharply as we fare south.'

Daliana measured his tension, unfooled. She knew his nature would not let him disclose the brute will he required to keep his composure. His fierce grasp of statecraft was too ingrained. He would not bend, or plead for help in resistance. The stalker's aggressive instincts were wakened, which made him hair-trigger dangerous. Pity could not appease his affliction, but only provoke the lethal response any predator showed towards weakness.

Unfazed, she approached his problem, prosaic. 'How long can your half brother run before he's exhausted? One day, two, perhaps? Three at the most? We only have to outlast his endurance to defend the bulwark of your integrity.'

Lysaer dismissed the suggestion, impatient. 'You speak of a man trained to mastery by mages. He can wield Shadow, even asleep. I've seen him withstand the need for rest, days on end through his filthy practices.'

'Not set to flight by fanatics, I'll wager,' Daliana insisted. 'He will break.'

'I will crack sooner,' Lysaer snapped, distressed. 'Do you think I can stay under siege for that long? Don't even try to trifle with card games. I'm pushed past the point where I can stay focused on trivia.'

'Then I'll send for hot brandy.' Her grin lit with mischief. 'What if you drink until you can't stand up? I'll shoulder the vigil. It can't be too hard to make sure you stay comatose.'

Lysaer inhaled, to a chatter of teeth. 'You don't know what you risk.'

'That's no reason to pack up before the pitched fight.' She stared down his fraught terror, unflinching. 'What chance for the victory if no one stays beside you to hold the line?'

'You don't know what you risk!' Lysaer repeated. Cornered, torqued still by stark desperation, he scrubbed a palm over his streaming face. 'I don't want you hurt.'

'Is this gallantry?' Daliana cut him no slack. 'If so, then you cannot afford it.'

That she dismissed basic manners, and even his deepest integrity, woke an ire that lifted his shuttered hand. Vision dissolved into perilous sparks. Jabbed by the murderous force of the curse, Lysaer breached the tissue-thin veil of civility first. 'Did you know that I raped my second wife?' He pushed on and killed her shocked interruption. 'Yes, in cold blood! With the help of a belt of strong brandy, beforehand.'

Recoil made her blink. Entrained on her person like a hazed lynx, Lysaer saw the clasped fist in the folds of her mantle clench to white knuckles. He pressed the cruel advantage to drive her from him before he shattered. 'Ellaine had your hair colour, child! Don't think Desh-thiere's geas will not prey upon that similarity. Go away, and don't martyr yourself over misfit kindness for my sake.' He drew in a shuddering tormented breath, at a loss when she did not retreat.

Her stiff silence ground out the deeper admission, wretchedly stripped to bare fact. 'Then don't dismiss my sorry attempt at protection. This is no banal platitude, Daliana. Never believe that I could abide such heroic abuse of your innocence!'

She swallowed. The tremulous glitter that clung to her lashes at last revealed her stifled weeping. 'I understand,' she said gently. Then moved, not to leave. Her hands shook very little as she unclasped the ring brooch that fastened her mantle. 'We'll disarm the dread in your worst fear, directly. Accept my consent. I am willing.'

'I'm not!' Lysaer shouted, aghast. 'Don't assume that I want you at all! I prefer my bed partners experienced.'

She laughed. 'Do you then?' Her challenge was brass. 'Let's put that blow-hard claim to the test.' Careless and quick, she drew her knife. The small blade flashed, a stroke that risked skin as she slashed through her bodice laces. Chin raised, eyes on him, she reached towards her throat. While his pulse slammed and raced, she nipped the draw-string tie at her collar. Her blouse slithered open. The loosened cloth slipped off her shoulders before he could react. Bared to view, her pert young breasts stole his senses. Like two rubbed pearls, tipped in delicate pink, with her eyes watching his transfixed entrancement black-lashed and golden: grace save him, *exactly like Talith's.*

Older memory resurged like an echo and threw him the wrenching flashback: of his lost beloved with her stays undone, poised in eager abandon before him.

The shock sheared him through. On his feet before thought, he groaned at the ache that flooded his groin. He had not touched a woman in far too long, never mind one with a shred of regard fueled by other than brazen ambition.

'Don't do this,' he pleaded. Unlike before, this time Lysaer saw through the shield of delusion the curse wove to blind him. He clung to clarity through assaulted nerves. If Daliana pressed him now and forced his heated need, *would* she not see? He could never outlive his redoubled shame for the grotesque necessity that poisoned the purity of his affection.

Daliana did not retreat. Instead, she repeated his name in a tone that terrified for its genuine mildness.

Rage overtook him, a wave of bleak, uncontainable savagery, that any woman should ever so dare to corner him beyond recourse. Through that torn breach, lent the foothold of anger, the Mistwraith's curse seized fell advantage. Jolted from restraint, hounded in spirit by the raw toll of hurts inflicted by his faithless mother, and Talith, and Ellaine, *all of whom had abandoned him,* he surged forward. The chit who annoyed him was a frail doll in his hands, a flower stem overdue for a well-deserved plucking. Lysaer wound his fist in her tumbled brown hair. He twisted her head back with aggressive fingers. Her soft lips parted anyway, ripe for his kiss, which was not going to be tender.

Her eyes stayed on him. She never blinked. He searched her face, sought the pain of resistance, and read nothing there but pity and sorrow, and love deep enough to embrace his most criminal failures.

The honesty behind that pliant surrender struck Lysaer like a cold-water slap. He loosened his death grip. Flung her away, turned his back, and cried hoarsely, 'Cover yourself. Leave the room. If you tempt me or taunt any further, your victory is certain to seal my bane. I will lose control. The curse shall tear me asunder and unleash the vicious side of my nature. Let me go before I destroy you that way. I would rather die like a cur on the run, before having to live like a coupling beast.'

He waited hard-breathing, gazed fixed on the lamp-flame, ears trained for the least scrape of movement. He heard the sigh of cloth over skin and hoped beyond the reach of salvation that she restored her unfastened clothing. Distressed over the fact she had slashed her laces, he untied his doublet one-handed. He tugged the sweat-damp garment over his head and extended the crumpled cloth like an offering. Face averted, eyes shut, he insisted, 'Borrow my points. I won't have you go out unseemly with your linen and bodice undone.'

The floor-boards creaked to her cautious step. He felt every riffle of air through his pores as the doublet was tugged from his fingers.

'I'm not leaving you,' she declared from behind. When she laid her cheek against his thin shirt, he quivered. A cry ripped from his throat. Wordless, he could not escape the weakness of his injury to fling off the velvet embrace she wound over his torso. Pressed close, she would not miss the tremors that raked him; or avoid the embarrassment, that he was weeping.

Firmly determined, she reached lightly and unstrung his shirt. 'I want this, liege. No matter how ugly you think Desh-thiere's curse might drive you to become, that horror's not real. I don't believe you are cruel at heart. More, I would be guilty of worse than neglect if I should abandon the passion I offer you, freely. Once, Sulfin Evend stood firm for your sake. He appealed to your better nature for love. Why should I do less for the blameless fact I am female?'

Tensioned to reject her by force, despite the handicap of his sore collar-bone, Lysaer argued, 'You know nothing of me! Or my forsaken sense of royal pride, that the curse would use beyond conscience to bring your destruction.'

Daliana firmed her ardent grip. 'I don't care what past nightmares, or what crimes your curse-driven weakness pushed you to commit! Those memories are yours alone, and the past. *This* is my present, also yours, free to choose. I am here at your side, alive, and no ghost. Let beauty and care forge the weapons tonight. Let us build a strong bridge between us, together. Give my steadfast devotion the chance to defeat the murderous urges that plague you.'

He shifted her clasp, then. Caught her warm hand, turned and pulled her close as he let himself face her. He was undone. Almost ripped beyond gentleness as he bent his head to hers and laid his wet cheek on her forehead. Her own ragged breaths fanned his throat as he stroked his unsteady palms downwards over the lustrous warmth of her. She straightened his chin with cupped palms and held his wide eyes. Trapped him with her gaze until he saw that she recognized all of his tortured depths. She did not pull away or deny his mortified stress, as the Mistwraith's geas continued to tear at him.

'My dear,' he said, ragged, 'you are much too brave.' Lost to his wracked need, but not past self-control, he raised unsteady fingers and smoothed down the tangles his abusive grip had rumpled through her hair. 'Please understand this! I can't trust myself. Not compromised, not this way. The treasure you offer to me without strings is too likely to crush you under the weight of my doom.'

Daliana leaned full length against him. The raced beat of his heart slammed like caged thunder beneath her pliant weight. 'You cannot trust yourself,' she agreed, bed-rock calm. 'Therefore, let go. Seize life and place trust in me.'

Her hands moved and lowered unasked, in an exquisitely urgent appeal for surrender. Where she touched, he shuddered, beyond turning back. Constrained for too long as the ruler, cut off by conscience from the sweet vulnerability of unconstrained union, Lysaer crushed his fists into her soft, unbound locks and let the wave of ecstatic sensation consume his awareness. He allowed her bold claim, cast adrift by desire that drowned out the siren's cry of Desh-thiere's design.

'Daliana?' Her name shocked a gasp that exposed his core agony, fast buried under a kiss that tasted of tears. Hers or his own: neither knew in the deluge which one of them, broken, was joyously weeping. The flash-point of fused passion rocked Lysaer off balance long before she unstrung his rifled trousers. To stay upright became an unbearable trial. The unleashed torrent built to a cascade that flooded him towards blinded ecstasy. Lysaer freed his sound arm from their twined embrace. He groped for the bedstead behind him. But the hand he flung out to cushion their dizzied plunge towards sublime release never found the surcease of the mattress.

In residence at Whitehold, entrained in rapport with her senior scryer, Prime Selidie fell back on the tactical counterstroke to heighten the assault by the Mistwraith's curse. Its ascendant hold *would* launch her planned triumph. Prepared against need, she sent word to the poised circle of Seniors on call at East Bransing. Received over distance, her command unveiled the wrought fetch, charged by a clipping of Arithon's hair preserved from his term of imprisonment. The black lock was twined through a second gold strand, secretively purloined from Lysaer centuries before. One word activated a drawn sigil, which in turn activated a fetch infused with the resonance of Arithon's direct presence . . .

The spell-wrought effect struck the compulsion of Desh-thiere's curse like a hammer's fall, ringing on red-heated steel. Run through in an instant, his grip on sane will ripped asunder, Lysaer screamed. A stricken animal lashed into madness, he stiffened, then shoved free of the woman whose clasped arms roped him down with insufferable constraint.

Equally desperate, thralled to the rip tide of shared passion, Daliana gripped his sleeve as his move in rejection burned through her grasp. Reflex pitted her wiry strength in a useless attempt to restrain him.

That thoughtless small error respun his perception and realigned her as his enemy.

Lysaer turned on her, reverted to savagery. The curse distilled the venomous pain of every prior betrayal. The crippled core left by a mother's desertion, then fat to the fire, the loss of a cherished first wife that bulwarked his vulnerable dread: the same defensive need to shield himself from intimacy also had poisoned the next bond of wedlock, made only to produce his lawful heir by Ellaine.

Reflexive self-loathing sparked hatred to flash-point. Lysaer raised his hands against Daliana. As though to fend off a mortal blow, he kindled raw light to destroy the threat she posed to his integrity.

The levin bolt struck her naked breast, tossed her head over heels, and torched the small chamber. Wreathed in explosive flame, her disheveled clothes smouldering, she slammed into the rug. A blue halo of warding spindled her form: the grace of Asandir's mark alone spared her from instant immolation. Yet the protection did nothing to cushion the violent impact. Tumbled over and over, Daliana fetched up against the rickety washstand. Slopped water exploded to steam. The crockery basin toppled and fell, bashed her forehead, and shattered. Lit cherry red, the half-smelted fragments shot through the crackling inferno. Blood welled through her hair, the mahogany strands despoiled and singed, but not burned to cinders.

Her survival lashed Lysaer to tormented fury. 'I should have guessed the Fellowship Sorcerers would send their string puppet to thwart me!'

Daliana's winded effort to move was seized short by the stab of burst ribs. Her cry strangled to a choked whimper.

'Was the curse of your lineage on me not foretold?' Lysaer ranted in demented agony. 'Was I not promised the arrow from the shadows, poison in my cup, and a knife at my throat from s'Gannley? I should have expected the underhand cruelty before any act of cold murder!'

Daliana stared into the face of stark madness, unable to help since his malign reference to some distant forebear escaped her. 'Lysaer!' she croaked hoarsely, 'Fight back. A work of dark spellcraft has clouded your mind.'

'Oh, yes,' he agreed, 'the enchantment of love!' Veiled in whirled cinders, soul-wracked beyond salvage, he clutched his hurt shoulder as though pain alone stayed him from battery. 'But never again. I won't be misled by female wiles. Your false trap of affection will tempt me no longer.'

Light discharged from his hand, pitched for wrack and ruin.

The dazzle deluged Daliana's last sight: of Lysaer's silhouette, stamped against a hellish curtain of fire. Horror undid her as consciousness wavered. She coughed, scalded by bitter ashes and smoke, and grieved for the scope of her failure. Desh-thiere's geas had triumphed. In a port town ignited by feverish zeal, the demonstrative outburst of Lysaer's gift would align the True Sect followers like a beacon. Willed choice had no chance: curse-bent impetus would cavil at nothing to wreak the Master of Shadow's destruction. Under thrall once again, reclaimed as the Light's avatar, the Divine Prince would rally the faithful to spear-head the Sunwheel cause.

Cleared awareness returned to dull pain and thick fumes, and a nearby voice that exhorted her with piercing urgency. 'Get up! Daliana, you must! The roof is blown off, and the fire has charred the support beams. I can't hold the floor under you, or save the plank stair when the walls collapse, without drawing hostile notice. Your escape must be masked amid the confusion before this building burns to the ground.'

A hacked cough grated snapped bones and knifed stabbing pain through her chest. Sickened by the reek of singed hair, Daliana moaned and stirred, the sting of salt tears like lye on her blistered cheek.

'On your feet! Now!' An icy gust dealt her an impatient buffet. 'Follow me.'

The maelstrom of red flame swirled and parted, a vortex of clear air drilled across the puddled expanse of scorched carpet. Daliana peered through the gap, apprehensive. 'Daelion's fist!' she croaked in frustration. 'I can't see you.'

'That's because I'm a shade!' shrilled her testy ally, past patience. 'If you don't rise and march, I'll be forced to take drastic action. That outright folly would see you condemned, and scare every witness in range to embrace the Light's godless religion.'

Daliana shoved herself tenderly upright. Wrist over her mouth, she gasped gruffly, 'Which Sorcerer?'

'Kharadmon, at your service, my dear. Step leftwards. The stair is still sound, only a few paces this way.'

Stumbling, wracked double by billowed smoke, Daliana tugged up her sooty chemise and winced as she trod on a coal. No word of thanks emerged from her lips, but a curse for her savior's tardy appearance.

'I could not spare Lysaer!' Kharadmon snapped, galled just as much by the chanting and shouts that hailed the Light's glory from the outside street. Mighty cheers praised the faith's restored avatar, loud even through the thunderous roar of the blaze that gutted the tavern.

'My liege is lost to the priests' unholy doctrine,' Daliana accused. 'He feared that downfall above anything. Could you do nothing to spare him, or shield the last shred of his besieged intellect?' Rattled past sense, she lamented, 'I had his better nature secured!'

Kharadmon cut short her agonized ranting. 'Our Fellowship cannot help since Lysaer's choice revoked charter law. His obstinacy forced us to cast him from the compact sworn as surety for Mankind's protection.' A chill breeze that harried her this way and that on an unsteady course towards the stair, the discorporate Sorcerer softened. 'Your staunch courage delayed today's deadly breakdown. In fact, you held out far longer than Asandir believed anyone could.'

A sob ripped from Daliana's raw throat, seized short by the wrench of cracked ribs. 'Was there never hope, Sorcerer? I've served only to fail?'

'Every hope survives, surely. You are alive, with no hurt to your body that cannot mend.' Limned in murk through a tunnel of flame, the landing loomed ahead like the gates of Sithaer's inferno. Kharadmon wrapped her battered form in a bracing draught that hastened her unsteady steps towards the tap-room. 'Don't short-change yourself. Your best years lie ahead.'

Tough enough not to dwell on self-pity, Daliana scrubbed blood and tears from her pummelled face. Sparks nettled her skin like flung acid. Reduced to a hobble by wrenched joints and bruises, she threaded her way through the vacated trestles, and took bewildered stock of her wrecked resources. Her scorched leathers were torn and scoured with holes. The rucked bodice cinched by her belt dangled, laceless, with the grimed rags that remained of her blouse unfit to cover her nakedness.

Kharadmon mimicked a polite cough. 'For your dignity, have I leave?'

'Too little, too late.' But her resilient spirit did not stand on pride. Her disconsolate nod gave permission.

Time stopped. The fringed tongues of fire that chewed through the tavern's exposed beams froze in place, while the clogged air momentarily brightened. Undone by heart-ache, beaten and sore, Daliana became enveloped in tenderness that dissolved her benighted distress. The torments that plagued her abused body melted. Soothed down by a tingle that sang through her bones, her battered frame knitted as though touched by light. Her purpled abrasions subsided. Remade, uplifted, she cried for the sorrows which ran deeper than hurt to the flesh. 'I should have known better than to try to hold him!'

'Perhaps. Though in truth, you were overfaced.' Kharadmon added in gentle reproof, 'Behold your worth, lady.' His airy conjury combed through the ravaged room and borrowed substance from the abundance of wreckage. Respun, the essence of ash became transformed to shining threads coloured robin's egg blue, and bright gold, and cinnamon. These replaced her torn linen, and re-clothed her form with artful abandon.

Daliana yelped with surprise, regaled in jacquard silk and tinselled brocade fine enough to bedazzle a queen. A girdle of stamped velvet held sheaths for her throwing knives, and the laced boots on her feet felt sturdy enough to withstand hard use in the stirrups. More, her singed hair was restored, its lustrous length twisted into filigree loops and fixed with fine pins, each strung with a jaunty pearl dangled on tiny gold chains.

'Are you quite done?' Daliana lifted an irritable hand to yank out the ball-room jewellery. When a rankled breeze batted off her contempt, the effrontery sparked her to outrage. How paternal, how *male,* to presume her distress could be tamed by flattery and vain fripperies.

'I've always preferred lavish gifts to adorn a beautiful woman,' mocked the Sorcerer, unrepentant. The illusion of his person shimmered into view: lean, dark, and dapper in emerald silk, he flicked out lace cuffs with wicked delight and bowed before her like a courtier. 'Are you not impressed?' The breeze mocked her outrage with buoyant laughter, while his last gallant's flourish unfurled a plain brown cloak overtop her extravagant finery.

Then, impervious to the rich slap he deserved, the discorporate Sorcerer snuffed out his dandified image. His pretentious levity vanished. 'Fair as you are, I don't act on a whim. Unruffle your feathers and look straight ahead.'

Beyond the smashed doors, the bucket brigade had abandoned their effort to quench the wild fire that consumed the tavern. Rather than address the risk the blaze posed to the adjacent shops on the thoroughfare, the gathered mob chanted the canon's litanies in rapturous praise to the Light. Still more joined the packed surge towards the dock side. Upended by the awe-struck excitement sown in the divine avatar's wake, young men and craftsmen abandoned their tools to fight for the Light's glory and take down the Spinner of Darkness.

To the watch-dog spirit attached as her escort, Daliana asked, heart-broken, 'Why did this happen? What evil design pushes Lysaer to embrace this rampant destruction?'

Kharadmon deferred her inquiry, terse. 'Pull up your hood. Let me see you away from here.'

She bundled her frown beneath nondescript wool, too stubborn to budge without answers. 'My liege mentioned a curse laid on him by s'Gannley. Did a past entanglement tied to my ancestry spur him over the edge?'

'No.' The flick of a gust urged her to quit the unstable shambles of the burning tap-room. 'Lysaer recalled the old sentence leveled against him genera-tions ago for his criminal execution of Tysan's *caithdein.* You know Desh-thiere's curse will use any expedient? But this time, his demise was created. Lysaer fell to the wiles of the Koriathain.'

Daliana stopped short again in stunned shock.

'If you please? I'll explain the particulars later in private, after I've taken you to safety!' Insistent, the Sorcerer chased her from the ruin, then whisked her seamlessly against the press of the tumultuous throng.

* * *

The stately, three-story town house lay in secluded silence behind a high wall, its patterned brick dormers and peaked slate roof surrounded by sumptuous gardens. Tulips and daffodils brightened the view through the lozenged glass of the casement window-seat where Daliana perched with a mug of hot tea. Her beautiful clothes matched the wealth of the setting: a comfortable study with a gentleman's antique desk, varnished wainscoting, and a dyed heirloom carpet. The fragrance of citrus polish masked the ingrained musk of ink and rare leather-bound books. Small carvings and unfinished children's toys lined the checkered inlay that patterned the sill. Daliana poked at a miniature chariot, the spoked wheels of which revolved to a flicked glint of gilt. The deep quiet bespoke a home without servants, cared for, but uninhabited. 'Who lives here?'

'Traithe most of the time, through the worst winters when the wet makes his scars ache.' Kharadmon's presence ignited the laid fire, while outside, spatters of rain streaked down the leaded rondels. A frosty zephyr wrung pensively still, he relented at last and resumed the tense subject left dangling.

'Daliana, I'm sorry. More cannot be done. Your liege has debarked on a galley headed for East Bransing. He will reach Havish within two days. Prime Selidie turned him as her deliberate ploy to impel the Light's war host across Lanshire. She intends the fury of the assault to pin Arithon down against the shores of Lithmarin, or failing that, to drive him at bay against High King Gestry's warding, which must be raised under charter law to keep the glades of Elkforest sacrosanct.'

Daliana set down her tea, scarcely tasted. 'Then give me a ship and your help to catch Lysaer.'

'I cannot.' Kharadmon roved the room with a gusty sigh that rattled the quill pens and rocked an enamel figurine stacked as a paperweight. 'The curse has engaged Lysaer directly with Prince Arithon's fate. To send you into the fray would abrogate our Fellowship's oath of nonintervention. Even if our hands were not strictly tied, your attempt to give chase would but compound the crisis. Your liege will enforce the True Sect Canon's mission to obliterate the old blood-lines. Your gifted lineage indelibly brands you as a minion of Darkness. Lysaer would see nothing of you as you are, but only the pawn of his enemy.'

Daliana looked up, to the glimmer of seed pearls that trimmed her brocade collar. 'I have to try!'

The sorrow that rippled through Kharadmon's presence held empathy wide enough to fill all the world. 'Sweet lady, you cannot untangle Lysaer's doomed fate. Koriathain have engaged a spelled fetch to seal him beneath the grip of Desh-thiere's curse. I suggest that you lack the main strength to prevail against the aggressive designs of Selidie Prime.'

Daliana swallowed, hands clenched in the lap of a tinselled silk skirt that heightened her beauty to sensual radiance. 'Have you foreseen that immutable future?'

The Sorcerer hesitated, as reluctant to foster false hope as to rend the frail haven of ambiguity.

Daliana gave his reticence her roughshod contempt. 'I will not be told to embrace desolation. Something could change that you haven't imagined! Lysaer might wake up to himself, or waver before battle is joined. *The curse is not his true self,* but a vile geas bound over him! At the last, if his half brother dies, he must come back to his senses.'

A discorporate could not console her through touch or offer a shoulder to lean on. Kharadmon answered with a regret to wring tears from the essence of moonbeams. 'Lady, your love cannot close this breach. Even restored to his natural mind, Lysaer will not bend before your steadfast courage. This day's failure will brand him with rage and self-hatred. He will recoil from humiliation. Should you pressure that wound, the venom of recrimination will gall him to the bittermost edge. Your best effort may not break his pride to remorse. Don't unleash the shame that cannot do other than seal his final undoing.'

Daliana blotted her cheek with her wrist, unselfconsciously weeping. 'You need not help, then. I will sail on my own, as I must.'

Kharadmon's sigh raised a shiver of cold that rimed hoar-frost across the drenched window-panes. While the intensity of his unseen survey scoured through her without quarter, he spoke gently. 'No one before you has ever succeeded.'

But her choice stayed adamant. 'I will not abandon him. Don't stop me from making the greater mistake because that is the only sad outcome he knows!'

The Sorcerer could not bear to add the discouragement, that the toll of past failures also lay at the feet of his Fellowship colleagues; and greater than them, had outstripped the limitless compassion of Ath's adepts.

Daliana was heart-set. To balk the purity of her determination surely would fracture her spirit. Clad in clothes that equaled her matchless magnificence, she would have towered among the past company of Tysan's most steadfast queens. Her love left Kharadmon no other course. Respun as a dapper image in silk, he bowed in homage and let her go.

Storm's Edge

Prescient dreams had disturbed Tarens's sleep for three nights when at last the family survivors of the Torwent massacre straggled to the end of their journey. The High King's encampment that promised them protection occupied the north bank of the River Lithwater, a grid of field tents huddled on the high ground above the seasonal flood, thrashed to spate from the melt off the mountain snowpacks. Only the royal war band remained. The combined strength of the garrison troops levied from the coastal towns had lately deployed along the ancient Paravian way to halt the invasion through Ghent and Carithwyr. The vacated ground displayed the raw scars: trampled turf, checkered by yellowed plots of pressed grass where pitched canvas recently stood.

Only Telmandir's immaculate guard defended the central command. The crisp array of the officers' quarters clustered like starched linen, offset by the layer-cake peaks of the royal pavilion, its scarlet-and-gold pennons and Havish's hawk standard whip-cracked at the windy crest overlooking the Paravian ruin at Fiaduwynne.

Tarens surveyed the site. No longer the hayseed crofter, he noted the purposeful movements of men, but no field drills. The pickets of destriers, not tied at rest, but saddled and bridled in full caparisons with attendant grooms at the ready. The scene thrummed with muzzled tension, pitched for the hair-trigger spring.

The grizzled campaigner whose task squad escorted the refugees' rag-tag approach took notice of Tarens's keen survey. 'Aye, we're spooked, sure enough. The wait chews at the nerves. The assault we expected ought to have hammered our centre by now.'

A fortnight gone, the outriding scouts' sent reports showed the enemy's

frontal advance slowed down to a crawl. 'Due to what seems a manic reinforcement of the enemy's eastern flank, though no one knows why.'

'Makes no tactical sense!' The patrol's dumpy sergeant mopped his florid
brow in acute frustration. 'Why should The Hatchet square off on Scarpdale?
The waste has nothing to offer but mud pots and treacherous geysers. Besides
volcanic hot springs sulphurous enough to singe a man's eyebrows, a thrust
through there will just pile his troops hard against the lake-shore of Lithmarin.
That's tactical suicide, penned by the Storlain glaciers on one side, and hemmed
by our High King's set wards to guard Elkforest's edge on the other.'

'If the Light-blinded fools don't drown themselves first,' another man cut
in, one burly arm steadied around the thin toddler perched on his saddle-bow.
For Tarens, he added, 'The white-water race of the river's a maelstrom not
readily forded in spring.'

Throughout the exchange of idle speculation, Tarens let the rough footing
excuse the fact he listened without comment. The mild descent from the ridge
top gradually unfolded the vista that cradled the ancient complex where, record
held, a magnificent healer's gardens had been nurtured by the vanished
Sunchildren.

But such marvels evaded Havish's armed war band. The telir orchards
whose purple fruits once fermented ambrosial brandy had faded from legend.
Mankind's memory was brief. None knew to mourn the lavender blossoms
that in bygone times had wafted an intoxicating fragrance, while the silvered
veils of spring showers unrolled the green carpet of grass across the wild steppe-
lands of Carithwyr. Only the remnant wealth imbued in the land recalled the
fertile past, where the rich acreage tilled farther south grew the malt barley
prized as gold by the brewers at Cheivalt. The view that opened before the
exhausted villagers, burdened down with their plaintive toddlers and bundled
children, offered no more than the haunted beauty of long-term desolation.
Centuries of neglect had overgrown the beds of cailcallow. Wild foxglove and
nightshade twined through the crabbed briar, while the tall, graceful towers
crumbled with storm and time, their cast-bronze bells silenced, that had tolled
at equinox for the mystical glory of the Riathan migration. Naught but roofless
stone captured the breezes this day. Only the remnant bones of the hollowed
stairwells fluted their mournful notes to the passage of seasons.

Except that the heart of the ruin was no longer dead. Nearer, the curve of
the slope fell away to unveil the old circle, crafted with purpose by the centaur
guardians to harness the flux. Tarens surveyed an array of stone slabs polished
clean of encroaching sod. The gleaming, offset rings had been fashioned of
pearl and indigo onyx, a concave conductor fused by grand conjury, which
crackled with the lightning-spark purl of focused lane force.

A concerned man-at-arms cautioned against the perilous fascination evoked
by the active circle. 'That is where the King's Grace will raise the wardings to
repulse the invasion. The overgrowth was cleared by those with old blood

talent, before Gestry engaged the attributes of his crown attunement. The site's latent resonance is dangerous even before the currents were raised to yon heightened state.'

The burly rider who minded the toddler qualified with a warning. 'Watch the children. See they don't stray within. The refined energy burns with an intensity to knock a grown man unconscious.'

Ozone spiked the stiff breeze like storm scent, the belt to human senses a tonic that laced the spirit to exhilaration. The freighted air shimmered, rainbowed with moisture thrown up by the foamed rush of the melt-waters, jewel-toned in pale aqua and blue by the moraine swept from Lithmarin's glaciers.

The proximity to Athera's mysteries also quickened the urgency of initiate sight. Tarens realized he dared not defer his presumptuous request. 'Who should I approach to ask for the king's ear? I have information, perhaps the reason behind the Sunwheel thrust to the east.'

The patrol captain reined in and questioned at once. 'What do you know?'

Pressured as the sergeant's mount also crowded him, Tarens stiffened, annoyed. Though reluctant to broach his affairs in the open, he took his chance to secure a direct audience. 'I've had Sighted visions and several dreams that link the realm's safety to the fugitive Prince of Rathain.'

The two officers exchanged a discomfited glance. 'Ath's sweet mercy, another!' the grizzled captain exclaimed in exasperation.

Tarens demanded, 'What's happened?'

The captain scraped at the stubble under his helm strap, recoiled to frosty evasion, 'The guard's first commander will hear you at need. You will not see the king. This war camp has seen trouble enough by way of a small party attached to Rathain's interests. I'll see you escorted to the royal guard. They'll settle you with the other delegates, where you'll stay for as long as you're with us.'

The shift to abrasive hostility shocked in the face of the volunteer service just given to succor Torwent's survivors. 'What's wrong?' Tarens asked. 'Has someone been murdered?'

'Not exactly.' The more affable sergeant glanced away embarrassed, while his senior officer stifled the subject. 'To our sorrow, you'll see why we've restrained your welcome once you've spoken with the Mad Prophet.'

Tarens was not asked to relinquish his sword. But the hackled speed at which the task squad's armsmen whisked him into isolation stymied his repeated appeal to be heard. Summarily bundled off to join the unknown kingdom envoys held in duress, and unnerved by his chilly reception, he was marched to a tent removed from the main camp, surrounded by taciturn sentries.

The king's guard kept their distance, too reserved to lay hands on him. But their alert posture suggested resistance likely would provoke them to drawn weapons. Annoyed by the stares raised by his broken face, Tarens glowered back, while his person was handed off with a terse distrust that left him estranged. He approached the tent's open flap alone, met at first encounter by the rushed whispers of a furtive conversation on-going inside.

'Ath, Khadrien! We must. The stakes are too grave! Do you think to play with live fire for the sake of a hare-brained prank?'

'No, Esfand. I'm not joking! If we told, they would take her away from us!'

Tarens lightened his step. As a timely cloud masked the sun and snuffed out his fore-running shadow, he peered into the sepia gloom of a tent whose hidden speakers fell silent.

Enveloped by the gamy musk of green deer pelts and smoke-tainted trail clothes, Tarens made out a row of field cots in varied states of disorder. The strewn assortment of personal belongings included a fringed jacket, and several sheathed knives with antler handles. The one folded blanket cushioned a horn bow, the gut string new enough to be yellow, and clamped with horse glue to set the wound silk that prevented frays where the arrows nocked. Tarens recognized the appointments of the woodland clans, civilized by the loan of bleached linen and woven wool. The turf floor was covered by a rush mat, and a table, furnished with leather-seat stools, held an unlit lamp and stacked pewter utensils.

Tarens ventured a cautious step forward. An athletic rustle from between the cots disclosed a lanky clanbred teen, old enough for a thin scruff of beard, and quick to raise challenge at knife point. 'Who are you?'

Which indignant assault lost impetus to the flush of the sheepishly guilty.

No fool when it came to the exploits of boys, Tarens craned his threatened neck. A timely glance caught the covert slither as two more youthful culprits scuttled out of a clandestine huddle beside a curtained alcove. 'Caught you eavesdropping, did I?'

The brutal scar across his mangled nose favoured him with a second's shocked hesitation: apt enough opening for the offensive strike borrowed from Jieret's trained reflex. The brash scoundrel found himself smartly disarmed. Scatheless, the divested blade in his possession, Tarens watched the chastised pup rub his wrenched wrist. While the dark-haired companion choked back girlish laughter, the tougher, broader knave at her side more wisely stood off before trying the prowess of a strange opponent.

'I am Esfand, heir apparent to s'Valerient.' Stepped forward, he offered neutrality, fists crossed at his heart in formal salute. 'My insolent cousin owes you an apology, and this is Siantra s'Idir.'

'Khadrien, here. If I cleaned your boots, might I earn back my dagger?' When servile flippancy won no reprieve, the redhead grinned to disarm the offence of his outfaced aggression. 'We were trying to follow the spellbinder's scrying since we're pledged to help locate the Prince of Rathain.'

'But I know where to find your missing prince,' said Tarens, the volatile content blazed through his dreams too dire to waste over small talk. 'If your spellbinder's in there and not deaf, I might solve the problem directly.' As all three pairs of eyes lit to avid interest, he reversed his grip and returned the disputed weapon. 'Iyat-thos Tarens. I'll share what I know if you explain why I'm stuck here with your disgraced company.'

'Oh, that's easy.' Khadrien thumped himself down on the nearest cot with satisfied relish. 'Dakar fell into a fit during a tactical conference with the royal war-captains.' Hide boots crossed at the ankles, hands laced through the ginger braid at his nape, the young scoundrel added, 'Tranced out of his wits, the Mad Prophet blurted a prophecy that forecast the death of the High King.'

'Shame on you, Khadrien!' Melted by Tarens's weary confusion, Siantra shoved forward and qualified. 'The *Caithdein* of Havish does not wish her liege to know since the advisors fear that King Gestry may lose heart and shrink from the course of crown duty. We've been restrained here until Dakar completes their charged task of sounding a fortunate outcome.'

'There won't be one.' The curtain stirred and admitted a pot-bellied fellow, the beard and mussed hair that framed his moon face faded nearly to white. His myopic blink and artless clumsiness exposed the muddled transition from the depths of an entranced vision just interrupted. Draped in a blanket overtop a night-shirt and laddered hose, he grumbled in grainy misery, 'It's the Fatemaster's curse on my talent. Those futures that burst through during unconscious fits are not known to be mutable.'

Come before the arrival's tall figure and squinting against backlit daylight, the mageborn prophet peered up and exclaimed, 'Ath wept! You cannot be Jieret!' He ground his dimpled fists into pouched eyes and looked closer, rebounded to civil regret. 'I'm sorry. You have the same carriage as a valiant friend who is more than two centuries dead.' But the vacuous daze of the moment before had resharpened to acute attentiveness. 'Who are you? How under sky can you bear the signature mark of the s'Valerient heritage?'

'*What?*' Esfand glared at the blond stranger with the crooked nose and denounced, 'I should know if my family lineage acknowledged a branch of outbred kinsfolk!'

'Long story,' said Tarens, disgruntled himself. Taxed enough by his thankless weeks on the march, he shrugged off the testy barrage. 'The clans in Caithwood were as fast to draw steel. But embraced by the amity of your prince, they were quicker to offer polite hospitality.'

Dakar's brown eyes widened. 'You were shown guest welcome in the company of Arithon Teir's'Ffalenn? Come with me.' A repressive frown deterred eager followers as the Mad Prophet hustled Tarens into his personal quarters.

The enclosure was warmed by a bronze brazier. Reprieved at last from the brutal spring damp, Tarens perched on a horse-hide hassock before the low table where a lit candle and basin sat inside a precision array of chalked lines.

Other tools of the seer's trade lay nearby: a stone pendulum affixed by a string, a hawk's quill, a tail feather plucked from a raven, and a clamshell silted with sand and the ashes of aromatic herbs. The frame bed piled with cushions and quilts breathed a residue of astringent scent that suggested a paste for aged joints. The ruddy boots tossed by the clothes-chest and the crumpled breeches hung up to dry revised that assessment: the fat man had hiked a long way before dawn, over trackless outdoor terrain.

'The guardsmen keep us apart from the king. We are otherwise given our liberty.' Dakar shuffled to the end of the table. He scrounged a plate with a halved loaf of stale bread and a near-emptied wine bottle, shoved the food within Tarens's reach, then parked his broad rump in the ox-leather camp chair.

When his famished guest chose not to eat, Dakar directed his piercing regard through the lambent flame's halo. 'Who are you, Tarens? What brought you here? Tell me everything. For the straits of far more than this realm surely hinge upon your information.'

'What do you know of his Grace?' Tarens hedged.

'Arithon?' Dakar laced pudgy fingers over his gut and groaned in exasperation. 'Nothing. That's my thorny problem. Every scrying I've cast that concerns Rathain's prince has gone dark as the damned since three days ago. Oh, please, sit back down! If he were dead, I'd have sounded the crossing where his shade passed the Wheel. Trust this much, I do know my business. I've borne the curse of erratic prescience throughout a very long life.'

Stonewalled by Tarens's wary reserve, the fat seer threw up his hands. 'Ath above! You'd be wise to speak openly. I was assigned as the Teir's'Ffalenn's close protector for nearly three decades, and more, a scar on my back from an assassin's shaft should have finished Rathain's royal lineage!'

'Then show me proof,' Tarens said.

'You sound *just* like Jieret.' Offended, Dakar made no move to comply.

'Strip your shirt to the skin, or this talk is ended.' Tarens snatched up the uneaten bread, tore off a portion, and let fly as he chewed. 'I hold Jieret's memories. If you took a wound in behalf of his liege, the evidence would be known to him.'

'I have a better way,' Dakar retorted. 'You have the iron stomach? Then give me your hand. Why not share the first hand experience?'

Tarens had never lacked stubborn courage even as a stoutly bred crofter. He laid down the bread crust, extended his chapped palm, and invited the Prophet's moist grip.

'Permission as granted,' Dakar confirmed. He took hold, then engaged his trained faculties.

A moment of swimming lightness fluttered Tarens's gut, followed by a tingle that raced his pulse. Then a jolt at his nape like a blow uprooted his natural senses. While he suffered in sudden white agony and gasped in extremis on the rain-runneled shale of a Vastmark slope, Dakar threshed into his opened mind and seized *everything else*. The rampaging sweep also rifled the dreams that had broken Tarens's peace for three nights and dissected their content in punch-cut clarity.

The remorse stung too harshly, that Arithon was alone, set on the run through desolate country with no haven in reach and no friend at his shoulder . . .

Wrung like a rag, then thrust with a sickening wrench back into his skin, Tarens felt the glass clink of a bottle thrust against his locked teeth. Someone's insistent grip parted his jaws. He choked, barely able to swallow as wine flooded into his throat.

A slap stung his back. He spluttered and breathed. As dizziness threatened to reel him prostrate, he heard Dakar's thumped tread, then the brisk movement of cloth as the mantled blanket was tossed off and replaced with a sober brown doublet. His sight cleared as the prophet tied off the laces and snatched up his belt.

'Finish the wine,' Dakar snapped, beyond rushed. 'I need you steady and lucid for an immediate audience before High King Gestry.'

'The armoured fellows outside will object.' Tarens swayed, unable to rise, in fact forced to lean on the table to fight down a queasy stomach. 'You have a persuasion to argue with halberds?'

The Mad Prophet seized his wrist without sympathy and hauled him unsteadily upright. 'I swear by the living grace of the mysteries, I'll flatten the royal guard to the man, who dares to obstruct the needs of this kingdom!'

Steered remorselessly back through the privacy flap, then raked in turn by the curiosity of the clan youngsters, Tarens had no chance to wonder how much they might have overheard. Dakar's mood brooked no questions: shaken to pale distress, he snapped orders to Esfand, 'You three stay here. Pack up your things. A forced march will be underway in an hour. Be ready to move.'

The order sparked a crazed thrill of excitement, with the brash adventurers too wildly eager to embrace a plunge into the throes of a fateful event.

'No, you young scamps!' the spellbinder shouted to douse the gleam of their recklessness. 'You'll be sent off by clan escort through Elkforest on a secure passage homeward.'

Dakar propelled the stumbling crofter on a ruthless course outside the tent. Desperation fuelled his haste: the man in his braced grasp could scarcely stand upright, far less interpret the rapid-fire speech delivered to placate the guardsmen. But even an unfocused awareness must bend before the urgent development that also lashed the sentries' bored postures up straight. The fastest one sprinted forthwith to report to his acting captain.

The rest dressed weapons and marched in tight step, shaken beyond thought of protest.

Dakar breasted the buffeting wind, bristled to chills and too pressured for time to smooth anyone's rankled feelings. Tarens deserved heroic admiration.

The fellow endured the brutal onslaught of ill treatment without a complaint past one token slur made for unkind hospitality. The Mad Prophet guided his unsteady step and relied on the brisk uphill walk to settle his shocked wits into grounded recovery.

No tonic of fresh air and exertion might ease the dreadful pitch of Dakar's anxiety. Ahead of him the grim news of the storm crow, to ask an inexperienced young sovereign to ride into lethal danger. Behind, like a hornet's stir through the king's guard, he sensed the realm's war-captain sprint and vault astride the saddled horse nearest to hand. His spurs raised a gallop that scattered the bystanding grooms from his path like blown smoke. While the man's break-neck rush angled uphill to intercept, and with Tarens dragged along as an unwitting catalyst, the Mad Prophet approached the tasseled awning at the entrance of the command tent. Eight crown armsmen in Havish's scarlet-hawk blazon stepped forward, determined to forbid his audience.

Dakar kept walking. 'Stop for nothing and no one,' he instructed Tarens. 'The details are already managed.'

Then the on-coming thunder of hooves shocked the turf. Pulled up at their backs, the war-captain's blowing destrier spattered foam from the yanked rings of its bit. Its ranked rider dismounted and turned the excited horse loose, too driven to care if an underling's hands took charge of the abandoned bridle.

Dakar set his teeth, prepared for any expedient to forestall drawn weapons and bloodshed.

'Let the Mad Prophet through!' bellowed the war-captain of Telmandir's elite company.

Advanced to stride abreast, the crown's first defender came to the crux unarmoured. His surcoat was belted, but lacked sword and baldric. The rapid summons had left him no chance to snatch up his crested helm. His authority still crackled. His scaled right gauntlet stayed poised within knife's reach, backed by the strength of a veteran retainer sworn to protect Havish with life and limb. Brimstone bitterness rode his broad shoulders: subject to the word of a Fellowship Sorcerer, he had already bowed his bull neck to issue the heart-sore command to withdraw the lines that defended the border. The face of the fighter yet reviled the necessity that mounted the kingdom's strategic stand here and abandoned an untrained rabble of crofters to face slaughter before the Sunwheel invasion.

'You'd better know what you're doing,' he warned Dakar. A testy glance granted Tarens a provisional tolerance for his brave service to Torwent's survivors.

Then the loom of the current disaster broke off further words. The sentries assigned to the King's Grace backed off and cleared the carpeted threshold. Both ill-starred petitioners were bustled inside, nailed close by the war-captain's escort.

Except for staked torches in pierced-metal brackets, the pavilion's interior did not glitter. Where the core of the realm's business was conducted, tradition kept every appointment functional. The central pavilion had field quarters on both sides, curtained off by tapestries slung from bronze rods. Their weave was plain wool and the dyes, unexceptional. Unlike the magnificent silk artifacts woven by Paravian workmanship once salvaged from Tysan's sovereign court, Havish's Second Age legacy had burned, the great hall at Telmandir sacked in the ruthless first blood of the bygone rebellion.

Yet the scenes reworked in these hangings depicted historic antiquity from First Year One, when the Fellowship Sorcerers had sworn surety for Mankind's tenancy under the compact. The pageantry commemorated the origins of charter law, that the bounds of human sovereignty on Athera should never be over-stepped or forgotten.

The austere furnishings included a trestle table for conference, swept bare of linen or cloth. The royal armour hung on a tree stand, a chain-mail byrnie and hauberk plain as any garrison officer's but for the surcoat emblazoned with the crown insignia. The leather wall chests were tacked with common brass studs, and the king's seat, just as unadorned as the chairs occupied by the unsettled stir of the realm's gathered councillors.

Framed by the blood-and-gold back-drop of Havish's hawk banner, High King Gestry stood up as the precipitous tumult swept past the honour guard into his presence.

A sturdy, unfinished lad clad in wine-dark leathers, not silk, he presented a face of inquisitive intelligence and a square chin with a dimple, clean-shaven. His dark brown hair gleamed with a reddish tint, tied back in a clan-style braid. Beyond a battered fillet of wire incised with Paravian runes, he wore no gold ornaments. No precious jewels but the massive state collar of rubies and the matched seal ring of his office. His sheathed sword on its cordovan baldric wore the storm-grim glint of tempered steel forged for war.

Tarens's forward step faltered, tensioned by dismay to be confronted by an old blood monarch without the expected pause for deferent courtesy.

'High kings are not raised to stand upon ceremony,' Dakar made haste to explain. 'Charter law appoints them as the realm's champions. Their forebears were the chosen speakers, bred of a lineage endowed to treat at first hand with the Paravian presence. They are the arbiters for equal justice, not any figure-head puppet of state costumed to raise awe on a pedestal. Their service is harsh, and too often short. You will nod in salute, right fist at your heart. Show the same respect given to Taerlin's earl if you happened to meet him in Caithwood.'

They had reached the verge of the rug by the trestle. Dakar made the genteel acknowledgement described, still softly speaking to Tarens. 'To his Grace's right, the care-worn old lady in black is Halika, the titled *caithdein*. She is the king's conscience, invested with the power to dethrone any sovereign who proves unfit. The blond coquette to Gestry's left, and still seated, is Princess

Ceftwinn, the throne's heir designate by Asandir's sanction and daughter of the late queen's youngest brother. She will inherit, whether or not his Grace should marry, or whether he sires blood issue.'

No more could be done to prepare the broken-nosed bumpkin beside him. Given the High King's flicked gesture of leave, Dakar addressed the assembly.

'The danger before you has turned for the worse, with a peril far beyond the True Sect's armed war host.' A sideward nod drew their attention to Tarens. 'This man carries proof! His prescient vision has seen past the dark wards that conceal a dire plot, which eluded the reach of my scryings. Your Grace of Havish, I charge you to stand at the battle-front to defend the weal of the compact! The Koriathain have used their black arts to awaken Desh-thiere's curse and drive Lysaer s'Ilessid to madness. Their meddling work has reforged his false cause. He's come south to spear-head the Sunwheel invasion in the pose of incarnate divinity.'

Against the ripple of aghast murmurs and horrified dismay, Dakar added, 'The bale-fire strike will fall on Lithmarin and destroy everything caught within range.'

'This is no threat!' The inevitable protest erupted from the elderly *caithdein,* thrust to her feet at her liege's shoulder. 'Elkforest will be well and soundly defended by his Grace's raised ward of protection. King Gestry goes nowhere. Our war bands hold their covert defense from the river-bank, while his Grace shields the groves from secure refuge at the Paravian focus! Those were Asandir's standing orders. Are you mad to suggest the reverse?'

Dakar's response became shouted down as the gaunt, beak-nosed seneschal banged the trestle in stark disbelief. 'Why should the Koriathain ignite the fanatics, and what earthly gain would the True Sect achieve through a thrust by the barrens of Scarpdale?'

Gestry quelled his *caithdein* with a touch, then raised his fists and commanded silence. 'No earthly victory!' His eyes were a pale, ethereal blue, focused to a raptor's intensity as he inclined his head towards the pair of petitioners over-shadowed by his war commander's armoured distrust. 'Surely the prize for the puppet-string campaign would be the Prince of Rathain?'

The Mad Prophet swallowed. No language existed to soften an impact fit to shatter the very foundations that secured Athera's deep mysteries. 'Koriathain desire Arithon dead if they cannot arrange his recapture. At all costs, I tell you, they must not succeed!'

Uproar and objection mounted to a clamour as *caithdein* and councillors overpowered each other in shouted opposition.

Dakar's irritable snatch uprooted the nearest torch stand. Heedless of stream-ered flame, he hammered the spike on the trestle. The iron clang did not quell the noise. But the burst of dashed cinders and flared bits of oiled rag forced several nearby councillors to beat sparks from their smouldering clothing. 'Gestry must take the field by force of arms and wield the High King's attunements directly against Lysaer's roused might!' Again, Dakar breasted the explosive tumult. 'Unless the wards over Elkforest are dropped to give Arithon a clean escape, our downfall will be inevitable.'

'We should risk our feal defenders to carnage for the sake of one life?' The *caithdein* pealed on, beyond incensed. 'To value a threatened royal lineage at such a cost is an outright, reckless insanity. More, any engagement against an assault backed by the false avatar's light would be suicidal, if not outright treason!'

Against the timbre of fear in her anger, Dakar shook his head and appealed, 'King Gestry, far more lies at stake than the welfare of Havish! Mark my word as a prophet, but do so in private where I can be heard!'

Again the royal hand rose for quiet. 'As you wish. But Halika stays for the closet council, and the princess. Also, my first captain at arms.'

The tent cleared, to many a grudging glower and guarded undertones of disgust. Since Tarens's unkempt appearance and smashed nose caught the undue share of repressed animosity, Dakar protectively hastened him towards the vacated side of the trestle. 'Don't mind their resentment. And don't misapprise Gestry. Despite his appearance of quiet distraction, he's engaged with the focus at the Paravian circle, slowly building the powerful charge needed to raise the ward curtain.'

'That duty would tend to unbalance the mind,' Tarens said. 'I saw more than I wished, immersed in the flux currents in Caithwood.'

Dakar dragged up a chair pushed awry by the disgruntled exodus and urged the shaken crofter to take his ease. 'Gestry's attuned to crown power, not initiate. His affinity isn't quite the same thing.'

The crown princess swooped into the empty seat opposite, her linen overdress a delicate spring green, with the yoked collar and the cuffs of her shift embroidered with mother of pearl that gleamed to her sprightly movements. Slender and fair with peridot eyes, and a saffron scatter of freckles, she smiled and reached across the boards and clasped Tarens's rough hand in welcome. 'We should be ashamed. You came only for help with Torwent's families, yes? Then take my promise that our poor hospitality will be redressed.'

'There may not be time!' Dakar broke in, as the inner council settled to listen. Faced by King Gestry and his *caithdein*, and hedged from behind by the cantankerous war-captain, he stiffened his courage and plunged. 'What I will reveal stays in strictest confidence! Swear by your lives you will not divulge what I say without the most dire reason. Once I delivered a prophecy which foretold that the Fellowship of Seven will never recover full strength if the Prince of Rathain dies untimely. The record was sealed in the presence of Althain's Warden and witnessed by four other Sorcerers. Arithon Teir's'Ffalenn was kept uninformed! But because of the crux that hangs on his fate, Asandir asked him to swear a blood oath that he would use every means to survive, no matter the cost or the consequence.'

The *caithdein*, Halika, turned utterly white. 'But no sanctioned heir has ever required such drastic measures—'

'Never before!' Dakar interrupted. He snatched a chair for himself, eyes locked on the High King, still standing. 'That should tell you the gravity of the hour! If the Seven should come to be broken, your charter law loses its backbone. The throne's sovereign purpose cannot be sustained, or the refuge that maintains the free-wilds mysteries in the first place.'

Gestry sat also. Under the sulphur glare of the torches, his pupils were black wells, rimmed by a pale sliver of iris. 'I am listening. Go on.'

But the captain at arms rejected composure. 'Do you know what this deployment is likely to cost?' he demanded, appalled. 'If you are wrong, spellbinder, if my men take on Lysaer s'Ilessid on behalf of the Master of Shadow, the alliance will inflame the True Sect past reason. And should doom overtake our affirmed king too soon? What then? Guaranteed, we'll have opened the breach that will disrupt Elkforest's resonance. The deep glades could burn if those dedicates break through! Would you press the unethical chance and dare risk the stroke that threatens Paravian survival?'

'I see no other choice,' Dakar said.

'On what grounds do we side-step a Sorcerer's wisdom?' Halika demanded, unsatisfied. 'Tell me why Rathain's prince cannot exert his sanctioned right to ask for Fellowship help?'

Dakar sighed, cornered into the shameful confession that placed the entanglement at his own feet. 'Once long ago, when Arithon's life lay in jeopardy, I bound Rathain's crown to an oath of debt to the Koriani Prime Matriarch, that one of their healer initiates might act to save him. That pledged claim was discharged on formal terms last autumn by a Fellowship stay of nonintervention. I can broach this matter only because my apprenticeship has been revoked as a punitive consequence. I no longer speak under the Sorcerers' auspices, but only on my human merit.'

Silence descended, loud with the hissed flutter of flame as draughts wavered the upright torches. Under the flickered penumbra of shadow cast by the starched disapproval of his *caithdein*, King Gestry stirred from reflection. 'History tells us that Arithon once raised the wardings that defended Selkwood. Asandir mentioned as well, that lately the bounds of Caithwood were made inhospitable to outsiders engaged in obsessive pursuit.'

Dakar crushed *down* the searing, distressed impression just stolen from Tarens's recent experience – worse than harried, Prince Arithon had looked lost. As if, under the uprooted threads of remembrance, his spirit sensed how sorely he had been forsaken by a steadfast friend once appointed as his defender.

A thump in the ribs, dealt by Tarens, broke the strangle-hold grip of regret. Dakar surfaced to find King Gestry's inquiry deferred to his cousin, the princess, who pursued in gentle remonstrance, '. . . could his Grace of Rathain not also tap the same arcane forces in Elkforest on his own?'

'No.' Dakar regretfully quashed that false hope. 'Arithon Teir's'Ffalenn cannot reweave such wardings again, even if he contrived to cross over the river alive. At Selkwood, he owned the full memory of his initiate mastery. The peace of the moment let him engage his masterbard's art without hindrance. He succeeded, yes. But the subsequent onset of over-extension left him incapacitated. An attendant liegeman pulled him clear of the marker stone's range before he succumbed to dissolution. The late triumph in Taerlin did not incur such a back-lash because he was guided. There Arithon reinforced the existing trace remnant of a greater past working, when Asandir raised the consciousness of Caithwood's trees for a prior defense.'

The gravel baritone of the war-captain broached the self-evident fact with reluctance. 'Rathain's prince is close-pressed by the enemy. He may not have the stamina to reach Elkforest, far less shoulder the subtleties of arcane talent. Though we broke horses and sent word to the woodland clans, he could be run to earth before their scouts find him.'

The *Caithdein* of Havish rejected the case, as she must, sworn to service as shadow behind the throne. 'Our king's line of defense will be overfaced! You know what will happen if that stay fails, stressed under a rear-guard retreat.'

'Yes.' Dakar sighed. 'The compact will be threatened in force, and perhaps break apart altogether.'

'Dharkaron's immortal bollocks!' the realm's war-captain swore in disgust. 'What strategic retreat? You will see an end to that fight in red slaughter hard on the Lithwater's bank. If Elkforest's glades become fired by Sunwheel fanatics, the covenant made to protect the Paravians falls in the breach.'

The Mad Prophet flung down that gauntlet himself to quench the next flare of objection. 'Yes, if the worst happened, the Fellowship would be compelled to step in for redress!' That horror engendered a thunder-clap silence. Every counselor present grasped the dread impact of chain-lightning consequence. Under their binding tie to the drakes, the Seven would be obliged to wreak Mankind's downfall before the loss of the planet's deep mysteries. If not by their own hand, to sorrow past requite, Atheran humanity would see massacre by the terrible might of Seshkrozchiel.

Dakar hammered home his unpleasant warning. 'I lived to behold the slagged stone and ash when Avenor was leveled by drakefire in Year 5671. Don't *ever* rest under the gross misconception that the will of a dragon might take pause to compromise.'

The Mad Prophet quaked under the burden of certainty: his recent scryings had shown him Luhaine, locked in the delicate knife-edged peril of argument with Seshkrozchiel. Engaged as spokesman in Davien's behalf, the Sorcerer's desperate, convolute debate strove day and night, without resolution. The dragon still snorted curled smoke in amusement. Such towering strength, quick to anger and supremely arrogant, deemed all other things to be figments, kindled to substance only through the power of her kind's omnipotent dreaming. Seshkrozchiel lacked the referent experience to conceive that such ludicrous two-legged beings were not *toys*, but intelligent *entities* animate and alive in their own right.

'The Warden of Althain well may have foreseen this terrible pass.' Dakar surveyed the poised authorities in place to determine the uncertain future: Halika, braced in her storm crow's black, her white knuckles laced on the trestle; Princess Ceftwinn, tautly perched as a jade-tinted porcelain, her eyes liquid and wide, and lines furrowed across her gold-dusted forehead. Chilled by the mute fury of the war-captain, behind, Dakar laid his final appeal before the sovereign will of the King's Grace. 'I may be the loop-hole Asandir created, with my disgrace prearranged to unravel the cascade of a misplayed future. I don't know for certain. Perhaps I am wrong. But Havish's resources are yours to spend. All choice on the outcome rests on your shoulders.'

Gestry broke the unbearable pause. 'If Asandir's last assessment was flawed by constraint, past question the compact that supports the Paravians claims precedence. The armed strength of Havish must take the field. I'll ride at the forefront, and wield the crown's attuned power against Lysaer's curse-driven assault.'

Halika stood with such force that her chair overset with a bang. 'What if the Mad Prophet's assessment is faulty? By law, as *caithdein*, I can forbid this! A king may be deposed. Past question, the weal of the realm is at risk if the direct charge of a Sorcerer can be revoked without founded evidence.'

'Then let me broach the debt that the Crown of Havish owes to my liege of Rathain.' The calm voice thrust into the stand-off was Tarens's. Arisen in courageous appeal and unabashed by welled tears, he told of the ruse, fashioned amid hunted pursuit, that had spared from the torch a locked barn jammed with terrified women and children. 'You would have no survivors from Torwent's debacle. Not an innocent family would live, but for the foolishly brave intervention of Arithon s'Ffalenn.'

King Gestry stood. He bowed before Tarens, the traditional gesture a sovereign awarded to confirm royal service to a feal liegeman. Bent on one knee, the unbroken fall of the torch-light underscored the humanity of the young man selected to bear Havish's sovereignty: from the fey gleam in his distanced eyes, to the anguished stamp of the caring ruler, to an exhaustion beyond the reach of what human flesh had been born to withstand. Yet with graven majesty, his self-honest respect and humility lifted his stature to greatness. 'I will go,' he affirmed. 'Let us hope that the striving of men will suffice to spare your liege from the net.' Against his *caithdein*'s aghast disapproval, he challenged, 'On your head be the ruin, Lady Halika, if you should twist your powers of office in selfish action to stop me.'

Flash-points

Between the whirlwind strike-down of tents and the tumultuous muster that sets the High King's war band on the march, Dakar discovers the clan brats confined to his quarters have scarpered; which minor disaster is shouldered by Tarens, who offers, 'Two of the young pests are Jieret's descendants; who better to track them? If their foxy tricks can be fathomed, I'm out-bound for Halwythwood anyway . . .'

Stymied at last in his grueling effort to nitpick a reprieve from a dragon's fixation, Luhaine plays his final, heroic card to stave off defeat, 'Since Seshkrozchiel deigns not to release my colleague from his ruinous bargain, I propose that Davien and I should change places, since as a shade, the indefinite span of drakish hibernation will not pose me a fatal inconvenience . . .'

Informed that the High King of Havish forsakes Fellowship orders to secure the realm's protections from Fiaduwynne in favour of marching headlong to meet the Lysaer's invasion by force of arms, Prime Selidie crows with exhilaration, 'Sisters, we've just been handed the demise of the compact, along with the downfall of Arithon s'Ffalenn . . . !'

XIV. Conflagration

T he cloud cover broke as the sun crossed the zenith. A ray of spun gold
sliced downwards through pine boughs and dissolved a whisper-thin
thread of Shadow, which in turn snapped a small stay of binding. Arithon
stirred. Aroused from the formless depths of sealed trance, he opened his eyes.
A brief surge of dizziness lifted his mazed senses clear of the turpentine flow
of spring sap.

Then terror resurged with a graphic jolt and shredded the unnatural languor
that shielded his warm-blooded orientation. He *no longer* knew the quietude
of deep roots, or danced to the whispered song of jade needles, combed through
by capricious wind. Awareness returned as a human fugitive, at present lodged
forty feet above ground, lashed by the wrist to the trunk of an evergreen
somewhere northwest of Scarpdale.

The chase that drove him to that perilous refuge would not have slackened
while he was immersed.

A parched mouth and the cruel pinch to his belly suggested his torpor had
lasted for days. *How many?* By the cyclical reckoning of the tree, Arithon counted
three nights. Separated to analytical recall, he also recalled that the tap-roots
beneath thrummed to no invasive animate vibration; nor had, for some time. Yet
if armed searchers did not beat the immediate bushes to flush him, a watchful
patrol might lurk in deep cover, poised in wait for the moment he stirred.

That anxiety chafed Arithon less than the loss, torn past conscious reach by
the rifts in his memory. The close threat of pursuit did not blind his heart.
Yearning blazed up *for her*, whoever she was: his agonized passion stayed

515

nameless. Arithon quenched his reckless urge to use *tienelle* to smoke out her elusive identity. If he tried, starved desire might blaze past his control, careless of all costs in consequence. As the irresistible lure, her very existence endangered his freedom. Yet to suppress the vital core of his attachment raised an ache that near strangled his heart-beat.

Arithon shivered and expelled a wrung breath. Alert and rebalanced, he risked careful movement and unbuckled the belt, lashed in place to prevent an untoward fall. The effort tugged at the scabbed gash in his thigh, price of an archer's blind shot through the dark just before the black stallion bore him beyond range. The wound hurt, but without the fever of infection, given the caustic sap from the pine smeared at need on his makeshift dressing.

Arithon delved into his satchel, extracted a dry shred of willow bark, and chewed on the raw, bitter remedy. While the juice numbed the edge off his pain and eased the complaint of stiff muscles, he filtered the reach of initiate senses back into the pith of the tree. Not to sleep this time, but to tap into the flux and sound after the rushed counter-measures left engaged in his stop-gap effort to mislead the hunt.

The first trick utilized the snatched floss from a pod, stripped on the run from a dried stalk of milkweed. A dab of his blood on the seeds had been fixed with the signal flare of his private affection, looped and amplified by a rune. The bits of fluffed down had sailed forth, simple constructs blown hither and yon by the wind. Such pig-simple spellwork – *who had taught him to craft such*? – had not fooled the skills of the temple's talent diviner. But the brutal conjury that drove The Hatchet's quartz construct whirled into conflicted circles, skewed awry by divergent attraction.

Arithon's cursory check found that his tinker's ruse no longer functioned at strength: the grounding douse of a rain-shower had almost rinsed out the ephemeral markers. Nonetheless, the shrill ripples of martial frustration trammelled the ambient flux stream. Arguments and confusion divided his trackers, well to the south of his perch. Which meant The Hatchet's lancers had split up in their rabid excitement and overshot the tree-top haven snatched here to foil the trackers' dogs.

The east-flank companies had not circled back. Surely *only* because he had left a clipped lock of his hair plaited into the stallion's mane. That trick would divert the intrepid diviner, at least until a more active, true presence overwhelmed the falsified signal. Cautiously, the pine borrowed this time as a shield, Arithon eased his probe outward. Soon enough, he encountered his precision conjury laid down in actualized Paravian. Blessedly, still, that power yet knitted his dilute veil of Shadow about the loose animal: a cloaking dense enough to cause fear and mask that it no longer carried a rider. Canny spirit, the horse eluded the chase with the same manic glee that had lathered the war camp's skilled grooms to annoyance.

Arithon trembled with gratitude. Past question, the spirited stallion had spared him. Granted his respite to bid for escape, he slid off the branch and climbed downwards. Memory tickled: *he had done this before.* But the wooded knoll that hosted these evergreens lay matted with pungent, shed needles: not the snow blanket on gravel suggested in flickered recall, bounded by a choked winter stream. Here the warm earth wore the musk of new spring, though the turf underfoot had been just as viciously trampled by enemy destriers.

Arithon stifled the flare of his yearning. Too risky, to seek out his prior experience since any spontaneous burst of high feeling might flag the vigilant diviner. His flight for survival hounded his nerves with an unpleasant sense of familiarity. Surely he had suffered such desperate straits through a man-hunt determined as this one. Stealth ruled his urgency as he crept to the verge of the trees and surveyed his limited prospects.

Beyond the spindly fringe of stunt saplings, the flat landscape unrolled a mottled span of burlap brush. Gusts hissed through hummocks of briar and gorse, and tossed the clusters of scrub willows, stitched like yellow fringe at the seams of meandering, melt-swollen gulches. Small game could be snared there, and water offered the clearest of conduits to sound the surrounding flux currents. Arithon ventured downwind, tensed for signs of pursuit as he ducked between pockets of scanty cover.

He laid traps for sustenance and tended his wound. Jumpy as a wild animal, he relied on initiate sensitivity to gauge the dedicates' frenetic activity, then wrung his fickle, ancestral foresight to cast the bent of their movements into the future. The shifting shadows of probability showed his choices cut off on three sides, with the eastward course his best option.

The breeze from that quarter wafted a sulphurous taint off the rugged waste of Scarpdale. The bubbling mud pots that riddled the volcanic seam at the Storlain foothills edged an unstable terrain, fraught with poisonous, opaline mineral pools and blow-holes that vented the steaming plumes of the geysers. A man on foot in that country could perish, scalded by the explosive seethe of the natural elements. But such hazards offered a back-handed advantage. Hounds scented poorly across heated ground tainted by brimstone and lava smoke. Danger also heightened uncertainty, pressure enough to exhaust oathsworn faith. Deprived of shelter and solace, the enemy war host could outreach its line of supply. If their quarry ran far enough to lure them astray, he might fray their endurance, perhaps even fracture their faith-based commitment.

But the sudden bray of a horn crushed such opportune hope. Launched to instantaneous flight, Arithon bolted flat out across the desolate terrain. He ran, unaware how his passage had always been dogged, each twist and turn of the Sunwheel campaign played against him on puppet strings by his most dangerous enemy.

Amid a trade caravan encamped alongside the dusty road north of Sanpashir, Elaira shut her eyes through a sudden onslaught of dizziness. Her white-knuckled grip scarcely salvaged her perch on the tail-board of a tinker's wagon. As her jolted senses upended, the care-free squeals of the pot-mender's raggedy children faded, overrun by the fierce awareness: *of a wrenching, unbearable outcry for love lost, and passion that pierced with the quicksilver spurt of Arithon's ungovernable longing . . .*

. . . alone in the desolation of Scarpdale, the Teir's'Ffalenn gasped aloud. Either his exhaustive vigilance had slipped; or his unseen captors barraged him afresh. The strong jolts of desire that wrecked his control were spell-driven seekings unleashed by an enemy's crystal aligned to run him to earth. *Whoever* she *had been, dead or alive, her remembrance posed him a fatal liability.*

Arithon smothered his ruthless need and still failed to curb his raced heart-beat. Hard-pressed not to weep, too aware his position was compromised, he snatched up a willing, rough pebble and sequestered the blaze of his private emotion into its mineral matrix. Then he ran, desperate, until his lungs burned. The first ditch he found with a muddy streamlet dropped him onto his knees. He tossed the stone into the water. Prayed the sluggish current could clear the vivid imprint quickly enough to erase the damning, bright signature that his outburst of passion blazed into the flux.

He moved on, pushed himself past exhaustion to distance the site since his fixated foes would be drawn like a magnet until the last trace ripple of his anguish faded . . .

. . . the rip tide of the errant vision shattered, dispelled by the touch of someone's warm hand. Elaira blinked, restored with a wrench to her proper orientation. Little time had elapsed. The tinker's vivacious youngest, age two, charged on stumpy legs and sat down on the contested ball, a wad fashioned out of wound string. Her gleeful antic fouled the game played with sticks by her elder brothers. Their whoops enlivened the day's last sunlit hour, barraged by yipped barks as the camp dog tore free of two more rosy girls, who chased, squealing, into the rumpus.

The gaunt father, who mended a broken tin lamp by the fire, kept whistling, long since deafened by their youthful exuberance. But his generous, black-eyed matron never missed anything. Her next oldest daughter stirred the forsaken supper pot while she attended the peaked distress of her female passenger. 'Has our noise caused a headache? Might want to lie down. I'll brew a tisane to ease you.'

Elaira patched together her shredded poise. 'No, thank you kindly. I'll take care of myself.' Before the good woman shouted to restrain her exuberant brood, the enchantress pushed off the wagon and stood. 'Let the little ones play. A brisk walk ought to set me to rights.'

The matron's searching glance remained dubious. 'I've marked your bouts of pallor for days. Might not be caused by the heat. You're not bearing, dearie, are you?'

Elaira laughed. 'No. Beyond question.' But a truthful note of aggrieved regret spiked through her casual humour.

'Ah, well, you're young yet,' the matron sympathized. 'You've got plenty of time in the world. There's a little stream a short hop through the wood with a peaceful spot on the bank. Take my small copper kettle from the family chest. I'll send one of my brats with a striker and kindling.'

'My own pannikin will boil tea well enough.' Elaira shouldered her satchel, anxious to duck the matron's nosy solicitude. 'Please don't put your child to the trouble.' She forced her unsteady knees to bear weight, then threaded her way past the raucous ball game and lost herself into the gaudy sprawl of parked wagons and picketed draught animals.

Need for quiet solitude pressured her urgency. She sensed *every time* when the Prime's ugly use of her personal, crystal-sent signature goaded her beloved to fraught exposure. Always, Elaira cringed to imagine which of the order's dark sigils ruled the vile construct created to spur The Hatchet's search. Her innate female instinct raised strident foreboding that the late bid to force Arithon's capture masked a manipulative strategy to advance Koriani ambition. Growing anxiety left her distraught, that Arithon had been driven near to the end of his resources.

Elaira hurried, dead-ended again in the tight maze of wagons and tethered livestock. Her rush scattered a bleating flock of goats, to insults from the rattled herd-boy. The spring caravan out-bound from Atchaz crammed the grass verge, the stale scent of oxen mingled with the seared fat dripped from spitted meat and the fragrance of crushed thyme and clover. Dogs yapped, while the mournful strains of a flute and two frenetic fiddles wove through the mingled, bickering folk settled down to their evening meal. Elaira forced her way through the clusters of drays, jammed with silk bales wrapped under tarpaulin. She could not distance herself fast enough from the crowded tents and raised dust. This encampment already held more than a hundred mixed wagons. By equinox, more would grind their sedate way by road towards the eastshore harbours, while galley trade slackened in the southern seaports before the onset of summer. Heat bred the pestilent fevers, with increased concern that sickness could run rampant as the Light's hysterical, back-lash cleanses stamped out heretical talent. True healers and herb-women with Elaira's knowledge stayed secretively scarce since the violent flux shift incited the fervent wave of mass conversions.

More than ever before, her arcane practice demanded circumspect caution. Masked in due course by the twilight wood, Elaira turned up-stream. When she found a remote pool undisturbed by the women and girls sent out to draw water, she settled herself on the mossy bank with her satchel unopened beside her. She never intended a fire or tea. Settled in privacy, surrounded by piping frogs and the scrape of night insects, she breathed in the heady tonic of tender greenery, forehead rested on her crossed arms. But on this fraught hour, even her iron discipline failed to restore any measure of calm.

Worry shredded her effortful focus. 'Beloved,' she whispered, then bowed under the torrent and wept.

Arithon's plight wracked her spirit without surcease. She knew he snatched his hazed rest in catnaps. No music or language soothed his strained ears. Only the lilted chirps of wild birds, and the cough of the night-hunting bobcat. He ate wild roots and boiled milkweed sprouts. When game fell to his snares, the uncured pelts patched the clothing ripped ragged on the wild briar.

No mortal was fashioned to endure countless days, spent immersed in the etheric surge of the flux tides. Arithon had little choice. To evade The Hatchet's relentless patrols, he tapped his deep mage-sight as compass and guidance, until his taut nerves flinched to each flash-point flare that rippled the lane current. Wrenched by the blaze of his animal needs, Elaira knew when he fled the search parties beating the brush. She startled to his sped pulse when the pheasants flushed in squawking alarm, and reflexive empathy whipped him to a sprint on the burst of their avian terror.

Such extended bouts of overtaxed focus distorted the balance of human senses. As Arithon's sounding-board, heart and mind, Elaira shared the intimate shock of assault as the war host's relentless advance inflamed his overwrought flesh. Shuddered under the throes throughout his bouts of rogue vision, she tasted the martial tang of the on-coming war: bitter as oiled steel and old blood, barbed in pain that howled for requital. Other times, she caught Arithon's panicked glimpse of the marching ranks of the vanguard: a distant shimmer that mowed like a whetted scythe across the mottled landscape of thicket and furze. She felt Arithon flinch to the pounding gallop of The Hatchet's mounted couriers. His recoil sawed into her quietude, while the thunderous mill of iron-rimmed wheels and yoked ox trains conveyed the invasion's supply to a chopped welter of mangled turf.

Always, Arithon threaded the needle's-eye gaps between the encroaching trackers. Only profound trust in his wily inventiveness sustained hope throughout the repeated, surprise thrusts aimed to snare him. But if the brow-beaten Sunwheel dedicates failed to capture him, living or dead, the insidious pressure behind tonight's assault catastrophically altered the stakes.

Burned dry of tears, centred at last, Elaira assembled her limited assets to fathom the Matriarch's secretive game plan. If the stone knife the Biedar left in her charge could tip the odds in Prince Arithon's favour, she would hang the consequences, break her life-term oath, and act without hesitation.

Never mind the stark folly that her resolve to pry into the order's Senior affairs posed a suicidal risk. The mere prospect prickled Elaira's nape and broke her into a cold sweat. The Fellowship themselves seldom dared to cross a Prime's will or meddled into the order's warded business. Since in a straight contest, the Sorcerers' power quite likely outmatched Koriani enchantments, the Seven might venture such perilous ground through cagy wisdom, if not dauntless force. But the contest outfaced a third-level sister restricted to charitable service. Elaira risked the high charge of betrayal, disadvantaged without the trained knowledge carried by Seniors endowed with administrative rank.

The tranquil night wood lent her no secure haven from her superiors' long reach. Elaira would be crushed on the instant if her rash intrusion drew notice.

'Powers of mercy forefend,' she whispered, committed past reason, and terrified. She had only a trick bag of hedge witch's skills, picked up from a crone during earliest childhood, added to the brief tutelage of Ath's white adepts, who taught only the pure precepts of healing derived from the grace of the prime source. To that scrounged patchwork of skills, she owned a clean crystal, gifted to her by a seller of simples and outside the provenance of the Koriathain. Also the empathic connection to Arithon, ceded to her for safekeeping. Barebones invention alone must fashion the strength of her strategy.

Elaira steadied her shredded nerves and immersed herself into the wider awareness of trance state. No untoward movement disturbed her surrounds. Only the wing-beats of night-flying moths and the rustles of four-footed predators. The velvet dark contained no hidden threat. Night breezes whispered of nothing else but the courtship of frogs and the liquid arias of a wakeful mockingbird.

For the greatest endeavour of her working life, Elaira enacted a cross of guard: a ward of concealment basic as dirt, whose rhymed cantrip charged the essence of four commonplace river stones with the virtues of the cardinal elements. Such a lowbrow technique once had raised the cross-grained surprise of Kharadmon, caught out in a stealthy act of intrusion. The protection *might* be as disdainfully missed by the order's tight circle of watch-dogs. Poised within her rote-formed construct, Elaira invoked her natural affinity to water and tapped into the electromagnetic stream of the flux. Then she unwrapped the cleared shaft of her quartz and engaged the precepts espoused by Ath's adepts. Granted a willing partnership with the mineral, she ran her awareness of Arithon through its enabled matrix.

Softly as a stalker, more silent than snowfall, she tuned her mind to receive. Then she touched the tip of the crystal to earth. She listened, stilled as the mirror flawlessly polished for passive reception, that her refined discernment might identify the tell-tale stamp of the sigils employed by the order. If the Prime shaped a malign thrust against Arithon, Elaira's cross-linked awareness through him sought to uncover the pattern.

An hour passed, uneventfully calm. Then another, disrupted by biting insects and a cramped leg, crushed bloodless from immobility. Elaira stretched, changed position and started again, while the night deepened and the overhead canopy stitched leaves like jet lace against the shimmered stars at the zenith. Owls hunted for mice. The frogs' chorus swelled and waned to gapped pockets of silence. Before dawn, about to lose heart and give up, Elaira detected the elusive ripple of wrongness: a ring of chained sigils surrounded Scarpdale in a wide-spread net that extended clear to the shore of Lithmarin. Deftly woven by multiple Seniors, the noose strung in wait was tempered to spring on the instant the lone fugitive encountered its boundary.

As the trap's select design filtered through Elaira's awareness, the unparalleled scope of the Prime Matriarch's cruelty shocked her explosively out of deep trance.

She wakened, crying with outrage and grief. For Arithon's ruin, the sisterhood spurned every limit of moral restraint! Revolted to hatred, seared by a bitter revilement that snapped final faith in the order's integrity, the enchantress who cherished the Prince of Rathain covered her face in despair.

Far worse than death, the brutal spells entrained for her beloved were pitched to revive the old pattern of Desh-thiere's geas. This, when the targeted man was alone and friendless, beset by a war host of zealots whipped onwards by Lysaer's fetch-driven madness. The ugly snare had been sealed into place with Arithon already surrounded. When he succumbed, the Mistwraith's rekindled design would torch off a massacre. Both Havish and Tysan would suffer the impact, thousands of lives destroyed at a stroke for the Prime's cold-cast plot to abolish the compact.

Elaira rocked in destitute horror. She could make no difference. In her hands, at long distance in Shand, the stone knife of the Biedar was useless. For all its potential to avert the holocaust, she could not reach Arithon's side or turn his despair on the fateful hour he would trigger the diabolical bane set to break him.

Spring weltered the wild steppes of north Havish in mud, transformed at a breath by floss shoots of pale green, which had burst beneath the sun's blaze before equinox into a leafed scrim of briar and willow. The thawed bogs baked dry. Reduced to clay hardpan that no longer pulled horseshoes and mired the supply wagons up to the hubs, the march of the True Sect invasion lumbered out of its nerve-wracked crawl. Gadded in turn by the swarming flies that savaged the flesh of men and harnessed livestock, the rank and file tramped in lock-step, while the white-and-gold standards snapped at the fore, and the officers' impatient outriders harried the dusty laggards in the rear-guard.

As the Light's hammer descended to strike its righteous blow against Havish's anvil, The Hatchet angled the armed jaws of his east and west flanks with the finesse of the master tactician. For two fortnights, his crack trackers had flushed their exhausted prey into repeated flight. Select companies of dedicate lancers and a steel hedge of weapons hazed him ever to the south towards the shore of Lithmarin. Given the avatar's power of light and sure means to ascertain the quarry's position, the elusive Spinner of Darkness could be pinned at bay against the sheer, rampart cliffs, reared above the melt-swollen lake. The campaign's high command jockeyed for the certain destruction of evil within three days.

Until the succession of lathered scouts reined in with reports that a pitched battle might hamper the victory. Late off the mark by The Hatchet's vexed estimate, Havish's royal defenders marched to take the field. At numbers, in strength, they pushed to oppose the southbound thrust of the invasion.

'It's a gang-up nuisance!' the True Sect commander summed up, his sweaty gauntlets flung at his cringing equerry. 'If the king's forces stand their hard ground, if they fight under punishment long enough, they might provide the Master of Shadow a narrow gap to slip through. Though by Light, they'll take withering losses with no guarantee they can buy his escape!'

Grim death itself underwrote the attempt. Gestry's advisors were not blind or sanguine. They knew a fixed stand to deflect the advance pitched Havish's forces against crippling odds. Where the High King's wards might back a defensive engagement on favourable terrain, this provocative rush to launch an assault placed the rocky ravine at the defenders' heels. The thundering spume of the river-course allowed no safe ground for retreat. Yet the nettlesome temper of the king's war chief held the sheer drop at the gorge as the least dreadful feature laid against his outfaced troops.

Which vivid truth Tarens encountered at once in his hot pursuit of three flit-brained clan youngsters. Though their hapless course threatened to grind him, and them, in the maelstrom once the implacable war hosts collided, he faced the uncanny array of entanglements surely plotted to muddle his course: for the miscreants led his chase down the old track carved out by Athera's Paravians.

The ancient way followed the crest of the ridge on the Lithwater's northern bank, its derelict presence an indented crease shadowed beneath the aged boughs of twisted, mossy oaks. Matted with leaves and wire-tough snarls of bramble, the great, fitted slabs of grained granite laid down by the centaur masons once connected a Second Age line of defense works. Its paved course bisected the continent, arisen at the buried focus circle beneath Jaelot, to wind through the southernmost pass in the Skyshiels, then plunged in reeling, stepped switchbacks to the shores of Daenfal Lake. At midpoint in the heart of Paravia, the route sliced between two massive, paired marker stones. The western leg threaded the volcanic gap in the Storlains, thence skirted the Lithwater's downstream plunge towards the Westland Sea. Though the mighty blocks might have supported a wagon, no wheels rolled here, nor ever had: charter law disbarred all trade use beyond Backwater.

Mankind rightly should fear to tread where even the Fellowship Sorcerers travelled lightly.

But not Cosach's young heir, selected for the *caithdein*'s seat after his father. Esoteric affinity for the free wilds was Esfand's born provenance, an advantage he seized to abet his companions' hair-raising intent to foil adult pursuit.

To catch them, Tarens must match their brash lead or abandon his charge altogether.

Thrust into rugged, uncanny territory, and truly alone, he began to encounter the profound changes wrought since the loss of his farm-steader's roots. The instant he trod, quivering, onto unquiet ground, the alarmed instincts of Jieret's bequest stabbed his nerves to a prickle of warning.

Tarens refused panic. Against the haunted, urgent unease that suggested the flicker of uncanny movement, he saw nothing. Only the busy rustle of squirrels disturbed the shadowy canopy. Slant sunbeams latticed the mild spring air like sheer ribbon and etched the spring ferns to translucent, chipped jade. And yet the strange quiver of *presence* persisted. Even the gentlest riffle of breeze puckered his skin into gooseflesh. As if strains of music teased his awareness just beyond natural hearing, he shuddered, raked by an exquisite desire to lose himself into beguilement.

Caithwood's experience taught him when not to listen too closely, where transcendent perceptions tickled the bounds of human awareness. 'Forgive,' Tarens murmured, awake to his peril. He roused himself enough to move on without fatal pause for reverie.

Jieret's clanbred imprint also cautioned him to avoid the glass-clear pools and to drink only water dipped from the swift race of the Lithwater. Tarens pressed forward with edgy care. He learned not to look each time something *other* flashed through his peripheral vision. The least intent to discern the disturbance invited the silver-point dance of a bygone era's inhabitants, fast followed by a swell of grief that threatened to unravel his mortal peace. Often the surfeit of residual emotion broke him to tears. Some things that were lost to the world had been far too exquisitely joyful to bear. Each of his blundering steps on the earth spoke through the ancient track and wakened the echoes of forgotten song. Beauty and wisdom whispered in stark lament for the sorrow evoked by the old races' passing.

Jieret's impressed background informed Tarens against the town-born's ignorant mistakes. He did not cut living wood, or light fires, or trap game where the springs welled through the rocks and unreeled in silver-thread falls to the Lithwater's thundering flood. When he needed to hunt, he turned north to forage, even as the clan youngsters he tailed must do also, too near where the lane forces rang with a spirited vibrancy that enthralled a man, body and mind.

At night, Tarens slept with his back to a tree. The deep plunge of roots in black earth, and the flow of live sap acted as a staid balm and helped him to settle. Even so, his dreams swirled like rainbow flame through his being, dazzling as the shimmer of opal. He heard the ephemeral trace of the sound and light chord that sourced life, and cried aloud for release. Under the moon, he often woke weeping, his heart-beat sped to a drum-roll that threatened to pound through the walls of his chest. He rose dizzy, and walked. When exertion failed to ground out his turmoil, Tarens soaked his clothes in the river and shivered with cold, the shock needful to anchor his senses.

He did not have Arithon's initiate mastery at hand to steer his strayed mind if his human wits wandered. When the breezes fluttered the greening leaves, and taunted with almost formed words, or when the graceful forms of the Paravians glimmered through time's translucent veil and beckoned him to step out of his skin and join their celebration under the moonlight, Tarens had no markers to measure whether he dreamed, or if he walked through a silken fabric of vision, captured while fully awake.

Had he been the same man his blood family recalled, he might have spun in crazed circles, overcome by the rip tide of pure exuberance: or else dropped into bewilderment, abandoned to the heady ecstasy of the unknown.

Yet the touch of a masterbard's art had steadied his unmoored perception amid the raised realms of awareness. The music lent by his own Name firmed his step, while the surge of the flux tides soaked through him. The bestowed heritage of a forestborn chieftain understood that he trod in the hallowed footsteps of the vanished Paravians. Whatever the grace of such creatures had touched, the residual glimmer illumined the colours like velvet, brightened by the preternatural flare of light-gilded embroidery.

Here birthright granted way-rights on sufferance to the blood-line of Athera's kings; and also, by tradition of lawful crown oversight, to the purview of the *caithdeinen*. Esfand was versed to the perils he broached, well enough to safeguard his companions. But a fortnight passed before the brat acknowledged that Tarens's determined course would stay unshaken. At which point, his deft evasion veered northward, a welcome relief with the volatile rise of the mysteries cresting towards the peak at spring equinox. If the pavane of the Paravian presence diminished, the currents still surged with reactive force anywhere near the stone way's proximity.

Tarens shivered, often hazed by the invasive tramp of armed troops in a place where no townsmen had trespassed for centuries. By day, his pulse throbbed to the thunder of drums that beat out the pace for the True Sect advance. He sensed the crack of silk pennons on the wind, and ached for the friend who ran, haplessly chased down the gauntlet as the gap narrowed between opposed factions. The flux keened to the advance of King Gestry's war band, pressed on forced march to wrest back the desperate hope of an intervention. They pushed from the west, singing to raise their defiant courage against the agonized certainty of the life-blood soon to be spilled. Death waited at the north shore of Lithmarin. Tarens's crude instinct could not predict when the unequal battle would become joined. The flux currents transmitted their imprint by intensity, with little regard for distance. The deflections unleashed by the line of advance could be far off or nearly on top of him.

King Gestry's doomed stand might come too late. Or worse, engage and fail to hold out long enough for the sacrifice to spare Arithon's life. As haplessly caught in the same deadly mesh, three clanborn youngsters determined past sense to act in behalf of their threatened crown prince.

Tarens tagged their back trail without mercy, thwarted by their insolent, trail-wise expertise, and hungry again for the pressure that shortened the time he needed to forage. Worn lean from the fortnight spent in hard chase, he cat-footed into a shady hollow curtained in the limpid streamers of sapling willows. The dimple left by a dried vernal pool showed a grey carpet of leaf mould, recently rumpled. Warned by that unweathered scatter of brown, Tarens paused.

His smile was as crooked as the scar on his disfigured nose. Jieret's distinctive experience marked the patch of turned leaves and disclosed the tell-tale signature of a laid trap. Tarens smothered his laughter. Fondly mindful of his nephews' lively antics, and the whispered conspiracies that had led to furtive fingers unbuckling harness straps, he took stock. Scratched at the dandelion growth of the beard he had not dulled his steel to keep shaved, until untoward stillness let him confirm the taut pocket of a nearby, watchful presence. Since the young rogues aimed to mock his demise, he chose on wry impulse to speed things along. He unsheathed the broadsword filched as a prize from The Hatchet's stolen chariot. Then he propped the bare blade against a handy tree and stepped four-square into the noose.

Rathain's clan children practiced their forefathers' crafts with particular vengeance. The trigger twig snapped at first touch underfoot. The sprung bough whooshed upright, freed of the deadfall fashioned as counter-weight. The noose whumped tight and yanked Tarens upside down with a force that knocked out his wind. Dangled in a slow spin, he waited, his loose jerkin rucked to his chin, while the rushed blood suffused his face and darkened his eyesight.

The black moment of faintness dissolved into sparkles, then melted into the *aliveness* of vision: Sight showed him Sunwheel banners and blood, and voices raised in praise of the avatar's glory to call down the destruction of Shadow. The destined moment approached: a battle of levin bolts and cruel steel, where the dying imprinted their final agony into the spring-tide flux. Which assault to wrenched senses hurt far too much, as violence unfurled blight and dissonance through a seasonal tapestry spun only for joyous renewal. There was Light and bleak death, and *light* that was life, until the appalling dichotomy threatened to rend the gauze fabric of reason.

Tarens's stressed outcry spluttered through the splash of cold water, hurled into his face. Another voice, stridently petulant, demanded, 'Iyat-thos, why are you tracking us?'

His vision cleared. Shaking, consumed with unnatural dread that the Sunwheel advance was *in fact* dreadfully close, Tarens met the blunt glare of the speaker, rendered upside down, and revolved into view by the spin of the rope. The eyes were hazel, set in a square-cut, tanned face, and contentious beneath the sleeked-back roots of a walnut braid, tinged to red glints in full sunshine. Esfand s'Valerient stood with arms folded, the leather-wrapped hilt of a shoulder-slung sword disregarded in favour of a cut pole fashioned as a crude javelin.

Tarens gave him the rebuff in clan dialect. 'I grant your insolence no civil standing.'

A prod dug his side from another hacked stick. The view turned, replaced by Khadrien's contemptuous disdain, dusted with freckles beneath foxy tangles of hair. 'You cannot lay claim to our people's courtesy. Your accent is town-born.'

In suspension, not helpless, Tarens twirled about, surveyed last by Siantra, her own seal braid repressively neat, with fey eyes, deep-set in her triangular face, the turbulent grey of a storm-cloud. Her rapt interest pierced beyond skin and bone. Surely talent perceived the left mark Jieret's touch had impressed on his spirit, since she pronounced unequivocally, 'Nonetheless, he is one of us.' Against Esfand's hissed protest, her rebuke was granite. 'Cut him down. He won't run, at my word.'

Tarens's view revolved to the patched green of the willow grove, while instinct spoke before reason. 'For Sidir's descendant, no need to stand surety.'

Come full circle, Esfand's earnest features crimped into a frown. 'Who are you? No one has pronounced her ancestral name that way for over two centuries.'

Steel spoke: a knife blade, unsheathed from behind. Esfand shouted, too late. Khadrien's hasty slash severed the rope and dropped their victim in a head first tumble.

Tarens caught himself on his hands, broke a fall meant to damage his neck, and flipped himself upright. Through fair hair tangled with musty leaves and senses upended by vertigo, he encountered the sharpened end of the stick, leveled at his throat by the shiftless braggart. 'Any of mine would be thrashed like a child.'

Abrasive with bravado to prove himself, Khadrien spat, 'Townsman, you trespass!'

The rustle of Siantra's outraged advance drew more steel and thrust in between. 'I'll speak for the burden of my friend's discourtesy!' To Esfand's appalled shock, against Khadrien's glower, she championed the pretentious stranger. 'Whatever this man tells you, however outrageous his claim, for honour's sake we must listen! True Sight has revealed him. His aura can't lie!'

Esfand's sturdy features went white. 'Siantra, what are you saying?'

But Tarens elbowed her protection aside. 'Stop quibbling! We haven't time. My charge matches yours: to see your liege clear of the True Sect's invasion and get him safely away to Rathain.'

'This liegeman does have the right!' Siantra insisted, fast enough to quash further objection.

'We'll talk on the move,' Tarens insisted, then reddened three faces by knowing *precisely* how to free the slip-knot that fastened his ankle. He hurled the rope towards Khadrien's chest, which forced the poised stick sidewards to field the surprise without catching the punitive lash of the follow-through.

When the crofter spun to retrieve his stashed weapon, he all but collided with Esfand, who snatched up the sword's grip ahead of him.

The youngster offered the weapon hilt first and conceded with striking aplomb, 'Who taught you the trap?'

Tarens burst into laughter. 'The man who perfected it. Your people knew him as Earl Jieret s'Valerient. But we have to move, or else forfeit the chance to hear me explain.'

'He's serious,' Siantra broke in, sharply urgent. 'Listen!' In fact, the sweet trills of the song-birds had faltered. The rustle of wind did not overwrite silence, but masked a bass rumble, ominous as the growl of an on-coming storm through the sultry back-drop of greenery.

'That isn't thunder,' said Esfand, alarmed. 'Drop it now, Khadrien. *We have to run!*'

Survival eclipsed the last, stubborn argument. The measured boom of the drums from the open warned of the True Sect's on-coming advance. Too soon, too exposed, and dreadfully vulnerable, the small party of four faced the outbreak of war, with the pitched battle almost on top of them.

Dakar stood within line of sight at the forefront of the king's war band. A shuddering bundle of nerves bathed in sweat, he shielded his eyes against the barrage of low, morning sun that bedazzled his vision. Before him, the massed host of the Sunwheel invaders shimmered against the bare scarp, a jacquard weave in thread-silver and gilt that seethed forward in lockstep formation. The blare of an officer's horn signalled the dedicate troops to close ranks. The brass notes drilled into his ears like steel bodkins. An initiate mage should be far removed from this field, given a feather-wit's measure of sense.

But the royal war-captain's challenge was just: the prophet who incited the Crown of Havish to attack at all costs should prove out his conviction beneath the king's banner.

'Dharkaron Avenger's black bollocks take honour!' Since Dakar could not get drunk, he hoped Sethvir was listening; more fervently, he wished the virulent sting of his saddle-sores and the sick flutter of nausea upon the absent person of Asandir. 'Once folly, twice fatal, you Sorcerers insisted throughout my apprenticeship.' The spellbinder had taken the arrow for Arithon before: stepped into harm's way and nearly perished of the Koriani binding wrought to ensure a fatality. After that narrow brush, today's bid for death ran beyond suicidal. Front and centre, King Gestry's forces stared down the maw of wholesale immolation.

'Regrets?' snapped a familiarly sarcastic voice, arrived on horseback beside him. 'You look faint of heart. Do you need to be propped upright before you slide from the saddle?'

Dakar shrugged off the brusque gibe. 'Speak for yourself. Only rank ignorance measures a man by appearances.'

Gestry's war-captain grunted. 'You look green enough to heave up your breakfast. No offence, if I hedge my bet.'

Dakar swallowed. He was in fact wrung to hollow distress *because* he had dared the unthinkable, outfaced by the horrific prospect of slaughter: dosed himself with narcotic *tienelle* leaves to augment his prescient faculties. For his nightmare forecast had come to pass: Lysaer's personal banner streamed over the white-and-gold Sunwheel of the religion. The day would be ruled by Desh-thiere's curse in the language of fire and blood.

Positioned as advisor at the High King's left hand, the spellbinder shouldered his reluctant role. Eyes squeezed shut, senses reeled by the scents of hot horse-flesh and oiled steel, and the sour sweat of his overcranked nerves, he absorbed the disturbance as the blunt war-captain reined his mount into stride on his Grace's opposite side. To the man's acid roil of distemper, Dakar said, emphatic, 'You must call the charge. Now. We have no other option but failure. It's too late to retreat.'

'Let them come to us,' the war-captain rebutted, annoyed to abandon surprise and commit his troops over a rise that lent even the semblance of minor advantage. 'What difference over a handful of minutes? Our losses already are fated.'

Dakar wrestled the drowning surge of stifled apprehension and fear, *not his own,* but the men's, clamped under discipline as the stilled foot-troops awaited in ranked formation. To the war-captain's molten seethe of reluctance, he said, 'The order's a tactical necessity, required as a diversion.' Scarcely able to think, Dakar bludgeoned his scattered wits to explain, 'Lysaer's entanglement with Desh-thiere's curse is infallible as a weathercock. He has pin-pointed Arithon's flight. The shift in the flux currents lets me extrapolate the near range of future probabilities. If you don't press the shock of engagement immediately, the Sunwheel light horse on the eastern flank will be ordered to move on a sighted disturbance. They are within reach to run Arithon down. Our strike from this vantage will draw Lysaer's attention, we hope, long enough for delay.'

The war-captain bit back his fierce despair. Mail jingled against the dull boom of the drums as he dismounted and knelt at the feet of his High King. 'My royal liege, only at your command.'

And as generations of greatness before him, Gestry Teirient's'Lornmein of Havish rose to the bleak hour and assumed the harsh weight of his crown. 'Sound the charge,' he affirmed, braced to challenge the disastrous fury of Desh-thiere's curse.

The war-captain rose, fist to heart, then departed to relay the order with lips clamped against bitter protest. Through the whispered cloth flap of the blazoned standard, the young man attuned to the weal of Havish softly summoned his page. The boy came, obedient, and silently unlaced and removed his liege's leather bracers. Laid bare on the wrists of a king whose dearest thrill once had been a common armourer's work in the forge, the gold bracelets gleamed, inset with matched rubies. The paired jewels served as master keys to the smaller gems in the state collar. Bestowed upon coronation, the stones had been mined on the far world beyond West Gate, cut and endowed by Paravian artisans to invoke the intent of the royal who defended the land.

A rustle of impetuous movement and the muted scrape of steel marked the keen stir of anticipation, as the war-captain's relayed directive stiffened the ranks poised on either side.

Dakar opened his eyes. He propped his queasy frame in the saddle, ripped open in spirit and bled beyond remedy, while around him what seemed the whole world came undone. As though set into motion by the cast of Dharkaron Avenger's Black Spear, the surge came without horn-calls. The signal that consigned the brave to the Light's slaughter stayed silent: a brief, scarlet flash of fluttered cloth as the standard-bearer answered the hour's exigency and dipped the crown's hawk blazon into a left-to-right flourish.

The immediate surrounds shuddered and heaved as the war bands of Havish burst through the bundled broom breastworks uselessly placed for concealment. Their forward rush to engage the enemy roused a shout from the throats of the Light's faithful. The noise resounded to the horizon, the voice of the vast northern host like the roaring thrash of a storm sea. Through the deluge of noise, the war-captain sent off a fast runner to dispatch his best troop of light horsemen to the right flank. Their task, tantamount to a suicide charge, must head off or engage any dedicates set after Prince Arithon's heels.

Their valiant intervention could not be enough, should the centre lines crumple too soon. At the forefront, where resistance meant death, the battle converged towards engagement.

One breath before the rending collision of armoured flesh and edged steel, ahead of the instant when the fraught shouts through the clangour shredded to soprano screams from the maimed, Dakar gripped his mage-sighted focus with adamant strength. He locked down his boundaries, altogether aware that Arithon's plight could no longer be saved by arcane observation. In contrary fact, the fury of Lysaer's cursed madness posed a seer's gift the most grave liability. Against unruly senses and buckling stress, Dakar aligned his augmented talent to assay the untried sovereign beside him.

Gestry sat his grey horse with straight bearing, his horseman's slit byrnie belted beneath the scarlet surcoat bearing the crown's hawk cartouche. The fist closed on his destrier's reins stayed rock steady. Bare-headed, at first glance boyishly casual with his conical helm hooked by the strap to his pommel, he presented the image of self-possessed calm under pressure.

But a glacial pallor tensioned his profile. Beneath the battered gold circlet borne by generations of s'Lornmein forebears, his youthful features had been reforged under the fires of sovereign might. The altered perceptions begun by the crown seat's attuned affinity to the elements intensified once the raw powers became invoked. The man consecrated as the land's living conduit now wore flesh and bone as though smelted into refinement. His last ounce of immature flesh lay stripped. As though a frantic vitality torched him from within, his pale blue eyes shone fever brilliant. From hollowed cheeks, to clean limbs pared down to muscle and sinew, Gestry assumed the carved grace of a master-worked sculpture. That unearthly stature, refined day by day, endowed him with a presence that near stopped the breath to behold, until the drape of the clothes on his form seemed a clumsy disruption of harmony. The shell talismans tied for luck to his belt by his littlest sister, and the favourite knife made through the armouror's tutelage now seemed the care-worn artifacts from a childhood cherished by somebody else.

A month since the invocation at Fiaduwynne, when the King's Grace had raised the Paravian focus and gathered the flux to prepotency with intent to ward the free wilds of Ghent and Carithwyr. The abrupt change in plan to restage for attack kept those volatile forces bound in reserve. Throughout the march, the uncanny charge built, a wound spring held compressed by bare-handed will. A feat royal character was fit to endure, but not without cost to the bearer.

Dakar mapped the heightened course of the strain ingrained in live flesh like a water-mark. As the human channel for the land's power, wound in check week upon week, Gestry had to be strictly reminded to eat. Under constant, pent pressure, his restless nights passed nearly sleepless. The least sound in his ears would ring painfully loud, while the impact of daylight flared hurtfully bright and dazzled his sight into shimmers and rainbows. He moved as a creature with one foot past the veil, strung up and suspended. The dichotomy he suffered estranged him from the comforts of commonplace fellowship.

Kings who invoked the unbridled might of crown power were, none of them, destined for long reigns. Dakar had been an indifferent historian. But longevity and exposure to Althain Tower's archives confirmed that no heir within living memory had withstood such a trial. The inked lines of the ancient record endured: near ten centuries ago, through the bitter effort to stay the Mistwraith's incursion at Earle, manuscripts detailed the graphic price bought in bone and blood by the royal lineages. Demand had expended the pool of available heirs until the choice of succession devolved to the handful of survivors: then that irreplaceable heritage had been brought to the brink of extinction by murder under the knives of revolt.

Which gravity of tradition did nothing to ease today's brutal burden.

'The wait can't be much longer,' Dakar encouraged. 'Your Grace, are you prepared?'

Gestry turned his face, skin burnished to an egg-shell patina that almost shone eerie silver with the corona of flux, even under full sunlight. His wide eyes were enormous, the tight, pin-point pupils fixed as starless night under unblinking lashes. 'Who could be?' His faint smile emerged, sweetened by an unbearable chagrin. 'Don't mourn the exigency. Asandir told the truth. I have been lifted quite beyond pain. My spirit will rise to meet whatever comes. End your fear. No shame will befall the name of my ancestry.'

'That never concerned me.' Dakar's voice failed, choked off by grief. Atheran high kings before this one had wielded their birthright and risked all they were to the crucible, unflinching. S'Lornmein forebears had stood beside Fellowship Sorcerers and stemmed the Mistwraith's incursion at South Gate. They had battled ravenous drake spawn, and died in the bale-fires of dragons gone rogue. But never before had a newly crowned sovereign risked the raw brunt of Lysaer s'Ilessid's mastery of elemental light. Twisted under curse for unbridled destruction, that potential for widespread disaster lay past the measure of Dakar's experience. Rightly or wrongly, the outcome for the endeavour lay at his feet.

The sting of regret could not stop the deadly commitment set into motion. Paralytic dread peaked like a stopped breath, filled by the inchoate howl of fury as both forces closed for the reckoning. The roar broke to a shattering crash of edged steel as the shock of first impact struck home.

Dakar was not brave. At the crux, he lacked the staunch nerve that shaped heroes. Nor was he sustained by the selfless service demanded of an old blood lineage. His coward's plea trembled between frail hope and prayer as Havish's mismatched assault smashed against the white gleam of the True Sect's locked shield wall. For agonized minutes, the wave battered and bowed the enemy's drilled formation. The clangourous din quavered with screams as lances struck home and blades rose and fell, clotted scarlet. Then the mass of sheer numbers steadied, and pushed, and ground Havish's centre backwards. Step by agonized step, while the ranks were carved down and trampled under the unstoppable pressure, King Gestry held back.

His effort must not stem the bitter retreat, fought by unbearable inches. No replacements remained to shore up the frayed lines, and no backup relief force existed to plug the breached gaps where the butchered lay fallen. Locked into a fight never staged for a victory, the defenders of Havish sustained the unconscionable trial of fatal attrition. How many died meant less than how long they could stem the True Sect's zealous slaughter.

Throughout, the horns wailed. If the drums boomed still, their rhythm was drowned by the dissonant snarl of combat. The sun burned above an arena of blood, and the wind blew corrupt with the abattoir reek of mass carnage. And still, Gestry stayed firm through the horror: watching his best and his bravest cut down without hope of quarter.

Dakar wiped his soaked face, teeth clenched against the visceral shudders that ripped him. The mage who loved peace should be far removed, where the plunge of cold steel rent vital organs and threshed the life essence of men in prime health, all untimely. Eyes opened to mage-sight would show the faint mist of shocked spirit light, torn ragged and streamed in a roiled half state of transition.

Aware of the near sounds of restive horses, and the staccato bursts of the war-captain's orders between the breathless sprints of the messengers, the spellbinder stationed at Gestry's side could do naught but endure the havoc that pummelled his stressed faculties. The *tienelle*'s influence proved a fatal mistake. He could not stay focused. The ruthless state of overload spurred his volatile talent out of control. With subtle awareness held in duress, Dakar overlooked the critical moment when the profound shift swept over the warfront.

Warned first by the sidle of the king's mount in response to a sharply gripped rein, he murmured, 'Steady. Hold fast, your Grace. If your sequestered might is released prematurely, all of your valiant fallen will have wasted their lives to no purpose.'

'Our tactical thrust to draw fire has failed,' Gestry stated without hesitation. 'Our best company of light horse cannot withstand the headlong blast from the avatar without my support.'

Dakar guessed which trial before the king rose in his stirrups and pointed.

Past the wracked commotion of snarled steel bloomed the first dazzling star-burst of light. The flare sheeted into a bale-fire plume for an impact targeted eastward. Lysaer's cursed directive had not been foiled by Havish's rush at the forefront. Already detached from The Hatchet's centre company, he struck to immolate the small band of cavalry, placed to thwart the east flank's breakaway charge to take down the Master of Shadow: a man Dakar once counted as his best friend, alone on the run and without any memory of whose broken trust had betrayed him.

If the hedonist's preference for comfort and life cried out to turn tail and run, Dakar's final chance to shirk fate became forfeit as Gestry released his mount's reins and lifted crossed wrists. A flare of caught sun rinsed the rubies coal red as he touched the bracelets together against the rune-marked circlet worn at his brow.

The Warden of Althain, perhaps, perceived what would happen: the crown's legacy responded to each individual high king differently. When the royal intent to stand guard for the land interlocked with the pooled reservoir pulled from the flux, force became manifest through the matrix the Paravian gem cutters fashioned into the crown jewels. Every sovereign to invoke the realm's might before this surely had a Sorcerer at his right hand, placed at need to temper the primal ferocity of the first full engagement.

Gestry had none but a master spellbinder, wracked witless, and expelled by the Fellowship for misconduct.

Dakar was not fit or prepared for the explosive, deafening peal of vibration. Power released with the galvanic plunge of a boulder hurled into a well. The concussive splash rippled outward beyond the speed of his mage-taught reflex. The pure burst of energy, past sight and sound, hit the Mad Prophet's chest like a shattering blow and hurled him straight into black-out unconsciousness.

Crescendo

A league from the site of King Gestry's defense, the concussive force of the conjured event burst with a shock to hurl a grown man off his feet. The firm ground did not shake. Not a leaf stirred. The blow that unstrung mortal nerves was etheric, and painless, a ripple that snatched at the heart-strings and stopped breath, then upended balance to whirling dizziness. Least endowed with born talent, Khadrien suffered scarcely an instant of black-out. Ears ringing, rattled to a summary burst of euphoria, he was the excitable first of his stunned companions to recoup his shocked senses and surge to his feet.

'Great Ath, what was that?' He swiped back the sweaty strands wisped from his clan braid and shed a caught flurry of twigs and dry leaves in his scrambled rush forward to peer past the verge of the trees.

'Idiot!' Esfand moved, at risk of upset equilibrium and launched after his impulsive friend. His testy grip snagged Khadrien's shoulder and tumbled them both in a heap. 'Jump towards the fire, one day you'll burn.'

'Not this time.' Siantra sat, groggy. She knuckled her forehead, thrashed her wits into sensible focus, and said, muffled, 'We're already caught inside of the threshold, and that was only the opening wave just unleashed.' She surveyed their surrounds, chafed to unease by the pent hush fallen over the greenwood. All bird-song silenced. Not a breath of wind trembled the glassine air. The sun streamed through the leaf canopy in welded rays, dusted with lit pollen, but no longer cluttered by the frenzied shimmer of swarming insects. 'Where's Iyat-thos Tarens?'

'Over here.' His deep voice emerged from the edge of the trees where he stood, his intent gaze trained outward. Upright and restored back to calm self-command, his fortified poise stayed the most firmly seated after the blast

534

of raised resonance. Fitter than most for uncanny encounters since his initiate ordeal in Taerlin, he added, 'Whatever's coming, it's too late to flee. High King Gestry's engaged the crown jewels of Havish.'

Rampant fascination made Khadrien jerk free of Esfand's restraint. Which callow outburst made Siantra wince: as if the suspension that locked the tense stillness might smash like a hammer-blow to a snapped stick.

Yet nothing upset the anxious, strung pause. Esfand rubbed his wrenched wrist, twitched his leathers to rights with a rueful shrug, then offered his hand to Siantra. 'We're neck deep, anyway. Might as well watch.'

She dropped pride, for once. Entrusted the welts on her newly healed palm to his clammy grip and let his sinewy strength tug her erect. Together for comfort against the unknown, they burrowed into the dense thicket beside Khadrien and the unfathomable stranger, Iyat-thos Tarens.

Through the dipped emerald window of shaded leaves, morning sun shone from a robin's egg sky. Day buffed the undulant nap of wild heath that textured Scarpdale's southern bounds in tasseled weeds of taupe and fallow gold. The weighted air smelled of ozone, cranked to the tension fore-running a violent storm front. Then a subliminal glimmer arose, most noticeable in the patched blots of shadow cast by the drift of wisped clouds. Like cracks shot through the glaze on old porcelain, the electrostatic oddity brightened, roused to the blue-violet shimmer of ground lightning as the raised flux lines crackled alive. The channels inherently laced through the landscape burgeoned into currents of visible light. Where the pathways converged, a fountained gush of hurled sparks merged into a torrent and swept towards the mercury glitter that marked the True Sect's armed advance. Where, in pockets, the bannered squares of ranked dedicates still chewed into the tossed wrack of Havish's blood-soaked retreat. The distanced, steel seethe of their pebbled helms suggested the hurly-burly contortion of battle. Yet the clangour of weapons, the raised screams, and the roar of engagement seemed wrung oddly silent, the boom of the drums not muffled, but mute. The brass horns of the officers nicked the tableau with sun-caught reflections, just as stifled to uncanny quiet.

That moment the witnesses at the side-lines noticed the ominous, bass swell of sound: a subliminal surge of vibration no longer below hearing but risen to a pervasive hum that utterly cancelled the tinker's din raised by the living. Power rolled through the solid earth underfoot, until the shock rippled through the scrub brush and the grass tips trembled as the bed-rock beneath rang under the excited flux like hammer-struck steel. Soon that singing cry razed through flesh and bone, and buzzed the clenched teeth of the poised observers.

'Hang tight,' Tarens whispered, instinctively braced.

For only the leading edge of the warfront stayed dead-locked. A stir quickened the True Sect's rear-guard as a sparkle erupted into a levin-bolt stab of pure light. The discharge cracked skywards to a report that slammed echoes like the clapped peal of close thunder.

Siantra cried out, seared to agony by the resharpened gift of her truesight. 'Lysaer, driven under curse by Desh-thiere! Gestry's doomed.'

'Cover your eyes,' Tarens cautioned. 'Protect your hands and faces.' Jieret's memory informed him: the unshielded backwash of such an assault could blister skin, even blind the unwary. But talented vision embraced no such frailty. Initiate awareness recorded the impact that naked sight could not withstand. Through the shimmer of stress-heated air, the glare of the false avatar's aggressive retort exploded to bale-fire brilliance. The flash scourged the elements to a luminous blast fit to raze everything in its path to flash-point immolation. Carbon and ashes would sublimate, with naught left but glazed slag, while a landscape carved over millennia came unravelled on the rage of an instant.

'Run!' Tarens gasped, terrified. 'Find the nearest stream and immerse yourselves!' For the recoil would ignite the forest like kindling: Earl Jieret had barely escaped such a wild fire, knocked down out of harm's way by a crossbolt in the grisly debacle that raked Daon Ramon's conflict several centuries ago.

Except back then, no crowned royalty had stood in defense against Lysaer's attack.

The electrical flare of Lanshire's flux lines glittered like earth-bound chained lightning, its power released through the pin-point focus that was High King Gestry, attuned by his sovereign ritual to the land. The pent stream unfurled, a geyser of force that pin-wheeled a nexus of gossamer streamers outward through the air. The tinted-rainbow veils netted over Lysaer's elemental assault. His raw light knifed that delicate stay of restraint and unravelled to a concussive bang that shocked like the grind of an avalanche.

Light died. For a smothered instant, the world quivered, snuffed to primordial darkness. Whether human senses momentarily failed, or if the wrench of stopped time unshuttered the deep of the void, no man knew.

The heart-beat of life resurged to reveal a sunlit vista, untouched except where adamant battle had reaped desecration, dimmed beneath a palled scrim of whipped smoke. The aroused blaze of the flux lines had quenched. Faint paths traced the scrub where the torrent had passed, scorched leaves and twigs left dusted in charcoal.

Poised at the immaculate verge of the wood, Tarens and the three clanborn youngsters remembered to breathe. Alive, disbelieving, they blinked dazzled eyes. The aftermath horror took seconds to register, that the threat of bloodshed was not ended.

Faint against the stunned quiet, the manic shouting of shocked men called the orders for Sunwheel troops to regroup. The break at their centre by an arcane conjury rekindled and fanned the fuel of religious conviction. Lancers and pikemen thrown down on the flanks were called to arise and close the gaps in the devastated main battle-line. A horn sounded. Then dogged, the drums picked up and firmed the beat to resume the advance.

Combat rejoined with a tinny clash. Dauntless, the True Sect fanatics stormed onwards to finish their righteous butchery of Havish's battered survivors.

No answering glimmer arose from the flux, which suggested King Gestry's held power was spent, courageously wielded to little avail matched against the inflamed faith of dedicate thousands. Worse, the unvanquished fitful flare, as Lysaer's gift spat forth a tentative levin bolt. Rallied into a partial recovery and cruelly cursed, he drove on to renew his assault. But not to march forward: the urgent blast of an officer's horn sounded a treble command to wheel the temple's unfazed reserves.

'They are turning!' gasped Tarens. 'East, surely guided by Lysaer's geas to close upon Arithon's position!'

Esfand responded, his *caithdein*'s heritage bred into his bones. 'Then we have to get there ahead of them.'

'Not possible.' Tarens cursed fate for the failure: the True Sect's vigorous reengagement cut off their approach. 'Even if we had a chance to get through, we're too few to make any difference.'

'We go nowhere,' Siantra broke in. 'Don't you hear the whine?' She blocked Khadrien's hot-headed reach to draw steel, and yanked Esfand's sleeve to catch his attention.

'You suggest the flux lines are active, still.' The blunt warrior's frown taken after his sire lifted into fierce hope. 'King Gestry's intent still directs the pulse of the land?'

Siantra shook her head, fighting tears for the heart-break. 'I'm not sure. Whatever he's doing, the response is weak.'

'No.' Tarens paused, intent. 'Not weak. His Grace is working too far above the range of our human senses.'

'He can't do that, and survive!' Esfand snapped in anguish. 'Such extreme frequency will burn out even his royal nerves, stop his heart, and arrest the reflex to keep breathing!'

'The master spellbinder's at the king's side,' Tarens cracked in restraint. 'We stay clear. His Grace must rely on Dakar's wise guidance.'

But if the Mad Prophet stayed fit to act, already the crested rush of fine energies raced unseen through the earth. Wrought and forged in the eerie registers of fast silence, the ripple tossed a sharp eddy of wind through the overhead branches. Plucked sticks pelted flesh hard enough to raise welts, whipped amid a fierce gyre of shredded leaves. Then the ferocious blast died to a breeze. Torn foliage winnowed downwards, soft as a sigh, while the air belled and shivered and sang to an unheard note that lifted the hair at the nape and buzzed bone and flesh to a shudder of uncanny harmony.

As if wakened by a summons, the land itself bloomed. Each rock, each plant, and the low swell of the hillocks shimmered, limned by a moon flare of slivery light.

Tarens stiffened, brushed to chills of epiphany by Earl Jieret's imprinted awareness. 'Cover your faces!' he cried. 'Do it now!'

But his timely words proved too clumsy and slow. That swiftly, the explosive torrent of wild energy crested and peaked into resonance. The belling peal raised the phosphorescent glimmer of the Paravian spectres from the ancient way. They came, a bright imprint called out of the past: not living, nor bound on this side of the veil, but the impressed echo of exultation that remained of forgotten, magnificent splendour. Manifest in the etheric shimmer of flux, their gossamer forms advanced like wisped smoke towards the strident chaos of the battle-field.

'Don't look!' Tarens shouted. Every hair on his body prickled erect. He shivered with an inchoate urgency, touched through the marrow by the tingling passage as the unearthly purity of the old races' remembrance rushed through the core of his spirit.

The intuitive impact of exalted beauty could not be shut out. Eyes closed or not, the summoned host dazzled, the fair stream of light written on *light*, inscribed upon cognizant perception. In silver-point form, or etched out in pristine white fire, they came: the Sunchildren dancing to crystalline flutes, and the Riathan, the unicorns, evanescent as the gleam on new pearl, gold horns raised and the pavane of their cloven hooves soundless.

Struck blind by joy, undone into rapt throes of ecstasy, Tarens clasped a tree trunk just to stay upright as waves of emotion flung down every bastion of human intellect.

He grasped the likely outcome. His shared memory of Jieret's death-wish in Daon Ramon knew the blast of the horn's call that had raised a congruent event from the past. The blood rage of battle and the cursed grip of madness on Lysaer had been wrenched into abeyance and paralyzed.

Today's grand summons would strike with more crippling force, magnified by the attributes of a High King's enabled crown jewels. Those in close proximity would be struck senseless, some surely never to rise again living on the worldly side of the veil.

Knowledge made the experience at the margin no easier to bear, clothed in the quick flesh of mortality. Ears ringing, and sweat-soaked as though sapped by a fever-dream, Tarens clung to rough bark and wept for such grace, unleashed amid wholesale carnage. The bitter wail, risen, had no animal voice. The twisted cry wrung from the killing field reverberated from thousands of steel weapons, forged and sharpened for purposeful maiming and death, that now denounced the form of their making. Which shattering utterance of horror and pain might have squeezed widows' tears from earth's bed-rock.

The grievous burden of remorse shouted shame, that a criminally blind ideology could reject the promise of birthright, then mangle the exuberant vigour of life, designed by nature to celebrate only creative abundance.

All the remorse in the world could not unmake the toll of desecration.

Harrowed by the need for sweet respite, Tarens crumpled. Undone, he clenched his forearms over his head, his salt-wet cheek pressed for comfort against the warm ground. A deafened part of him dimly registered the clanborn youngsters felled beside him in whimpering knots.

'Rise!' The deep voice boomed almost on top of him. 'One liegeman among you must stand!'

That imperative command could not be gainsaid, short of death. Tarens stirred to a shuddering breath. Confronted by a massive pair of cloven hooves wisped by flaxen silk fetlocks, his awed sight lifted, then took in the massive legs, four-square and tall as pillars in front of him. Quaking, undone, he picked himself up. Erect and trembling, nose to muscled chest, he squinted upwards, dwarfed and dazzled by the flame-presence of an Ilitharis – a centaur guardian – arrived before him.

The creature towered, wrapped in sheets of gold light, his antlered head crowned in glory to burn mortal cloth past the flash-point of sanity. The broad straps of his harness glinted with jewels. His mane tumbled over his back and shoulders like sunbeams spun into corn-silk. No human eye could endure the brilliance of his naked countenance: fierce enough to stop the heart and reweave the drum-beat of living pulse to the purest, unbearable strains of compassion.

Yet dark as cut shadow, a loose stallion walked in the creature's presence. Bare of bridle and saddle, tail and mane snarled with the burrs and tangles of a creature gone wild, the horse rolled a ghost eye and dropped its neck to graze at the guardian's feet.

'One must draw the black blade, Alithiel,' the Ilitharis intoned, alive with infinite gentleness. 'The one fated among you must rise to the moment.'

Esfand knelt, shamefaced with hesitation. 'I daren't.' Scarlet yet from the recent rebuke of a Sorcerer, he unyoked the slung baldric and offered the sword, upraised across his outstretched palms. 'Let your greater wisdom take her, exalted.'

The centaur did not move. Pale turquoise, his eyes, piercing with regret. 'Young man, I cannot.'

Siantra's appeal emerged, quick with pain, her scarred hands cradled protectively to her breast. 'Exalted, we are, none of us, fit!'

Tarens ventured, torn breathless, 'The guardian can't. You may not realize, real as he seems. We behold only a sending. Not solid in our shared existence. His hooves leave no track. The weight of the sword would pass through such a semblance, insubstantial as smoke in this place.'

The centaur's antlered majesty shifted, perhaps with impatience, or sorrow. 'One must bear Alithiel. In truth, I cannot.'

Tarens moved, willingly courageous.

But Khadrien's impulse leaped faster. His nimble hand snatched the sheathed weapon from his cousin's numbed grasp. The instant the sword's wrapped hilt had been claimed, the centaur apparition flicked out, vanished like a gale-snuffed candle. Dizzied senses recorded the tender spring turf *in fact* left unmarked by its passage.

The desolate, stark impact of separation pierced the soul to the quick: that only the jet stallion with the ghost eye remained, warm and breathing. A stamped hoof and an impatient tail switch suggested an imperative invitation. Before anyone else rebounded from shock, Khadrien sprinted forward. Ever the bold opportunist, he tossed the loop of Alithiel's baldric as a noose and captured the horse. Sword sheath gripped left-handed, he closed his other fist in the animal's mane and vaulted astride.

'No, boy! Hold hard.' Tarens sprang and locked his ploughman's two-handed grip on the strap cinched over the stallion's neck. 'Your liege's defense is better off handled by a grown man.'

Khadrien snarled and clapped in both heels. 'You don't understand! I was chosen for this!' While the horse plunged and sidled, he yanked the sheathed sword in an upward arc and battered at Tarens's left wrist. Shouted protest rang through the drum-roll of hooves as the stallion wheeled to dislodge the crofter's determined hold.

Tarens held on tenacious, dragged into an unbalanced stagger.

'This is my task!' Khadrien shouted. Red head turned, insistent, he struck again. 'Let me go! I was called to the sword since the very beginning.'

'No!' Esfand cried, voice split by anguish.

But Siantra blocked her friend's distraught charge. 'Khadrien has to! There's no other choice. Don't you realize? Esfand, as your father's heir designate, you're needed!' Her gentian eyes eerily fey, and backed by a truth-sighted lineage, she also exhorted the blond crofter. 'Iyat-thos, let Khadri go!'

No true clanborn might argue bare fact: not when Khadrien's Sighted dream had incited Alithiel's theft from Halwythwood's armoury in the first place.

Even so, Tarens continued resistance; in conscience, he must. 'No lad under my charge will ride alone into uncanny peril.' The loss of his nephews and a brother's bereavement had shown him the horror of children who died untimely before their parents. He spun with the bravest intent to mount up and ride pillion behind.

But no man's strength could outmatch the stallion's ferocity, abetted by Khadrien's wildcat recklessness. The horse reared, broke away and galloped, tail streaming. Showered by the gouged clods thrown off its hooves, two friends left behind stared in distress, joined by Tarens, who cradled a purpled sprain and a friction-burned palm. The large man hunched over, unabashedly weeping.

'You could not go, Iyat-thos.' Siantra grasped the crofter's hide jacket, as pale as he with shared agony. When Tarens recoiled, she berated his anger with a mature sorrow past her tender years. 'You could not! Stand tall. As the gifted bearer of Earl Jieret's legacy, you carry the stamp of the ancient past. There will come the hour your liege needs that guidance! Esfand understands this, as well. Even though Khadrien's larking idiocy shrugs off the gravity of the risk, we're too late. His own mother would tell you. Once he's hard set, nobody ever has managed to keep him at heel.'

Yet the cold douse of reason left Tarens wretchedly unconsoled. He had one duty now, placed ahead of his liege by the dictates of his upright character: to see two clan youngsters safely back to Halwythwood, and worse, to explain his failure to guard a distraught family's feckless son. There would be worried kinsfolk left disconsolate by this day's toll of disaster. For Khadrien's life, no excuse could suffice. Apology bought no forgiveness.

The black horse was away with an untried boy, a puny retort to adult strife and ruin, quickly lost from sight in the glare of the heath and the dismembered wrack of the battleground.

Spring 5923

Diminuendo

The Mad Prophet wakened from the debacle at Lanshire, already burdened by the aggrieved awareness the High King's spirit had made final passage over Fate's Wheel. For the initiate mage, visionary perception often stayed manifest while the body languished in supine unconsciousness. Even out of his senses, Dakar had been aware of the rarified note carved out by Gestry's green intent. His Grace's sovereign charge, enabled through the crown jewels, shaped the plea to spare every feal liegeman his power might salvage and still hold the weal of the land. Among the sprawled wrack of breathing survivors, some individuals in Havish's war band were spared from the coil of certain doom. Even a few companies of the True Sect host might arise unharmed from the debacle. A chastened minority would forsake their misguided pledge to break the realm's tolerance for mystical knowledge. In repentant remorse, the bravely defeated might find their true heart and go home.

But the feat that had called the Paravian spirits from the old way to end strife had been bought without thought for personal consequence.

High King Gestry lay in a crumpled heap, unblemished and stilled in the scarlet splendour of his silk surcoat. His smith's hands rested open in the soft grass, unmarked and tensioned with care no longer. The outflung wrists, clean as white bone, still wore the gold bands of the ruby-set bracelets. Beneath the ancient runes in the wire fillet, fronded under a spray of brown hair, his wide-lashed gaze glinted with sky-caught reflection, the slack pupils unresponsive. The sunlit arch of his brow showed no more furrowed stress. Instead, the unearthly youth of his features remained sculpted into sublime beatitude.

Dakar choked on the futile apology owed for the misfit failure of his desertion. Left no inspired eulogy for the loss of a majesty that left a noble blood-line diminished, he stooped beside the departed, blind with tears. His saddened care gently straightened the rucked folds of the royal tabard and smoothed down the gold circle of Havish's hawk device. Last of all, he stroked Gestry's lids closed and veiled the peace that stared out of unseeing eyes.

Nearby, the royal trumpeter stirred in fitful agitation. The plump banner bearer slumped over the pole of the toppled standard rasped and twitched, painlessly snoring. Every elite armsman in the king's company lay winnowed like chaff, prostrate forms strewn across the swept gorse like tossed rags from a dismembered puppet stall. There would be dead among them: spirits hurled through the far side of the veil by the resonant surfeit of ecstasy.

Dakar shivered. Somewhere, oblivious, their Named essence would be singing still, borne past the bounds of mortality on the crested wave of wild harmony.

The spellbinder left to behold the razed aftermath was wrung too pithless to mourn. His heart weighed too heavy to measure the tally of bloodless casualties. He lingered only to place a hand on the sinewy, tanned neck of the realm's irascible war-captain. The bullish, impetuous muscle of him remained sprawled, steadfast at his sovereign's right side. The pulse beat strongly beneath Dakar's touch. The man's chest rose and fell with the calm of deep sleep. Disinclined to be caught on the field when the adversarial brute reawakened, and not yet prepared to shoulder just blame for the tragedy of the royal demise, Dakar stood. Let Gestry's feal liegemen bear up his Grace and take responsible charge of the kingdom's crown jewels.

The Mad Prophet turned his gutless step from the knoll, braced to pass score upon score of dropped bodies, knocked senseless and scarcely breathing, or else shocked beyond life by the blasting pulse of the land's higher mysteries. More men would be bled white, gutted by wounds. But unlike other fields of war before this one, the strident, rasped calls of the first carrion crows sliced through naught but the peace of clear air. On every side, the atmosphere hung untrammelled by the shocked steamers of etheric distress. No torn remnants lingered in the aftermath of violent slaughter.

Shades did not walk here, confused and disoriented from the shock of untimely doom. The glorious working of Gestry's last testament had cleansed all unsettled disharmony and borne the newly deceased without fragmentation through a swift crossing.

Dakar dared not pause to marvel in mourning, nor even to succour the wounded who languished in the throes of stupor. Some would perish anyway, reaped by the brute stroke of cold steel. More would gasp their last before their hale comrades could stir and regain the wits to bind their hacked flesh into dressings.

Weeping, conflicted by pity, Dakar forced the stern strength and strode past. He stepped over the sticky gleam of dropped swords. Picked his way through the muck of pooled blood, and skirted the grotesque, tangled toll of the fallen from both sides. He abandoned a man who choked with filled lungs, anguished beyond thought of stopping. The lapse on his part was not callous, in fact. He made haste, sore-hearted and driven by the most dire necessity. Someone must handle another concern: the frightening peril that still ranged at large, with no one else restored to clear sight or warned by the aware foresight to attend.

The individual he sought with such urgency should be found a league distant from the carnage at the front line, sprawled amid what remained of the Sunwheel light horsemen dispatched on their fever-pitch chase to pin down the Master of Shadow. Dakar had no choice but to locate Lysaer s'Ilessid before the dedicate troops who survived recouped their shattered awareness.

The ground rose again past the desecrate vale where the centre ranks had clashed in grim slaughter. Pushed to the next crest with his pounding pulse loud as a hammer-stroke in ringing ears, Dakar shoved through the stand of socketed banners that marked the True Sect's central command post. Two high priests sprawled there, fine white-and-gold robes rumpled like snow upon trampled earth. One shuddered in a mindless, fetal curl. The other lay still, a vacant corpse with a face seized into a rictus of stupefied dismay. Their talent diviner flopped face-down nearby, alive and gasping like a beached trout, but etherically blasted to infantile witlessness and soiled with puddled urine. The Hatchet's charioteer had lost consciousness, also. A swathe of snapped poles and maimed corpses marked the trail mown down where his harness team bolted. The carnage left halberdiers with staved-in chests, and more men bled white by arterial gashes, cut down by the iron wheels or trampled to oozing pulp. Settled now, the loose animals grazed a stone's throw down the rise, with the senseless, short frame of the Light's Supreme Commander of Armies felled on the platform like cast-off armour across the heaped form of his reinsman.

Mage-sight revealed that the murderous flare of ungoverned rage had been rinsed from the willful man's aura. But the grace instilled by the Paravian presence in this case was destined not to last. Dakar shuddered under the prompt of the seer, forewarned that the Light's testy commander would arise and rebuild his wounded pride through black hatred. The day's brief epiphany would be crushed under denial and not realign the warped pattern of a stubborn character.

Before The Hatchet recovered the will to give orders, come what may, Lysaer must be gone, far enough to outdistance the curse that inflamed him beyond reason within Arithon's proximity.

Past the hillock with its forlorn straggle of banners, Dakar waded into the field tents pitched behind the wracked field to attend the mauled casualties. There, soaked in sweat under shimmering noon sun, he commandeered a double team hitched to a flatbed dray, stocked with litters and blankets to succour the wounded. He added a store of supplies and provender, then raided the officer's picket lines for a half dozen fresh mounts, readied with saddles and bridles to replace the ones killed or spurred to exhaustion. Dakar selected only the best horseflesh. He knotted their head-stalls to the dray's baggage strap, clambered onto the driver's box, and reined eastward at a smart trot.

Spoked wooden wheels jolted over mossed stones and gouged a crushed track through the broom. While the rhythmic swish cut through laced canes of briar, and the shear severed crushed stalk from set flower, the spellbinder engaged his trained faculties. He plumbed his high art for every sly trick to bind his activity under concealment. For that reason, he became first to discover that he was no longer the sole opportunist who ventured amid the grotesque tableau of the prostrate.

Someone else walked upright through the burnished glare, haloed in the floss sheen of fluffed seeds scythed off by a cut switch of pussywillow.

Dakar took pause and halted the lumbering dray. While the horses he towed behind the flat wagon jibbed and jostled the stance of the harness team, he reined them back to a jingle of bits and snubbed their nervousness with a firm grip. Then he studied the figure's limping approach and identified the carrot head of the lanky clan brat, for some flit-brained scam parted from his companions and jaunted off on his own. The knave appeared plagued by the ache of thumped joints. Closer at hand, Dakar noted the grazed cheek; then the bent forearms which gingerly cradled brush-burned palms, both skinned raw. The lad's fox braid was stuck with gorse shreds, and the leathers that sported a tear in the seat wore a green, foamy splatter of horse slobber.

Rather than laugh, Dakar eased the skeined spells woven for invisibility. As his presence leaped stark to the heedless boy's eye, he challenged, 'Just what are you doing here, Khadrien s'Valerient?'

The miscreant startled half out of his skin. Stopped in his tracks, hand slapped to the antler haft at his belt sheath, he *almost* threw his knife for the jugular.

'Don't,' admonished the spellbinder. 'Bared steel at this pass would be most unwise.'

Nailed under authority's jaundiced eye, Khadrien swore under his breath. He shrugged and relinquished his gripped blade with an insolence that knew when not to beg for a remount. Dared not, despite the evident fact that Dakar's purloined string seemed excessive.

The spellbinder addressed the lad with the smug calm of a mage who read guilty minds. 'Lost your horse, did you? And got bitten to boot?'

'The damned black devil ducked a shoulder and tossed me off,' the rogue snarled with injured affront.

Dakar raised his eyebrows with ironic amusement. 'A dark stallion, no markings? With a ghost eye?' Fixed by Khadrien's resentful glower, the spellbinder slapped the rein ends across his knees and laughed. 'Dharkaron's own Vengeance! What did you expect? That animal was bred as a Sorcerer's mount and dreamed back to life by a dragon! Of course it rejected your foolhardy bidding.'

'Sounds like you've bit the dirt, riding him, too,' the sprat fired back in rejoinder.

Dakar snatched the aplomb not to rise to that bait, no matter the hard grain of truth at the core. Brown eyes sharpened enough to raise sweat, he measured the stripling from tousled head, to scuffed palms, to the stains and dust smutched into his crumpled shirt. 'Tell me what's become of the heirloom sword you clan bravos smuggled out of the Halwythwood armoury?'

Khadrien's mouth opened. Then shut fast with a click. He scraped his stubbled chin with the back of his wrist to prevaricate, his nonchalance spoiled by the violent flush that pinked his freckled fair skin to the forehead. Words failed to frame the inadmissible truth: his fault entirely that the great blade, Alithiel, had been tossed to perdition attached to a feckless, loose horse. 'The stallion—' he mumbled, terrified to outface the punitive presence lodged on the wagon seat.

'Oh, quite!' Dakar rolled his eyes in forbearance. 'Dharkaron's almighty bollocks, don't admit that a horse has more brains than you on a good day. Since you're grossly incompetent at everything else, you will kindly scavenge the belts off some corpses, then follow and lend me a hand.'

The spellbinder clucked the draught geldings forward without a glance back to see whether Khadrien honoured his peremptory instructions. He let the wagon tow his recalcitrant hoofed captives another half league into the shadow cast by the brass sun, tipped past noon, and now angled westward.

Nothing spoke for an interval. Only the rumbled grind of the wheels and the whisper of breeze flicked through the wild gorse. Freshened wind brought the high, ranging flocks of spring swallows, and also, at distance, the outraged bicker of a disturbed murder of crows.

Dakar steered his stolen vehicle that way. Disrupted from gorging, the birds flapped and cawed, settled again like judges at an assize on the dead limbs of a snag. Beneath, spilled like mannequins dressed out in mail, sprawled the slack bodies of The Hatchet's finest company of dedicate horsemen.

Surprised again, Dakar found he was not the first two-legged figure abroad on the scene. Alone, upright, and grunting, a slender young fellow wrestled to haul an inert body into the brush. The drag of spurred boots had ploughed a parallel furrow of broken stems and trailed bracken, determinedly aimed for the sweated horse left hobbled in the skeletal shade of the barkless tree.

Rife panic flared next. The towed corpus was blond, the tipped-back, noble features unmistakably Lysaer's. Mage-sight captured the imprint of his abductor's subtle aura: *a female*. Recognition exploded to blinding relief. The Sunwheel surcoat and mail coif disguised none other than Daliana.

Fat and beyond tired, the spellbinder secured the reins of the team. He called out her name and jumped down. The tell-tale crows dispersed as he stumped down the rise, gushing in awed incredulity. 'How in the name of Ath did you get here? And what device under sky kept you standing through Gestry's defense?'

Daliana glanced over her shoulder and grinned. 'Possibly the protection of Asandir's spirit mark?' Spun back to her interrupted travail, she growled in frustration and released her grimed hands. Her salvaged male burden thumped into the dust and lay still, a magnificent, loose-limbed heap of insensate majesty. Lysaer would have been furious were he aware, and not dealt the excoriating insult of helpless unconsciousness.

The intrepid woman stood guard for him still, ferocious with love's dedication. 'I swiped a dedicate's trappings and rode as a squire behind the lancers. But truly, I dared not approach my liege to attempt human contact before this.'

Her face lifted. Dakar noticed the tears striped in shining tracks down her hollowed cheeks.

For some time, she had been quite as busy as he: Lysaer s'Ilessid already lay bound, wrists and ankles lashed tight in the strap leather cut from a strayed horse's bridle.

Daliana squinted against the harsh sun, prompted to a gruff defense by the spellbinder's pensive silence. 'You plan to object to the indignity, surely? But as I know my liege, he is better off held in duress.'

Dakar broke in quickly. 'If he wakens to memory and finds his hands free, the despair of personal dishonour will quite likely drive him to harm himself.' Weary beyond care, the spellbinder nudged her aside, then bent and hefted the slack weight of Lysaer's shoulders. 'Take his feet. And don't worry. If you had not addressed the necessity yourself, I intended to do the same thing.'

A wry nod to his left acknowledged Khadrien, just arrived with his pillaged collection of belts.

'Let's be going.' Dakar ceded his place to the clan youngster's muscle, then with resigned gallantry, assumed one booted half of the load that weighed down Daliana. 'Minutes count. We cannot take chances. Those belts can be used for added restraint once we've loaded your liege in the wagon-bed. Lysaer must be taken far from this place before his stupor wears off.'

'What of The Hatchet's war host?' Daliana inquired. 'They're not muzzled. Won't they press the invasion?'

Teeth flashed through the Mad Prophet's beard as he swore. 'Dharkaron's Black Vengeance! They can slaughter themselves off, or starve themselves to stripped bones for the sake of their godless delusion.' Paused sharply to crush near-hysterical grief for the fact the young King of Havish had fallen, Dakar blinked, then resumed his breathless course. 'Asandir will be called here. He must attend the crown princess's coronation at speed. Trust his hand will clear out the True Sect's presence on the instant that Arithon crosses over the border.'

Daliana's sucked breath pocked the effortful pause while the three of them hefted Lysaer and rolled his limp weight onto the bed of the dray. She admitted, as her hands moved on to make nooses of belts, 'I fear there could be complications.'

Before Dakar spoke, and while Khadrien tracked every movement and phrase with agog fascination, Daliana paused and wiped damp palms on her filched surcoat. Then she cracked under her anxious dread, and confessed what Kharadmon had sorrowfully told her concerning dark practice and the Koriathain's vile use of a fetch.

Before she faltered through the last line, Dakar's lowered frown rivaled a thunderbolt. 'That won't happen again,' he promised. 'On my life, by Dharkaron's witness, I shall take steps and make certain that Lysaer does not wake up to encounter that horror.'

No sweet thanks met his pledge, but instead a crazed lunge in assault. *That* fast, Dakar swallowed against the chill prick of Daliana's drawn blade at his throat.

'Move and you die,' she warned, quite possessed by the fury of the cornered lioness. 'You'll not murder my liege! Even under such threat, I will not let you kill him!'

Dakar shut his pouched eyes. Somehow through the sick pangs of *tienelle* withdrawal, he clung to the rags of his patience. 'Put up your rash steel. Bloodshed won't be required! A spelled potion will knock your liege out well enough. Since I suffer from a bad stomach, and the dreams after wars wreck my sleep, I've stashed an adequate store of valerian with the supplies.'

Eventide melted into a moonless, cloud-lidded vista of lonely darkness. Alone once more on the Lanshire heath, Dakar sat cross-legged before a small fire, tucked into a secluded hollow beside the gurgle of a freshwater streamlet. The wagon bearing Lysaer was gone, driven north through the night by Daliana. She was charged to keep her distance for safety, until the ugly business attached to the spellbinder's promise found closure.

Distressed to be on his own to shoulder a binding of such delicate gravity, Dakar scraped at the welts left by swarming gnats. He flicked off something hard-shelled and six-legged that burrowed under his frayed sleeve, and cursed the fact the straight conjury to foil pests taxed his resource too dearly to waste. The Mad Prophet flexed his bare toes. Relieved of his hose and caked boots, his feet ached. Too much to tramp in search of the sweet fern whose pungent oil repelled biting insects.

The clan brat might have been tasked with the chore. Except that Khadrien had scarpered again. Who cared where the feckless young scamp fared, now? The lad had conveniently vanished when he was dispatched to fetch kindling at sundown.

Which perfectly suited Dakar's intent. In truth, he wanted no witnesses. Dug in like a tick to risk the fell wrath of the Koriani Prime Matriarch, a disgraced master spellbinder must swallow pride and accept the demeaning sop of cold comfort: only Sethvir would know if tonight's effort failed. The Warden of Althain likely sat poised with dipped pen, prepared to inscribe the embarrassing record of fool's luck in victory, or finish a lonely epitaph.

Hardened to bitterest patience, Dakar braced for the ebb in the flux that occurred past the nadir at midnight. The Prime would strike then, when vitality paused, and life's boundaries thinned through the hours before daybreak. She would waken her spider's mesh of spelled snares and engage the fetch imbued with Arithon's imprint. The vicious work of one fatal second, and a twisted sigil's wrought influence could ascertain that Lysaer's shocked spirit stayed bound to the madness of Desh-thiere's curse.

'Dharkaron Avenge, and against my last breath!' Dakar vowed with dangerous anger. But the quaver that marred his resolute oath exposed the naked fear in him. One tiny slip, the least whiff of suspicion that he meddled inside the Prime's close affairs, and he would be dead, struck down in an instant, with Lysaer left broken past salvage.

Best not to dwell on the unpleasant stakes as the final minutes streamed by. Dakar steadied his nerve and pronounced a clipped cantrip. Cast across distance, he invoked precise skills and retested the strength of the ward rings left sealed around Lysaer's drugged person. Should those stringent protections give way, his best effort here would spark off the whirlwind and reap the sure course to disaster.

The last, tensioned seconds spun past, inexorable. Dakar broke into sweat, chilled by the fickle spring air on his skin, and too well aware of the crickets whose songs hushed into an ominous silence. He checked his own guard spells. Poised, he prepared to unveil the meticulous construct cradled in his unsteady palms: a tattered bit of cloth, torn from Lysaer's shirt, stained with a let drop of s'Ilessid blood, then rolled up and knotted with a plucked strand of gold hair.

A second filament of Lysaer's hair, braided into a ring, wound his left, little finger. When the looped strands tingled with sudden roused power against the spellbinder's damp skin, the sensation forewarned him that Selidie Prime invoked her raised fetch.

Dakar released his pent breath and engaged the rune for *an*, one, left scribed by permission in air. The figure glowed blue, then crackled active, and wakened the tailored artifact he had already framed in retort. Its signature pattern pealed through the flux as a shout, wrought to mirror the Named essence of Lysaer s'Ilessid.

Selidie's diabolical sent trap locked into that amplified, unguarded target. For a heart-beat, Dakar held the malevolent thrust of her warped energies captive within his bare hands. He locked his grip. Sealed the noose with the rune of ending, *alt*, spoken in frantic exhilaration. Which decisive obstruction conjoined the duel, beyond revocable.

His bold move threw the Prime's Seniors off stride. Surprised, never powerless, they had a split-second chance to react. But a tranced circle thralled into subservience through crystal required a half beat more effort to shift course in pursuit of the Matriarch's will.

Dakar acted first. He doused the sealed construct into the streamlet. Natural current stripped away charge and dissolved the layers of fine energies.

Protections and stays came unravelled at speed, hastened along by Dakar's aligned partnership, worked through permission with the four elements. His core of laid runes embedded in wait unleashed and flared, by reactive design activated through running water. Four of the six primal runes of unbinding arced and countered the eightfold sigils the Koriathain enacted to halter free will.

Far off at Whitehold, the fetch made to maim Lysaer unravelled into an explosive gout of white flame. Selidie's riposte raised only screams as the sisters she managed recoiled and broke contact with the quartz matrix that focused their power. Scalded to blisters, then deafened and blinded, they lost their tranced poise and reeled in disarray from the violated connection.

Dakar sealed the finish. His shout in actualized Paravian split the night and called on the living flame of the cardinal element: *'Fiadliel! Ei lysien cuen shed-uanient i'an!'* <Fire-Light! I entreat you to cleanse this!>

He was no crown prince; not any longer a Fellowship agent to command the mysteries for Athera's need. Nonetheless, the response echoed through him. He felt the summoned forces rush into release with a roar down the tenuous spelled line, fast fading, but anchored yet to the sisterhood's doings in Whitehold. His intent stayed adamant, final and swift as the cut of the surgeon's knife: anything *anywhere* in the Prime's possession that resonated to Prince Arithon or Lysaer hit flash-point and went up in smoke. The effusive burst of wild ecstasy wrought as his act of grand conjury reached completion stung bone and flesh with fierce joy in swift passage. Dakar panted, slumped, his face masked in soaked hands. Droplets spilled down his wrists. The salty scald of his tears mingled with the icier runnels of wet splashed back into the streamlet.

In afterthought, diminished to distanced faint ripples cast through flux, he caught the howl of Selidie's curse to inflict her balked vengeance upon the mind and person of Arithon Teir's'Ffalenn.

Spent to lassitude, Dakar ground out a weak laugh. Then he steadied his reeling wits and erased his spelled lines of protection. One by one, with reverent gratitude, he freed and dispersed his borrowed ties to the might of the elements.

Morning waited but hours away. By then, the Prime's promise of retaliation would be too late to enact.

The vision of seer's talent already flowered, exuberant with the forecast proof: Dakar *sensed* the black stallion's disgruntled annoyance. Prompted to fury, at last driven mad by the itch of chafed skin, the horse stopped trying to scrape off the baldric and sword left noosed to its neck by Khadrien's impetuous presumption.

Straight as the shot arrow, Asandir's stallion made for the nearest trusted, friendly hand to ease its rankled discomfort. The horse would find the Master of Shadow stretched prone in light sleep, tucked in a dry gulch for concealment. It would nose his clothes and lip at his hair until he honoured the need to awake.

For once, errant talent bestowed the requital: Dakar viewed the stallion beneath the late-risen moon, one ear cocked back for the singer's voice that addressed its true spirit in musical tones of endearment. Tender fingers eased the caught burrs from its mane. Gentle, they moved and scratched the satin hair whorled with dried sweat at its crest. Pleasure sang in twined partnership, man's and beast's, as the black leaned into the caress and shuddered with bliss. The horse heaved a bottomless sigh of content at the last, when Arithon's touch unbuckled the baldric slung from its neck and restored it to freedom. His Grace did not know yet that his small act of kindness had reclaimed a vital piece of his forgotten birthright.

Once more, the Teir's'Falenn bore up the heirloom sword, Alithiel, bestowed on his royal lineage as a past gift of gratitude.

Soon enough, his curiosity would prompt him to unwind the wrapped leather and unmask the blade's emerald-set hilt. Rathain's prince would recognize the unearthly grace wrought into the sweep of dark quillons. The talent in him could not do other than recapture the whispered secrets instilled in the runes on the blade. As Athera's Masterbard, he was fit to recognize the latent presence of the grand chord once spoken by the Paravians to Name the winter stars. Which promise offered him potent defense for the hour he needed protection . . .

Roused back to himself from the depths of tranced prescience, Dakar arose stiff and tired, but oddly calm. He would let sleeping dogs lie, for tonight. Rathain's prince could be left undisturbed to complete his escape on his own. The lonely, fat spellbinder's cowardice chose not to address the raw wound of betrayal that had broken a difficult, long term of service and reduced a cherished friendship to ashes.

In the grey mist just prior to dawn, ravenous enough to consider eating the stolen gelding he untied and mounted, Dakar reined around and picked the less tangled course to redeem his mistakes. He kicked the hack under him to a smart trot. The easier fate lay ahead of him, surely. One that sent him to safeguard the slow journey northward and committed his steadfast help to secure Lysaer's sanity with Daliana.

Spring 5923

Defeats

Days later, come to the far verge of Scarpdale, a dark-haired royal fugitive strips to bare feet with intent to leave Havish by wading through the shallows at the north shore of Lithmarin; but one step from freedom, he shivers, brows hooked to a troubled frown: decisive through the instant's warning of threat, he draws the black sword, whose pealed note unfurls light and song with a beauty that severs the grotesque ring of enemy spells laid to debase his hard-won autonomy . . .

Set back yet again, her late effort smashed by Alithiel's pure note as she seeks to bind Arithon back under the coils of Desh-thiere's curse, Prime Selidie never blinks, but calls on the last Senior sister held poised in waiting at Deal: 'The time's ripe to engage my alternate plan made in reserve against today's failure . . .'

On the very hour that Asandir travels to treat with The Hatchet and clear Havish's border of the remnant war host, Davien departs on foot from the mountain cave where Seshkrozchiel sinks into a dragon's encapsulated hibernation; and perhaps, Sethvir dares to guard renewed hope, to journey back to Althain Tower and answer the debt bought by Luhaine's act of self-sacrifice . . .

GLOSSARY

A'LIESSIAD—a wholeness of balance between all beings.

    pronounced: ah-less-ee-ahd

    root meaning: *a'liessiad* – balance, with the prefix for the feminine aspect.

AFFI'ENIA—name given to Elaira by an adept, meaning dancer in the ancient dialect of the Biedar tribe, but carrying the mystical connotation of 'water dancer,' the wise woman who presided over the ritual of rebirth, celebrated on the spring equinox.

    pronounced: affee-yen-yah

    root meaning: *affi'enia* – dancer

AIYENNE—river located in Daon Ramon, Rathain, rising from an underground spring in the Mathorn Mountains, and coming above ground south of the Mathorn Road. Site of the ruinous battle between Earl Jieret's war band and the Alliance war host under Sulfin Evend, which enabled Arithon's escape to the north in Third Age 5670.

    pronounced: eye-an

    root meaning: *ai'an* – hidden one

ALESTRON—city located in Midhalla, Melhalla. Paravian built with warded defenses. Once ruled by s'Brydion, placed under entailment by the Fellowship Sorcerers after the siege in Third Age Year 5672.

    pronounced: ah-less-tron

    root meaning: *alesstair* – stubborn; *an* – one

ALITHIEL—one of twelve Blades of Isaer, forged by centaur Ffereton s'Darian from metal taken from a meteorite, and sung by the Athlien with the arcane endowment for transcendent change. Passed through Paravian possession, acquired the secondary name Dael-Farenn, or Kingmaker, since its owners tended to succeed the end of a royal line. Eventually was awarded to Kamridian s'Ffalenn for his valor in defence of the princess Taliennse, early Third Age, and held in the heritage of the s'Ffalenn royal line.

    pronounced: ah-lith-ee-el

    root meaning: *alith* – star; *iel* – light/ray

ALTHAIN TOWER—spire built at the edge of the Bittern Desert, beginning of the Second Age, to house records of Paravian histories. Third Age, became repository for the archives of all five royal houses of men after rebellion, overseen by the Fellowship Sorcerer, Sethvir, named Warden of Althain since Third Age Year 5100. Warded by the Ilitharis Paravian spirit of Shehane Althain.

    pronounced: all-thay-in

    root meaning: *alt* – last; *thein* – tower, sanctuary

    original Paravian pronunciation: alt-thein

ANGLEFEN—swampland located in Deshir, Rathain.

    pronounced: angle-fen

    not from Paravian

ANIENT—Paravian invocation for unity.

    pronounced: an-ee-ent

root meaning: *an* – one; *ient* – suffix for 'most'

ANSHLIEN'YA—name given to Meiglin s'Dieneval by the desert tribes of Sanpashir, prior to her conception of Dari's'Ahelas, crown heir of Shand, who would bear the rogue talent for far-sighted vision.

pronounced: ahn-shlee-yen-yah

root meaning: *anshlien'ya* – Biedar dialect, ancient word for 'dawn;' idiom for 'hope'

ARAETHURA—grass plains in south-west Rathain; principality of the same name in that location. Largely inhabited by Riathan Paravians in the Second Age. Third Age, used as pasture land by widely scattered nomadic shepherds.

pronounced: ar-eye-thoo-rah

root meaning: *araeth* – grass; *era* – place, land

ARIN—abbreviated diminutive for Arithon, taken from his faulty recall.

pronounced: ah-rin

ARITHON—son of Avar, Prince of Rathain, 1,504th Teir's'Ffalenn after founder of the line, Torbrand in Third Age Year One. Also Master of Shadow, the Bane of Desh-thiere, and Halliron Masterbard's successor. First among Mankind to tap the transcendent powers of the sword, Alithiel, and also responsible for the final defeat of the Grey Kralovir necromancers. Taken captive by Koriathain in Third Age 5674, and held under crown oath of debt with a stay on his life bought by Fellowship intercession for the purpose of setting his Masterbard's title to use to subdue the free wraiths from Marak.

pronounced: ar-i-thon

root meaning: *arithon* – fate-forger; one who is visionary

ARWENT—river in Araethura, Rathain, that flows from Daenfal Lake through Halwythwood to empty in Instrell Bay.

pronounced: are-went

root meaning: *arwient* – swiftest

ASANDIR—Fellowship Sorcerer. Secondary name, Kingmaker, since his hand crowned every High King of Men to rule in the Age of Men (Third Age). After the Mistwraith's conquest, he acted as field agent for the Fellowship's doings across the continent. Also called Fiend-quencher, for his reputation for quelling *iyats*; Storm-breaker and Change-bringer for his past actions when Men first arrived upon Athera.

pronounced: ah-san-deer

root meaning: *asan* – heart; *dir* – stone 'heart rock'

ATAINIA—north-eastern principality of Tysan.

pronounced: ah-tay-nee-ah

root meaning: *itain* – the third; *ia* – suffix for 'third domain' original Paravian, *itainia*

ATCHAZ—town located in Alland, Shand. Famed for its silk.

pronounced: at-chaz

root meaning: *atchias* – silk

ATH CREATOR—prime vibration, force behind all life.

    pronounced: ath

    root meaning: *ath* – prime, first (as opposed to *an*, one)

ATHERA—name for the world which holds the Five High Kingdoms; four Worldsend Gates; formerly inhabited by dragons, and current home of the Paravian races.

    pronounced: ath-air-ah

    root meaning: *ath* – prime force; *era* – place, 'Ath's world'

ATHILI—proscribed region located at the border of Havish and Rathain, between the principalities of Lanshire and Araethira, which bounds the grand portal created by Ath Creator when the Paravian presence was made manifest in the world.

    Pronounced: ah-the-lee

    Root meaning: *ath* – prime force; *i'li* – a state of self-aware exaltation.

ATHIR—Second Age ruin of a Paravian stronghold, located in Ithilt, Rathain. Site of a seventh lane power focus; also where Arithon Teir's'Ffalenn swore his blood oath to survive to the Fellowship Sorcerer, Asandir.

    pronounced: ath-ear

    root meaning: *ath* – prime; *i'er* – the line/edge

ATHLIEN PARAVIANS—sunchildren, dancers of the crystal flutes. Small race of semi-mortals, pixie-like, but possessed of great wisdom/keepers of the grand mystery.

    pronounced: ath-lee-en

    root meaning: *ath* – prime force; *lien* – to love, 'Ath-beloved'

AVENOR—Second Age ruin of a Paravian stronghold. Traditional seat of the s'Ilessid High Kings. Restored to habitation in Third Age 5644. Became the ruling seat of the Alliance of Light in Third Age 5648. Located in Korias, Tysan.

    pronounced: ah-ven-or

    root meaning: *avie* – stag; *norh* – grove

BARACH—former Earl of the North, second son of Jieret s'Valerient and older brother of Jeynsa; Presided over the trial of Eriegal for betrayal; brokered a lawful peace treaty with Mayor Lysaer s'Ilessid in 5688; died Third Age 5712; forebear of Cosach s'Valerient, Esfand, and Kadrien.

    pronounced: bar-ack

    root meaning: *baraich* – linch-pin

BARISH—coastal town on Mainmere Bay in south Tysan just north of the border.

    pronounced: bar-ish

    root meaning: *bar* – half; *ris* – way

BIEDAR—desert tribe living in Sanpashir, Shand. Also known as the Keepers of the Prophecy. Their sacred weaving at the well produced the conception of Dari s'Ahelas, which crossed the old *caithdein*'s lineage of s'Dieneval with the royal line of s'Ahelas, combining the gifts of prophetic clairvoyance with the Fellowship-endowed penchant for far-sight.

pronounced: bee-dar

root meaning: *biehdahrr* – ancient desert dialect for 'lore keepers'

BISH—fisherman from Torwent.

pronounced: bish

not from the Paravian

BITTERN DESERT—waste located in Atainia, Tysan, north of Althain Tower. Site of a First Age battle between the great drakes and the Seardluin, permanently destroyed by dragonfire.

pronounced: bittern

root meaning: *bityern* – to sear or char

BRAGGEN—one of the Fourteen Companions who were the only child survivors of the massacre at Tal Quorin in Third Age 5638. Stood proxy for Jeynsa s'Valerient's absence upon High Earl Barach's oath swearing to Prince Arithon in 5671, which obligated him to execute Eriegal's sentence for crown treason in 5674.

pronounced: brag-en

root meaning: *briocen* – surly

CAINFORD—town located in Taerlin, Tysan.

pronounced: cane-ford

root meaning: *caen* – vale

CAITHDEIN—(alternate spelling *caith'd'ein*, plural form *caithdeinen*) Paravian name for a high king's first counselor; also, the one who would stand as regent, or steward, in the absence of the crowned ruler. By heritage, the office also carries responsibility for oversight of crown royalty's fitness to rule.

pronounced: kay-ith-day-in

root meaning: *caith* – shadow; *d'ein* – behind the chair 'shadow behind the throne'

CAITHWOOD—free wilds forest located in Taerlin, southeast principality of Tysan.

pronounced: kay-ith-wood

root meaning: *caith* – shadow – shadowed wood

CAMRIS—north-central principality of Tysan. Original ruling seat was the city of Erdane.

pronounced: cam-ris

root meaning: *caim* – cross; *ris* – way 'cross-road'

CAOLLE—past war-captain of the clans of Deshir, Rathain. First raised, and then served under, Lord Steiven, Earl of the North and *Caithdein* of Rathain. Planned the campaign at Vastmark and Dier Kenton Vale for the Master of Shadow. Served Jieret Red-beard, and was feal liegeman of Arithon of Rathain; died of complications from a wound received from his prince while breaking a Koriani attempt to trap his liege in Third Age Year 5653.

pronounced: kay-all-eh, with the 'e' nearly subliminal

root meaning: *caille* – stubborn

CARITHWYR—principality in Havish, once a grass-lands breeding ground for the Riathan Paravians. Now produces grain, cattle, fine hides, and also hops and wine.

    pronounced: car-ith-ear

    root meaning: *ci'arithiren* – forgers of the ultimate link with prime power. An old colloquialism for unicorn.

CASCAIN ISLANDS—rugged chain of islets off the coast of Vastmark, Shand.

    pronounced: cass-canes

    root meaning: *kesh kain* – shark's teeth

CAYTE—a female deck-hand on a smuggler's sloop.

    pronounced: kay-ta

    root meaning: *ka'itha* – fifth girl

CEFTWINN s'LORNMEIN—princess and heir apparent of the royal line of Havish.

    pronounced: kef-twin slorn-main

    root meaning: *kef* – jasper; *tuinne* – rose; *liernmein* – to centre or bring into balance

CHAIMISTARIZOG—Elder dragon standing as keeper of Northgate.

    pronounced: shay-mist-tar-ee-zog

    root meaning: *chaimistarizog* – Drakish for fire gate keeper

CHAN—crofter's child from Kelsing who died of summer fever, brother of Paolin, son of Saffie, nephew of Efflin, Tarens and Kerelie.

    pronounced: chan

    not from the Paravian

CHEIVALT—coastal town in Carithwyr, Havish, known for its refined lifestyle.

    pronounced: shay-vault

    root meaning: *chiavalden* – a rare yellow wildflower which grows at sea-side

CILADIS THE LOST—Fellowship Sorcerer who left the continent in Third Age 5462 in search of the Paravian races after their disappearance following the rebellion.

    pronounced: kill-ah-dis

    root meaning: *cael* – leaf; *adeis* – whisper, compound; *cael'adeis* colloquialism for 'gentleness that abides'

COSACH S'VALERIENT—current Earl of the North and *Caithdein* of Rathain, husband of Jalienne, father of Esfand.

    pronounced: co-sack s-val-er-ee-ent

    root meaning: *val* – straight; *erient* – spear

DAELION FATEMASTER—'entity' formed by set of mortal beliefs, which determine the fate of the spirit after death. If Ath is the prime vibration, or life-force, Daelion is what governs the manifestation of free will.

    pronounced: day-el-ee-on

    root meaning: *dael* – king, or lord; *i'on* – of fate

DAELION'S WHEEL—cycle of life and the crossing point that is the transition into death.

    pronounced: day-el-ee-on

    root meaning: *dael* – king or lord; *i'on* – of fate

DAENFAL LAKE—lake that bounds the southern edge of Daon Ramon Barrens in Rathain.

    pronounced: dye-en-fall

    root meaning: *daen* – clay; *fal* – red

DAKAR THE MAD PROPHET—apprentice to Fellowship Sorcerer, Asandir, during the Third Age following the Conquest of the Mistwraith. Given to spurious prophecies, it was Dakar who forecast the fall of the Kings of Havish in time for the Fellowship to save the heir. He made the Prophecy of West Gate, which forecast the Mistwraith's bane, and also the Black Rose Prophecy, which called for reunification of the Fellowship.

    pronounced: dah-kar

    root meaning: *dakiar* – clumsy

DALIANA sen EVEND—descendant of Sulfin Evend chosen by Asandir to stand heir to lineage.

    pronounced: dah-lee-ahn-a

    root meaning: *dal* – fair; *lien* – harmony; *a* – feminine diminutive

DAON RAMON BARRENS—central principality of Rathain. Site where Riathan Paravians (unicorns) bred and raised their young. Barrens was not appended to the name until the years following the Mistwraith's conquest, when the River Severnir was diverted at the source by a task force under Etarran jurisdiction. Site where a combined Sunwheel war host led by Lysaer sought to corner the Master of Shadow, and met defeat against clan war bands under Jieret s'Valerient in Third Age Year 5670.

    pronounced: day-on-rah-mon

    root meaning: *daon* – gold; *ramon* – hills/downs

DARI S'AHELAS—crown heir of Shand who was sent to safety through West Gate to preserve the royal lineage. Born following the death of the last Crown Prince of Shand, subsequently raised and taught by Sethvir to manage the rogue talent of a dual inheritance. Her mother was Meiglin s'Dieneval, last survivor of the old *caithdein*'s lineage of Melhalla, which was widely believed to have perished during the massacre at Tirans. However the pregnant widow of Egan s'Dieneval had escaped the uprising and survived under a false name in a Durn brothel.

    pronounced: dar-ee

    root meaning: *daer* – to cut

DARKSHIEL—river located in northern Lanshire in the Kingdom of Havish.

    pronounced: dark-sheel

    root meaning: *dierk* – drake; *shiel* – tears

DAVIEN THE BETRAYER—Fellowship Sorcerer responsible for provoking the great uprising in Third Age Year 5018, that resulted in the fall of the high kings after Desh-thiere's conquest. Rendered discorporate by the Fellowship's judgement in Third Age 5129. Exiled since, by personal choice. Davien's works included the Five Centuries Fountain near Mearth on the splinter world of the Red Desert through West Gate; the shaft at Rockfell Peak, used by the Sorcerers to imprison harmful entities; the Stair on Rockfell Peak; and also, Kewar Tunnel in the Mathorn Mountains. Restored as a corporate being following Asandir's interaction with the Great Drake, Seshkrozchiel, in the banishment of the Scarpdale grimward in Third Age Year 5671. Bound into the dragon's service ever since.

pronounced: dah-vee-en

root meaning: *dahvi* – fool; *an* – one, 'mistaken one'

DESHIR—north-western principality of Rathain.

pronounced: desh-eer

root meaning: *deshir* – misty

DESH-THIERE—Mistwraith that invaded Athera from the splinter worlds through South Gate in Third Age 4993. Access cut off by Fellowship Sorcerer, Traithe. Battled and contained in West Shand for twenty-five years, until the rebellion splintered the peace, and the high kings were forced to withdraw from the defence lines to attend their disrupted kingdoms. Confined through the combined powers of Lysaer s'Ilessid's gift of light and Arithon s'Ffalenn's gift of shadow. Currently imprisoned in a warded flask in Rockfell Pit.

pronounced: desh-thee-air-e (last 'e' mostly subliminal)

root meaning: *desh* – mist; *thiere* – ghost or wraith

DHARKARON AVENGER—called Ath's Avenging Angel in legend. Drives a chariot drawn by five horses to convey the guilty to Sithaer. Dharkaron as defined by the adepts of Ath's Brotherhood is that dark thread mortal men weave with Ath, the prime vibration, that creates self-punishment, or the root of guilt.

pronounced dark-air-on

root meaning: *dhar* – evil; *khiaron* – one who stands in judgement

DIER KENTON VALE—a valley located in the principality of Vastmark, Shand, where Lysaer's war host, thirty-five thousand strong, fought and lost to the Master of Shadow in Third Age 5647, largely slaughtered in one day by a shale slide. The remainder were harried by a small force of Vastmark shepherds and clan scouts from Shand, under Caolle, who served as Arithon's war-captain, until supplies and loss of morale broke the Alliance campaign.

pronounced: deer ken-ton

root meaning: *dier'kendion* – a jewel with a severe flaw that may result in shearing or cracking.

EAST BRANSING—town located on the coast of Instrell Bay in Tysan.

pronounced: bran-sing

root meaning: *brienseng* – at the base, at the bottom

EFFLIN—a croft holder near Kelsing, and older brother of Tarens and Kerelie.

pronounced: eff-lin

root meaning: *e* – prefix for small; *ffael* – dark; *en* – suffix for 'more'; *effaelin* – a dark mood

ELAIRA—initiate enchantress of the Koriathain, currently serving the order as a wandering independent. Originally a street child, taken on in Morvain for Koriani rearing. Arithon's beloved, became handfast to Rathain in Third Age Year 5672.

pronounced: ee-layer-ah

root meaning: *e* – prefix, diminutive for small; *laere* – grace

ELKFOREST—free-wilds forest located in Gent, Havish. Site of the Queen's Glade.

ELLAINE—daughter of the Lord Mayor of Erdane, once Princess of Avenor by marriage to Lysaer s'Ilessid, and mother of Kevor s'Ilessid, who became an adept of Ath's Brotherhood.

pronounced: el-lane

not from the Paravian

ENNIE—a young woman from Kelsing.

pronounced: any

not from the Paravian.

ERDANE—originally a Paravian town given over to Mankind's rule; became the seat of the old Princes of Camris and the s'Gannley blood-line until the uprising that followed Desh-thiere's conquest in Third Age 5015. Became an iniquitous nest of necromancy in the years following, then the site of the True Sect High Temple of the Light since the Great Schism in 5683, and where the conclave of priests signed the doctrine into the First Book of Canon Law in 5691.

pronounced: er-day-na with the last syllable almost subliminal

root meaning: *er'deinia* – long walls

ERDANI—from Erdane.

pronounced: er-day-nee

root meaning: *er'deinia'i* – being of the 'long walls' – colloquial suffix for identity.

ERIEGAL—second youngest of the fourteen child survivors of the Tal Quorin massacre known as Jieret's Companions. Renowned as a shrewd tactician, he was ordered to serve Jieret's son Barach as war-captain in the Halwythwood camp rather than fight Lysaer's war host in Daon Ramon Barrens in Third Age Year 5670. Tried and executed for Crown Treason in 5674.

pronounced: air-ee-gall

root meaning: *eriegal* – snake

ESFAND s'VALERIENT—heir designate to the *Caithdein* of Rathain, son of Cosach s'Valerient and Jalienne.

pronounced: es-fand s'val-er-ee-ent

root meaning: *esfan* – iron; *'d* – suffix for behind

ETARRA—trade city built across the Mathorn Pass by townsfolk after the revolt that cast down Ithamon and the High Kings of Rathain. Nest of corruption and intrigue, and policy-maker for the North. Lysaer s'Ilessid was ratified as mayor upon Morfett's death in Third Age Year 5667. Site where Arithon defeated the

Kralovir necromancers in Third Age Year 5671. Also the former seat of the Alliance armed forces. Ruled by acting elected mayor Lysaer s'Ilessid, in residence since the Great Schism in Third Age Year 5683.

    pronounced: ee-tar-ah

    root meaning: *e* – prefix for small; *taria* – knots

FALLOWMERE—north-eastern principality of Rathain.

    pronounced: fal-oh-meer

    root meaning: *fal'ei'miere* – literally, tree self-reflection, colloquialism for 'place of perfect trees'

FATE'S WHEEL—see Daelion's Wheel.

FELLOWSHIP OF SEVEN—sorcerers bound to Athera by the summoning dream of the dragons and charged to secure the mysteries that enable Paravian survival. Achieved their redemption from Cianor Sunlord, under the Law of the Major Balance in Second Age Year One. Originators and keepers of the covenant of the compact, made with the Paravian races, to allow Mankind's settlement on Athera in Third Age Year One. Their authority backs charter law, upheld by crown justice and clan oversight of the free wilds.

FFEREDON-LI—ancient Paravian word for a healer, literally translated 'bringer of grace' and the name given to Elaira by an Araethurian seeress on the hour of Fionn Areth's birth.

    pronounced: fair-eh-dun-lee

    root meaning: *ffaraton* – maker; *li* – exalted grace

FIADUWYNNE—site of a Second Age focus circle, and a once vast complex of healer's gardens and telir orchards, located in south Lanshire, Havish, at the banks of the River Lithwater.

    pronounced: fee-ah-dew-win-e – with the last syllable nearly subliminal

    root meaning: *ffiadu* – to make whole; *wynne* – orchard

FIATH—deceased croft holder from Kelsing, husband of Saffie, uncle to Efflin, Tarens, and Kerelie.

    pronounced: fee-ahth

    root meaning: *ffiath* – a verity, a truth; *ff'i'ath* – giving identity to that which is Ath

FORTHMARK—city in Vastmark, Shand. Once the site of a hostel of Ath's Brotherhood. By Third Age 5320, the site was abandoned and taken over by the Koriani Order as a healer's hospice.

    root meaning not from the Paravian

GESTRY s'LORNMEIN—heir designate of Havish, crowned High King of Havish in Third Age Year 5922.

    pronounced: guess-tree slorn-main

    root meaning: *geies* – obligated duty; *tieri* – steel; *liernmein* – to centre or bring into balance

GLENDIEN—a Shandian clanswoman, wife to Kyrialt s'Taleyn, formerly the heir designate of the High Earl of Alland; mother to Arithon's bastard daughter, Teylia, conceived in the confluence at Athir in Third Age Year 5672.

    pronounced: glen-dee-en

    root meaning: *glyen* – sultry; *dien* – object of beauty

GREY KRALOVIR—see Kralovir.

GREAT WAYSTONE—see Waystone.

GRIMWARD—a circle of spells of Paravian making that seal and isolate the dire dreams of dragon haunts, a force with the potential for mass destruction. With the disappearance of the old races, the defences are maintained by embodied Sorcerers of the Fellowship of Seven. Of seventeen separate sites listed at Althain Tower, thirteen are still active.

GRISMARD—a wealthy townsman from Kelsing.

    pronounced: grease-marred

    not from the Paravian

HALIKA—Caithdein of Havish in service to High King Gestry s'Lornmein.

    pronounced: ha-lee-kah

    root meaning: *hal* – white; *lie* – note struck in harmony; *ka* – girl

HALWYTHWOOD—forest located in Araethura, Rathain. Current clan lodge of High Earl Cosach's band.

    pronounced: hall-with-wood

    root meaning: *hal* – white; *wythe* – vista

HAMMON—a fisherman on a lugger from Torwent.

    pronounced: ham-mon

    not from the Paravian

HATTSEY—a bar maid in Etarra, friend of Daliana sen Evend.

    pronounced: hat-see

    not from the Paravian

HAVISH—one of the Five High Kingdoms of Athera as defined by the charters of the Fellowship of Seven. Ruled by a queen, succeeded at death by Gestry s'Lornmein. Crown heritage: temperance. Device: gold hawk on red field.

    pronounced: hav-ish

    root meaning: *havieshe* – hawk

HELDA—a fourth-rank initiate in the Order of the Koriathain.

    pronounced: held-a

    root meaning: root meaning: *huell* – one who protects; *da* – by/next to

HIGHSCARP—city sited near the stone quarries on the coast of the Bay of Eltair, located in Daon Ramon, Rathain. Also contains a sisterhouse of the Koriani Order.

ILITHARIS PARAVIANS—centaurs, one of three semimortal old races; disappeared after the Mistwraith's conquest, the last guardian's departure by Third Age Year 5100. They were the guardians of the earth's mysteries.

    pronounced: i-li-thar-is

    root meaning: *i'lith'earis* – the keeper/preserver of mystery

INNISH—city located on the southcoast of Shand at the delta of the River Ippash. Formerly known as 'the Jewel of Shand,' this was the site of the High King's winter court, prior to the time of the uprising.

    pronounced: in-ish

    root meaning: *inniesh* – a jewel with a pastel tint

INSTRELL BAY—body of water off the Gulf of Stormwell between Atainia, Tysan, and Deshir, Rathain.

    pronounced: in-strell

    root meaning: *arin'streal* – strong wind

ISAER—power focus built in the First Age in Atainia, Tysan, by the Ilitharis Paravians, to source the defence works of the Paravian keep of the same name.

    pronounced: i-say-er

    root meaning: *i'saer* – the circle

ISFARENN—etheric Name for the black stallion once ridden by Asandir. Died in the Scarpdale grimward in Third Age Year 5671.

    pronounced: ees-far-en

    root meaning: *is'feron* – speed maker

ISSING—river located in Havistock, Havish, arises in the Storlains and flows south to Redburn harbour at Rockbay.

    pronounced: i-sing

    root meaning: *yssing* – spindrift

ITHISH—city located at the edge of the principality of Vastmark, on the southcoast of Shand. Where the Vastmark shepherds ship their wool fleeces.

    pronounced: ith-ish

    root meaning: *ithish* – fleece or fluffy

IYAT – energy sprite, and minor drake spawn inhabiting Athera, not visible to the eye, manifests in a poltergeist fashion by taking temporary possession of objects. Feeds upon natural energy sources: fire, breaking waves, lightning, and excess emotion where humans gather.

pronounced: ee-at

    root meaning: *iyat* – to break

IYAT-THOS—clan dialect name for Tarens.

    pronounced: ee-at thoss

    root meaning: *iyat* – broken; *thos* – nose

JAELOT—city located on the coast of Eltair Bay at the southern border of the Kingdom of Rathain. Once a Second Age power site, with a focus circle. Now a merchant city with a reputation for extreme snobbery and bad taste. Also the site where Arithon s'Ffalenn played his eulogy for Halliron Masterbard, which raised the powers of the Paravian focus circle beneath the mayor's palace. The forces of the mysteries and resonant harmonics caused damage to city buildings, watch keeps, and walls, which has since been repaired.

pronounced: jay-lot

root meaning: *jielot* – affectation

JALIENNE—wife of Cosach s'Valerient, current *Caithdein* of Rathain.

pronounced: jah-lee-en

root meaning: *jia* – binding, tie together, intertwine; *lien* – to love

JESSIAN OATHKEEPER—historical sister of the Koriathain, prior to settlement on Athera, when the order was a secret society, sent to the planet Scathac to treat with the Biedar, and witnessed the tribal rite that preserved the planet from Calum Kincaid's Great Weapon. Subsequently came to trial and imprisonment when she refused to break the silence sworn to the Biedar matriarch never to reveal the experience. Her secret was kept until she was executed, but the mystery it concealed launched the Koriani Order on a search that eventually resulted in coercive disclosure and theft of the ancient Biedar knowledge.

pronounced: jess-ee-an

not from the Paravian

JEYNSA s'VALERIENT—daughter of Jieret s'Valerient and Feithan, born Third Age 5653; appointed successor for her father's title, *Caithdein* of Rathain. Married Sevrand s'Brydion.

pronounced: jay-in-sa

root meaning: *jieyensa* – garnet

JIERET s'VALERIENT—former Earl of the North, clan chief of Deshir; *Caithdein* of Rathain, sworn liegeman of Prince Arithon s'Ffalenn. Also son and heir of Lord Steiven. Blood pacted to Arithon by sorcerer's oath prior to the battle of Strakewood Forest. Came to be known by head-hunters as Jieret Red-beard. Father of Jeynsa and Barach. Husband to Feithan. Died by Lysaer s'Ilessid's hand in Daon Ramon Barrens, Third Age Year 5670.

pronounced: jeer-et

root meaning: *jieret* – thorn

KADIERACH—Ilitharis Paravian, or centaur guardian, who was called forward by High Earl Jieret's transcendence. Also appeared to Arithon s'Ffalenn during his passage through Kewar's Maze in Third Age Year 5670.

pronounced: kad-ee-er-ack

root meaning: *kad'i* – to quicken etherically, or bring to blossom throughrefined awareness; *era* – place; *ch* – suffix for attached to or rooted to a site

KATHTAIRR—barren land-mass in the southern ocean, across the world from Paravia.

pronounced: kath-tear

root meaning: *kait-th'era* – empty place

KELHORN MOUNTAINS—a range of shale scarps located in Vastmark, Shand.
pronounced: kell-horn
root meaning: *kielwhern* – toothed, jagged

KELSING—town located south of Erdane on the trade-road in Camris, Tysan.
pronounced: kel-sing
root meaning: *kel* – hidden; *seng* – cave

KERELIE—crofter's daughter from Kelsing, sister of Efflin and Tarens, niece of Saffie and Fiath.
pronounced: care-ah-lee
not from the Paravian

KEWAR TUNNEL—cavern built beneath the Mathorn Mountains by Davien the Betrayer; contains the maze of conscience, which caused High King Kamridian s'Ffalenn's death. Arithon Teir's'Ffalenn successfully completed the challenge in Third Age Year 5670.
pronounced: key-wahr
root meaning: *kewiar* – a weighing of conscience

KHADRIEN s'VALERIENT—clanborn second cousin to Esfand s'Valerient, friend of Siantra s'Idir.
pronounced: cad-ree-en sval-er-ee-ent
root meaning: *val* – straight; *erient* – spear

KHARADMON—Sorcerer of the Fellowship of Seven; discorporate since rise of Khadrim and Seardluin leveled Paravian stronghold at Ithamon in Second Age 3651. It was by Kharadmon's intervention that the survivors of the attack were sent to safety by means of transfer from the fifth lane power focus. Currently working the wardings to defer a minor invasion of wraiths from Marak.
pronounced: kah-rad-mun
root meaning: *kar'riad en mon* – phrase translates to mean 'twisted thread on the needle' or colloquialism for 'a knot in the works'

KORIANI—possessive and singular form of the word 'Koriathain'; see entry.
pronounced: kor-ee-ah-nee

KORIATHAIN—order of enchantresses ruled by a circle of Seniors, under the power of one Prime Enchantress. They draw their talent from the orphaned children they raise, or from daughters dedicated to service by their parents. Initiation rite involves a vow of consent that ties the spirit to a power crystal keyed to the Prime's control.
pronounced: kor-ee-ah-thain – to rhyme with 'main'
root meaning: *koriath* – order; *ain* – belonging to

KRALOVIR—term for a sect of necromancers, also called the grey cult, destroyed by Arithon s'Ffalenn in Third Age Year 5671.
pronounced: kray-low-veer
root meaning: *krial* – name for the rune of crossing; *oveir* – abomination

LAITHEN s'IDIR—clanborn woman from Fallowmere, descended from Sidir's lineage, mother of Siantra s'Idir.

pronounced: lay-then see-deer

root meaning: *laere* – grace; *thein* – tower; *laerethien* – pillar of grace; *s'* – of the lineage; *i'id'ier* – almost lost

LANSHIRE—northernmost principality in the Kingdom of Havish. Name taken from the wastes at Scarpdale, site of First Age battles with Seardluin that blasted the soil to slag.

pronounced: lahn-sheer-e

root meaning: *lan'hansh'era* – place of hot sands

LAW OF THE MAJOR BALANCE—founding order of the powers of the Fellowship of Seven, as taught by the Paravians. The primary tenet is that no force of nature should be used without consent, or against the will of another consciousness.

LEYNSGAP—narrow pass in the Mathorn Mountains, Rathain, famed site of Braggen's stand, where the clan Companion single-handedly fought and held off a troop of Sunwheel soldiers in pursuit of Arithon Teir's'Ffalenn.

pronounced: lay-ens-gap

root meaning: *liyond* – corridor

LIRENDA—former First Senior Enchantress to the Prime, Koriani Order; failed in her assignment to capture Arithon s'Ffalenn for Koriani purposes. Held as a passive servant under the Prime Matriarch's sentence of punishment since Third Age Year 5670.

pronounced: leer-end-ah

root meaning: *lyron* – singer; *di-ia* – a dissonance – the hyphen denotes a glottal stop

LITHMARIN—glacial lake located in between Lanshire and Ghent in Havish.

pronounced: lith-mar-in

root meaning: *lieth* – flow; *mieren* – mirror

LITHWATER—river

pronounced: lith

root meaning: *lieth* – flow, current

LORN—town on the northcoast of Atainia, Tysan.

pronounced: lorn

root meaning: *loern* – an Atheran fish.

LUHAINE—Sorcerer of the Fellowship of Seven – discorporate since the fall of Telmandir in Third Age Year 5018. Luhaine's body was pulled down by the mob while he was in ward trance, covering the escape of the royal heir to Havish.

pronounced: loo-hay-ne

root meaning: *luirhainon* – defender

LYRANTHE—instrument played by the bards of Athera. Strung with fourteen strings, tuned to seven tones (doubled). Two courses are 'drone strings' set to octaves. Five are melody strings, the lower three courses being octaves, the upper two, in unison.

pronounced: leer-anth-e (last 'e' mostly subliminal)

root meaning: *lyr* – song; *anthe* – box

LYSAER s'ILESSID—prince of Tysan, 1497th in succession after Halduin, founder of the line in Third Age Year One. Gifted at birth with control of Light, and Bane of Desh-thiere. Also known as Blessed Prince since he declared himself avatar for the following known as the Alliance of Light. Elected Mayor of Etarra in 5667. Declared apostate to the Light at the Great Schism in Third Age Year 5683; retired to his seat at Etarra, signed Treaty of Law with Rathain's clans in 5688.

pronounced: lie-say-er

root meaning: *lia* – blond, yellow, or light; *saer* – circle

MAENALLE s'GANNLEY—former Caithdein of Tysan, put on trial for theft and outlawry on the trade-road, condemned and executed at Isaer by Lysaer s'Ilessid in Third Age Year 5645.

pronounced: may-nall

root meaning: *maeni'alli* – to patch together; *gaen* – guide; *li* – exalted, in harmony

MAINMERE—town at the head of the Valenford River in Taerlin, Tysan. Built on a site originally kept clear to free the second lane focus in the ruins farther south.

pronounced: main-meer-e (last 'e' mostly subliminal)

root meaning: *maeni* – to fall, interrupt; *miere* – reflection/colloquial for disrupt continuity

MARAK—splinter world, cut off beyond South Gate, left lifeless after creation of the Mistwraith. The original inhabitants were men exiled by the Fellowship from Athera for beliefs or practices that were incompatible with the compact sworn between the Sorcerers and the Paravian races, which permitted human settlement on Athera. Source of the Mistwraith, Desh-thiere, and the free wraiths that threaten Athera.

pronounced: maer-ak

root meaning: *m'era'ki* – a place held separate

MATHORN MOUNTAINS—range that bisects the Kingdom of Rathain east to west.

pronounced: math-orn

root meaning: *mathien* – massive

MATHORN ROAD—trade-road running just south of the Mathorn Mountains.

pronounced: math-orn

root meaning: *mathien* – massive

MEIGLIN s'DIENEVAL—the legitimate daughter born to the widow of Egan s'Dieneval in Third Age 5019, just after his death in the slaughter of the rebellion. Heart's love of the last High King of Shand for one night, just prior to his death while fighting the Mistwraith. A weaving by the Biedar of Sanpashir, done at the behest of the last centaur guardian, ensured the union would bring conception, and the birth of Dari's'Ahelas. Also named Anshlien'ya in desert dialect, as the dawn of hope.

    pronounced: mee-glin s-dee-in-ee-vahl

    root meaning: *meiglin* – passion; *dien* – large; *eval* – endowment, gifted talent

MINDERL BAY—body of water inside of Crescent Isle, off the eastshore of Rathain.

    pronounced: mind-earl

    root meaning: *minderl* – anvil

MIRALT HEAD—point of land on the north coast of Camris, Tysan, with a port town by the same name.

    pronounced: meer-alt

    root meaning: *m'ier* – shore; *alt* – last

MISTWRAITH—see Desh-thiere.

MORVAIN—city located in the principality of Araethura, Rathain, on the west coast of Instrell Bay. Elaira's birthplace.

    pronounced: mor-vain

    root meaning: *morvain* – swindler's market

NARMS—city on the coast of Instrell Bay, built as a craft centre by Men in the early Third Age. Best known for dye works.

    pronounced: narms

    root meaning: *narms* – colour

NORTHSTRAIT—narrow passage from the Westland Sea into the Gulf of Stormwell, located in the northwest corner of Tysan.

ONYA—a townswoman of Kelsing.

    pronounced: on-ya

    not from the Paravian

ORLAN—pass in the Thaldein Mountains in Tysan where the clan seat has a hidden outpost.

    pronounced: or-lan

    root meaning: *irlan* – ledge

OSTERMERE—coastal town in Carithwyr, Havish, once a smuggler's haven.

    pronounced: os-tur-meer

    root meaning: *ostier* – crumbled; *dir* – stone

PAOLIN—crofter's child who died of summer fever, son of Saffie, brother of Chan (also deceased), and nephew of Tarens and Kerelie.

    pronounced: pay-oh-lin

    not from the Paravian

PARAVIA—name for the continent inhabited by the Paravians, and locale of the Five Kingdoms.

pronounced: par-ay-vee-ah

root meaning: *para* – great; *i'a* – suffix denoting entityship, and raised to the feminine aspect, which translates as 'place inclusive of, or holding the aspect for greatness'

PARAVIAN—name for the three old races that inhabited Athera before Mankind. Including the centaurs, the sunchildren, and the unicorns, these races never die unless mishap befalls them; they are the world's channel, or direct connection, to Ath Creator.

pronounced: par-ai-vee-ans

root meaning: *para* – great; *i'on* – fate or great mystery

PENSTAIR—Second Age ruin on the north shore of Deshir, Rathain.

pronounced: pen-stair

root meaning: *pensti'era* – watch point, place for beacon fires

PRANDEY—Shandian term for gelded pleasure boy.

pronounced: prandee

not from the Paravian

RATHAIN—one of the Five High Kingdoms of Athera, ruled by descendants of Torbrand s'Ffalenn since Third Age Year One. Device: black-and-silver leopard on green field. Arithon Teir's'Ffalenn is sanctioned crown prince, by the hand of Asandir of the Fellowship, in Third Age Year 5638 at Etarra.

pronounced: rath-ayn

root meaning: *roth* – brother; *thein* – tower, sanctuary

REDBURN—town located in a deep inlet in the northern shore of Rockbay Harbour in Havistock, Havish.

pronounced: red-burn

root meaning not from the Paravian

REIYAJ SEERESS—title for the Seeress sequestered in a tower in Shand, near Ithish. Her oracular visions derive from meditative communion with the energy gateway marked and measured by Athera's sun. Born sighted, but practice of her art brings blindness. The origin of her tradition derives from the mystical practices of the Biedar tribe in the Sanpashir desert.

pronounced: ree-yahj

root meaning: *ria'ieajn* – to touch the forbidden

RIATHAN PARAVIANS—unicorns, the purest, most direct connection to Ath Creator; the prime vibration channels directly through the horn.

pronounced: ree-ah-than

root meaning: *ria* – to touch; *ath* – prime life-force; *an* – one; *ri'athon* – one who touches divinity

ROCKBAY HARBOUR—body of water located on the southcoast, between Shand and West Shand.

ROCKFELL PEAK—mountain containing Rockfell Pit, used to imprison harmful entities throughout all three Ages. Located in West Halla, Melhalla; became the warded prison for Desh-thiere.

    pronounced: rock-fell

    root meaning not from the Paravian

ROCKFELL PIT—shaft built by the Sorcerer Davien in Rockfell Peak to contain harmful entities; currently sequesters the Mistwraith, Desh-thiere.

SAFFIE—deceased croft mistress from Kelsing, wife of Fiath, aunt of Efflin, Tarens, and Kerelie, mother of Paolin and Chan.

    pronounced: saf-ee

    not from the Paravian

s'AHELAS—family name for the royal line appointed by the Fellowship Sorcerers in Third Age Year One to rule the High Kingdom of Shand. Gifted geas: far-sight. Also the lineage that carries the latent potential for the rogue talent for far-sight and prophecy, introduced when the *caithdein*'s lineage of s'Dieneval became crossed with the royal line in Third Age 5036, resulting in Dari's birth in winter, 5037.

    pronounced: s'ah-hell-as

    root meaning: *ahelas* – mage-gifted

SANPASHIR—desert waste on the southcoast of Shand. Home to the desert tribes called Biedar.

    pronounced: sahn-pash-eer

    root meaning: *san* – black or dark; *pash'era* – place of grit or gravel

SANSHEVAS—town on the south shore in Alland, Shand, known for citrus, sugar, and rum.

    pronounced: san-shee-vas

    root meaning: *san* – black; *shievas* – flint

s'CRIADIEN—an older, outbred clan lineage arisen from past liaison between Torwent fishermen and Caithwood's clan blood-lines.

    pronounced: cree-ah-dee-en

    root meaning: *cor'ia'dreien* – a shipmate or shipping partner

SCARPDALE—waste in Lanshire, Havish, created by a First Age war with Seardluin. Once the site of the Scarpdale grimward, banished by Seshkrozchiel in Third Age Year 5671.

    pronounced: scarp-dale

    not from the Paravian

s'DIENEVAL—lost lineage of the *caithdeinen* of Melhalla, the last to carry the title being Egan, who died at the side of his High King in the battle to subdue the Mistwraith. The blood-line carried strong talent for prophecy, and was slaughtered during the sack of Tirans in the uprising in Third Age Year 5018, with Egan's pregnant wife the sole survivor. Her daughter, Meiglin, was mother of Dari s'Ahelas, crown heir of Shand.

pronounced: s-dee-in-ee-vahl

root meaning: *dien* – large; *eval* – endowment, gifted talent

SECOND AGE—Marked by the arrival of the Fellowship of Seven at Crater Lake, their called purpose to fight the drake spawn.

SELIDIE—young woman initiate appointed by Morriel Prime as a candidate in training for succession. Succeeded to the office of Prime Matriarch after Morriel's death on winter solstice in Third Age Year 5670, at which time an unprincipled act of possession by Morriel usurped the young woman's body.

pronounced: sell-ih-dee

root meaning: *selyadi* – air sprite

SELKWOOD—forest located in Alland, Shand.

pronounced: selk-wood

root meaning: *selk* – pattern

SESHKROZCHIEL—name for the female dragon who was mated to Haspastion. Forged a bargain with Davien, who borrowed on her powers while she was in hibernation in exchange for his term of service, for however long she required it. Her wakening in Third Age Year 5671 incurred the debt, still on-going.

pronounced: sesh-crows-chee-ell

root meaning: *seshkrozchiel* – Drakish for blue lightning

SETHVIR—Sorcerer of the Fellowship of Seven, also trained to serve as Warden of Althain since Third Age 5100, when the last centaur guardian departed after the Mistwraith's conquest.

pronounced: seth-veer

root meaning: *seth* – fact; *vaer* – keep

s'FFALENN—family name for the royal line appointed by the Fellowship Sorcerers in Third Age Year One to rule the High Kingdom of Rathain. Gifted geas: compassion/empathy.

pronounced: s-fal-en

root meaning: *ffael* – dark; *an* – one

s'GANNLEY—lineage of the Earls of the West, once the Camris princes, now bearing the heritage of *Caithdein* of Tysan. Iamine s'Gannley was the woman founder.

pronounced: sgan-lee

root meaning: *gaen* – guide; *li* – exalted or in harmony

SHAMSIN—a dedicate lancer in the True Sect Guard stationed at Kelsing.

pronounced: sham-sin

not from the Paravian

SHAND—one of the Five High Kingdoms of Athera, located on the south-east corner of the Paravian continent, originally ruled by the line of s'Ahelas. Current device: purple-and-gold chevrons, since the adjunct kingdom of West Shand came under high crown rule. The old device was a falcon on a crescent moon, sometimes still displayed, depicted against the more recent purple-and-gold chevrons.

pronounced: shand – as in 'hand'

root meaning: *shayn* or *shiand* – two/pair

SIANTRA s'IDIR—clanborn daughter of Laithen s'Idir, of Sidir's lineage.

pronounced: see-an-tra see-deer

root meaning: *sian* – spark; *tier* – to hold fast; *a* – feminine diminutive

SIDIR—one of the Companions, who were the fourteen boys to survive the massacre at Tal Quorin in 5638. Served Arithon at the Battle of Dier Kenton Vale the Havens in 5647, and at the siege of Alestron in 5671. Second in command of Earl Jieret's war band. Married Jieret's widow, Feithan, in 5672.

pronounced: see-deer

root meaning: *i'sid'i'er* – one who has stood at the verge of being lost.

s'IDIR—lineage of Sidir. His descendants derive from a youthful liaison with a clanswoman in Fallowmere.

pronounced: see-deer

root meaning: *i'sid'i'er* – one who has stood at the verge of being lost.

SILBERNE—river that runs southward from Tornir Peaks and empties into Mainmere Bay, Tysan.

pronounced: syl-burn

root meaning: *shiel* – tears; *biern* – memorial

s'ILESSID—family name for the royal line appointed by the Fellowship Sorcerers in Third Age Year One to rule the High Kingdom of Tysan. Gifted geas: justice.

pronounced: s-ill-ess-id

root meaning: *liessiad* – balance

SITHAER—mythological equivalent of hell, halls of Dharkaron Avenger's judgement; according to Ath's adepts, that state of being where the prime vibration is not recognized.

pronounced: sith-air

root meaning: *sid* – lost; *thiere* – wraith/spirit

SKYRON FOCUS—large aquamarine focus stone, used by the Koriani Senior Circle for their major magic after the loss of the Great Waystone during the rebellion.

pronounced: sky-run

root meaning: *skyron* – colloquialism for shackle; *s'kyr'i'on* – literally 'sorrowful fate'

SKYSHIELS—mountain range that runs north and south along the eastern coast of Rathain.

pronounced: sky-shee-ells

root meaning: *skyshia* – to pierce through; *iel* – ray

s'LORNMEIN—royal lineage of Havish, founded by Bwin Evoc in First Age Year One. Gifted geas: temperance.

pronounced: slorn-main

root meaning: *liernmein* – to centre, restrain, bring into balance.

SOUTHSHIRE—town on the southcoast of Alland, Shand, known for shipbuilding.

pronounced: south-shire

not from the Paravian

SOUTH STRAIT—body of water and passage from Rockbay Harbour into South Sea.

STORLAINS—mountains dividing the Kingdom of Havish.

    pronounced: store-lanes

    root meaning: *storlient* – largest summit, highest divide

SULFIN EVEND—son of the Mayor of Hanshire who held the post of Alliance Lord Commander under Lysaer s'Ilessid. Spared Lysaer from his dark binding to the Kralovir necromancers, and in the course of that awakened the talent of his outbred clan lineage: of s'Gannley descent, through Diarin s'Gannley, who was abducted and forced to marry his great grandsire. Bound to the land in Third Age 5670 when he swore a *caithdein*'s oath at Althain Tower as part of his bargain with Enithen Tuer, who in turn imparted the ceremonial knowledge and the Biedar knife used to sever the etheric cords the cult used to enslave victims. Named the Heretic Betrayer by the True Sect in the belief he corrupted the avatar, Lysaer. Ancestor of Daliana sen Evend.

    pronounced: sool-finn ev-end

    root meaning: *suilfinn eiavend* – colloquialism, diamond mind 'one who is persistent'

SUNCHILDREN—common name for Athlien Paravians, see entry.

SUNWHEEL—heraldic symbol adopted by the religion of Light, and the device of the True Sect.

s'VALERIENT—family name for the Earls of the North, regents and *caithdeinen* for the High Kings of Rathain.

    pronounced: val-er-ee-ent

    root meaning: *val* – straight; *erient* – spear

TAERLIN—southeastern principality of Tysan, also a lake in the southern spur of Tornir Peaks.

    pronounced: tay-er-lin

    root meaning: *taer* – calm; *lien* – to love

TAFE ALEMAN—innkeeper in Kelsing, Tysan known to give work to destitutes.

    pronounced: tayf

    not from the Paravian

TAL QUORIN—river formed by the confluence of watershed on the southern side of Strakewood, principality of Deshir, Rathain, where traps were laid for Etarra's army in the battle of Strakewood Forest, and where the rape and massacre of Deshir's clanwomen and children occurred under Lysaer and head-hunters under Pesquil's command in Third Age Year 5638.

    pronounced: tal quar-in

    root meaning: *tal* – branch; *quorin* – canyons

TALITH—Etarran princess; former wife of Lysaer s'Ilessid, estranged from him and incarcerated on charges of consorting with the Master of Shadow. Eventually murdered by a conspiracy of Avenor's crown council, when an arranged accident caused her fall from Avenor's tower of state in Third Age 5653.

pronounced: tal-ith – to rhyme with 'gal with'

root meaning: *tal* – branch; *lith* – to keep/nurture

TALLA s'CRIADIEN—a countrywoman healed by Asandir.

pronounced: ta-la

root meaning: *tal* – branch; *a* – feminine diminutive; *cor'ia'dreien* – a shipmate or shipping partner

TARENS—town-born crofter from Kelsing, brother of Efflin and Kerelie, nephew of Saffie and Fiath, uncle to Paolin and Chan.

pronounced: tar-ens

root meaning: tirans – *tier'ain* - protect

TEIR—masculine form of a title fixed to a name denoting heirship.

pronounced: tayer

root meaning: *teir's* – successor to power

TEIREN—feminine form of Teir.

pronounced: tear

root meaning: *teiren* – female successor to power

TEIRIENT—queen.

pronounced: tear-ee-ent

root meaning: *tierient* – female successor to power in the emphatic form

TEIR'II'DAEL—Paravian title given to a Fellowship-sanctioned crown prince.

pronounced: tay-er ee'eh die-el

root meaning: *teir'ii'dael* – the emphatic form of colloquial 'successor to power'

TELIR—a rare fruit once cultivated by Paravians that made fine brandy.

pronounced: tell-leer

root meaning: *telir* – sweet

TELMANDIR—seat of the High Kings of Havish in Lithmere, Havish. Ruined during the uprising in Third Age Year 5018, rebuilt by High King Eldir s'Lornmein after his coronation in Third Age Year 5643.

pronounced: tel-man-deer

root meaning: *telman'en* – leaning; *dir* – rock

TEYLIA—bastard daughter of Arithon Teir's'Ffalenn and Glendien, widow of Kyrialt, born in Third Age Year 5672, sworn into the Order of the Koriathain by her own will at three years of age.

pronounced: tay-lee-ah

root meaning: *tien* – dream; *lie* – note struck in harmony; *a* – female diminutive

THALDEIN—mountain range that borders Camris in Tysan, site of the Camris clans west outpost.

pronounced: thall-dayn

root meaning: *thal* – head; *dein* – bird

TIENELLE—high-altitude herb valued by mages for its mind-expanding properties. Highly toxic. No antidote. The leaves, dried and smoked, are most potent. To weaken its powerful side effects and allow safer access to its vision, Koriani enchantresses boil the flowers, then soak tobacco leaves with the brew.

pronounced: tee-an-ell-e (last 'e' – mostly subliminal)

root meaning: *tien* – dream; *iel* – light/ray

TORBRAND s'FFALENN—founder of the s'Ffalenn line appointed by the Fellowship of Seven to rule the High Kingdom of Rathain in Third Age Year One.

pronounced: tor-brand

root meaning: *tor* – sharp, keen; *brand* – temper

TORNIR PEAKS—mountain range on western border in Camris, Tysan. Northern half is actively volcanic, and there the last surviving packs of Khadrim are kept under ward.

pronounced: tor-neer

root meaning: *tor* – sharp, keen; *nier* – tooth

TORWENT—fishing town and smuggler's haven located on the coast of Lanshire, Havish, just south of the border. Descendants of many outbred clan lineages live there since the exodus to escape persecution under Lysaer s'Ilessid the pretender in Third Age Year 5653.

pronounced: tore-went

root meaning: *tor* – sharp; *wient* – bend

TRAITHE—Sorcerer of the Fellowship of Seven. Solely responsible for the closing of South Gate to deny further entry to the Mistwraith. Traithe lost most of his faculties in the process and was left with a limp. Since it is not known whether he can make the transfer into discorporate existence with his powers impaired, he has retained his physical body.

pronounced: tray-the

root meaning: *traithe* – gentleness

TREY—diminutive of Traithe.

TRUE SECT—offshoot branch faith of the religion of Light formed after the Great Schism, when the avatar turned apostate to the doctrine in Third Age Year 5683.

TYSAN—one of the Five High Kingdoms of Athera as defined by the charters of the Fellowship of Seven. Ruled by the s'Ilessid royal line. Device: gold star on blue field.

pronounced: tie-san

root meaning: *tiasen* – rich

URMALA—town-born croft woman from Kelsing.

pronounced: ur-ma-la

root meaning: *urmala* – cow

VALENFORD—town located in south Tysan, on the barge route at the River Valendale.

pronounced: va-len-ford

root meaning: *valen* – braided

VASTMARK—principality located in south-western Shand. Highly mountainous and not served by trade-roads. Its coasts are renowned for shipwrecks. Inhabited by nomadic shepherds and wyverns, non-fire-breathing, smaller relatives of Khadrim. Site of the grand massacre of Lysaer's war host in Third Age 5647.

pronounced: vast-mark

root meaning: *vhast* – bare; *mheark* – valley

VERRAIN—master spellbinder, trained by Luhaine; stood as Guardian of Mirthlvain when the Fellowship of Seven was left short-handed after the conquest of the Mistwraith.

pronounced: ver-rain

root meaning: *ver* – keep; *ria* – touch; *an* – one

original Paravian pronunciation: *verria-an*

WARDEN OF ALTHAIN—alternative title for the Fellowship Sorcerer, Sethvir, who received custody of Althain Tower and the powers of the earth-link from the last centaur guardian to leave the continent of Paravia in Third Age Year 5100. Prior to then, the titled post was held by a Paravian.

WAYSTONE—spherical-cut amethyst used by the Koriathain to channel the full power of all enchantresses in their order, lost during the great rebellion that threw down the rule of the high kings, and recovered from Fellowship custody by Lirenda in Third Age Year 5647. Currently useless to the order, due to Arithon's arranged sabotage, which has infiltrated a stray *iyat* into the stone's matrix in 5671.

WESTLANDS—originally a term for the western kingdoms of Tysan, Havish, and West Shand. Evolved to mean a specific set of mannered customs mostly practised in Tysan after the great uprising that threw down the high kings in Third Age Year 5015.

WHITEHOLD—city located on the shore of Eltair Bay, Kingdom of Melhalla.